THE ENTERPRIZE

Hardback ISBN: 9798990651104
Paperback ISBN: 9798990651128
ebook ISBN: 9798990651111

APOCORE PRESS

Cover art and design by Brian Barraza of Ink & Echoes Creative
Interior map art by Brian Barraza of Ink & Echoes Creative
Interior chapter artwork by Brian Barraza of Ink & Echoes Creative

For those in the midst of their greatest struggle.
May your toughest challenges inspire your most creative ideas.

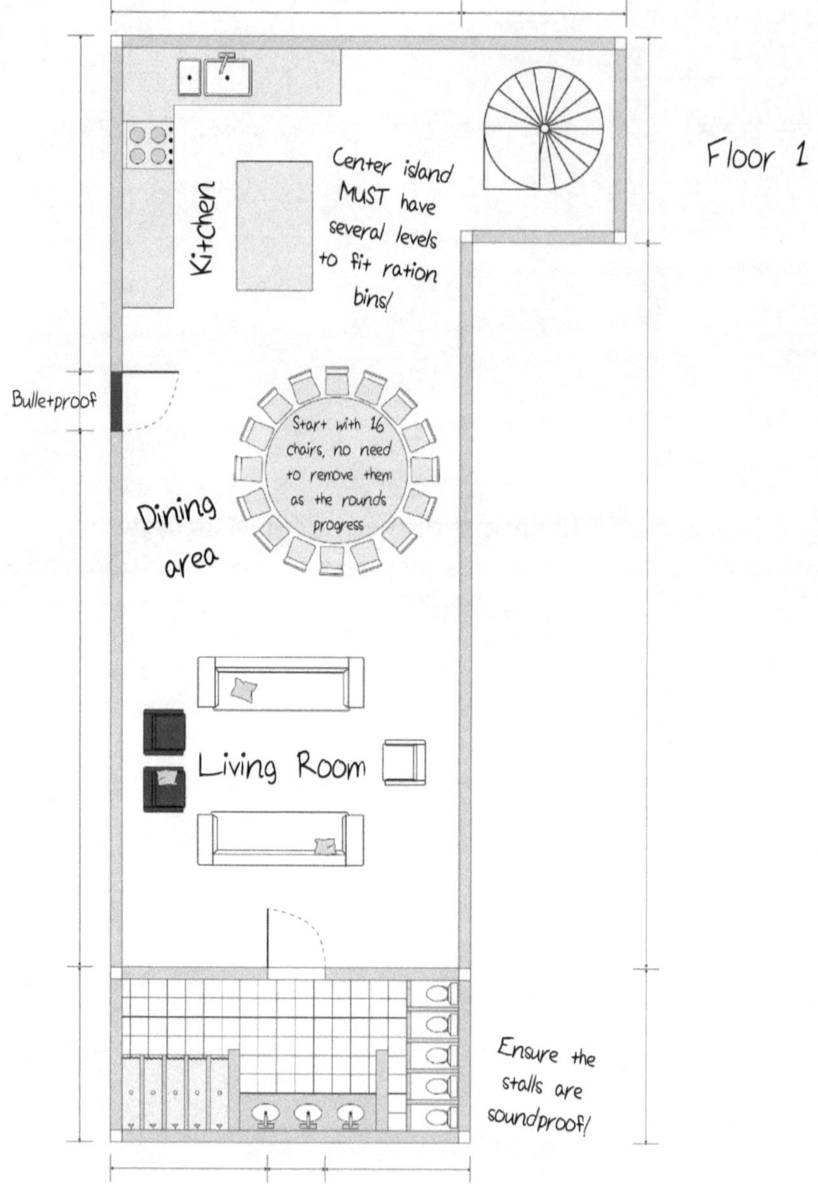

Floor 1
Kitchen
Center island MUST have several levels to fit ration bins!
Dining area
Start with 16 chairs, no need to remove them as the rounds progress
Bulletproof
Living Room
Ensure the stalls are soundproof!

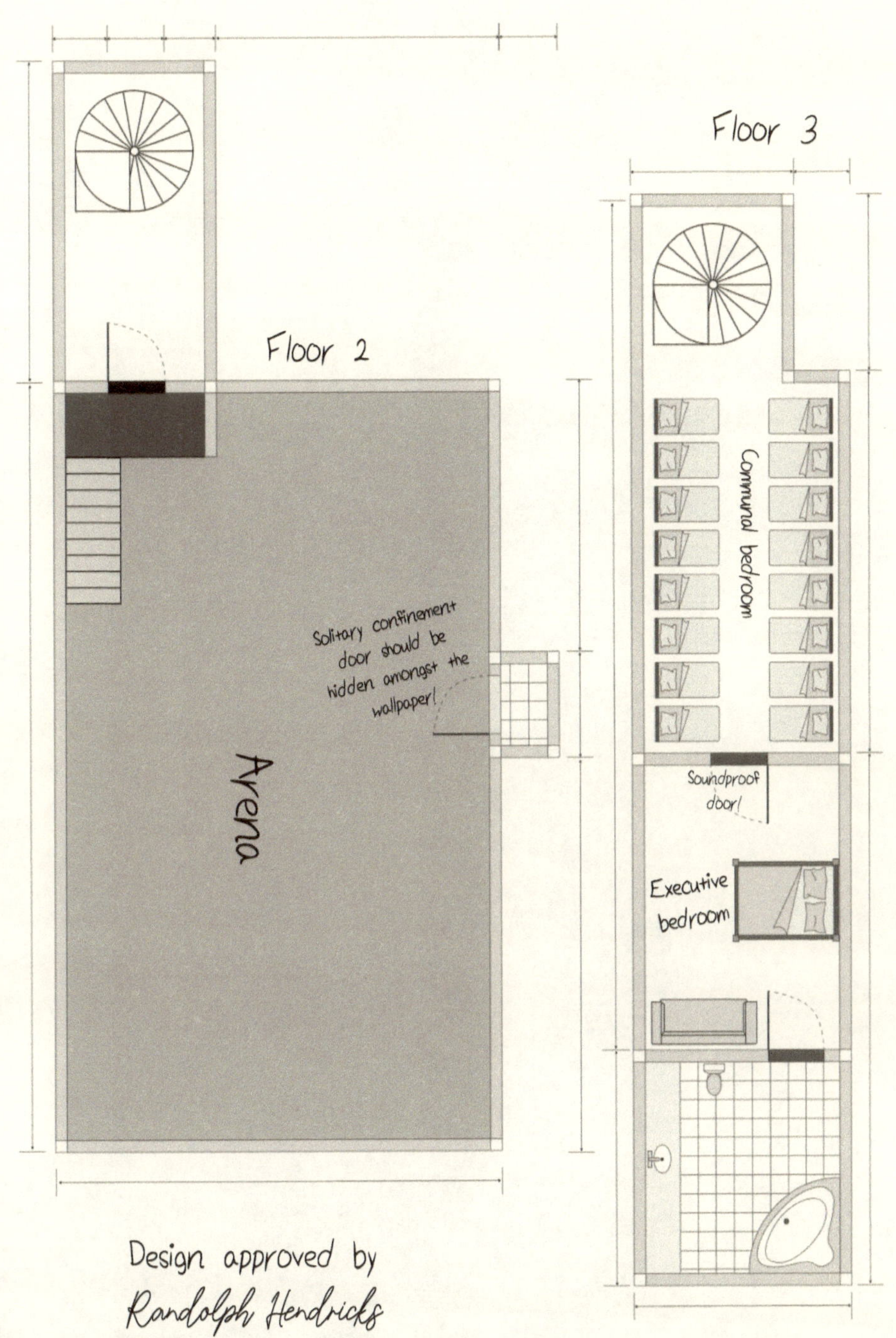

Floor 2
Floor 3
Solitary confinement door should be hidden amongst the wallpaper!
Arena
Communal bedroom
Soundproof door!
Executive bedroom
Design approved by
Randolph Hendricks

Prologue

My eyes shoot open. I bite my bottom lip hard, having learned long ago that screaming is a death sentence. The alternative may bring pain, but at least it keeps me alive.

BANG BANG BANG.

I wrap my legs around my brother and put a hand over his mouth. He knows how serious his silence is to our survival, but I take the extra precaution to be safe.

BANG BANG—

The front door slams to the floor, shaking my floorboard ceiling. Even with the gaping hole, it's still pitch black in my quarters, the sun not shedding a single ray between the wooden cracks.

Prime time for a night raid.

My eyes widen with desperation, urging Lunar to be brave. His body trembles, so I squeeze him tighter against my body to keep his shaking from bringing attention to our hiding spot.

Five Authority agents storm into our home, boots booming on the flimsy wooden floor. My arms wrap tighter around Lunar, prioritizing his silence over my own terror. Pushing away my trauma isn't ideal, but it helps keep me steady in these terrifying invasions.

"Can I help you?" my father questions the agents with a deep voice.

My vision is obstructed, but I've been trapped long enough to rely on my ears. I don't have to see to know that my six-year-old sister sits atop her attic bedroom ladder, bawling hysterically. The Authority agents will attribute the cries to her young age. They would never suspect that her screams crescendo higher than innocent children because she's terrified her illegal siblings will be found.

But we know better.

"The Miasmis Central Ascendency Corporation thanks you for your patience and sacrifice. Your home was randomly selected for inspection of stolen rations," an agent with a baritone voice announces. The declaration is the same every raid, the empty words long lost on us.

"There must be some sort of mistake," my father argues. "This is the third time this week…surely that's against Miasmis doctrine?"

My body jolts when our dishes crash to the floor. Our view is obstructed, but the sounds confirm they've begun their raid. Plastic and glass tumble to the ground, landing in a cascade of shards. I turn my back against the kitchen, protecting Lunar and me against the sharp debris shooting toward us. My father continues defending my family's honesty and integrity, but the Authority ignore him as they run to the master bedroom.

Not daring to speak, I rub Lunar's innocent bowl-cut hair and will him to be brave. My own ability to remain silent doesn't worry me until the agents storm the attic, shoving Curi so she falls toward the hardwood floor from the second story.

My mother grabs her just in time, saving her delicate head from splitting open on the floor. My mother screams desperately, Curi's cries intensifying the porcelain massacre.

"This is brutality! You can't do this!" my mother shouts. Curi's screams are suddenly stifled, so she must be pressed against my mother's chest. My father sits beside her on the floor, trying to comfort them while the raid continues.

The agents descend the attic ladder as my father rises from the floor. He balls his fists tightly and lets his voice bellow across the home. "I assure you, men, there is nothing here to find! We work for the rationing office. Why would we hoard? Surely, there's something I can do for you to exempt us from this raid."

For the first time, an agent acknowledges my father. "Are you suggesting we compromise our integrity and dedication to Miasmis for *your* convenience? We are not that type of organization, *sir*, and if you want to go as far as to offer some sort of bribe to keep us from raiding, then I'll have to report you for obstruction of justice. Is that something you'd like to be punished for?"

My body freezes, and a tear falls from my eye. Lunar's lips quiver against my hand, so I press harder to ensure his whimpers aren't audible.

My father takes a shaky step back, and his voice raises an octave. "I—I apologize for any confusion. Please…take your time."

The agent spins away and joins the others at the entrance. Relief washes over me before being replaced with terror. The agents aren't leaving.

They're getting their batons.

I clench my teeth together and pray that my pounding heartbeat isn't echoing through the floorboards. The agents spread amongst the floor, whacking segments of the wood. Sometimes, when suspicion is high, the Authority are permitted to destroy the home in search of hollow areas where rations may be illegally stored. No matter how many raids we've survived, the brutality never gets easier. For the fifth time this month, I'm overcome with so much terror that my consciousness detaches from my body. Every limb is frozen, and I'm helplessly waiting to be discovered and murdered for my illegal existence. The batons get closer and closer to my hiding spot, and I brace for impact. An agent steps onto my floorboard ceiling, baton raised.

And keeps walking.

The agents abandon their search and head for the door, having destroyed nearly every inch of our tiny home.

"Miasmis thanks you for your cooperation," spits the deep-voiced agent in charge of the operation. They evacuate through the open area where our front door once stood and leave my family sitting in silence, awe, and horror.

Bugs fly into our home, oblivious to the atrocities committed. I take a deep breath and open my eyes slowly. Lunar's face is wet with salty moisture, and the unmistakable waft of urine fills the air. I wipe Lunar's tears and let out another sigh of relief. But one thought prevents my nerves from ever subsiding.

How long will we be locked indoors, never allowed to feel the light of day?

4 YEARS LATER

PART 1

Chapter 1

When I wake, my arm is numb under Lunar's limp body. This isn't uncommon considering how cramped our sleeping quarters under the floorboard are. I shake my arm free and watch Lunar turn over slowly, still in a deep slumber. From the shade of light peeking through the cracks of our splintering timber ceiling, I predict it's dawn. I already hear Curi's faint shuffling of papers and stacking of book as she meticulously gets ready for school. All ten-year-olds are required to regularly attend classes until they reach the *mature* age of sixteen. That's when they leave for the *Assessment*.

But not for Lunar and me. Most days I'm grateful we've been in hiding all our lives. At fifteen I'd be required to leave home next year to be tested against all the other sixteen-year-olds to determine if I'm "worthy" of joining the Authority or if I would have to relocate for work on genetic modification.

The Assessment hasn't always been like this, but desperate times call for desperate measures.

My eyes squeeze shut from the silent yawn stretching from my left ear to my right. I stop abruptly when a new source of light is glowing behind my eyelids, then relax at the sound of static.

Another Authority holograph. It takes all of two seconds for me to know the information is useless. I ignore the usual horse manure but freeze when a new line is added to the regular script.

"The unofficial redistribution of assigned rations is hereby FORBIDDEN. Any citizen caught sparing rations for others will be punished accordingly. Do your part to fight this famine..."

I glare at the picture projecting on the floor above me. I don't have to locate the iron disk bolted to the floor to know it's rigidly anchored in the center of the living room. A woman in a dingy flat lab coat is cast in three dimensions from the holograph, rocking back on her heel as she recites the teleprompter outside the picture. I shift closer to Lunar to get around the floorboard blocking my vision and connect all the slivers of the hologram into a single image. When I finally do, I scoff at the woman towering over me.

Full cheeks. Bulging stomach. Healthy red locks bouncing around her chest. The woman hasn't missed a single meal in her privileged life.

I wish we could turn the dang thing off. How can that woman preach fighting the famine as a team when she's ignorantly flaunting her wealth to the millions in Miasmis forced to watch? I shake my head because I'm too old to think sheer prayer will end the hologram. The Authority won't shut it off until the announcement is complete. They ensured we couldn't ignore their words when they barged in and bolted the dang thing to the floorboards. It took a few days for reality to set in after installation, but we've tried everything.

Authority holographs project without user instruction. There's no switching the image off or flicking between channels, and no obstruction is possible. Not unless you want your brain split apart from the ear-piercing screeches that the tiny platform blares from a simple porcelain bowl blocking its mission. In our testing phase, we did find that partial blocks were permitted.

But only because holographs find a way.

It's ridiculous that the Authority spent such an absurd amount of money and technological resources to exert control over their population. But without installing immovable holographs in every home, how else could they force us to watch the evening executions?

After her casual addition to the laundry list of rigid laws plaguing our country, the woman returns to her usual script. Having lost interest, I relax against the floorboards and sigh. It doesn't take long before I block out the rest of the useless propaganda. Instead, I focus on the dust particles floating in each beam of light through my floorboard ceiling, revealing my current collection of novels. The topics often vary, but the logic booklets with complicated puzzles have always been my favorite, as evidenced by the ripped-out pages bulging through the edges, with "Iris" scribbled on their tops in black ink. Something about reasoning through seemingly impossible problems makes the hours living amongst the shadows of my home fly by.

Most of the time.

I try not to resent my parents for hiding my brother and me. My mother was too young to have children, a crime punishable by death.

Everything is punishable by death these days.

As long as I've lived, the Authority have always been more than happy to pull the trigger. The Authority insist it's because of overpopulation and diminishing natural resources. That's why there's a single child policy in place and why every woman must be thirty years old to give birth to a child. It's also why every mother is forced to submit to a hysterectomy once labor is complete and fathers are chemically castrated. My mother claims it's just another excuse to exert their barbaric power.

Stacked atop my treasured novels, one of Curi's school textbooks mocks me. The juxtaposition of free thinking and reason against the doctrine of the Authority would be comical if it weren't so chilling. I reach for the black and gray spine and gag at the seal of the Authority, a hearty tree with equally plentiful roots. The background is the same symbol, pixelated and repeated to camouflage the barren wasteland of Miasmis. This is the signature design for Authority-issued equipment and educational material, so it's plastered on all of Curi's school books. It's barely noticeable with the sparse light stretching through the cracks in the musty floorboard. But I've become so accustomed to seeing this design on my sister's course materials that sufficient light isn't required to identify the atrocious pattern. I position the cover in a sliver of light and read *Miasmis: Assessment and Genetic Modification.* I roll my eyes at the irony of calling a nation Miasmis when all the Authority do is relish in our struggle.

I wish Curi's assigned readings didn't consist entirely of Authority propaganda, but I'm lucky to have a consistent source of volumes to sift through. Still, I prefer the ones my parents bring me from the reading room.

I flip through the dry, creased pages and recite the preface by heart.

"Because of the hard, honest hours put in by Misamis's top scientists, medical advancement in the treatment of age-restricting terminal ailments like cancer and Alzheimer's led to their official extinction in the year 234 DM. Average natural mortality has proudly risen to one hundred and thirty years of age. But with great achievement comes great sacrifice," I read, moving the book across the light to highlight the words on the page.

"As always, focus on one area results in neglect of another, leaving Miasmis with an already fatal shortage of food." I turn the page and start scanning through the first chapter for the third time this week.

"So concerned about terminal mammalian disease, scientists were unprepared for the virus that ravaged our lands and destroyed any vegetation within reach. This phenomenon was branded The Hage."

Footsteps descend. Shifting to find the source in the floorboard cracks, I find Curi stalking toward the kitchen, ruffling papers and gathering her notebooks for class.

"Lunar." I close the textbook and nudge my brother's side. "Time to get up and help Curi get ready for school."

"Hhhhmmmmmmm," Lunar moans back as he pushes even further from me, seemingly trying to expand this small space to get as far away from me as possible. "She doesn't need my help, and isn't it too early for us to be in the house? Couldn't we be seen?"

Night raids ensure no family is hoarding more food than their rations allow. But other rules can be broken, like having two undocumented children living underneath your floorboards for the past fifteen years. That's why we hide; we've had too many close calls for us to be roaming about the house before work hours.

Before I can answer, my mother's fist taps lightly on our "bedroom door." That's what *she* prefers to call our floorboard ceiling.

"You two can come out," she whispers. "The blinds are closed. They'd be crazy to raid twenty minutes before their shift ends."

I unlock the rusty metal latch on our ceiling and open the wooden square above me, still clutching the Authority hardback. My eyes take a moment to adjust to the sun's brightness that slices through the cracks in our blinds, but I don't mind. The older and larger my brother and I become, the more I detest our sleeping arrangement. The light has become an increasingly welcome sight.

I reach down with my book-free arm to help Lunar out of the pit we call our bedroom. He reluctantly takes hold while shielding his eyes with his other palm. At thirteen, he's got a lot to learn about the beauty of working hours.

"Come on, Lunar, your mother didn't fake pneumonia for four months for you to sleep your life away," my father reminds my brother while emphasizing the virus my mother never had. Despite our nation's best efforts against the more gruesome terminal illnesses, pneumonia has persisted and grown in prevalence. It was the perfect ruse—pneumonia's quite common in my town.

With the brutality of the winter months and widespread malnourishment, more and more people are debilitated from this infection. Most perish with medical attention no longer being a priority of the Authority. They rarely check on home-quarantined patients, hoping they won't make it through the night. The Authority would murder half the planet if they could ensure there wouldn't be a rebellion.

That's how my mother hid my birth. My brother's was much easier. Even more common than being infected with pneumonia is having a second bout. It sounds crazy that the Authority would pass over our home for inspection in the midst of her suffering. But when you're desperate to cut the population, you don't offer assistance.

"Yeah, it's almost like the thirteen *years* I've spent living in a glorified ditch because you two couldn't keep it in your pants. But I appreciate your sacrifice." Lunar condescendingly bows at our parents, golden-brown hair ruffled about at odd angles. His resentment of our life sentence of house arrest consumes him more entirely than I ever experienced, and he often takes it out on our parents. But he offers a valid point; we've suffered in hiding our entire lives, having only ever communicated with those in our family. But hostility guarantees nothing more than a screaming match, so I disdain conflict. And I'm not willing to begin our morning with this decade-long, unresolved disagreement.

"Hey, it has its perks. I've read more books than this entire town, thanks to you two," I say gleefully to my parents as I kiss my mother's soft, freckled cheek. I've learned to be quick in situations like this. Otherwise, we run the risk of another one of my mother's emotional breakdowns. Ever since Curi was born, my mother's sensitivity has been unmanageable. I'm confident it's guilt. While Curi has grown up having friends, sniffing fresh lily-of-the-valley in the summer breeze, and scribbling notes in class with her purple crayons, Lunar and I have lived in the shadows, sentenced to a life of nonexistence. Our grandparents raised us in their dinky, rotting attic until our sister was born.

Ever since she arrived, Curi's gotten to live the life we've always wanted.

As I make my way to the kitchen, I slip the propaganda our government calls "history" into Curi's frilly purple knapsack and smile. She's the cutest little girl on the planet; even though I've never seen another, I'm sure of it. Her long, golden-brown hair always manages to lay straight, except for the few stray strands peculiarly framing her face. I've always loved them because the imperfection exemplifies her youthful innocence. To complete the picture, her two front teeth are missing, and she can't help peeking her tiny pink tongue through their gap. I can't imagine there are more adorable children strolling the roads of the Central Ascendancy.

I plop myself comfortably onto a rickety stool and find our typical breakfast strewn across the table: slimy, overripened watermelon chunks, and three whole grain bread buns, hard as rocks. This setup is meant for the three people documented to be living under this roof, but having our parents has perks.

"As always, thanks for your breakfast rations, you two." I smile at my parents.

"It's no problem, sweetie. You know we have a stash of croissants at the office from the Christmas ration." My father smiles, knowing Christmas was two months ago and those croissants are far from edible. I feel terrible that they are constantly undernourished to support us, but this is the price of having illicit children. Stashing food is a felony, but when you work for the rationing division of the Central Ascendancy and you are the head of food delivery, The Authority tends to ignore what you hide in the office.

Unluckily for us, this doesn't apply to the home.

"Why can't you ration us more food like you did last month? I'm *starving*," Lunar snaps.

Sacrifice remains a concept he's too immature to comprehend.

"You know we have to be careful with that, Lunar. If it happens too often, the Authority will get suspicious. You can only assign those officials so many extra rations before they start investigating what you take for yourself," my mother says patiently. If it weren't for my father's hand on her back, her temper would have burst far earlier from Lunar's blatant unappreciativeness.

"I'm going to start walking to class!" Curi calls from the door, skipping right through the image of the lab coat ginger. No matter. The image rotates around her, refusing to be obscured.

"Have a great day sweetheart!" my father calls as he chases after her, holding my mother's hand.

As they bearhug, I hurry to my little sister and stress the importance of studying hard: to get top results on the Assessment.

"We've been through this a thousand times, Iris! I'll work hard, I promise," Curi complains, rolling her eyes.

"Pinky swear?" I smile at her, pinky finger outstretched.

"Pinky swear," Curi smiles back, green eyes sparkling. We lock pinkies and kiss our thumbs together, sealing the unbreakable oath.

"Now have a great day little one, I love you," I say to my best friend before shuffling back toward the kitchen table.

"Love you, Iris!" Curi sings as she excitedly slides open the slab of wood we call a door. She shuts it behind her quickly and skips off to school.

I'd be more jealous of her life if I wasn't so close with my sister. She never knew my grandparents, since she was only two years old when they passed from heart conditions. Seven years of providing us with most of their food rations caught up with them, and their sacrifice ensured our survival. Without enough nutrients to sustain normal heart functions, they didn't stand a chance. Life after my grandparents was spent either reading or raising my sister with Lunar. We spent a large portion of our time teaching her the importance of family and the consequences of exposing our existence. We've taught our little sister to be the perfect little liar, but when your entire existence is confidential, being dishonest isn't sinful.

It's survival.

When your life is one massive lie, a moral check keeps a clean slate. That's why pinky swearing has become such a sacred practice. If you aren't loyal to anything, trust cannot exist. Promises to deities are empty; pinky swears are sacred.

Pinky swears are not to be broken.

My parents peek through the shutters and watch Curi skip across the yard. I can see their love for her in the way they pack her books, prepare her meals, and watch her dance. She's the best thing that's ever happened to my parents — a pregnancy at age thirty. But I don't hold their favoritism against them — not when I love Curi even more than they do. I'm okay to live in the shadow of my sister if it means she can have a better life than the one Lunar and I were cursed with.

"We have fifteen minutes before we leave for the rationing office. Want me to do up your hair Iris?" my mother asks.

I'm far too old for my mother to braid my hair, but I know how much comfort it brings her. I may not be her favorite in the family, but that doesn't mean the love isn't there.

Besides, I don't have any other plans.

I sit at our filthy kitchen table, splintering at the sides. My mother's cold, fragile hands shakily section my wavy, dark brown hair and she adjusts her wedding band to avoid pulling on me. She loves to fishtail my hair down my back and tie it off with a few loose strands at the end.

Halfway through my fishtail, my brother drops onto a neighboring stool and shoves down his roll one monstrous bite at a time. Lunar has never learned to chew with his mouth closed, but our life is not one where manners are relevant.

A disturbing thought occurs to me when my mother's hands slow at the larger sections of my hair. "Mom, what was the Assessment like for you?"

My father sits beside me on the floor since my mother, Lunar, and I are occupying the only three raggedy, fragile stools. He takes a deep breath and then answers for her.

"Well Iris, the Assessment is a lot different now than it was a hundred years ago."

I laugh as my father pretends to be older than he is.

"Dad, you took the Assessment nearly thirty years ago, how much could possibly have changed?"

"How do you spend all that time reading yet still not understand how the Assessment has changed?" Lunar snaps at me. "It used to be a way for the Authority to divide us all into the job that fit us best based on our education and physical skill," Lunar says as monotone as possible, like he's reciting from a textbook. "For *some* reason they don't think we can figure out what's best for ourselves."

"Yes honey, but it's not that simple," my mother says as she shakes out my hair to start over.

I know she made no mistake, but I don't make a fuss. Her glimpses of affection are oddly comforting, even though they always leave me wanting more. They're like an insatiable craving that needs a feast to be pacified but is constantly left with only the appetizer.

"There are too many of us. The only way to make sure we pursue something that we are actually qualified for is if the Authority assign it for us. Otherwise, we might make the mistake of picking something we merely enjoy doing."

"And what a crime that would be," I joke. Sometimes it's best to laugh about how lousy our situation has become. At the very least, it keeps us sane.

"Exactly," my mother fits through a chuckle. She's halfway through my hair once again, seemingly more confident this time around.

The room falls silent, so I break it. "Right, but it's not like that anymore."

My father takes a deep breath. "Well, with how long our natural lifespan is, it's not necessary to replace teachers or general workers. Employees in those professions can work for a hundred years," he explains. "Ever since the Hage, the Authority decided to commit all resources to Genetic Modification."

My mother cuts in as she reaches the bottom of my braid. "Now the Assessment sorts you into what Genetic Modification sector you are most qualified for. I was luckily the last to pass through the system before this adjustment, and that's how I met your dad," she says, sending an affectionate smile to my father.

"Does it ever bother you that when Curi leaves for the Assessment we'll never see her again?" Lunar ignorantly interjects to provoke my mother.

This is a certainty we ignore, but Curi leaving in six years is as much of a reality as me and Lunar having to hide for the next hundred. We can disdain the cruelty of our world, but nothing will change it. Not until there is a cure for the Hage.

A depressing silence fills the air as we each consider what an appropriate response could be to the dreadful inevitability of Curi's eventual parting. Without conversation, it's impossible to ignore the Authority puppet, yapping in the newscast. Her voice travels to the forefront, disrupting my train of thought.

"See something? Say something. Report to your local agent any suspicious rationing in your neighborhood and be rewarded handsomely."

I bite my lip and gulp, hoping the broadcast was enough to distract my mother from Lunar's outburst.

But when she reluctantly utters, "Hey Iris?" I'm confident it didn't do the trick.

"Yeah?" I ask quietly, trying not to turn around and mess up her work on my fishtail.

"Thank you," she says slowly, holding onto the end of my hair a little too long.

"For what?"

"I just—"

"Can you spit it out? We don't have all day," Lunar complains as his roll is returned to his plate through sloppy crumbs he can't manage to keep in his mouth.

"I'm sorry I brought you into this cruel world. I haven't given you the life you two deserve," she whispers, tying the end of my fishtail into a knot.

I turn around slowly and watch as glittering tears fall down her cheeks.

"I'm so sorry. You deserve so much more. And I wish I could give it to you. There's just *no way out*."

"Mom," I say delicately, bringing her into a hug. "Stop. We're okay. It's okay."

She sniffles and releases me. "I love you two so much. If there was *a way out of this*, I would—"

The pounding begins before she can finish her sentence.

We turn as my father looks at the lazy slab of wood with wide eyes, then shoots his stare back at us.

These eyes can't belong to the man I know.

These are not the eyes of my fearless father, always stoic in crises.

These are the eyes of a hopeless doe, waking to the drool of a starving tiger over her sleeping body.

These are the eyes of *terror*.

"CENTRAL ASCENDANCY SERVICES AGENCY. OPEN UP!" the other side of the slab shouts, three more fists pounding on the door.

"Iris, take your brother out the backdoor and *RUN!*" my mother whips at us, sending her stool to the floor in a desperate lunge toward my father.

I turn my attention to Lunar, who has finally stopped eating. "Well don't just sit there, *run!*" I shout, taking his hand.

I don't let my mind wander to where we could possibly hide, because there's no time. Instead, we race toward the back of our home until the front door crashes to the ground. Three Central Ascendancy service agents rush into the house with their black and gray camouflage fabric stretched head to toe, identical to the one on Curi's textbooks. My eyes scan their automatic rifles, with enough bullets to wipe out a room of two hundred people.

I've heard the Authority mere inches from me countless times but seeing them with no barrier between us flips a switch in my nervous system. Now, there is no denying they know we exist. With this reality crashing down on my shoulders, my fight or flight response shuts down entirely, and I'm frozen in my place.

"IRIS! WE HAVE TO *GO!*" Lunar shouts, yanking my hand. Despite my impulse to flee, I cannot move. It's like I'm trapped in a terrible dream, legs replaced with cinder blocks. Lunar tugs harder and harder, unable to break my position. Only when the gunshots sound does he finally halt to watch the blood of two of the only people we've ever known splatter on the ceiling of our bedroom floorboard.

Chapter 2

"*R*eady or not, here I come!" I sing, opening my eyes and sliding my palms back down to my sides. I spin to face the combined kitchen and living space and find Curi's favorite pink and silver polka-dotted blanket haphazardly strewn across the empty wooden floor. I jokingly tiptoe toward the obvious ploy and continue in my sing-song voice, "Is this where the birthday girl is hiding?" I gently lift the fabric off the rough floor and feel it catch on a loose splinter of wood. "Not under here! Where could she be?"

High-pitched chuckling echoes from the other side of the room as my little sister tries to stifle her giggles. Hide-and-seek is Curi's favorite game, so an occasion like her birthday is the perfect time to bring out the crowd-pleaser. I always search the entirety of the house before finding Curi in her famous refuge between the raggedy, mud-stained cloaks in our parent's closet. I've found it's best to build the suspense; this achieves the most laughter possible from our little 8-year-old angel.

I make my way to our parent's bedroom and effortlessly walk through the open doorframe. Doors are a commodity few in this town can afford, so naturally, my family gave up the right to privacy long ago. I peek under their bed as I continue to sing, "No, not under the bed," and move on to the closet. I shuffle through the garments as slowly as possible before yanking the last bit behind me for the grand finale. Only this time, Curi is nowhere to be found.

Where is she? I've exhausted her favorite places to hide. Our home is quite insignificant, so hiding locations are limited.

I hear another snicker across the room and scratch my head with my nail stubs. Nail biting is a filthy habit I've completely succumbed to, but with little else to do and the constant anxiety of getting caught existing, I imagine there are worse obsessions I could adopt. I follow the high-pitched laughter and trace it to my floorboard. It's a mystery how it's taken this long for Curi to pick Lunar and my bedroom as a hiding spot, but I imagine it was bound to happen eventually, considering the few secret areas our home has to offer.

I reach for the hatch and lift it open, singing, "There she is! There's the birthday girl!" I lift Curi in between bouts of her laughter and swing her around before bringing her in for a hug. "What were you doing in my room, little one?" I ask, releasing our embrace with a smile.

Curi tugs on my trouser leg and answers as innocently as possible, "I wish I could live in a fort and have secret slumber parties every night, just like you and Lunar. You're so lucky," she concludes; far too young to understand the power of her words.

I keep a smile plastered upon my face and play along with her misunderstanding, but my heart breaks a thousand times over. "We sure are, Curi. We sure are."

"Hands where we can see them!" shouts the larger of the two agents as he points his rifle square at my chest. Lunar drops my palm, and our arms shoot into the air. Lunar shakes in my peripheral vision, making it remarkably difficult for me to remain calm. I try to keep my gaze on the agents, but looking away from the two lifeless figures on the ground is impossible. My knees buckle, and I fight from collapsing. The momentary comfort sourced from Curi being absent for their murders is quickly replaced with all-consuming terror. My mind flashes through horrifying scenarios about what graphic punishment may lay in her path for being complacent in our existence. Tears well in my eyes, but I fight them from flowing over for her sake. We're submitting so quickly and easily to the powers of the Authority; the least I can do is put on a brave face.

My visions stop abruptly when the two agents, nearly seven feet tall with biceps larger than my torso, approach Lunar and me with weapons held high and fingers floating on the triggers.

"Hands behind your backs! Move and Ethan will shoot, do you understand?" the larger agent demands more than requests.

Lunar and I whip our hands behind our backs, and the enormous human forces us into handcuffs. His violent motion pains my arms as he grabs them with unnecessary force to hold them still. *Why be so aggressive when there's a gun pointed at me? What am I going to do, fight back?*

"Offenders 12 and 13 are secured," Ethan reports on his radio. The weightier agent, obviously a relative of the Sasquatch, pulls Lunar and me by the chains of our handcuffs, burning my wrists. He drags us backward out of our home while Ethan points his rifle at us, his finger still resting on the trigger. Fury courses through my veins when I catch the lab coat woman's smirk. It nearly convinces me that she knew our fate the second she projected into our living room. But of course, that's impossible. If the holographs doubled as spyware, we'd have been dead years ago.

Right?

The second we cross through the threshold of our home, my eyes sting with the power of the natural light. I've only been outdoors twice in my childhood to travel to my grandparent's house and back, so this foreign light holds a painful power to my fragile eyes. To distract myself from the awful chafe of the handcuffs and difficult adjustment to the sun, I bravely and curiously turn my head to see where we're going, and my heart drops to my stomach.

Rovers. No, not just Rovers. *14 Rovers.* I've only ever seen them in textbooks. Of course, I've only ever seen *most* things in textbooks, but situations consisting of Rovers have never been pleasant for captives. Like anything sanctioned by the Authority, the vehicles are plastered with the gray, branchy tree-and-root seal, designed to resemble camouflage against the matte black background. That wouldn't be so terrifying if each vehicle wasn't fit with eight oversized wheels, requiring a step on each side to open the doors.

It's humorous that they thought 14 Rovers were necessary to secure my brother and me, but the brutal murder of our parents and Curi's imminent doom loom over me, keeping me from laughing. When we reach the dirt before the closest Rover, I see the number 12 etched over the front right tire in chrome silver writing. Sasquatch yanks open the back door, shoves me into the ride, and I land painfully on my side. While recovering from the attack, I'm further assaulted with Lunar's body being flung on top of me. We look at each other with annoyance and horror and hear the enormous doors lock shut beside us.

Taking advantage of our five seconds of privacy before the agents join us in the Rovers, I rapidly whisper to Lunar, "Stay quiet, do what you're told, and don't give them any reason to shoot." His eyes bulge, his limbs stiffen; his terrified gaze meets mine. I can tell he understands how essential our obedience is to survival.

Ethan and Sasquatch enter our Rover, and the train of vehicles takes off, away from our home and away from our slaughtered family. Lunar and I rigidly and quietly look out the windows at the world we have only ever read about. As extraordinary as the outside world is, I can't help but feel an overwhelming sense of disappointment. Even though this is obviously not how I pictured myself touring the world; I never imagined how drab the wasteland surrounding us would be.

We drive for hours on dirt roads sandwiched between barren patches of failed farmland, as I desperately convince myself that Curi is not in danger. I distract from my violent visions of her doom with the foreign views that leave me swaying in my seat in disbelief. I've learned that vegetation used to be green and vibrant, even growing between cracks in abandoned structures. But where roots used to prosper, disease-bearing rodents and near-extinct insects reign. I watch from my window as a desperate farmer excitedly hoists a decomposing snake carcass, bursting with delight to show his family this luxurious addition to their evening meal. I scrunch my face in disgust and confusion. *If scientific advancement can expand human life by 50 years, why can't we extinguish the Hage?*

We drive for several more hours before our Rover slows to a halt at another home. Lunar and I exchange confused looks but maintain our silence. Despite being hours from our house, we gaze upon an identical structure. If it weren't for the barren forest surrounding the area, I'd think we had done a circle around town. The agents from the vehicle ahead of us lazily climb off their Rover and stroll toward the front door. Steps from the entrance, the left agent covers a yawn with his free hand; the nonchalance is nauseatingly foul.

We wince as they pound on the door before them, using the same procedure our captors followed. I keep my eyes from the altercation when gunshots and high-pitched squeals break the painstaking silence. Terrified screams echo throughout our Rover, so I gaze back to the struggle as a teenage girl is dragged out of her home in handcuffs. She's more beautiful than any girl I've ever seen in a photograph, with blonde hair extending to her waist and body clearly developed from years of overindulgence. I mentally urge her to stop disobeying commands and once again force my eyes away from her when the agent yanks the chain on her handcuffs, making her tumble to the ground.

After several aggressive kicks to her abdomen, the agent again tows her by the chain of her restraints as she silently, barely conscious, accepts her fate.

Her blonde locks disappear inside the Rover marked *13* in the same silver writing decorating on our ride. Only when Ethan's radio rings in with, "Offender 14 secured," does our Rover continue its journey forward.

It isn't long before we arrive at our next, and hopefully final, pickup destination. If our abduction and this new girl's kidnapping correspond to the numbers on our Rovers, we should only have to witness one more scuffle. I initially notice how far from civilization this next location is, even despite being within thirty minutes of our last stop. We take windy stretch upon windy stretch of dirt before off-roading completely in an utterly desolate forest. The sun has begun to set when we finally reach a clearing, and our Rover comes to another halt.

I'm astonished at the sheer extravagance of the tower before me and completely unprepared for the ignorant greed. At least three stories tall, this was obviously the home of an Authority member. The larger part of my heart sympathizes with the occupants and their impending arrest. A smaller piece struggles with jealousy at their full bellies and the actuality that most laws don't apply to them.

The fraud is birthed from the mandates allowing the Authority to oversee the minuscule rationing of civilians outside of governing entities. So, even if my parents had wanted us to eat like kings, the Authority would've put an immediate stop to it.

Then to our lives.

It's all so the ones in charge can overindulge. Ordinary civilians cannot take more than their share because it directly impacts the Authority's ability to over-ration themselves.

And that simply won't do.

That's why success in the Assessment is vital – so one can comfortably live without concern over starvation or the death penalty. But when three agents exit the Rover marked *14* with uncompromising intention, it's clear that this immunity can only take a family so far. Despite the government being able to get away with nearly anything, this structure is a blatant flaunting of wealth; the ensuing struggle will likely match the excessiveness of this lifestyle in callous consequence.

This raid seems more significant than the last two as the three rifle-bearing agents sprint to the front door and shatter the glass entryway with a single hoist of their weapons. After minutes of silence, our ears pierce with the unmistakable discharge of a firearm. The shots must last twenty seconds before there's total silence.

Three agonizing minutes later, two agents return, each hoisting the handcuff chain to one of two teenage boys. Lunar and I exchange a curious look, realizing we weren't the only forbidden children in hiding. These two boys look identical but are greatly different in size. The one in front has muscles similar to the agents and could no doubt put up a fight if there wasn't a several-inch height difference and rifle at his back. The two boys have the same dirty blond hair, long enough to curl at the bottom of their necks. Both sport jeans torn at the knee and gray t-shirts, loose on the smaller twin and fitting on the meatier. It's almost impossible to tell them apart.

Lunar and I watch the brothers get dragged toward the Rovers. Steps from the caboose vehicle, the rear agent collapses and fumbles with his rifle. I gasp, watching the skinnier twin fight for his life, kicking the agent in the temple twice before awkwardly sprinting away. The handcuffs make it impossible for him to keep his torso squared in the direction he's targeting, but he flails his legs as he desperately tries to escape.

I silently root for the boy and clench my fists in anticipation. But just before he turns the corner, he tumbles to the dry, dirty land, and red liquid expands around his torso. Screams penetrate the otherwise calm evening, and I focus on the source. Face first in the dirt, the heavier brother lies helpless, tears streaming down his cheeks. The guard previously in charge of him seemed to have shoved his prisoner to the ground before turning his rifle on the brother, eliminating one more hostage than intended.

Once the boy is heaved into Rover 14, the agent walks back to help up his colleague. Black eye already developing, the beaten agent furiously marches to the Rover and takes his place opposite the driver's seat. Our rides begin rolling forward, and I take a final glance at the lifeless corpse lying stiff beside the luxurious mansion. I snap from my trance when I hear the familiar static of the radio.

"Agent 25 killed in action. Offender 15 secure. Offender 16 early expulsion. Directing our route to the Enterprize."

Chapter 3

My stomach rumbles me back to consciousness. It's been half a day since the twin boy's capture, and I regretfully yearn for the untouched whole-grain roll left behind at my parent's murder site. Unfortunately for us, Ethan and Sasquatch seem to have no intention of feeding us or stopping to convenience us "criminals" any time soon.

I'm haunted by the last words projected from the radio. *Early Expulsion? Enterprize?* There's no telling where our destination will be or what sentence awaits us, but I fear it could leave us wishing we were dead.

We finally abandon the dirt roads and embark on a several-mile stretch of gravel. It's impossible to sit still through the rough terrain and countless potholes over which our Rover maneuvers; Lunar and I are constantly crashing into each other since our hand restraints are restricting our balance more than ever. Despite the pain and the annoyance, we both know better than to complain.

Where are they taking us? I urgently search my brain for anything that may hint at our fate. The two we saw abducted were obviously some sort of criminals. Whether they deserve the death penalty is still up for debate. The overly developed blonde girl has obviously been fed far more than her fair share of rations; Lunar and I are illicit children; and the last boy had obscene wealth and an illegal twin (who lawfully should have been *disposed of* at birth as the younger child). *But why wouldn't they just kill us too? If all crime is punishable by death, why go through this hassle?*

My shallow breathing quickens as I realize how far we are from home. Assuming she hasn't been captured, Curi will have come home by now, distraught from the sight that awaited her. The only thing keeping me sane is that our parents have spoken positively of our neighbors for years, particularly their fondness for my little sister. Squeezing my hands to calm my anxiety, I desperately hope our neighbors heard the gunshots and cleared the area before Curi's arrival home. I can't stomach imaging she had to see our parent's stiff and purple bodies sprawled across the floor.

Despite today's chaos, my mind is clear enough to be certain that I must find my way home and back to my little sister while keeping Lunar safe. But that's seeming more and more impossible by the minute. We've taken so many turns and crossed so many foreign territories that it'd be a miracle for me to find my way back.

We travel so far that a salty scent wafts into the vehicle. Looking out Lunar's window, the coastline envelopes the entirety of the transparent square. The ocean is easily four hundred miles from my hometown, a several-week journey on foot. I watch the fishermen wheel in empty nets, desperately trying to salvage what little is left. When the Hage began its reign over the land, Miasmis turned to the sea. After decades of overfishing, fishermen are lucky to catch two or three bass a day.

We shoulder the ocean for several hours until black tints abolish our view; the agents must have activated some masking mechanism that makes us completely blind to our location.

"Fifty miles from the Enterprize; offenders' sight is obscured," an agent chirps through the static on the radio.

Lunar and I exchange concerned looks, and he's holding back tears. With the excitement of our kidnapping, neither of us has had time to completely process the terror that unfolded hours earlier. We've also been too afraid to make a sound. I gesture to Lunar to put his head on my shoulder, and we spend the rest of our drive in this position, trying to comfort one another over our deceased parents and abandoned sister.

Two of the only people I've ever known: dead. Lunar and I have lived alternatingly boring and terror-filled lives, but our parents made our situation easier to bear. Despite my frustrations with our life sentence of invisibility and underlying envy of Curi, I never wanted revenge on my parents. Now, in the Authority's eyes, they got exactly what they deserved.

The thought makes me shiver.

Just as I start to process the day's horrors, another agent chimes into the radio.

"Welcome to the Enterprize, gentlemen."

The train of Rovers halts, and our agents flank the sides. Before pulling me out of the vehicle, Sasquatch yanks open the door so violently that it flings off its hinges. Haunted by how willing the other agents were to shoot a teenager yesterday, I obey his guidance. Lunar is beside me moments later, dragged by Ethan and wincing from the pain of his handcuffs. All the other agents follow suit, pulling their offenders one by one. Some of our fellow prisoners try walking with their captors to lessen the pain. Others refuse to cooperate and are dragged across the floor.

Taking in the others, I count fifteen of us. The average age would be sixteen if not for the man in his seventies. His age sharply contrasts the young group surrounding him, and I wonder what he could have done to land him a position amongst us outlaws. He is obviously underweight, his grey t-shirt hanging limply from his sharp shoulder bones, eliminating the possibility of food hoarding or ration robbery. Besides malnourishment, he looks healthy, measuring about six feet in height. The only thing connecting Lunar and I to this man is that we are obviously a different age from the mean. My brother and I are the smallest and youngest ones here. At fifteen, I blend in more with the others. Still, my undernourishment has stunted my growth, so I look even smaller than a teenager should. Quite a few others appear malnourished, but none more than Lunar and me.

I turn around at what appears to be the Enterprize towering over us in all its elegance. Pristine white and three stories tall, the Enterprize is easily the largest, most beautiful building I've ever seen. When our Rover stopped at the twins' home, I thought I'd never see a more extravagant structure. But craning my neck to examine the tallest floor of the Enterprize, I realize the world is much bigger than what can be written on paper. There's a daunting entrance before us: a massive metal door for the highest security. It's a sharp contrast to the rest of the building; it's the only feature that makes it feel like a prison.

The structure could fit six of my house. The extravagance causes an involuntary rush of excitement to wash over me. I may have no control over what is in store, but it appears I'll have a luxurious experience while imprisoned.

We're lined up according to the numbers etched on our Rovers. To my right is Lunar, eyes wide and trembling in his medal restraints. To my left is a brunette female with freckles and a bob haircut; she's just a few inches taller than me. I notice her pale skin, and her fists clench and unclench in rhythmic beats as she whispers numbers under her breath. *What happened to her?*

"Offenders," we hear from behind. We're all still being detained by the Agent assigned to us, so we must turn our heads against the direction of our bodies to identify the source. The thin, lengthy figure slowly walks around us before finding his place on the stage before the house. His hands rest on his hips in a wide stance, and he exudes strangely opposite vibes from the uniformed agents behind us. He sports a silky white button-down with the top two buttons undone. He's paired this obvious attempt at sex appeal with black slacks and shiny black pointed shoes, seemingly dressed for a special occasion while having a nonchalant ease about himself. The Agents bow their heads respectfully, undoubtedly in positions lower than this warden figure.

"Each of you is a criminal or has associated yourself with one, making you equally guilty," the warden begins with a cheeky grin. "As such, you will *not* be sent to the Assessment. For most of you, your road ends here." Silence ensues throughout the captives. The urge to glance at the expressions of the others is insurmountable. Nonetheless, I resist and keep my focus on the warden.

"Instead, all sixteen," the warden catches himself, letting out a quick, malicious laugh when he recalls the twin brother's death. "Excuse me. All *fifteen* of you are given a wonderful opportunity. A second chance at life.

"But only one of you will be exiting the Enterprize alive."

Thinking about what that insinuates for the future of my brother and me, my hands tremble in their cuffs. *If I am to see Curi again, Lunar will have to die.* Refusing to show weakness, I fight back tears and glare firmly at the warden.

"Whichever of you that is will be fast-tracked into an Authority career, with your selection of Ascendency placement." He smiles lightheartedly and cracks his knuckles before his waist. "Which means, of course, that all crimes will be pardoned."

In my peripheral vision, I catch several of my future housemates gasp.

21

"Who will that person be? That's the fun part." He dances excitedly. "*You* get to decide."

My eyes narrow on the warden in horror. *How are we supposed to decide who lives? We all want to make it out alive; how can we make judgments on people we don't know?*

The warden clears his throat, and his eyes narrow more seriously, all lightheartedness having dissipated. "You've all violated the Authority to grant yourself some advantage or…*overindulgence. Finally*, you will confront the consequences of those actions."

This cryptic explanation for our position gets my mind racing. So many thoughts circulate that I can't grasp a single idea that could expand upon this justification. Biting my lip, I abandon rationalization and focus again on the warden's monologue. His rigid body dissolves back into his originally giddy manner, and a toothy smile stretches across his lips.

"The rest of you will leave the Enterprize greeted with a punishment fit to your crimes. Fail to follow instructions, and you will be treated…*accordingly*."

Dozens of men step forward from behind him, only now visible since coming out of the shadows near the building. Each is outfitted with the tree and root camouflage uniform of the Authority and an identical automatic rifle to the ones pressing into our backs.

The urge becomes too great, so I observe the others as the news sinks in. Some are rigid apart from their trembling hands. Others sweat profusely, fighting the redness that consumes their faces. Overpopulation in Miasmis has become such a disaster that prison systems have been inactive for decades. All crimes are now punishable by death for the sake of the nation. You serve your country with your end by providing fewer mouths to feed.

The warden seems to have no remorse for the position he is forcing us into. He stands solid on the stage before us and continues with the same animated smile stretching across his lips. "Confusion is expected, but further instructions will be provided. And when in doubt," he snaps his fingers, forming both hands into playful handguns, "smile for the cameras!" He takes a deep breath, then gestures with a wide arc of his arms toward the Rovers behind us. Our restraints loosen so we can get a glimpse, but once we do, we wish we hadn't.

Projected in front of the row of vehicles is a hologram of the warden, leaning back to inhale every molecule of oxygen in the air. It swiftly disappears to show each prisoner twisting around to see the picture. I gasp for air when the pieces click together.

We're being projected on every holograph in Miasmis.

I whip around at the realization but am greeted with an even more horrifying image. Because finally, the warden stares directly into my eyes, and despite his plastered grin, there is nothing but malevolence.

"Ladies and gentlemen, welcome to the Enterprize."

ROUND 1

Chapter 4

Sasquatch yanks my restraints, and I oblige to lessen the pressure on my wrists. Regardless of cooperation, he has no intention of being gentle, so the skin under my cuffs continues to burn. One at a time, the fifteen of us are escorted to the massive iron door, and our cuffs are removed. The firing squad stares hungrily at the group, so none of us make an escape attempt. Instead, my fellow prisoners go willingly, stumbling clumsily in defeat.

My cuffs are removed at the front of the line, and I'm shoved into the Enterprize. I fall trough the entrance and wave my arms to catch my balance to no avail because, seconds later, Lunar tumbles in and pushes both of us onto the floor from the force of Ethan's massive shove.

"Lunar," I gasp, lifting myself off the carpet. Once my stability is established, I reach out my hand and lift him into a hug. "Are you okay?"

"Iris, have you seen the others?" he whispers, eyes darting side to side. "There's no way we're making it out of here alive."

I was so focused on listening to the instructions I hadn't taken much time to assess those accompanying us. Apart from the few very distinct members of our group, everyone melts together in one large blur.

"Lunar, that's not true. We don't know how this works," I reassure him as we separate. "Who cares about strength? It's probably more about making a good impression. One of us can make it out of here; we just have to lay low." Terror threatens to dominate my senses, but Lunar's panic triggers my protective instincts. "Make friends, and don't bring too much attention to yourself. Then we—" I'm cut off when the beautiful blonde from Rover 13 staggers into the room.

She's way prettier than I previously gathered. Her blue eyes look into mine, and her *M* necklace sways to a stop as she catches her balance. Taking my own advice, I approach her slowly, trying to make a good first impression.

"Are you okay?" I ask, trying to catch her gaze. I reach out my hand, and she stares at it nervously.

After a few brutally long seconds, her face contorts into a grimace, and she spits back, "What do you think, skank?"

She marches toward the right of the entrance, and I stand frozen in shock. I rub the back of my neck anxiously, biting my lip. *Getting out of here will be even harder than I originally feared.*

I opt not to wait for our next guest and grab Lunar's hand. "Come on, let's find the others," I bemoan as we march to the left.

Lunar's face breaks into a weak smile, and he lets out his first chuckle since our capture. *"It'll be great, Lunar! Lots of fun! We're going to make so many friends. It'll be easy!"* he sarcastically quips in his best impersonation of my voice.

"Oh, shut up," I say, passing the kitchen area. I'm relieved Lunar can joke about our predicament. Still, I remain on edge about the potential for his eventual meltdown. We rush so quickly through the kitchen that it blurs into a mess of blue. Hurrying to the staircase, I mentally note to investigate the kitchen further once we locate the others.

From the bottom of the steps, I hear voices above and make my way up the two flights of winding stairs circling over themselves. The clean white carpet cushions my march, giving every step a false sense of comfort. I find myself slowing to enjoy the luxury. Sky blue paint covers the walls, and the colorful innocence blinds me to the seriousness of our situation. The home contrasts with our fate, giving us an illusion of safety and comfort amongst the chaos bound to ensue.

I've let go of Lunar by now, understanding that he doesn't need me as a forceful guide. When we reach the top, we fathom how little privacy we will get in this house.

The staircase opens into an expansive room where the cameras and microphones are camouflaged to blend in with the blue walls, likely to help us forget that people are watching. There is no door dividing the rest of the building from the bedroom, and no barriers separate the beds from one another. Despite the discomfort of sleeping next to thirteen strangers, I'm excited about the luxury of having a bed. I briefly scan the blue sheets with matching pillows, eight on each side of the room. I'm overwhelmed by the grandiosity of this room but am brought back to reality when I locate the large group of residents gathered at the other end.

I look to Lunar and signal him to follow me to the group. The white carpet matches the plushness of the stairs, and I fight the urge to kick off my shoes and squeeze my toes in the gentle fabric. We approach the group and realize they are surrounding another steel door; it's the same material as the front door but much less significant. One appears to be pushing against it and trying to turn the knob, only to find it locked.

"Dude, I told you. It's not gonna open," we hear from the left side of the group.

"It was worth a try," the red-headed pusher whines, giving up.

Lunar and I skim around outside the circle, trying to avoid bringing attention to ourselves. We hear the same voice as earlier from the left side of the group, commanding exactly what we tried to avoid.

"Hey, open up the circle. It's the illegal kids," the boy says calmly but commandingly.

The crowd opens, and everyone turns to face us. I get a first look at the boy in command and feel a subtle arrogance about him. He's about as tall as everyone else, but his stance exudes confidence. His brown hair frames his flawless face perfectly, and his clean eyebrows and green eyes complement his razor-sharp jawline. If his arms indicate his physical ability, he appears to be in incredible shape. He has a blatant handsomeness about him, one that most women would swoon over.

But I've never been much of one for arrogance, let alone a distinct jawline.

"What's your story, *convict*?" He grins.

I gaze out at the crowd before locking eyes with this mystery man in charge. I scan my brain for a way to approach this question and decide to match his sarcasm. "I heard winning awards you the *pleasure* of meeting the warden. Wouldn't miss that chance, would I?" I flirt with the same smile the question was asked with. My anxiety fades as the room fills with laughter.

My questioner looks at me gleefully as another one chimes between cackles, "Yeah, what was that guy's problem?"

"Had a real stick up his ass if you ask me!" a beautifully olive-skinned, dark-haired girl exclaims.

Our laughter heightens as we each try and cover our discomfort at the awfulness of our situation. Finally, the original brown-haired leader interrupts with his hand outstretched to meet mine. "The name's Destry. And you are?"

"Iris," I say with a smile, accepting the friendly gesture. I drop his hand and motion to my right side. "This is my brother, Lunar."

Lunar gives a tense smile and reaches for Destry's hand.

"My God, you can't be older than twelve!"

"Thirteen, actually," Lunar replies.

"Geez, if you're a kid, anything's free game." Destry shrugs.

It's a sad reality we live in that kids are murdered for their mistakes.

"Forget about us?" a voice calls from the staircase. We all turn to watch the six others join us, finally completing the group of convicts. I recognize the blonde girl who threw me a snarky comment and avoid her gaze. It's great to know that some of my new housemates are friendly, but she's an important reminder to be wary of whom I offer my trust.

"What do you say we sit down for some introductions?" Destry commands more than asks, an egotistic grin still stretched across his lips.

"There are couches downstairs. Shall we get comfortable down there?" one of our new members suggests.

I find the seventy-year-old hiding in the back of their group and notice he's one of the only guys with them.

"Let's do it," Destry calls back, and our group heads to the staircase to merge with the others. Voices murmur as the group convenes, but I'm focused on the silence of the single twin. Most of this crew had plenty of time to process the events which unfolded to land them here, but that boy was the last to join us. I'm pushing away the pain threatening to destroy me in front of these newcomers, but he's had even less time to process everything. It's no surprise he has yet to match the misguided enthusiasm of the rest of the group.

I glance back at my new bedroom when I reach the top of the stairs. *Sixteen beds*. That has to be challenging for the twin to consider.

I start turning my attention back to the staircase when I catch somebody watching me. A boy, six feet tall, with ruffled brown hair. He's not particularly attractive but is redeemed by his charming blue eyes. Blue eyes that stare directly into mine.

The second I meet his gaze, he looks away, but there is no mistaking his intention. Whomever this man is, he was surveying me, and he doesn't want me to know. *What is wrong with people?* I ignore this awkwardness and focus on the task before me.

I climb steeply down the plush white flight and pass by the kitchen again. My stomach rumbles in defiance at my decision to delay eating, but first impressions are way more critical to my survival right now than satisfying my momentary appetite.

We move past the massive iron entrance and make our way to the right, where the rude blonde initially set her path. We immediately find ourselves in the same peaceful setup as the bedroom, only this time with couches. I've now concluded that white carpet stretches through the entire building, this room being no exception. The blue walls continue to engulf the house and match the sky blue of the couches. The sofas are organized in a rectangle, with two long settees extending on the longer edges but two different setups on the shorter. At the head of the rectangle sits an oversized loveseat that could fit two people but seems to only be meant for one. The opposite end offers two identical loveseats, just a touch smaller than the single one, so both can fit in the area. The only parts of this organization that do not live up to the peaceful aesthetic are the two loveseats sitting next to each other at the tail end, which are a deep black color.

I avoid the intimidating single seats and pick a spot on one of the blue couches next to Lunar. The witty olive-skinned girl sits on the other side of me, and a wave of calm rushes through me. This girl doesn't look aggressive like some of the others, so I feel at ease.

Once we've all made ourselves comfortable, the only empty spot is the single chair at the head of the rectangle. Nobody wants to look blatantly like they are taking command, so it sits unoccupied for now. Predictably, Destry stands up from the couch across from me and begins his introduction.

"I'm Destry, I'm 18 years old, and I'm innocent," he smiles as he sits back down. A light chuckle surrounds the room, and I can already see how big of a threat Destry will be. Nobody will touch him if he's this likable, and his humor has solidified his invincibility. Despite this disturbing certainty, a realization washes over me. If I team up with the invincible, I could make it far. *We get along well. Why not?* I make a mental note to keep him in my circle.

Destry is sitting on the furthest left of the couch, so there is only one option for who goes next. A petite male with bright red hair rises, and I urge my lips not to smile. His resemblance to the fictitious Leprechaun is astounding, and I swear I've seen him before in one of Curi's illustrated children's books. He's an inch shorter than me, with freckles painted throughout his body, most noticeably on his face. His blue jeans are the only feature that separates him from the fictional elf.

"My name's Finian. I'm seventeen, and what do you know? I'm also innocent," he smiles with his humorously red lips, deeply contrasted against his pale skin.

The laughter continues as Finian returns to his seat, and it becomes apparent that we will all assert that we are innocent. One by one, people go around the room claiming their innocence, laughter building higher and higher as the introductions go. The seventy-year-old man is named Eno, and the shy, tall, brunette woman standing beside me outside of the Enterprise is Sola. She was particularly nervous in her introduction, and her shaking had not calmed down. She stayed seated for her mumbled monologue and didn't take a single glance off the floor. It hits me that no laughter has been sounded from her thus far. Most of us may be in denial, but she is in full panic.

Another man named Cypher stands up and reveals himself to be sixteen. He's monotone and awkward and carries his body as stiffly as possible. His declaration of innocence is the funniest one yet, seeing that the power behind his words is almost nonexistent.

I recognize the next boy who stands from when he stalked at me on top of the steps. His blue eyes sparkle in the synthetic light, and he nervously smiles at the group while avoiding my eye contact.

"I'm Artemis…sixteen years old." He says as he wipes his sweaty palms on his khakis. He sits back down, and I notice just how giant his hands are. I suppose it's unsurprising, considering how tall he is. Still, I imagine the struggle it is for him to fit his paws in those khaki pockets and stifle a laugh. There are a few moments of silence until Finian finally interjects, "…and?" Laughter spreads through the group, and Artemis clumsily shoots back up to, what we can only assume, declare his innocence.

Except he doesn't.

"Yeah," Artemis chuckles, "you're all better than me. I probably deserve to be here."

Laughter erupts as he sits down, and Destry reaches over to touch his arm.

"Hey!" Destry calls. "You can't say that and leave us hanging!"

The group continues to laugh until Artemis sits up straight, says, "Yeah, maybe one day," and smiles as he slumps back into the couch.

By now, any pit in my stomach Artemis produced has vanished. The ease of his humor is exciting and attractive and makes me want to trust him. My first impression of him may not have been pleasant, but I don't count him out as an ally.

Next is the person I've been dreading from the second she walked in. I gulp back any grudge toward her initial name calling and remind myself that she's in just as much trauma as the rest of us…if not *more*. If I had gone through the arrest alone, without Lunar to trigger my protective instincts, I may have an attitude as well. So, when the snarky blonde rises confidently and declares, "This is ridiculous," I take a deep breath to soothe any potential prejudices that may grow from her outburst. "Why act like friends?" she spits, throwing her hands up in distress. "We're screwed!"

The laughter stops, and the awkwardness is palpable. This is the reality none of us wants to confront. Every person here experienced something horrific in the past twenty-four hours, and there's only worse to come. *But how far will it get us in the game if we take time to grieve?*

I gaze at the floor and shift my weight uncomfortably on the couch. The tension-filled silence is unbearable, because there's power in her words. Fostering relationships here will only end in tragedy. Therefore, the wisest way to avoid heartbreak is to do away with the pretense that any friendship can be meaningful in the Enterprize. *She could be the smartest one here.* But one scan of her sturdy body reminds me that she has an advantage that I do not.

Strength.

Her physical advantage may allow her to get away with hostility and brutal honesty. But as a frail, undernourished con artist, those are not anchors I can afford to be burdened with.

I've trained Curi in the art of deceit for the past eleven years. Even before she could speak, I'd reward her with hugs or games if she successfully convinced my parents she hadn't yet eaten. Mercedes may have the physique to make it far. But eleven years exploring the intricate art of duplicity has left me with one thing the others couldn't possibly have:

An unbelievably trusting facade, and a talent for telling others exactly what they want to hear.

I don't take pride in my deceitful talents. But if it comes down to saving Lunar or falling at the hands of a stranger, I'm not afraid to utilize my ability.

Finally, a familiar voice breaks the silence.

"So do you have a name or…?"

The house bursts into laughter; even Sola breaks from her trance and stops trembling through the giggling roar. I scan Artemis and can't believe how much he's come out of his shell in the last thirty seconds. He smiles at the success of his joke and, for the first time since the top of the stairs, locks eyes with me.

My stomach drops, and this time I'm the one that looks away quickly. I'm unsure what it is about Artemis, but I immediately take to his humor.

The girl's face transforms into what's become her signature grimace, and she shoots a death stare at Artemis. "Mercedes, smart ass." She collapses back into her spot with a frustrated *humph*, making it clear that she has no intention of sharing her age or denying her crime.

The ensuing sight is hilarious. Unfortunately for Mercedes, Artemis sits directly to her right, so she can't escape her aggressor. Instead of switching to the empty seat at the head of the group, Mercedes stubbornly crosses her arms around her plentiful chest. Her plop into the cushion was so aggressive that her long blonde hair landed haphazardly on the couch, with an exceptionally long section taking sanctuary on her neighbor. Artemis makes a dramatic yet silent display of removing Mercedes' locks from his left arm, acting as if it's the most disgusting thing he's ever had the displeasure of touching.

Mercedes' eyes make a hostile roll. Despite having the same eye color as Artemis, the two couldn't look more different. Artemis's eyes have a welcomeness that invites you to relax and trust. Mercedes' has a mark of evil, starving to slap opponents for even the slightest step out of line.

Since the opposite couch has finished their introductions, the miniature monologues move on to those occupying the black armchairs. The girl closest to Mercedes rises and projects a similar declaration to the group.

"I'm Crescentia. And like Mercedes, I'm not an idiot. This friendship crap is absurd, don't you understand? We're *voting* on our survival. *We* are responsible for who gets killed. You don't see the cruelty in this?"

This is the first time I get a clear look at our new roommate. Her black hair stands out against her ashen skin. If not for Finian, she would claim the prize as the palest person here. She can't be any taller than I am, making her one of the shortest in the group. She's also the least feminine girl here, holding herself in a boyish stance and wearing the same jean and t-shirt combination as some men in the group.

Her attitude confirms that she's not my first choice for an ally, but I can't refute that Crescentia's words have power. Not only will we be fighting to convince others that we deserve to live, but we are also deciding the fate of those around us. It would be much easier for the Authority to kill us with our families. But where's the psychological torture in that? They want us to singlehandedly be responsible for the deaths of people we just met.

They're not doing this for entertainment.

They're doing this to make an example out of us.

"You can pretend this is a vacation and laugh all you want. But if you're the one that survives, everyone else is dead. And their blood is on your hands."

"Don't you think we know that?" Destry interjects. "But what use is there griping about it? You heard the warden. We can't get out of here. Anything we try will get us killed. We don't have a choice."

For the first time, I hear the mechanical sound of a camera moving. I look at the blue walls and find another camera camouflaged against the painted structure. Its only tell is the red blinking on its lower corner, flashing every other second. It adjusts its view to center Destry in the frame, and I shiver as I envision his seated figure blabbing across every holograph in Miasmis. The red blinks are just another chilling reminder that the entire country is watching us.

Curi is watching us.

Destry continues, "So why don't you just tell us your age, what you did wrong, and sit your ass back down? We don't know how long they're keeping us here. Let's make the most of it."

Crescentia's eyes shoot daggers at Destry, and she throws her hands up in frustration. "Fine, wanna be friends? Let's be friends!" She paints a fake smile on her lips and directs her gaze at the entire group. "I'm sixteen. I'm here because my parents fucked up, and I'm being punished for them." Her ingenuine grin is so haunting that I prefer her scowl.

She situates politely back into her chair and mockingly turns to the man beside her. "Your turn, *buddy*!" she exclaims with her hideous sneer.

We have finally landed on the wealthy boy whose home we stopped at last. He slowly grips the sides of his chair, and his biceps bulge as he hoists himself to a stand. He runs a delicate hand slowly through his dirty blonde hair and begins his introduction.

"My name's Lagiacrus, I'm sixteen years old, and I'm here because I have—" he stutters before correcting his mistake. "Had a twin."

The group stays respectfully silent, and a few others bow their heads in reverence. We all witnessed Lagiacrus's family massacre because he was the last to join the Rovers. Of the two detainments I watched and one I partook in, his capture was the most brutal from the outside looking in. He nods stoically and returns to his spot in the menacing chair.

Our couch is the next to go, and the boy sitting closest to Lagiacrus rises.

And he is the most handsome man I have ever seen.

The way he holds himself...his light brown hair flips over his brow, and his violet eyes twinkle in the light with a sparkle of kindness. I don't know how I missed him. He must have been a part of the large group in the bedroom when I was riddled with making the perfect first impression. His brown boots have a hardened layer of dirt on the heel, so he must have been working outdoors before his capture. He carries himself with subtle confidence, not arrogant like Destry or needing approval like Artemis. It's an effortless yet gentle sureness that accentuates his attractiveness to surpass his already dashing looks.

He begins his monologue by elevating the right side of his mouth into a sexy half-smile. He scans the room and projects his voice over the crowd, "My name's Mace, and I'm sixteen years old. Like most of you," he gestures to the group, "I'm completely, unequivocally, undeniably, innocent." He sends a wink through the crowd, and my heart swoons. This is the most blatant attempt at lust, but with him, it's effortless. How he annunciated his words and deepened his voice to emphasize *innocen*ce is completely, unequivocally, undeniably sexy.

My cheeks burn as I shrink into the cushion. Shame replaces my attraction, and one terrifying thought dominates my consciousness. *Mace's charm is a significant threat to my safety.* Lunar and my survival will always be my top priority, so I mentally curse myself for fawning over my new housemate. Far from feeling guilty about their lust for Mace, Mercedes and Crescentia exchange a look of admiration. Finian leans over to Destry, hand covering his mouth to conceal a whisper, both fascinated by their new roommate's introduction. Destry is glowing as Mace sits down, and I can feel the dynamic shift. Destry may be in charge, but Mace is the one admired.

And that yields significantly more power than some artificial sense of command.

I'm so absorbed with my housemates' reactions and my own internal conflict that I don't notice Lunar stand. I am awakened from my trance when he announces, "I'm Lunar, I'm thirteen, and I'm innocent!" Beaming, he plops back onto the sofa, insinuating it's my turn. I slowly rise and think of a way to continue my positive first impression from the bedroom.

I direct my sight first at Destry, then at the rest of the group, a delicate smile painted on my lips.

"I'm Iris. Fifteen years old." I make a dramatic pause before pointing at Lunar and continuing, "And I don't know what the hell he's talking about; we're *very* undocumented," I laugh, reclaiming my seat.

The crowd receives the joke well, but I don't get the reaction I hoped for. *How does Artemis make it look so easy?* I'm partially deflated but guiltily filled with butterflies when I catch Mace laughing at the declaration.

The last three girls introduce themselves in a blur. All are sixteen, and none reveal how they earned a stay at the Enterprize. The olive jokester beside me introduces herself as Ashlea, and I mentally repeat her name to ensure I remember it. She's undoubtedly somebody I want to partner with, and it would be a shame if I forfeited her trust by immediately forgetting her name.

Kylah is next, followed by Jade. Both are unremarkable, and I struggle to retain their names. Kylah has curly red hair and looks significantly older than her age. Wrinkles contour her face, and she's as tall as Artemis. Her monotone introduction gives me no indication of whether I can trust her or not, and Jade is the same. She has stick-straight, jet-black hair with tan skin. She's average height and gives a straightforward introduction, returning to her seat without a sound from the group.

Seemingly on cue, Crescentia jumps from her black settee and spreads out her arms, pale skin pink with annoyance. "Whelp, now that we're familiar with the faces we're killing, shall we vote?" Several eyes roll in the crowd, and others look to the floor nervously. "Nobody knows what's going on, so somebody should get this started."

"I propose we kill Artemis," Mercedes smiles mockingly, arms still crossed over her chest. She sends an aggressive side-eye to Artemis, and he sits up straight, appalled.

"And I thought we were just starting to hit it off!" he cries mockingly, and my lips stretch back into the smile he so effortlessly gets out of me.

In my peripheral vision, Mace stands slowly. "Nobody is killing anybody," he announces. "So you can just sit your ass back down, Crescentia, and wait for the warden to give instructions."

I should be appalled by his outburst, but his attractiveness makes me giddy. I hide the involuntary smile his rejection of Crescentia has threatened to give me.

Crescentia puts a hand on her hip and laughs. "Oh, ho! Didn't mean to upset you, big guy. By all means, you make the first vote." Mace stands firm, completely undisturbed. He crosses his arms impatiently until Crescentia sits down, her face slick with sweat. Her infatuation with Mace conflicts heavily with her frustration at the situation, and her embarrassment makes it hard for me to keep a straight face.

"Right, thanks for that," he responds jokingly. "I don't know the rules any more than the rest of you. But I overheard the agents in my Rover talking…and it sounds like we'll be here for a while."

The group of us stay silent, desperate to hear what information Mace has. Delicately, Jade whimpers, "What did they say?"

Mace drops back into his seat and leans forward. "I couldn't catch everything, but they mentioned two voting options. Maybe somebody picks two people to select from? And the loser...*you know.*"

"Then what?" Ashlea questions. "Somebody else picks the next two options?"

Mace shakes his head quizzically. "I guess we'll find out?"

Crescentia rubs her face with the heels of her hand before opting for a calmer, more understanding tone. "Well, even if that's true…who decides who those two people are?"

Mace shakes his head and runs a hand through his hair until a familiar voice sounds over some intercom system.

"Convicts," the voice echoes from the front of the room.

We all turn our attention to the front despite there being nothing material to look at. My stomach churns with dread as the instructions pour out.

"Make your way to the second floor." The warden pauses before making one final, daunting memo. "Don't forget the consequences of disobedience."

Chapter 5

Crescentia slowly rises from the black settee and slides her right hand into the back pocket of her jeans. "Let's get this over with," she directs at the wall in front of her, leading the march to the second floor.

The rest of us follow suit, some darting their eyes back and forth while Lunar trembles so hard he can't stand straight. I squeeze Lunar's hand and smile.

"It's gonna be okay," I whisper to him.

He smiles back, but his palm hasn't stopped shaking.

"We'll get through it together...whatever it is," I continue, squeezing his hand three more times.

My brain spins through the endless possibilities of what may await us, and my breathing quickens. The group has become completely silent, and the laughter from earlier seems a distant memory. It takes everything in me to resist hyperventilation.

We ascend the white plush steps, and my parents' murders fight for the attention they deserve. *Not now. Please, not right now.* I fight back the grief and clear my mind. Whatever lies on the other side of that door, I have little doubt it will require all my strength to come out alive.

I walk in the middle of the group and stop a few steps from the second floor as the leaders reach the entrance. I hadn't noticed earlier in the excitement of locating the others, but the second floor looks as haunting as the two black chairs in the living room. It's the only place in the house without carpeting. In its place is a shiny black hard floor, extending only a few meters before ending at another massive iron door.

Crescentia pushes the door open, and it loudly creaks along the floor. Once gathering her confidence and controlling her fear, Crescentia presses through, and the group orderly follows.

Lagiacrus brings up the caboose, and the enormous door slams shut the second he enters. I jump in surprise but quickly cover it with a nervous smile. Several mechanical locks bolt, isolating us from the rest of the house.

Before us stretches an arena with vibrant grass covering a 50-yard field. Natural vegetation hasn't thrived in decades, so it's obvious the surface is AstroTurf. The walls extend into a light blue cube painted with white and gray clouds. The objective was clearly to make this hellhole seem like a welcoming outdoor scene, except that the ceiling is the same metal surface as the doors in the house. I get a shiver down my spine when I catch the rotating cameras, plastered with the repeated tree-root seal of the Authority, hanging down from the top of the stadium and off the walls. The mechanical equipment and the penitentiary-like roof are the only features that expose this sanctuary for what it is: a prison.

We descend a rusty metal staircase, my legs wobbling more intensely with each step. Once stepping onto the ground floor, we approach a large, black structure planted in the center. I stand back from the group, heart pounding in my ears, and study the circular mechanism. It's easily twenty feet tall and towers over us. Silver chains hang down from the roof of the contraption, evenly spaced apart from one another and swaying three feet above the ground. Getting closer, the minuscule disk-shaped seats come into focus. At the bottom of each metal line sits a white, plastic disk, sixteen spread amongst the mechanism. My heart painfully twists when Lagiacrus hangs his head, avoiding the reality of his deceased brother. A plasma screen is placed on the wall behind the structure, illuminating bright red numbers reading *00:00:00*.

Just before reaching the edge of the apparatus, we discover a large, laminated card leaning against the chain of the closest seat. Crescentia aggressively swipes it from the hanging disk and turns to project to our crowd. She lifts the card to her eye line so the rest of us see the camouflage Authority seal painted on the back.

"*Convicts,*" reads Crescentia, eyebrows raised. "*Each of you will seat yourself on a disk of your choosing. If any part of your body touches the ground, you are eliminated. The final criminal will be crowned the first Executive.*

"*We begin once every convict has mounted their disk.*"

"What the hell?" Mercedes questions. "Executive? What's that supposed to mean?"

"Maybe it has something to do with what Mace overheard," suggests Destry. "Even if it doesn't, I don't want to be shot for disobedience," he announces, hopping onto the nearest seat and twisting his legs around the chain.

"Let me see that," demands Finian, grabbing the card from Crescentia. He scans the paper with a hard swallow, then glances around at us, shrugging his shoulders.

"Thanks for the trust in me," Crescentia groans, rolling her eyes.

Artemis crosses over to stand beside Finian. "It's not about trust," Artemis says halfheartedly. "We're just trying to figure out what all this means."

Crescentia sighs. "What is so confusing about it? Be the last person hanging." She folds her arms across her chest and stomps to the opposite side of the apparatus, deciding on the seat furthest from the group.

My palms quiver as I consider the potential consequences of failing. I reject the possibility that the fallen convicts will be killed. The warden mentioned that we will be voting, and Mace overheard as much. That also insinuates that winning would not be a death wish, although I can't rule out the possibility that it may qualify you as one of the murder choices.

The rest of my housemates make their way around the mechanism, choosing their positions as they go. I guide Lunar to neighboring disks with a reassuring hand on his back. He drags his feet toward his chain and wipes his sweaty palms onto his pants before climbing onto the circular seat. Like the others, I grab the chain to successfully hoist myself onto the disk. My bottom hangs off the sides of the Frisby-like mount, so I feel like I'm sitting on a quarter. I cross my legs around the metallic rope above my disk to strengthen my hold and involuntarily lean back, making my steel cord sway. Unfortunately, balance on this torture machine requires constant muscle flexion from both my arms and legs, so even the most convenient position yields immediate exhaustion.

On my opposite side, Sola nervously takes her chain and hoists herself up but struggles to hold her place. Her flimsy momentum causes her chain to fling her disk and body backward, so she fights to keep her pedestal upright. Sola tries to stay airborne as her chain whips her about and eventually establishes enough balance to bring her disk to a light sway. Seconds after she relaxes, the clanking of chains booms above us. I frantically shift my focus left and right, searching for the source. I grip tighter as the chain in the center of my tiny seat retracts, raising me several feet off the ground. Sweat slickens my grip and I squeeze my eyes shut, hoping for my disk to come to a halt. When it finally does, I search the others and confirm that the adjustment was made for everyone. A fall from this height would not be life-threatening, but that hardly eases my anxiety. My sight dizzies as I imagine the severity an injury could be from this high up, and I grip my chain harder to calm my nerves.

The plasma screen starts counting up from zero. Another thunderous screech sounds from the center, and we begin to rotate. The speed is pedestrian, hardly increasing the difficulty of this task. But as time passes, the pace quickens. Before long, our chains fan out at ridiculous angles, pushing us away from the center. The longer we last, the faster we spin and the further away from the center we get. Within minutes, my quads ache, and my palms burn.

In an unsurprising turn of events, Sola crashes to the ground, triggering a horn. "CONVICT: SOLA. ELIMINATED AT 00:03:07," a robotic voice chimes in from the intercom. I grip my chain tighter and wait for gunshots, but as I suspected, nothing happens. I sigh with relief that failure will not provide immediate consequences, then wince at Sola's poor performance. Given her struggle to mount her disk at the start, I knew she wouldn't be a threat, but I hardly expected her to last less than five minutes. My heart hurts knowing she has nobody to grieve her loss with, but I can't help wondering why she's faring worse than the others – especially considering that Lunar and I are the only ones with something to go back to.

Seconds later, the horn blares again, and the robotic voice announces Eno's elimination. I didn't witness his tumble, but with his towering height and decrepit age, it's easy to find him sprawled on the artificial pasture. It takes him several minutes to find his feet, and he immediately collapses once he does.

"My legs," he chuckles from the turf. I don't risk my balance by watching his fragile figure below me; instead, I keep my eyes forward until I catch him sitting beside Sola against the far-right wall of the arena, establishing that as the elimination sector. As soon as Eno reaches his destination, the speed of our swings levels out, but it's already fast enough to give me a headache. Soon enough, Sola's hushed counting joins the pounding in my head, and her shaking intensifies. I eventually drown out her routine muttering when I focus on the mechanical exertions of our spinning contraption.

As time passes, my legs ache from the tension of holding me in place, and I understand why Eno struggled to stand. The muscle strain keeping me solid is exhausting my limbs, and my head spins with dizziness. The only advantage I have over the others is that my sleeping quarters under the floorboards had little space to stretch out. Probably unlike my competitors, I've been used to my legs numbing from stiffness for the past fifteen years.

When vertigo takes over ten minutes later, my training in cramped lodging is moot. I wrack my brain for ways to keep from getting woozy and think back to my long days at home with Curi, spinning her around by her arms until we couldn't stand straight. *How was I able to do that for so long?*

I close my eyes and focus on the darkness of my eyelids. My headache exponentially increases, and I nearly fall off my disk. Abandoning that useless idea, I search for a consistent point to direct my attention to. I gaze at the fake sky brushed on the wall, painted with clouds in varying shapes, sizes, and shades. One threatening cloud stands out from the others, medium size and uniquely dark. I can easily spot it through every rotation, so I use it to anchor my focus. Finally able to shake off the threat of dizziness, I spend the next ten minutes locked on the thunderous cloud.

A third horn blast jolts me from my anchor, and it takes a moment to locate it again. The robotic voice announces that Kylah has been eliminated just after fifteen minutes. Excitement courses through me as I get closer to victory. Even if I don't win, I need to stay in as long as possible to show I'm a worthy ally. Being in the first half of eliminated contestants would not solidify my desirability. I keep my eyes glued to that cloud and only remove them when I hear the fourth horn blast and a robotic voice announcing, "COVICT: LUNAR. ELIMINATED AT 00:22:59."

Fear washes over me, and my heartbeat races as I locate the empty disk ahead of me and curse myself for not checking in on my brother. He peels himself from the plastic grass and stumbles three or four times before crawling to join the others. His long brown bowl-cut hair, short enough to keep from his shoulders but long enough to have the innocence of a child, is jutting out at odd angles, clearly disheveled from the plummet and half an hour of rotations.

He finds me watching him and gives a supportive thumbs-up. "You've got this, Iris!" he shouts from the wall. Relief flushes through my body when he shows no sign of injury, and I nod gently in his direction before gluing my eyes back to my cloud.

My thoughts start trailing, and I get nervous about Lunar's weakness. *He's only a child.* But then again, if the rest assume he can't compete well, they won't view him as a threat. Nobody in their right mind would waste their vote on taking out such a weak player. *Lunar's disadvantage could guarantee his survival.*

I then worry about his declared support for me when cheering me on, but let it fade when I consider that everyone already knows we're related. Of course, Lunar is going to root for me. It would be suspicious if he didn't.

The horn returns to announce Crescentia's failure at just over thirty-eight minutes. Pitied curiosity has me gazing down to check her condition, but her black hair curtains around her, obstructing my view of her face. She jerks back and forth, the revolting noise coming from her throat enough to prove that she's violently retching on the turf. The second I spot the chunky vomit on the grass, I shift my attention back to my thundercloud.

Despite her outburst during introductions, my chest tightens at her failure and my inability to assist her. Still, I can't help but feel relieved that one of the most outspoken convicts here will not have the power to send me to my death. The more I question the Executive position and what earning the title may bring, the more I confirm that it's a desirable reward. If being the last person standing was a death sentence, why would any of us try? Cameras follow our struggle, and regardless of who is watching, the Authority will want to put on a good show. I resolve that the winner of this spinning frenzy will have the power to determine who will die. How that will play out stands as a mystery, but I know that Crescentia being out of the competition is good news for my survival. I note that if Mercedes, the beautiful blonde, is eliminated, my odds of survival may increase drastically. Those two were the only ones that didn't seem to reciprocate my forced enthusiasm, so I can't imagine either will be rooting for my success. I grit my teeth with resolve. *If nothing else, I have to outlast Mercedes.*

"One hour in! Great job, everyone!" shouts Eno from the elimination sector. He smiles and waves at us, likely working to get on our good side.

Another fifteen minutes pass without any elimination. My hunger pains me so severely that I curl my body onto the chain, somehow still managing to keep my balance. It's been twenty-four hours since I last ate, and over thirty since I had more than a *bite* of sustenance. I try and embrace my ability to go long periods of time without fuel. From previous experience, I know that the hunger will subside if I fight for another ten minutes. Besides, those doors aren't opening until an Executive is named, so I may as well sit up here instead of with those eliminated.

As my stomachache settles, I distract myself by counting the remaining competitors. *Ten contestants to go.* My arms ache, and I bite my bottom lip to absorb the pain. I've lost all feeling in my legs, so they stay locked where they've been, straddling the chain. Being used to the numbness, it's the least of my worries. Still, I'm surprised more people haven't dropped out yet, but I suppose that once you establish an anchor to focus on, the time passes quickly with mental ease.

"Ninety minutes in. Great job, you guys," shouts Eno again, embracing his aged role as group father. As if on cue, a mechanical noise booms throughout the arena. I wobble briefly as a large medal pole rises from the turf.

The rod climbs until it reaches the height of our apparatus. It's close enough to our trajectory that as it gets higher off the ground, we start crashing into it with every spin.

"Jesus Christ," Destry complains, colliding with the pole. The impact feels like we're repeatedly slamming into concrete. The harder you brace yourself, the more painful the collision. Every time I gather myself from a crash, I'm back at the barrier for another hit. It's now impossible to keep my eyes on a target as the pole spins me around in differing directions every few seconds. With this new twist, we start dropping like flies.

The horn honks four times within fifteen seconds, announcing first Finian's demise, then Jade and Ashlea's. Destry completes the group of collapses at ninety minutes and fifty seconds.

The elimination is chaos. With each collision against the pole, my housemates are flung from their disks, landing in a heap of bodies upon the unforgiving turf. The crashes amplify with intensity, worsening with each consecutive blow. Just as one tries to gain balance, they're struck by the next contestant. Finian groans from the bottom of the dog pile until the four finally separate. Some roll away from the apparatus, unable to get feeling in their legs or arms. Others crawl slowly from the popular drop point in opposite directions.

I grip my chain until my fingers lose color, urging myself to outlast Mercedes. I start jerking my swing just before the pole to avoid a serious collision, but eventually mistime my lurching and smash my shoulder into the rod. It takes the entirety of the blow, and I let out a silent whine. Tears fill my eyes, and I will them into place. *Do NOT let them see you cry.*

I cross my legs tighter, adrenaline bringing feeling back into them. A collective shout of surprise distracts me from my pain, so I turn around to find Artemis hanging onto his disk by his enormous fingertips. A rod collision knocked him off his circular seat, and he desperately hangs on. His palms cover the surface area of the entire disk, and his body crouches to keep from touching the ground. The eliminated cheer him on until he nearly regains his position on the circular seat. He is almost back on, but the pole whacks him from behind, and he plummets to the turf.

Most of the group applauds his effort as his demise is announced. There's an eruption of laughter when he kneels from the grass and performs a dramatic and colorful bow for his supporters. I smile at the silliness of the gesture and slam again into the immovable iron pole. I cling to my seat, managing to keep my balance and glance downward just in time to witness several eliminated participants offering Artemis a reassuring pat. Eno helps him walk to the elimination sector, smiling supportively.

I watch Artemis for a second too long and get ambushed by the pole. I lose my grip and flip upside down off my seat. My legs are still wrapped around the chain, but my arms hang with the rest of my upper body toward the turf. I try to flip myself over but lack the strength to succeed. Overturned, I watch the metal post approaching my face. I close my eyes and wrap my arms around my head, bracing for the crash.

Just before the collision, a surge of terror courses through me, causing my legs to relinquish their grip on the chain. I hurtle toward the ground, headfirst, the world spinning in a dizzying blur. I shift my arms to protect my neck and land on my left side, back slamming into the pole. A shock goes through my spine, and my limbs burn from their exertion. The world spins, and I squeeze my eyelids shut, worsening my light-headedness.

HONK. "CONVICT: IRIS. ELIMINATED AT 01:32:45."

Lunar hoists my torso up, and I let out a groan.

"I'm such an idiot," I say, clutching my back. "I lost focus."

Lunar's lips curl into a playful smile. "Yeah, you're pretty useless, huh?"

I chuckle weakly, but my pride remains damaged. Mercedes continues rotating, blonde hair flying about like a horse mane. I'm beyond annoyed about the inevitable doom I'd face with her at the helm, but I try to push it to the back of my mind.

I take a few minutes to rub the feeling back into my legs and straighten the chunks of hair falling out of my braid. We approach the others, and I pretend to be in good spirits. "Quite the show you had out there, *Arty*," I flirt. For whatever reason, his sense of humor makes me feel comfortable around him.

He laughs from his seat on the ground and smiles back, eyes glinting with curiosity and amusement. "Arty, huh?"

My annoyance at being eliminated fades, but before I can respond another horn blares. I pray that Mercedes has fallen, but I remain disappointed.

The voice announces Cypher's downfall, and a metallic taste fills my mouth. I slump my shoulders as Cypher starts to peel himself from the ground. I hide my grimace, watching Mercedes easily swing on the apparatus, but a disgusted shout brings me back to the turf.

"EW!" Cypher exclaims, throwing up his palms. He rolls over, revealing his spoiled blue t-shirt, caked with dried chunks of Crescentia's barf. "DISGUSTING!" he shouts.

Artemis and Destry laugh, and Crescentia interjects with a feral sneer. "Is something funny?"

"*Obviously*," Destry smiles, pointing at Cypher, and he and Artemis burst into laughter.

The cackling fit is impossible to fight. Lunar and I join in, Ashlea chuckling beside us.

I plant myself next to Artemis, sitting in order of elimination. Lunar dismisses the precedent and situates himself on the opposite side of me. Lagiacrus, Mace, and Mercedes continue spinning, but I focus on Artemis and Destry, whispering in my periphery.

"Dude. It's like, she's hot but psychotic," I eavesdrop from Destry as he watches Mercedes spin.

"And that's a problem because…?" Artemis responds, triggering light laughter from the two. "Don't knock it 'till you try it, right?"

The two continue to giggle silently, and I'm appalled at their crudeness. Even more so, I'm disturbed at the ease with which I communicate with Artemis. He's likely showing off in front of the others, but I still question whether he's the genuinely nice, funny guy I initially thought. I wipe this interaction from my consciousness and stop listening to their private, immature conversation.

The spinning apparatus makes another one of its mechanical clamors, and the spinning picks up speed.

"Christ," Lunar exasperates beside me. "They're gonna kill 'em."

"Yeah, I suppose that's the point," I reply, suppressing my shock.

"I guess they want this to end?" Finian questions.

"The grand finale," Ashlea says with alarm.

The swing gets faster until their chains are nearly perpendicular to the center of the apparatus. The remaining contestants pound against the pole one by one, wincing in pain. Mercedes strikes the iron with such force that a crack echoes off the elimination wall. The brutality finally ends when she tumbles to the floor screaming, holding onto her ribcage.

The swing slows to a stop, with the final two hanging limply on their disks. Mace and Lagiacrus are far enough apart that communication requires yelling, ensuring that any possible conversation would be audible to the rest of us. They hang silently while Mercedes shuffles toward the elimination wall, clutching her side and leaning over in pain. Predictably, she sits separate from the rest of us and positions her head between her legs. Destry and Artemis exchange a smirk, and Artemis shrugs, signifying his unaltered interest in the blonde bombshell.

My stomach twists with a terrible idea, but I can't help myself. Mercedes left a dreadful first impression, but can I blame her? Tensions were high. I wasn't exactly in the best condition when Sasquatch shoved me into the Enterprize. I sigh because Mercedes is not a monster – she's a grieving orphan like me. I stare at the plastic blades of grass around my shoes and shake my head, resolving to do whatever I can to salvage her spirits and prevent her worldview from turning entirely pessimistic.

Tapping Lunar on the shoulder, I adjust to a squat. "Stay here. I'll just be a sec." Artemis watches me in my periphery as I shift in Mercedes's direction.

Lunar jumps to his feet the moment he senses my path. "No, Iris." He grabs my wrist. "It's not worth it. You heard her in the living room. She wants to go at it alone." He pulls me toward him. "Just leave her be."

Searching for words, I find myself glancing back at Artemis. His eyes are on mine, curiosity swimming at my intentions. Looking away, I take a deep breath and gently slide out of Lunar's grip. "Nobody wants to be alone. We were all a bit riled up at the start. It couldn't hurt to offer some support."

This time, Lunar yanks the back of my shirt. "Yes, it could, Iris. It *really* could."

I offer a soft smile and rest a delicate palm on my brother's shoulder. "Well, I guess I'll just have to find out for myself then." I flip on my heel and take a couple large steps to clear some space from him. I know he's only trying to protect my spirit, but he's too young to understand that no human is truly rotten. There are only souls which have been corrupted through consistent injustice and betrayal.

If I can crack Mercedes and prevent her from crossing over the edge, her spirit may be liberated before it's too late.

When I approach, she's still burying her face in her knees. Silently, I squat to her level and tap her knee with a single finger. "Hey, are you – "

She flattens away from my touch and bares her teeth. "I swear to God, if you ask me if I'm okay one more time, I will slit your throat with a toothbrush."

I press my lips into a thin line and force a sympathetic grin.

It only hardens her glare.

"I'm dead serious. I will *fuck* you up."

I bite my lip and force myself to settle beside her on the turf. "Look, I know you must be going through a lot right now. I just wanted to – "

"To what? Get on my good side so you could stab me in the back in two weeks?" She lets out a humorless laugh. "I don't know what gave you the impression that I had any interest in making friends here. But if you had any wisdom at all, you would drop it. I don't want your pity, and I sure as hell don't want to be your ally."

Mercedes stares daggers at me, and my heart pounds in my ears. I bite my lip and nod, not wanting to add any more fuel to the fire. Instead, I rise and dart away from her gaze, desperate to deflate the newfound tension.

"Understood," I say to the ground, using all my strength to lift one foot in front of the other. I've only made it two steps when her voice returns, sending a shiver down my spine.

"Oh, and lady?"

Of course, she doesn't know my name.

I turn around and smile, eyebrows raised. Mercedes's lips are stretched into a mischievous grin, and her hands are clasped in her lap like she can hardly contain her excitement.

"If you ever touch me again, I will make sure it's the last thing you do. Do you understand me?"

She cocks her head with her wild grin. Discomfort boils in the pit of my stomach. I cannot contain it for long, so I respond with an awkward chuckle when it pops over the edge. Otherwise, I don't acknowledge her comment as I grip my fists and stalk back to Lunar, fighting the urge to curl into a ball right where I stand. The impulsive piece of my soul wants to tell her *exactly* where she can shove her words. But the overwhelming majority has me slumping in defeat, because I can't ignore the fact that Mercedes is nothing but injured, scared, and alone.

And there's *nothing* I can do to help her.

Once I'm finally sliding against the back wall and back onto the turf, I let out an anxious sigh. Tipping my head back to rest against the rampart, I shut my eyes and force deep breaths through my lungs.

"That go how you planned?"

Artemis is smiling on my right, a relaxed elbow resting against his bent knee. His eyes shine with something I can't quite place, but instead of wasting my time cracking the nature of this stranger's gestures, I simply shake my head.

"She just needs time, that's all."

Lunar laughs. "To what? Carve a shiv to stab your eyes out with?"

Despite my defeat, I smile. There's a cackle from Destry and Arty's direction, soothing my nerves until I can relax against the rigid structure at my back. Nobody dares to speak another word, so Sola's counting tick climbs back to the foreground, filling the space with her strange variation of white noise.

The arena remains silent for what feels like forever, so I examine the final two more seriously. Neither struggles nor has any intention of quitting. Starvation has finally taken control over my body, but it's clear I'm not the only one. Lunar holds onto a stitch in his side and squeezes his eyes shut, making his hunger obvious. I tap on his arm and let him lean his head on my shoulder, feeling safer being close to him. We sit like this, crunching ourselves over to stifle the hunger and wait patiently for one of the men to drop and end our suffering.

When Eno announces that three hours have passed, I jolt awake and shake Lunar. Neither Mace nor Lagiacrus have moved, and the eliminated are starting to gripe. Angrily, Crescentia moves to speak for the group, standing up to project her voice to the final competitors.

"Seriously, how long do you expect us to wait? I haven't peed in *hours*."

The two turn their attention to the whiner, but Lagiacrus remains cold. He's a man with few expressions, the most prominent being stoicism. Her announcement has not impacted his intention; he continues to hang motionless. Mace, on the other hand, makes it clear that he does not negotiate with terrorists. Or, in this case, cranky teenage girls.

"There's plenty of space to mark your territory, *sweetie*. Pick a spot, any spot. You have my word that I won't watch."

I smile at his effortless comeback, and Artemis has no remorse holding back his laughter. Mace doesn't take being messed with, which may be his sexiest feature yet. He hangs onto his chain with his dirty boots crossing over one another, reminding me of yet another layer of his attractiveness. Despite the hours of spinning, his messy brown hair has remained untouched, continuing to curl over his brow. The rotations have added volume to the 'do and have somehow enhanced his appearance. Albeit for the circle of sweat that has formed on the back of his grey long-sleeve, it's difficult to tell that he's been involved in this competition for the past three hours.

His arms flex from hanging onto the chain, and each vein outlines his curves. His sleeves have no problem staying rolled up to his elbows, and I'm so drawn to his burly figure that I jerk back when Crescentia yells her response.

"Fine, enjoy the show," she yells, walking several yards away from us and removing her trousers.

"Christ," Destroy laughs under his breath, triggering another cackle attack from his newest friend, Artemis. I direct my attention to the opposite direction of Crescentia and widen my eyes as the cameras focus on her. *The Authority are disgusting.*

Just as I accept that we may be sat here for the better part of a decade, Mace extends his loyalty to end this torture and boredom.

"Hey, man. Seriously, good job. This isn't easy." I'm unsure how sincere this compliment is, seeing that neither has shown any struggle since the competition began. But Lagiacrus nods and speaks for the first time since his introduction.

"Give me your word, and if I have anything to do with death selections, you have nothing to worry about," he offers, getting right down to business. It's obvious how much Lagiacrus wants to win this. I'm unsurprised, considering the terror he has faced today; I imagine even this small victory would be a vengeance for his brother. And after the rumors Mace heard in his Rover, it appears we're all under the impression that being the last one standing will be rewarded.

"Hey, you're good on my end. If I get any power, then you're safe."

"How long?" Lagiacrus questions, expression still stoic.

Mace responds without hesitation. "Three rounds, man. You keep me safe in your reign, and you're good in my book for ages."

I drop my jaw at this offer and don't see how Lagiacrus can refuse. I wonder why Mace would agree to this, given how early into the Enterprize we are. *What if something changes? What if Lagiacrus is insane?* My nerves calm when I remind myself I'm not involved in this negotiation. It's an agreement that Mace is committing to, with the entire house bearing witness. *He may look perfect, but Mace could be the biggest idiot here.*

A short silence follows the offer, and Lagiacrus gives in.

"Deal," he says, nodding to Mace. "Shake on it?"

"It would be my pleasure," smiles Mace, letting go of his chain and landing on his feet.

The robotic voice returns to announce Mace's elimination after three hours and fifteen minutes, then strays from its regular script.

"CONGRATULATIONS: LAGIACRUS. YOU ARE THE NEW EXECUTIVE."

Chapter 6

Lagiacrus slides off his disk, landing gracefully on his feet. The two meet under the apparatus and pull their handshake into a masculine side hug, solidifying their agreement. The rest of us rise from our seats on the far wall to congratulate the man who may have the power to decide our fates.

Destry is the first of us to reach the two, giving Lagiacrus that same hand-pull, side-hug as Mace had.

"Insane, man. Big congrats," he smiles before complimenting Mace on his performance. The rest of us follow suit, with the women shaking Lagiacrus's hand and the men doing the precedented side-hug. When it's my turn, I follow a similar script.

"Good job, man. You deserve it," I say, smiling at Lagiacrus. We shake hands, and Lagiacrus nods, still stoic despite his accomplishment. I turn my attention to Mace and freeze when he's already smiling at me. I return the grin and reach out my hand.

"Impressive performance, *soldier*," I joke as he accepts my hand. Butterflies flutter about my stomach when our palms make contact.

"Impressive performance yourself, *sergeant*," he flirts, winking.

I'm entirely flustered by Mace, especially his violet eyes sparkling in the artificial light. My interest doesn't feel one-sided, but I have no way of knowing. This is my first-time meeting people outside my family, so relationships are entirely foreign.

The butterflies in my stomach suddenly halt and drop to my gut. My infatuation with Mace pains me, given how much more important it is to keep Lunar and me alive. My mind wanders to how we got to be in this position in the first place. Curi was trained to keep us a secret; seeing how well we've guided her in the art of deception, I don't see her being the rat. Somebody sold my family out, and when I get out of here and find my sister, I intend to find out who.

I make my way to the back of the group and wait for everyone to get their chance to congratulate the Executive. Embracing his new role, Lagiacrus leads the rest of us back up the flimsy, iron staircase. When he reaches the robust entrance, the mechanical locks clank open, and we exit the arena.

Lagiacrus leads us to the kitchen, indicating that I am not the only one on a mission for food. When we arrive, I examine the room more seriously.

The carpet is white like the rest of the house, but every surface is blue, from the countertops to the cabinets. There's no food in the cupboards, and my housemates share in their confusion until Mercedes opens a cabinet on the center island and huffs, slamming her fist on the table.

"Oh, you have *got* to be kidding me."

"What's up, *princess?*" Destry spits back, grimacing.

Clutching her side, Mercedes pulls out blue plastic bins with our names etched on the sides. Each container holds rations to last the day: a white roll with a cup of peanut butter for breakfast, cantaloupe slices, and a turkey-cheddar wheat bread sandwich for lunch, and freeze-dried chicken breast with a cup of rice and broccoli for dinner.

It's the most food I've ever seen. I'm in paradise with this stockpile of cuisine, but the bulkier convicts look at the bins nervously. It's safe to assume the more developed houseguests violated some food rationing law to earn their place here, making traditional rations seem meager. Having to share three of these bins for five people for the better part of ten years, Lunar and I have become accustomed to surviving on less than the government provided. *But the others might struggle.*

After she winces a few times from the strain on her ribcage, Destry helps Mercedes place the bins on the counter. Then panic erupts.

"How am I supposed to survive off this?" Mercedes complains, then points at me. "Who do they think I am? Little miss twig-bitch, over here?"

The others stare nervously at Lunar and me, anticipating our comeback. Many forms of retaliation cross my mind, but I swallow my pride and retrieve my plastic bin. Taking it by the handles, I smile at Mercedes and say, "Happy eating," flipping on my heel before she has a chance to respond.

Lunar follows me to the blue dining table, just a few feet from the kitchen island. We melt into the plush cushions of our matching blue chairs before unpacking the contents of our cases. Not knowing how long the contents will last, we decide only to dine on the lunch ration and store the rest for later.

Lunar devours his turkey sandwich so quickly that he nearly inhales the plastic wrap. I'd reprimand his horrific manners if I weren't so hungry myself. Within minutes, most of the others join us, and the room falls silent, albeit for the crunching of bread and swishing of saliva.

To Lunar's right sits the ancient-looking, curly-haired giant, Kylah. She picks at her food slowly, opting for the rice and broccoli mixture. She delicately tilts the contents of the container into her mouth, gripping the cantaloupe slice in her opposite hand. To my left is the witty, olive-skinned girl, Ashlea. Her black hair is still matted from the competition, but she ignores the mess, stuffing her face with a peanut butter-plastered roll.

Jade and Cypher sit across from me, the latter of whom eating shirtless to escape the stench of his vomit-spoiled t-shirt. The two whisper and laugh between bites of freeze-dried chicken. The rest of the group has dispersed throughout the house, and I'm relieved to be as far away from Mercedes and Crescentia as possible.

I finish picking at my sandwich and break the silence. "I guess we should pick out our beds then?"

Ashlea looks up from her bin and nods. "Yeah, I wouldn't mind joining you."

We rise from our chairs and pick up our baskets. I wait for Lunar to join, but he dismisses us. "You go ahead and pick a bed for me. I'm gonna hang out here a bit longer."

"You sure?" I ask, nervous to leave him alone with these strangers.

"Need me to hold your hand? Be brave, Iris. I know you can climb the stairs yourself."

I laugh, happy to see a glimpse of his old personality coming back. Proud of my little brother, I ascend the stairs, leaving him to converse. When Ashlea and I reach the top floor, we hesitate at the sight before us.

The locked iron door from earlier is ajar.

"Who do you think opened it?" Ashlea asks.

"The Authority?" I shrug. "Maybe they were waiting until the competition was finished?"

We walk to the room's far end and place our baskets on the two back left beds closest to the new entrance. We push open the door to the most extravagant room in the house.

The walls are blue, and the carpet is white, just like the rest of the Enterprize. But the resemblance stops there. This room is the size of the living room, and the bed could fit at least four people comfortably. The frame has four wooden posts on each corner, and the sheets are a soft grey, not harsh like the clouds in the arena, but welcoming and soft, like a cashmere sweater. There's an iron door on the opposite end which leads to a master bathroom, with floor-to-ceiling mirrors covering the wall directly to my right. A granite shower, constructed like a waterfall, sits opposite the mirror, accompanied by various soaps and shampoos of floral scents. Even the toilet is luxurious with the granite seat and accompanying four-ply toilet paper.

"Holy crap," Ashlea gasps beside me. "I've never seen anything like it."

"Me neither," I respond, flabbergasted at the grandiosity of the room. I turn to leave the bathroom but stop abruptly when I catch myself in the mirror.

I don't recognize myself. My brown hair sticks out of the fishtail braid in dramatic chunks, the top detached from the knot. The spinning competition has done a number on my appearance, and my eyebrows fan out from their usual steady lines. My face is pink, and my black t-shirt is twisted around my body. I adjust it around my torso and straighten my brows, taking one final look into my hollow hazel eyes. I smile weakly in the mirror, willing myself to feel joy. But all I can summon is the emptiness I feel at my parents' murders and the anxiety surrounding where Curi may have ended up. Careful to force my emotions down, I exit the bathroom to join Ashlea on the bed, convincing myself everything will work out.

We lay together on the plush, and exhaustion washes over me. "If I fall into a coma on this bed, don't pull the plug."

"Don't get too comfortable," a masculine voice announces. I jump off the mattress as Lagiacrus walks in smiling, the first time I've seen the man make any such expression.

47

Behind him is Destry, followed by Artemis and Mace. The four of them sit with us and sink into the mattress, making relaxing groans as they settle in.

"What is this place?" asks Ashlea, directing her question to the man in power.

"I went upstairs and there was a sign with my name on the door," Lagiacrus explains, pointing to the laminated card now sitting beside his bed. The tree and root seal covers the back in the same camouflage pattern as usual, and the front reads *LAGIACRUS*. "I guess it's some sort of reward for the Executive."

"Well, that's pretty nice!" I exclaim, trying to get on his good side.

"Gives the big man some privacy to make the important decisions," Destry says jokingly, obviously buttering up to Lagiacrus.

"Did the card say anything about what this means? What…what happens now?" I wonder out loud.

Lagiacrus takes a deep breath and stares absently at the ground. "Nothing I didn't already guess myself." He fidgets nervously on the bed. "Whatever Mace heard was right. In three days, somebody here will die. And, well…I decide two people for you all to vote between."

Silence passes over the room, and I press my lips together.

"Well…have you given it much thought yet?" I ask, looking in his general direction and nervously twisting loose strands of my hair between my fingers.

"Honestly," Lagiacrus starts, "I'm just trying to figure out what is the fairest. I don't want this first round to be about me or who I dislike. I want it to reflect on what everyone's done so far."

I consider what he's saying and make sense of it. A fair decision would have the most negligible backlash on him, so I can't blame him for this line of thinking.

"I just don't know what would be best," Lagiacrus admits. "I'll have to think about it tonight. The card says I have 24 hours to choose, so I'll sleep on it."

I look back at his card and find some smaller text below his name that I missed before. Getting closer I can finally read, "EXPULSION RISK INDIVIDUALS ANNOUNCED IN 24 HOURS."

The conversation dies down, and I rise before anything gets awkward. "Well, I'll leave you to your throne," I smile at Lagiacrus. "Again, congratulations. Let me know if I can help with anything."

"Thanks," Lagiacrus smiles. My heart warms despite our circumstances, knowing he's caught a break. After his day, I'm glad he can have some privacy.

Ashlea and I enter the main bedroom, shutting the iron door behind us. When I don't hear anything from the other side, I conclude that the room is soundproof, giving the Executive a massive advantage.

"I guess we should make ourselves comfortable?" advises Ashlea.

"Not a bad idea," I say back, sinking into the bed closest to the Executive room. Ashlea takes the cot next to me, and we save the one next to her for Lunar. We store our food containers under our bedframes and get comfortable.

"Wow," Ashlea calmly exclaims as she lays her head down. "You know, it's nothing compared to the bed next door, but I've never slept on a real mattress before."

"Really?" I ask. Of course, I've never slept above ground, but I forget others may had similar struggles.

"Yeah, we slept on hammocks," she shrugs.

"Wow," I say, shaking my head. "I've never used one before. Lunar and I…we slept under the floorboards. Not the best arrangement, but we made the most of it.

There are a few moments of silence before Ashlea asks softly, "How did you go so long without being found?"

I take a deep breath and respond as simply as possible, "We got used to confined spaces."

Ashlea smiles. "I'm sure you did." Her gaze wanders to the rest of the room, so I prompt her to bring her back.

"So, what's your story?" I ask.

Ashlea turns to me, teary-eyed. It takes a moment for her to muster up the strength, but she eventually whispers, "I fell in love."

I sit still before answering. "And that's against the law?"

She looks straight ahead at her feet before answering. "It is when they're a married man in the Authority."

I gasp. "You did not!"

Ashlea laughs. "I did too! He was twenty, married to this twenty-five-year-old wench."

I hold my stomach from the laughter.

"She was!" Ashlea defends herself. "Like Mercedes, but four-foot-*nothing*."

I laugh when I imagine Ashlea trying to compete for a man against a four-foot gremlin.

"She was in the Authority too. I'm from the Western Ascendancy. It's highest in security."

I think back to Curi's textbooks and remember reading about crime in the Western Ascendancy. Authority security members were stationed at all schools and streets to execute for misdemeanors.

"Sometimes they'd work together." She says about the mystery man and his wife, touching my shoulder to add effect. "Those days he wouldn't even look at me. It's like I didn't exist.

"But most days, he would be alone," she says more happily, sitting up straighter. "He worked security at the school, so I'd see him every day."

"What was his name?" I interject.

"Seb," she smiles. Sighing, she adds, "We'd joke around together a lot until one day, we couldn't help ourselves."

I lean in jokingly. "You give him a little smooch?"

Ashlea bursts out laughing, and I join in. "I guess you could say that."

Our laughter dies down, and the room falls quiet. "Then what happened?"

Ashlea sighs. "I don't know…things got complicated. I'm sixteen, you know?"

"Yeah," I respond. "I remember from the living room. But what's that got to do with anything?"

"I was being sent to the Assessment," Ashlea says plainly. "I wasn't going to see him ever again."

I can see the pain in her eyes and regret prying. I don't pressure her further, but she continues anyway.

"Something isn't right, Iris. He didn't want me to go to the Assessment. Like, *really* didn't want me to go."

"What do you mean?" I ask. "Of course, he didn't. He'd lose you."

"It was more than that," Ashlea says hesitantly, looking around at the cameras and bringing her voice to a whisper. "I…I feel like there's something they aren't telling us. He was so desperate that I avoid the Assessment that he —"

The iron door leading to Lagiacrus's room whips open and the boys pile out, ending Ashlea and my conversation abruptly.

"Time to leave the boss man alone!" shouts Destry to Lagiacrus as he shuts the door.

"Decided to stop ass-kissing?" jokes Ashlea to the boys, swiftly changing our subject.

"Ha, ha," responds Destry sarcastically before claiming the bed straight across from Ashlea. Moments after he settles into his new spot, Artemis claims his cot across from mine, also closest to Lagiacrus's room. I'm disappointed when Mace takes the bed across from Lunar's but I convince myself this arrangement doesn't matter. If all that's happening here is sleeping, the layout is irrelevant.

We hang out for several hours before Lunar joins us with Kylah and Eno. Eno tells stories from his childhood and imparts some old-man wisdom. We laugh about his and his friends' fun in their early teenage years and grow to enjoy his company.

Throughout the night, the group of us become more comfortable with each other, and I find myself connecting with Mace more than the rest. Artemis takes to Destry well, but the three boys together keep Ashlea and me gasping for breath between howls of laughter. When the rest of our roommates finally come to bed, we retire for the night.

When the lights darken, I close my eyes and try to keep the pleasant ending at the forefront of my mind. But no matter how hard I try to relax, I lay awake from Ashlea's story. Why was Seb so adamant that she avoided the Assessment? I attempt to get some rest, but one thing Ashlea said repeats over and over in my mind, haunting me. *There's something they aren't telling us.*

Chapter 7

Screams echo off the Enterprize walls, waking me with a start. I spring out of my bed with most of the others, surprised and fearful. My mind clears up enough to identify that the shrieks are coming from the kitchen. Ashlea and I exchange confused looks before putting our shoes on and heading for the staircase.

"Another day, another bitch fit," Artemis laughs. I'm too tired to engage, but I smile anyway. I start descending the steps, Ashlea in the lead and Artemis behind me, when the screaming becomes coherent.

"YES, YOU DID!" shouts Mercedes at the top of her lungs. Whatever rib pain she experienced from her competition collision appears to have evaporated, considering the force with which she screeches. She certainly doesn't seem to be caring about the pain now.

"Dude, you need to calm down." Cypher backs away with his hands up, still without a shirt. His skeletal frame is gaunt from malnutrition, and I can count every one of his ribs every time he exhales. He continues to carry himself awkwardly, but it is overshadowed by his anger as he backs toward our group.

"What's your problem, Mercedes?" Artemis calls down from the second floor as we descend toward the scene. I feel Jade's unsteady breath as she shifts beside me on the stairs, concerned about the predicament of her new friend, Cypher.

"They refilled our bins last night, and this *fat-ass* STOLE MY RATION!" she yells to Artemis.

"I'm not even a hundred pounds!" Cypher argues. "What makes you think I did it?"

"You were the only one down here when I woke up! Who else could it have been!?"

Cypher puts his hands up defensively. "Look, I don't know who took your food. But it wasn't me!"

"YOU BETTER WATCH YOUR BACK," Mercedes screams at Cypher, starting to charge him. "You better believe you are FIRST on my hit list!"

Mercedes winds up her right arm for a punch, but Destry grabs her from behind. "LET GO OF ME! DON'T TOUCH ME!"

"Calm down, and I'll release you," Destry says firmly, trying to diffuse the situation. Mercedes winces from her still fragile rib cage and bites down on his arm as hard as she can muster.

"JESUS CHRIST!" Destry exclaims, pushing her to the floor. "What's wrong with you?"

Lagiacrus strides into the room, and Mercedes turns to him from the carpet, out of breath and spazzing her arms. "Put up Destry and Cypher, or I swear to God!"

"You swear to God, what?" Lagiacrus shouts, baring his teeth. He marches toward her and towers over her, begging her to threaten his authority. Only then does Mercedes finally quit yelling. Instead, her body shrinks in on itself and her skin flushes.

"Right. So, you *will* sit in the bathroom until you've calmed down. You understand me?" Lagiacrus demands.

Groaning, Mercedes stomps past the living room and toward the bathroom stalls, kicking a trashcan in her path. We located these toilets and showers last night before settling in for bed; they're significantly less luxurious than the Executive's private suite, but they're functional.

"You alright, man?" Lagiacrus asks Destry, blood dripping down Destry's arm. Mace rushes from the bathroom with paper towels to stop the bleeding, hair bobbing up and down, and laser focus in his violet eyes.

"This has got to stop. Somebody has to put Mercedes in her place," Destry replies. "That bitch is already making our lives miserable."

"Oh, like you're a ray of sunshine," shouts Crescentia from the living room. She enters the kitchen furious, pale skin transforming into deep pink. "If you have something to say, why don't you say it to her face?"

"I'm not afraid of you!" shouts Destry, holding the paper towel to his arm, red bleeding through the flimsy fabric. "Come here and we can talk, man to man, *bitch*."

Crescentia sprints into the kitchen, black hair straight but sticking out wildly. "WHAT DID YOU JUST CALL ME?"

"GUYS, STOP!" shouts Lagiacrus, standing between them and putting his arms out to separate them. "This isn't your fight. Just let it rest."

Cypher, finally having removed himself from the situation, sits at the kitchen table with his head down. Jade slides in beside to him, rubbing his back slowly, whispering something incoherent into his ear.

I can't imagine getting into a fight this early into our stay, but many of these people have never experienced hunger. A stolen ration means no food for 24 hours, so it would only have been a matter of time before somebody was hungry enough to lash out. It's not lost on me that the Authority could be responsible for this mishap, trying to stir up drama to see how criminals act in desperate situations.

Crescentia accepts her defeat and stomps toward the bathroom. Deeming the kitchen safe, I descend the final steps and retrieve Lunar and my ration bins. Ashlea and I have been given new containers, signifying that hiding previous ones won't impact new rations. We opt for the couches, leaving Cypher and Jade alone to wallow in today's events. Lagiacrus and Artemis settle in beside us, and I rest Lunar's bin in the middle of the floor for when he finally appears.

We all dig in, making small talk to diffuse the tension. Once his wound has stopped bleeding, Destry joins us and whispers to Lagiacrus, "I'm okay with whatever decision you make, man. But don't you think it would be fair to pick the two most insufferable people for Death Row?"

Lagiacrus chuckles softly. "Death Row…I like it." He takes another gigantic bite from his peanut butter roll, ignoring Destry's selection suggestion.

The rest of the day is filled with my housemates filing in and out of Lagiacrus's chambers, begging for safety. It appears that he's giving every person the same speech, judging by the mutterings of "fairness" around the house. I can't help but laugh when Crescentia and Mercedes climb the stairs, intent on bargaining with Lagiacrus as a pair.

"You've got to be kidding me," Ashlea says, rolling her eyes as the two girls reach the final floor and proceed to Lagiacrus's room. The rest of us at the table laugh, and Artemis jumps at the opportunity for attention.

"Bitchy and bitchier up there, as far as I'm concerned."

I'm unsure of the genuineness of his insult, considering his earlier interest in Mercedes. Still, his need for attention outweighs his attraction to the feisty blonde. Despite this, I don't completely dismiss his chances of spending more time with her.

Several hours pass as the others make their way to speak with Lagiacrus. I opt to give him some privacy, seeing as I briefly talked with him yesterday. However, I encourage Lunar to speak with him and offer to vote out whoever Lagiacrus wants this round. I make sure he mentions that I'm willing to do the same and trust Lunar to make the offer for both of us.

An hour from Death Row selections, I slump into one of the side couches, Ashlea by my side.

Ashlea and I have spent nearly the entire day together. Unfortunately, she hasn't expanded much on her love affair, but I've managed to tell her a bit more about Lunar and my upbringing. Ashlea is becoming a fast friend, making my stay at the Enterprize much less miserable.

We're eventually joined by Mace and Artemis, two people I've managed to inadvertently avoid all day. Anytime we've crossed paths, the two have been together. They are occasionally joined by Destry, Finian, or Jade and Cypher. But regardless of who joins them, the two have become inseparable. Mace and Artemis sit beside us and begin making small talk.

"So," Artemis says suggestively. "What's your type, Mace?"

My ears perk up, and Mace laughs at the question. His violet eyes lock with Artemis's blue as he replies, "Well, my mother's blood was B, and my father was A, so what does that make me? O?"

Ashlea and I clutch our stomachs from laughter, and Artemis sarcastically rolls his eyes to the ceiling. "First of all, no. Not even close. Second," he says, lightly slapping Mace's arm, "What's your type of *woman*?"

Ashlea and I smile, looking over at Mace and awaiting an answer. Mace effortlessly quips back, "Oh, woman! Occasional Neanderthal, but primarily Homo sapiens," he says, sending me a wink. A squeaky laugh escapes my throat, and immediate embarrassment flushes my cheeks.

"What was that?" Artemis exclaims, pointing at me in my bashfulness.

"What!" I shout, trying to recover.

"Was that a cat?" Artemis laughs.

"Oh, shut it," I say between cackles. "What's your type, *Arty?*"

"Predominantly those who don't call me Arty," he responds, smiling. He looks at me a second too long before the room quiets, and a shiver runs down my spine. Our humor is highly compatible, and I love that my comfort around him allows me to show Mace my true colors. I snap back out of this line of thinking when Shaela, Lunar, and Eno sit on the other couch, reminding me that one of us is days away from being killed.

One by one, the rest of our housemates join us on the couch and get comfortable, some more anxious than others. Sola's nervous shaking is at an all-time high, and her whispered counting has sped up drastically from her usual rhythm. She sits on the opposite couch from mine, clenching and unclenching her fists in tempo with her counting. Finian sits beside her, pale skin now pink, and orange hair drenched from sweat. The conversation dies down, and I hear Ashlea's heart pound beside me.

Eventually, fourteen of us smush onto the couches, avoiding the two black chairs at the tail end of the room. Apparently, they are reserved for those on Death Row, so we all avoid them like the plague. I'm not feeling particularly nervous until I'm hit with a gut-wrenching revelation.

My stomach drops. *How could I not see it?* Paranoia clouds my senses, and I can't stop myself from turning to Ashlea in a panic.

"Ashlea," I harshly whisper. "He said he's basing it on what's fair, right?"

Ashlea looks at me wide-eyed, disturbed at my sudden urgency. "Yeah, he told everyone that."

I look at her desperately and grab her arm. "Do you think he'll put me and Lunar up? Because we were a team before this even started?"

Ashlea opens her mouth to gasp but quickly closes it and whispers back supportively. "No, I don't think he'd do that. He was supposed to be here with his brother, too. I doubt he would punish you for having yours."

My stomach calms at this, but I sweat so much that I drench the collar of my shirt. Ashlea reaches for my hand before squeezing it and gazes into my hazel eyes. "Iris, you don't have anything to worry about. He likes you, and Lunar is hardly an advantage. He's young…he's weak. Don't sweat it. You're going to be okay."

She smiles at me weakly, and I return the expression, thankful for my new friend.

Lagiacrus finally descends the stairs, hands stuffed in the pockets of his ripped jeans. His face contorts in remorse at the position he finds himself in.

He plants himself at the front of the room, opting to stand rather than sit in the giant solo chair behind him. He awkwardly removes his hands from his jeans and clasps them behind his neck. The room is hauntingly silent, and most people stare hollowly at the floor.

"Hey guys," Lagiacrus starts.

Most of us look up from the floor in respect, but Sola can't seem to escape her empty trance.

"This is obviously…uncomfortable. I wish I didn't, but I have to pick two of you for Death Row," he starts, embracing the term Destry suggested. "I've spoken to everyone here about my intentions. I'm going to make this as fair as possible."

I look to Ashlea for reassurance, and she returns a smile.

"Your past doesn't define you; I'm not interested in that. I'm making this decision as unbiased as I can. So…I've thought a lot about it…and the only thing I can fairly judge you on is your performance yesterday…in the competition."

This is the first time I've seen Mercedes and Crescentia look nervous. The two once confident and menacing women now show immense respect for Lagiacrus, telepathically willing him to keep their names out of his mouth.

"That being said…Sola and Eno," he slowly announces, turning his attention to them. "You were the first two eliminated yesterday." He gestures his hands to the daunting black chairs across from him. "Please…take a seat on Death Row."

Chapter 8

Screams erupt, and I deflect my gaze to the walls, away from Sola's horrific screeches. Eno lifts himself from the overcrowded couch and gradually makes his way to the left Death Row settee. The rest of my housemates are silent, allowing Sola's screams to reverberate.

For the first time since entering the Enterprize, Mercedes and Crescentia soften their gazes and contort their faces in pain. Finian, sitting directly beside Sola, rocks back and forth with his ears covered, holding back tears. Usually firm and fearless, Destry has turned green, sick with sympathy but flooded with relief.

I exit my trance and reach for Lunar. My stomach drops when I notice his hyperventilation. His eyes have widened in horror, and he's crunched his body into a ball of fear. I want this moment to end. I *need* this moment to end.

Lagiacrus shifts uncomfortably from side to side before shuffling up to Sola and offering a hand. This heightens her screams, and they crescendo toward the kitchen, leaving us little room to escape her terror.

I can't take it anymore. I launch to my feet and yank Lunar's hand without a word of explanation. He willingly takes it, running behind me as we shoot for the stairs. I don't know where I'm going, the floor ahead of me blurring into a fuzz. But I intend to get as far away from Sola as possible.

We stride up the white steps, skipping plush platforms to reach our destination quickly. The walls around me start closing in, and the once-luxurious home becomes a nightmare. The white carpet has turned from an optimistic, comfortable hue to an inescapable, petrifying prison. The blue walls transform from a welcoming beacon of hope to a taunting metaphor of freedom and opportunity, which are forever out of reach. I hate this place. I hate everything about it, and I am determined to get out of here.

We barge into the bedroom and sprint to my corner. Opting for the floor, we curl up with the wall at our backs, letting my mattress block our view from the rest of the room. Lunar seizes my pillow and buries his ears, his body shaking uncontrollably while tears stream steadily down his face. He rocks back and forth, so I fight back my tears and fully commit to my role as Lunar's protector.

"Shhhh, it's okay. It's okay," I whisper to him, rubbing his back and forcing my voice to be steady.

Lunar is now bawling. I bring him into a hug, continuing to whisper encouragement. I speak desperately, just as much trying to calm myself down as my little brother.

He lets a loud whimper escape his throat just as Kylah crests the steps. Looking around frantically, she calls for my brother. "LUNAR?" Her voice shakes but is direct.

"Back here!" I shout from our hiding place. At this moment, I wish nothing more than to have a singular moment of privacy to grieve and cope. Instead, ten cameras point at us, focusing on my brother's meltdown. Hatred boils within me as I picture those who trapped us here, circled around a television screen and drunkenly howling with laughter. I ball my fists so hard they lose color and rise to destroy the cameras around us. But Curi pops into my mind, and I tell myself to stay strong. If not for me, for her and my brother. *The only two people I have left.*

Kylah rounds the corner and covers her mouth with her hands.

"Oh, Lunar," she says softly, voice breaking. She hurries the last few steps and buries Lunar into a hug. He cries in her arms, and I'm thankful my brother has yet another person to offer protection. I continue rubbing his back softly, and Kylah and I sit quietly, waiting for his sobs to run out.

"I…I can't do this," Lunar cries, covering his face with his palms. "Our family, gone! We…we're next!" He sniffles. "What are we gonna do…and Curi!? *There's just no way out!"*

My breath catches in my throat.

"I'm so sorry. You deserve so much more. And I wish I could give it to you. There's just no way out."

"Mom," I say delicately, bringing her into a hug. "Stop. We're okay. It's okay."

She sniffles and releases me. "I love you two so much. If there was a way out of this, I would—"

I break from my daze as Lunar enters a fresh bout of sobs. Sola's screams echo throughout the bedroom, and my anger boils so violently that I can't take it anymore. I rise from my squat beside Lunar and rip my blankets from the mattress. I throw them against the wall but get little satisfaction. I feel this foreign, intense desire to slam something. *My mother: dead. My father: dead. My sister: alone. My brother: suffering. And there's NOTHING I can do about it.* I can no longer stifle my trauma and feel a rush of urgency overcome my senses. Punching a wall will only hurt my chances of succeeding in any physical competition, so I search desperately for an alternative. I'm seconds from screaming at the top of my lungs, but I hold back when he materializes at the top of the steps.

Violet eyes stare into mine, so potent they glow across the room. Mace runs his fingers nervously through his hair, cresting at the end of the curve over his brow. This is the first time he hasn't exuberated confidence, adding terror to my already shaken demeanor. He shuffles toward the group of us, sorrow in his eyes.

"How is he?" Mace asks.

I feel deeply uncomfortable, my attraction to him attempting to distract me from the matter. But Lunar's sniffles keep me authentic, and I push aside Mace's allure, accepting his concern.

"Her screams are frightening him," I say, looking back to Lunar as Mace hurries over. Once behind my bed in our makeshift hiding place, we crouch to my brother's level.

Kylah lets go of Lunar, and he matches Mace's gaze. Tears continue to stream down Lunar's face, but the shaking has slowed.

"It'll be over soon, I promise," Mace whispers to Lunar. "You're going to be okay! You saw her when she entered this place, didn't you?"

Lunar nods, but he can't stop hyperventilating.

"She looked like a Morphflux addict!"

Lunar cracks a smile, but his eyes continue to glisten with moisture.

I'm surprised he's even heard of the addictive painkiller, but I won't question him. I never thought I'd be so relieved that he's familiar with illicit drug names.

"It's not going to be like this every round, Lunar. It's not. She was already fighting demons before stepping foot in that Rover."

A shiver runs through Kylah, and her body briefly shakes at this admission. *What happened to Sola?*

"She has to stop soon," Mace continues. "If not, her voice will run out soon enough. Right?"

Lunar nods his head, and Mace extends his left hand.

"Are you going to be okay if I leave you with these two beautiful ladies?" Mace asks my brother with a hint of reassurance.

Lunar nods and wipes the tears from his face. Sola's screams vanish as if on cue, and we finally sit in silence. Mace rises and starts to exit the bedroom, and I chase after him.

"Hey, Mace!" I call, his name feeling strange coming from my mouth. I'm so infatuated with him that even acknowledging his title makes me uneasy. He turns around and raises an eyebrow.

I finally reach him and have no idea what to say. We stand silently for a moment, and Mace smiles at my apprehension. "I just…how…why did you do that?"

I look back and gesture toward a calm Lunar, speaking quietly with Kylah.

"Do what?" Mace smiles back at me.

"Help my brother…why'd you run up here and help us?"

Mace smiles and raises an eyebrow. "First off, I didn't *run*." He lets a soft chuckle escape his lips. "Second," he pauses and points at Kylah. "He has two great women in his life. But sometimes a thirteen-year-old needs an older brother.

"Besides," he says, softening his voice. "Why did you try and comfort Mercedes when you knew she was a lost cause?"

I step back and examine his face more clearly. "How – how did you know about that?"

Mace smiles, inching closer to me. He traces a gentle thumb down my forearm, making my skin erupt in goosebumps. His breath is hot against my temple, and I gulp back the urge to pull him against my waist. "You act like I wasn't stranded on a metal swing with nothing to do. You really think I stared at the turf when, all the while, the most beautiful woman I've ever seen was making a hopeless yet…*touching* display of compassion?"

My back starts arching, and my eyes are inching closed when Mace turns around and walks down the steps, leaving me still in the center of the room. I hear laughter behind me and turn to see Kylah giggling uncontrollably at something Lunar said, his face painted with a smile.

I shake my head and call out to them, "Just what do you think you're laughing about?" I stroll back to my bed and sit on top, beaming at the two of them.

"Nothing!" Kylah and Lunar yell simultaneously, causing a fresh bout of laughter.

I chuckle and pick up my sheets from where I threw them on the floor. I slowly make my bed while Lunar and Kylah chat quietly, laughing on occasion. Lunar's sobs are distant memories, so I trust him alone in Kylah's company.

Smiling, I start heading toward the staircase.

"I'm going to check on how things are going downstairs," I call over my shoulder. Lunar and Kylah nod, and I enter the battle zone.

When I reach the living room, I don't find Sola. Apparently, Jade and Cypher escorted her to the bathroom, so any restroom urgencies have been put on hold for the night. The house's ambiance has transformed into a depressive grief zone, with most others sitting quietly with their heads in their hands. I force myself to stop a grimace when I see Artemis with his arm around Mercedes as she cuddles up against him. I can't help but feel a twinge of anger at the sight, especially considering how well he and I get along. His humor is intoxicating, and despite our friendship being new, weak, and barely established, I feel oddly protective of who he spends his time with. Perhaps it's because I want to spend more time with him. Maybe it's because of how close he is with Mace, and Mercedes could sour Artemis's perfect friend. Whatever the reason, I don't like how interested he appears to be in her.

I join Ashlea on the blue settee, which I am suddenly repulsed by, and regret joining the others. Beyond Artemis cuddling up with his malevolent acquaintance, the scene before me is dispiriting. Eno eventually rises and mumbles something about turning in early. He shuffles past the kitchen without a flinch, even though he skipped dinner. He nods at Crescentia, who sits alone at the dining table, and continues his journey to the bedroom. Destry and Finian speak quietly on the couch across from me, soft enough that I can't eavesdrop.

"What if I give her my room for the night?" Lagiacrus asks, interrupting our dejected trance.

"It's up to you, man. If that's what you want to do," Destry responds, careful with his words.

"If it blocks out her screams, it could be a good idea," Mace suggests from the sofa across from me. "Just to keep people calm."

"I feel like it's the least I could do," Lagiacrus responds, walking to the bathroom to share the news.

The rest of the night is gloomy and slow. Before Death Row selections, the certainty of our fates hadn't completely set in. Having been hidden for fifteen years, I was admittedly excited to meet new people. I blocked out the circumstances of our situation in my quest to make friends and avoid foes. I have no doubt that the excitement of the past forty-eight hours had the same effect on a lot of the others. No longer with anything to distract me from my nearly inevitable fate, I am terrified.

I speak with Ashlea half-heartedly, but we produce no meaningful conversation. The night's events were too horrific, so my only option is to sleep away the terror.

A few of us turn in for bed shortly after Eno, Ashlea and Destry included. I twist and turn for an hour, replaying Lagiacrus's announcement on an endless loop. I focus on my last-minute panic. The proclamation of fairness. Sola's nervous twitching before the decision. *Her screams after.*

I'm frozen in my bed with fear until Artemis and Mercedes enter the room, hushing their laughter. Mercedes slaps his shoulder softly and cackles; my fear quickly subsides as annoyance takes its place. They are the last two upstairs, so I imagine they've been alone for the past twenty minutes. My head hurts when I consider why their new friendship annoys me so much. Perhaps it's because he speaks so poorly of her to the rest of us. Perhaps because I know he can do better.

Several restless hours pass while my trauma slams down upon me. Images of my parents sprawled motionless on the floor flash behind my closed eyelids. I see blood splattered across the peeling wood. Then there's Lagiacrus, wailing with his face smashed into the dirt. I'm even flashing back to when the Authority kicked Mercedes into cooperation. None of the horrors make any sense. Why put up this production when they could have just shot us with our parents? Why, amongst all the criminals in Miasmis, are *we* being tortured? I shiver thinking about Curi and where she may have ended up, praying that our neighbors took her in.

My stomach drops and twists in my torso when I hear the cameras whirl, reminding me that we're being broadcast to the entire country. Whether families want to watch our suffering or not, we'll be holographic residents in millions of homes until this competition has reached its conclusion. The shock our neighbors must feel, watching Lunar and me on television and realizing our parents' crimes. I take a deep breath and commit to being brave for Curi. I bury my fearful spiral of where she may have ended up and comfort myself with the knowledge that our neighbors don't have a child and wouldn't be punished for taking Curi in.

The longer I lay, the worse my imagination becomes. So, when another hour passes like this, I accept defeat. Rising from my cot, I quietly hike down the spiral staircase, going round and round until I reach the bottom floor. Then, I stride through the kitchen and plant myself on the closest sofa.

I lay down with my head closest to the Death Row settees, feet settled near the Executive couch. Relaxing with my eyes open, my pupils adjust to the room's darkness. Turning the lights on would be a death wish, so instead, I locate the blinking red glow on the cameras above me and count the cameras around me, trying to pass the time while simultaneously attempting to induce sleep. *Fourteen cameras.* I move on to the blinking lights and watch the clock. *Thirty-two blinks per minute.* My process is working, and my eyelids grow heavy. I'm moments from shutting them when I see a tall, muscular figure on the other side of the room.

"Can't sleep?" Artemis asks, plopping onto the couch across from me.

"No way," I say quietly, concealing how startled I am. "You?" I feel another twinge of anger at him over his sudden closeness to Mercedes, but I do my best to hide my childish grudge. The last thing I need is to make myself a target over something trivial.

"No chance," Artemis replies, lying on his couch as I am, our heads on the same ends so we can look at each other.

We sit in silence for what feels like an eternity. Knowing my history with Lunar, only muteness can hide bitterness, so I have no intention of keeping our discussion alive. Unaware of my irritation, he breaks the ice.

"How are you holding up?" he asks, turning to face me. The red blinks on the cameras light enough of his face that I can see the genuine concern in his eyes. One look into those blue eases and I can't hold back from cooperation.

How can a single look make me trust him so deeply?

"As good as you'd expect, I guess," I say without feeling. We stare at each other for a few quiet moments, and I can't help but succumb to my friendly adoration for him. Deciding this cold shoulder act goes against my best interest, I continue with more emotion. I shrug and expand, "Lunar's taking all of it pretty hard."

"Yeah, I saw that," he replies, rubbing the side of his head. "Is he okay?"

"He'll be alright," I answer. "Mace really helped him out. Sola's screaming just set him over the edge."

Artemis nods. Silence passes between us before he gets the courage to speak again.

"I should have checked on him."

"Stop," I respond quickly. "He's okay now. Mace knew exactly what to say."

"But I could've helped."

An awkward tension fills the air. Artemis directs his gaze to the ceiling, and I regret bringing up Mace. Despite their solid friendship, there appears to be an odd sense of competition between them. I can't identify why, but I want no part in the immature feud.

We sit without conversation for several minutes, and the horrors threaten to haunt me again. I push them back as hard as I can, but the awkwardness consumes me. Wanting nothing more than to joke around with him, I extend a truce. "Tell me a story."

"A what?" Artemis laughs, blue eyes once again beaming into mine.

"A story, something funny," I request. "You're funny, right? Make me laugh."

Artemis chuckles. "Okay, I can do that." He racks his brain before beginning. "You know I pranked the Authority once?"

I turn in shock, making the couch shake. "You *what?*"

Artemis laughs. "Probably not my best idea."

I join his laughter and inquire for more.

"Well, it was a couple of years ago. I was fourteen, so just older than Lunar," he says, gesturing upstairs at the sky-blue ceiling toward my brother. "And…well, there was a particular officer…and we didn't mesh well."

"Well, don't just leave it there," I exclaim, tossing my hands up. "Why didn't they like you!"

Artemis laughs. "Me and two of my friends would hang out a lot, right? Well, this government prick didn't like us *loitering*. I mean, come on. *Loitering*. How else are we supposed to hang out? I mean…whatever. So anytime he saw us together, he'd yell and chase us home…sometimes with the beating rod."

"Western Ascendency?" I ask, knowing the violent history of the region.

"Oh yeah," Artemis says. "One day, we had enough. I mean, come on. *Beating children?* Give me a break. So, when the time came, we skipped class. Got in big trouble with our parents for that one," he notes lightheartedly. "But that was the only time we knew he wouldn't be home."

"Oh god," I smile. It's exciting for me to imagine life outdoors. Even now, I'm still trapped inside a house, just a much larger and more luxurious one than before.

"We all came prepared, mind you. I brought my honey ration, Anthony had poison ivy remnants from his backyard, and Jeremy had his black bean allotment for the month. We got lucky; he left his hovercraft at home that day.

"I mean, it was a simple enough prank. Honey in the mailbox, poison ivy on the door handles, and beans in the Plastygas tank."

"Beans in the *what?*" I smile, eyes bright and glossy. Centuries ago, Miasmis replaced fossil fuels with liquid plastic, transforming waste into an energy form. Thus, Plastygas was created.

"Beans in the Plastygas tank, of course! Haven't heard of that?"

"No, of course not," I laugh. "We didn't plot many pranks under the floorboards."

Artemis pauses, embarrassed at forgetting my background. "Well, it was hilarious. Imagine his face when an ant colony took residence in his mailbox. Or how he was out with poison ivy for a week. Or my favorite—"

"His car not working and finding the beans in his Plastygas tank?" I ask expectantly.

He laughs. "Yes, that was the best one. We waited hours outside his house to see his face. A very long twelve hours, but worth every second."

We chuckle together for several long minutes. Once we've caught our breath, I ask something that's been admittedly bothering me.

"Does that have anything to do with why you're here?"

His lips stretch into a frown. He looks at the ceiling and replies, "Yeah, not quite."

Several moments pass before I realize he won't share without prompting.

"You said the first day that you probably deserve to be here. What did you mean by that?"

He laughs. "The first day? You mean yesterday?"

I pause. "Has it really only been one day?"

He laughs. "Feels like a lifetime." He looks back at me and stares, a smile plastered on his face.

"What?" I say back, matching his smile, familiar with his habit of lingering eye contact.

"Nothing," he says, beaming.

"Are you going to tell me anything?" I question him. "Like…what's with you and Mercedes?" The question escapes my lips before I can stop myself. But I'm so curious, angry, and *frustrated* with their relationship that I can't help myself.

Artemis bursts into laughter, almost loud enough to wake the others. "What about it?" he says with his cheeky grin.

"I don't know…one second, you hate her. The next, you're connected at the hip. I mean, honestly. Pick a lane," I quip with my palms to the sky.

Artemis continues laughing, flattered that I care. "Okay, what about you and Mace? What's up with that?"

My breath catches in my throat. "Come on, don't joke about him."

"Why?" Artemis says with a grin, showing off his crooked teeth.

"Because I actually really like him."

Artemis pauses. He presses his lips flat, and his eyes turn sullen. "Well…then you should tell him."

"Right, like that would ever happen," I laugh.

"Why not? If you like him, why not do something about it?"

"Come on, this is hardly the circumstance for romance," I say regretfully.

"I guess," he responds, clenching his teeth. His attitude has completely changed from the start of our conversation, so I attribute it to his need for sleep.

Matching his fatigue, I feel a rush of exhaustion. I rise from the couch and direct my voice back to Artemis. "I should get some rest. I finally feel up for it."

"Glad I had that effect on you," Artemis retorts with a smile.

I laugh back and shoot, "Good night," in his direction. I step away, but Artemis's voice cuts my stride.

"I was a part of a covert refugee operation."

I stop in my tracks and spin around. "A what?"

He gulps. "Don't worry about it," he says, shaking his head. "I just wanted you to know that I'm not here for hurting anybody. I just…I was trying to protect people."

"From what?" I ask quickly.

"Really, Iris. It's nothing. I just…I'm not a bad guy, okay?"

I stand still, overcome with confusion. "I didn't think so," I say back uncertainly. "But why do you care what I think about you?"

"Just…please remember that, okay?" he responds mysteriously. I'm so confused, but my exhaustion makes me resign my efforts.

"Okay."

I turn back around to make my way up to the bedroom, but I'm halted once again by his delicate voice.

"Goodnight, Iris."

"Goodnight, Artemis," I respond. Then, I quietly stride up the steps.

Chapter 9

"*If you ask me, she isn't helping herself.*"

Cypher's whispers travel toward me, and I wake with a gentle start.

"It's like she's given up," Jade contributes quietly. "It's probably best to put her out of her misery."

I squint my eyes, but it is pitch black in the bedroom. Laying perfectly still, I can just make out Jade's hair, straight as a pencil. Ashlea is on her side, conversing with the duo. They clearly don't know I'm awake and probably assume I wouldn't be able to hear them with how quiet they are. But living in the silence under the floorboards has spared my ears, so I can hear everything.

"Have you spoken to anyone else about it yet?" Ashlea pipes in. "I just want to vote with the group, so if everyone's voting out Sola, I'm in."

I fight my shock and keep completely still. I've never seen Ashlea speak to the pair, so the entire dynamic is utterly confusing. I decide she'll either fill me in on their conversation later or is playing harder than I realized. Ashlea is the only person I trust outside of Lunar, so I pray she's not making deals behind my back.

"Not yet. We were going to start spreading it around tonight. The voting is tomorrow, so we don't have much time to waste," Cypher answers.

Ashlea shifts uncomfortably. "Well, keep me in the loop. If anything changes, just make sure you tell me."

After some hushed assurances, Jade starts to prompt Ashlea.

"Are you feeling safe for Round 2?" she asks, voice raising an octave.

"I mean, I don't see how I could?" Ashlea responds carefully. "Unless I'm Executive, I don't think it's possible to feel comfortable."

"I guess…" Jade replies with a heavy sigh.

"I'll just say if Mercedes wins, we're screwed," Cypher says plainly.

"You want her out?" Ashlea asks so quietly I nearly miss it.

"She's public enemy number 1," Jade responds. "The way she walks around like she runs the place? Insufferable."

"And that whole ration thing? Give me a break," Cypher interjects. "I didn't take her goddamn food." He leans in closely to Ashlea. "We want her out, *badly*."

Ashlea just nods her head and shrugs. But Jade and Cypher won't accept neutrality for an answer.

"Who are you going after if you win next round?" Jade pokes. "Mercedes?"

Ashlea squirms. If she says she supports Mercedes, she's pinning herself as a target for the duo. But agreeing with them could incriminate her should Mercedes come into power. Ashlea contemplates her response while Jade and Cypher lean over, nearly bouncing off their toes.

"It's hard to say," Ashlea responds. "We haven't been here long, so I really don't know what I'd do. We have two full days for things to change. So honestly, I have no clue."

Cypher nods before pushing further. "You wouldn't put up me or Jade, right?"

I continue to hold my body still despite my racing heartbeat. I become less suspicious of Ashlea having a secret alliance and grow concerned that they're setting her up in a trap.

"No," she replies. "Unless something drastically changes, I'm not targeting you two."

"So, you're targeting Mercedes, then?" Jade quips back. Their eyes glow as they lean over her.

"As I said," Ashlea begins, "I don't know what I'd do."

Jade and Cypher slouch with disappointment. Before they can push any further, Ashlea shoots back, "I'm going back to bed. Let's just talk more later, okay?"

"Sleep well," Cypher says, crossing his arms and turning for the stairs. The pair march away, and Ashlea cuddles back up for sleep.

I close my eyes to prepare for slumber but lay awake in paranoia.

Can I trust Ashlea?

Chapter 10

The kitchen table erupts in laughter. Today's entertainment consists of Eno's old man stories enhanced by Mace's dramatic facial expressions. The cameras focus on the two, zooming in and out to ensure complete focus. Our rations are identical to the past two days, but I'm not picky. I nibble on my grainy turkey cheddar sandwich as I have been for the past half hour, chewing in between laughs and savoring every bite. I supplement my meal with a little extra from my stored bin the first night; the staleness doesn't bother me, considering the sheer quantity of food.

"But how did you get away with that?" Mace exclaims.

"Wait, what happened? I missed it!" Lunar whines, taking the seat beside me.

"Well," Eno begins, abandoning his sandwich to focus on storytelling. "You have to remember; this was thirty years ago!"

"Oh, so crimes were forgiven then!" Mace announces, putting his hands up in a grand gesture to emphasize his sarcasm. The table consisting of Eno, Mace, Ashlea, Artemis, Destry, myself, and now Lunar erupts into another bout of laughter, Lunar having no idea what the joke is about.

Eno turns to Lunar to catch him up. "I was born into the Authority. Both of my parents were members, so they had their company-issued hovercraft. When I was a child, probably ten or eleven years old, they ran out of Plastygas right when they dropped me off at school.

"Well, they were arguing about what to do, and I'm in the back seat now twenty minutes late for reading time!" Eno exclaims with a smile. "Mind you, our hovercraft is now dragging on the concrete, no fuel keeping it afloat. And they wouldn't let me in the school until this whole debacle was sorted, so I took their siphon, went to the only other hovercraft in the lot, and emptied their Plastygas tank."

The table continues their laughter, and Lunar kicks off in a more extravagant bout of cackling.

"What?" Eno questions with a wide grin, "It was just the school's Authority officer's craft, so not a big deal."

"Um, how did they ride home?" Mace questions, smiling.

"And why did you have a siphon in your car?" Ashlea chimes in.

"You see," Eno begins with a grin stretched across his lips, "that's on a 'need to know' basis." Eno leans back in his chair, hands clasped behind his head.

"Any advice for us young'uns?" I ask with a snort. "Or just delinquent tales?"

Eno laughs and directs his attention to me. There's a short pause before he jokes, "Don't break the law. You might have to swing around on a quarter for two and a half minutes."

I laugh so hard, I hold my stomach to soothe the ache in my abs. It takes a full minute to catch my breath. The others are in similar positions, struggling to breathe through their gasps of glee.

"There's more where that came from," Eno jokes as he rises, giving a boastful bow. "Keep me here, and I promise to last about that long in all future competitions."

We're all smiling as he rises from his chair, holding his back and shaking while he shuffles to the sink. His gigantic display of elderliness is even funnier because he's only middle-aged. But being more than twice as old as anyone here establishes him as the old man, and it's great to see him taking his label in stride.

The rest of us talk around the table for another half hour, saying nothing important but making the time pass. One by one, my neighbors pack up their trash and move on to a different space in the house, trying to diversify who they converse with. But I sit motionless, mesmerized by Mace and his ability to make anyone feel like the world's most important person. With every passing discussion, Mace watches the speaker with focused eyes, holding onto their every word. Desperate to learn more about him, I stick around until we're the final two at the table.

Mace turns to me with a bounce. "So, what do you want to talk about?"

He beams at me, and I laugh. I shake my head and try to match his energy.

"Oh, wow. If I had to pick *anything*," I start with a playful eye roll, "how about the weather? Wonderful weather we're having, isn't it?"

He laughs, admiring the plain walls. "Oh yeah, not a drip of rain in the forecast!"

We chuckle together, and despite how depressing it is that I've never felt a drop of rain in my lifetime, Mace makes me feel like I can laugh about anything.

"You know, I've never felt rain before," I state the obvious. "We weren't allowed outside, so I've only seen it through holes in the window shades."

Mace nods and draws his eyebrows together, fully engaged in our conversation shift. "What was that like?" he asks. "I can't imagine being on house arrest."

"Oh, it wasn't too bad," I joke. "Every day's a vacation, right?"

Surprisingly, Mace doesn't entertain my sarcasm. Instead, he puts his chin in his hands and directs his full attention on me before prying, "No, seriously. How was that?"

There's silence between us, and I contemplate my response. His violet eyes gaze into mine before he continues. "I heard the gunshots, Iris."

I flashback to my parents, motionless on the wooden floor. "I mean…," I try to control the shakes in my voice but can't contain my anguish when bringing back my trauma. His stare sends a chill down my spine. "I just did what I had to do...to not get shot, I mean." His eyes focus on mine, and my stomach jumps from the tension. Regardless, I push through. "And keep my brother and sister safe."

"Sister?" Mace asks, lips stretched in a line across his perfect skin.

"Curi," I croak. "My little sister. The only one who is supposed to live."

"Iris, what are you doing here?" Mace asks, making me feel as if nothing else in the world matters. "What was your crime?"

"I mean, I guess it wasn't really *my* crime…" I begin, immediately regretting putting the blame on my deceased parents. "I could ask you the same thing," I pivot, smiling. "Why are you here? What did you do, *criminal*?"

Mace doesn't laugh. Not even a smile spreads over his face as he continues to pry.

"This isn't about me," Mace says, leaning in. "I asked you first."

Finally, Mace smiles at me, and I'm overcome with the urge to speak.

"Well…my parents were too young. When they had me, I mean." I twist my thumbs under the table and continue. "My mother wasn't thirty yet, but she managed to have me and my brother just a few years apart."

Mace nods.

"Obviously, if she said anything, we would all be dead. So…I don't know. We lived in secret. Under the floorboards, where nobody would find us. Well…finally, a few years later, Curi was born. And not just born, *legally* born.

"I mean, my parents were thrilled," I begin. "And honestly, so was I. She's everything to me…everything Lunar and I couldn't be."

"Because you had to be a secret?" Mace interjects. His eyes stay wide, unblinking. I start picking at the underside of the table, feeling the wood flakes ricochet off my thighs as they fall.

"Yeah," I begin, stumbling over my words. "I resented my parents for years over it. But after a while…once you realize nothing's ever going to change…" I shrug. "I guess I just learned to push back my emotions. I learned to put on a brave face for them."

Mace rests a hand on my knee and leans closer so I can hear him whisper. "That's not fair, Iris. You shouldn't have had to bottle everything up to keep them happy."

I stop picking at the table and freeze. My stomach flips upside down with how close he is. My instincts tell me to back away, but I lean into the tension.

"I needed to teach Curi to lie. The best way to do that was to understand it myself." I'm watching his lips with such intensity that I shiver, and he scoots closer from his concern. I scoot to the back of my chair and smile, nervously pushing a strand of hair behind my ear. "The trick is to convince yourself that it's the truth. I kept telling myself that they tried to give us everything they could, given the circumstances. It's just…there's only so much you can do when your kids shouldn't exist. You know the rationing laws…food was sparse. Really, this is the most food I've ever seen."

"What is she like?"

"What?" I ask.

"What is Curi like? Are you two close?"

"Oh yeah," a smile takes over my lips and my legs cross onto the chair. "Curi is everything to me."

There are a few moments of silence between us as I imagine Curi. "Tell me about her," Mace leans back in his chair, as attentive as before.

I chuckle, squeezing my arms between my legs. "I don't even know where to begin."

"What is she like? Start there."

Mace's interest sparks electricity in my heart. His genuine concern about my life, about my family…it's impossible to keep myself from sharing. And to be honest, I don't want to hide it from him.

"She's the funniest, cutest, smartest little girl in the world."

"Now, how could you know that if you lived in the floor?"

My muscles tense at the words. Swallowing hard, I turn around to a plain-faced, mid-bite, angry as-always Crescentia.

"Can we help you?" Mace asks, rolling his eyes.

"Just living on planet Earth if you care to join me on the couch." She winks at Mace and stalks to one of the empty sofas, flipping her hair so dramatically she has to claw it out of her eyes. She recovers and tries to be graceful, but her feet are clumsy as they stomp across the carpet.

"Well?" I smile at Mace, raising my eyebrows and gesturing over my shoulder at his admirer.

"I'd rather stick pins in my eyes, Iris. *Pins.*"

I laugh as Mace rolls his violet pupils and takes the seat next to mine, forcing Crescentia out of his view. He grips the sides of the table and pushes his chair closer, making the table sway. "Now I'd love to hear about how smart and cute and funny Curi is. Please, flatter me." His smile is genuine, and his eyes sparkle with admiration. I rack my brain for something relevant and let out a small chuckle.

"Well, there's that time a bird got in the house. Curi chased that thing like a cat." I laugh. "She's always had this love for animals, and when we had an avian visitor, she went nuts.

"My Curi time was exclusive to the indoors, so her love for creatures, insects even, is something I rarely got to see. I mean, how often does a bird fly through your front door?"

Mace smiles and nods for me to continue.

"When my mother got the broom…Curi was distraught. She cried for half an hour, *begging* our parents to leave it alone. When they finally did, Curi was in heaven. She chased that thing for hours. Wouldn't shut up about its colors."

"What were its colors?"

I smirk from surprise. "Surely you don't care?"

"Curi isn't the only one who admires animals."

Time slows as I recall the beautiful creature. "It was blue…light blue. Like the sky."

Mace smiles but doesn't speak. I blink hard to relieve myself from the pain. "We had that bird for hours…named him Stephen." Mace laughs but still doesn't interrupt.

I want to be alone, but his lure intrigues me enough to stay. "That's it, really. Curi chased the bird, got water for it, and brought some seeds into the house. Pretty sure it was just a pile of dirt, but the girl tried." I smile at Mace and am flushed with embarrassment. "Probably not that great of a story…I'm sorry to disappoint."

"What are you talking about?" Mace asks, eyes wide. "I loved it. What happened to Stephen?"

I smile at the name but turn solemn, staring down at my hands. "He eventually got out. Probably flew back to wherever he came from."

"Maybe he was changed? Maybe her love made him want to stick around?" I look up and meet his gaze and feel as though we're the only two people in the world.

"I guess I wouldn't know," I respond in a daze. Silence passes between us.

"I'm sorry…" he says, biting his lip. "I'm sorry that she's gone. Not like…gone-gone. But you know. I'm sorry that you're here. And that you've never felt rain."

I look into Mace's eyes and feel the electricity. His honest concern and the kindness emanating through those violet oases. His love for anything and everything human.

"Why are you at the Enterprize?" I ask, tilting my head.

Mace smiles and shakes his head, grabbing the edge of the table. "I can't wait to hear more about you and your sister, Iris." Still grinning, Mace hoists himself up and saunters up the plush white steps.

Ten minutes later, I'm still blushing.

Chapter 11

Hours pass with me staring at the iron slab that separates Lagiacrus from the rest of us. I ran on the high from my conversation with Mace for several hours, but now that it's worn off, I dread my decision between Eno and Sola's death. And it is not a decision I take lightly.

Equally as daunting, a new Executive will be crowned just after the execution. Lagiacrus has received written instructions from the Authority on tomorrow's schedule and told us that we will be voting secretly. We'll have one button for each name and must press the title of the person we wish to…eliminate. We'll have ten minutes to decompress, or as they wrote, for the Authority to "dispose of the remains" before we begin the next competition. Staring at the barrier between the communal bedroom and Lagiacrus's chamber, breathing becomes a chore, and eating is impossible. Knowing it can't get much worse, I finally approach the iron slab to communicate an elimination consensus.

And do my best to convince him to keep Eno alive.

My knuckle hits the hard surface, and the door cracks open, revealing only a sliver of light from the neighboring room. Destry's face pokes through the hole and, upon recognition, whips open the iron blockade, inviting me inside.

I stumble into the extravagance when I see Destry, Mace, Artemis, Lagiacrus, and Finian already gathered. I could have assumed the first four would hang out alone, but *Finian* is a surprise. Despite his Leprechaun-like appearance, he has done an exceptional job of lying low. Apart from the quarter-hanging circus ride, I've barely seen the man in my three days in this prison. "Am I…interrupting anything?" I ask, eyes wide.

"No, you're just in time," Destry begins. "We're making a plan for tomorrow."

"You mean who to vote out?" I ask, taking a seat on the floor. I'm careful to get an unobstructed view of the others without bringing attention to myself.

"Bingo," Mace says, turning to me with a friendly smile. I fight a blush as butterflies flutter in my stomach. My redness starts to burn when I remind myself that somebody will die. I force back my foolish feelings for Mace and replace them with disgust at our position.

The room is still, everyone nervous to take charge of the conversation. Finally, Artemis breaks the ice.

"Well…I feel like we can all agree that Sola is a trainwreck."

The crowd nods, most tightening up or turning pale. Artemis, forcing back a tremble, continues. "But you're the Executive this round, Lagiacrus. So, you should have the final say on the vote."

"Thanks for that," Lagiacrus starts. "But I don't want it to be all on me. A group decision would be best, and if we can talk to the others and make it a unanimous vote…that would be great. No need to split the votes this first round if we can prevent it."

"That's fair," Destry butts in with support. "All in favor of Sola?"

Artemis and Finian raise their hands, but Lagiacrus and Mace keep their arms stiff at their sides.

"Wait," Mace interjects. "I feel like we need to discuss this a bit before voting. Agreed?"

Artemis and Finian drop their hands before nodding.

I've been motionless throughout the exchange thus far, trying to find a natural way to suggest Sola's expulsion. *Not execution.* Expulsion makes this more bearable.

Lagiacrus is the first to speak his mind. "We all agree that Sola is a bit…unstable. But we shouldn't just give Eno a free pass. You saw him at breakfast this morning. The house loves the guy. Isn't that kind of a threat?"

"But what is he ever gonna win?" Mace asks. "The man is as athletic as this tabletop," he says, motioning to the glass table his legs rest on.

"But what if it's not just physical competitions?" Destry asks. "If they throw something mental in there, he could have a shot."

"Yeah, and Sola is so unstable she wouldn't be able to win regardless of what we have to do," Destry responds. "We know Sola is alone in this game. Why don't we capitalize on that?"

The conversation favors Eno's execution, and I won't let that happen.

"If you're scared of his intelligence, why not team up with him?" I suggest.

The five boys turn to me, some having forgotten my presence, and silence passes over the group.

"That's not the worst idea I've ever heard," Mace smiles, looking to the others for support.

Destry tilts his head, holding his chin between his forefinger and thumb. "Go on."

I pick at my fingernails, not wanting to get overly involved in case word gets out that I want Sola expelled. But I know I can't shy away from expanding; weakness is never well-respected. So I drop my hands to my sides and project my voice to the room.

"It's not like you'd have to be best friends with him…you could just get to know him more so that he's in your back pocket in case you need him. Like you said, having Sola on your side would do nothing to advance your game. But with Eno's social game, he might save you from expulsion without you having to lift a finger."

Destry raises his eyebrows and turns to Lagiacrus. Both smile wide before Destry turns back toward me.

"Hell," Destry laughs, clapping his hands together once. "I don't have a buddy yet…I can try and get close to him. Like Iris just said, it'd steer him away from targeting us."

The others nod, and I finally realize what's happening. *This is a team.* And not just any team. An all-male team that *I am a part of.*

"Wait," I interject, shifting the attention back to me. "Is this an alliance?"

All five guys burst into laughter, Artemis howling louder than the rest. "I'm glad you were able to gather that, *detective.*"

I scrunch my face at Artemis to match his sarcasm before taking a deep breath and bowing my head. *I am in an alliance. I am safe.*

"Wait," I realize. "What about Lunar?"

Destry raises his eyebrows. "Based on your suggestion, you already know the answer."

I squint at the others, tilting my head. Finally, Lagiacrus catches me up to speed.

"The other night, the five of us met up. We got to talking…and we think you'd be a great addition to our crew."

A smile spreads across my face. I take advantage of this inadvertent reaction and joke back, "Well, I'm happy to bless you with my presence," and curtsey with exaggerated form. I get some chuckles from the group and continue, "But I don't see how that has anything to do with Lunar?"

"You do, though," Lagiacrus starts. "You see, the six of us alone…we're not that dominant. But the six of us *plus* everyone having somebody on the side? That's unbeatable.

"You have Lunar, who you can persuade to do anything. If you vote a certain way, it's probably safe to assume he will, too." He waits for my reaction, and I nod in agreement.

"So having you on board is great for the whole group! And we can keep you and your brother safe until the final seven…but you can't tell him about us."

"What?" I gasp.

"The second we're exposed, we're screwed," Destry interjects. "Our collective strength is also our weakness. The second our side alliances gain wind that they're not in the main bubble, they *will* retaliate."

"I hate to say this, Iris, but if you tell Lunar, he'll probably just tell Kylah," Mace says. "I know it sucks to lie to him, but being honest could ruin the entire operation."

It takes me a second to comprehend the importance of this secret, but if keeping it from Lunar will help him survive, I'm willing to lie, cheat, and steal.

"I'm in."

The others clap, and Artemis gets up to pat me on the back with his giant palms. "What's even better is you've got Ashlea under your wing," he says. "So, it's three for the price of one! Maybe even four if you count Kylah."

"What about you guys, then?" I ask the others. "Who are you getting on board?"

"Well, Artemis obviously has Mercedes," Destry suggests. Artemis nods his head, and my stomach gets an uneasy rumble.

"Mace is working on Ashlea," Lagiacrus announces. "Which should be easy enough…you two hang out a lot." *You two hang out a lot.* Who is he talking about? Me and Ashlea? Me and Mace? *Is Mace only hanging out with me to get close to Ashlea?*

"We're working on the last two but keeping Kylah could make things interesting. And now that you've pointed out Eno…we've got our missing piece."

Lagiacrus does some calculations in his brain. "Yeah…that could work. Destry, you get close to Eno, and Finian, you get close to Kylah. Start planting seeds now, keeping us safe. But above all…we keep the core together. We come first."

The others stand and put their arms in the middle, watching my next move. I look from Mace to Artemis, both encouraging me to rise and join. But the reality is…I don't have a choice. I want Lunar safe, and the core six does *not* involve him. But I'm doomed if I refuse the offer and branch out now. This core controls the house, and regardless of how Lunar fits into that right now, I have to go along with it.

I rise and put my hand in the middle. The others smile at me, and I summon the courage to look Destry in the eye.

"Until the end."

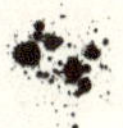

We test potential team titles and finally land on Dial FM. It combines the first initials of our names, so we settle on it to make time for more meaningful discussions. *Like who to send to their death.*

"It's decided, isn't it?" questions Lagiacrus. "There's not much need to keep discussing if we want Eno on our side."

We reach a consensus on Sola, and I'm ready to put the conversation to rest until Destry sighs.

"Yeah, probably best to put her out of her misery."

This is far from the first time somebody has spoken of Sola's complicated past, and being out of the loop frustrates me to no end.

"What do you mean by that?" I ask, the others staring at me blankly. "Everyone keeps talking about putting her out of her misery or her fighting demons. What do you know that I don't?"

My new team members look at the floor or shift their eyes from mine, uncomfortable sharing their knowledge. Finally, Lagiacrus gives me something to work with.

"I mean…I only found out yesterday. And I was in the last Rover, so I'm just taking everyone's word for it."

Lagiacrus looks at Destry, holding his breath. Destry continues gazing at the floor, so Lagiacrus continues with deflated encouragement, blonde hair shaking from the discomfort in his body.

"Destry, why don't you tell her? And I'll do a final recon of the living room and see what everyone's up to. Start planting some seeds." He rises slowly from the enormous mattress. "I really don't think I can stomach hearing about it again."

The others sit in silence before jumping in line to leave. One at a time, Artemis and Finian rise and follow suit, each shooting back some form of "me neither" or "I'll catch you guys later."

Mace is the last to leave, eyes glossing with moisture. I can feel his regret when he shuts the door, leaving me alone with Destry.

Destry rises and sits across from me on the floor. It's in a friendly way, to comfort me at whatever terrible news he has to share. But there's a personable way about how he interacts with me. Like there's no romantic interest, no genuine care. It's almost like everything he says is…

Transactional.

"Iris," he begins. "You know how you and Lunar were some of the last ones captured?"

"Yeah, I was there," I say plainly, frustration building from this dramatic revelation.

"Well…Sola was picked up right before you. Remember?"

I think back to the warden and remember standing alongside my brother, shaking arms restrained behind our backs. To my left was a mortified, muttering Sola, completely inconsolable from whatever terror she had escaped.

"Yeah," I say, "she was freaking out before we even made it in here. What are you getting at?"

Destry takes a deep breath.

"Iris, I was the first one arrested."

I gulp, having not even thought about who may have been first. Considering this, his calmness at the start finally makes sense. The way he took control of the situation, comforting the others, it's obvious now that he had more time to process the abduction than the rest of us.

But my heart also wrings with this reveal. Destry being in Rover 1 means that he had to watch every kidnapping that took place. Every execution, every emotional eruption, and every struggle for the inhabitants of the Enterprize to avoid the competition they are in now. I experienced two other kidnappings. Destry experienced them all.

He shyly smiles at the shock on my face and methodically contorts his expression into remorse.

"Nearly everyone saw what happened to Sola, Iris. The only ones who didn't are Lagiacrus, Mercedes, Lunar, and you."

He takes a deep breath before continuing. "Remember our introductions? She's sixteen years old. The girl is a kid, just like the rest of us. When the Authority came, Sola was outside…sitting beside a barren oak tree in her yard, nearly dried to a twig. When she stood up…"

Destry pauses, reliving the story. I wait patiently, considering what could have happened when she stood up. *She tripped? She was tased?*

"She was holding a baby."

Chapter 12

My mouth falls open. I try to blink, but my eyelids won't shut. My chest thuds hard, my heart trying to break through my ribcage. When I finally gain enough strength to speak, I stutter. "Sh…she…she what?"

Destry shakes his head. "Don't make me say it again, Iris."

I swallow hard, feeling like there's a rock lodged in my windpipe. "But…that doesn't make any sense…who's baby was it?" I ask. "She's *sixteen.*"

"Iris, it was *Sola's,*" his voice shakes. "It looked *exactly* like her…it couldn't have been anyone else's."

"But…" I jerk my hands above my head. "She's *our* age? It's *illegal.*"

Destry jumps from his spot across from me and starts pacing the floor. "Ever wonder how she ended up here?"

Silence passes between us. "Sola's…a mother?"

Destry nods, eyes locked on the ground. He answers quietly, almost soft enough for me to miss it. "*Was.*"

I plant my hands on my head and try to rise, but my legs won't cooperate. The horror and shock quickly dissolve, leaving room for a more prominent, all-consuming feeling.

Pure, unequivocal *fury.*

"You mean to tell me," I spit at Destry, "The Authority *murdered* Sola's *newborn infant?*"

Destry stands in silence. Frozen in his horrifying memory, he's lost the strength to communicate.

But I can't back down.

"You're saying," I grimace, finally forcing myself to rise, "that the Authority…showed up to her house…*murdered* her few-month-old child *in her arms*…and *dragged* Sola's body into the Rover?"

Destry stays frozen for several moments before closing his eyes and giving the slightest nod of confirmation.

I whip my head back and forth. "Where does it *stop,* Destry? How can they do this?" I start pacing. With each word, my volume intensifies. "We're going to kill this girl…*just* like they killed her child! What makes us any different from them? We're *just* like them if we go through with this!"

My lapse in judgment snaps Destry back to reality. His eyelids shoot open, and he grips my shoulders. "Iris, stop! We've been over this!"

"What are we gonna do? How are we gonna get out of here?"

"IRIS!" Destry yells, saliva hitting my cheek. "Get yourself together! We need you…stop talking nonsense! If we don't cooperate, they'll just kill us too! You need to hold yourself together!"

The shouting distracts me from the iron door opening behind us. But when Mace walks into my field of vision, my muscles loosen, and I scrunch my eyes to hold myself together.

"Iris," he says, eyes wide. Destry backs away from me, inviting Mace to approach. "Are you okay?"

"How can they do this to us, Mace?" I say, forfeiting any effort to gain his fancy. I squeeze my hands into fists to fight the urge to yank on the Enterprize front door and run for freedom.

"Hey, hey, hey! Iris, *look* at me. LOOK AT ME!" Mace says, grabbing my shoulders like Destry had. But unlike Destry, I feel a sensitive touch with Mace. An intention to help, not for a transactional purpose but rather a heartfelt one.

I meet his violet gaze and freeze from my attraction. My nerves soothe at his tender touch, and his body language calms me enough to speak clearly. "What are we gonna do?"

"We're going to take it one day at a time," he starts, loosening his grip. "We've got Dial, right?" It takes me a second to remember Dial FM, and I finally nod in recognition. "It'll be impossible for us to get…*voted out*…at least in these first few rounds."

I nod and notice Destry on the bed, head in his hands. His distress would be contagious if not for Mace's calming gaze. My nerves finally vanish, and I'm left with only admiration for him. I'm seconds from surrendering all my fear, but one final concern holds me back.

His violet eyes give me the strength to voice it. "And after that?"

Mace looks back at Destry before meeting my eyes again. He takes a deep breath, squeezes my left arm delicately, and whispers soft enough for only me to hear.

"We navigate this game together. I'm not going to leave you. I give you my word."

"Your word?" I smile at him, the corners of my mouth barely curving.

Mace's right hand floats toward me, pinky finger outstretched. My breath catches in my throat. I've only ever known one person to seal a promise like this.

"Pinky swear."

Chapter 13

With life moving slowly in the house, I have several hours to process how I will fight for Eno's safety. But as long as I stare at the blue walls, an answer doesn't come. How can I tell people who to kill? If I'm the one securing the votes for Sola, doesn't that make me responsible for her death? My stomach turns, and my anger intensifies at the role I've been given. As a last-minute addition to the alliance, it's not beyond my notice that I'm being taken advantage of for having to secure two extra votes instead of one. But focusing on this only distracts me from the pain of ending someone's life.

How am I to turn easygoing conversations into ones revolved around murder? What gives me the license to tell Ashlea who to vote for? Getting Lunar on board is easier…his safety is my top priority. If he votes against the group, he'll be the next target. When it comes to Lunar, my desperation to keep him alive outweighs my terror of murder.

I flashback to last night's hushed conversation between Ashlea, Jade, and Cypher. The duo didn't seem to mind advocating for Sola's execution and pressuring Ashlea to hop on their bandwagon. Whatever Jade and Cypher went through before the Enterprize must have done a number on their concept of life and death. But it's still too real for me…would it mean my soul is corrupted if I pushed for Sola's death too, given the circumstances?

Perhaps I can avoid the action all together. If there's one benefit to Jade and Cypher's evilness, it's that they've already pushed Ashlea to vote out Sola. It occurs to me that I don't *need* to control Ashlea. Because even if the duo's murmurings weren't enough to persuade her, Jade and Cypher have made their position clear. With them voting out Sola…the result is secure.

I shiver and bring my knees to my chest. *Sola is going to die tomorrow.* I hate having the responsibility of controlling her fate. I may only be one vote of twelve, but that does little to stop the stream of sweat pouring down my back. Trying to calm myself, I start flashing through the black-and-white details. I am not the person pulling the trigger. She had a chance to keep herself safe and failed. And surely…this decision is for the best. *Right?* Soon, she will be reunited with her child. The two will lay below a fleshed-out, deep green pine tree, cold wind rushing through their hair.

Somehow, the thought makes everything worse.

"Hey," Lunar says, joining me on my bed. "How's that wall lookin'?"

I'd usually smile at the quip, but it takes everything to keep myself from trembling.

"Everything okay?" Lunar asks. Tomorrow's reality hasn't set in on him yet. He's still using humor as a distraction, and his lightheartedness stings me.

I shake my head and whisper. "How are we going to kill somebody tomorrow?"

Lunar's energy shifts and his body deflates. He shakes his head in unison with mine.

After taking a deep gulp of air, I lean into his ear. It destroys me to speak about murder this way, so I rip off the Band-Aid to quicken the horror. "The house is voting out Sola tomorrow. So are we."

He drops his head, putting it in his palms. "So…that's it then? That's how we decide death around here?"

I stare blankly at the blue wall ahead and nod. "It's barbaric." A tear threatens to fall, but I sniff it back.

Knowing my standard method of stifling emotions, Lunar puts a hand on my back. We sit together in silence, letting our breaths heave together.

After my tantrum in the Executive room, I stopped asking how the others ended up here. As it turns out, most have merely avoided going to the Assessment. I assume this concerns the fear of abandoning their lives and families. I'm empathetic to this, especially when imagining how I would have dealt with Curi leaving for the Assessment.

Since Lunar left me hours ago, I lay alone in my bed, left to my thoughts. Before long, Destry's experience looms. My throat tightens, imagining him watching every murder and kidnapping in a row. Through the grapevine, Ashlea heard that Destry avoided the Assessment, much like Jade and Cypher. She didn't reveal her source, but I didn't bother to ask.

After tossing and turning for an hour, I abandon sleep and make for the bathroom. Shuffling down the steps, I bump into Eno coming the opposite way. We nod and smile at one another, and I'm relieved that my vote has a positive aspect as well. I…may be aiding in Sola's murder…but at least I'm saving this man's life…. *even if it's just for another round.*

My body shakes, so I grip the railing to descend the final steps safely. Finally, on the ground floor, I freeze when Jade and Cypher disappear behind the ration counter. Curious, I trek close to the island and hear the unmistakable sounds of laughter and kissing.

Rolling my eyes, I back away from the counter and beeline for the bathroom. *Kissing? Already?* I shake my head and complete my journey to the restroom stalls.

Before I can open the door, Mercedes bursts through, howling with laughter. Pretending I don't exist, she slams the door into my side. Taking a quick look behind, she skips toward the staircase, arms swinging back and forth like a windmill. "Good night, Artemis-*sweetums!*"

My eyes widen, and despite the emotional stress I've dealt with today, I can't stop a grin from spreading across my lips. Artemis has an effect on me…no matter what is going on around me, I can be myself and have fun when I'm with him. I'm thankful his friendship distracts me from the horrors of the Enterprize.

When I open the bathroom door, I catch Artemis with his hands pressed across his forehead. He looks up and meets my eye contact, electrifying me. With today's toll and tomorrow's daunting task, I don't completely open back up. But enough of my personality returns to give Artemis a suggestive eyebrow raise, forcing him into a burst of cackles.

Artemis rolls his eyes. "Shut up."

I chuckle back, more of my character returning. Opening my arms into a dramatic shrug, I widen my eyes and smile brighter. "I didn't say anything!"

Artemis's blue eyes sparkle, and he can't erase his blush. "You didn't have to."

I let a soft laugh escape my lips before approaching the sink. I catch him watching me in my periphery, but I ignore his gaze. I turn the nobs and splash the lukewarm water on my face, prepping myself for another attempt at sleep. Turning the water off, I gaze to my left and right, searching for something to dry my face. Finally, I look at Artemis, who has watched the entire scene.

"Um…do you have a towel?" I smile, eyebrows scrunched together.

Artemis laughs and reaches to remove his shirt. Adrenaline shoots down my spine, and I wholly forget my responsibility tomorrow. "Woah there, mister! Let's not get naked now, alright?" I back up smiling, hands up in surrender.

Artemis laughs even harder, then stops and stares at me, blue eyes glossy and bright.

"What?" I ask. "Don't laugh much with Mercedes?"

He lets out a few more cackles before responding, "Yeah, something like that."

His lips press together in a soft smile. I shake my head, wafting my face dry with my hands. Grabbing the edge of the grey marble, I hoist myself onto the sink and let my feet hang. Artemis watches and laughs.

"You really are something else, Iris."

He keeps chuckling, enjoying my awkward sense of humor. Once dry, a coldness flows through me; the reality of his role as the 'Mercedes vote wrangler' sets in. The toll she is taking on him is clear, and my heart pinches that he's been entrusted with being around her.

"Can I ask you something?" I try to make the question as casual as possible, but I'm desperate to hear his honest opinion on Mercedes.

Artemis smiles. "You just did."

I roll my eyes. "Ha, ha." He laughs before meeting my eye contact again more seriously. "I just…why are you doing this?" I ask, pursing my lips to the side.

"Doing what?" Artemis asks.

I lean forward. "Pretending to like Mercedes? It's clearly taking a lot out of you. Why don't you just pick somebody else?"

Artemis's eyes get cold. "It doesn't work like that, Iris."

"What do you mean?" I urge. "You shouldn't have to do this."

"Let it *go*, Iris," Artemis complains, turning his back to me. His aggression surprises me, so I do my best to backtrack.

"Sorry. It's just…*I'd* be fine with you switching. Why would anyone want her vote, anyway?"

"Iris, there's a reason for everything around here. *Don't you understand?*" Artemis's breathing picks up, and when he turns to face me, his nostrils are flaring.

He leans closer with a whisper that cuts through my skin.

"What if none of us win Executive next round? Then what? If we keep someone around who people hate and is a big target, not only do we have their vote, but we can convince the others that she needs to go. People don't just do things around here for no reason, Iris. *How do you not understand that?*"

I wince at his words and back away. I search for any way to salvage this friendship and grasp at straws. "Artemis," I stumble, "I'm sorry! I'm sorry if I hurt you…I didn't know things were that calculated." I throw my hands up. "That's on me!"

Artemis takes a deep breath. "There's a lot of things you are oblivious to around here, Iris."

"Okay, Arty! I'm sorry," I begin, talking so fast that I'm holding my breath. "Can we forget about this and move on? I'll never question your actions again, okay? *Please* don't be upset with me."

Artemis raises his eyebrows and then plants his eyes on mine. His ocean eyes gloss over, and he hangs his head. "Sorry. It's just…taking a bit of a toll on me. I mean…the voting tomorrow."

I nod and tap the counter beside me, inviting him to sit. "Me too."

We sit in silence, our breath the only noise in the room.

He sighs. "It just isn't fair."

"Life isn't fair," I shrug. "We just have to try and do the best with what we have."

He shakes his head. "You know…I had a good life outside of here. Friends…a family. All gone. And now…any friend I make in here is temporary. Because if I make it out, they're all dead. If any of *you* make it out…well, then *I'm* dead."

"That's not all true," I start, resting a hand on his back. "You still have Anthony and Jeremy." I made an effort to remember his friends' names—the ones that helped him prank the Authority.

Artemis's breath catches in his throat. He turns to me slowly, eyebrows scrunched together. "Iris," he says. "*They're all dead.*"

"Wha—what?" I stumble. I know the Authority are cruel, but they rarely kill for sport. Whatever crime his friends have committed, he's failed to mention it to me. "Why? What happened?"

Artemis takes a deep breath. "We've got a big day tomorrow. Maybe…I could tell you some other time. Honestly, going forward…anyone in my past is dead…understood?"

His eyes twitch, holding back tears. He abandons my gaze and looks back at the floor, done with the conversation.

I shift closer to him and wrap my arm around his torso. "I'm so sorry, Arty." The sarcastic nickname has turned from a flirtatious mocking to a mark of friendship and trust, deepening the sentiment. We sit motionless, but my fingers twitch relentlessly. The silence makes me itch to find something, *anything* to brighten him up. Finally, I hit the jackpot.

"Hey," I say, backing away from him with a shy smile. "This might cheer you up."

"What?" Artemis asks, raising his eyebrows. His frown remains, but his eyes are hopeful.

"You'll *never* guess what I saw on my way down here," I begin, a crack of laughter in my voice.

"What*ever* did you see, Iris?" he asks. His eyes match mine, and the corner of his lips now point in a smile.

"Everyone's favorite Enterprize romance, Cypher and Jade, swallowing each other's faces."

Artemis laughs, exhilarating me.

"You're joking, right?"

"No!" I smile, throwing my arms up. I lower my voice to a hyper-soft whisper. "They were hiding behind the ration counter!"

He continues to laugh, and our bodies sway from our amusement. Feeling more confident from his reaction, I continue.

"I mean honestly," I smile, "why would you kiss somebody you met *three* days ago?"

Artemis's laughter halts. He sits completely still, turning away from me and gazing at the floor.

"What?" I ask Artemis, hitting his forearm. "What is it?"

Artemis finally meets my gaze, and his eyes twist in deep regret. He might be a swift liar, but I'll always be able to read through those ocean eyes.

I wrack my brain for what could have him so remorseful. When it finally hits me, my stomach twists with a deep ache.

"You didn't."

Artemis can no longer handle my gaze, so he turns his head away. Confident he can't see me, I make a snap decision on how to react.

I laugh.

Artemis looks at me with flushed cheeks. Once he realizes I'm not angry, he sinks his body back against the wall in relief.

"You," I laugh, "kissed," my cackling builds, "*her*?" I burst into a crescendo of laughter, sure that he will feel better knowing I don't view him differently. It's incredibly forced, but I'm a good enough liar to pull it off. *This* is why he wanted me to know he's a good guy. *This* is why he was so angry when I suggested he ditch her. He doesn't want me to judge him for pretending to have a relationship with Mercedes when it's for the benefit of the group.

Artemis laughs and smiles, one eyebrow raised. "You don't care?"

"Why would I care?" I laugh, "You're doing what you need to survive…to protect your team. Really…I couldn't care less, Arty."

His cheeks flush with relief. After a few minutes of giggling, I shake my head and match his gaze.

"You do what you need to," I say, climbing down from the sink. "But tomorrow's a big day…and I need some sleep."

He smiles, eyes glistening. Nodding, he lets out one final laugh. "Goodnight, Iris."

"Goodnight, Artemis." I roll my eyes with a grin and bounce out the door.

But the second I reach the living room, my gate slows. The further I get from the bathroom, the more my feet drag on the carpet. My smile fades with every stair ascended, and when I finally reach the bedroom and tuck into my sheets, my energy is depleted. Tomorrow's vote lingers, but this depression is different. It peaks when I spot Mercedes on the opposite side of the room, whispering to Crescentia with a smile showing all her teeth. Rolling my eyes, I pull the covers over my chest and watch the wall separating me from Lagiacrus's bachelor pad. Despite every trauma I've faced today, only one thing runs through my mind.

Artemis and Mercedes kissed.

And for hours, I don't sleep a wink.

Chapter 14

Curi's oversized shirt envelopes her skeletal frame, and she tugs on the sides relentlessly. She hasn't aged a day since our pinky promise, but her usual pluckiness has drastically shifted to agitation.

"It's swallowing me!" she shrieks. "Can't I wear some of Iris's old clothes?"

My mother strokes her arm, hushing her. "Sweetheart, you know that could risk our secret. If you wear her old clothes, people will wonder where they came from! We can't endanger the family. I'm sorry, but you must wear your father's work shirt."

Lunar and I exchange a confused look, tilting our heads and squinting our eyes. "Well, that doesn't make any sense," Lunar retorts. "How would that give us away? Explain that to me."

My mother opens her mouth for rebuttal but immobilizes when the pounding begins. Our bedroom floorboard shudders from the hammering within, and we all stand frozen in fear. Our eyes search the room, counting our family, concluding that we're all already here.

"Mom?" Curi's voice shakes as she runs into our mother's arms.

The floorboard bangs thrice before flinging off the hinges and shooting forward. We're all statues, frozen from terror, waiting for the creature to unveil itself.

A gigantic hand plants itself into the light. The figure hoists itself from the shadows, and I gasp.

"Artemis?"

He fades into darkness while another, less inviting figure takes his place.

"LISTEN TO ME!" Sola shouts, violently shaking my shoulders and forcing me into consciousness. It takes a moment to gather my bearings, but my vision no longer blurs at the edges, confirming I'm awake. Sola's grip slips down the length of my arms, my sweat making it impossible to keep a steady grip on my body. Her eyes are wild with animalistic desperation, pupils dilated and hungry for brutality.

"What's going on!? What do you want!?" I shout, completely forgetting the Enterprize and forfeiting any previous conception that I am an emotionally stable individual.

Her brunette hair is soaking wet, knotted, and sticking to her face in clumps. Her grasp has slid all the way to my wrists, her body on top of mine to prevent escape. She screams at the top of her lungs, and my eardrums vibrate at the limit of their capacity.

"DON'T VOTE ME OUT. YOU CAN'T VOTE ME OUT! DON'T VOTE! THAT'S WHAT YOU SHOULD DO! DON'T VOTE AT ALL!" She starts sobbing, her body heaving. Instead of releasing me, her grip on my wrists tightens. "DON'T KILL ME! I DON'T WANT TO DIE, PLEASE DON'T KILL ME!"

Her weight on my diaphragm starts to aggravate my breathing, and I no longer have the air to protest. The world around me blurs. The only thing I can concentrate on is her terrifying transformation from horror to manic laughter. Her hold on my body vibrates from her bizarre cackling, and I brace for faint as her feral eyes fade from my consciousness.

Suddenly, my stomach is released, and Sola slams against the wall beside me. I catch my breath in time to see Mace towering over my aggressor, violet eyes unrecognizable from their dilation. He picks her up and pins her against the wall.

Spit flings from his mouth when he speaks. "What the *hell* do you think you're doing? Are you out of your goddamned mind?" he shouts at her, still pinning her to the wall.

Sola bursts into demented laughter, losing sanity by the second.

"Iris, run downstairs! *Now!*" Mace directs at me as I scoot away from Sola. I nearly fall off the bed but catch myself, clumsily regaining my balance and sprinting across the bedroom.

I fight to stay up as long as possible, but my hurried pace keeps me stumbling along my path. When I finally reach the staircase, I grip the handrails and hop down three steps at a time. The world around me distorts, but I focus on the ground ahead. When I finally reach the bottom floor, I stride past the kitchen and living room before yanking open the bathroom door.

The door slams shut behind me, and I have no recollection of trapping myself in one of the accompanying stalls, each having its own iron slab, ensuring my protection if Sola were to attack. The iron door before me, usually ice-cold and daunting, feels like a haven since it's the only thing keeping me from murder through maniac suffocation. The turn of events is lost on me as tears stream down my face. The whole experience is out-of-body, the dissociation causing me to watch myself from above as I have a panic attack on the cold hard tile.

I gasp for air, but nothing's entering my lungs. I choke on my tears and bury my face, waiting for my respiratory system to surrender. *At least my demise will put an even smaller target on Lunar's back.*

I rock back and forth with my head between my knees but halt when I hear pounding. Much like the vibrations of the floorboard in my dream, the door throbs with fists bashing, and I cover my ears to lessen the terror.

"Iris, it's Ashlea! Open up!" my newest friend shouts through the door, begging me to let her in.

I'm frozen on the ground, unable to comprehend her intentions. She continues smashing the barrier, trying to convince me to let her in. Only when I hear Lunar's voice do I snap out of my dissociation and reach for the handle.

Ashlea and Lunar pile into the room, unprepared for me to obey. They collapse beside me but rebound quickly, bringing me into a hug and rocking me back and forth.

It takes ten minutes of hushed encouragement before I can comprehend the situation. I look up out of my hands, finally calm enough to string words together.

"What…just…*happened*?"

"Iris…I don't even know what to say," Ashlea stutters.

The composure I've managed to hold since my parents' murders finally *cracks*. "She's a lunatic!" I exclaim. "Where the *hell* did that come from? I wake from a nightmare, and she's *choking* me to death?"

"Shhhh," Ashlea urges. "She's lost her marbles, Iris. From what she's been through…"

"I DON'T GIVE A *FUCK* WHAT SHE'S BEEN THROUGH!" I yell. My frustration at their pity blows me over the edge. Whatever anger I felt at the Authority for her child's murder has wholly transformed into rage against *her*. I try to remind myself that she's not in control of her actions…she may be having a psychotic episode. But it's difficult to convince myself it *wasn't* intentional when I can feel the bruising already coloring my neck. Perhaps I'll feel for Sola's loss once the excitement of her attack has worn off. But being seconds from death has temporarily emptied me of any empathy toward her. "We've all been through hell! That doesn't mean she can strangle me!"

"IRIS!" Lunar yells, grabbing my face and forcing it to look at his. "In four hours, she's out of here…*gone*! You have to calm down. Everyone saw what happened! Nobody will keep her now!"

The tears pour once again, and my body trembles harder. *Who else will descend into madness?* Ashlea and Lunar comfort me until I calm down entirely. Once my tears have dried and I find my voice again, I beg for answers.

"What…happened?" I ask once more, this time with clear intention.

They look at each other and shiver before deflecting their gazes to the ground. Ashlea twirls her fingers on the tile before answering. "It's like…his life depended on saving you."

Lunar nods but keeps his eyes on the ground.

"Who? Mace?" I ask. "I mean, thank *God* for him. I'd be dead without him!"

Ashlea shakes her head but doesn't say a word. Lunar and her shiver once more, and my heart rises to my throat.

"Is somebody going to tell me what's going on!?" I shout, not caring if the rest of the house hears me.

Ashlea continues drawing circles on the floor, so I finally burst.

"Sola woke me *in a chokehold*," I yell, "and Mace saved my life."

"But Iris," Lunar begins, "we're not talking about Mace."

I look between the two of them and throw my hands up. "Then who *are* you talking about?"

Ashlea stutters. "We…we're talking about Artemis."

"Art— Artemis?" I ask, narrowing my eyes on them. "What does he have to do with anything?"

"Iris," Ashlea starts, "When you ran downstairs…Mace was trying to calm Sola down. He didn't want her to hurt you…you know. He was just trying to protect you. But Artemis…" she looks at Lunar who puts his head in between his knees again.

"What? What did Artemis do?" I plead.

"Iris, he just went in," Ashlea tells me, biting her lip. "Mace was trying to protect you; Artemis…he was trying to *avenge* you. He ran to Mace…pushed him to the side. Sola…he just smashed her into the wall…over and over…"

"What do you mean? Is she hurt?" I ask, scrunching my eyebrows together.

Ashlea winces at her flashback. "I mean…yes? We ran down before the worst of it, but Iris…it was terrifying."

"He was out of control," Lunar shares. "He didn't stop until Mace and Destry pinned him down."

My mouth falls open. "But…why would he do that? I got away…what was the point?"

"I don't know." Ashlea shakes her head. "But Iris…I don't know about him."

I tilt my head to the side. "What do you mean?"

Ashlea and Lunar exchange a look.

"You weren't there," Lunar shutters, taking my hand. "I just…I don't know if he's as good of a guy as you seem to think."

"Guys, I've known him for three days," I say, rolling my eyes. "I barely know him! But you have to make friends here if you want to make it out. You *know* that!"

"Iris, you're misunderstanding us!" Ashlea rebuttals. "We're just saying…try and keep your distance, okay? The guy is a maniac. You can't trust him…he hangs out with Mercedes for crying out loud!"

"Yeah, but that's only because—" I catch myself before revealing Dial FM.

Ashlea leans forward. "See, Iris? You're trying to make excuses for him. Just…be careful, that's all."

"Yeah, seriously," Lunar interjects. "I want to make it out of here too, Iris. But he's not the answer."

Leaning against the concrete wall, I press my palms against my forehead. *Why is everyone so against Artemis? What's so terrible about him? He came to my defense! Doesn't that just prove his loyalty?*

I shudder at how much this fiasco has caused me to marginalize Sola's oncoming demise. My throat thickens when I consider what the Enterprize has already done to me. *And on Round One!*

A camera whirls, drawing my attention. I glance at the ceiling at the single-stall camera. It's nauseating that the bathroom stalls are being recorded, but how else would our private panic attacks be captured? *Am I becoming just as immoral as the Authority? Defending Artemis's violence…supporting a mother's demise?* Nausea consuming me, I let the severity of what Artemis had done set in. Finally, I wipe the sweat from my forehead and squeeze Lunar and Ashlea's hands. "I'll keep my distance...okay? I *will*."

The two nod and stay beside me until my trembles fade. Eventually, they lead me to the sink area to scrub the dried-up tears from my cheeks. They now sit with me, like Artemis had last night, while I fishtail my hair behind my back like my mother did, seemingly a lifetime ago. It was a time when she was alive, and circumstances were very, very different.

Chapter 15

"Iris?"

Destry peeks his head into the bathroom, where I have taken up residence for the past three hours. During this time, my housemates have come and gone, all eventually having to complete their morning bathroom routines. But I remained beside the bathroom sink. Dead-eyed and frozen.

Ashlea eventually left Lunar and me, and we've been sitting in silence ever since, feet dangling off the cold granite countertop. I know we're minutes from voting, but I'm far from eager to reserve my spot on the couch for a front-row seat to Sola's execution. And admittedly, I'm terrified of what will happen when I see Artemis.

Should I…thank him? Be disgusted with him? The possibilities run through my mind, and I resort to hoping the beating was far less severe than everyone made it out to be.

Destry walks further into my focus and repeats my name.

"Iris…we need you in the living room. Voting is in five minutes."

Destry rubs his trembling hand through his ruffled brown hair, biting his lip while shifting his weight back and forth. Allegedly, Destry prevented Artemis from Sola's premature murder, so I can imagine he will be walking on eggshells around me. It's funny, really. How, within a couple hours, Artemis has gone from a comedian to someone people don't feel safe around. I can only imagine what our friendship will do to my reputation.

And that's not something I will allow him to tarnish.

"Thanks…we'll be out in a sec," I say in return, avoiding his gaze. Destry nods before shutting the door behind him, leaving me alone with Lunar.

I take a deep breath before looking Lunar directly in the eyes. "If we don't vote…they *will* kill us." Lunar nods, holding back tears. I bring him in for a hug, rubbing his back. "Take three deep breaths, okay?" I instruct. We breathe together, allowing the air to expand our diaphragms and deflate our lungs. Once the simple task has been completed, I grab Lunar's wrists. "It's just a button…right?"

He nods but can't get a response out. I don't force him. Because without him, I couldn't hold it together either. But knowing he needs all the bravery he can get forces me to be strong.

I hop off the bathroom countertop and help him slide down. Holding his hand, I lead him to the living area where everyone is already in attendance, albeit for Lagiacrus, Destry, and Sola. Lunar and I sit in the two empty spots beside Mace. I situate between him and my brother, keeping hold of Lunar's hand.

I scan the others; my adrenaline spikes when I spot Artemis on the opposite couch, Mercedes beside him. Being as far from the Death Row cushions as possible, he stares blankly at the floor. I ignore Mercedes' arm around his shoulder, but my heart rate slows as he rubs the outer surface of his clasped hands. He jumps at every sound, eyes darting wildly around the room.

Don't trust him.

"You doin' okay?" Mace whispers to me, breaking me from my silent vow.

"Wha—oh. Yeah…yes." I smile. "Thank you…for saving me," I stutter. "I owe you."

"You don't owe me anything," he smiles as he rubs my arm. My stomach settles, and a slow smile spreads across my lips. "I'd do it again in a heartbeat."

Just as he finishes this declaration, there's a booming from the stairwell. The entire house spins toward the noise, but Artemis keeps his eyes on the floor. Curiosity winning, I follow the direction of the turned heads, and my jaw drops to the ground.

Destry and Lagiacrus descend the staircase, holding onto a slumped figure, keeping it upright. It's challenging to recognize the individual, stained with red and barely conscious. But when I finally do, a shiver runs down my spine.

Sola.

Dead.

Or seconds from it.

Wanting to shield my eyes from the horrific sight, I whip my head back to the center of the room and instinctively take Mace's hand. Embarrassed at my gesture, I try to unlatch my grasp, but Mace squeezes tight. Ensuring my safety. Silently promising to protect me.

Artemis, on the other hand, has completely buried his face in his hands, trying to escape the consequences of his impulsivity. Mercedes rubs his back to console him, but the damage has been done. Sola is so wrecked she can't walk on her own. Her breathing sounds like a chore. Even if we didn't vote Sola out, she'd be dead within the hour.

Destry and Lagiacrus place her on the Death Row couch furthest from Artemis and take their seats among us. The pained moans and gargling sounds from Sola's direction are the only things piercing the silence. I squeeze my eyes shut, mentally begging for something, *anything* to distract us from her misery. Finally, the same robotic voice that refereed our Executive competition returns.

"CONVICTS," it starts. Most of us search to see where the voice is coming from. There's no specific speaker we can identify, so we let the directions ring out. "YOUR VOTING ORDER HAS BEEN SELECTED BY RANDOM DRAW. WHEN YOUR NAME IS ANNOUNCED, MAKE YOUR WAY TO THE SECOND FLOOR. INSTRUCTIONS WILL FOLLOW.

"MERCEDES."

Mercedes looks up at the ceiling and nods with determination. She rises off the couch, removes her arm from Artemis's back, and treks up the staircase.

One by one, my housemates leave when their names are called. Some return distraught, like Finian. Others are unfazed, like Crescentia. I imagine this has to be some sort of act…an intimidation tactic. *Surely*, nobody can feel that nonchalant about murder.

"IRIS."

Mace squeezes my hand, wishing me luck. After he extends an encouraging smile, I rise off the couch, shaking.

I focus on the carpet ahead of me and hear the cameras rotating to catch my movement. My stomach curls, and I have an intense urge to sprint out of the Enterprize. But I know that ends with a bullet through my skull, so I focus on taking one step at a time.

I finally reach the second floor and find the arena door slightly ajar. Gently nudging the slab open, I recognize the flimsy metal staircase that once led to the spinning apparatus…the contraption that put Lagiacrus in charge. I take hold of the railings, keeping myself steady as my body trembles. The rickety structure can hardly withstand my quivering, so I'm relieved when I reach the AstroTurf, away from the metallic echoes.

This time, there is no spinning apparatus. Instead, white velvet railings lead me to a podium at the other side of the arena. I hold onto the velvet as I walk, trying to keep myself from falling. The trembles have now reached Sola status, and I fear I won't make it to the buttons.

When I finally reach my destination, a reflective, jet-black podium stands before me, slick to the touch. On the left lies a blue button reading "Eno." To the right, a white button is marked "Sola." The consistency with the Enterprize color scheme is haunting.

The robotic voice returns. "PRESS THE BUTTON OF THE PERSON YOU WISH TO EXPEL." I wipe a bead of sweat off my brow, flick my fishtail braid over my shoulder, and take another long, deep breath. The decision itself isn't difficult, and I'm lucky that my vote has essentially been cast for me. My only part in this is the button-bashing.

It should be simple, but I cannot bring myself to lock in the vote. I stare at the white button sporting Sola's name for half a minute and can't press it down. My body stands frozen in fear, and I curse my entire situation.

Why are they doing this to us? Why can't they just kill us like every other convict in Miasmis? The psychological torture is unbearable, and it's sickening that they're broadcasting it to the entire country. I stand as I have, frozen, while the power of this game sets in.

They aren't doing this for entertainment. They're doing it to inflict fear, just like they have done with the evening executions for years. By now, it's clear that the death penalty isn't enough to force cooperation. The results are the same: executions commence, illegals are born, rations are stolen from the wealthy, and the Assessment is avoided. The Authority know there *must* be more on the line. Their desperation has increased the stakes. Because the death penalty won't stop people from defying them.

But the public psychological torture of children might.

93

"TEN SECONDS."

The mechanical voice wakes me from my epiphany. Whipping my head up, I find the giant clock counting down, oblivious to my internal crisis.

I watch the numbers decrease to nine, then eight, then seven. My heart begs me to listen to it, urging that this isn't who I am. But my brain knows what will happen if that clock hits zero.

With five seconds remaining, I locate Sola's white button and smash my hand down. Just as it collides, a robotic voice broadcasts from the button.

"VOTE: SOLA."

I have the simultaneous urge to curl into a ball and launch the midnight podium across the arena. But neither of these options will change what has been done, so I bunch my hands into fists and stomp to the metal staircase. Pumping my arms, I angrily leap to the top, keeping my face contorted into a determined, vengeful glare as I reenter the house, descend the stairs, and sit back next to Mace.

The next few minutes blur into one another. The remaining names are called. I give Lunar a comforting pat when it's his turn to vote, and Sola continues to choke on her own blood. Jade is the last to be summoned, and when she returns to the couch and slouches back into the sofa, the voice returns.

"WHEN ANNOUNCED, THE EXPELLED CONVICT MUST EXIT THROUGH THE FRONT DOOR WHERE EXECUTION WILL COMMENCE."

How pleasant.

Eno shifts, his brow furrowed. His safety is evident, but I can't imagine anyone would feel comfortable on Death Row. Sola's eyes roll to the back of her head. The gargling worsens, proving that her lungs aren't giving up without a fight.

"BY A VOTE OF TWELVE TO ZERO: SOLA IS EXPELLED FROM THE ENTERPRIZE. YOU HAVE THIRTY SECONDS TO EVACUATE."

We all turn to the bloody slab of human we still ignorantly call Sola. Oblivious to reality, she doesn't move an inch. Seconds pass without movement, so we start darting our gazes at one another.

"What do we do!?" Finian shouts, voice shaking. "In twenty seconds, they're gonna burst through that door and *open fire!*"

"You two picked her up before! Can't you drag her out?" Crescentia suggests, glaring at Destry and Lagiacrus.

"You're kidding, right?" Destry quips back. "Helping her down the stairs and dragging her to the firing squad are two *completely* different things. You want her out of here? *You* haul her out."

A bang reverberates outside the Enterprize, taking my mind back to my parents *screaming* at me to run. My hesitation may have cost them their lives, causing us to get caught red-handed. The image of their blood staining the floorboards jolts me into action, so I snatch Lunar and jolt him off the couch. The reality of the Authority barging in with automatic rifles is closing in faster than a freight train, and I'm far from wanting to witness another public execution. Or worse, face the consequences of getting in the Authority's way.

"Come on!" I yell at Lunar, pulling him as I run. Mace pushes him from behind, blocking his vision and getting him as far away from the commotion as possible. Steps from the bathroom door, the iron entrance to the Enterprize groans open. Still in a sprint, I turn and see five members of the Authority, covered head to toe in their black and gray camouflage.

My housemates scatter out of the way, some racing to the bathroom and others rushing up the staircase. The Enterprize is in chaos, and I can barely see the commotion in the living room.

But it would be impossible to miss the twenty bullets exiting Sola's body, painting the blue wall behind Death Row with blood.

PART 2

ROUND 2

Chapter 16

"Oh my god, oh my god, oh my god!" Lunar holds onto the bathroom wall, forcing himself upright while his chest heaves. "They did it! They actually did it!"

"Of course, they did! When have they *ever* been bluffing!?" Crescentia smashes through the door behind us, wiping Sola's splattered blood from her forearm. Finian sneaks in behind her, throwing up bread chunks onto the bare tile. Kylah shoves him to the side before pouncing on Crescentia.

"Do you *ever* shut the hell up!?" Kylah shouts in Crescentia's face, spit flinging from her chapped lips. She towers over the pale, black-haired monster, her auburn curls flinging across her face as she yells.

Crescentia rolls her eyes, unfazed. But from the way she perches herself on the counter and flings her feet into the sink, I can tell that she's not immune to the horrors of what she's done. Turning the nob for hot water, she avoids Kylah's gaze and starts rubbing her temples.

"In here!" calls Mace from the stall furthest away, and the group of us pile in, leaving Finian alone with Crescentia. Lunar collapses to the floor and curls his legs to his chest, trembling. I rub his back and Kylah takes his hand; we whisper empty reassurances to keep his mind from crossing into traumatic territory he may never come back from.

Mace stands still, his eyes darting back and forth. His silence alarms me, so I finally croak at him, fighting my closing throat. "We have ten minutes until we have to compete! What are we gonna do!?"

"Hey," Mace starts but I can hardly hear him. My stomach twists as I realize the impossibility of winning this next Executive competition. In my current state, there's no chance I can keep my composure. Beyond that, Lunar is gone. My need to protect my little brother currently dominates my own terror, but what will happen when that fades? "HEY!" Mace shouts, forcing my attention to his violet eyes. They offer comfort…care. But most of all, protection.

"Everyone here is just as scared as we are, okay? You saw them scatter. Every person out there ran as far away from that living room as possible." He shakes his head. "I don't *care* how strong Crescentia pretends to be; we're all afraid! We're all competing with adrenaline; we just have to control it!"

I nod mechanically while tears form in the corners of my eyes. "Mace…" I choke back the oncoming sobs. "If Curi's out there…she'll be watching…she'll have seen it *all*…"

Mace puts his arm around my shoulder and lowers his volume to a whisper. "Yes, and she wants to see you be *strong* and win Executive this round." He takes his other arm and wraps it around me. "Whoever she's with will have diverted her attention. She won't have seen the worst of it. But now she's watching *you*. Can you be brave for her?"

A tear drops down my cheek and he wipes it off, not breaking our eye contact. I bite my lip, holding back sobs, and nod as he gives my face a delicate stroke.

He turns away, touching Lunar's knee to get his attention. When Lunar finally looks up, Mace declares, "We're going to win this for you, okay? Just try to get your head on straight. If there's a chance to put yourself in danger, avoid it. We don't know what we're gonna have to do, but we can win this. We just have to breathe…calm our nerves! Okay?"

Lunar nods and Mace continues. "In a few minutes, we're expected to be on that second floor. *Listen to me very carefully,*" Mace looks directly into Lunar's eyes with urgency. He knows Lunar only heard the gunshots and missed *seeing* the massacre, so he makes his instructions clear. "The second we leave this bathroom I want you to look down at the floor until we hit the stairs. *Only then* can you look up." Mace is completely serious, any humor from before this morning having completely disappeared. He talks to Lunar as if his life depends on it. "And when you do look up, I want you to look directly in front of you. Block out everything but my back. Do you understand me? Under *no* circumstances can you look at Death Row. *Do you understand?*"

Lunar nods, jolting his head up and down. Regardless of the Authority's disposal of Sola's remains, it'll be impossible to completely sanitize and remove the blood from the walls. I'm sure they won't even try to, considering how little they care about our comfort. The last thing Lunar needs is to be retraumatized, seconds from having to compete.

Mace shakes Lunar's knees with both of his hands. "You're going to get through this, Lunar. It's going to be okay."

I put my head between my legs and block everything out. My few private moments end when Mace's gentle touch reaches my shoulders and a rush of safety flushes over me. I look up and find his eyes, gazing intensely into mine.

"You can do this, Iris. You *can.*"

I nod my head and see Lunar doing the same, supporting me for what's to come. After a long, deep breath, I adjust into a squat and take Lunar's hand. The four of us barge out of the stall with a newfound determination.

When we reach the sinks, Crescentia is still absentmindedly cleaning her feet. Luckily, she doesn't acknowledge us. Finian is nowhere to be found, so I assume he's already made it to the second floor. After the production the Authority put on in the living room, I don't want to find out what will happen if I'm late to Round Two.

We get in a line, Mace at the front, Kylah in the back. Lunar stands immediately behind Mace, so I keep my hands on my brother's back in case his legs fail him again. Mace rests his palm on the iron bathroom exit and looks back at the group. Grabbing Lunar's shoulder, he repeats his instructions.

"Right ahead. Eyes on the ground. *Nowhere else.*"

Lunar nods. "Nowhere else."

Mace gives a final nod. "Let's win this."

He opens the door, and we sprint across the living room. I push Lunar to make sure he's moving and block his side view to ensure he's not peeking at the massacre to his left. We make it to the staircase with no issues and reach the iron slab on the second floor. With it already ajar, Mace yanks it open, and we tumble back into the plastic arena.

Mace shakes Lunar's shoulder, letting him know it's safe to look up. We descend the rickety metal staircase one by one and find that the velvet rails and podium on the turf have been removed. Now, a massive glass structure sits in the center of the arena. It forms a ring, leaving an open circle of turf in the middle. It is divided into thirteen compartments, with transparent walls separating each one. Within the chambers are waist-high black buttons sticking onto the walls facing the center.

Being four days since the Enterprize began, the creators have made the necessary adjustments to eliminate Lagiacrus's brother's existence from the games. They probably assumed others would drop for reasons besides expulsions, so it makes sense that future competition designs would be flexible. I shiver, considering the possibility that voting isn't the only way we are expected to die. Imagining why separate chambers would be necessary makes my trembles worse. I quickly remind myself that now is *not* the time to contemplate the morality of the Enterprize and center my focus on the AstroTurf ahead.

Circling the structure, we notice that the others haven't arrived yet. A few yards away is a white stool, a card folded on its top. We inch closer to the seat, finally close enough to recognize the tree root-camouflaged pattern on the note. Lagiacrus's name is printed on the front, but Mace flips it over and reads the instructions to himself.

"It's…riddles."

"What?" I ask. My dread is transformed into excitement, and a smile spreads across my lips. *Riddles*. Fifteen years in the floorboards, and all I have to show for it is my strength in logic.

"That's…well, that's good news, right?" Lunar asks, shaking my nervous arm.

"Yeah…yeah, I guess so," I smile at him, trying to contain my elation.

Mace doesn't change his expression. Instead, his stare deepens, confirming that he's read the directions correctly.

I lean closer to him, biting my lip. "What is it?"

He shakes his head. "There's…punishments."

My mouth falls open and I grab Lunar. "No…what…what kind of punishments?"

He shakes his head again, still reading. After a deep breath, he shrugs. "It doesn't say."

I grip onto Lunar tighter, his unsteady breaths picking up. Noticing his distress, Mace kneels at Lunar's height. "Hey, it's okay. You're gonna be okay. It's nothing we won't be able to handle." He ruffles Lunar's hair. "Just gotta stay alert."

Lunar's muscles loosen, so I shut my eyes, trying to soothe myself. Mace's abrupt chuckles disrupt my daze.

"Apparently, Lagiacrus can't compete."

My eyebrows raise to the ceiling. "What?"

He wipes a bead of sweat off his forehead, smiling. He flips the card over and smashes it back down on the stool. "Apparently, you can't win twice in a row."

"Yes!" I whisper, tilting my head to the ceiling with a grin. It strikes me that without Lagiacrus competing, we will have one less alliance member on our side. But his absence increases the odds of Mace or me winning, so my relief trumps the blow on Dial.

Before the others reach the turf, Mace smiles at me and offers his hand. "You ready?"

The violet fires in his pupils force a smile on my face. I nod, squeezing his hand. "We're gonna win this."

"This is a test of logic," Lagiacrus reads to the group, standing beside his stool. All his weight leans on his right leg, and he holds the card with a single palm. Since finding out he can't compete, he's had a noticeable shift in attitude, now having no patience for the Authority's games.

I try to focus on potential questions that could be asked, but I can't stop glancing at Artemis across the group. I'm dreading the moment we finally talk about Sola. But when I genuinely consider his attack on her, my heart twists in a deep sadness at the isolation he must feel from his mistake. Before he notices my lingering gaze, I stare at the turf. His existence is already so conflicting for me; the last thing I need is his presence to distract me.

"You will be asked a series of riddles, all of which have *only one* correct answer," continues Lagiacrus, tapping his foot. "The first *convict*," he reads, rolling his eyes at the label, "to press their button, gets to answer the question. Press before the completion of the question, and the remainder of the reading will be terminated." Having read the card myself, I know what direction comes next. I brace myself for the reveal.

"Answer the riddle correctly, and you get to…" Lagiacrus's eyes widen, "*select one convict to punish.*" The tension in the air grows, everybody stiffening up at the instruction. There's murmuring as the others guess what punishments will be inflicted. I close my eyes, trying to block out their ruthless speculation.

"The first person to answer three riddles correctly will be crowned the Executive. Buzzing in and answering *incorrectly* will eliminate you from the competition."

He places the card down at his side. "Any questions?"

Nobody answers. The second Lagiacrus puts the card back on his stool, each compartment door slides open, causing a loud boom to echo throughout the arena. Shaking, I approach the glass structure with the others, silently entering through the cell. I keep Lunar to my left, and Mace positions himself to my right. I tap my podium nervously, examining the glossy black button level with my waist. The silence is deafening, only disturbed when Crescentia blurts out, "Well, who's reading the questions then?"

On cue, the glass doors slam shut, locking us in our chambers. Lunar turns around, testing the door, but it doesn't budge. His arms tremble, and when he turns toward me, his face lacks all color. I mouth reassurances, and the robotic voice from the first-round returns.

"QUESTION 1." I'm caught off guard at the promptness of the start and nearly miss the beginning of the question.

"WHAT IS THE SINGLE THING ALL MEN, REGARDLESS OF RELIGION, AGREE IS BETWEEN HEAVEN AND EARTH?"

I feel like I'm choking on the air. Despite my hours studying under the floorboards, I'm entirely unprepared for the pressure of this competition. Losing could mean death, but winning would mean murder. I freeze as the flashbacks strike. Sola, eyes reduced to slits, slumped on the couch, too paralyzed to move. Lagiacrus's brother... sprawled on the dirt with blood pooling around his chest. My parents...*my parents.*

"CONVICT: JADE."

I blink away the images with a jolt. Jade looks up from her perch, lip quivering. "The sky?"

A buzzer booms around the arena, making us all jump. "INCORRECT. CONVICT: JADE. ELIMINATED."

Destry stifles a cackle while Jade pounds the glass wall. Her jet-black hair frays about as she throws her temper tantrum, but all movements stop abruptly when a metal showerhead lowers from the top of her compartment. She watches the structure, wide-eyed when a gray gas falls into her cell. Within seconds, the vapor reaches her forehead.

And she screams bloody murder.

I back away from my button, covering my mouth. *What are they doing to her?* Destry's smile disappears instantly, and my housemates erupt into a panic.

"Somebody, help her!" Cypher shouts, pounding on the back of his glass prison. Jade ducks on the floor now, hiding her face from the poisonous cloud and viciously pushing at the door, screaming. But it doesn't budge.

I turn to Lunar, putting my hand on the wall that separates us. "Don't answer anything!" I demand. "Stay away from that button!"

He backs away, leaning against the glass wall and holding his ears to spare himself from Jade's screams. I whip my head left and right, desperate to protect him but stuck to the confines of the prison.

A *ring* brings me back to the competition.

"CONVICT: MACE."

I twist to my right in awe. Mace's eyebrow twitches as he tries to ignore Jade, but his words are barely perceptible beneath Jade's shrieks. Regardless, he straightens his back and shouts his answer. "THE WORD: AND."

Ding. "CORRECT. CONVICT: MACE, ONE POINT."

I let out a sigh of relief. Instead of celebrating, he nods and stares at his podium, preparing for the next instruction. His lack of excitement confuses me, but the robotic voice makes his stoicism clear.

"SELECT A CONVICT FOR PUNISHMENT."

Mace stares at the ground, itching the back of his head. I watch, my eyes twisting in pain as he announces, "Cypher!"

The second the name leaves his lips, a compartment from the ceiling opens. Expecting the gas, Cypher throws his hands up. "What the hell, man?" When no sprinkler descends, he looks up at the ceiling, searching.

Just as a metal screw launches into his eye.

The shouts are instantaneous. He's directly across from me, so I get a front row show. He covers his eye, a clear liquid spewing out of the socket. Mace backs away from his button, mouth ajar. Suddenly, I understand that the directed punishments might be even more deadly than the penalties for an incorrect answer. Jade lies on the floor, body heaving for clean air, but Cypher's entire torso is painted with the liquid spewing from his eye.

"QUESTION 2." I reach for Mace, but he stays focused. I close my eyes and make a split decision. If I want any chance at protecting Lunar, I need to participate. And I *need* to answer correctly.

I widen my stance, stretching my neck. A glance at the ceiling reveals a scoreboard projected on all the walls. A bright red "X" hangs below Jade's name, and a Roman Numeral I is cast below Mace's.

I shake my head to wake my mind. *No more distractions.*

"IF YOU HAVE A CUBE, EACH EDGE TWO INCHES LONG, HOW MANY TOTAL SQUARE INCHES ARE THERE AMONG ALL EIGHT SIDES?"

The whispered counting of my competitors fades to white noise under Jade's screams. My palm trembles as I draw imaginary numbers on the glass wall ahead of me, trying to block out Jade's pain. I jump back when there's a *ring* and brace for impact.

"CONVICT: ARTEMIS."

I widen my eyes at Artemis, and he's squirming at his podium. He looks up at the ceiling, his blue eyes twisted in insecurity, and stutters, "Um…SIXTY-FOUR?"

The buzzer returns, eliminating him from the competition.

Just as with Jade, a metal structure descends from the ceiling, flooding his compartment with gray gas. He pulls the collar of his shirt to his nose and ducks to the corner of his pod. Terrified of what will happen to him, I return to my imaginary work, my finger stabbing the wall so hard that the vibration of the glass banging echoes around me. When I reach the seventh side, I abruptly stop my writing and smash the button. My name is announced, so I shout, "TRICK QUESTION! CUBES HAVE SIX SIDES."

Ding. I give a subtle fist pump at my side, smiling. But when I'm prompted to serve a punishment, I freeze.

No…I can't do that to someone. What if…what if they die? But just as this hesitation descends, I realize that refusal would likely inflict punishment on me or somebody I cared about.

So, instead of selecting someone new, I solidify Cypher's probable hatred toward Mace and myself.

"Cypher," I shout.

Now, Cypher ducks, covering his other eye. He cowers away from the ceiling but realizes it's unnecessary when his black button abruptly switches to a deep, glowing red. He stares at the neon curiously but stays away from it. Hoping the punishment is complete, I sigh. Mace sheds his competitive exterior in my periphery and sends me a thumbs-up. I nod before squinting my eyes in focus. I hover my hand over the button for the next question, bending my knees to prepare to pounce.

"QUESTION 3: IT OCCURS ONCE IN A MINUTE, TWICE IN A MOMENT, BUT NEVER IN AN HOUR."

Ring.

"CONVICT: MERCEDES."

The bombshell flips her hair over her shoulder. Manipulating vocal fry to sexualize her tone, she answers. "That would be the letter M."

Ding.

I can't stop my eyes from rolling. Her confidence and unapologetic honesty have my stomach hardening with a hideous rage. I gulp back the heat rising to my throat, because I can't let her divert my attention for long. But it's a lost cause, because the robotic voice doesn't even have to finish asking her who to punish when my name leaves her lips.

I dart my eyes at Mace. He signals for me to take deep breaths, moving his hand up and down from his chest. I nod, trying to let my lungs push air into them. I don't have to look at what's being released when my ceiling compartment opens. Because when the hordes of centipedes start to layer around my ankles, I know they won't stop coming.

I tense my muscles, standing as still as possible. The centipedes rain down on me, landing in my hair, around my shoulders, and into the crevices of my clothes. They crawl on me, their legs tickling my skin, causing goosebumps to erupt throughout my arms and legs. I shake, getting the sensation of scraping my fingernails on a chalkboard a thousand times in slow motion. When one of the insects starts crawling into my ear, I shake it loose, throwing my hair back and forth.

Artemis's screams finally start, and I watch him curl onto the ground, his skin blowing up several sizes. I take a deep breath, convincing myself that the bugs are nothing I can't handle, and try not to cringe when they layer up to my knees.

"QUESTION 4." I take a deep breath, directing all my focus on the question and shying away from the millions of legs crawling over my skin. "IS IT LEGAL FOR A MAN TO MARRY HIS WIDOW'S SISTER?"

I squirm, trying not to let the bugs divert my focus. Widow's…*sister*? So, the man was married, and his wife died? I scratch the bugs out of my hair, shaking from the sensation of their furry legs, and try to focus. My eyes dilate in concentration and abruptly widen when I realize my misunderstanding. *The wife is a widow.* Which, of course, can only mean that the man is dead.

I bash my button, flinging off a dozen centipedes, but I'm too late.

"CYPHER."

I almost can't hear his name because he screams so loud he nearly blows out my eardrums. One hand still on his pierced eye, he aggressively shakes out the other before squeezing it between his knees. I glimpse his palm and bite my lip when I see the third-degree burn.

The button. His button is flaming hot, burning him every time he answers a question. I squint my eyes, hoping he'll get it wrong so my punishment on him can end.

Between cries, he answers. "NO, BECAUSE HE'S DEAD."

Ding.

There's no celebration. Instead, Cypher's shouts intensify as he pulls the long metal screw out of his eye socket. He tosses it on the floor, specks of blood mixing with the clear liquid bursting from his socket. So, when he selects who to punish, I'm far from surprised that it's Mace.

Mace takes a deep breath as his ceiling opens. Water launches on him, flooding his compartment. I'm relieved it's not worse until it dawns on me. Just like the bugs, the water isn't going to stop. If this competition goes long enough…Mace will drown.

I look at the scoreboard, confirming the four-way tie for first between Mace, Mercedes, Cypher, and myself. The centipedes now bunch to my waist, hundreds crawling around my neck and through my hair. Nausea twists my stomach, and the urge to hurl is overwhelming. But when the voice announces the fifth question, my panic shifts to the water now accumulating at Mace's shins. *I won't let him die.* So, I take a deep breath and hover my centipede-caked arm close to the button.

"IS IT CORRECT TO SAY, 'THE YOLK OF EGGS *IS* WHITE' OR 'THE YOLK OF EGGS *ARE* WHITE'?"

I smash the wall but miss the button. I'm shaking so hard that I can't even hit the target. I launch for it again, ignoring the cacophony of screams between Cypher, Jade, and Artemis, and finally catch a *ring*, indicating that I've failed.

"CONVICT: CYPHER." I deflate as a centipede crawls into my nose. I huff out heavily, launching the bug into the pile around my stomach.

"YAARRGG!" he shouts, his hand glowing red from the double burn. "Neither!" he calls, spit flinging from his lips. "The yolks are yellow!"

Ding.

Cypher enacts the perfect revenge before the voice can question the punishment recipient. "PUNISH LUNAR!" he yells between pained yelps, hunching over his burnt hand.

I whip my head to my left, eyes widening. Lunar scrunches into a ball on the ground, cowering away from the descending sprinkler system. "LUNAR!" I shout, quivering at what horror awaits him. Slowly, his chamber clouds up to a point where I can barely see him. I wince, waiting for his screams, but they don't come. Staring at his ceiling, I realize that the gray vapor sent to the eliminated contestants is much different from what's filling his chamber. From the look of things, nothing is being released into his pod. It's not until he wipes the ice away from a section of our conjoined wall that I realize what's happening.

They're freezing him.

"Take your arms out of your sleeves!" I demand. "Hug yourself tight and stay away from the walls!"

He nods before his chamber walls ice back up. *This needs to end before he freezes to death.*

We are running behind, with Cypher at two points and Mace, Mercedes, and me at one. I run my fingers through the top of my fishtail braid, shaking the centipedes out and shivering. If I wasn't covered in these pests and had quicker reflexes, I'd have won this competition by now. If I lose to Cypher…who knows if Lunar and I are safe? He won't want me to stay, especially now that I've burned the guy. I take deep breaths, trying to calm my nerves.

"QUESTION 6: IF A ROOSTER LAYS AN EGG ON THE EXACT PEAK OF A BARN, WHICH SIDE—"

Ring.

"CONVICT: MERCEDES."

I gaze at the blonde, dropping my jaw to the floor. She buzzed in early, terminating the rest of the question. Artemis's screams come to a halt as his body trembles on the ground, and he watches her between a sliver in his hand. Her original arrogance has extinguished, her hand shaking as she twists a string of hair around her finger. "It's on neither side…it's in the middle!"

The buzzer blares, making me jump. "INCORRECT."

"NO!" Mercedes smashes the back wall, not making a dent. The gray substance rains down on her, and her screams join the chorus of Jade and Artemis.

Seeing her whither in pain, Artemis bangs on their connecting wall. "BREATH THROUGH YOUR SHIRT!" He starts coughing, then stuffs his top collar back over his mouth. She follows suit, the two huddling into adjoining corners. My heart feels a brief twist of insecurity that's wiped immediately from my mind when a centipede sinks its sharp teeth into my flesh.

Ring.

"CONVICT: MACE."

I wince from the bite but turn toward Mace regardless, praying he knows the answer. The water is at his chest, so the button is underwater. Not wasting time, he shouts to the sky, "ROOSTERS DON'T LAY EGGS!"

Ding.

I let out a sigh of relief, a centipede willing itself into my mouth. I spit furiously, shaking my head as thousands of the creatures storm around me. The hoard is up to my ribs, making it impossible to see my button.

The voice prompts Mace to assign a convict for punishment. Without hesitation, he shouts Cypher's name. "COME ON!" Cypher yells, punching a wall with his healthy hand, causing his empty eye socket to spew a mixture of clear and red liquid more heavily than before. As expected, a sliver of his ceiling opens, but just like Lunar's punishment, nothing visible is released. I glance at the wall conjoined to Lunar's compartment, but several layers of ice prevent me from seeing through. A tear builds in the corner of my eye, so I alter my gaze back to Cypher, his chamber starting to steam up. The heat is so unbearable that he kicks the wall to the exit, screaming when it won't open.

When the next question starts, I look away and allow the shrieks around the arena to fade into white noise. "QUESTION 7: A COWBOY RIDES INTO TOWN ON FRIDAY. HE STAYS THREE DAYS, THEN RIDES OUT OF TOWN ON FRIDAY. HOW?"

I push my hand through the bugs, causing several to attack. I still manage to bash the button, yelping from the pain, and scream my answer as quickly as I can when my name is called.

"The horse! The horse's name is Friday!" I talk so fast it turns into a single word.

Ding.

I sigh in relief, watching my score rise to "II." The projection confirms a three-way tie between Mace, Cypher, and me. If any of us answer the next question correctly, the competition is over. I glance back at Cypher's chamber, trembling as he screams from his series of ailments. I bite my lip, terrified that another jab at him could end his life. His life will have to end eventually if I want to make it out alive…but I don't have it in me to deliver the final blow. Anxiety building from the furry creatures burying me alive and wishing I could return to favor to Mercedes, I do the next best thing. "PUNISH CRESCENTIA!"

In seconds, she's doused in water to her ankles. Her entire body is soaked, but the water stops pouring. The hose retracts into the ceiling, so she stands with her arms out, darting her eyes back and forth. I pray that the extent of it was a splash of ice-cold water.

I'm sorely mistaken when her body shakes, her teeth chatter, and her hair stands on end.

Her entire cell lights up yellow, and she can't stop shaking. Her body is electrocuted in pulses so quickly that she doesn't have time to yelp. I urge myself not to watch as the bugs reach my neck, and I focus on Mace, swimming to the top of his compartment to breathe.

"QUESTION 8." The words come out in slow motion, so I put my hand closer to the button, centipede teeth piercing me from every direction. "WHAT COMMON ENGLISH VERB BECOMES ITS OWN PAST TENSE BY REARRANGING ITS LETTERS?"

I wince, closing my eyes to ignore the flashes of electricity reflecting off Crescentia's chamber. No matter how long I consider the question, no answer comes. The others are also stumped because, apart from the screams and whimpers of the eliminated contestants, there's silence all around. I shake my head, fighting the centipedes from crawling into my eyes. Mace swims to the top of his cell, stealing his last few breaths.

Ring.

"CONVICT," the mechanical voice starts, and I cross my fingers, hoping it's not Cypher.

"DESTRY."

I'm not expecting his participation. I'd forgotten that anyone besides Mace, Cypher, and myself were competing. But I'm so far from caring about his addition to the fight that I mentally urge him to quicken his answer. Destry opens his mouth with insecurity and shouts to the sky, voice shaking, "EAT AND ATE?"

Ding.

My eyes widen with awe. I'm shocked somebody figured it out and relieved that it was a member of Dial. He shouts Kylah's name before the voice even asks for a punishment recipient, and a twelve-foot snake launches from her ceiling, knocking her to the ground.

It slithers around her, flaunting its fangs. She backs away on the ground, putting her hands up and keeping as still as possible. Her auburn curls twitch from her trembles as the serpent wraps itself around her torso.

"QUESTION 9." My stomach boils with nerves. Cypher has a gleam in his remaining good eye and bunches his burnt palm into a fist. Mace takes a deep breath as the water consumes him and presses his ear to the top to hear the question. Two mere inches separate the water from the roof of his chamber, so he hovers his foot by the button, preparing to kick. I breathe through my nose, fighting against the bugs, ready to suffer more teeth punctures for the win.

"IT'S ALWAYS IN FRONT OF YOU BUT CANNOT BE SEEN."

I bash the button until I'm sure it's broken. Even then, I hold it down, crushing bugs against it and willing the voice to announce my name. But when it returns, it doesn't say Iris.

It says Mace.

"THE FUTURE! THE FUT—" The liquid bubbles his words, but his answer is clear. He falls to the bottom of his chamber as the water envelopes the top. The centipedes are up to my nose when the *ding* finally sounds.

"CONGRATULATIONS: MACE. YOU ARE THE NEW EXECUTIVE."

Chapter 17

The chamber doors open, unloading both victims and terrors onto the AstroTurf. I sprint out of my compartment, shaking off the centipedes that cling to my skin. I take only a moment to whip my hair around, releasing the bugs from their grasp, before striding to Lunar's cell. Everyone else has crawled from their jails, but Lunar remains frozen on the floor, trembling. "Lunar!" I shout, pulling him from his prison and hugging him tight, letting my body warmth soothe his frigid limbs. I wince, the centipede bites having made my skin fragile to the touch. But his icy body distracts me from the pain, cooling me faster than I can warm him. He's so chilled that our bodies struggle to part, his skin freezing against mine. Instead of panicking, I grip him tighter and watch the others stumble along the turf.

My heart twists, watching the water from Mace's section burst out of his cell. He hacks out his lungs, gasping for air, and it takes everything in me not to run to his side. Cypher rolls on the ground, holding onto his various ailments, his shrieks making my ears ring. Lagiacrus and Finian, being two of the only healthy housemates, tear the snake off Kylah, working together to distract and unravel the beast. Crescentia falls to her knees, wrapping her hands around the back of her neck. But the worst is the eliminated contestants, crawling out of their prisons, scrunching up on the turf as they hack for air.

Artemis's body convulses, working to rid itself of the toxic gas. His enormous hands have swollen to twice their size, and the exposed areas of his body bulge so large he defies normal human proportions. Jade is worse, bawling and punching the ground, aware of how close she was to cardiac arrest. The remaining healthy convicts get to work: Destry slaps Mace's back to eject the water from his lungs, and Ashlea joins my and Lunar's frozen huddle.

"What can I do?" she asks, eyes dilated and voice urgent. Her arms surround us both, rubbing Lunar's back to generate some friction heat.

"Get some bed sheets!" Kylah shouts, running toward our group. Finally, out of the grasp of the boa constrictor, she's doing damage control. "I'll steam up the shower room…Iris, carry him to the bathrooms, but *don't put him in the water.*" Her last words are louder than the rest, her face getting closer with each order. "If you do, his tissues will burn. Just…keep him in the steam until I figure out what to do!"

Before anyone can object, she sprints out of the arena, flinging the iron door open and letting the sturdy knob bang into the wall. The clash echoes through my bones, and goosebumps erupt on my arms.

Ashlea rises, eyes wide. "Get him as close as you can to the bathrooms…I'll grab the sheets and find you!" I nod, shivering from the icicles hardening Lunar's hair. Ashlea leaps up the metal staircase, her pounding steps making the rickety structure sway.

"You heard them…we have to move…" I direct myself more than Lunar. He doesn't acknowledge me. Instead, he rubs his arms within his shirt, willing them to warm.

When I stand, I realize how much of his temperature I've absorbed. Finally separate from him, I shiver hard, trying to grab his arm but struggling to keep a firm grasp on the fabric of his shirt. He doesn't budge, shoving his arm away from me as he rocks on the turf. I run my fingers through my hair, prompting a rouge centipede to sink its teeth into my skull. I yelp, pulling it out and smashing its lengthy body in my fist. Lunar is entirely out of touch with reality, unaware of how vital his cooperation is to his survival. I abandon pulling and try to lift him, squatting beside his frigid body to get a solid grasp. I succeed, carrying him a few meters across the turf before collapsing under my own frozen legs. Laying on the slick turf, I accept my defeat. I rub my fingers through the plastic blades of grass, and a thousand images jump through my mind. Artemis's swollen limbs… Cypher's empty eye socket…but apart from Lunar, only one person lingers beyond a single image as I shut my eyelids and stretch my arms.

Water drips on me, seeping into my wounds, making me recoil into a tight ball. I'm immediately unwound as Lunar is lifted off the ground, and my arm is tugged. Despite the pain, I feel a rush of safety and let this mysterious figure transport us. Only when I look up do I recognize the brown locks, sexily slicked back from the drenching he got from his underwater compartment.

"Mace?" I whisper, trying my best to oblige with his urgency.

He ignores me and collides with Ashlea in the kitchen. Blankets in her arms, she opens them wide, Mace setting Lunar into the middle. They wrap him up together, making sure to cover every inch of his body. Once only his mouth is visible beneath the blanket shell, Kylah bursts from the communal restroom. "In here!" she shouts, jolting Mace and Ashlea into motion. This time, instead of my arm, Mace clasps onto my hand, holding my palm tight by interlocking his fingers in mine. Ashlea pushes us all from behind until we reach the bathroom floor.

"What now?" Mace asks Kylah with insistence, rocking back and forth on his heels. I can barely pay attention, the cool tile sapping the remaining warmth out of my body. I bring my knees to my chest, wrapping my arms around my legs, and nestle in my nose as I tremble.

Kylah looks both Lunar and me up and down before settling her eyes upon my figure. "Get her in the water. Lunar needs more time to thaw…she'll be fine to start the showers." She points to the various shower heads, directing her attention to Ashlea. "They're in order from coolest to warmest…start her in the closer ones and move her up as she warms." Ashlea nods, grabs my hand, and takes me behind the dividing wall between the sinks and the showers.

"I'm fine…really, I'm not even that cold," I plead with her, trying to stop my shivers and hide my pink skin.

"After two minutes of hugging that icicle?" Ashlea scrunches her eyebrows together. "I don't think so." My warmth has drained, trying to keep Lunar alive. I know Ashlea's right, but it doesn't make cooperating easier.

She shoves me in the shower room, not bothering to remove my clothes. It's the best technique to flush all the centipedes away, so I don't mind. Besides, with Mace around the corner…it's better this way.

The second the water touches my skin, my screams begin. The lukewarm liquid pounds against my bite lesions, making me jump back from the searing pain. Ashlea holds me in the water, forcing me to face the discomfort at the benefit of my eventual warmth. Her apologies harmonize with Mace's, the latter's echoing across the bathroom into the shower space.

The cuts are eventually clean enough that they stop throbbing, and I'm able to focus on the process before me. Finally used to the lukewarm temperature starting to chill me, I plead with Ashlea to graduate me to the hotter showerheads. It's not until the third step that I feel relief. I sigh, enjoying the warm water running through my hair and down my back. But unlike Lunar, I'm far from frostbitten. I cooperate to speed up the process. Because despite warming up, I'm stuck with the image of Lunar shivering beside Mace and Ashlea.

Once Ashlea wraps the towels around me, I rush to the sinks. Lunar's finally communicating, but only in short bursts. Mace and Kylah pick him up, readying him for the process when I block their path.

"No!" I shout. "I can do it…I can help him."

Kylah shakes her head. "No, you need to get *dry*," she objects. "He'll be fine."

I shake my head wildly, not ready to give him up. Finally, Mace grabs my shoulders and stares into my eyes with his violet oases.

"Hey, you can trust me, okay? I promise." He gestures toward Lunar. "He'll be alright." His grip tightens, and he leans closer to me. "Do you trust me?"

My breath catches in my throat. A tremble shoots through my spine while his eyes stay steady on mine. I consider our pinky promise…that he would be with me until the end. So, when all is said and done, and his urgent focus moves consecutively from my left to my right eye, I bite my lip and nod, letting go of any doubt I had about Mace's loyalty.

Mace touches my chin and grins with the side of his lip. He directs his attention to Kylah, who explains the procedure, then flees with Lunar behind the barrier. Ashlea and I lean our backs on the concrete separating us from the showers, and she gives my hand an encouraging squeeze. Kylah paces, less concerned about my safety and more distraught over Lunar's. I close my eyes, willing Mace to hurry.

Before long, the two approach the sinks, Lunar wrapped in a pile of towels.

I'm on my feet in seconds, rushing into Lunar's warm arms. "You scared me to death," I whisper, relieved to feel his muscles working again. The cuts along my body burn from the pressure of our embrace, but my heart swells so large that I barely notice.

"I'm so glad you weren't eaten," he whispers back, breaking me into laughter.

I shake my head and back away. "It's okay…we're okay."

He smiles, and we hug tighter. I push back my tears, wanting to be strong for my brother. Only when the restroom door opens at Mace's hand do I release from Lunar's arms.

"Wait!" I shout. Mace turns, and I leave my brother, rushing toward the bathroom exit with my towel pile weighing me down. Silence passes between us as Mace looks me up and down. Taking in the towel monster that I am, he laughs.

"You know…I'm *also* glad you weren't eaten."

Our eyes meet, lifting a bout of butterflies through my stomach. We've held in so much emotion that I can't help but laugh at the juxtaposition of his flirtation. I black out, coming to while hugging the man who helped save my brother. I smile, overwhelmed with relief.

"Thank you," I whisper, nudging my head in the crook of his neck.

His arms tighten around me. "I'd do it again in a heartbeat."

As hard as I try to avoid Cypher, it's impossible to get away from his screams.

Throughout the night, I moved from room to room, trying to escape him. But avoiding him invited other horrors.

Moments after my group left the showers, the eliminated discovered cold water as the only effective remedy against their pained swelling. Even so, it offered negligible release, causing Jade, Artemis, and Mercedes to let out a chorus of screeching cries. Needing an hour to eliminate the inflammation, their shrieks became a background noise, even breaking through the soundproof bathroom door. Evading their agony just brought me to the kitchen, where Cypher worked on tearing a piece of fabric with his teeth and healthy hand, trying to create an adequate eyepatch. Despite his focus, he was still intent on glaring at me with his remaining good eye.

Trekking up the spiral staircase brought me face to face with Crescentia, hunched on the second floor with her back against the shiny arena door. Her hair twists into dreadlocks, and she holds her face between her knees, rocking on her tailbone. She's not aware enough to acknowledge my presence, and I'm thankful for it. Because when she finally comes to…she'll remember who selected her for that torture. And nothing about her history shows that she'll let it go quickly.

Now, lying in bed with the plush sheets pulled up to my neck, I try to leave the terrors in the past. But thousands of furry legs seem to crawl within my skin every few minutes, making me shiver and jump out of my sheets.

"The bugs?" Ashlea asks, curled up under her own covers.

It takes a moment for me to register her question before I can answer. "Yeah…" I start, shifting to the edge of my mattress. "I can't help but feel like they're still surrounding me. Like…they're crawling *inside* me."

Her green eyes shift to the ground before landing back on me. "If it helps…I saw them wash away. There's no way there's any still lingering."

I nod, pulling my knees up to my chest. Silence passes over us as I draw circles on my knee with my fingernail, watching the white marks disappear as the pressure is removed. My right arm aches from bite mark sores, and I take a deep breath before considering Crescentia and Cypher's possible retaliations against me for inflicting their punishments on them.

"They're gonna kill me."

Ashlea tilts her head. "Who's gonna kill you?"

I stuff my head between my knees, letting my speech distort from the barrier. "Crescentia. If Cypher doesn't get to me first."

Ashlea shakes her head. "Not if Mace has anything to say about it."

I huff, balancing my head on my knees and directing my attention to the foot of my bed. "But what about the one who remains? Whoever's left will go after me…or maybe Lunar, just to hurt me." I straighten my back with newfound determination. "Maybe I should go talk to her."

Ashlea's eyes widen. "Who? *Crescentia?* You mean the girl that sat in the sink after Sola's execution, completely unfazed at the bloodbath in the living room? The girl who's best friends with Mercedes? Mercedes – the one who basically told you to go fuck yourself? Yeah, I wonder how that would go."

I let out a sigh as Ashlea's words sink in. Sensing my defeat, she rises from her cot and joins me on mine, touching my shoulder with her soft palm.

"Iris, I know it's hard to believe that somebody could hate you for no reason."

I shake my head. "I must have done something for those two to act like that. I just don't understand what."

Ashlea hugs me with one arm. "There's nothing to understand. Sometimes, good people do horrible things. And other times, they're just evil human beings. Not everybody has good in them, Iris. It's something you learn in the real world…you just didn't get the chance to see it."

I tense up, because I refuse to believe her claims have validity. But a part of me struggles to justify why Sola tried to murder me in my sleep. I never spoke to her, and I barely campaigned against her. Yet somehow, she hated me so much that she wanted me *dead.*

"There's a lot of people in this house, Iris. Crescentia wasn't even close to winning. And Cypher?" She blows out air. "He's so beat up I doubt he stands a chance at winning *anything* in this game. Truly…I don't think you have anything to worry about."

Her words soothe my anxiety, so I put my head on her shoulder and let the silence wash over us. Now that the screaming has ceased, the quiet feels foreign. I'd be uncomfortable if I wasn't so dialed in on my trauma.

We watch our other housemates come and go, some stopping by Mace's Executive room to beg for their safety. As much as I'm dying to pay him a visit, I prioritize giving him time to consider tomorrow's Death Row selections.

I'm almost tired enough to shut my eyes when Ashlea's voice floats in my ear. "How were you so good at that, anyway?"

I turn to face her, backing away. "Good at what?"

Ashlea shrugs. "The questions…the riddles. How did you know so many?" She shakes her head. "I actually *went* to school and didn't know a single one."

I let out a laugh. "That's your problem right there. Don't go to school."

She smiles with a soft chuckle. "No, seriously! How were you so good?"

I shake my head. "My parents always brought home logic and puzzle books so I'd have something to fill my time. So…that's what I did. *Every* day." I lean back and smile. "What else was I supposed to do? I lived in a floor."

Ashlea laughs, this time with genuine joy. She shakes her head with a grin, so I lean back in satisfaction. I don't show emotion about my inner horrors, but the reality is that potential torture brought an entirely different element to that challenge. I may have been the smartest contestant out there, but when Lunar's life was on the line? I could hardly hold myself together.

Ashlea slides off my sheets and plops back onto her bed, oblivious of my inner turmoil. So, when she steals a quick glance at the ground and her lips stretch into a suggestive grin, I let my disappointment dissolve.

"How do you think Mace was so good at them?" Ashlea whispers. She caught on to my attraction to him long ago. Still, Mace's urgency in helping Lunar and me has solidified that the feelings may not be one-sided. I may have left Mace alone to converse with the others and allow his win to set in, but that did little to staunch my eagerness to get a proper private celebration with him.

"Honestly, I have no idea." I shrug. "I feel like I've known him forever but know nothing about him." I frown and stare at the ground, disappointed that I haven't had more time to bond with him. But success in this game requires much more than having a single ally, so I've had to spread my time amongst the others to ensure my safety for upcoming rounds.

"Well…maybe this round could change that?" Ashlea grins, poking me in the stomach. I give a weak laugh and crunch up as she continues. "Honestly, with that private room, you two could get to know each other a lot…if you know what I mean…"

Despite the circumstances, I burst out laughing. Maybe it's because of all my pent-up anxiety, but the suggestion sends me to another realm of amusement. "Shut up!" I shout, grinning at Ashlea.

She cackles hysterically on the bed beside mine, and we're left smiling until the giggles fade to a distant memory.

Ashlea and I sit opposite each other for the next hour, distracting ourselves from the Enterprize with stories from home. I get lost in our conversation, letting the pillow absorb my stress one feather at a time. But when Artemis exits the Executive bedroom, I can't help but straighten my posture. I imagine he's been in to discuss basic safety and strategy, so I don't think twice about his visit. But having healed from the toxic gas, leaving only red scars from where his skin once stretched, he has returned to the same gloomy posture he's sported since his…*encounter* with Sola. Strangely, it sends a dagger through the center of my heart. Finally, away from the physical pain of the swelling, his misery and regret consume him all over again. It destroys me to watch this once humorous and cheery man now slouch across the bedroom, long arms hanging limply at his sides. I watch as he shuffles down the steps without glancing in my direction and rashly decide to follow him.

"I'll be back," I say, patting Ashlea on the shoulder. I smooth my hair behind my ears and rise, trying to hide the urgency with which I stride to the stairs. I'm only a few steps away from the spiral staircase when Ashlea calls after me.

My heart skips a beat as I turn around to face her. "Yeah?"

"I know what you're doing."

Silence passes between us. When I can't stand the awkwardness any longer, a laugh escapes my lips. "What do you mean?"

She doesn't match my smile. Instead, she takes a deep breath, biting her lip. "Just…be careful, okay?" She gulps. "You *can't* trust him."

I nod and continue walking, rolling my eyes once she can't see me. *Why doesn't anybody trust Artemis?* In a house full of strangers, he's become my friend. Is it that terrible to check up on him? Or make sure he isn't beating himself up inside? Even though it feels like decades ago, and my brain tells me he shouldn't be forgiven for his actions against Sola, my heart hurts seeing him so distraught. His brutality may demonstrate his true character…but what does that have to do with trust? Sola never had any sort of trust in him, to begin with. Nothing was broken by his mistake.

Except her bones, of course.

I climb down the stairs, holding onto the smooth rails. When I reach the bottom, Artemis sits on the final step, smack dab in the center. He stares at the blue wall ahead but turns around once I'm a few steps behind him. Recognizing me, he gives a slight nod before returning his attention back to the opposite wall.

I know I should be disgusted with him but seeing his lifeless eyes…I struggle to catch my breath. I'm desperate to bring back the soul I know he has, so despite the tension, I step closer. Finally, one stair behind him, I raise my eyebrows, grasping onto a sarcasm that I know will lift his spirits. "Now, how do you expect me to get around you? *Pick a lane, man.*"

Artemis looks back at me and smiles, moving to his right so I can get past. But instead of walking around him, I position myself to his left, squatting down to join him on his step.

"*Great* job in that competition," I say with wide eyes, lingering on the colorful marks along his neck.

Artemis snorts back. "I did *so* bad, Iris. How does somebody do *that* bad."

I give a slight chuckle. "It's just one competition. You know you're safe with Mace anyway, so what does it matter?"

"I just wish I could show that I'm worth keeping around."

I nod, this time landing my eyes on the stretch marks covering his hand. They cover his entire body, most noticeably painting his neck with various pink and purple lines. I swallow away the lump in my throat and whisper. "I think you've done a decent job showing everyone you're a team player…protecting me, I mean."

Artemis meets my gaze, and the world freezes. His ocean eyes have the power to trap any onlooker in, me being no exception. Despite the wounds stretching across his skin, his athleticism makes me squirm with desire. His sleeves are curled up to his shoulders, showing off his chiseled arms, defined even against his swell scars. But they're impossible to see, given how entranced I am by our eye contact.

"I…I don't know what got into me." He looks down at his laces and starts fiddling with them, ending the moment. His face contorts in regret, and his body slumps in shame. No longer frozen by his gaze, my heart aches.

"It hurts me to see you like this." He lets go of his shoelaces. Despite his lack of acknowledgment, it's clear that he's taking every word to heart. I take a deep breath before continuing. "We all make mistakes; you clearly feel terrible about it. If it helps…" I lean forward, turning to face him. "I don't view you any differently."

He looks back into my eyes, and I get lost once more. "How?"

I shake my head, still entranced. The words come out in a whisper. "I just don't."

We sit silently, eyes locked, and I get a strange feeling in my stomach. Unsure of the source, I ignore it and seize the opportunity to lighten the strange tension. "Maybe don't do it again, though?"

He laughs, shaking his head. "Deal."

I pat his back as our laughter dies down, and I'm struck with an idea. One that, despite every person telling me would be suicide, my instincts urge me to follow. Ignoring my better judgment, I take advantage of the opportunity to form a stronger friendship and alliance. "You know…if you want me to help you with the logic stuff, I'd be happy to teach you."

Artemis's eyes widen. "Are…are you serious?"

"Yeah, why not?" I shrug. "Living in the floorboards had its advantages. I never had anything else to do but study and…become logical, I guess?"

His eyes contort into genuine appreciation. I keep gazing at him with a smile until his eye contact becomes so intense, I have to look away. His silly smile remains plastered on his face through the silence, making my heartrate quicken. "What?" I ask, tilting my head.

"It's just," he starts and pauses. Finding his words, he continues. "Nobody's ever really cared about me that much. To like…help me…you know?"

I smile and give him a pat on the back. "Well, Arty," I rise off the step. "That's what friends are for. Right?"

He looks back down at his shoes with a nod. I take a few steps, then turn around with a smile. "We start tomorrow." I keep walking, but not before catching the smile stretched on his lips.

Chapter 18

As the Enterprize residents complete their nightly routines, Dial members slowly file into Mace's bedroom for the selection meeting. Once Destry leaves the living room, I wait another five minutes before ascending the staircase, trying to avoid raising suspicions of a large group convening at once.

Steps from the towering Executive door, I take a few seconds to redo my braid and adjust my brows. My fingers get caught in the knots of my stringy locks, so I abandon straightening them out and throw them into a makeshift braid behind my back. The seriousness of the subject being discussed behind that door weighs heavily on my shoulders, so I distract myself with trivial physical matters. And if Mace is impressed with the outcome…that's an unintended benefit.

When I finally enter the room, I'm warmly welcomed. "Iris!" shouts Mace with a smile. He pats the bed space beside him, signaling for me to accompany him. I'm slightly taken aback by his enthusiasm but blush as I squeeze into the hospitable warmth of the covers. Clearing my mind from the dozens of fantasies that surface, I narrow in on the conversation before me.

"I think she's the obvious choice," Destry starts. "You put her on Death Row, and we have the numbers. She's gone."

"I just don't know how Artemis is going to take it," Lagiacrus starts. "We *could* just plop Jade and Cypher up there to keep him happy."

"Yes, but if we do plan A, Cypher will be so thankful for our mercy that he might forget about us." I squint my eyes at the suggestion. Surely Mace isn't naïve enough to think Cypher will forgive us for impaling him by giving him a round of safety? Oblivious of my shock, he continues. "With Mercedes and Crescentia, the only person we upset is the person voted out. So that's even less blood on my hands," Mace says plainly. He winces when he realizes the irony of his word choice but lets it pass and carries on. "I spoke to Artemis earlier, and he proposed Jade and Cypher too. But if we do what I'm thinking, then sure, Mercedes will be mad that she's in a compromising position. But there's *no* chance she accidentally gets voted out."

I straighten my back against the bedframe and tilt my head toward Mace. "Why aren't you targeting Cypher?"

Lagiacrus puts his hands up to emphasize my question and slouches against the back of the couch. Licking his lips, Mace turns in my direction and crosses his legs. "He's weak, Iris. His dominant hand is out of commission, and his depth perception is down the drain.

The odds of him winning anything in the future are slim to none. But with Crescentia getting electrocuted and the likelihood of her making a full recovery…it's safe to assume she's not gonna stop until you're dead."

The suggestion makes me tremble, so I nod my head against the shakes. I'm not entirely convinced Crescentia is the best target. I'm even more nervous about how Artemis will react to Mercedes being on Death Row. But before I can consider the repercussions further, the iron entrance to Mace's room opens, and Artemis peeks through the door. Destry waves for him to come in, and Artemis nods, shuffling toward the furthest-most crevice between the floor and the wall. I offer him an encouraging smile that he reciprocates before his lips return to neutral.

"Just in time," Mace drags out his words, delaying the inevitable. Artemis watches the violet-eyed beauty in silence. He keeps his expression as neutral as possible, in sharp contrast to the Leprechaun beside him. Finian, also leaning against the crevice, picks at his nails, face turning a bright shade of pink. Finian's never contributed much to our discussions, so I don't expect that to change now. Being of little more use than a vote to us, I ignore Finian and turn my attention back to Artemis.

Mace bites his lip, rubbing his hands together. "I thought about what you said…but we have a better idea. And I'm not sure you're going to like it."

Artemis makes a slow and loud gulp before answering, "Hit me with it."

Lagiacrus stands up to make the proposal. "I know this isn't…*ideal* for you. But we're thinking about putting Crescentia and Mercedes on Death Row."

Artemis shifts uncomfortably. "The target?"

"Crescentia, of course," confirms Mace. "There's no reason to get out Mercedes. She's a number for us."

"And a *lover* for you," Destry jokes. The others laugh, some more genuinely than others, but I stare in the opposite direction, twiddling my thumbs. I'm not surprised by Destry's crudeness, but it still makes my skin crawl. I'm entirely uneasy about the entire Mercedes situation. It doesn't sit right with me that the Dial men are forcing Artemis to engage with her romantically for the group's betterment. Both the morality of it…and something much more profound. Seeing the two together makes my stomach churn, and I can't entirely determine why.

It's not until Artemis speaks that I realize he never laughed. "If you value her so much, why not put up Jade and Cypher? Since neither of them are with us?"

Mace interjects, "If we do that, one of them stays. And whichever one is here will do anything in their power to avenge the other."

"But who's to say they aren't planning to do that already?" asks Destry. "By keeping both of them, you could just be making your chances of survival even worse."

"Especially after you two targeted Cypher in the competition," suggests Artemis, gesturing toward Mace and me.

I crane my neck forward. "But apart from that, are we really their biggest target?"

The room turns to face me, and I give a nervous gulp. Just two nights ago, Cypher and Jade were complaining about Mercedes to Ashlea. My shoulders tense, knowing that their intentions may not have been pure. But everything that's happened at the Enterprize up to today's Executive competition confirms that Mercedes is their target. And if I must wait until everyone else leaves to divulge that information to Mace, I will.

I shift my line of sight from Mace to Destry, then explain. "I mean…if I had to guess who they are after, it's Mercedes. So even if they put Mace on Death Row next to her, we'd have the numbers to keep him safe."

"Who's to say Mercedes won't come after *you* next round if you put her up?" Artemis asks, a twinkle of desperation in his eye. I fidget with the blanket beside me, gliding my fingers along the silky fabric to calm down. I would've thought Artemis would be eager to get rid of Mercedes, not fight for her safety. I look up at the camera pointed in my direction and give the slightest shake of my head, ashamed of my ignorance. *Elimination isn't just elimination. It's death.* Of course, he doesn't want Mercedes to die. He is her closest ally, and she'll likely do whatever it takes to keep him safe. Why would you want to risk somebody that could be your savior?

"I doubt she'd do that," Mace starts. "You've told me before that she *hates* Cypher and Jade. They are the ones she's after. The way I see it, why eliminate them for her if she's going to do it herself? And we have *you* in her ear." Mace opens his palm and points it at Artemis. "Even if she *is* hellbent on putting me on Death Row, she's probably willing to hear you out on who to pair me with. And from there, we'd have the numbers to get out our target."

My eyes widen, a stroke of fear pulsing through my stomach. "What if she puts me up there?"

Mace and Artemis turn, so I continue before they can interrupt. "When she got her question right, she could have chosen *anybody* to punish…but she picked *me*."

Artemis shakes his head so fast his cheeks shake. "No. She's not after you; that's not why she picked you."

My eyes contort in confusion. "Why else would she choose me?"

His head doesn't stop shaking as he speaks. "Jade was already eliminated, and Cypher was impaled. She wasn't about to share the blame for that."

"So…what? I'm third on her hit list?"

Artemis puts his arms out, trying to diffuse my anxiety. "No! Mace is right…I have an influence on her. She'll listen to me." He leans forward, putting his hands together as if in prayer. "She won't go after you; I promise you that."

It's like he's forgotten her safety was ever at risk. Before I have a chance to process his shift in behavior or respond, Mace jumps in. "It's settled then. We put Crescentia and Mercedes on Death Row and tell Mercedes she isn't the target. Hell, we'll even tell her the plan before the selection announcement." He locks eyes with Artemis. "You bring her up here tomorrow morning, and I'll give her the news. I'll need you here to comfort her but be careful not to give away the alliance." Artemis nods, so Mace continues. "I'll strike some sort of deal with her…*whatever*. The point is that Crescentia is out, and there's nobody left behind to avenge her. With Jade and Cypher…we knock out one, the other is after us." Mace leans back and nervously slides his hand through his glossy brown hair, ending with the long piece that flips over his brow. "Whether they can manage to win anything or not, they would be a threat if we draw the line in the sand."

Artemis nods, but his paling fist reveals his defeat. After a series of nods, Destry stands up and solidifies the plan. "It's settled then. Mercedes and Crescentia."

It's so quiet I feel like the air has been sucked out of the room. Finally, when I can't take it any longer, Artemis stands up, looks at the lot of us, and mumbles, "Sounds like a plan." Slumping his shoulders, he adds, "See you in the morning," and walks out the giant metal door.

Destry raises his eyebrows before settling his gaze on Lagiacrus. "I guess he took it well?"

"As well as you'd expect," Lagiacrus shrugs. "I know he doesn't like being around her, but when you spend that much time with anybody, you have to end up caring at least a little bit."

The comment drops a pit in my stomach, and I can't stop my cheeks from flushing. The sensation is short lasting as I remember the circumstances we're in. But no matter how far we steer away from the topic of Artemis and Mercedes, my brain can't stop flashing through scenarios of the two snuggled together in various crevices around the house.

The conversation shifts more than a few times, my alliance members filing out with each topic transfer until I'm left with Mace and Lagiacrus. My eyes focus in and out as I fight against slumber, the flickering red lights on the cameras threatening to plunge me into REM.

Lagiacrus stretches his arms over his head, watching Mace. "Why did you say you're here?" My muscles stiffen at the question. I've been so exhausted that I've missed the point where the conversation turned to our crimes. Suddenly, it's not the least bit difficult to stay awake. I straighten my back against the bed frame, clasping my hands together to keep still. There's mechanical whirling as the cameras focus on Mace, and I force down a deep gulp, struggling to breathe normally.

Mace runs a relaxed hand through his brown locks. "It's nothing, really." He shrugs. "I just didn't go to the Assessment."

"Why?" I interject. Having forgotten about my presence, the two jump. Mace gives a brief chuckle at the shock before turning to include me.

"Well…my parents." His lips return to a frown. "They may not have been that old, but they *were* weak. They needed me…and I couldn't leave them. Especially not indefinitely and with nobody else to look after them."

I bite my lip, letting silence grip the room. Lagiacrus just nods, then shrugs. "Well, it's for the best that you didn't go."

Mace whips his head toward Lagiacrus, beating me to the punch. Lagiacrus stares at the ground until his eyes widen, realizing the gravity of his declaration. There's radio silence until I break it. "What do you mean it's for the best?"

Lagiacrus sits motionless, face turning a light shade of pink. He shifts uncomfortably, biting his lip until Mace reiterates my question. "Best that I didn't go…because my parents needed me?"

"No," Lagiacrus shakes his head, avoiding eye contact. "No, that's not what I meant."

We sit silently until the temptation to break my fresh rule about prying into my housemate's pasts is too overwhelming to refuse. "Lagiacrus…what do you know about the Assessment?"

He freezes to formulate his response. Finally, he slumps, whispering, "It's complicated."

Mace leans forward. "I'm sure I can keep up. I did win the logistical comp."

Lagiacrus nods. "Well…it all started when I was born." He takes a deep breath. "You guys know the rule about twins?"

We both nod mechanically, wincing at the brutal law for multiple births. Regardless of twins, triplets, or separate births, every couple is allowed a single child. Without exception, only the firstborn is permitted to live. All children that follow must be…disposed of. Not having the power to eliminate twins in utero, parents are not punished for their births; however, only the oldest child can survive. But suppose a woman illegally avoids the required hysterectomy and a father bribes his way out of chemical castration, leading to multiple children being born at different times. In that case, both the parents and the youngest child must perish for the intentional violation of Miasmis doctrine.

"I was born first. My brother, Aurelius…he wasn't supposed to live. But my parents…they're in the Authority." Lagiacrus pauses, trying to be intentional with his words. "Well…they're not just *in* the Authority…they're at the *top* of the Authority." He shifts his gaze from Mace to me. "They're big decision-makers in Miasmis. So, when we were born…they had the connections to keep Aurelius alive. The others at the top…they agreed to keep our existence a secret. They approved my parents' request to have our family relocated." He picks at his fingernails, keeping his attention on the floor. "So…we were moved. Somewhere nobody would stumble upon us. That way, Aurelius and I could live relatively normal lives."

I'm shaking my head as I flash back to Lagiacrus's kidnapping. The grandiose home in the middle of the barren woods, with enough coverage and distance from others that the family could live in private. *And show off their wealth by any means possible.*

"It's amazing what Authority families can get away with," I whisper, immediately turning red.

"To a point," Lagiacrus says, raising his eyebrows. "They oversaw a lot, but the Assessment was out of their jurisdiction. *Until* the head of Assessment operations passed. Age 124." He nods as if this point is obvious. "Being in the Authority for thirty-five years, they promoted my father to Assessment management."

Lagiacrus takes a deep breath. "Guys…I don't know what he saw. But whatever it was…" He gazes into my eyes, sending a fearful shiver down my back. "It was bad enough that he risked our lives to stop it."

I lean forward. "But…what does that even mean?"

Lagiacrus licks his lips. "He threatened to expose the Assessment…he threatened to end it. In fact, he *tried* to. He and my mother spent *weeks* organizing a plan to stop the operation. But once the others caught on to what they were doing…"

"They came."

We turn to Mace, who is slumped in defeat.

"Exactly," Lagiacrus answers. "We had some warning…a friend of theirs tipped us off about the ambush. That's why my parents were prepared to fight." He shakes his head. "But they told us not to resist. They didn't want us killed." He bites his lip, blinking to prevent tears. "I tried not to fight back…and my parents…they really *did* put up a good fight. But Aurelius…"

"I'm so sorry," I whisper. "That must have been terrifying."

Lagiacrus nods but quickly takes a deep breath, puffing out his chest. "I mean…we've all been through hell, haven't we? Everyone we know…*gone*." We sit in silence, and I can't help but let my mind wander to Curi. My heart aches, hoping she's safe. Afraid that tears might start if I keep my thoughts on her, I force the conversation forward.

"Did they know about the Enterprize?" I ask carefully, not wanting to trigger him further.

He shakes his head, eyes wide. "They had no idea."

We sit motionless, letting the information sink in. *His parents were the head of the Authority but didn't know about the Enterprize? Or the Assessment?*

"Anyway…I should be going." Lagiacrus rises and walks toward the door. Just before opening it, he turns back to us. "They never told us what's *really* happening in the Assessment. So, I couldn't tell you. But whatever it is…we're better off dead."

Chapter 19

I sit frozen beside Mace, hiding my torso under the covers that once provided me so much warmth and comfort. Now, they do nothing to combat the goosebumps running across my flesh. The iron slab shuts behind Lagiacrus, so I open my mouth to speak, but no words come out. My life has been filled with little more than Authority propaganda, so the Assessment being anything other than what it has been advertised as drives me mad. Finally, my frustration boils past my awe.

"Why does everyone know about the Assessment but me? It's not like my parents were in hiding. I feel like they would've mentioned something or…or tried to protect Curi."

Mace locks his violet eyes onto my hazel ones. "I don't think you're the only one in the dark." He taps the back of my hand gently. "I had no idea. I just didn't want to leave my family. As far as I knew, the Assessment tested what genetic modification faction I'd be sent to work in."

I shake my head. "It just doesn't make any sense. If it's a secret, why does everyone know about it but us?"

"I think the Enterprize is making it look like more people know the truth than they actually do." He keeps eye contact, making my heart stir. I ignore the sensation, the severity of the conversation helping me hold on to his words. "Think about it. Everyone here has committed some type of crime, right? Whether they avoided the Assessment, had a twin, or their parents had them too young. The ones who know about the Assessment are *here*. The ones that don't…well, they *aren't* here."

I flick my eyes to the nearest camera and pause, a rush of adrenaline coursing through my veins. The red flickering has disappeared from every camera in the room, indicating that the recording has halted. The cameras sit motionless, and it dawns on me that I haven't noticed the blinking since before Lagiacrus mentioned the Assessment. The producers must have switched the footage to another room to avoid audience suspicion. I shake my head as my body shivers, my brain aching from curiosity at what the Authority could possibly be hiding.

Mace leans back, staring at the ceiling, letting an oblivious smile poke through his lips. "We're all just filthy criminals."

I laugh, forgetting the lights and leaning my head on his shoulder. But instead of feeling comfort, my mind wanders to a place of regret and horror. I back away, puckering my lips to the side. "You know…I almost couldn't bring myself to vote this morning. But…I was terrified about what would happen if I didn't."

Mace stares at the foot of the bed for a while before answering. "Me too."

I take a deep breath and flinch as the red blinks return, further reminding me of our circumstances. "Millions of people are watching us *right now*, Mace." I gulp. "I can't imagine what they're thinking about all of this."

Mace takes a deep breath. "I just don't get what the point of it all is. Why not just kill us like every other criminal in Miasmis?"

I lean my head back to the ceiling. "To scare people into following the rules." I tilt my head in his direction, locking onto his eyes. "They're torturing us to raise the stakes. If they just killed us, nothing would come of it but fifteen fewer mouths to feed. But throwing us in here…"

"It might actually get people to listen."

I nod, blowing air out slowly. Mace runs his hands through his hair, but a gleam in his eye shows me that even the greatest evils can't make his confidence falter. His steadiness slows my heartrate a touch, but nothing could entirely eliminate my guilt at participating in these games.

"Mace…we killed her." My voice quivers, and he gives a gentle nod. We have no choice but to compete, but that doesn't change the fact that the only thing we've accomplished through voting out Sola is having one less person to murder. And this round…Mace is responsible for who is killed.

I rub my temples so hard I see stars. Mace stretches his arm around me, whispering in my ear.

"We just have to look forward and keep our friends close. It's all we can do."

He rubs my back softly, calming me. But no matter what comfort he brings, I can't stop reflecting on the murders we'll have to commit if we want to survive. I crave an escape, if not physically, then mentally, for just a moment in time. Like with Artemis a few nights ago, I prompt Mace to take me away from the Enterprize.

I nestle my head closer to his ear and whisper. "What was it like?"

Mace turns to me with his head tilted, his beauty radiating even through his raised brow. I scan his face, memorizing the divot in his cheeks and freckles on his nose.

"Living a normal life…with friends and rations and…sunlight and school. What was that like?"

Mace looks at me seriously, but his eyebrows droop in sorrow. He shifts in his spot above the sheets and removes his hand from my back, once again sifting it through his light brown hair.

"Sure, parts of it were great. But others…" He takes a deep breath. "As I said…my parents were old and…frail. My mom…she suffered from cyclical pneumonia for years. My dad…he tried to help, but he was also on his last legs." He shrugs. "I just did whatever I could to keep them alive. If not for me…I doubt either would've survived very long."

I nod, watching him carefully. "How old were they?"

He looks at me, his eyes mourning. "They were sixty when they had me so…seventy-six?"

My eyes bulge at how old his parents really were. With medical advancements made before the Hage's destruction, it's not uncommon for births to happen after sixty years of age. But with my isolation, I've never truly known what the traditional maternal age was. Authority propaganda, as I am understanding, is often deceptive.

"They were amazing, Iris." He looks down at his feet at the other end of the bed, squeezing his palms. "My dad…he did whatever he could to help my mother, but the Authority forced him to work. So, I was really the only one that could help her." He bites his lip, forcing himself to stay strong. "School is required in the Midwestern Ascendancy, just like everywhere else. But…they're more lenient with attendance. It seemed to be the only things they were relaxed about. So…I stayed back a lot. And with more time at home, I actually got a lot further than the others in my class."

I lean closer. "That's why you're so good with the riddles?"

He nods. "I mean, probably. I'd heard of a lot of them already. And if you know the patterns, it's not all the hard to figure the rest out."

I nod with a soft smile. It's humorous that home school is often more beneficial than the standard Miasmis education. Still, this conversation is hardly one that warrants laughter. Not wanting to trigger his trauma further, I change the subject.

"What was the sunlight like? And the weather…the warmth and the cold?"

He looks back at me with a grin, his violet eyes beaming. "It was incredible, Iris. Even the rain…running home through the pouring water, laughing as you try and stay dry…" His eyes glisten, and he sighs with a smile stretched across his lips. "But nothing can top the sun's heat on your skin." He perks up, making the bed shake as he jumps. "And the sunsets! Have you ever seen a sunset? Maybe through the window shades?"

I smile at his enthusiasm and close my eyes, imagining the feelings and senses. My heart warms with both the sunshine and rain but fades at the mention of sunsets. "Kind of. Well…not really." I shrug. "Once it's dark, it's easy to see inside windows. So once the sun would start to set, we'd have to hide." My smile disappears, and I rub my fingers together, letting the friction warm the tips. "But from what Curi has described, even as young as she is…it's the most beautiful sight in the world."

Mace puts his arm around me, and I feel his body adjust as he turns to face me. "Well, in a few weeks…when you *win*…" He nods. "You and Curi will get to experience it all. *Together*."

I back away, tilting my head. "What makes you think I'm going to win? What about you?"

Mace gazes into my eyes, making my cheeks tingle. "Iris…you have something to live for. Me…they're *gone*. Everyone is gone." He places a delicate hand on my cheek, inching closer to my face. "You're gonna make it out because Curi needs you. And you have a team…a team that's gonna get you out of here. I…" he breaths out. "I'm gonna get you out of here."

His eyes make me freeze. The violet is so deep, so intense, that I hear my heart pounding in my ears. His eyes flash slowly between my lips and my eyes, giving the butterflies in my stomach more fuel to fly. He leans closer, and I follow my instincts, closing my eyes and allowing myself just this moment to follow my heart and pretend like I'm away from the Enterprize, somewhere safe with the man I've so quickly started to fall for.

My eyes flash open when the knocking sounds, and the fluttering stops instantly. My face flushes, and I look away, but not before catching Mace's shaky hand, fixing his hair over his brow. The knocking continues, oblivious of our lost moment. Mace coughs awkwardly before shouting, "Come in!" I sit uncomfortably beside him, subconsciously trying to hide myself beneath the blankets.

Crescentia shuffles in with her arms crossed against her chest. I soften my gaze as she mechanically moves one step before the other, her coldness piercing through the bedspread. When she trips over the even ground, catching herself before she falls, I realize her discomfort has little to do with her personality and all to do with her torturous punishment. She grips her biceps, forcing her trembles to calm down, but they're still visible despite her desperate attempts to hide them.

She flashes a quick, hopeful look at Mace before focusing on me. Locking onto my face, she deflates, her chest getting hollow and her cheeks drooping to her jaw. Her presence frustrates me in layers. I'm most angry about my magical moment with Mace being interrupted, replaced by a tangible and embarrassing tension. Once I clear my head and gain my bearings, my throat thickens, and I feel even guiltier about electrocuting her.

"What's up, Crescentia?" Mace's voice is monotone, and he doesn't look her in the eye. Instead, he slumps forward, showing no interest in a conversation with Crescentia.

"Um, nothing…I was just hoping to speak with you…in *private*?" She glares at me, and I raise my eyebrows, stretching my back against the bedframe.

"Surely, if it's *nothing*, Iris can stay?"

I smile and look down at the covers. Despite my guilt at her ailments, my stomach flutters at Mace's gesture.

Crescentia gives a deflated chuckle. "Well…it's game-related."

Mace nods and sits up straight, ignoring her request for me to leave. "Alright, what can you offer me?"

My grin is unmistakable, but it's brief. Because as the conversation commences, I can't think of anything but her pending murder. Dial made Crescentia the expulsion target, so her negotiations are pointless. My stomach churns, watching her bargain for her life. But I will not be safe while she's at the Enterprize, so Mace and I have no choice but to endorse her death.

She flicks her eyes in my direction and opens her mouth to speak, but Mace interjects, waving his hands above his head. "Hey! I'm over here."

Crescentia whips her attention back to Mace, and my grin returns. She lets out a puff of frustration. Her dark brown hair lays flat over her shoulders, looking as dejected as she feels. "If you keep *me* here, I'll keep *you* here."

Mace nods, pretending to take her words into consideration. His actions are calculated, but I can sense no cruelness behind them. He can't reveal his Death Row selections before speaking with Mercedes, so despite the pinch I know his heart feels at lying to a walking tomb, he keeps his body steady and leans forward.

"How long?"

Crescentia turns her head, squinting her eyes. "What?"

"How long will you keep me here?" Mace puckers his lips to the side. "One round, or until I win?"

Crescentia widens her eyes, backing away. "Umm…I mean…if you keep me off Death Row this round, I'll keep you off for…" she bites her lip. "Let's say the next four."

Mace contorts his face into a fake consideration so convincing I catch myself falling for it. Finally, he shakes his head. "Not good enough."

Crescentia's eyes dilate with rage. "Look, is there *anything* I could say to keep me alive? If that offer isn't good enough for you, you obviously have your mind made up already." She storms closer to the bed. "You two have had it out for me since day 1. *Why?* What have I ever done to either of you to make you want to…" She takes a deep breath, letting her words ring out in our ears. "To make you want to *kill me.*"

Silence engulfs the room. She stares at us for so long, unblinking, that I can't stop myself from looking away. My heart pounds in my ears until Mace clears his throat.

Finally, he lowers his voice and gives a weak nod.

"Look…I'll think about it, okay? Is that all?" I know that he won't change his mind, but with the way he rubs the sheet between his forefinger and thumb…it's clear he's not taking this decision lightly.

Crescentia doesn't reciprocate his kindness; instead, she rolls her eyes and marches for the door. She opens it wide before turning around, whipping all her slick brown hair behind her shoulder. "You know only *one* of us gets out of here, right? If Iris makes it to the end, she'll take the pardon for herself without a second thought about what'll happen to you. There isn't a single person here that will roll over and let you win."

My breath catches in my throat. Any consideration to apologize for her punishment vanishes as Ashlea's advice flashes into the forefront of my mind. *Not everybody has good in them.* Crescentia is urging Mace not to trust me while I'm *in the room.* Who's to say what she says behind my back? I nervously gulp, because I'm starting to understand what Ashlea meant by the concept of good versus evil. As much as I want to fix the situation between us, there may be nothing I could say to Crescentia to get on her good side.

My skin threatens to perspire when Mace diffuses the tension with a soft giggle. "You have the most amazing night as well, Crescentia. Please…*do* sleep well."

She rolls her eyes once more before slamming the door behind her.

Mace shakes his head, a grin still plastered on his lips. "Well, that went well."

I smile, laughing under my breath as I slump against the bedframe. Finally, away from Crescentia, my nerves soothe. An entirely new tension replaces the sensation when I notice Mace watching me. I match his gaze, and we stare at each other longingly, my stomach fluttering despite Crescentia's brief and disturbing interruption. But with the initial moment having passed, I have a sudden urge to flee from the potential of further awkwardness.

So, instead of leaning into him, I remove the sheets from my legs, my arms clashing with one another as the blankets get caught on my toes. "Well," I say, laughter under my breath, "I guess I should go…long day tomorrow." The comforter finally frees my legs, so I rise from the mattress and stumble around the bedframe toward the exit.

Once I reach the door, I rest my hand on the smooth surface and smile, hiding my teeth. Mace grins and chuckles, his violet eyes entrancing me into a fantasy. "You have a great night, Iris." My heart leaps as he says my name, and I blush instantly.

"You too, Mace. Enjoy the room." We watch each other, and I flash back to everything he's done for me thus far. I think about him throwing Sola off me without a second thought, regardless of what repercussions could follow. My chest warms, remembering his calming touch when he soothed Lunar's panic after the Death Row Selections on the second day. The butterflies in my stomach sour as I reminisce on Mace inspiring Lunar and me to be strong for Curi. My heart is falling for him at an unprecedented pace, every moment with him speeding up the process. Perhaps this is because I've never had the chance to be in love before, and I worry that my lust is a misattribution of arousal. It's also impossible to ignore that only one of us can make it out of here alive, and putting faith in him could be a drastic strategic mistake. But something within my heart urges me to trust the man with the sparkling violet eyes, so I happily accept.

Chapter 20

Lunar's fingers are interlocked in mine, and I give his hand a reassuring squeeze. On my right, Ashlea leans forward from the blue living room sofa and smiles, slowing my brother's anxious breaths. Kylah rounds out the crew on Lunar's left, rubbing his back while frantically darting her eyes around the room. Aware of my connection with Mace, Lunar knows that he's safe. But that does little to calm his anxiety about the potential aftermath of the Death Row selections. If it's anything like Sola's reaction last round, we're in for a horrorfest.

My eyes flicker toward the black Death Row chairs, and I squeeze Lunar's hand tighter to fight off my own trembles. A bead of sweat falls down my chin as my eyes trace the trails of Sola's blood up the walls, thinning as the ramparts creep toward the ceiling. Subconsciously protecting my panic, I avoid the large blot of blood around the head of the Death sofa.

My breath comes out in a shaky puff, and I silently curse myself for not having even attempted to clear the living space of the atrocity. Of course, no amount of cleansing could possibly remove the bullet holes from Sola's chair. But somebody could have *tried* to clear the ricocheted blood off the surrounding settees. Scanning the rest of the room, my other housemates smush as far away from the Death Row couches as possible, further establishing the universal discomfort at the massacre evidence.

I glance at the clock above the Executive chair and watch as it nears five minutes remaining. Mace, Artemis, and Mercedes are the only ones missing, the boys waiting until the last minute to conduct their courtesy meeting with her. As much as I'd love to be a fly on the wall when she finds out she's a pawn in this vote, I know I'm safer away from it all. I can only imagine who she'll lash out at when she finds out, and the further away I am from her, the less likely I'll be the one to take her rage.

Closing my eyes, I bring Lunar closer and take a moment of gratitude for our safety. Last night was the first complete cycle of sleep I've had in days, the comfort of Mace's victory responsible for it. For the first time since entering the Enterprize, my eyes don't droop, and the cots *don't* beg for my company.

Lunar also slept through the night, but the neon countdown is enough to raise anybody's heart rate, no matter how safe they feel. Across from us, Destry flicks his gaze from the clock to the staircase, unsure of what to watch more intently. Despite knowing who Mace is selecting, Finian sweats profusely, his pale face the darkest shade of pink he's had yet. Beside him, Eno gazes at the carpet, his hands folded neatly in his lap.

Crescentia sits next to Eno, balancing out his serenity. Her dark hair is drenched in sweat, her stringy locks sticking to her face and chest in large chunks. Considering how poor her conversation with Mace went last night, she must know she's in danger. My stomach twists, recognizing how numbered her days really are, but I remind myself that if it must be somebody, it's got to be her.

A door slams shut on the top floor, the force reverberating through the living room. I whip my head around but avert my eyes when Mercedes marches down the steps, her chest puffing with each exaggerated breath. Mace and Artemis are a stride behind her, speaking quietly with wild hand gestures. But a quick look around the room confirms that all the attention is on Mercedes.

Sweat drenches her pits, and her face is as flushed as those around me. But unlike the others, her teeth are clenched in fury, and her eyes shoot daggers. At the bottom of the steps, she slams her hand against the wall, causing another loud echo to settle around the room. The others look away, not wanting to trigger her further, and she drops onto the couch opposite mine, Destry to her right. Her left leg shakes rapidly as she glares at Mace and Artemis, who are whispering in the kitchen. With sixty seconds left on the clock, the two shuffle to the living area, their calmness making Mercedes grunt with frustration.

"Take your time, why don't you?" Spit flings from her mouth as she shouts. "We'll all wait. Don't you even worry about that."

Mace looks at her wide-eyed and quickens his shuffle. But it doesn't calm her fiery rage.

"Gotta follow the rules, don't you? Don't wanna announce selections late! Why take the bullet for us when you can deliver it, right?!" Her arm extends toward the clock, just missing Destry's nose. "Why risk it and wait? Announce them now! Everybody knows who you're gonna pick, so just say it!"

Artemis squeezes next to Mercedes and puts his arm around her shoulder, whispering calming reassurances. Unfortunately, it has the opposite of the intended impact.

"You were in on it too, weren't you?" She backs away from Artemis, smashing Destry against the others. "I trusted you!"

"What are you talking about?" Artemis says in a panic, giant palms opening to the sky. "I don't want this either! Why would I want this?"

Jade stifles a laugh at the other end of their couch, her black bob bouncing through her silent cackles. Mercedes rises from the sofa and launches an inch from Jade's purple and red stretch-scarred face. "What the hell are you laughing about? You've known too, haven't you!"

Jade snorts, not backing an inch. "Get over yourself, Mercedes. How would I know who's going up there?"

For the first time in ages, Cypher laughs. "But if things go how I think they will, I'm sure there'll be reason to celebrate."

"SHUT UP!" Mercedes rages, saliva flinging against Cypher's plain eyepatch. "How about I tell the house where you two *really* met?!"

Silence engulfs the room. Jade and Cypher lock their eyes on each other and open their mouths to defend themselves, but nothing comes out.

"Cat got your tongue?" Mercedes shouts, backing away. I straighten my posture, suddenly desperate to find out their secret. But when the clock strikes zero, and a buzzer sounds, there's nothing left to be said. The room is at a standstill, half of us scared to death about what's to come, the other half eager for Mercedes's accusation.

"Umm…" Mace stutters, unsure of where to begin after Mercedes's outburst.

"Say it, Mace! Be the Authority's puppet, you coward!" Mercedes is screaming now, her blonde locks flying like a mane behind her back.

"Jesus Christ!" Mace shouts, scrunching his hair between his fingers. "Fine! Mercedes and Crescentia, pop a squat!" His eyebrows are raised, wrinkling his forehead. He points a solid finger at the black sofas, signaling them to relocate to Death Row.

Crescentia tilts her head to the ceiling, squeezing her eyes shut. Mercedes stretches her lips into a wicked grin, bowing at Mace. "Now, was that so hard?" Mercedes stomps to the black chair Eno was sitting on yesterday and drops into it, crossing her arms around her plentiful chest. After a few deep breaths, Crescentia rises from the blue cushion and stomps to Sola's bullet-pierced throne, hands squeezed into fists. Lunar shivers as she plops down, so I squeeze his palm to calm him. But before we can react, all hell breaks loose.

"What the hell, man?" Crescentia leans forward, fingers clenching the hair near her temples. "What do you have against me? What have I ever done to you?" Her face is glowing red, and she stumbles over her words. "You…you could've had…" She takes a deep breath, but it doesn't stop her trembling. "I would have been *so* loyal…" She closes her eyes and covers her face with her palms. Finally getting her strength back, she breathes slowly and raises her head, eyes so dilated only the black is showing. "You." She whispers to Mace before finding her voice again. "You're gonna regret this decision, I *promise* you that. When I stay, I'm after you. And I will not *stop* until you're *dead*."

"I understand," Mace responds, his voice steady. His arms are limp at his sides, and he clenches his jaw, but I can see the remorse hidden in his eyes. He knows she has no chance of surviving this and takes no pride in delivering her to her death. So, instead of fighting back, he relaxes in his Executive cushion, melting into the plush. Just as I think he's about to apologize for the circumstances, he looks her dead in the eyes with a raised eyebrow. "Game on, Crescentia."

"AAARRRGGG!" Crescentia shouts, leaping off her cushion and stomping toward the staircase, kicking every chair and trashcan in her path. She bounds up the spiral steps two at a time, shouting violent threats and crude obscenities that gain severity with each passing stride. Only once she crests the top is her rage out of earshot, leaving the living room in tense silence. Mace takes a deep breath and shakes his head, frustrated with how poorly the operation went. Lunar is rigid beside me, pale with terror at the anger unleashed in the house. Artemis rests his head in his palms, and Mercedes taps her foot impatiently at the foot of the room. I clench my hands, fighting the overwhelming urge to flee. When I can't stand the tension any longer, Destry leans forward off the couch, palms turning toward the ceiling.

"So, are we going to ignore what just happened?"

Glaring at Mercedes, it's obvious Destry's not talking about Crescentia's tantrum. He throws his arms up and shouts to ensure we're all on the same page. "What do you know about Jade and Cypher?"

"They grew up together!" Mercedes yells. "I heard them talking last night—their memories, their mutual friends…they came in as a pair and lied about it to all of us!"

My jaw drops to the floor. In hindsight, it all makes sense. But I'm frustrated that I hadn't connected the dots earlier. It isn't entirely surprising that two criminals from the same Ascendency knew each other before the Enterprize. But with how close they are…how had they hidden their relationship so well at the start?

"Why should anyone believe you, Mercedes!?" Cypher defends in a panic, sweat pouring down his face. "You're the biggest *bitch* in the house! Stop…stop making things up to deflect attention from yourself!"

He hugs his shoulders, clenching his teeth. His desperation to change the topic to Mercedes's flaws is a dead giveaway of his lies. The last person I thought I would agree with is the blonde beauty queen, yet I find myself believing her.

"Why would we keep that a secret?!" Jade shouts, her voice cracking. "How would that help us?"

Mercedes laughs manically. "Are you serious right now? *How would that help you?* HA!"

"Dude," Lagiacrus says to Cypher, unable to look him in the eye. "You came in as a pair…and you lied?" He leans forward, finally facing the fraud. "I lost my brother, and you just sat there, saying nothing?"

Mercedes continues laughing, leaning back into her chair and opening her palms to the sky. Despite their failure and the negative backlash, I understand why they kept their connection a secret. I would have considered a similar strategy if Lunar wasn't my brother and we weren't captured together. But I wasn't offered this option, so their lie infuriates me.

Jade searches the room frantically, desperate to save her credibility. She punches the couch, unable to contain her aggression. "Mercedes, I don't know why you're attacking us when you were never even on our radar." She wipes a bead of sweat from her brow, and it launches to the floor. "Ashlea's the one going around the house telling people to gun for you!"

For the second time this afternoon, I audibly gasp. A few nights ago, I woke to Jade and Cypher pressuring Ashlea to declare war against Mercedes. Despite their accusation, she evaded their questions while they awkwardly campaigned against the bodacious blonde. Their last-ditch effort is based on another outrageous lie, confirming to me that they have known each other for years.

"*Are you kidding me?* You psychopath!" Ashlea launches from the couch, closing the gap to Jade in a second. Jade steps closer, getting inches from Ashlea's face. My muscles freeze on the sofa as the two girls scream over one another, and my housemates struggle to keep their jaws off the floor.

"You *BEGGED* me to tell you who I was after, and I said I wasn't sure because I do *NOT* lie!"

Jade pushes into Ashlea. "*YOU* approached me and Cypher in the middle of the night, *SCREAMING* about how much you hated Mercedes!"

"THAT'S A LIE AND YOU KNOW IT!"

"Don't be a coward, Ashlea!" Jade continues pushing into her, only a couple of centimeters separating their faces. "OWN UP TO YOUR MISTAKES!"

The urge to step in dominates my senses; I open my mouth and take a breath to intervene. Just before I can speak, Mace appears in my peripheral, shaking his head so quickly his hair sticks up. His violet eyes lock onto mine, urging me not to get involved. He might not know about my presence in that midnight conversation, but he knows my friendship with her could bring me to her defense. My stomach churns, knowing there's nothing I can do to help her. I consider whether to speak with Mercedes in private, but my thoughts are distorted by the growing screams.

"I swear on my *life* you said that!" Cypher shouts at Ashlea, joining the mayhem.

"You think I'm scared of you?!" Ashlea shoves Cypher. "I am *NOT* scared of you!"

The entire scene is chaos. The three push each other relentlessly. Cypher screams at the top of his lungs, and Finian's face pales until he's close to fainting. Apart from the Leprechaun, my alliance members sit back against the sofa cushions with varying degrees of enjoyment in their eyes. As we hoped, we avoided the mayhem and faded into the outskirts. Our silence keeps us safe, and I'm grateful that Mace signaled for me not to get involved.

Surprisingly, Mercedes leans forward, beaming with her chin resting in her hands. Despite the conversation being about her, the shouting is directed in the opposite direction. Her eyes twinkle with satisfaction that the biggest issue in the house is no longer her problem with Mace but rather her biggest targets digging themselves deeper graves.

"Everyone, please calm down! This isn't you!" Old man Eno finally rises from his couch, putting himself between the two girls. Ignoring his presence, Cypher continues shouting at Ashlea, drowning out Jade's vile insults.

"If you want to shout at a girl, that's fine!" Ashlea backs away from Cypher, putting all the blame on him. "Show the audience how you *really* treat women."

The moment it leaves her lips, I know it's a mistake. Cypher launches at her, but Eno jumps in the way at the last second. Cypher strikes Eno to the floor, now rageful about his interference. He extends a foot over him, attempting to move onto his primary target, but his violence strikes a nerve with the other men in the house. After the Artemis debacle with Sola, the house has unofficially committed to preventing the intentional harm of another houseguest. Destry and Lagiacrus break the laissez-faire tactic they've employed throughout this argument and jump onto Cypher, holding his arms behind his back and pinning him to the floor.

"This isn't over, *bitch*!" he shouts as the two men drag him into the bathroom.

Following their initiative, Artemis and Mace separate the girls from one another. Mace pulls Ashlea toward the stairwell, so I leap from the couch, towing Lunar. Kylah follows suit, our posse rushing to Ashlea's side as she's pulled to the communal bedroom. Artemis escorts Jade to the kitchen, and Finian falls to Eno's side to check the damage. When we finally reach the staircase, the entire house has scattered, leaving Mercedes alone on her black Death Row cushion. Before ascending the steps, I catch her flip a large chunk of blonde hair behind her shoulder, cross her legs, and laugh. Just before I am out of earshot, I see her lock eyes with the nearest camera, lick her lips, and smile.

"Let the games begin."

Chapter 21

"They're a pair, and they *lied* about it!" Ashlea pounds her fists on the mattress, dried tears crusted on her cheeks. "They've been lying this entire time!"

I rub Ashlea's shoulder gently, careful not to apply too much pressure. For the entirety of the night, she screamed about Cypher and Jade, insisting that she was telling the truth. Any efforts to calm her have been to no avail, her shouting still reaching new octaves despite the fight being separated hours ago.

"You guys *have* to believe me! I've never said a word about Mercedes! To them or anyone!"

Lunar and Kylah sit silently on my bed, nodding their heads between bites of dried chicken. Ashlea's tantrum has extended so long that our crew's taken turns delivering our evening rations. It's unlikely anyone's missed anything in the retrieval process—Ashlea's cycling through her same set of grievances on a loop. "Why are they even here, huh? Is anyone else even the least bit curious as to what they've done?"

Mace squats on the floor between my bed and Ashlea's and pats his hand on my friend's pillow. "Does it really matter?" Mace's words are soft, but I know he's holding back frustration at how long Ashlea's rage has lasted. "The numbers were against them, to begin with. And with their credibility gone, I doubt a single person here would protect them."

Kylah swallows her chicken and nods, leaning forward to touch Ashlea's knee. "And Ashlea, we believe you." Kylah smiles.

Ashlea takes a deep breath, rubbing the salt from her cheeks. "Nobody that desperate to deflect is ever telling the truth."

Finally having a chance to get a word in, the group of us validate her frustrations and reassure her of her safety. Her anger subsides when our housemates start filling in for bed, so we complete our night routines one at a time, careful to keep Ashlea company. She eventually tucks herself into her sheets and shuts her eyes, satisfied with how far Jade and Cypher's beds are from hers and exhausted from yelling.

I collapse onto my bed beside hers, eyelids fluttering shut and muscles melting into the blankets. But not two minutes later do I shoot off my pillow, remembering my promise to Artemis. With the Death Row anxiety and chaos, I've completely forgotten my offer to tutor him. Leaning against the bed's backboard, I sigh, debating whether to ditch tonight's arrangement. I toy with the thought of abandoning him, emphasizing to myself that tomorrow is reserved for decision-making and could be the perfect time to pull him aside for training. A sinking feeling fills my chest as I consider this, my brain and heart aligning that I must follow through on my promise. After all, if my word isn't good for something as simple as this, how can I ever be trusted?

Rolling my eyes, I rise from my mattress and fight off its magnetic pull. I scan the cots, searching for Artemis, but only find his empty bed directly across from mine. Taking another deep breath, I kiss Lunar on his forehead and descend the spiral staircase, yawning three times on my way down.

Steps from the bottom, Artemis's voice stops me in my tracks. The words are whispers, but they're unmistakably his. I step back to avoid his and his friend's notice, my stomach dropping from the close call.

"You're gonna be fine, Merc. But *only* if you lie low." I lean past the edge of the wall and see Artemis holding Mercedes by her shoulders, his grip gentle. "Mace guaranteed your safety, and I know him—he's good for his word."

Mercedes whispers back, her voice shaking. "But…how can he know that? He doesn't even get to vote." I bite my lip, never having seen Mercedes so anxious. There's a slight tremble in her arms. Her rage at the selection ceremony has vanished, anxiety at her position taking up its residence.

Artemis positions his fist under her chin, his thumb lingering close to her bottom lip. "Can you just trust me? I trust Mace, so…if you trust *me*, you'll trust him too."

There's silence between them, and Mercedes nods, prompting Artemis to continue. "Good. Now, please…no more fighting. If you keep your cool, you'll be safe. You've made your hatred for Jade and Cypher clear…the others won't touch you because they know who you're after. You've done your part…now it's time to sit back."

There's no response for several seconds, so I pick up my leg to close the distance and steal Artemis for our lessons. But before I can place it on the floor, Mercedes's words freeze me to the step.

"I love you, Art."

Frozen in place, my eyes widen in horror. I clench my fists and scrunch my eyebrows together, my vision turning red. It's hard to believe I considered abandoning Artemis tonight. Right now, I want nothing more than to get him alone, far from Mercedes's grasp.

My body acts of its own accord, my brain protecting my heart from the possibility of Artemis saying the words back. Without instruction, my legs smash down the final steps, preventing Artemis from developing a response. Startled, Artemis's eyes widen in horror, and he instantly breaks his hug with Mercedes. Watching him fluster, Mercedes steps away from the embrace with her head tilted. Once spotting me, she stomps her leg and sets her hands on her hips. She rolls her eyes so hard they nearly pop out of her head, and I struggle to find an explanation for my interruption.

"Uh—umm…" I stutter, lips twitching. "Sorry…I just…" I glance in Artemis's direction. "I'm here for the tutoring?"

Artemis lets out a shaky breath and nods, a lightbulb going off in his mind. He breathes in and turns to Mercedes, placing a soft hand on her forearm.

"Remember what I told you yesterday?" He squeezes her wrist. "About Iris…offering to help me with the riddles?"

Mercedes nods slowly, not taking her eyes off me.

He moves into her line of vision. "Well…I guess it's that time?"

Mercedes flicks her gaze between the two of us and rolls her eyes again. "Fine. I'll keep *our* bed warm." She smirks at me with squinted eyes before pulling Artemis in and locking onto his lips. She feels him up, one hand trailing up and down his torso while the other forces his face into hers. I stare at the ground, puffing out a single cheek, counting the seconds until the production ends. Occasional glances confirm that the passion is one-sided. Artemis's arms lay limp at their sides, only his lips committing to the act.

When they finally separate, Mercedes smirks in my direction while running a hand through Artemis's hair. She skips up the steps, blonde locks flying back and forth with each jovial jump. Once she's finally out of earshot, I lift an eyebrow, unable to mask my disgust.

The words escape before I can stop them. "How…charming."

He palms his forehead while his head shakes back and forth. Avoiding eye contact, he shifts his enormous hands, wiping the sweat off the bridge of his nose. "I'm so sorry. You know Mercedes…she just—"

"What are you sorry for?" I cut him off, forcing a grin. "Your girlfriend's just being your girlfriend…what's there to be sorry about?"

He bites his lip, eyes shifting to everything but me. "You don't understand…how hard this is…"

Guilt and shame eat away at my stomach lining. Artemis's vulnerability helps me identify my earlier rage as childish jealousy. No matter how much I fight it, I yearn for the attention he gives the voluptuous firecracker. This acknowledgment makes the room feel like it's boiling; it's foolish to feel such a way when our predicament is deadly. Beyond this, their relationship isn't real. Artemis is being forced to engage with Mercedes romantically for the group's advancement. Confusion mixes into my thoughts, so I push my feelings away and nod, letting him off the hook.

"Don't worry about it," I whisper. "You don't have to explain yourself. We're friends…right?"

He winces at 'friends' but nods, nonetheless.

Artemis follows me to the living room, and we settle on opposite sofas. I lean forward with my hands clasped in front of me, thinking of a way to begin, but I'm quickly distracted by the beaming red clock at the head of the room, reading, "23:03.17". With Death Row selections already being announced, the time of day has replaced the countdown until the last day of this round, where a descending timer for the vote will start. I forget Artemis is across from me, my mind swimming with how I'll have to concede in killing off yet another housemate who doesn't deserve it. I imagine Crescentia fighting the guards when the vote is revealed, refusing to leave…*being shot to death on Sola's cushion.*

"Iris?"

I jump, meeting Artemis's eyes. My cheeks flush with embarrassment, and butterflies mysteriously flutter into my abdomen. His ocean pearls fill me with a strange sensation, and I shake my head, forcing myself to ignore it.

"Sorry," I smile, breaking our eye contact.

He doesn't miss a beat. "Nervous?"

I lock my gaze back onto his instantly, and goosebumps erupt along my legs. I tilt my head, baffled at how he can sense the hold he has on me. Before I can respond, he blinks three times and then continues. "I mean…about next round?"

I breathe out, flushed with relief. Quickly recovering, I bite my lip and kick my legs out slowly, one at a time.

A thousand thoughts fight for my attention. But shallowly, my safety comes at the forefront. And despite my studies, I can't begin to imagine what kind of horror awaits us. "I mean…all of this…it's a lot." I deepen my gaze. "We don't really know what to expect for the next competition, do we? And after the punishments this round…what could be next?"

He nods, stretching the left edge of his lips into a comforting smile. "Yes, but we've got a strong team, Iris. Whatever they throw at us…we shouldn't have a problem securing the win."

I shake my head. "That's not *really* what I'm nervous about."

He raises his eyebrows, encouraging me to continue.

"Think about it." I rub my hands forcefully, the realization and terror hitting me all at once. "After being on that swing for a while, they brought out the metal pole…making it dangerous. And then…what looked like riddles became a battle royale." My throat burns, urging my voice to quiver. But I force it to stay steady. "Who's to say the comps won't keep getting worse as we go?"

Artemis scrunches his eyebrows together. "There's just no way to know. But thinking about it…it's gonna torment you." Silence engulfs the room, so he pokes my leg with the toe of his shoe, eyes determined. "But whatever it is…we'll all take it on. Together. We've got each other's backs, right?"

"For a while," I say in a daze. "But what about a few rounds from now? When the numbers dwindle down?" I shake my head. "Then what?"

Artemis considers this question, and I can almost see the gears running in his head. He scratches the back of his neck, glancing at the floor. Finally ready to answer, he locks back onto my gaze.

"We just need to focus on the now, Iris. And…not allow ourselves *any* regrets."

His pupils narrow, and the streaks of darker and lighter blues in his eyes reveal themselves against the ocean hue. This time, the butterflies in my stomach take full flight. I squeeze my right palm, fighting my urge to ask what he's insinuating. Quickly flashing back to reality, I force the sensation to dissipate and change the subject.

"Speaking of the now…" I run my fingers along the sofa's plush, letting the soft fabric distract me from our previous conversation. "Ready for the first lesson?"

The transition is unnatural, leaving an awkward tension in the air. Nonetheless, Artemis smiles, showing off his crooked and gapped teeth, putting my butterflies to rest. Artemis folds his hands into his lap and sits straight, resembling a student in a classroom. "I'm all ears."

I wrack my brain, searching for a place to begin.

"Well, for starters…you suck at riddles."

He laughs and shakes his head. "I'm glad to see you've gathered that much."

I smile. "Well, I'll give you some advice in that realm, but I don't think it'll be entirely helpful. I doubt they'd do the same competition twice. But if there's anything like it, it's worth considering a few things." I take a deep breath, then stretch out my arms as a teacher would, emphasizing important points. "It's really about practice. Think about the riddles in the comp." He nods politely, but the purple streaks along his neck make me confident he ignored every question after his gassing. Regardless, I continue. "Most of them had the answer within the question. For example…didn't you get the number one wrong?"

He nods his head, focused on me. I bite my lip, treading lightly. "You were thinking about it too hard. There was maybe a question or two that required outside knowledge. *All* the others told you the answer. Just focus on what you're given and work from there. Don't think about it too much."

We get into the nitty-gritty of solving riddles, using examples for practice. After twenty minutes, I switch directions.

"We should also consider other mind-related puzzles and start studying for those."

Artemis clasps his hands into his lap, still sitting up straight. "Like what?"

I pucker my lips to the side, thinking. "Well…this house has a ton of details, right? What if we're quizzed on that? Like…how many steps there are, the number of drawers in the kitchen…we should count the microphones in each room-stuff like that. And what if they ask us stuff about time? It could be worth remembering how long everyone has lasted in the other competitions. Or the order they were eliminated."

His eyes widen, and his lips stretch into a smile. "How do you think of this stuff, Iris?"

I match his grin and shrug. "Well, *Arty*…a lifetime in the floorboards will get your mind moving."

We spend the next half hour reviewing times and elimination orders from the first competition. Then we count cushions and doors on the bottom floor before diving into even more specific details, like the number of screws holding each cabinet in place. We make a game out of it, racing around the bottom floor and blocking the other's routes, forcing each other to guess before counting. The session naturally progresses from a mission into a playful contest until we collapse from laughter on the kitchen chairs.

"There are thirty steps to the top! Not a doubt in my mind," Artemis leans back in his chair with his arms folded, letting the back pegs take all his weight. His proximity to me makes it even funnier, so I slam the table with my palm, mouth wide.

"Are not! There's gotta be less…no more than 25!"

Artemis leans closer, touching a single finger to his smiling lips. "Shhh," he drops off his tongue, sending me into a fresh bout of howls. He presses a hand to my mouth as we laugh, pointing upstairs so that I quiet down. Rocking back and forth from the giggles, I whack his palm from my face and scrunch my eyebrows together.

Once we can finally breathe, Artemis gets the words out. "If you're so confident, let's bet on it!" He leaps from his chair to block my view of the staircase. "If I'm closer…" He places a thumb on his chin, and I hold my stomach to soothe the laughter aches. He smiles, struggling to get the words out. "If I'm closer…" He waves his arms, ensuring I can't see behind him. "Then *you* have to go a *week* without showering."

I gasp and choke at the same time. "No way! I'd smell terrible!"

He laughs back manically. "Then you better win!"

I shake my head and consider an equally disgusting punishment. Finally striking gold, I grab his arm and poke him in the chest. "If *I'M* closer…" I rise from my chair and inch toward his face, eyes wide. "Then *you* have to drink the toilet water!"

Artemis booms with laughter. "No, not a chance!"

I smile, straining to keep my volume from waking the others. "If you don't want to do it, then win!"

He shakes his head and raises a single eyebrow. "You strike a hard bargain." He stares at the ceiling for a moment, considering the deal. Finally, his gaze settles on mine. "Closest?"

I smile. "Without going over."

He rolls his eyes but can't wipe off his silly grin. Finally, he extends his palm. "Deal."

I grab his hand and shake, electricity pulsing through my body the second we touch. We both freeze, gazing into each other's eyes. My smile fades, the moment pausing time. Suddenly, I'm aware of every physical feature, from his muscular forearms to the veins running down them. My grip slackens, the length of his thick brown hair suddenly sending a powerful urge through my abdomen. He raises a single eyebrow as my smile completely disappears. Disrupting the tension, he turns around, pulling my hand as he sprints to the bottom steps. I shake my head, relinquishing the moment for the present, his energy powering back my excitement. I laugh, letting the brief connection fade, and match his level of anticipation.

Our hands quake as we calculate each step, smiles plastered on both of our faces. We reach the final step at the same time, and I gasp in delight.

"No frickin' way," Artemis shakes his head, but he can't hide his smile. "Twenty-nine steps."

I back away with my palms open to the ceiling. "What did I say, Arty?!"

He laughs and shakes his head. Letting out a large and miserable exhale, he stares at the back wall and whines, "Get me a cup, you witch."

I skip to the kitchen, laughing all the way to the bathroom. To his credit, he drinks an entire glass of toilet water, sending me to my knees in eccentric howls. He doesn't look up a single time from his cup, but when he finishes, he scrunches his face like he's tasted something sour. I slap him on the back, and he joins my screeching chorus. Not only do we forget about the Enterprize and the consequences tomorrow could bring, but for a moment in time, we are the only two people in the world. The bathroom being soundproof, we let our cries ring out into the night, only going back to the living room so Artemis can escape the taunting toilet waters. We plop onto the couches, and my breath catches in my throat when the red numbers flash with "1:32.00."

"Arty…we've been down here for nearly three hours," I point out. We laugh again, and he shakes his head as silence consumes the room.

"Iris…" Artemis's blue eyes glisten in the light. "Thanks for this…seriously."

"For helping you?" I ask, unable to contain my smile. "It's the least I could do after how *terribly* you performed yesterday. *I* was embarrassed *for* you!"

He rolls his eyes, then lets his face soften. His features become kind, no longer sharp or demanding. He shakes his head and settles his gaze on me, freezing me to the couch. "No…no. Thanks for *tonight*. *All* of it."

My hand starts to tremble, and my stomach drops four flights. I can't deny that I've never laughed this hard in my fifteen years of life…but the emotion behind those words…

It brings me back to the moment we had in the kitchen. The electricity I felt from his touch. Surely, that went both ways? But when he smiles at me, teeth caving in at odd angles, giant palms lifting strands of hair from his face…

All I can think about is how much I wish Mace could be the one sitting in front of me.

The thought of Mace encompasses my body in a mixture of joy and guilt. Sweating, I make an exit strategy, unwilling to let this night go even further. Possibly, past a point of no return…

Forcing a smile, I rise from the couch and match his gaze. "Anytime, Arty." I flip around toward the staircase, forcing my stride to slow enough to erase suspicion of my conflicting feelings.

"And Iris?"

I stop in my tracks and turn back, careful not to show too much interest. "Yes?"

He gulps before answering.

"She's not my girlfriend."

A shiver goes down my spine, the words confirming my suspicion. I frown as his blue eyes shift up and down my body, examining every inch and lingering around my pelvis. Suddenly, everything about Artemis clicks. His overreaction to Sola's murder attempt. The constant apologizing for his relationship with Mercedes. The wincing when I call him my friend. I flashback to his insistence that he's a good person. *He's not trying to be my friend.* He's not even trying to show me that I can trust him.

He's doing so much more than I could have imagined.

Careful to stay friendly, I force my lips back into a smile and whisper delicately, "Okay." Then I make my way up the steps two at a time, my stomach twisting in guilt and my mind running a million miles an hour.

Chapter 22

"There's no way that's washing out," Crescentia barks. "Even if it would, you're not sewing up those bullet holes."

Lagiacrus looks back from scrubbing the blue sofa and glares at her. "That doesn't mean I can't try."

With many of the houseguests getting weak stomachs at yesterday's selection ceremony, Lagiacrus took on the responsibility of the cleanup crew. All morning, he's scrubbed the walls of Sola's expulsion remnants, erasing evidence of her murder from the ramparts. However, his efforts at scrubbing the bloodstains from the carpets and surrounding settees have shown little success, Lagiacrus mostly just spreading the stains into the surrounding fabric.

"How 'bout I give you a hand with that?"

Beside me in the kitchen, Eno sets his bowl of bland oat cereal down (this round's breakfast ration), grips the table determinedly with both hands and gives a large, elderly "humph" as he rises. Lagiacrus and I roll our eyes and chuckle at Eno's pathetic attempts, relieved from the humorous exaggerations of his age. Even Crescentia hides a smile at the display, looking the opposite way to avoid being associated with us.

Since dawn, the four of us have silently accompanied each other on the ground floor, tending to our own dull tasks. Whether picking at oats, cleansing the living room of Sola's blood, twiddling our thumbs, or organizing our thoughts, we all have the same intention: getting the time to pass. Despite the comfort of my safety, I didn't catch a wink of sleep. Opposingly, when Artemis flopped into Mercedes's arms, his immediate stillness confirmed that he fell asleep in seconds. His ease of slumber is no surprise to me, given the events he believed to have occurred between us last night. But I laid awake, hating myself for even giving him a sliver of hope that he was anywhere close to my number one ally. Even if his brief and gentle touch stopped time…

I tossed and turned last night, Mace and Lunar competing for attention in my dreams. Ashlea was always in my mind to pick up the pieces, and it took everything in me not to reach out to her in the night. My trust in them is justified and strong, and nobody around me questions their loyalty. But with Artemis…

Mercedes is the only one who feels the same way as I do about Artemis. She is hardly the company I want to associate with, so I know Artemis can't be good news. However, the more I consider Mercedes, the more I recognize that she may be the only genuine person in this house. She wears her emotions on her sleeve, and she's only cuddled up to a single ally. In the meantime, I'm pretending like half of the house is going to make it out alive. When it comes down to it, befriending as many houseguests as I have will make this game so much more difficult to navigate – not to mention the heartbreak waiting in my path. As much as I hate to admit it, Mercedes may not be as cruel as she portrays herself…she could just be protecting her heart. And any sane person would respect those motives.

So, why won't my stomach stop *burning* with jealousy?

Twirling my oats around their bowl, I decide to distance myself from Artemis—at least until his feelings have dissipated. *Embrace the people you trust entirely. Disregard the rest.*

And don't get voted out.

My other housemates start filing into the kitchen as the morning develops, and I give each one a halfhearted smile and nod. Finally, Lunar and Mace descend the staircase side by side, making my smile come naturally.

"Sleep well?" I ask as Mace ruffles Lunar's brown mop of hair at the bottom of the steps.

"Yeah, mind telling me what year it is?"

I grin at Mace and feel a touch of envy at his luxurious bedroom. With my lack of sleep, I'll have to take advantage of this commodity with a nap by the end of the day.

Lunar plops down beside me and kicks my leg playfully. I hug him, releasing him when Mace drops his and Lunar's rations onto the table.

"We miss anything?" Mace asks.

"Just that old man draining his last bit of physical strength to get out of this chair." I point to Eno, on his hands and knees in the living room, and the floor erupts into a chorus of laughter.

"I'm telling you guys, I'm a *legitimate* physical threat in this house," Eno jokes, still on all fours. "You'll probably want to get me out of here while you still can!"

We keep laughing, Mace moving his chair an inch closer to mine. Instead of matching his gesture, my mind mysteriously wanders to Destry. A few nights ago, my alliance members agreed to start pursuing friendships outside of the group to cover our bases and control the votes. Destry was supposed to start a serious friendship with Eno, but I haven't once seen the two together. Perhaps I should take Dial's allegiance with Eno into my own hands. That way, Destry's laziness doesn't get us all—

"Hey, have a sec to talk?"

I turn to my left as Crescentia pulls a chair between Lunar and me, having to forgo the nonexistent gap between Mace's and my chairs. My breath catches in my throat, shocked by her sudden urgency. I gulp back my anxiety before answering. "Yeah, sure. Right here?"

She scans the three of us, eyes lingering on Mace. "Yeah, that's fine. You three are a trio anyway."

Mace squints. "Says who?"

Crescentia's mouth falls open with regret. She puts her hands up defensively. "No, sorry, I didn't mean…can we start over?"

The three of us look at one another before I nod, encouraging her to continue.

She leans closer, rubbing her forehead. "Look…obviously, the vote is tomorrow. I just wanted…to get a feel for where you are." She takes a deep breath. "Is there anything I can do to get your votes?"

One glance at Lunar confirms his discomfort. He's out of commission, scratching his fingers on the back of his chair, causing shards of wood to fall to the floor. I deflate, realizing my once sassy, witty brother is being transformed by the Enterprize into a nervous, panicked shell of what he once was. With the safety of the floorboards gone, he's lost his edge. I lick my lips and turn to Crescentia, ready to get the conversation over with and get Lunar out of here.

"Have anything in mind?" I ask.

"All I have is my word…I'm alone in this game. Mercedes…she doesn't really pay much attention to me since…*you know*. So…I have no allegiance to anyone. There's no reason for me to make empty promises to you guys. Who would I run to?"

"You make any deals with anyone else?" Mace interjects.

Crescentia glances at him before answering. "You're the first people I've spoken to."

"And you expect us to believe that?" I ask, strangely eager to hear her offer.

She shrugs. "Like I said, I have *nothing*. Either believe what I say or don't. There's really nothing I can do at this point to change your mind. But if you are open to making some sort of deal…"

She turns to see whether Eno or Lagiacrus are listening, but both are absorbed in their own scrubbing and chitchat. Crescentia lowers her voice to a barely audible volume.

"If you two vote to keep me, I'll be in debt to you. If I win executive next round, the three of you are safe. I'll even keep Ashlea here if you want." She softly nudges her head toward me.

"Who are you after?" Lunar asks, voice shaking. We turn to him, stunned that he's spoken to her. He quickly shifts his gaze to the floor and whispers, "If you don't mind me asking."

Crescentia nods and takes a moment to gather her thoughts. Finally, she whispers back, "It depends on who votes against me. That's who I'd be after."

"For how long?"

She stares at Mace, lips pressed together.

"*How long* would you work with us, Crescentia?"

She gulps, resting her hands on the table. "Until the end, if that's what it takes."

Silence falls between us, and I take the opportunity to get out. "We'll think about it, alright?" I say carefully, wondering if her word is trustworthy.

There's a crash on the stairs, and hyenic laughter travels into the kitchen. I turn to the spiral structure and find Artemis and Mercedes, hand in hand, swinging their arms back and forth like children on a playground. Mercedes's smile is beaming, but her eyes narrow maliciously onto mine. Artemis's lips are painted with a smirk, but he directs his gaze away from my table. He sweeps their rations from the cabinet, and Mercedes jumps excitedly.

"Thanks, Art, Art!" She stands on her toes, kissing him on the cheek. His eyes droop in misery, but his limbs flail in content. The urge to roll my eyes fills every inch of my being. They skip to the living room and settle on the opposite side of the disinfectant squad, Mercedes practically lying on Artemis's lap.

Crescentia notes my staring and leans close, just inches from my face. She licks her thin lips quickly, then whispers so only the three of us can hear.

"And look…I like Mercedes as much as the next person," she starts, overestimating Mercedes's popularity. "But that right there," she barely nods toward Artemis and Mercedes so only we can distinguish the motion, "that's a duo. You keep them in here long enough, and they'll pick you all off one by one. If you vote *me* out tomorrow, fine. But you're gonna have a *really* tough time taking those two down. You'll have to break them up at some point…I suggest you do it before they're too strong."

I stare at the pair as Crescentia sits back, arms folded. Artemis's vulnerability last night confirms he doesn't love Mercedes, but it's difficult to ignore the picture painted before me. Artemis laughs, gazing his kind blue eyes into her nasty, hate-filled ones. He reaches an oat-filled spoon toward her mouth but misses, causing milk to splash onto the settee. The two ignore Lagiacrus's aggravated huffs, Mercedes slapping Artemis's arm and triggering more of his laughter. My eyebrows droop as I question whether I was too exhausted last night to make a conclusion about the way he feels. But as he reaches the spoon toward her mouth for a second round, I swear that for a second, just *one* second, he watches me in his periphery, studying my reaction.

Chapter 23

"When I was your age, food was everywhere. It was coming out of my ears!" Eno jokes, making his voice sound older than it is.

Ashlea leans back on her bed, smiling, and snarks, "How *old* are you, Eno?"

Eno shifts onto his left foot and looks to the ceiling in wonderment. Mace and I sit beside one another on my tiny twin bed, Lunar in front of me. I rub my brother's back to calm his nerves for tomorrow, and Eno finally addresses the question.

"How old would I have to be for that story to be true? Three hundred?"

We howl with laughter, Lunar giving the biggest holler of us all. Destry may not be fulfilling his role as Eno's friend, but I'm happy to take on the added ally. Apart from Kylah and Mace, Eno has been an important influence in Lunar's sanity at the Enterprize. He's been entertaining us for hours with stories from his childhood, and Lunar is finally gaining enough confidence to share his experiences.

"One time, our dad tried to cut an old biscuit for Iris and me to share, and it was so stale that the blade broke off the knife."

Mace chuckles, and Ashlea smiles; I sit back and laugh at the memory, now fond of a time when we had safety and freedom, albeit artificial.

"You ever think you'd long for the floorboard days?" I joke as I lightly push Lunar forward.

"No, but now I'm feasting!"

I fold over in laughter. "That's how I feel!" I joke with Lunar. We laugh until Eno interrupts.

"Lunar, how did you spend your free time back home? Iris said she took on reading…what about you?"

Lunar tilts his head before responding. "I'd watch her read."

The group laughs in unison. Eno leans forward. "No, what did you *actually* do? I know a bit about Iris and nothing about you."

"He wasn't always like this," I start. "He used to give my parents quite the trouble back in the day."

"*You*? A troublemaker?" Eno gasps.

Lunar laughs. "No! Not really…I just…Iris!"

I sit back and laugh, Mace smiling in my periphery.

"Honestly, I was good! I was just more into the games, athletics, that kind of stuff."

"What could you have done athletically in your house?" Kylah laughs as she crests the stairs to join us.

"Kylah!" Lunar shouts. She sits beside Ashlea on the cot. Her curly, auburn locks billow around her so much they nearly merge with Ashlea's dark strands.

"I'd just do flips and stuff. Nothing crazy."

"He's super flexible!" I point at Lunar, coming to his defense from his own self-deprecation. "I'd read, he'd cartwheel. A force to be reckoned with."

Mace watches me and smiles, taking in every word. Eno shifts left to right before sitting on Ashlea's cot, officially overcrowding the two beds. Mace takes the opportunity of silence and probes Eno.

"Eno, why are you here?" My eyes widen at the blunt questioning. "If you're way older than us, why are you here?"

Eno shakes his head slowly and shrugs. "Your guess is as good as mine. I figured they'd have just killed me with the others."

"It's weird," Mace takes a deep breath. "There's got to be *some* reason."

We sit and ponder but nobody comes up with anything. Finally, Kylah breaks the silence. "So...what *did* you do?"

Eno shrugs again. "Fudged some numbers, helped feed families. Mostly illegal children. I guess somebody found out and snitched...and now I'm here."

My stomach twists, his crimes setting in. My parents were responsible for over-rationing us straight from the rationing offices, so there's no way Eno had anything to do with my family's feeding. But my heart swells with respect, knowing he was helping people like Lunar and me. In some sense, I feel an even deeper connection with him.

I look at my shoes, unable to match his gaze. "That was really noble of you, Eno."

He smiles, understanding exactly why his crimes mean so much to me. "It's nothing. Just did what any decent person would have done."

I smile and grab his arm, thanking him with the gesture. He nods in acknowledgment, and the exchange ends with a deep breath from Ashlea.

"What are we gonna do tomorrow, guys?"

We're all dreading the Executive competition but, even more so, the voting. Not wanting to announce any decision ourselves, we look to Mace.

"It's tough because like...I don't like either of them. But killing them...it's just tough."

"What do you think happens if we don't vote before the timer ends?" Lunar's arms are stiff, and he doesn't look to anyone specific. I wrap my arm around him, recognizing the gravity of the decision no matter whose life is at stake.

"Let's not find out, okay?" Kylah pats his back to calm him down and keep his mind straight.

"Who are you guys leaning toward?" Eno asks the group, clearly wanting to vote with the house.

Mace opens his mouth but is interrupted when Jade and Cypher enter the bedroom. They sit on the bed furthest from us, ignoring our presence and speaking in hushed voices.

Mace leans forward, dragging his words out. "Why don't we move this conversation to my room?" We nod and follow Mace to his glamorous suite, filing in and settling around the room. Lunar and I join Mace on his massive bed, my brother and I kicking the comforter to until it covers our feet.

Eno starts by suggesting we split Artemis and Mercedes up, but Mace makes the same argument as he did with Dial, explaining that we know Mercedes's intentions. The entire conversation is a repeat from yesterday, the others considering Mercedes a more significant threat. Fighting back, Mace and I explain why Crescentia should go.

"But Iris, you're close with Artemis," Kylah points out. My cheeks burn, but I resist the urge to hide under the covers. "He has Mercedes under his wing, so she's not gonna touch you."

"Hey, if you feel safer with Crescentia here, be my guest," Mace points out. "It's really up to you. We'll just see how the votes turn out tomorrow."

A knock sounds on the door, and Mace rises to unlock it. Destry and Finian march in, Destry enthusiastically fist-bumping every one of us, Finian hiding behind him closely.

"Hey guys!" Destry smiles. He looks at Eno and shakes him, "How's my old man doing?"

Eno raises his eyebrows and responds hesitantly, "Always a pleasure, Destry."

Destry plops onto the couch so hard it quakes with aftershock. "What's up?"

"Just talking about votes," Mace shares, shutting down the enthusiasm.

"Oh." Destry calms a touch. "What're you thinking?" He's hiding the alliance and Dial's prior decision to vote out Crescentia surprisingly well, and the two discuss the pros and cons of keeping Mercedes or Crescentia in the house.

As the conversation carries out, my eyelids grow heavy with exhaustion. Everything being discussed is old news to me, so it feels like a broken record: *vote out Crescentia; Mercedes hates Jade and Cypher.* I gradually wrap myself in the blankets as housemates pile in and out of the room, discussing strategy or making meaningless conversation. Slowly but surely, nearly all my housemates exit. Lunar waving at me with his tongue hanging out is the last thing I see before everything goes dark.

Chapter 24

I grip the edges of the long, blue sofa and grab Mace's right hand tight between my palms. Sweat pours down my face, and tears blur my vision as I scan the Death Row cushions, left to right: Lunar versus Curi.

Curi twists and turns in her chair, the sofa so tall her feet don't touch the floor. The bullet holes from Sola's expulsion have vanished, and her blood has been completely erased from the living room. I don't give it a second thought when my eyes land on Lunar, bawling into his hands.

I jump when the mechanical voice sounds, indicating the voting has concluded. I grip Mace's hand even tighter and feel a tear crest my bottom lash before it drops to the floor.

"BY A VOTE OF SIX TO FIVE: CURI IS EXPELLED FROM THE ENTERPRIZE. YOU HAVE THIRTY SECONDS TO EVACUTE."

I break as Curi rises from her cushion, searching for the voice's source.

"Where am I going, Iris?" she asks, her smile stretching to her ears. "Did I win something?"

I struggle to breathe as I embrace my little sister. "Yes, Curi, that's exactly what's happening. I promise you're going somewhere much safer than here. You're going to be so much happier; I promise!"

"I wish you could come with me," Curi whines. "Why can't you come too?"

I crumble as she pulls on my sleeve, urging me to follow. The floodgates crumble, and I embrace Curi, convulsing through my tears. She hugs me back, moving her arms very slowly around my torso.

"Iris…what's going on?" Curi asks, voice muffled through the fabric of my shirt.

I don't have the heart to tell her. I can't tell her. So, when she releases me, I fall apart. I take off sprinting to the nearest camera. One aggressive leap later, I'm on the kitchen stool, gripping the device with all my strength. "TAKE ME INSTEAD!" I scream, shaking the camera so hard I'm surprised it doesn't detach from its mount. "PLEASE! JUST TAKE ME INSTEAD."

"But Iris," Curi whines, "Why can't we go together?"

She tugs on the end of my top, so I turn slowly and squat on the stool to hug her again. My tears soak her silky locks as a bird soars past her ear, blue feathers shedding to the floor. Curi smiles and wipes the tears from my cheeks. "Don't cry, Iris," she says, voice squeaking. "You'll be with me soon! And we'll have a great time together. I pinky swear."

The door bursts open, and hordes of guards burst into the living room. Mace grabs me from behind, yanking me from Curi. I won't let her go, making him pull the two of us to the other side of the room. I scream as I shield her from the guns, cocooning her in my arms to protect her. "DON'T TAKE HER! TAKE ME INSTEAD!" I scream at the top of my lungs, my voice catching as I run out of air. "YOU STAY AWAY FROM HER!"

I flee to the second floor with Curi in my arms, seeking refuge in the arena. I don't even make it to the kitchen before a guard punches me square in the face, knocking me to the carpet.

Leaving Curi vulnerable in the center of the kitchen.

"What's wrong, Iris?" Her voice cracks on the second word.

"CURI!" I wail, ridding my lungs of their remaining air. I reach out to her, but I'm too late. Dozens of bullets shoot through her chest, and her lifeless body thumps to the floor.

"Iris! IRIS! It's okay! It wasn't real!"

I'm screaming at the top of my lungs, sweat drenching my clothes. Mace shakes my body back and forth, his violet eyes dilated in fear, but his face flexes with strength and confidence. Despite the security he provides, my heart rate skyrockets, and I start a fresh bout of screams.

"They killed her! They killed her, Mace, and they're going to kill us too!" My hair sticks to the moisture on my neck, and tears stream down my face. I hide my eyes in my palms and let out an insane mixture of crying and screaming. The image of Curi falling to the floor replays in my mind on a loop, and closing my eyes only develops the image more on the darkness behind my eyelids. My body shakes with my sobs, and I choke. I struggle to breathe, feeling like I'm at the bottom of an ocean, not knowing which way is up.

"IRIS!" Mace yells above my screams. "It's okay! IT'S OKAY! Curi is safe. She's safe with your neighbors, remember?"

"WE DON'T KNOW THAT!" I scream. "What if they got her? What if they killed her too!?"

"IRIS!" He continues screaming over my sobs. He shakes me harder, his grip strong on my shoulders. "LOOK AT ME IRIS! LOOK AT ME!"

I spread my fingers so I see a sliver of reality and locate his violet pupils, widened with concern.

"Iris, if they wanted to kill her, they'd have done it already! Do you understand me? They would have done it in front of your eyes to torture you! They killed Sola's baby *in her arms*! The neighbors will have taken Curi in—you know this! Iris, please break out of this. It wasn't real!"

"But it may as well have been!" I scream back. I finally remove my hands from my eyes and grab Mace's forearms, shaking him into my reality as he just did to me. "If it's not Curi, it's Lunar. If it's not Lunar, it's Ashlea. If it's not Ashlea, it's you! It never *ends*, Mace! We're all dead—none of us are making it out of here!"

"Iris!" He pleads. Mace grabs my arms until we're mixed into a pretzel, each trying to get the other to understand the severity of each other's realities. "You listen to me right now. Please, listen to me!"

I hold my tears back and search his eyes. His violet pearls focus on me so hard I can't see anything else. They're filled with desperation. Filled with compassion. And filled with…something else. Something I can't place my finger on. But they draw me in, giving me the strength to stop my fit and listen. Above all…they make me trust everything coming from his mouth.

"You're going to make it out of here, Iris. Not because you want to but because you *have* to. Curi needs you. You are going to go home, Iris. There's *nothing* that will stop me from making that happen."

I sniff back another bout of sobs and stay locked onto his eyes, searching for what else they portray. Putting the mystery aside, I finally dare to squeak out what I've been dying to say for days.

"But what about you?"

Mace squints his eyes, and I swear he's holding back tears. He gulps and finally asks, "What *about* me?"

I sniff once more. "How will I go on without you?"

Mace looks at me seriously, and my heart swells, reality clicking. His eyes don't call me a friend. They're not simply caring for me as a teammate.

It's love.

We stare at each other for a single second before everything goes dark. I feel his left hand on the back of my neck, caressing my hair while his right palm holds my back. Our lips interlock, and my back arches, wanting every part of me to rub up against him. I grip his biceps and feel his heartbeat racing in his veins. Fireworks burst in my stomach as our lips move together, his leading mine and pulling me in for more.

My heart erupts when he pulls away, eyes focused on mine. I smile because, for the first time, I can read him all the way through. And now, despite the nightmare…despite the terrifyingly unfair situation I'm in and the uncertainty of the future….I know one thing for sure.

Mace loves me.

And I love him, too.

Chapter 25

Crescentia sits quietly in her bullet-pierced, jet-black sofa, eyes pink from hours of tears. Mercedes touches her shoes to the floor, circling her ankles in a nervous twitch. Artemis sits on the blue couch directly to her left, holding her hand tight and watching the clock.

Everyone is gathered in the living room as the clock glows red, with ten seconds remaining. I hold Mace's hand on my right, reaching over the gap to the Executive couch he'll give up within the hour. Nobody speaks, a mixture of tension and nerves filling the silent air as people shift uncomfortably in anticipation.

Finally, the clock strikes zero, and the robotic voice returns.

"CONVICTS," the voice begins as last time, reciting an identical script. "YOUR VOTING ORDER HAS BEEN SELECTED BY RANDOM DRAW. WHEN YOUR NAME IS ANNOUNCED, MAKE YOUR WAY TO THE SECOND FLOOR. INSTRUCTIONS WILL FOLLOW.

"DESTRY."

Destry shifts beside Artemis, grabs his own knees to create momentum, and rises off the couch. His sharp jaw is clenched, and he shuffles toward the second floor, brown hair bobbing with each step.

As the names are called, Crescentia's torment builds. She's gripping her chair's sides so intensely that her knuckles turn white. Her usually pale face is bright pink, and her hair is pushed to the back, getting slicker and sweatier from the perspiration running down her spine. My leg trembles against the carpet because she *doesn't* deserve this. Regardless of this reality, I'm going to metaphorically march her to her death. Mace notices my shakes and extends his leg until his shoe pins mine to the floor. When I glance in his direction, he sends me a gentle smile. I scrunch my eyes and muster a weak grin but can't stop my leg from quivering under his.

Crescentia isn't the only houseguest panicking. Mercedes isn't confident either, especially when Jade and Cypher are called to cast their votes. I give Lunar an encouraging pat on his back when it's his turn and grip Mace harder, tortured by the possibility that Lunar doesn't vote in time. Once he returns, I also grab his palm, steading myself on either side.

As the names are called, my eyes can't help but flicker to Mercedes and Artemis. Arty whispers desperately to his partner, trying to calm her. She nods as he speaks to her, his volume so quiet that nobody else can eavesdrop.

When Artemis finally leaves to vote, I know I'll be the last to push my button. My legs shake while I wait, and I watch Mercedes grow in discomfort. Her blue eyes start glistening with tears, and I'm summoned just before one drops.

"IRIS."

I rise from my spot, Mace giving my hand an encouraging squeeze. Shuffling to the staircase, I do my best to ease my body tremors. I focus on each step with my eyes glued to the ground, so I nearly run into Artemis as he descends. I look up just in time to make eye contact. Like when we first met, he immediately flicks his gaze to the ground, embarrassed that I saw him catch my eye. I get a strange feeling in my stomach about the encounter, but my nerves hide the confusion and push me forward.

I finally reach the door on the second floor and push it open. The scene is familiar, metal steps directing me toward the AstroTurf, where velvet railings lead me to a podium. I move as I did last time, making the railings shake as they support my body weight. Once I finally reach the shiny black podium, I examine my choices. A blue button on my left reads, "Crescentia." The white one on my right says, "Mercedes."

The same instructions as last time are announced as I hover a hand over Crescentia's name. I stop and consider my options for the first time, considering whether this is my best move. Dial has been controlling my decisions, but that isn't necessarily bad. Crescentia *is* a wild card. And Artemis and I are such solid friends that the possibility of Mercedes putting me on Death Row is relatively low. It's almost like Artemis having an ally provides me with one as well. Isn't that the point of Dial?

But as much as I hate to admit it to myself, a tiny part of me thinks about what life at the Enterprize would be like without Mercedes. Without her attitude, without her drama erupting the house in chaos. Without the constant displays of physical affection, Artemis finally free from the medal shackles of their relationship…

My moment of selfishness leaves me embarrassed and ashamed. *I made an agreement with my alliance, and I will stick to it.* Dissociating the vote as much as possible from the result it brings, I press down on the blue "Crescentia" button well before my time is up. I shake out my fishtail braid, rub my face until I see stars, and strut back to the living room.

The second my bottom molds into the blue plush, the robotic voice returns.

"WHEN ANNOUNCED, THE EXPELLED CONVICT MUST EXIT THROUGH THE FRONT DOOR WHERE EXECUTION WILL COMMENCE."

Mercedes's left palm has lost all circulation, now just as white as Crescentia's. Artemis scrunches his face in pain from Mercedes's firm grip on his palm. Crescentia's eyes are pink from her tears as she senses her impending doom. Everyone else is silent, bodies frozen to the cushions.

"BY A VOTE OF NINE TO THREE: CRESCENTIA IS EXPELLED FROM THE ENTERPRIZE. YOU HAVE THIRTY SECONDS TO EVACUATE."

Mercedes collapses into Artemis's arms, him stroking her back and hiding his face in her hair. Crescentia's body explodes in a crescendo of agony. She hides her eyes in her palms, bawling as the clock ticks down. She finally rises from her bullet-filled Death Row cushion and embraces Mercedes, hugging her tight. Nobody else stands, all keeping their eyes glued to the floor.

"I'm so sorry," Mercedes pleads. "I'm so, so sorry, Crescentia."

Crescentia sniffs her sobs and responds, "You get to the end, Mercedes. You can, you really can." They embrace again, and the two walk toward the front door, Artemis trailing behind.

Finally, Crescentia smooths her hair, wipes her tears, and gives Mercedes a final nod. "Goodbye, friend." The two may not be as close as they were at the start, but the sentiment is special all the same. Mercedes holds back tears, and Artemis stretches his arm around her as Crescentia reaches for the doorknob.

She pushes it forward and walks over the threshold of the house. For just a moment, the world is still, almost peaceful. But when the door finally locks, gunshots echo through the deafening silence of the Enterprize.

ROUND 3

Chapter 26

Silence.

That's all there is when the shots finally end. In sharp contrast to Sola's expulsion, my houseguests rise from their couches and shuffle absentmindedly to different areas of the house, most opting to be alone. No guards extract an uncooperative corpse. There are no blood stains on the wall behind Death Row. The world is strangely still, not even a sniffle among us.

Mace settles beside Lunar and me on the couch. Once the room is fully evacuated, he whispers under his breath. "Who was that third vote? It was Jade and Cypher, obviously…but who else?"

With the competition looming, the rouge vote is the least of my concerns. I try to entertain Mace's looming conspiracy, but my voice still comes out flat. "I guess someone thought Mercedes was the bigger target…or Crescentia made some absurd deal. It wouldn't be the first time." I shrug, my lack of focus blurring my vision. "There's thirteen of us here, right? She must've gotten through to somebody."

When the cushions start vibrating, I think I'm hallucinating from panic. But a quick glance confirms Lunar's trembles. He stares at the ground, grabbing the edge of the couch so hard his knuckles pop out in peaks. Mace traces my vision, catching onto Lunar's anxiety. "Hey," he pats Lunar on the back, making my brother jump. Mace smiles. "There's nothing to worry about. Maybe this competition is made for shorter people? They'll be eating your dust!" His words are delicate, his lips barely moving when he speaks.

Lunar gives a halfhearted smile and nods. My stomach pricks, nerves fighting their way to my exterior. I only have the strength to let out a weak chuckle. "Yeah, let's hope," I say.

We break for the bathrooms before journeying to the second floor. When we arrive, Ashlea, Eno, and Lagiacrus block the door, the former two exhaling shaky breaths. Lagiacrus stands firm, arms crossed over his chest, biceps bulging through the end of his short sleeves. Ashlea's the only one that acknowledges us, offering a gentle smile.

I nod at my friend before shuffling past the group, moving closer to the iron slab. Before I can pass Lagiacrus, he nudges me to the side. "It won't open."

"What?" My stomach drops to the floor. "What do you mean it won't open?" Images of death flash through my mind, the Authority combining thousands of torturous punishments for our non-compliance. My voice cracks. "What if we're late?"

"I…maybe they aren't finished?" Ashlea gulps. "Setting up, I mean."

"We've still got a few minutes," Eno says, fiddling with the doorknob. "Should be any second now…"

I close my eyes and take a deep breath, letting my diaphragm expand until the point of exhaustion. I focus on breathing, desperate to calm my nerves before being thrown into the arena with whatever horror awaits us.

The others gather behind us, making my heart rate faster than I thought possible. "How much time is left?" Destry asks, panic in his voice. Cypher strides down the steps and announces the three-minute mark when there's a loud click, making several of us stumble in surprise. The slab cracks open, and Lagiacrus grabs its edge. One deep breath later, Lagiacrus announces, "Here goes nothing," and presses the door open.

One glance at the turf makes my teeth chatter. I look away and grip Mace's hand, and he squeezes tight. Like Lagiacrus experienced three days ago, Mace cannot compete for Executive this round. Luckily, he's taking on his role of coach in stride, drawing circles on the back of my palm with his thumb.

I descend the frail metal steps, one hand in Mace's, the other on the railing. When we reach the turf, I hold Lunar on my right and force myself to look directly at the transparent, house-like structure in the center of the arena. The formation comprises four clear, thick plastic walls and a transparent roof. There's a single clear door facing the staircase, but no windows exist. Twelve clear buttons surround the inside of the structure, evenly spaced along the walls at hip height.

"What the hell?" Mace whispers as we close the distance to the building.

A single black stool rests in front of the structure, hoisting the tree and root Authority instruction card. With sixty seconds remaining, Mace grabs the sheet and reads aloud.

"The last convict holding their button will be crowned the Round 3 Executive. Release your button, and you are eliminated from the competition. But there's a catch…"

"A catch? What catch?" Destry asks, inching closer to Mace to read over his shoulder.

Their eyes widen simultaneously. "When eliminated, you will earn either a punishment or a reward, which will be announced immediately upon exiting the structure. But the stakes are even higher…" His breath catches in his throat. "The winner will *also* have a chance to compete in next round's competition for power."

"What?" Kylah asks, jaw on the floor. A newfound tension fills the air, everyone even hungrier to win. Usually, there is a risk with winning Executive—you don't get to compete the following round. But this reward…it changes *everything*. If anyone was trying to hide their strength before, they certainly won't be doing it now. *Especially* not with the risk of punishment looming.

"One last thing," Mace reads. "Don't get too comfortable. For every hour that passes, the temperature and humidity will be raised within the chamber…and…and…"

Destry finishes the sentence, chest deflating. "You can expect more surprises surpassing your wildest dreams."

"That can't be good," Ashlea whispers.

I press my lips together, trying not to show weakness. But my lip quivers when Ashlea looks my way, sweat running down her jaw.

I squeeze my eyes shut, allowing a moment of fear. Lunar and Curi immediately pop into my vision, revitalizing me with the strength to fight. Opening my eyes, I puff out my chest, tighten the knot at the end of my braid, and wait for the final instruction.

Just before Mace can finish the card, Destry's eyes widen to twice their size on the final words. "Shit!" he shouts, racing for the plastic house. The rest of us stand rigid, some looking around helplessly while others clasp their hands in preparation for a fight.

Mace gasps a second later, and his voice heightens an octave in panic. His words come out in a single breath. "You have ten seconds to enter and begin holding down your button. Fail, and you're eliminated!"

I sprint to the structure, the mob pushing me from behind. Lagiacrus yanks the door open and launches to the other opposite side of the plastic box. I'm knocked into the door hinge and spin, never letting go of Lunar's palm. We have no time to strategize positioning, but I manage to pick a button the has Lunar to my left. Destry is on my right, smashing his button with both hands. We hold down our buttons firmly, Eno reaching his with a single second to spare. A buzzer booms, indicating the start of the competition.

"Welcome to the 'Suffering Sanctuary'." Mace reads from the card, looking up and meeting his violet eyes with mine from the other side of the plastic wall. There are no words, but his eyes say everything. Even without speech, I feel his terror.

Because the person he loves is about to endure a fate that may be worse than death.

"God damn, it's hot."

Sweat pours down my face as I turn reluctantly to the bare-chested Destry on my right, who, despite his complaints, is holding firm. The moment Mace announced the hourly increase in temperature and humidity, Destry and Lagiacrus stripped off their shirts and wrapped them around their heads. However, they didn't realize that our chamber is heated by UVA radiation.

In other words, the "Suffering Sanctuary" is roasting us alive.

"Feel free to drop if you can't handle it," Mercedes responds without looking away from her button. "I'm sure the air is lovely out there."

Destry shakes his head in my periphery. "Not a chance. I'm here 'till the morning."

"CONVICTS," says the robotic voice. "YOU HAVE COMPLETED: ONE HOUR."

Not only is there a noticeable temperature rise, but a loud rumbling noise reverberates throughout the chamber. The ceiling vibrates very subtly until, finally, there is silence.

I scan the others on my wall: Destry, Lunar, and Cypher. They look up expectantly, so I follow their vision and see my reflection. I tilt my head, my reflection doing the same. *The ceiling isn't transparent.*

It's mirrored.

"What the—" starts Eno, but the buzzing of a thousand bugs cut him off.

"Ew!" Mercedes screams as she whacks her leg with her free hand. "Mosquitoes!"

I bite my lip and tense my arm to keep from letting go. But I can't stop squirming when hundreds of mosquitoes crawl around my moist legs, injecting their saliva into my skin.

"Ever wonder what mosquitoes felt like?" I joke to Lunar, forcing a smile across my lips. He looks back at me with a frown, wincing.

"I could've gone without finding out."

A single chuckle leaves my lips when Mace approaches from the opposite side of the glass.

"How you holdin' up?" he asks, quiet enough not to draw attention to himself. I give a weak smile and an enthusiastic thumbs up. The heat's uncomfortable, and my skin glows pink from the developing sunburn. Despite these inconveniences, the competition isn't that difficult. The mosquitoes are annoying but far from detrimental, so my time in this competition is just getting started.

Half an hour later, I take back everything I thought about the bugs. My legs begin to shake, the bites refusing to be ignored. The intense sensation covers so much of my body that I dig into my skin desperately, urging it to stop. Blood streaks down my legs, and I ignore it until Mace knocks on the other side of the chamber. He motions to my legs and shakes his head, urging me to stop scratching. I deflate, wanting nothing more than to relieve the feeling. I glance at Lunar, wondering if he's experiencing a similar struggle. His fist, whitening from how intense his grip is, confirms that he's straining.

As the next half hour progresses, the compounding heat and humidity give me a splitting headache. Communal body odor now heavily fragrances the unventilated house. Instead of avoiding it and covering my nose like others, I waft in the scent, willing my nostrils to adjust. My arm aches from the effort of holding pressure on the button, so I occasionally use my opposite arm to help hold up the important one.

The chamber is silent, and time passes by excruciatingly slowly. The hardest part would be the boredom if it weren't for the heat and dehydration. We're all bored out of our minds but unwilling to risk entertaining others by speaking.

That'll just make the competition last even longer.

Yawning, I scan the others, surprised by how badly some of their skin is already peeling. Destry's t-shirt headband is now completely drenched from sweat, and his exposed torso is spotted with blisters. Finian is shaking, pale face barely recognizable from the burns.

Why are they fighting so hard when they have no home to return to? I have Curi, who could be wandering the back allies of the Central Ascendency for all I know. And if I can't outlast the others in the Enterprize, I can at least protect Lunar for as long as I live. But my competitors…without their loved ones, they have *nothing*.

I get a stabbing pain in my side as I fight the shame that accompanies the thought. I'm just so desperate for them to hand me the win that I'm trying to rationalize why they should drop out. Why should any of us compete to win when quitting would save so much torture? I shut my eyes and sigh, accepting the reality that the others won't just lay over and let me be the lone survivor. It's the same reason why desperately starving humans variably turn to cannibalism.

The will to live is too high. If people are willing to tear others apart and eat their remains to stay alive, of course they'll keep their hand glued to a button. Their families may be in the grave, but the warden has offered them the potential of a new life. And I know as well as the others that a life in the Authority could grant security and eliminate the need to hide for survival.

It's the life everyone dreams of having.

I wince, my sweat now stinging my sunburns. Shaking my head, I silently curse the Suffering Sanctuary.

"CONVICTS, YOU HAVE COMPLETED: TWO HOURS."

I stiffen up when the mechanical noises return and immediately look to the ceiling for our next surprise. There's a crash, and I shut my eyes.

But not soon enough to avoid the maggot dropping into my eye socket.

I shake my head violently as the maggots fall, and I gag at the unmistakable scent of decomposing flesh. A large chunk of rotting fish slams onto my cheek, and I lash at it, desperate to rid myself of this nauseating concoction.

Screams erupt around the arena. I claw at my hair, picking maggots and flesh from my skull, and suddenly envy Destry and his makeshift headband. I shake my body to rid it of detritus and shove the collar of my t-shirt over my nose, abandoning my method of smell adaptation. My stomach twists in nausea, the horrific odor still finding a way past the fabric and into my nostrils.

"CONVICT: JADE. ELIMINATED."

Violent hurling echoes throughout the chamber as Jade throws up the entirety of the contents in her stomach. She continues to chunder for nearly two minutes, Mercedes screaming at her the entire time to throw up outside the sanctuary, where the scent won't circulate around us for the next ten hours.

Jade crawls out of the door, maggots clutching onto the fabric of her clothes as she slides on the floor. The door slams behind her automatically, and the robotic voice returns, announcing that she's been assigned a punishment.

Jade rolls over, limbs flailing around her on the turf. She takes a deep breath and shuts her eyes when the voice returns.

"NO RATIONS FOR ROUND 3. ACCEPTING OTHER CONVICT'S RATIONS WILL RESULT IN PREMATURE EXPULSION."

My eyes widen and gasps rebound against the walls of the chamber. The entirety of Jade's stomach has just been ejected onto the floor of the Suffering Sanctuary. Likely, Jade will suffer from her punishment far after the completion of this contest. Despite this, she barely comprehends the announcement. She continues chundering, even as she's sprawled against the floor. I wince as maggots eject themselves from her clothing, feasting on her puke.

"Oh, screw this!" Kylah shouts as she pulls maggot after maggot out of her auburn curls. They have really taken to her nest of hair, so she releases her button and digs both hands into her mane while her elimination is announced.

She rushes out of the chamber, clawing through her hair. Clusters of maggots fall to the floor as she exits the building, whipping her hair around hysterically. She only stops when she's assigned a reward.

She looks up expectantly with a flicker of excitement in her eyes. Her face is still coiled in disgust as the waste waterfalls off her body, but the prospect of some prize softens her features. The voice returns.

"YOU ARE SAFE FROM DEATH ROW FOR ROUND 3."

Kylah smiles, raising her arms above her head before dropping them to continue her bug extermination. Jade slams her fists against the ground, being so close to safety but falling short. Cypher lowers his head and shuts his eyes, and the rest of us continue shaking the waste from our bodies. The maggots pay particular interest to our insect wounds, clinging onto our exposed blood. I scrape my shoes against my legs, digging hard to release the bugs. I'm so concentrated that I fight for balance when Lunar's whisper reaches my ear.

"What?"

He makes a stomping motion and demonstrates his method of killing the maggots around him. He points to me, encouraging me to follow suit. I nod, then target the fallen larvae to lessen their impact and pass the time.

Another sweaty hour passes and my throat dries so much I can't swallow without pain. I've steadily been dehydrating for hours; now, my thirst blurs my vision. When I shut my eyes, I'm transported to a highlight reel of horror. My parents' murders replay, the bullets entering and exiting their bodies a hundred different times. My nightmare mixes in, and I start to tremble as I watch Curi collapse to the floor in a motionless heap.

"CONVICTS: YOU HAVE COMPLETED: THREE HOURS."

I squeeze my free fist and focus on the button ahead of me. Instead of fearing the visions, I use them as motivation to *keep going*.

As expected, the heat and humidity intensify. The UVA rays boil my skin, and my shoulders peel. My cheeks are so swollen with blisters that they obstruct my vision. I wish I thought of the headband method until I glance at Destry and Lagiacrus. Their faces may be shielded, but their torsos are scorched. Their discomfort is hidden behind their stoic exterior; neither wince nor shake, their fingers frozen to their buttons. I take a breath of relief when nothing is released from the ceiling with the hourly announcement.

Within seconds, I wish the punishment were that simple.

Instead, a varied, ear-piercing ring sounds in and out at frustratingly different intervals for diverse lengths of time. At no point can you pass the time by preparing for the next ring as there is no say when it will sound. Some beeps are as short as three seconds. Some are as long as two minutes. Mace sits on his stool, plugging his ears every time the beeps begin. The rest of us plug one ear and lean the other against our shoulder blades, desperate to block out the noise. Thirty minutes in, it's clear that the intermittent ringing will not stop.

"I'm out," mumbles Eno, letting go of his button and plugging his ears with both hands. As he exits the structure, a few contestants mumble congratulations, stunned that he held up for three and a half hours. I nod in his direction when he looks back at the Sanctuary, proud of the old man for fighting so long.

Eno holds his fist up high, playing up to the compliments. But when he's assigned a punishment, his arm goes limp at his side.

"PUNISHMENT: ONE WEEK WITHOUT SHOWERS OR CLEAN CLOTHES."

Eno rubs his hand through his hair, hanging his head. I wince when roasted maggots stick to the sweat on his palms.

Mercedes stomps her feet but keeps her mouth shut. As much as I value Eno's friendship, I can't blame her for her frustration. Because this punishment wasn't just designed for him. Yes, his comfort level will plummet as the stench follows him. But the man may get used to the grime. But the rest of us…

This will still be an unpleasant week for us all.

Artemis scoffs.

"What?" Mercedes asks, squinting. He shakes his head and waves his hand dismissively, but I instantly catch on and smile. *Our bet.* Had I lost, I would've had Eno's punishment. How was it just days ago that we made that bet? I know we're both feeling lucky that I was the victor now.

Eno joins Kylah and Jade as far from the stink as possible. I smile at Mace, impressed with how close he is despite how revolting we are. He jokes with me on the other side of the plastic, plugging his nose and pretending to wipe our smell from his vicinity.

If nothing else, he helps pass the time.

"Seriously…good job guys," Destry grumbles. "This isn't easy."

I turn to him and gasp at how severely his torso is burnt. Now, nearly four hours since the start, he's shaking, jaw clenched as sweat pours into his open wounds. He stares at the eliminated and shakes his head, so I follow his line of vision. Eno, Jade, and Kylah are crunched against the back wall, guzzling from Authority-logoed water bottles, forgetting to breathe between gulps. I'm amazed at how delusional I am from dehydration; I hadn't even noticed the bottles being delivered. I salivate and bend over, desperate for a sip to soothe my aching throat. I imagine downing five bottles at once and jolt when the robotic voice returns.

"CONVICT: DESTRY. ELIMINATED AT 00:03:57."

Destry marches to the end of the chamber as the door opens wide. "I *need* water. I can't do this." He walks out and strides for the stockpile of bottles by the eliminated contestants.

"CONVICT: DESTRY. REWARD. BURN ELIXER."

A panel of the arena ceiling slides open, and a medicinal bottle drops directly into Destry's palms. In an instant, the blisters on his torso are irrelevant. One dose of that elixir, and he'll be pain-free. Destry tilts his head to the sky and mouths thanks, shoves it into the waistband of his shorts, and downs two water bottles at once.

I sigh, desperate for relief. Now that I've missed the opportunity for it, my skin pulses with agony. I gaze at those around me, seeking refuge, and focus on the likelihood of my safety. Finian, Lagiacrus, Lunar, Artemis, Ashlea, and I still stand firm against Mercedes and Cypher. The temptation to put the responsibility on my friends and team makes my knees buckle.

I wipe the river of sweat pouring from the sides of my forehead and take another glance at my allies. *If they're looking strong…there's no need for me to keep fighting*. But when I linger my gaze on Finian, my breath catches in my throat.

The Leprechaun is dry a desert.

There's no moisture on his skin, and no sweat stains on his t-shirt. If I didn't know any better, I'd think he was extremely well adjusted to tropic conditions. But hours under the floorboards with nothing but my studies have taught me that dryness, after hours in direct heat, is not a good sign.

Finian is facing the first tell-tale signs of heatstroke. If he doesn't get out of here soon…a vote won't be needed for his demise. The Suffering Sanctuary will eliminate him before any of us get the chance.

My instinct to give up dissolves as quickly as it was created. With Finian fighting on his death bed, I can't fold. So, instead of falling to the floor, I hold myself in a squat and shake my head. *My allies are relying on me.*

I will push through for the win no matter how long I must suffer.

I force my hand into the button with more determination than before. I focus, waiting for the fourth hour to pass, when my nose twinges, making my face scrunch.

"You have *got* to be kidding me," Mercedes shouts. I flip around as Cypher pulls his pants up with a single hand, having emptied his bowels in the corner of the chamber. I groan, watching him kick his feces toward the center of the Sanctuary.

"You two are nuts!" Mercedes shouts. "You had to go *in here*? Where everyone has to smell it?"

"Mercedes, you can say whatever the hell you want. But I'm not letting go of this button."

"And you think I am? I'll hold this button for the next four days if I have to. As long as you're here, I'm not moving."

The bickering intensifies, but I'm thankful for the entertainment. Having some distraction from my boredom gives me the strength to stand tall, so when the mechanical voice finally returns to announce that we've completed four hours, my knees are uncurled, and my spine is upright.

"Hey," I whisper, smiling at Lunar. "Good job, kid."

He smiles back. Our grins instantly disappear when the transparent building vibrates, gears cranking. I stretch my neck to get a look at the source and hold my breath as the center of the porcelain white floor opens, revealing a dark pit beneath. We don't search the depths for long.

Because a hidden sector begins to rise.

Once it reaches floor level, my heart stops. I quit breathing, willing myself not to make a sound.

A fifty-legged creature emerges, huffing so angrily its body elevates several feet off the ground with each breath. I watch myself in its glossy exoskeleton, jaw opening wide as it pinches its massive claws. It's vicious, genetically modified for size and strength, and starving for its next meal.

And it's staring directly at me.

Chapter 27

Mace rises from his stool. "Iris…*don't*…move…" His voice is steady…soft…*desperate*. My eyes widen but I keep completely still, terrified movement will spring the creature into action. I let my breath out slowly through my nose as I examine the beast, eyes lingering on its bulbous tail. A stinger sticks out like a foot-long needle. But instead of the tail springing up high over its body, it rests on the floor, the end too heavy to lift. But where the stinger lacks in function, the jaw more than compensates. Fangs extend so long they can't fit inside its mouth. I take a shaky breath and instead focus on the space beside the monster. *Anywhere but the eyes.*

A scorpion. I've only seen them in textbooks, but their hunting method has always been straightforward. *Sting. Let the poison kill.*

And I'm the only one in its vision.

One look at the tail confirms this beast is an anomaly. Given its towering height, there's no telling what the Authority have done to it. I never expected to see one of the Authority's genetic mutations in my lifetime. But here it stands with five times as many legs and two hundred more pounds than any scorpion should have. It tilts its head at me, sizing me up as a threat. The silence confirms that every person in the Sanctuary has frozen their stance, terrified about the monster's intention.

Despite my fears, I stand my ground, refusing to forfeit and run. Tears drop down my face, melding with the sweat that never seems to stop. I control my breathing, trying to keep my chest level. Almost encouraged by my efforts, the arachnid paces toward me, all fifty legs moving in pairs. The closer it gets, the more I quiver. I keep my eyes glued open, terrified even a blink will trigger an attack.

One moment, there's silence. The next, the ringing returns. The scorpion clicks its claws together, rageful at the ear-piercing addition.

It continues inching toward me as the ringing persists, past the point it's gone before. The monster only stops once it's inches from my foot. Another tear starts to fall, but I stand firm, letting it conjoin with my sweat.

Determining that an attack is unavoidable, I make a plan. A stupid, ridiculous, *desperate* plan that twists my stomach into a knot. I have a brief thought about how gut feelings are always right.

And unfortunately for me, they *always* are.

The second the ringing stops, I yank my left leg from the floor, ready to smash it into the center of the beast's body. Before I get the chance, the monster opens its jaw wide and clamps its razor-sharp fangs into my shin, engulfing my leg from my calf to my shin. I scream with every ounce of my being and release the button, struggling to free the creature from its grasp.

"CONVICT: IRIS. ELIMINATED AT 00:04:03."

I pull my leg out of its mouth, and the entire jaw sheds with the force. The monster lays dead on the ground, separated from the mandible now lodged into my flesh. I roll on the floor, writhing in pain as maggots inch toward me, desperate for blood.

"Iris!" screams Lunar, so loud it vibrates in my bones.

"NO!" I shout back. "DON'T MOVE! We need you, Lunar!"

His jaw is quivering as he shakes his head, tears in his eyes. Mace pounds on the plastic walls, begging the Authority to let him into the Sanctuary. My heart beats in my eyes with each thunderous bang, and I scream as I drag myself out of the chamber, the jaw still lodged in my leg. Mace wraps me in his arms the second I roll onto the turf.

"Stay with me!" he urges, pushing my hair back. He pulls his shirt over my face, wiping the sweat and tears from my cheeks.

"CONVICT: IRIS. PUNISHMENT."

I wince, and Mace's grip on me tightens. I don't have the energy to be rageful. Because right now, with my head resting in Mace's lap and my vision a mixture of black and stars, I can only focus on my terror of death.

"SOLITARY CONFINEMENT FOR ROUND 3. EFFECTIVE IMMEDIATELY."

"WHAT?!" Mace and I shout simultaneously.

"Solitary…solitary…where are they taking me? What am I gonna do?!" I'm wincing from the pain of the bite and hyperventilating from the prison that awaits. The jaw is completely lodged in my leg, the creature's death making it immovable.

Mace rubs the blood from my leg, and I wince, clutching onto him tighter. "You're going to be okay, Iris. You will! You *have to* be strong. I'll be waiting on the other side, I promise you!"

"But what if they put you on Death Row?! What if they vote you out!?" My breath catches in my throat, and the floodgates open. "What if I never see you again!?"

"IRIS!" Mace shakes my torso, urging me to listen. "Look at me…LOOK AT ME!"

My eyes lock onto Mace, and despite the tears blurring his image, my heart swells with the same love I felt this morning. He takes my head in his hands, and his violet eyes gaze into mine.

Like I'm the only person in the world.

"Iris…I love you."

I cry, salty tears burning my skin.

"I love you, too."

He presses into my chapped lips with a kiss so passionate I forget my pain. My hands instinctively reach for his neck, pulling Mace in deeper to feel every bit of him. My fingers latch onto his hair, clumps bundled between my nails as I straighten my back for more.

The strands slide through my fingertips as I'm yanked from the ground, both of my arms hooked behind my back.

"MACE!" I scream at the top of my lungs. My voice breaks as the fangs dig deeper into my shin, the turf pulling it at new angles.

"IRIS!" he screams back. "It's going to be okay! I'll be waiting for you!"

I kick with my healthy leg and choke on my squeals. Two gloved hands grip my armpits, digging in so hard that I gag. I'm dragged across the arena, far away from the Sanctuary and even further away from Mace. With every breath, I shriek, desperate to be rested on the floor. Finally getting my wish, I'm thrown onto the turf. The jaw lodges deeper, making me see stars. Shaking, I turn to a blue door indistinguishable from the wall. The guards press a button in the paint, revealing a keypad. I moan on the AstroTurf as they type, my lungs burning too much to scream any longer.

When the door finally cracks open, the guards yank me from the ground and fling me into the chamber. I land on my shoulder and roll onto my back, trembling so hard that the two guards turn into four.

The two on the left shout in unison. "If not selected for Death Row, you will be summoned when it is time to vote."

"But…" I stutter, wincing through the pain in my leg, "What if I *am* selected for Death Row? And…and voted out?" I hold back tears as blood pools around my calf.

The two guards on the right that I know realize are one chuckle an evil snicker. "Then you will be summoned and escorted when it is time for execution." They slam the door.

I take a breath, but it deepens the pain. I lie freezing, dehydrated, and trembling in a totally bare room.

Completely and utterly alone.

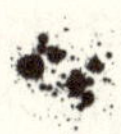

I can't feel my leg.

But that's not even my biggest concern. Because as I lie on the cold tile, chest heaving, it hits me. *I may never see Lunar or Curi again.* I smash my fists into the ground and yell at the possibility. I pound even harder when I realize I won't have gotten the chance to say goodbye. Even if I do survive past this round, there is no guarantee that Lunar or Mace will. My rage transforms into despair as I let the tears fall. I reach for my face to rub away the anguish, but the blisters throb at my touch, and I nearly pass out from the pain.

Black surrounds the outside of my vision. Desperate to distract myself, I examine my tiny cell. White tiles line every inch of the chamber. Even the door is made of them, so it camouflages into the wall. The room could fit four of me lying vertically and horizontally across the floor, but the prison shrinks the more I look at it. What was once four of my size turns into three, then two, and eventually less than one. I hyperventilate, getting the sensation that I'm being smashed into a box. Back home in the floorboards, I could watch through the cracks in the wood; I knew there was an escape. But here, in solitary confinement…there is no refuge.

I wheeze, struggling to get air into my lungs. Instead of focusing on my predicament, I envision who's left in the Suffering Sanctuary. *Lagiacrus, Finian, Artemis, Lunar, and Ashlea against Mercedes and Cypher.* The odds may be in my favor, but knowing my little power and influence in this prison makes the hyperventilation start all over again.

I take deep breaths in and out for what feels like ages and finally gain the courage to examine my wound. I blindly roll up and rip the cuffs of my pants, wincing as the jaw shifts. Finally freeing my pant leg from the area, I take a deep breath and close my eyes. On the count of five, I open them.

I nearly pass out.

My calf rests in a pool of blood, the edges soaking through my clothes. The jaw looks lodged in my shin bone. I wail, tears falling into my leg as I assess the damage.

"I'm going to die," I whisper. It won't even matter if Cypher or Mercedes wins Executive.

The blood loss may kill me first.

I'm limited in medical knowledge, but it's obvious I won't be able to compete with a jaw lodged in my leg. I bite my lip, mortified about my next move. *The mandible must be removed.* Only then can I thoroughly assess and treat the area. I close my eyes and curse. Several deep breaths later, I count aloud.

"One…" I wipe sweat from my forehead. "Two…" I extend my fingers around the jaw. "THREE."

I try to pull the mandible apart as hard as my muscles can take.

It doesn't budge.

Pain shoots through my leg and into my chest, and I scream at the top of my lungs. Every inch of my body trembles, my teeth chattering as I whimper. The black around my vision pushes in further, making my image of the room a tiny dot in the center. The walls close around me, and I give up, fanning my limbs out and willing death to take me in its ruthless and unforgiving clutches.

"I'm so sorry," I choke out, shutting my eyes and loosening my fists. Only when the images appear in the darkness do I smile. Curi dances amongst a colony of blue jays. Her yellow dress fans out as she spins, a smile extended across her lips. She waves me toward a bright light in the distance, extending her hand. I reach for it, tears streaming down my cheeks as I get closer. Closer. *Closer.*

Just as I touch her fingertips, a loud creak brings me back to consciousness. My eyes shoot open, but I don't move an inch. The guards return, so I reach out to them, hoping they're here to help me. Instead, a large figure is dumped beside me, extremities bright red with blisters scattered throughout. I feel his sweat fling onto me as he collides with the cold, hard floor, and the guards give a callous, bloodcurdling snicker.

"If not selected for Death Row, you will be summoned when it is time to vote."

The door slams so violently that I swear it shakes the room. I take a deep breath, force myself onto my side, and look directly at the face of my new roommate.

Deep ocean blue eyes stare back into my hazel ones, and my breath catches in my throat.

"Iris."

Artemis's smile drops, jaw widening in horror when he glances at the blood still pooling out of my leg.

Chapter 28

Relief rushes through me first. But seconds later, my stomach heats with rage. *Another one of my allies has fallen.* Oblivious to my mental war, Artemis leaps from the floor and races to my leg, arms shaking as he hovers above me. He stretches his lips into a straight line, concentrating on my injury. Through it all, his eyebrows arch in worry.

Delusion twists my mind. *How could he give up when we're relying on him?* So, instead of embracing him and thanking the heavens I'm not alone, I slap his torso, forcing him to step back.

"Iris?" His voice cracks as he raises his hands. "What's wrong?"

This time, I shove him. "How could you drop out!? We *needed* you, Arty. Now…now, we're screwed!"

"Iris, calm down!" he urges. "You're delusional right now! We need to sort out your leg before you lose any more blood."

"Jade's gonna win it all!" I screech. "And when she does…she's gonna go after us! *All* of us!"

"IRIS!" Artemis shouts, holding back tears. "Jade got out hours ago! You need to take a deep breath! I can fix this. You just have to listen to me! Do you understand?"

I mutter gibberish as I try to comprehend the situation and fight from blacking out. I can only keep my focus once Artemis's face is square in front of mine. Blue eyes urgent, he whispers. "Do you trust me?"

The words send a shiver down my spine, and I force a nod. I lay back and allow him to survey the damage. A million thoughts pool in my mind, but I fight them off for Artemis's sake. Finally, he crouches over my face. His upper half is completely bare, his shirt hanging from his hands. In my delusion, I linger on his torso, the lines defining his chest drawing me toward his chiseled stomach. He squeezes his shirt dry in my periphery, and my vision blurs on his upper body, every defined element becoming one jumbled mess of tan skin. Finally, a massive hand waves over my face.

"Can you hear me?" His eyes are dilated and urgent, and I shake my head to regain focus.

"Wha…what did you say?"

"I'm going to get the jaw out of your leg, and it's going to hurt like hell." His usual flirty manner has disappeared. Now, he's giving me instructions like a drill sergeant. He reaches the shirt over my head before continuing. "It won't taste good but put this in your mouth. Grip it with your teeth…it's not ideal, but it's the best we've got."

I nod slowly, still dazed. My eyelashes obstruct my vision, flickering closed until he snaps his fingers inches from my face.

"IRIS!" he shouts. "No matter what, you *have to* stay awake. No matter how bad this hurts or how tempting it is to rest…you can't! Do you understand me?"

This is the most serious I have ever seen Artemis, and I nod to oblige. He places the shirt in my mouth gently, and I nearly gag at the sour and salty mixture of sweat and body odor. He repeatedly whispers how sorry he is until I forget where I am and his mission.

Then, the pain begins.

I scream at the top of my lungs, louder even than before, this pain being much more intense than when I attempted the task. I bite down as hard as I can on the shirt, surprised when my teeth don't rip through the fabric. Tears stream down my face in a steady flow, and I whimper between my shrieks. Artemis vocalizes how it's almost over, but I can't concentrate or comprehend anything. Instead, I force all my might into staying awake. The pain is so unbearable I slap Artemis to get him to stop. His voice cracks as he fights back, apologies spilling out like a waterfall. Another pinch slices through my flesh, and I start pleading for him to stop.

"I *promise* you're almost done! Stay with me, Iris! Please, stay with me!"

I writhe in pain when there's one last pierce. Suddenly, the agony subsides.

The operation is complete.

I lie on the tile, taking deep breaths, my teeth still piercing the cotton in my mouth. Artemis jerks back into my sight, covered in blood.

"Iris, I'm gonna take the shirt back. We need to get your leg covered. It's not gonna feel good, but I *promise* this is the last of it. The sweat and the pressure…it's gonna hurt, Iris. But it'll help the healing…it'll save the leg. Okay?"

My jaw releases the shirt, and I watch him readjust it into a bandage. I close my eyes to prepare for the pain but feel his hand graze my cheek.

"Please…*please,* don't close your eyes. Please stay with me, Iris…I'm so sorry. I'm so, *so* sorry."

I nod, bracing my teeth, as he leans over my leg. There's a single moment of peace before the anguish returns. I scream again as he ties the shirt around my leg, and I can't help but inch away from him, trying to escape.

"Please stop moving. It's gonna hurt worse! *Please* stay still. You're doing so good!"

I freeze as he wraps my leg and completes the tie, screeching until my throat is raw. Finally, he steps back with his hands open, suggesting the procedure is finished. Blood paints his hands and dots the crevices in his torso as he compliments me on a job well done.

"I'm done! All done, Iris. See!? No more pain!" His smile is forced. He leans his back against the wall, relief flushing over him.

"It…hurts…so…*bad*…" I grimace, my leg throbbing beneath the bandage. My voice is hoarse; it feels like there's a handful of gravel in my esophagus. But Artemis is partly right…my calf is admittedly less painful now that the jaw has been extracted. The sweat on the bandage stings the wound further, but it's nothing compared to the pressure. I grip my fists and take deep breaths as the pain fades and my vision returns. I turn my head to the left and see the scorpion's mandible, completely dismantled into the top and bottom halves of the jaw. How Artemis managed to dislodge the bones from one another is a mystery, but I accept it as a miracle. I take several minutes to regain my breath before summoning the strength to communicate.

"I…hate…scorpions…"

Artemis chuckles before running his hand through his brown hair, face contorted in relief. "Come on…what have they ever done to you?"

I force a weak smile and shake my head. "How bad is it?" I croak. "The wound…I saw…I saw *bone*…"

This time, Artemis doesn't hold back his laughter. "What?" I ask, eyes wide. "How bad is it?"

"Iris," Artemis says between bouts of laughter, "You didn't see bone. That was tendon."

"TENDON?" I shout. "Will I ever walk again?"

Artemis laughs even harder this time. "Yes, Iris. You'll be able to walk. There wasn't any real damage to the tendon. Just a *lot* of blood." He raises his hands, painted with plasma. The cuffs of his pants are drenched from kneeling in the blood pool, but there's only a little bit splattered across his abdomen. "You're gonna be fine. And you made quite the masterpiece on the tile, right?"

I shake my head and smile. "I suppose so." I glance at the puddles of my blood, painting the floor into a haunting massacre. I tilt my head to the ceiling and shut my eyes, letting the exhaustion consume me. I begin to count who is left in the competition and abandon the task when I realize Arty may have the answers. I open my eyes and see him staring at me. His smile is soft. His knees are now to his chest, and he hugs them, his hands spreading red liquid over his pant legs.

"Arty…" I stutter. "How many hours did you make it? Five? Six?"

Artemis tilts his head. "Iris…I was eliminated five minutes after you."

I gasp. "But…that's not possible. I've been alone for hours."

"No, you weren't, Iris. Your head is just messing with you…the dehydration doesn't help."

I scrunch my eyebrows as the reality of solitary confinement sets in. The bland walls make minutes seem like hours and hours feel like *days*. My breath catches at the thought of being here for days, knowing it'll feel like weeks.

My anxiety starts spiraling, so I abandon the thought and move on to the next pressing question. "How'd you get eliminated?"

Artemis gives a weak, emotionless smile. "It was one of the high-pitched rings. I don't know…I guess it took me a little off guard. I wasn't the only one, though. Ashlea and

Lunar couldn't handle it either. Whatever it was knocked all three of us out at once." He shakes his head, smile having faded to a frown. "I lost control over my body…my hands shot to my ears without any registration." He kicks the wall weakly. "Such a waste of seven hours."

My heart races as I count who remains. Lagiacrus, a strong competitor, and Finian, who was on his last legs when I left. And the other two…Mercedes and Cypher. My chest deflates. "So, I have a fifty-fifty shot that I'm on Death Row."

Artemis raises an eyebrow. "What are you talking about? Who's after you?"

"Can I seriously trust that Cypher and Mercedes won't put me up?" I spit.

"Iris, you're being irrational. You said yourself that Mercedes is after Jade and Cypher. You don't have to worry about her. Besides…even if they weren't in the picture, I *know* she wouldn't go after you."

"How can you know that, though?" I shoot back. "Has she *ever* mentioned that I'm safe with her? I felt good about it earlier…but now that she might *win* the dang thing? I…I'm doomed!"

Artemis shakes his head. "Iris, look at me." I move my eyes toward his, breath catching in my throat when I lock on. "Mercedes isn't going to go after you because *I'm* not going to go after you. She won't intentionally remove somebody who could help her biggest ally stay in this house. She's much smarter than you give her credit for."

I take a deep breath, not letting his praise for Mercedes pierce my pride too deep. "And if Cypher wins?"

Artemis sits quietly, deflecting his gaze to the ground. My voice quivers as I continue. "What if I lose somebody? What if…what if I have to choose between two friends? What if it's you and Ashlea?"

Artemis gulps. "Then I guess you'll have to pick who's more valuable to your survival."

I shake my head so fast that my braid whips the sides of my face. "No…no, I can't do that. I *won't* do that."

"Iris," Artemis pleads, his voice suddenly urgent. "Just…promise me that whatever happens, you'll vote. It sucks…but we *have* to play their game. I don't want to lose you because your heart can't take it."

"But it's not fair!" I shout back, his last sentence striking a nerve. "And I…I shouldn't be alive." I gulp. "Arty, why did you save me? You could've let me die in here…you'd be another step closer to getting out alive."

Artemis rolls his eyes. "Iris, why do you insist that I don't care about you?" He grabs my arms and shakes me. "Do you have *any* idea how much you mean to me?"

His grip burns, but his desperate stare distracts me from the pain. His eyes shoot from left to right on my face, investigating my pupils with an intensity that sends a shiver down my spine. I match his gaze and find passion and kindness in his blue oases.

Suddenly, there's no doubt in my mind that this man would never cause me harm.

He would never betray me or do anything to hurt my chances in this game. Because Artemis cares about me. Perhaps…more than he's *ever* cared about anyone.

He finally loosens his grip and lets out another sigh. "You'll probably never know how much you mean to me."

My heart sinks because I know *exactly* how much I mean to him. But vocalizing it would shatter our fragile friendship, destroying our delicate balance as allies. And a friend like Artemis…

He will *never* be worth losing.

I wrack my brain for a topic change, but nothing feels natural. Any switch would seem like a reach to escape the moment. But I *can't* confront his feelings for me. *I refuse to.* So, instead, I stare at the blood that's pooled around my leg and follow the trail to where Artemis lies, his head now tilted toward the ceiling. His bare torso rises and falls as he breathes, abs contracting and releasing. His pant legs are rolled up to his knees, showing off the protruding veins in his calves. Artemis crosses his arms, making his biceps harden across his naked chest.

I've never found my ally handsome. But with the blood caking his body and sweat streaming down his abdomen…

I'm undeniably attracted to him.

Artemis chuckles, whipping me back to reality.

"What?" I ask, instantly blushing.

"Nothing." He shakes his head, and despite his earlier frustrations with my doubt in his game intentions, there's a smirk painted across his lips. His arms ease, and he lays down, closing his eyes but keeping the grin. "I'm going to get some sleep. You're safe to do the same. Now that the blood's stopped, you should be fine."

I watch as he relaxes, arms clasping behind his head. I scoot a few paces away from him and follow suit, cupping my own hands behind my neck. Just as I shut my eyes, Artemis's voice returns.

"Goodnight, Iris."

I open my eyes and find that same smirk on his lips. I shake my head before shutting them one final time.

"Goodnight, Artemis."

And despite my worries about the future and my anxiety about Artemis, exhaustion devours me until, finally, sleep whisks me away.

Chapter 29

*H*ONK.

    The horn jerks me awake. Artemis and I search for each other and shrug until we see the bright red instructions and countdown spanning the wall across from me.

24:00:00
EXPULSION VOTE

I blink several times as the numbers count down and finally register that it's a timer. *We have twenty-four hours until the vote and execution.*

Artemis yawns as he rises, squinting at the clock. I open my mouth to question why the vote is happening so quickly when we've only been here for…*how long?* However long it's been, it can't have been three days. Surely, we weren't asleep for that long. *Right?*

Just before Artemis starts the conversation, a loud *bang* makes him jump. When he looks behind me, his pupils dilate so wide I can't see the blue in his irises. When I turn toward the noise, my chest drops through the floor.

A section of the tile wall had swung open, leaving us completely vulnerable. Three men stare back at me from the other side, eyes hovering over their holographic computer screens.

I lean closer, narrowing my gaze into the room. Projectors span every inch of the wall. There's footage of the Enterprize, with my housemates milling about various rooms. But the largest and most prominent picture is the one zoomed on me, tilting my head and narrowing my gaze. I gasp, astounded that I hadn't realized it immediately. The solitary confinement chamber isn't just an attachment off the side of the arena.

It connects to the film crew's headquarters.

"Wha—" I start, but I'm cut off when the rations start falling from the ceiling. They burst upon impact and scatter around us, stealing my attention. When I glance back at the film room, the tile is locked back into place, as if the hidden sector of the house never existed.

"You're kidding!" Artemis shouts, piling the supplies into a bloodless corner. Bottles of water rain down from the ceiling, some exploding and showering us with freezing cold liquid. Too dehydrated to give the secret room a second thought, I reach for the intact water containers and gather them beside the rations, unable to contain my excitement.

"Oh my god!" I shout in a mixture of bewilderment and elation. My voice has returned, but my screech instantly shoots pain back up through my esophagus. I rub my throat as I flip into a crawl, but immediately fall onto my back, a bout of agony shooting through up from my calf. My left leg throbs in anguish, and I feel every individual beat of my heart travel through the gash across my shin. My skin burns from the sunlight, and blisters cover my legs, arms, and face. Spots of red paint my body from my mosquito bite scabs, at least a hundred scattered throughout my lower half. I peel my braid from the dried sweat on my back and lean against the wall, finally evaluating how disgusting I both look and feel.

"You, okay?" Artemis asks, reaching toward me. He abandons the food, all attention on me.

"I'm fine. Just…sore from yesterday." The pain settles, and I glance at all the food he's stacked. My mouth instantly fills with saliva, just the presence of the rations sparking my appetite. Artemis grabs a bottle of water and tosses it before opening his own. I thank him and finally sit up, guzzling the water as he continues sorting out our rations.

"I guess somebody won then, huh?"

Artemis turns back to me, slightly taken aback. "Yeah…I guess so."

I gulp loudly. "Who do you think it was?"

Artemis shakes his head, slowing down his ration organization. "No clue. But when I got out, Lagiacrus was looking strong. Maybe him?"

I nod but struggle to convince myself that Cypher was not victorious. The thought sends a shiver down my spine, so I search my brain for anything else to think about. Artemis tosses me a baguette, and I chew on it slowly, my stomach rumbling in pain from the prolonged absence of nutrition.

"How's the leg feeling?" Artemis asks between bites.

"It's fine, I guess." I shrug. "I mean, it hurts. But it's a thousand times better than last night."

He nods patiently before asking to take another look. I open my palms to encourage him, so he abandons his bread and readjusts beside me. Holding one of the water bottles, he points to it with raised eyebrows. "We just have a day left in here. Mind if I use some of this to clean that out?" I quickly oblige, and he gets to work. He slowly unwraps the wound and begins to clean it, and I look away, wincing from the pain.

"Hang in there," he encourages. "It's a world better than yesterday, so you probably won't lose the leg."

"*Probably*?" My eyes widen. "Probably!"

Artemis laughs as he pours more clean water onto the gash. "Iris. It's called a joke. Ever heard of one?"

I roll my eyes and hit his arm. "Not the time, Arty."

We laugh before the pain returns. I wince as he apologizes, but the process never seems to end. "How do you know what you're even doing, anyway? Where did you learn this?"

Artemis twitches at the question. "I," he pauses, unsure whether he wants to reveal the entire truth. We lock eyes as we so often do, and he opens up. "I was the makeshift 'doctor' at the refugee camp…I made sure the others were okay."

My eyes widen. *He's finally talking about his crimes.* He had mentioned the refugee camp to me ages ago, but never expanded upon its existence: neither why it was necessary nor what it was for. With just the two of us, I finally get an opportunity to pry.

"Arty…why won't you tell me where you came from? What you did?"

He stops washing my wound and watches the ground. He pushes his hands together as a distraction, forcing some dried blood to peel from his palms. "It's just really painful…and confusing…I don't know, it's a lot."

I touch his arm, barely touching his skin. "Do you trust me?"

His eyes lock onto mine. "Of course I do, Iris."

"Then you can tell me, right? You can tell me anything, Arty."

Artemis' eyes shift into a deeper adoration, erupting my stomach into butterflies. Confused at what's causing this sudden attraction toward him, I shake my right leg, ridding myself of the feeling. Luckily, Artemis ignores it. "Well…what do you know about the Assessment?"

Images of everything I've heard since entering the Enterprize flash through my mind. Lagiacrus's parents died for the secret of the Assessment. Many of my housemates are here because they avoided participation in the test. Ashlea's love urged her not to go…

"I mean…not a lot, really. I know it's supposed to determine what we are all best at…so we are employed in the positions that best suit our strengths. But now, I guess the careers are isolated to genetic modification? I don't really know anymore, though. The things I've been hearing here make no sense. What could be so bad about the Assessment that people will risk the death penalty to stay away from it?"

Artemis shakes his head. "It's complicated."

"Then explain it to me," I urge, leaning toward him. My head gets foggy from the sudden movement, and I'm forced to lie back on the cold, hard ground. Artemis lays a hand on my forehead, checking my temperature.

"No fever. That's a good sign."

I stare at him with urgency, willing him to continue.

He sighs. "To be honest with you, Iris, I don't really know either. But despite every barrier, my parents kept in touch with some classmates they went to the Assessment with thirty years ago. I don't know how…but they did. And…their classmates ended up in the Authority." He puckers his lips to the side, summoning the strength to continue. "Specifically, their classmates worked in the Assessment division.

"When I was fourteen, my parents sat me down and told me the Assessment's changed…that's it's not right. Nothing specific, but that we have a duty to protect those around us…those we love." He searches my eyes and quickly looks back down, starting to wash the blood out of the t-shirt once wrapped around my leg. "They started a refugee camp. Kids around the neighborhood…a few days before their sixteenth birthday, my parents would speak with their family. A couple days later, we had three more people living in our basement. This went on for years. I mean…I'm sixteen now."

I shake my head. "But how—"

"—did the Authority not find them?" Artemis finishes the question for me. "Connections."

I squint my eyes and find that I'm more lost than ever. Luckily, this prompts him to expand. "We had somebody on the inside…he'd fudge the numbers, say that our home was already inspected. And if anyone asked, well…he would suggest going there himself. And sometimes, he actually did." He nods. "That's when I realized…not everyone in the Authority is evil. They all started out just like us, getting tested and sorted." He shrugs. "Don't get me wrong, most are cruel in an Ascendancy like the one I'm from. But this guy…well, this was a diamond in the rough. In the end, forty people were living in our basement."

I gasp. "FORTY? How did you even have the space for that? The rations…"

Artemis shakes his head. "Iris, it was an entire operation. We had a ration guy fudging the numbers. For every new family that moved in, we'd dig further into the ground and make renovations together. Everyone had a role. Mine was in the medical field."

My jaw is still on the floor. "But if you're so good on the medical side of things, why can't you do the logic stuff?"

Artemis shakes his head with a weak smile, amused that of all things, that was one of my first questions. "If you're so good at logic, why can't you do the medical stuff?"

I nod my head with a slight smile. Finally, I ask about the end. "How did you get caught?"

Artemis shrugs shyly. "How did *you* get caught?"

We lock onto each other's eyes, and I'm entranced by his beautiful blue ones. I say, almost hypnotized, "I guess we'll never know."

We continue to stare at each other until I break it. Solitary confinement has me every type of confused, and I can't afford for my feelings to be disordered further. I twist my thumbs together as the silence sets in, waiting for Artemis to bandage me back up. When I finally look up again, his eyes are glistening with moisture.

"They killed every last one of them."

One hand instinctively covers my mouth. Slowly, I put the other on his back.

"Right in front of me, Iris. They killed them all. And *forced* me to watch." He takes a deep breath. "Why me? Of all people, why save me?"

I scoot closer and lean my head on his shoulder. He flinches from the burn but doesn't back away. "Aren't we all asking ourselves that same question?"

He sniffs back the tears and shakes, refusing sadness. We sit in silence, both staring blankly at the wall ahead of us. Finally, his voice cracks. "Iris…I have nothing left. No one…no one left."

I stiffen up, realizing what this means. "So…Anthony and Jeremy?"

Artemis nods. "Killed right in front of me."

I bite my lip as he trembles, holding him closer. A million questions float through my mind, but he answers them before I can ask.

"We pranked the Authority the day before my parents talked to me and started the operation. From that moment on…everything was different."

I hold his hand, and he squeezes tight. We sit there, side by side, on the cold, bloody ground as the clock ticks down, minute by minute, toward someone's demise. When I think there's nothing left to say, Artemis's voice floats back into my ears.

"There's nobody left that cares about me."

I lean off of his shoulder and look him dead in the eyes. "That's just not true."

He stares at me blankly, waiting for me to expand. I switch my gaze to the floor before starting. "You have Mercedes."

Artemis snorts. "Yeah. I've got Mercedes."

"Well, she…*loves* you, right?" I cringe at the word and mentally gag at the thought of them making out in the kitchen.

Artemis gives that same weak chuckle and responds, "Sure."

Finally, I turn to him, still holding his palm. "And you obviously have me, right?" Artemis freezes and stares into my eyes. I shift uncomfortably before continuing. "You're my best friend. You said it before…Mercedes knows I'll protect you. I'm going to fight to keep you safe, Artemis. Because people care about you." I blink. "*I* care about you."

There's a long string of silence until Artemis nods. When he finally shifts, I back away, watching him fold his old t-shirt into a makeshift bandage. "On that note, let's get you bandaged up."

I nod and smile as he cleans out the blood from his shirt, painting more of my plasma onto the tile. He soaks the top with fresh water before applying it back to my leg, securing it with a loose knot. "Good to go." I smile and return to my baguette, savoring every last bite. Just as I think our conversation is over, Artemis whispers over his shoulder.

"You're my best friend too, Iris."

Chapter 30

11:59:59
EXPULSION VOTE

"Cheers!" We shout in unison, clinking our water bottles to celebrate the clock striking halfway. We may be counting down to some horrific activity that could lead to the demise of either one of us, but after twenty hours in solitary confinement together, the two of us are losing our marbles. We laugh hysterically with one another, landing one joke after the other. I can't catch my breath before the next bout of laughter begins.

"Okay, your turn," Artemis laughs. "You and one other person are the last two people on earth. Would you rather have—"

"Oh god!" I shout back, laughing, head tilted to the ceiling.

"I haven't even given the options yet!" he defends. "You have to wait! I promise they're good!"

I cackle and point at Artemis with raised eyebrows, encouraging him to complete his question. He laughs uncontrollably before continuing. "Okay... okay! You're the last person on earth, and you get one buddy. Would you rather have Mercedes or the *Warden*?"

"WHAT?" I shout back. We burst out laughing, and I double over from the aches in my stomach. I must take deep breaths before I can even think about speaking again. I shake my head and stretch my arms innocently between my straight legs, holding my hands together with fingers locking them into place. I squirm, still shaking my head, and whine. "I can't answer that!" The answer, of course, is clear. But the exhaustion has powered us both to the point that anything is hilarious, and I can't keep myself from cackling every few seconds.

"Come on, you *have* to!" Artemis shrieks. "There's no getting out of it!"

I laugh, bending my knees and putting my head between them to show my deliberation. I'm smiling and cackling into my legs, building the anticipation as much as possible. I continue to squirm until Artemis gives a proper burst of laughter.

"Ha! I love you!" I look up quickly, about to make fun of him for the slip-up. Instead, my heart skips a beat as I realize the gravity of his words. Artemis doesn't seem to notice that he's said something significant because he just continues laughing. "I love that you do that! It's so cute!"

"Do what!?" I stammer, thankful he avoided mentioning his slip-up. I take a shaky breath and convince myself that it was a mistake. That he really meant to tell me that he loves this *conversation* and not *me*. I quip back quickly to avoid any awkwardness and ignore the gravity of his mistake.

"Okay, now understand this," I say in hysterical laughter. "This is *only* my answer because I'd have to build back the human race, and Mercedes and I couldn't procreate."

Artemis roars with laughter, louder than ever before. "SO, YOU'D PICK THE WARDEN!"

I stretch my arms further down my legs and bend forward, squirming in defense. "I'd have to! I couldn't just let the human race *die*!"

Artemis barely hears me over his laughter. "I knew you were into the Warden! You act like it's a joke, but I knew it!"

I hit his arm playfully. "Stop! What is he? Like, four times my age!?"

"So, you're into older men, then?"

My laughter rolls back to match his. "Shut up, you know what I mean! It's your turn now. Enough with me!"

Artemis holds his palm out to suggest he's not finished. "Okay, no. Since you cheated, we have to do it again. Between two guys!"

I shake my head in disbelief that he's still going and chuckle. "Okay, fine! What are my options?"

Artemis looks up in wonderment and then stares me dead in the eyes.

"The warden…or the most attractive man in solitary confinement?" He flicks his fingers from the top of his head to his shoes, smiling. "Mwah?"

My eyes narrow on him, my laughter dying. "Come on…you can't do that."

"Why not?" Artemis cackles. "Answer the question!"

I roll my eyes, putting Mace at the forefront of my mind. Up until this point, our jokes have been playful…innocent. But the second the question leaves Artemis's lips…guilt flushes through my chest, my heart stopping in rejection. "You're just flirting with me now, Arty." I put my hand up and lower it to simulate the volume being turned down. "Tone it down a notch."

Artemis punches my shoulder playfully. "Oh, come on, Iris! It's a joke. You can't joke around anymore now that you've kissed Mace?"

I raise my eyebrows, shocked that he's the one bringing up Mace. Instead of confronting him about it, I joke back. "Fine. Who would you pick: Kylah or Crescentia?"

Artemis chuckles lightly. "Okay, well, that's not hard. One of them is *dead*. Kinda narrows it down, don't you think?"

My smile disappears, knowing he took it too far. We've been bordering on some gray territory but laughing at the fallen…. it's uncalled for.

"Yeah, I guess it does." I sit back quietly, emotionless. Artemis senses his mistake and quickly gets on the defensive.

"Oh, come on…I didn't mean….I'm sorry, Iris. I just got carried away. Please, give me another one…I promise…I won't say anything like that again."

I shake my head with a weak smile. "Okay, fine. New choice: Jade and Kylah."

"Hmmm…" Artemis deliberates, touching his chin with his enormous left palm. "That's tough…" he leans over as I had, clasping his hands and arms between his legs. Mirroring my previous actions, he squirms innocently, playing up how difficult the decision is. Despite how cute he felt I looked in this vulnerable position, I don't find any form of the same attraction toward him.

Since being locked in solitary confinement with Artemis, my mind has been spinning out of control. One moment, he saves my life, and I'm overwhelmed with gratitude. Another, his bare torso makes my stomach twirl with attraction, dried blood peeling off of his abs like some formidable gladiator, fresh from battle. But between these brief moments of intrigue, he reveals a level of vulnerability that only a woman head over heels in love with him could find enticing.

And unfortunately for him, I am no such woman.

This is rather ruinous because when he jokes back, "Jade because her spicy attitude would probably translate to the bedroom," and I laugh from discomfort, his eyes glow with that same passion that Mace had before our first kiss.

The room grows silent, Artemis staring his blue eyes into mine, a vibrant smile on his lips and a nervous one upon mine.

"What?" Artemis asks with a laugh.

He watches me, and the feeling in his eyes intensifies. Only one other person has ever looked at me this way before…but this time, there's desperation. It's a delicate mixture of longing, joyousness, and deep compassion.

The unmistakable eyes of a man in love, desperate to feel it back.

My smile widens as I realize he possibly has the realization at the exact moment I do. And just for a moment, the world stops, and I can swear…Artemis is going to lean in for a kiss.

"Nothing," I say playfully, looking the other way, determined to freeze the moment in its tracks. And it's all because my previous doubts are instantaneously voided. Now, despite the circumstances and relationships he has outside of this room, I know exactly how Artemis feels for me. Because I feel it, too.

But it's for somebody else.

Regardless, my heart swells knowing how much I mean to the person in front of me. My best friend. I ponder my feelings toward Artemis as we sit in silence, seemingly for ages. *He makes me laugh like nobody else.* But he also frustrates me above all others with his manipulation of Mercedes, then ignorance and lack of compassion toward the Enterprize fallen. But along with all these other feelings, my time so far with him in solitary confinement has shown me his true character. Reflecting on who he is and what he means to me, I am brought to a single conclusion.

I love him.

I'm just not *in love* with him.

My heart tells me one thing, and my mind tells me another. I've been searching long and hard to identify why my stomach gets queasy around Artemis, how I can be myself so effortlessly around him, and why I care so much about his relationship with Mercedes. Finally, with him looking into my eyes the way that Mace does, I understand why.

I do have feelings for Artemis. But whatever romantic feelings I'm developing for him are no competition to what I feel toward Mace. Despite this, along with everything and everyone telling me to stay away from him, a harsh reality falls upon me.

I can't live without him. And I don't ever want to.

Chapter 31

00:18:23
EXPULSION VOTE

My hands clench through my brown locks, still secured into my fishtail braid. Because of my fidgeting, they now spill out of the knot haphazardly in chunks. My stomach feels empty yet full at the same time, nerves encompassing my entire being. My heart beats in my ears, and I grip my braid even tighter. Artemis and I sit side by side across from the bright red numbers, silently watching them tick down to either our casting of votes or our imminent demise.

"Hey," Artemis bumps into my left shoulder. "It's gonna be alright…we just need to keep cool. Get in there, push a button, get out. Convince yourself that's all it is."

I squeeze my eyelids shut as my stomach takes another tumble. "Unless I'm the one voted out."

Artemis looks down and shrugs. "You're not gonna get voted out. If anything, I'm the one that's in trouble."

I turn to face Artemis, my breath catching in my throat. "Why are you concerned?"

"Do you honestly think Cypher cares about you? Mercedes is the one he doesn't like. Why wouldn't he put her up against her closest ally?"

"Stop," I say, crunching my hair harder as I shake it back and forth in denial. "Don't say that. I…I can't deal with…just stop."

The idea of losing one of the first and strongest friendships I've ever had terrifies me. I try to convince myself that we're both safe, that this is just a game, and that there is nothing to lose. But my brain won't accept these tricks and instead flashes images of Sola and my parents, bullets shooting through their deceased bodies.

We sit in silence until the clock strikes five minutes. A buzzer blares, and the numbers triple in size, taking up the entirety of the wall. Each second, the numbers flash in warning, like a countdown to an atomic bomb. I stand up and start pacing, pain shooting up my left leg every time it strikes the ground. Artemis doesn't move a muscle.

The pain distracts me, but when it's too much to bear, I take out my fishtail and braid it meticulously. Despite this practice, the time seems to slow until only two minutes remain.

Artemis rises from the floor and grabs my arm to stop my fidgeting. "Listen to me, Iris. And *please* don't interrupt." I face him and watch his facial expression, direct and intentional. His sternness is surprising, but I lock onto his blue eyes and listen to his words like my life depends on it.

"If you're voting, they'll call you first. That just makes the most sense. But if you're on Death Row, they'll wait until after the votes are cast. Once that happens, I'm doubtful they'll let you out. They'll probably just execute you right here."

I glance at the clock.

00:01:34
EXPULSION VOTE

Artemis shakes me by the arms. "PLEASE. I need you to listen!" I shift my attention back to him, and his pupils scream desperation. "I don't know what'll happen if we're both up there, so that's unimportant. But if you go first, I very well may not make it. I just need you to understand…you're trusting a *lot* of people in there. If I don't make it out of here…please. Promise me you'll be careful about who you trust. You won't stand a chance if you trust like you are now."

"Wha—?"

"DON'T INTERRUPT." Artemis shakes me once again. "You can trust me, Iris. You have my word on that. I need you to understand…you mean *everything* to me. But if I'm voted out…you won't agree with me, but Mercedes is a straight shooter. You know where she stands. *Trust her*. Keep your friends close but promise me you're careful."

"Why are you telling me this?" I whisper. "Who…who shouldn't I trust?"

Artemis locks eyes with me, and I get the familiar feeling that he will try to kiss me. I back away from his grasp slightly, concerned about his next move, but he remains silent, unwilling to reveal the information he holds. A loud horn blares like it's begging us to evacuate, and I bring my attention back to the numbers on the wall.

00:00:10
EXPULSION VOTE

I take a weak step back, terrified of what's to come. Artemis and I glance at each other quickly. Despite the brief moment of awkwardness between us, we forget everything and embrace each other in a hug. My body trembles, and my nerves consume me so entirely that I can ignore the strange position this interaction leaves me. Artemis towers over me, and I stand on my toes to keep my arms around his shoulders. I hate how unnatural it

187

feels. But I fight to ignore this feeling and instead hold on to this wholesome moment with my best friend.

The last chance I may ever get to be with him.

PART 3

Chapter 32

"CONVICT: IRIS. EVACUATE FOR VOTING."

BANG.

The white tiled wall cracks open, revealing the entrance we've long forgotten existed. My body goes limp in Artemis's arms. *I'm safe.* Despite this, my stomach and chest tingle as I envision what this might mean for my ally.

We release our hold, and Artemis grabs me at arm's length. I open my mouth to say something, *anything* that could make this moment easier. But I can't squeak anything out of my vocal cords, so I stand frozen in terror as tears well up in Artemis's beautiful blue eyes.

"Hey," he says, stretching his lips into a weak smile. "I'll see you soon. It's going to be okay."

I nod as he releases his grip. Turning toward the exit, my eyes linger on the splotches of blood painting the bottom quarter of the door. My stomach drops to my knees. *Artemis is the reason I am alive.* My simultaneous anxiety and heartbreak distract me from my limp, and adrenaline leads me to the exit. I grip the cold tile separating me from the arena and glance one final time at Artemis. His sunburn blisters swell on his cheeks, and his blue eyes shine brightly against their charred canvas. His sculpted midsection is still exposed, as his t-shirt continues to bandage my scorpion wound. He's cleaned off most of the blood on his torso, but his khakis are still painted red at the cuffs. He doesn't seem to mind the discoloration because the only thing he appears to see or feel in this moment is me. Even though this may be the last I see of Artemis, I can't bring myself to say anything. No last words are found. Even if they were…my heart couldn't handle revealing them to him.

How he means the world to me. How I won't last much longer without him. How he's a bright light in my life that I could *never* forget.

And that I love him and will forever be indebted to him.

He smiles shyly and nods, encouraging me to leave the room. Holding back tears, I reflect his smile and shuffle over the threshold.

The door locks behind me, making me flinch. I quickly direct my focus forward and find the scene as it always has been, metal staircase and velvet ropes alike. Whatever comfort the familiarity brings deteriorates the second my eyes land on the giant red numbers counting down my fleeting opportunity to vote. As always, I'm only given three minutes to vote. But being on the opposite end of the arena with a debilitating injury, the time limit isn't nearly enough. I bite my lip and start hiking across the turf on my bad leg, my heart rate picking up with each step. At the rate I'm moving, my decision will have to be quick.

I limp across the arena, the turf vibrantly mocking my agony with its artificial lust for life and enthusiasm. With each passing stride, my heart thumps harder, anxiety blooming at my Death Row options. Half a step from the podium, I glance at the time I have left. *Two minutes.* My eyelids flutter shut, and my chest inflates as I let in three deep breaths. Nerves settled, I open my eyes to the blue button on my left and the white button on my right.

My eyes narrow, reading the names.

"JADE" in blue. "CYPHER" in white.

"*Yes,*" I whisper, falling to my knees. Somehow, someway, somebody outlasted Cypher in the Suffering Sanctuary. And by some miracle, none of my allies were targeted.

I let out a shaky breath and whisper, "*Thank you,*" into the turf. My hands settle behind my neck, and my smile widens as I stand. Lunar and Mace are safe, and Artemis will live to see another day. I raise my arms half an inch before there's a twist in my chest.

Somebody has to die.

And *I* have to pick who it is.

My mind spins as differing scenarios swirl, competing for my attention. But no matter what I consider, it's inarguable that Cypher is the stronger player. It boldens with every passing argument.

Jade is the head of the snake, spreading the lies he supports.

But Cypher is the stronger player.

Jade is the least likable of the two.

But Cypher is the stronger player.

Despite every argument against Jade, my gut tells me that Cypher has to go. I brace myself and wince as I press his button. It kills me, having to decide his fate like this. But as badly as my stomach aches, and as much as I try to convince myself otherwise…

Voting is getting easier.

I shake my head, willing this realization *far* back into the deepest and dustiest files of my brain. The nervous sweat on my brow stings my sunburn, and I wipe it hastily as I turn to exit the arena. My limping is consistent, but the pain eases with my excitement at returning to the Enterprize and celebrating my group's safety with Mace and Lunar. My pace quickens until I reach the metal staircase, where I summon enough strength into my arms to hoist me up each step. This offers a slight disruption to the pain in my leg. I take advantage of it, using the support of the railings until I reach the large iron door separating the area from the Enterprize.

I rest my hand on the cold, smooth surface of the iron slab, take a deep breath, and push forward. One step across the threshold, I'm slammed into Lunar's arms.

"We…thought…you…were…*dead!*" He can barely get the words out. He puts all his energy into squeezing my torso harder than I ever imagined possible. Lunar's force knocks the wind out of me, and the heat from his sunburns radiates off his skin. We both wince from the pain but bear it, unable to hold back our relief. His grasp tightens, and I hold back tears.

Because Lunar's never shown this side of himself to me before.

But three rounds into the Enterprize...it changes people.

"Well, I'm alive!" I finally joke, matching the intensity of his embrace. "I'm okay! It's all okay!"

When we finally release, my eyes gaze a few steps above us, and my lips break into a smile. Mace stands with his hands clasped behind his back, a romantic and grateful grin on his lips. His violet eyes sparkle, and I can't help but run into his arms, ignoring the piercing pain that shoots up my leg. He embraces me, lifting me off the floor and squeezing my torso.

"I meant every word I said to you," he whispers in my ear.

He kisses me on the forehead, his gentle lips lingering for a second longer than usual. My heart swoons as I wrap my legs around his hips. Without hesitation, the words leave my mouth. "Me too."

We finally descend the staircase, Mace and I hand in hand, with Lunar leading the way. Mace rests his opposite hand on Lunar's head, ruffling his hair. Mace's hand is soft, and with each subsequent circle his thumb makes on the outside of my palm, it's obvious he's been unperturbed by the Suffering Sanctuary. Because he was the Executive last round, he was the only one who avoided its horrors.

The others, however, faired about as well as I expected.

Lunar only lasted a few minutes longer than me, so he's just as burnt and barred as when I last saw him. Blisters bulb on his cheeks from *seven hours* in the solar chamber. With each peppy step, his sleeves bump up to his shoulders, revealing harsh tan lines where the cotton ends. There are half as many scabs on his legs as mine, his self-control against the mosquito bites having paid off. He hides his pain well, allowing me to reserve my mental torment for his agony for a later time.

Steps from the living room, reality hits. Because despite being punished in solitary confinement for the past twenty-four hours, I've forgotten that other penalties were assigned. So, when we finally reach the end of the kitchen, and I notice Finian's bald head, my eyes widen in horror.

His ginger hair is gone, and his bare skull shines bright as if the follicles were melted away. But the cosmetic change isn't isolated to his upper quarter. Finian's eyebrows, arms, and legs are also naked of hair. Where a clean shave would've left a smooth and pleasant exterior...

His skin instead glows with the unmistakable wounds and scars of chemical burns.

Noticing my eyeline, Mace whispers, lips so close they tickle my ear. "They showered him with chemicals...they burned it all off."

I shiver at the cruelty.

As we get closer, Finian doesn't move an inch. I imagine any slight movement would trigger insurmountable pain. When staring at him gets too uncomfortable, I search the others, narrowing on the roasted beauty-queen sitting cross-legged on the luxurious Executive cushion.

Her skin is charred. Blisters stack on one another, stretching the red and purple scars from the gassing she got in round 2. Her long blonde hair lays limb at her side, and she intently watches the staircase, her blue eyes longing for my solitary confinement roommate. Mercedes glances in my direction and stretches her lips into a sly smile that screams, "*You owe me.*" When she turns back to the staircase, Mace shakes his head. I tilt my head, and he mouths, "Later." So, for the moment, I'm just thankful my intuition about Mercedes's targets was right.

I settle between Mace and Lunar on the furthest couch, still clasping Mace's hand. Ashlea reaches over to squeeze my knee, and I smile.

"Punishment?" I mouth, eyes narrowing.

She grins and shakes her head. "Reward. Safety for the Round!" Her whispers are barely audible, but I catch them, nonetheless. My grin stretches wide enough for my teeth to show, and I nod, grateful for her luck.

I take deep breaths, mentally thanking the Authority that her and Finian's punishments weren't reversed. I bask in my relief, leaning against the back of the couch and counting my remaining allies. An immediate pang of guilt shoots through my heart when I watch the Death Row cushions and see Jade and Cypher huddled together, holding back tears.

My smile disappears, and my lips tremble. Because all at once, I realize that my happiness radiates in an egotistical shower of ignorance.

I've been so consumed in my welcome back that I've ignored the oncoming execution. My eyes flick between Jade and Cypher, who grasp onto each other for dear life. Any trauma the two have endured from the Suffering Sanctuary seems minor compared to the state they are in now. Jade's emotions finally pile over, and she bawls on Cypher's shoulder. He sniffs, keeping the tears away, but trembles against her, eyes squeezed shut.

I divert my gaze to the floor and deflate, ashamed of my inconsiderate celebration of survival. Mace squeezes my hand, and despite the gesture's comfort, my stomach still twists with regret.

But, when the arena door slams shut and Artemis's steps echo off the Enterprize walls, my shame disappears, replaced with my earlier relief at his survival. I straighten my back and steady my feet on the carpet, preparing to jump into his arms when he hits the ground floor. I smile, readying myself to be the first person he approaches when he reaches the bottom step. I imagine our embrace, and my heart does a cartwheel. *Two friends who went through hell together…making it out the other side alive.* We nearly said our goodbyes…I *really* thought he might get expelled. My smile widens as I let go of Mace's palm, priming myself to stand and accept Artemis's embrace.

But when he reaches the last step, he doesn't run for me. Instead, he screams, "I KNEW IT! That's my girl!" and lifts Mercedes off the ground, spinning her around the kitchen.

He digs his gigantic fingers into her hair and kisses her so passionately that the two gasp for air when he sets her on the ground. The pair harmonize their triumphant screams, only taking breaks to lock their lips in a sexual frenzy. Between kisses, they give romantic whoops, Mercedes shouting, "I did it for you, Art-Art!" while the towering, shirtless man shrieks, "I knew I could count on you, Merc!"

I clench my aching stomach as she wraps her legs around Artemis's waist, rubbing his naked torso with both palms and tracing her lips from the top of his neck to the center of his stomach. My disappointment and disgust only disappear when Mercedes finally screeches, "I love you, Artemis!"

My teeth clench when the words leave her lips. Even worse, Artemis whispers something imperceptible in her ear, causing her to breathe him in with her lips, grasping his body with a tighter embrace than before. They continue celebrating, and I suddenly doubt everything.

What happened in solitary confinement? Had I imagined Artemis's love for me? The way he talks to and acts around me both insinuate his true feelings. But his actions around Mercedes scream a completely different story. I review everything that happened between us from the first moment we entered the Enterprize. *When I caught him staring at me in the communal bedroom*, did I misread his intentions? Perhaps I imagined everything he felt. But no matter how confused I am, one detail remains that I cannot dispute.

The way he looked at me in solitary confinement was true, unconditional love. Whether he realizes it or not.

My chest tightens as I question why I'm so troubled by Artemis's love life. I slide my hands along the plush beneath me, wiping the sweat from my palms to calm my nerves. I grab Mace's hand, and he squeezes it three times, oblivious to my turmoil. He scoots closer to me, and his pant leg brushes my thigh, making my heart fuzzy.

I am in love with Mace. But as much as I try to convince myself that nothing else matters, my heart pounds with jealousy. I shake my head, reminding myself how ridiculous it is to feel this way. Only *one* of us is making it out of the Enterprize alive. My conflicting feelings are irrelevant because people are *dying*. And I need to make damn sure they aren't the ones I care for.

When all else fades, my jaw goes stiff. I clench my teeth, watching Artemis carry Mercedes by her waist and drop her onto her Executive cushion with a kiss that lasts far past the awkwardness threshold. The couple's insanely ignorant and impertinent celebration in the face of somebody else's death makes me grimace. My hypocrisy makes my face heat up when I consider my celebration just minutes ago.

The robotic voice returns, and the air thins. Jade's cries intensify to wails, muffled by Cypher's tightening hug.

"WHEN ANNOUNCED, THE EXPELLED CONVICT MUST EXIT THROUGH THE FRONT DOOR WHERE EXECUTION WILL COMMENCE."

Jade's sobs halt, but her breathing is unsteady. Her grip on Cypher tightens, and his hand starts going purple. They close their eyes, and I look away, unable to witness their pain.

"BY A VOTE OF FIVE TO FIVE: THERE IS A TIE."

What? Why on earth would anyone vote to expel Jade? She's clearly the weaker player. Why take her out now when she'll be easy to get out later?

There's silence as we stare at one another, unsure what to do. *Are both expelled at the same time? Do we need to vote again until one has more votes than the other?* Just as Eno opens his mouth for clarification, the voice returns.

"WHEN FACED WITH A TIE, THE EXECUTIVE MAKES THE FINAL DECISION ON EXPULSION."

Mercedes's jaw falls open, her smile having vanished. She drops Artemis's hand, and her temples break out in sweat.

"CONVICT: MERCEDES. YOU HAVE SIXTY SECONDS TO CAST YOUR VOTE AT THE HEAD OF THE ROOM."

Red numbers appear on the wall above her seat and count down from sixty, just as the voice commanded. Mercedes starts shaking her head in a panic, all joy extracted from the room.

"No…no, that's not fair."

Artemis puts a hand on her shoulder. "Merc…you've gotta do it. If you don't, they'll kill you."

"But that's not fair!" She yells, shooting up from her cushion. My heart twists with an odd mixture of confusion and respect. Mercedes may be cruel and conniving, but this is where she draws the line. "I have to decide who dies…me? Only *my* vote matters?"

Even considering her flamboyant arrogance moments ago, I can't help but feel sorry for her. Private voting gives the sense that no *one* person is responsible for the murder of another. Our collective compliance with the rules is what ultimately kills them. I can face it because my vote may never matter if everyone else votes the other way. There's still insurmountable guilt, but not enough to sacrifice my own life. But when there's a tie, and your vote becomes the only one that matters…that's much closer to pulling the trigger.

Cypher leaps from the couch and kneels before Mercedes with his hands in prayer. "Please, Mercedes. *Please.* Keep Jade here. For god's sake, vote me out!"

Jade shoots up from her Death Row cushion, jet-black hair floating up from her speed. "No! Cypher, don't do this!" Her sobs muddle her words. "I—I—can't—I can't live—without you!"

Mercedes pulls at her hair as the clock reaches twenty seconds remaining. Artemis rises from the couch and shakes her shoulders to get her attention, amplifying his volume so she can't ignore him.

"Mercedes, it's not fair. I *know* it's not fair! But you *have* to say a name. Just say a name—don't think about it. You can't die because of this!"

It's hard to distinguish one word from another once everyone starts shouting. A cacophony of yelling echoes off the living room walls, Jade and Cypher begging for each other's safety. At the same time, Artemis pleads with Mercedes to make a decision. Underneath the noise are Mercedes's distressed murmurs about how she can't do it. With five seconds remaining, Artemis's voice booms over the rest so loud that my ears ring. "PICK A NAME, NOW!"

Blue eyes wide, Mercedes grips her palms and shouts to the ceiling, "I vote to expel Jade!" before collapsing into her chair with her head in her hands.

"BY A VOTE OF SIX TO FIVE: JADE IS EXPELLED FROM THE ENTERPRIZE. YOU HAVE THIRTY SECONDS TO EVACUATE."

Cypher falls to his knees and screams, "WHAT HAVE YOU DONE?!"

Jade dry heaves, snapping Cypher out of his rage and making him remember the time limit. Cypher sweeps Jade off her feet as she cries and carries her toward the iron exit. Once there, with twenty seconds remaining, the two embrace and whisper desperately, unable to let go.

I squeeze Mace's hand tighter and reach for Lunar's to keep him steady. The living room is stunned into silence. Nobody watches the couple at the exit, opting for a view of the carpet instead. Artemis squats in front of Mercedes and grips her arms, whispering assurances that she did the right thing. But she keeps shaking her head, and for the first time since entering the Enterprize, I see her tears fall to the floor.

I practice incredible restraint by ignoring the scene by the entrance and pray it never happens to me. It isn't until the door slams and the *bangs* ricochet throughout the living room that I completely comprehend the gravity of what has been done.

ROUND 4

Chapter 33

There's approximately three seconds of silence.

Then there is chaos.

"*You.*" Cypher's voice sends a chill down my spine. His eyepatch is wet from Jade's sweat and tears, and his remaining eye dilates so wide it's only black. He points to Mercedes and stomps murderously toward the living room, quickening his pace with each passing stride.

"I didn't have a choice," Mercedes pleads, her voice quaking in fear. "They would've killed me!"

"THEN YOU SHOULD HAVE DIED!" He rushes into the living room, fist wound with intent to kill. Mercedes shoots off her cushion with her hands protecting her face, but Artemis pushes her aside, blocking her from the one-eyed criminal.

"Back away!" Artemis shouts. His torso is still bare, showing off his sharpening muscles. He bunches his hands into fists, unintentionally flexing his biceps so hard that the veins pop out. His body makes my stomach roil with attraction before dropping with humiliation that I ever thought I was the only one he'd endanger his life to protect.

Cypher shoves him forward. "You *did* have a choice, Mercedes! You *know* that! And you *chose* to kill an innocent life! You're a *monster!*"

Mercedes cowers behind Artemis but narrows her eyes with his accusation. She clenches her teeth, straightens her back, and steps forward to fuel the fire. "Nobody here is *innocent*, asshole. And I did what I had to *survive*, just like everyone else here does *every time* we compete, campaign, and vote. You had *no* problem voting against me last round when you had the chance!"

Her confidence builds with every sentence until she's inches from Cypher, only Artemis's body blocking her path. Noting her closeness, Cypher pushes Artemis toward the side, trying to get a clear view of Mercedes. Artemis fights back, struggling to stay solid but unwilling to relent. The rest of the living room sits in awe, too scared to walk past the altercation and too curious about how it will end.

"If you hit the girl, then we hit you," Artemis spits at Cypher, phlegm bubbles sticking to his opponent's eyepatch.

Cypher steps back with a nasty smirk. "Is that a threat?"

Artemis stays silent, hands frozen in front of Cypher to keep him from Mercedes. Artemis doesn't flinch at the accusation, solidifying his intent.

Cypher's smirk transforms into a chilling grin. "Do you seriously think I'm afraid of you because you beat some traumatized, frail girl into a pulp? If you want to fight, big guy, then let's fight! I'll beat the crap out of you!"

Cypher winds his fist but pauses when Destry and Lagiacrus jump to either side of Artemis. They stand in solidarity, arms extended for battle. Cypher falters his form but keeps his fist wound, blind confidence contaminating his reality.

"That's fine…I'll fight all three of you, then!"

"Cypher, you need to calm down!" Lagiacrus steps forward, reaching out to his opponent. "Or did you forget that Mercedes and I did you a favor in that chamber? The *least* you could do is keep your hands away from her."

"A FAVOR? You did me a *favor*?" Cypher laughs without humor. "By striking a deal to put me on Death Row with my partner to end the competition. *That* was your favor?"

"If it wasn't for that deal, you would've been dead twenty-four hours ago!" Lagiacrus shouts, veins popping out of his neck. "Ten minutes on that electric chair, and you would've been done!"

My eyes widen in horror. I search Mace for answers, but he shakes his head. I know he'll brief me later, but I can't help picturing the sadistic punishment. I imagine Cypher drooling, barely conscious. Jade screaming, pleading for the abuse to end. *Lagiacrus and Mercedes negotiating Cypher's survival.*

Understanding his disadvantage and the fight's imbalance, Cypher steps back with his hands up in surrender. "Then you should have just let me die."

The ensuing silence is agonizing. Artemis, Lagiacrus, and Destry stand solid in their faceoff against Cypher, with Mercedes a safe distance away.

Cypher lowers his palm and shakes his head with a sigh. "You all know as well as I do that none of us deserve to be here. And if you think for a *second* that they will be true to their word and *actually* let any one of us live at the end of this, you are kidding yourself. Play their games if you must. But from this moment on…I'm done. If you want murder on your conscience, that's on you. But *I'm* not doing this anymore. They're gonna kill us all anyway. What's the point? Die with a corrupt soul like Mercedes. Or die with a clean one."

The group of men continue their stance, unmoved by Cypher's monologue. Resigning to their power, Cypher faces the group on the couches. His facial features soften, genuine concern lining his lips.

"Don't let the Authority do this to you, guys." He locks his eye on the nearest camera and stretches his arms to the sky. "Don't participate. Screw them and their entertainment! We make a stance, and they either yield or kill us all. We participate, and they'll kill us all anyway. I'm willing to take the chance that they'll let us free. Who's with me?"

I avoid his gaze, diverting my eyes to the ground. The silence confirms everyone else is doing the same. Twenty seconds pass without noise, everyone avoiding Cypher. Because the reality is that they wouldn't put us through all of this just to kill the winner on live television…*or would they?* I give the slightest shake of my head. We have to *hope* they're telling us the truth. Without hope…we have no chance. The only guarantee is that refusal to participate leads to execution, as evidenced by both Lagiacrus's brother when he ran from capture and Sola when she was incapable of evacuating the Enterprize on her own. Cypher's proposal is a death wish, and the rest of us refuse to collaborate on such a fruitless delusion.

Cypher *tsks*, and I just see him tighten his palms into fists.

"You're all just as bad as the men who put us here. You're just as bad as the men who designed this place and the men who killed Sola's infant child *in her arms*. You *disgust* me." He turns and points at the cameras, blinking red in unison. "And I *promise* you, I'm not the only one who sees you for who you truly are." He marches out of the living room and slams his feet on the steps until he's far away from the rest of us.

Quietly, the living room disperses until only Mace, Lunar, Ashlea, and I remain. I tremble, only steadying my exhales when Mace's arm settles comfortably around my shoulder.

"Hey," Mace urges, "don't listen to him. We all expected this to happen. It's why so many of us voted against Jade."

"You voted out Jade?" I straighten my posture, eyebrows creased. "Why?"

Mace takes a deep breath. Careful not to expose Dial to Lunar or Ashlea, he speaks cautiously. "Originally, I wanted to vote out Cypher. He's the stronger player…it made more sense."

I nod. "Right, that's why I voted against him."

Ashlea and Lunar confirm their votes against Cypher as well. The three of us shake our heads, more confused than ever.

Mace puckers his lips to the side and lowers his voice to a whisper. "I just…I thought about it some more and started keeping an eye on Cypher…the way he panicked when Jade was in danger." He bites his lips, delaying the final blow. "I feel awful about it…but I knew he'd have a mental breakdown without her."

My eyes narrow with disgust. "That's barbaric."

"It wasn't just me, though. It hurt me to do it, I hate having to vote at all!" He throws up a hand in defense. "But so many people agreed with that logic that it just…made sense. As horrible as it sounds…a fragile Cypher is much easier to handle than a vengeful Jade."

My heart breaks that Cypher is only here because of how much he loved Jade. But it shatters even more when I agree with Mace's logic. Reading between the lines, it's clear to me that Mace wasn't in control of the decision. For all I know, he may have been completely against it, but he had to vote with the alliance to keep us both safe.

"Shoot, we've gotta go," Ashlea panics, rising from the couch. I glance at the clock and my stomach does a cartwheel. The conflict in the living room took so much valuable time away from us that I barely have four minutes to collect my thoughts and discover everything I missed in solitary confinement.

The rest of us follow her lead, but I stay a few paces back with Mace and tug his shirt sleeve. "Wait. Before we go…what did I miss?"

Mace chuckles. "We hardly have enough time to cover all that, Iris."

"Well, just the important stuff, then. Like…" My breath catches in my throat, and I hobble to catch Lunar. I tap his shoulder, mortified that I forgot to ask. "Lunar, were you punished when you were eliminated?"

He stumbles, shocked I'm delaying our departure to the arena. "I…they rewarded me. I got to choose the length of Round 3."

My eyes widen. "You *what*?"

He smiles. "Yeah. They listed twenty-four hours as the shortest option…so I picked that." His eyes narrow in sincerity. "I just didn't want you to suffer…I wasn't sure how long you would survive…that bite…"

I smile and give him a delicate pat on the back. "You really are somethin', huh?"

He nods with a cheeky grin, and I thank him before returning to Mace.

"What did they do to Cypher? For his punishment?"

"Electric torture." He gulps. "When he was eliminated, it was down to Lagiacrus and Mercedes. So…Cypher was strapped to an electric chair." He bites his lip, avoiding eye contact as we climb the stairs. "For every minute the competition continued, Cypher was electrocuted. And every minute, the intensity increased. He made it about five shocks before Lagiacrus cut the deal to end it. And to her credit, Mercedes held up her end of the deal by putting up Jade and Cypher."

"Oh my god," I gasp. "That's…ruthless."

"That's the Authority." Mace shrugs. "But if you ask me…I'd have taken Cypher's punishment over Lagiacrus's any day."

Ashlea and Lunar jolt, making Mace and I stumble back a step. Once they finally start walking again, I whisper in Mace's ear. "What punishment did Lagiacrus have?"

Mace shakes his head. He keeps his eyes glued to the ground, barely glancing at me in his peripheral. "They locked him in a room…and made him watch body cam footage from the captures." He winces, finally pausing to look at me. "Every. One. Of. Them." He returns his gaze to the ground and grabs my palm, squeezing tight. "His own…he said they played his arrest three times."

I stop dead in my tracks. "Wha—wha—wha—?" I can't get the words out. He watched my parents' murders. He watched Sola's baby die in her arms. He watched all forty refugees in Artemis's home fall to the ground in a frenzy of blood and screams...

He watched his twin brother get shot to the ground over and over and over.

Logically, the worst punishment *should* be reserved for the first loser…but what Lagiacrus was subject to was out of line. Send out a giant scorpion…electrocute our bodies…deprive us of food. But *don't* use our loved ones to torture us.

I'm numb as we climb the last few stairs and open the iron door to the arena. I try to get a glimpse at whatever mechanism awaits us in the center, but my view is obstructed by Lagiacrus's dirty blonde shoulder-length hair.

And despite failing to notice it before, he's trembling.

"Convicts," Mercedes reads from the camouflage notecard. "Congratulations on making it to the top twelve. Everyone is eligible to compete in this Executive competition."

Most of my housemates are restless, shaking their legs and arms to calm their nerves. Others search the metal wall before us, desperate to see behind it. Unlike the previous competitions, an iron partition separates the front of the arena from the back, preventing us from getting a peek at our latest torture. I glance at the staircase and lock on Cypher, whose defiance against participation keeps him slumped on the bottom step, chin resting in his hands. I clench my jaw, frustrated by his complete carelessness for his life. I quickly revert my gaze to Mercedes, lingering on Artemis behind her. He avoids my eye contact and, as if aware of my desperation for his attention, inches closer to the blonde warrior.

"Your objective is not to last the longest but to drop out as close to the one-hour mark as possible. The closest convict to one hour *without going over* will be the new Executive. If every convict goes over, the one closest to one hour will be the new Executive." She lowers the card and glances at the partition, but it stays solid, blocking our view.

Seconds pass while we stare at one another, waiting for further instructions. Finally, Kylah steps forward. "Okay, but what are we doing?"

"I don't know, it doesn't say," Mercedes quips back, narrowing her eyes on Kylah. She flips the card to investigate the back, groaning when there's no additional writing. Just as Lagiacrus marches to the wall to find a way around it, a mechanical noise blares, and the metal barrier starts lowering into the ground.

Slowly, the iron slab retracts into the floor, inch by inch, revealing the odd assortment behind. Twelve flat, metal tables are strewn about the AstroTurf, each the same size and height, evenly spaced out in a straight line. The uniformity and order are haunting, providing yet another juxtaposition for the chaos that is the Enterprize. Only five-meter patches of empty turf separate the three-foot-high tables from one another, and my stomach twirls, sending shivers through my extremities. The competition appears too calm, too easy, and above all else…

Too good to be true.

"So…we just pick a table then?" Destry asks, shuffling forward. My lips part to answer, but I freeze, finally getting a clear look at him. His tan is glowing, with no remnants of a sunburn lingering on his skin. Against the varying degrees of blistering amongst the rest of my housemates, it's as if Destry never even participated in the last competition. I hadn't realized just how effective his burn relief reward would be. My chest burns with jealousy, the throbbing pain in my leg momentarily subsiding, so I feel the full force of the heat radiating from my burns.

"I guess? And lay there for an hour?" Mace responds, bringing me back to focus.

"Seems easy enough," Mercedes chimes with fake enthusiasm. She drops the card and takes Artemis's hand, skipping toward adjoining tables. She swings his gigantic palm in high arches, like a child approaching a playground.

I swallow back my second-hand embarrassment and turn slowly to face Mace. He bites his lip and widens his eyes, causing us both to choke back laughter. The lengths Artemis is going through to gain Mercedes's trust are pitiful. I certainly don't respect his gameplay, and each passing moment he ignores my presence sends me into a deeper pit of rage. But having Mace on my side, in clear agreement that Artemis is acting pathetically, replaces my resentment with hilarity.

We all shuffle toward the tables, Finian lingering in the back. He walks slowly and mechanically, moving each limb robotically through the pain of his chemical burns. I limp with each passing step, frustratingly aware of the piercing ache in my calf. I settle on a table between Mace and Lunar as the clock counts down from thirty seconds. Both in position, I reach out to Lunar, and we touch hands, which gives me a new sense of urgency. *I have to win.* My mind wonders about strategy, and I try not to consider how difficult this hour will be. *At least I'm comfortable.* I consider how shockingly relaxed this competition is as I sink into the table with relief and smile until the clock strikes zero.

That's when the nails eject, stabbing my skin as screams echo off the arena walls.

Chapter 34

With only a desperate whimper escaping his lips, Finian rolls off his table and crashes onto the floor, putting up no fight to stop his fall. I hear him cry from his burns and imagine him curled into a ball, writhing in pain.

"CONVICT: FINIAN. ELIMINATED."

Mercedes's scream vibrates in my bones. Artemis offers hushed encouragement, but they can't do much to soothe her pain. Being in the Sanctuary the longest, Mercedes has the worst sunburns in the house. As painful as I feel, I cringe at her predicament.

I tremble from the piercing nails in my back. Luckily, they extended slow enough to avoid impaling me, but that does little to soothe the shooting pain jolting through my limbs. Slowly, I adjust my neck to steal a look at Mace. He's elevated on his table, nails extending from the surface at varying heights, making it impossible to distribute one's weight evenly. His hands ball into fists so tight that the skin on his knuckles burns white. A tear falls from my eye as I squeeze it shut, regretful that I can't be ignorant anymore of how our limp bodies look, slumped over the nails. My burnt skin scorches with the discomfort of the sharp metal tips. I expect my left leg to tear apart, but instead, find that the varying needle heights provide somewhat of an advantage to my predicament. Despite making the competition more difficult for the others, they displace my pain from the injury by elevating my leg in the proper position to prevent any nails from incursion.

"Iris." Mace's voice drifts toward me. "Try to relax. It disperses the pain. After a couple of minutes, we'll be fine. Just focus on counting."

I mouth, "Okay," before turning my neck to watch Lunar. Despite my anxiety about his potential discomfort, he surprises me with a smile.

"This is nothin'," he laughs, totally unfazed by the spikes. My jaw drops. *His weight. Of course,* he's in less pain; he has less weight for gravity to force against the nails. I chuckle without moving, careful not to deepen the nails into my skin. Lunar is just as sunburnt as I am, but his position on the table puts all his weight on his back, which was covered in the Suffering Sanctuary. Despite this, he certainly can't be comfortable. But his smile suggests that *this* round, he will be a worthy competitor.

When the screaming stops, all that's left is cold, hard laughter from the arena's entrance.

Cypher dances closer to the row of nail beds and claps slowly, as condescendingly as possible.

"Don't you see?" he shouts maniacally. "If you just *listened* to me, this wouldn't be happening!"

"Cypher shut the hell up," Kylah yells through pained whimpers. "You might have a death wish, but don't make that our problem."

"You're all dead, anyway," Cypher says calmly, the words flinging effortlessly off his lips. His footsteps fade until he hovers over Lagiacrus. "How you holding up, buddy? Feelin' comfortable?"

My breath catches in my throat. *His back.* Lagiacrus was the only other person who took his shirt off in the Suffering Sanctuary. Without Destry's burn elixir, he suffers on the table in agony, the piercing combination of needles on sunburn making him mute. "Nothing to say, big guy?"

Lagiacrus stays completely still, ignoring his terrorizer. In my periphery, Cypher leans over Lagiacrus's table, and I can feel the malicious grin behind his voice. "Who's capture was the most *thrilling* to witness? The death of my parents? Sola's child? Or perhaps your precious twin brother…"

Images of Curi swim through my vision, and my heart races as I imagine being forced to watch her suffer. "ENOUGH!" I shout, unable to keep my emotions in check. My heart beats in my throat as Cypher straightens from Lagiacrus's table. Seconds later, he struts toward me. I grip my hands into fists like Mace had and squeeze my eyes shut. *What have I done?*

Finally, hot air swirls into my ear, and a whisper spreads between him and my consciousness. "This one finally has something to say, huh? Little miss, 'Pretend I'm sleeping'? You eavesdropping, little miss *innocent*. You're not fooling anybody, and you're *especially* not fooling me." There's a cackle and a breath before the whispers return. "I've been watching you, Iris. You're not as *innocent* as they all think."

My stomach drops as I consider his words. How did he know I was awake when he and Jade confronted Ashlea? *Is that all he knows?* What else could he possibly be referring to…my relationship with Artemis? But how would he even know about that, and even if he did…what's wrong with it? We're friends and allies…it's wholly innocent. *Isn't it?* My stomach twists when considering my relationship with Artemis and allegiance to Mace. *What would Mace say if he knew how much laughter we shared in solitary confinement?*

"One little slip of my hand," Cypher begins louder, "and I could knock you off this table. Your time would be *finished,* and you'd be right out the door." He leans in again, letting his warm breath hover over my eyelids in a chilling whisper. "I know your secret."

My stomach drops to the floor and falls five more flights.

"See you in hell, Iris." I prepare myself for his physical attack, but it never comes. Instead, Cypher's shoes squeak against the turf as he abandons us. I take a deep breath and say a mental thank you to whatever stopped Cypher from going through with his sabotage. Despite being safe from his physical threat, I'm consumed with paranoia. *What is my secret?* What has he been told? My mind flashes back to solitary confinement with

Artemis. Does Cypher somehow know something about our time together? Even so…was there anything wrong with it?

"Mace," I whisper, "I…I don't understand. What did I do?"

"You didn't do anything, Iris." he whispers back. "He's lost his marbles. He doesn't know what he's saying. He's still in shock." He takes a loud gulp. "We have to ignore it and focus. Start counting. I'm at five minutes."

I take a deep breath and try to adhere to Mace's advice. Instead, I stumble over the numbers countless times, unable to focus past the threat Cypher poses. I wrack my brain, desperate for any information he might have to incriminate me. Biting my lip does little to calm my frustration because no matter how hard I try to steer away from the topic…my thoughts settle on Artemis.

Before long, I forget Cypher entirely, my anger toward Artemis too all-consuming to focus on anything else. *Why has Artemis been ignoring me?* After our moment in that prison together, I'd think he'd at least offer me a smile or show some form of relief at our mutual safety in round 3. My heart pierces with betrayal when I flashback to Ashlea and Lunar pleading with me not to trust Artemis…and I ignored them.

His words echo against the darkest crevices of my mind.

You won't stand a chance if you trust like you are now.

Who could Artemis have been referring to? Ashlea rarely hangs out with anyone besides me, so if she's preparing to betray me, she'd isolate herself from her only ally. And if he's referring to Mace, then he doesn't know what he's talking about.

Mercedes is a straight shooter…Trust her.

My brain screams that I could be a pawn in his ploy to get out of here, or worse…to get Mercedes further in the game. After all…if he'd string Mercedes along to get to the end, why would I be any different?

Ashlea's words float back to me. *You can't trust him.* Could she have been right?

No. She's wrong. Because despite Artemis consistently proving how dangerous he is, and his drastic change of behavior around me versus the others…my heart knows that our connection is real. So, who cares that my brain says his love in solitary confinement must have been a fluke…a way to bamboozle me into trusting him?

Because my heart knows it was real.

I force my eyes open, not letting exhaustion distract me — *as if I could fall asleep on these spikes anyway.* At Mace's suggestion, I dispersed the pressure throughout my body. It eventually made the nails less intrusive, but no adjustment could relieve me from the anguish of my sunburn against the sharp tips protruding against my skin.

I take a deep breath and bite my lip, amazed that not a single person has fallen since Finian's dramatic elimination. I hope that's a good sign because as much as I hate to admit it, I have no idea how long we've been lying on these tables. Despite my fruitless efforts to count, there are only so many times I can reach sixty seconds without losing my mind. The eerie silence helps my focus, but makes the time go by even slower. *How long is a second, anyway?* I've counted so many times now that my numbers slow and quicken, trying to reach some equilibrium around the correct length of a second.

My back muscles ache from my awkward pose, so I adjust my position, wincing as a newfound pain shoots through my back. I curse myself for forgetting, yet again, that movement only worsens the suffering. Exposure to new areas of my skin causes the discomfort and numbing process to start over. As much as my muscles strain to keep my body steady, it's preferable torture to the alternative. Desperate to distract myself, I whisper Mace's name.

"Iris?" His voice is melodic.

"What time are we at?" I ask. I can't tell him I haven't been counting, but it's better to start helping now than never.

"Close to fifty minutes," he whispers back, quiet enough that nobody can eavesdrop.

"Should I drop soon? Just in case we're off by ten minutes?" I offer. I know my body can handle more, but this competition is less about endurance and more about precision.

Mace takes a few seconds to consider this proposal. "Drop right after the next person. Then you'll be just over their time and closer to sixty minutes than they are."

"Okay," I agree. I lay still, waiting for another person to fall. *But nobody does.* Not for the five or six minutes since the plan was established. My consideration that Mace is a genius fades as I realize that every person here may have the same idea. But when I hear the elimination buzzer, there's no time to think. *Just time to act.*

"CONVICT: ENO. ELIMINATED."

I hurl my body to the left, the force hard enough to overcome the varying heights of nails. The newfound pressure digs into my skin, and I hold back screams as my leg is pierced before dropping to the AstroTurf. My reflexes are too slow to catch myself, and I collide with the ground face-first. Stars flood my vision as a chorus of elimination buzzers are triggered.

"CONVICT: IRIS. ELIMINATED."

"CONVICT: DESTRY. ELMINATED."

"CONVICT: ARTEMIS. ELIMINATED."

"CONVICT: KYLAH. ELIMINATED."

"CONVICT: LAGIACRUS. ELIMINATED."

Crap. Being right in the center of the mix of names, it's unlikely that I will have snuck in the closest time to an hour. If anyone from this grouping of eliminations wins Executive, it'll be Lagiacrus.

"Iris!" Lunar shouts. My heart beats in my leg, but I drown it out, desperate for Lunar to stay in. He looks almost comfortable. If he can endure the longest, it covers another base for our alliance if we all dropped well before the hour.

"Don't worry about me!" I shout, rolling onto my back. "You keep fighting! I'm fine! I'm okay."

Lunar responds with a childish grunt and keeps still, so I focus on my ailments. I struggle to stretch my limbs out and take my time wiggling my extremities, getting feeling back into each muscle. Once I can finally bear my own weight, I rise from the AstroTurf and scan the remaining contestants. *Mace, Lunar, Mercedes, and Ashlea.* My stomach twists with nerves. Despite Artemis's pleas to trust Mercedes, her presence in the fight makes me uneasy. Even if she kept me safe, I'd be naïve to think she'd keep my entire group of friends, from Ashlea and Eno to Lunar and Mace, alive. I shake my head of the thought and crouch beside Mace's nail bed.

"What're you at now?" I whisper.

"Fifty-six minutes," he answers. "I want to drop at fifty-seven but don't want Mercedes to scalp my win."

I glance at Mercedes a few beds over. Her eyes are squeezed shut, and her limbs are so tense I doubt she'll be able to move without pain for days. *She can't last much longer.* I inch closer to Mace and cup my hand over my mouth. "Lunar looks great. What if he's the last to drop? It would be you, then probably Mercedes and Ashlea. Lunar will just go last, so we cover all our bases."

There's a moment of silence before Mace agrees to the plan. I back away and prepare for him to drop, taking inventory of those around me. Those from my grouping of eliminations lie limp on the turf beside their nail beds, some only now rotating their wrists to regain circulation.

Only Artemis has regained his feet.

He kneels beside Mercedes's bed, whispering to her frantically, blue eyes wide with concern. I convince myself they're merely strategizing when my eyes freeze on Artemis's back.

Hundreds of scratch marks line his backside, blood flowing and gathering at the waistband of his pants. With his shirt still tied around my leg, he had no protection against the spikes, having to take the full force of them on his way off the bed. Despite my frustrations with him, my heart pierces, imagining his pain. *And it's all because of me.*

"CONVICT: MACE. ELIMINATED."

I whip back to Mace and find him sprawled on the ground. Just as I predicted, the others react.

"CONVICT: MERCEDES. ELIMINATED."

"CONVICT: ASHLEA. ELIMINATED."

"Now Lunar!" I urge my brother. He yanks his body off the bed, and Mace has just enough time to roll under my table and catch Lunar on his way down.

"CONVICT: LUNAR. ELIMINATED."

"That a way, Lunar!" Mace smiles. They hug on the ground, and I smile with them, certain one of us has secured the win.

I squat onto the turf and join their hug, prematurely celebrating our win. A loud *bleep* echoes through the arena, making us break away from one another. A black screen appears where the timer usually projects on the wall, and we help each other up as names and times appear in descending order from longest time to shortest time lasted in the competition. Every single name and adjacent time are in red, except for one.

"CONGRATULATIONS: FINIAN. YOU ARE THE NEW EXECUTIVE."

Chapter 35

My stomach plummets to the turf.

"Wha…what?" Mercedes stammers.

The projection reads, "Finian: 4 seconds," at the bottom of the list. Each name is presented in the order of elimination, the next one being Eno and the last name being Lunar, with a time of one hour and twenty-five minutes. I shift my eyes frantically, locating my name in the sea of red. *One hour and eighteen minutes.* How could we all have been so far off? My raised eyebrows and momentary confusion quickly transform into rage as my hands clench into fists.

When I turn around, Mace is already approaching Finian's nail bed. I grab Lunar's hand and follow Mace's lead, glancing at the bright red figure who's been lying beside his nail bed for the past hour and a half. Upon closer inspection, Finian's body is rat-like, his usual pale skin bright red from the chemical burns. I pity him, watching as Mace extends a hand to lift our ally.

"Congratulations, man. Well done."

Finian cowers at the outstretched hand before locking on Mace's eyes, nodding, and accepting the gesture.

"Tha — thanks," he stammers out, taking Mace's hand and flinching from the pain of the handshake. He winces as he hoists himself up off the ground.

Destry runs from his nail bed, clapping hysterically. "Well done, my man!" he shouts. "Your first time in power! How's it feel?"

Finian offers a pained smile and a brief thumbs-up before slouching with his hands on his hips.

"Undeserved," Mercedes shouts from her bed, not bothering to walk over. "How do we know this wasn't rigged? How can we be certain these times are legitimate?" Artemis rubs her back as blood drips down his own but flinches at her outburst.

"Does it really matter?" Kylah spits, auburn curls strewn about her shoulders. Her face ages a few years every day that passes. But even amongst the wrinkles, her anger is unmistakable. "Even if they're fake, there's nothing we could do about it. We're completely powerless."

"Now you're catching on," Cypher smiles from the staircase, chuckling at his feet.

Destry leans into Finian. "Just ignore them. You won that fair and square."

Finian keeps his pained smile, but the strain is obvious. Even the slightest movement of his facial muscles is agonizing because of the chemical burns. I force my lips into a smile, pity radiating from my contorted eyes.

There are mixed reactions amongst the rest of my housemates, but Eno is wildly enthusiastic.

"Way to go, kid! You outsmarted us all. That's something to be proud of."

I involuntarily cower at his approach, his foul punishment already catching up with him. Eno's stench slams into us like a brick wall, making everyone waft their noses in disgust. I'm also without a shower, but Eno's body odor exceeds mine and Artemis's tenfold, worsening the stink. In too much pain to notice, Finian simply nods at Eno.

Lunar and I congratulate Finian, careful not to touch him. One glance over his shoulder confirms that Mercedes is on her way, Artemis dragging her by her palm. They're flinging complaints at one another in a heated argument that no doubt stems from her objection to Finian's victory. Opposing the round Executive is a death wish, so I sigh, knowing that Artemis's frustration is justified.

Pounding her feet the last three steps, Mercedes whips her long blond hair behind her right shoulder and stretches her lips into an obnoxious smile.

"Congratulations, *big guy*," she spits. "What a *fight* you put up. That was a totally *well-deserved* victory."

She flips to Artemis and throws her palms to the sky. "Happy?" she whispers, then stomps to the metal staircase alone. Halfway there, she locks eyes on Eno and shouts over her shoulder, "And for god's sake, would you keep your stench away from the rest of us!"

Artemis runs a hand through his hair and takes a deep breath, urgent to separate Mercedes's actions from his own. He mouths an apology to Eno, then extends a palm to congratulate Finian. "I'm sorry, man. It's like working with a toddler."

I chuckle under my breath, accidentally attracting Artemis's attention. He locks eyes on me for the first time since solitary confinement and smiles, sending my stomach into a curious flurry of butterflies. Finally, he closes the distance between us and pulls me into a side hug.

"Good to see you made it out, *kid*."

"Kid?" I laugh. "I'm a year younger than you!"

He smiles, but the affection stops there. He ends the hug as quickly as it started and moves beside Destry. *What is his problem?* He's obviously developed some issue with me but won't communicate it. I bite the inside of my cheek, intent on hiding my disappointment at our underwhelming reunion. *He can't hide from me forever.* I care too much about our friendship to let it disintegrate.

Walking back to the Enterprize behind Finian, a sensation of unease rumbles through my stomach. Finian's in my alliance…I should be *celebrating*. So, why is there a pit of dread in my gut, forcing my steps to slow as we climb the stairs? *Is Finian the one Artemis was warning me about?* Of the alliance, Finian is the biggest wild card. I've never truly known where his loyalties lie but have been forced to blindly trust him against my own judgment.

I can't begin to fathom how he will use his power this round, but I flutter my eyelids shut and pray that it's in my best interest.

Finally, through the iron door, the crowd dissipates. Half of us are drawn to the promise of rations in the kitchen while the other half climbs the stairs for sleep. My crew descends for the kitchen, separating from the Executive and his *persistent* shadow. Still within earshot of the two, I internally gag as Destry guides Finian along the staircase and obnoxiously encourages him to take advantage of the privacy of his new luxurious suite.

"We need our newest leader in tip-top shape for the Death Row selections tomorrow. And that's *you*, bud!"

I glance at Mace as his eyes roll so hard they nearly pop out of their sockets. I hold back a laugh and smile as we stride for the rationing cabinets. Eno takes the lead in distributing the ration bins, but I'm far more interested in water. Wincing as I limp toward the sink, I change my priorities, desperate to get my gash cleaned. Seeing Artemis's bloodied shirt reminds me to find a better bandage alternative. *Is that why he's ignoring me?* I bite my lip. *Is he blaming me for the scrapes on his back?*

Leaving Lunar in Kylah's care, Mace half-carries me into the bathroom so we can tend to my injury.

"He's driving me nuts," Mace complains the second the door shuts. "Destry's the biggest kiss-ass I've ever seen. If he doesn't shut up soon, I'm gonna lose it."

"Was he this bad yesterday, too?" I ask, gripping my fists and flinching as Mace unties the end of Artemis's shirt.

"Sorry," he smiles, slowing his hands. He takes a deep breath and continues. "It's like he's done a complete one-eighty. His insecurities are starting to show…now he just sucks up to whoever's in power. I know he's close with Artemis, but he almost never left Mercedes's room yesterday. It's just sketchy…if people don't catch on soon, he might win this whole thing."

The tie undone, Mace unwraps the shirt around my leg carefully, pausing every time I wince. He lifts the makeshift bandage from my wound and stares blankly, careful not to react.

"How bad is it?" I ask, cold air rushing into the gash.

He stammers before sharing, "Nnnn….not bad…"

I let out a single chuckle. "That was convincing."

He looks up and forces a smile. "It's lucky you had Artemis in there with you, I'll say that much."

The comment sticks with me, and I nod, careful not to show too much interest in the subject. He carries me to the sink and lifts me to sit beside the bowl with my leg dangling under the faucet. Mace turns the sink on and lets the water rise, the cold liquid inching toward the damage in my calf. The silence does dangerously little to staunch my curiosity.

"What do you think of him?" I gulp. "Of Artemis?"

Mace's violet eyes connect with my hazel ones. He shrugs and tosses Artemis's shirt in the neighboring sink, turning the faucet to let out cold water. "Seems okay to me. We hung out a bunch in the first round, but that was before he really connected with Mercedes. I don't think you can fully trust anyone here, but I guess he's one of the best we've got." He squeezes Artemis's shirt and watches the blood spray into the drain. "We ought to return this shirt to him, though. No need for him to be strutting about topless."

I laugh, and Mace matches with a chuckle. "I don't know," I joke. "I think he likes the attention."

Mace scoffs. "Don't get me started on that man's *desperation* for attention."

We laugh until the water reaches my wound. The second it touches, my reflexes take over, and I whip my calf from the liquid so fast I nearly fall from the counter. I lock my arms around it and put my head between my knees, trying to calm my racing heart.

"Hey. We'll get through this together, okay?" Mace rests a hand on my shoulder and smiles. "Grab onto me and squeeze through the pain. I've gotcha." He holds out his hand, and I take hold, squeezing fiercely as the water engulfs my lower leg. He rubs the gash with his free hand, not complaining about my grip despite his fingers losing color. Eventually, when the pain finally subsides, I groan from relief.

Mace washes his hands in the opposite sink, letting the soap launch onto the mucky fabric of Arty's shirt. Then he kisses my forehead and walks backward toward the exit.

"I guess it's time to get some fresh fabric on there, huh?"

"Where are you going?" I ask.

Mace stops for a beat, running his hand through his hair and ending with the piece that sits over his brow. "There's…a few free beds now. I don't think anyone would miss a sheet if I took one."

Oh. I nod as he leaves the bathroom to retrieve blankets. His hesitation to abuse the belongings of those who've been eliminated makes my heart swell. His kindness and softness are some of the reasons I've completely fallen for him.

They're also in sharp contrast to Artemis, who takes joy in joking about those killed.

I bite my lip, disgusted by Artemis's comment in solitary confinement. Every conversation with Mace reassures me that Artemis could never be more than a friend to me…no matter *how* much my heart speeds up when we're in the same room together.

I twiddle my thumbs until Mace returns with long strips of makeshift bedsheet bandages. He places a bundle of them in the midnight black cabinet below the sink before settling beside me with two.

He points to the cabinet beneath me. "Those are for reapplication…it'd be smart to get some clean bandages on there every few hours." He lifts one stream of the sheet with his left hand. "This is to help clean it out." Lifting the other with his right hand, he instructs, "This is to wrap it up when we're done." I nod as he begins the procedure, cleaning my leg like an amateur, his brows creased with uncertainty.

I watch him meticulously wipe the gash, ridding it of blood as it appears. His eyes scan back and forth between the water and my leg, fumbling through the motions until I break the silence.

"Thank you for this." He flinches, so I grab his arm and smile. "I can't believe you care this much about me."

He abandons his medical mission and locks his gaze onto mine. I focus on the violet of his pupils, singling out each purple sliver. Segments circle in varying shades of indigo and magenta, spiraling around the midnight center. I try and memorize every shard, not caring that it's a hopeless quest. I don't even flinch my gaze when the words leave his lips. "I meant what I said the other day…before they locked you away."

His words stop time. The thumping in my chest becomes so great, I can't hear myself speak. "I meant it too."

His eyes twinkle in the light as he grabs my left cheek and kisses me, launching my heart into my pelvis. I lock my fingers behind his neck and move my lips with his, letting his tongue sweep the back of my teeth while a moan escapes my lips. Mace moves his hand to the back of my head, grabbing onto my hair and pulling me in deeper, sucking on my tongue until I relent to his urgency and melt into his chest, forgetting the pain throbbing in my leg and wanting nothing more than to have *every* piece of him. His opposite hand rests on the bottom of my spine, and his fingers swirl as they move toward my hips, lingering on the protruding bone. I press into his exploring palm, inviting him deeper with a confirming moan. He obliges, gently touching my skin as he adjusts his hand and I tremble, desperate for his fingers to move *exactly* where I want them to.

When his lips adjust into a smile, I retreat my own tongue from his mouth and back away with a gentle laugh.

"What?" He beams, his lips only inches from mine.

I shake my head, entranced by his violet eyes. "You have the most beautiful eyes."

His smile stretches wider. "So do you."

He glances at my mouth, and I lean in, smiling, giddy from his love. Just as the softness presses into my chapped lips, the door cracks open, and we turn our heads quickly to our visitor. Ashlea struts in with her eyes on the floor, unaware of our presence until she's mere steps away.

"Jesus!" she shouts, jumping back several feet. Mace and I laugh, Ashlea joining in once she gains her bearings. "You nearly scared me to death!" she yells, hitting Mace's arm.

"We were just sitting here!" he replies, smiling and throwing his hands up in defense.

"Whatever," she laughs. "What are you two doing in here anyway?" She nudges me with her elbow and raises her eyebrows suggestively. "Getting some *privacy* behind the soundproof walls?"

"Shut up," I joke back.

"It's good to see you again, too, Iris." She glances at my wound and frowns. "You hangin' in there?"

"Yeah, just need to get it wrapped up." I glance at Artemis's shirt in the neighboring sink and lift it with two fingers. "And somehow get this cleaned up for Artemis."

She yanks it out of my hand. "Don't worry about that. You just worry about *staying alive*." She winks and sets the shirt back in the sink before entering one of the private toilet rooms.

Looking around the corner to make sure the door is shut, Mace dries my leg and leans into my ear, his whisper tickling my neck. "We need to get to the Executive room as soon as possible. At least before any decisions are made."

I nod as he starts wrapping my leg and shiver as my pulse quickens. "Mace," I whisper, avoiding his eye contact. "I have a bad feeling about this round. I know he's in our alliance…but something doesn't feel right."

He ties the ends of the sheet together, securing my wrap in place. "We just need to go along with whatever they say and stay calm…" Mace gulps. "You weren't here last round…I know it was only a day, but…things are different. Think about it. Remember Round 1, when Lagiacrus and Destry were demanding side alliances?" He throws his hand up, palm pointed to the ceiling. "Whatever happened to that?"

My eyes widen as I stretch my neck forward. "Right? Destry's never made *any* attempt to get close to Eno, let alone talk to him. I feel like us and Artemis are the only ones pulling our weight."

Mace bites his lip. "It's almost like we're on the outside. Doing their dirty work for them."

I shake my head. "But if anything, it's just backfiring on them because we have more relationships in the house. They only have Dial, and it's just a matter of time before that falls apart."

There's painstaking silence as the anxiety grabs hold. Finally, Mace grabs the end of my chin with his forefinger and thumb and tilts my head to look into my eyes. "This round will be tough, Iris. We *have to* stay strong…and fight for the people we love."

"Okay," I whisper. He plants another light kiss on my lips before helping me off the counter. We exit the bathroom, and my feet sink into the plush carpet, my toes trying to ground me in the present. But with each step we take, my knees threaten to buckle as I mull over what these next three days may bring.

I have a feeling no amount of preparation could ready me for the hell that was about to crumple my world.

Chapter 36

Inches from Finian's door, Mace shakes my shoulders. "Remember...stay under the radar. We don't really know where we stand with these people right now, so we have to be patient and hear them out." I nod before he knocks three times.

Before long, Destry is at the entrance, letting us in. One look around the room confirms we're the last to arrive. I mentally curse myself but force my frustrations to the back of my mind so I can treat this meeting with all the sincerity I can muster.

"Welcome, welcome," Destry says, avoiding eye contact. It's not lost on me that despite Finian being the Executive, Destry answered the door *and* greeted us. Others may think he's just being nice. But I know better. *He's trying to control Dial.* I was skeptical of Destry from the moment I saw him at the top of the stairs on the first day. Now that Mace has planted doubt in my mind about the guy, I can't get past the feeling that he's trying to manipulate us.

"What did we miss?" Mace asks, settling onto the floor with me, the wall at our backs. "We got here as fast as we could. We just couldn't get an opportunity to sneak away without being suspicious."

"Probably because you two have so many allies outside of the group that they want to know what you're up to," Destry spits.

I tilt my head and squint at Destry. "Excuse me?"

"You two have yourselves spread pretty thin, that's all," Lagiacrus chimes in, blond hair slick with grease and grime.

"Whatever you have to say, can you just say it?" I ask, fighting my temper.

Destry stretches his neck left and right, then leans forward. "Look, we wouldn't be bringing this up at all if it wasn't relevant. But it just happens to be *very* pertinent to this round."

My stomach drops to the bottom floor, and Mace's hand flies to my back, rubbing circles against my shirt. My mind races as I envision the worst possible scenario. "Wha...what are you talking about? I thought you wanted us to get close to the other houseguests. That way, we have the votes. And because of *my* efforts, we do."

Lagiacrus sighs. "Iris...it's nothing against you. It's just...we're running out of people to put on Death Row. Sooner or later, we'll have to put one of your friends up."

"But why now?" My voice rises, but I fight it from shaking. "There are twelve people left in the house! Just put up Cypher and get him out of here. Why do you need to target my friends, who are, *by the way*, under *this* alliance's control?"

"Iris," Mace whispers. "Calm down."

"*Again*, Iris. We're not doing this to piss you off." Destry says, throwing his hands up. "But when all is said and done and it's just us and our side alliances, we're all alone in this game. But you…you're gonna have protection from so many people…we need to level the playing field."

I grind my teeth and turn toward Artemis, who avoids my gaze. I take a deep, shaky breath and silently pray for Lunar's safety. "What did you have in mind?"

"It's really not as bad as you think," Lagiacrus starts, trying to soften the blow. "Seriously, you'll probably be okay with it anyway."

"Just tell her," Artemis grunts. "You're just making it worse."

Destry and Lagiacrus shake their heads at one another. Finally, Destry takes a deep breath and looks me straight in my eyes.

"Death Row will be Eno and Ashlea."

I blink rapidly, trying to summon strength. I refuse to cry amongst this group of men. But my outrage refuses to be contained. This decision *only* hurts me, *and* it was made in my absence. *That couldn't speak louder volumes.* Before I can respond, Mace speaks in my honor.

"The target?"

Lagiacrus gulps. "Ashlea."

I shake my hide wildly. "No," I say to them. "*No.*"

"Iris—" Destry starts.

"No!" I shout, losing my temper. "Why was this decision made? Who is responsible? Because *Finian* hasn't spoken *once* this entire meeting." Finian is cowering in the corner of his bed, still frail from his burns. "Isn't this Finian's choice? Why are *you*," I point in Destry's direction, "hijacking his Executive run?"

"Iris, it's a *team* decision—" Destry objects.

"If it's a team decision, why were Mace and I excluded?" I turn to Artemis. "Did you agree to this?"

Artemis looks down, keeping his voice barely above a whisper. "Only one of us is making it out alive, Iris."

My jaw drops. "After *everything* we've been through, Artemis? You *still* don't have my back?"

He bites his lip, avoiding my direction.

I shake my head rapidly, refusing to look away from him. "You're a fucking coward."

Artemis looks into my eyes and *grimaces*. The blue orbs contort in heart-wrenching *pain*. "Don't *ever* call me a coward. I've never run from a goddamn thing in my life. You, of *all* people, should know that."

I throw my hands in the air and groan. "Artemis is *in love* with Mercedes. You think he's gonna protect *any* of you over her? Why not target Mercedes this round? Before it's too late?"

Finally, Finian sits up. His voice is gnarled, every word sounding more painful than the last. "We're not putting Mercedes up when she kept every one of us safe last round. We're *not* doing that."

I jump to my feet. "Okay, then Cypher! Put up Cypher!"

"He's self-destructing as we speak!" defends Destry. "He's already declared he won't be voting this round. Why would we kill him if the Authority will do it for us!?"

I grip my hands through my hair and lean against the wall, squeezing my eyes tight. "Why Ashlea? Why *her*?" I open them, scanning the room. "What has she done to any of you?"

"Honestly, Iris. You're lucky we aren't putting *you* up."

I straighten my back to the wall, eyes wide at Destry. "*What?*"

Destry shakes his head. "You want me to say it again? You're protected on all sides, Iris! There's no *person* we could put on Death Row next to you that would end with you getting eliminated. We'd be *fools* to keep every one of your alliance members safe!"

"They aren't *alliance* members, Destry. They're *friends*. And I'm only friends with them because half of you fell through on your end of the bargain. Tell me, Destry. Have you ever even *spoken* to Eno?"

"Enough of this," Lagiacrus demands, his voice slicing the air. "The decision has been made. Want something else? Get here earlier."

Everyone looks at Lagiacrus, not daring to speak. I've never seen him lose his cool like this. *His punishment must have struck a nerve.* Witnessing all those deaths, especially that of his family…it must have turned a switch in him. I want to give him the benefit of the doubt, but I'm so furious I can't hold it in.

"So that's it, then?" I ask, my voice catching on the last word. "There's no changing your minds?"

Finian shakes his head. "I'm really sorry, Iris."

I look at the floor and swallow hard, quickly deciding to backtrack. Nothing I could say would change anything. So, now…*it's time for damage control.* "Don't be." I shrug. "Only one of us makes it out alive, right?" I direct my last comment at Artemis, who keeps his eyes glued to the floor, avoiding confrontation like the coward that he is. Finally, I level my voice and approach the edge of the bed where Finian sits, Mace following suit. "Dial comes first. We all in on that?"

The others look around at one another and nod before approaching Finian. Trying to make up for my outbursts and remind them that I'm still in this alliance, I put my palm in the middle. "Until the end?"

The others follow suit hesitantly, each stacking their hands on top of one another. I stand in silence until Destry agrees for the group. "Until the end."

We drop our hands together and I nod, letting the agreement set in. Then, without another word, Mace and I flee for the living room. Fury enrages me so far that I barely feel a twinge of pain in my bandaged leg. When we finally sink into the giant blue sofa, plush cushions desperate to calm our frustrations, I turn to Mace and let my feelings out in a hushed shout, only audible to him.

"He just sat there, Mace. Completely compliant with whatever his *master, Destry,* wanted. I thought he cared about us."

Mace cracks his knuckles and shakes out his shiny brown hair. "Numbers are running thin. We knew it wouldn't be long before they turned on us…we just have to keep close the ones that we trust."

"But I trusted *him!*" I huff. "He even *warned* me when we were in solitary confinement. He cautioned me about committing to the right people…and he goes and does *this*?"

Mace tilts his head. "Do you think he was referring to himself?"

I throw up my hands and match Mace's eyes. "He basically declared his loyalty to me. Practically *begged* me to trust Mercedes if he's eliminated."

Violet eyes widening in surprise, Mace leans back into the neck of the couch. "You're kidding me."

"No, I'm not! He said, 'Watch who you trust, but *not* me or Mercedes! *We're* on your side.'"

Mace shakes his head. "Well, that's why he's treating you like this, Iris. He's manipulating you."

I stretch my back while my stomach churns. "Why—what do you mean?"

Mace winces, astonished I haven't caught on myself. "Iris, he's doing everything he can to get you on his side because he wants to bring Mercedes to the end. The more faith you put in him, the longer you keep him in the house…and the longer he gets to be with Mercedes."

I shake my head, refusing to believe it. "No…*no*, he wouldn't do that…I thought he didn't even like her. That it was a forced relationship? For the sake of the alliance."

"Iris…you can't spend that long alone with somebody and not end up liking them to *some* extent." His face blotches with red, and his lip curls. "You should have heard the perverted way he would talk about her in the beginning…at the very least, he cares about her now."

My chest tightens. Every inch of my body is overheating, and a boulder lodges in my throat. "But why would he…how could he do this to me?"

Mace rests a hand on my arm, trying to relax me. "His real priorities are starting to show…just like the rest of them." He pulls me into a hug and rubs my back. "I know it sucks, but you *can't* trust him. He beat one of our housemates to death on the fourth day, for Christ's sake. *He's dangerous.* And he tricked you."

I keep shaking my head, still in denial. "No…I can't believe it."

Mace presses his lips into a flat line and removes his hand, backing away from me slowly. "I'm sorry, Iris. But…why does he matter to you so much, anyway?"

My heart stops. Because of all the questions Mace could ask me, this is the only one I *cannot* answer. What would I say? *I love Artemis, but not in the way that I love you? If he's killed, my heart might stop permanently?* But that's not even what hurts me the most. The urge to kick the nearest trashcan until it's beyond repair doesn't come from my inability to tell Mace the truth. It comes from the heartbreaking reality that I truly *believed Artemis loved me, too.*

Was everything we've experienced together from day one a lie? Did he *ever* care about me? My brain yells at me that Mace is right that Artemis is and never has been more than a liar and a coward. But my betraying, foolish heart screams otherwise. That there is *no* way I mistook the way he looked at me in solitary confinement. That there's no way I misinterpreted our friendship. But if everything that Mace says is true, then of course I would think that…

Because Artemis manipulated me.

I surrender my love for Artemis and run my hands through my fishtail braid, now clumped from the sweat of this stressful evening. I shake my head, take a deep breath, and tell the most selective truth I can muster.

"I just can't believe I fell for it. I can't believe he would manipulate me. I know that's a part of this game, it's just…I never thought *he'd* betray me."

"Come here." Mace stretches his arms around me, and I rest my head in the nook on his shoulder. "This isn't the first betrayal you'll see…we need to be on watch. Keep our friends close…don't risk associating with the ones we aren't one hundred and ten percent confident in."

I nod, holding back tears. My chest is numb, and my mind fogs, drowning out any rational thoughts. Because not only have I lost my best friend, but I can't figure out if I ever really knew him at all. Beyond this, his betrayal terrifies me. If I can't trust Artemis, somebody I believed loved me beyond the bounds of this game…who *can* I trust?

I take deep breaths, trying to dislodge the boulder in my throat. When I finally break from our embrace, Mace takes my hand and holds it between his. His hands are perfect. *Warm and dry.* I lean my head on his shoulder, and we rest in silence while I attempt to process and internalize the full brunt of Arty's betrayal. As much as I try to convince myself that this makes everything easier, my heart won't let him go.

I am so deep in meditation that I miss Lunar's approach from the bathroom. He hides a yawn with his hands, closing his eyes to embrace the full sensation. He sits beside Mace and leans his head on his shoulder as if to snooze.

I lean forward and catch Mace smiling. "Sleepy?" I ask Lunar in a childlike voice.

Lunar nods, whispering, "Couldn't sleep with you trapped." My heart warms and I reach for my brother, squeezing his hand three times. I keep silent as he falls asleep on Mace's shoulder, and smile at both of them.

"I'll carry him to bed," Mace grins, rising from the couch. I nod as he picks him up, Lunar slinging his arm around him. He makes for the staircase, and I run after him before he reaches the first step.

"Mace?" I whisper, pulling on his sleeve.

"Yeah?" he whispers back, eyebrows raised.

I clear my throat. "We're not letting Ashlea die, are we?"

Mace smiles and winks.
"Not a chance."

Chapter 37

"Tell me about him," Ashlea says, smiling. Her eyes beam on the bed across from mine, and her legs dangle from excitement. I match her cheeky grin, but a pit forms in my stomach; she's blissfully unaware that within the hour, she will be sitting on Death Row, her life in the hands of nine teenagers. It's killing me not telling her. Because of my loyalty to Dial, she won't get to plead her case to Finian before selections. But it's not worth the potential backfire. In the best-case scenario, she would have talked her way off Death Row. But in the worst-case scenario, she could have accidentally talked my way *on*.

My chest tightens. *This is wrong.* I shouldn't be gushing about Mace with her when she's moments from imminent danger. Biting my lip, I justify my behavior, reminding myself that Mace and I will fight until the end to keep her alive.

So, I resort to the lessons in deceit I've spent countless hours teaching my sister and force a laugh.

"What do you want to know?"

She giggles, poking me in the stomach. "How did you know you loved him?"

Her playfulness destroys me, but I commit to my role. "Isn't that a dumb question coming from you?" I joke. "Aren't you the expert?"

She laughs harder, raising her eyebrows. "I'm hardly the expert." Taking a deep breath, she enters a romantic trance. "For me, it's just something that you *know*. It hits you out of nowhere—sometimes in the weirdest places or at the strangest times. If you doubt it or have to ask yourself if it's true…well, then you aren't in love with them."

I nod, her explanation hitting the mark. Nothing specific made me fall in love with Mace…it just happened. I never questioned if it was real because I *knew* that it was. But with Artemis, *nothing* is straightforward.

Solitary confinement distorted my feelings for Artemis. Starting to fall for him…it was misguided. He saved my life. Anything beyond that was a misattribution of arousal.

I lose myself in his flaws. First, how quickly he discarded his loyalty to me when Finian's selections were so clearly targeted at me. Second, how he flaunts his lust for Mercedes and utilizes violence as a love language. But when I'm honest with myself, none of that truly matters to me. Because behind all the fog of flaws, one blatant betrayal shines through.

Artemis has been using me this entire game.

For the past twenty-four hours, I've been relentlessly convincing myself that I never meant anything to him. But no matter how hard I try, I can't wholeheartedly believe that he loves Mercedes. *So why does he fight for her safety and not mine?*

Mace's revelation about Artemis's true intentions spoke volumes to me, but my brain refuses to accept it unquestioningly. Questions swim through my mind, but the reality is that he could vote me out *to my face*, and I would *still* feel like I needed more evidence that he's a monster. The only thing I know for sure is that any feelings I developed for him before weren't real. The fact that I sit here now, doubtful, is more than enough confirmation that I don't love him.

I think.

"Iris?" Ashlea asks, waving a hand in front of my face.

My cheeks heat at how long I've been lost in my thoughts. "S—sorry," I stutter. "What were we talking about?"

Ashlea laughs as Eno crests the staircase.

"What did I miss?" he asks, trenchant odors almost visibly wafting from his skin.

I pinch my nose to fight the smell, making him chuckle. "Nothing at all," I reply with a distorted nose-plugged voice, a pang of guilt hitting my heart that he'll soon be on Death Row for the second time. As before, I bury it deep inside my gut. "Say, Eno, do you have a partner outside the Enterprize?"

Eno sits on the ground a few feet away and rubs his hands together excitedly. There's silence, and his smile fades. "Nope." We all burst into laughter, not expecting that answer given how eager he was to respond.

"How?" Ashlea asks between laughs. "You're a funny guy! Smart. Kind. What stopped you?"

"Geeze, Ashlea! Date him already!" I say, Eno's humor making it easy for me to engage. His presence outweighs the severe stench that trails him, making it virtually unnoticeable as we converse. Eno's face melts into a deep blush, and he looks to the floor in embarrassment.

"She's kidding," Ashlea clarifies. "I have somebody waiting for me on the outside."

"Oh?" I ask. I knew she was in love with Seb, but I hadn't realized that he was the beacon of hope getting her through the Enterprize. She nods giddily before turning back to Eno.

"So why then, old man? Surely there was somebody?"

He shakes his head. "I decided long ago to help those hiding from the Assessment. My mission…I just couldn't bring anyone else into danger. There was too much to lose."

We nod, smiles fading. "Eno, who exactly did you help? And why?" I ask. "I mean…you went through the Assessment. Why would you believe so quickly that it's dangerous?"

"Well, things have changed quite a bit since I was tested." Eno rubs his hands together, sifting through his thoughts. "And I wasn't the only one involved in the operation. I just controlled what was shown in the official records. It was up to my partners to initiate the actual distribution of rations. It was one of them that got me involved…I guess they knew a family hiding refugees. From my understanding, someone in the Authority tipped them off about the changes to the Assessment. I was never given details, but the Authority were always clear that it was going to be different. I guess it's changed for the worse. But it didn't take much convincing to get me involved. This is *children* we're talking about. It's really not as much a sacrifice as a moral philosophy."

I nod but stop abruptly when my stomach gets queasy. I tread my next question carefully. "Eno…how did you get caught?"

"Well, that's the question, isn't it?" He leans back in a stretch, then huddles forward again, face hardened with serious intent. "A lot of possibilities run through my mind, but one makes the most sense. The family in charge of the operation…they had a son. Once he turned sixteen and didn't show up for the Assessment, I assume there wasn't much left to keep the Authority off their trails."

My stomach drops in unison with my jaw. *Artemis*. "Wait…a son? Turning sixteen?"

"Yeah, I guess. Why?"

My eyes widen, and the realization begs me to get confirmation. "Eno, what Ascendency were you in?" Artemis lived in the Western Ascendency…if Eno was there, too…

He opens his mouth to answer but is cut short by Mace peeking his head into the circle. We all give a slight jump at his sudden appearance. The conversation was so intense we hadn't even noticed him entering the bedroom.

"Am I interrupting something?" Mace asks, smiling.

"I mean, yes," Ashlea replies bluntly, sending Mace and me into a light chuckle.

"Sorry guys…it's just…*that* time."

The two of us shrink deeper into our beds, Eno melting into the floor. I bite my lip to hold back from forcing an answer out of Eno. But it *kills* me. Surely, our past will be an off-limits subject for the several days he may need comforting. Now, I've missed any opportunity to clarify a connection between his conviction and Artemis's. I take a deep breath, expanding my diaphragm while I try and wipe Artemis from my mind. He won't even look at me anymore, let alone talk to me. If Eno has some connection to Artemis's refugee camp…it's not my responsibility to care. I straighten my back, trying to convince myself I'm above this worry. But the pit in my gut proves my efforts to be futile.

Mace takes my hand, lifting me off my cot. A ghostly silence has fallen upon the group as we trek across the white carpet, the plushness no longer comforting to the pads of my feet. Ashlea and Eno follow us down the spiral staircase, and my stomach threatens to hurl out every last scrap of its contents. If everything goes to plan, my best girlfriend in the house will be pitted against the kindest man I've ever known. A man who's dedicated his entire life to helping teenagers survive. Regardless of the Assessment, Eno abandoned his innocence to help provide for kids in refugee camps. He forfeited any individual happiness to supply for others.

And I'm about to rally a vote to murder him.

Using the cold, white railings to keep weight off my left leg, I support myself through each step toward the living room. When we reach the bottom, my chest is drenched in sweat. My earlier shame at keeping Ashlea in good spirits is replaced with paranoia. Contemplating the potential consequences of my outburst last night sends me into a spiral of terror. Perhaps they've had a change of heart, and I'm the new target? Destry and Lagiacrus seemed quite interested in my side alliances…what if they skipped trimming the bushes and went straight for the trunk? I grow faint as we pass by the kitchen and have to use Mace's hand to steady myself. The living room is cryptically silent, every person frozen to the couches. The clock counts down from a minute and fifteen seconds as the four of us take our seats on the nearest sofa.

I can't afford paranoia, so I fight back thoughts of potential blindside and stay optimistic. I send Finian a reassuring smile at the front of the room, but he's stoically still on his Executive chair, exposed skin glowing bright red while his eyes gloss over in a trance.

Mace squeezes my palm, easing my apprehension as the clock nears zero. I mistakenly glance in Artemis's direction, blood boiling at Mercedes sitting on his lap, rubbing his bare chest with her scabbed knuckles. Artemis avoids my gaze and whispers in her ear, making Mercedes smile with all her teeth. She pulls his face toward hers and plants a kiss on his lips, completely turning away from the rest of the room to straddle his hips. I can't stop myself from rolling my eyes as his tongue pokes into her mouth, and Mace cuddles closer to me, trying to soothe my rage. When they finally separate, Artemis rubs his nose on Mercedes's nose, and I suddenly want nothing more than for Mercedes to be *dead*.

The two jump and separate when a buzzer confirms that the clock has hit zero. Finian lets out a long huff before grabbing the arms of his entirely undeserved Executive cushion, using it to support his weight to stand. After watching Finian struggle for several seconds, Destry springs out of his place on the sofa and sprints to help him. *Just when I didn't think he could kiss Finian's ass any harder.*

"Let me help you up, buddy. That's it…"

Mace and I look at one another and roll our eyes to the stars. Despite the seriousness of the situation, I can't help but stretch my lips into a smile. His violet eyes always seem to send me into the most elegant trances, so I feel a momentary sense of relief that he's *mine*.

"Thanks," Finian nods at Destry while the latter scurries back to the long sofa. Destry springs up straight like a puppy eager to please its owner, and my lip curls, a bitter taste settling in my mouth. He's so irritating that I almost miss Cypher slouching beside him, head supported by his fists in boredom. I'm surprised he's even attending the meeting after his grand announcement that he won't be participating in Enterprize-sanctioned events. But here he sits, brown eyes scanning Finian with utmost disrespect. If nothing else, his presence contradicts his monologue. He's potentially the most dangerous of us all, able to fly under the radar with the pretense that he will no longer cooperate with this game. He's certainly not a threat to me and my strategy; I'm sure the others feel similarly.

Finian stands with perfect posture and is robotic in his movements.

"There's really not much to say here," he begins. "I've chosen a great competitor. The other person is unanimously liked in the house and, therefore, equally dangerous. Only one of us can make it out alive, and the loved make it far."

A few of my housemates look at one another or tilt their heads, and all the air is sucked from the room. I squeeze Mace's hand, and he reciprocates, drawing circles on the back of my palm. My stomach twists with nausea, and I look down at the floor, forcing myself to breathe.

Finian opens and closes his mouth several times in my periphery, trying to get the words out. He finally coughs, then looks his selections in their eyes. "I'm...*so* sorry...Ashlea and Eno, please take a seat."

Ashlea chokes on her breath. I release Mace's grip and shove my head into my hands, blocking my vision. It's impossible to watch two of the only friends I've ever had drop into the bullet-pierced death sentence furniture behind them. My throat aches, tears threatening to budge. I force a deep breath and refuse the temptation to cry. *Don't show them weakness. Don't give them the satisfaction.*

When I finally remove my hands, it's as if time has stopped. Not a single person moves a muscle. The tension feels like a solid object in the air. Finian clears his throat as his posture sags. "I'm so sorry. I'm *so*, so sorry."

Eno shakes his head and shrugs. "Nothing to be sorry about. Someone's gotta go up."

I risk a look at Ashlea and shiver, the hairs on the nape of my neck lifting.

Her eyes contort in complete, utter, *inhuman* rage. She *never* rolls over in defeat, and the way she puckers her lips confirms that this situation is no different. She breathes steadily, keeping her olive skin from losing color. Ashlea finally locks onto Finian's eyes and stretches her lips into a smile.

"Game on," she says. Her smile is anything but sweet. Without another word, she rises from the couch and marches up the steps, leaving the room in awe. Even Mercedes hugs her trembling arms, yet again reminding me that she's human. She likely doesn't care about either of the nominees, but after being the sole vote that solidified Jade's death, the game must have a newfound gravity for her. She curls up to Artemis, this time in fear instead of lust, and I risk a look at his face.

He's watching me, sending a shiver down my back. It's a mystery what his blue gaze is trying to communicate, but the way his face wrinkles confirms there is remorse. I look away quickly, terrified of how this simple gesture may spiral my thoughts.

Cypher claps slowly, distracting me from my mental crisis. He rises from the sofa with his lips stretched into a malicious smile. "Very well done, Finian! How did that blind compliance feel, bud?"

Cameras around the living room whirl to Cypher, and he eats up the attention. "You're giving them *quite* the show, huh?" He points to the cameras and does a quick spin. "You must be so *proud* of yourself, Finian. Really. It takes guts to send innocent people to the firing squad. It really does."

"Oh, come off it, Cypher," Destry shoots at the vigilante. Cypher's eyes widen as he turns to Destry. His next two claps echo off the living room walls as he steps closer to the puppet master, smiling.

"You're right, Destry. Really, I should be congratulating you, shouldn't I? Or are you so far up Finian's ass you wouldn't be able to hear me anyway?"

I catch a laugh in my throat and cough loudly to cover it up. Destry's been playing a very dangerous game, and it's about time somebody stuck it to him. Nobody acknowledges my outburst, but I don't dare sneak a glance at the others for confirmation.

"Whatever, dude. You've got your own death wish—don't make that my problem. Come on, Finian." Destry offers Finian a hand and helps him off the couch, leading him to the staircase without looking back.

"That's right. You two have a good night," Cypher calls, cupping his hands to magnify his voice. "Maybe one day Finian will learn to think for himself!"

I bite my lip, forcing my smirk to disappear. Mace is doing the same, so when we lock eyes, it's even more difficult to conceal our laughter. Before the ensuing silence lingers too long, Eno rises and scurries from his black sofa.

"I'm gonna check on her," he says, itching the back of his neck. I let out a deep breath, my heart shattering all over again. Even in the face of plausible death, Eno prioritizes others. My smile vanishes as the ache in my chest grows, knowing Eno will die from *my* blindside.

Am I doing the right thing?

My housemates vacate the living room one by one, and Artemis and Mercedes stroll to the bathrooms hand in hand. I imagine he'll see his shirt hanging up and relieve us all from constantly having to ignore that he's half-naked with Mercedes attached to his hip. Mercedes won't be leaving his side anytime soon, but at least now he'll be completely clothed.

Lunar scootches closer to me, Kylah's arm around his shoulders in a comforting side-hug. Mace ruffles his hair and gives him an encouraging smile. "Way to be strong, kid. We made it another round."

Lunar nods with a half-hearted smile, but his scrunched cheeks confirm he's anything but comfortable with the selections. No matter what we do…one of our friends will die in two days. With Lunar being younger than the rest of us, he'll no doubt be taking it harder.

I pull him into a hug and tap his back, doing anything I can to soothe him. "It's all okay. We're okay…we're okay…"

I rub Lunar's back until his breathing normalizes. Once it finally does, the silence is agonizing, my heart thumping in my ears. I grab Mace's arm and search his eyes. "I want to check on her…on Ashlea. To see how she's holding up."

Mace nods, and Lunar takes my hand to follow. We leave Kylah and Mace on the couch, and despite the circumstances, I blush at the awkward duo. *He'll* absolutely *have to tell me how this conversation goes.*

Hand in hand, I lead Lunar up the staircase and into the communal bedroom. On her bed facing the opposite direction is Ashlea, head in her hands. Eno sits on my cot, leaning into her space and whispering reassurances. Two others are dispersed throughout the bedroom, but I'm beyond caring about their presence. There's no privacy in this house, so if I have to comfort my friend in front of the entire Dial alliance, I will. Upon second look, Lagiacrus and Cypher are the extras, lying on their beds with their eyes closed, so I walk straight past them and stop at the head of Ashlea's bed.

"Ashlea...I don't know what to say."

She turns to me, tears running down her face and black hair sticking to her chin. Even in distress, she's beautiful, and my body leads me to embrace her, taking Lunar with me. Eno joins in, and the four of us hug in a huddle, grieving this loss together.

"I just...I can't...what did I..." Ashlea cries harder, unable to form a coherent sentence. I hold back tears and let her weep, too concerned about her well-being to generate any pity of my own. I remain speechless, a thousand thoughts bouncing around my head and competing for attention. Above all else, my stomach twists, knowing that this nomination has nearly nothing to do with Ashlea and *everything* to do with me. The only reason they care about her is because she's my ally. If they tried to vote *me* out at this point, I'd have the votes to stay.

The only way to get to me is to go through my allies.

I always knew the point would come when somebody in my alliance would take the first punch. But the subtlety in which they are cutting me is infuriating. If I alter the votes and rally enough to eliminate Eno, *I* will be the one betraying and subsequently cutting off Dial. As Ashlea weeps, I ponder how this is precisely what Destry wants. *Technically*, these nominations keep the alliance safe. So, theoretically, he and Finian have the best interest of the group at the forefront of their plan. But I see past Destry's facade of unwavering loyalty for the advancement of the group. These decisions are not best for Dial. These nominations aren't even what's best for Finian.

Every decision has been made to advance Destry's game. He's just genius enough to make his advice look like it positively progresses whoever is in power.

I want to reassure Ashlea that we will do whatever it takes to guarantee her safety. But I have enough self-awareness to shy away from these promises in Eno's presence. Instead, we rally around her, agreeing that this decision has no justification. Slowly, my rage fuels enough that I can't keep it from bursting. I lean in and lower my voice to a whisper, the determination of war in my eyes.

"Like you said, Ashlea. If they want to play, then game on."

The three around me search each other, nervousness swimming in their eyes. "Please don't do anything stupid," Eno starts. "Not for us, at least. You'll risk your game."

"What game?" I whisper. "We can't ignore it anymore, guys. You *know* there's two sides of the house right now. Destry, Lagiacrus, Finian, Artemis, and Mercedes against us, Kylah, and Mace. And with two of you on Death Row...this round, we're on the wrong side."

Ashlea presses her lips into a flat line, and Eno deflates.

"From the way I see it," I whisper even quieter, aware that Lagiacrus is at the other end of the room, "the other side is solid. But there's a weak link, and if we play our cards right, we could steal his vote…maybe get his loyalty."

"Who?" Ashlea whispers back.

I lean in close and whisper so quietly I can barely hear myself speak. "Finian." I lean back while I gather my thoughts, then get close again to hide my words. "They think they have him in their grasp, but I have a gut feeling we can get him on our side. He's been floating this entire time. He just keeps to himself, careful not to ruffle any feathers. I bet he didn't even *want* to win Executive this round. Mercedes is an ass, but she was right about that. It was a cheap, bogus win." I shake my head, then cup my hands over my lips. "He's weak…he's just doing Destry's dirty work for him. If we can talk some sense into him…maybe get him to see where we're coming from, then *maybe* we can get him on our side next round. And get his vote this round if it comes down to a tie."

"But Iris, how would it come to a tie? Nine people are voting," Eno argues with a gentle stare, careful not to falter my confidence.

"Not if Cypher doesn't vote. If he refuses…the vote could be decided by eight people." I sigh. "It's worth a shot, isn't it? Besides…I don't want either of you gone. The conversation would really just be for the purposes of future planning…to get him on our side come next round."

"Okay," Ashlea mouths, cheeks soaked with moisture. Eno and Lunar nod, validating the plausibility of my plan coming to fruition. I watch Eno but look away when my throat burns with guilt. *He has no idea what this proposal will mean for him.* I swallow back a lump, justifying my behavior by considering that no matter the voting result, having Finian would strengthen our side of the house. The only thing standing in my way is getting Finian alone and trusting that he won't repeat the bounds of our betrayal to the rest of Dial FM. Knowing how much he cowers from confrontation, I don't believe this to be a legitimate threat.

"It'll happen tonight. When I can get him alone, I'll get him on our side. I *promise* you that I'll do my best." I lean back on my cot, retie my fishtail behind my back, and prep myself for battle.

A decision I fear I will regret for the rest of my life.

Chapter 38

The ceiling cracks, sending blue paint chips on my shoulder and revealing the harsh metal surface beneath. Several rounds in, the peaceful facade of the cheerful skyline and plush comfort of the once blemish-free carpets are faltering. The Enterprize is decaying, revealing the authentically stoic interior that encapsulates this prison. Railings and carpets are staining black from Executive competition detritus, bullets curse the comfort the couches once offered, and rations are becoming less of a luxury and more of a curse, exposing the nutrition Lunar and I should have been provided had the Authority been less firm in their penalty for young parents.

A calm has washed over the house, one side having a newfound hope while the other lives in blissful ignorance. I've waited hours for Destry to vacate the Executive bedroom, but his persistence with Finian is problematic. Even while chowing on my meatloaf dinner ration, I've kept my eyes on Finian's door, waiting for Destry to leave. Biding my time.

Mace and Kylah joined us for dinner, oblivious to my anxiety. They laughed about how much they'd learned about one another, which was a pleasant distraction from my intimidating mission. Really, it sounds more like they just sat in awkward silence, unsure of how vulnerable they wanted to get with one another. This visualization made us chuckle more than anything, far surpassing their realization that they have nothing in common. While we ate together, I felt an urgency to reveal my plan to Mace, but there was a lack of opportunity. I imagine he'd have found it a fine proposition and would have encouraged me to go forward with it anyway, which eased my nerves.

"Maybe call it a night? He practically lives in there now," Ashlea whispers to me as she tucks herself into her sheets. With how late it's gotten, several of my housemates have already nestled into their beds, with only a few stragglers shuffling about the first floor. Mace and Lunar left for the bathroom ages ago, so Ashlea and I have been sitting quietly in the darkness in our neighboring cots. I shake my head and sigh.

"What could they possibly be doing in there?" Time is precious, and my impatience is getting the better of me.

"Who knows? Do you think—"

Ashlea's cut off with the suddenly melodic grating of iron. The gigantic metal door creaks open slowly, and Destry shimmies out. He struts across the bedroom before descending the staircase with a bounce in every step. Ashlea's eyes widen as she gestures to the door, urging me to take advantage of his absence. I nod seriously, roll from my bed, and shuffle to the doorway only three paces away.

My heart pounds as I knock, seconds seeming to take hours. My leg trembles as I wait uselessly for somebody to answer the door. When nobody shows up, I take the initiative and turn the cold, silver doorknob. It budges easily, so I step through the doorway and push the giant slab closed behind me.

"Finian?" I shout, my voice shaking. There's no telling how he'll perceive my uninvited entry, so it's impossible to keep steady. Scanning the room, I can't locate the chapped Leprechaun, so when I see a light shining beneath the bathroom door, I float closer and knock, sure he's hiding in there. My knuckles drive the door open, so I step back, embarrassed that I accidentally forced entry.

I clear my throat before pushing further.

"Hello?" I step forward and jump when I see *him* sitting on the edge of the marbled bathtub, his blue eyes focused on mine.

"Oh—I'm sorry," I say to Artemis, flustered by his presence and Finian's absence. His t-shirt has finally been returned to its home, blood stains running across the fabric that stretches around his torso. "Um…" I stumble for words. "H—have you seen Finian anywhere?"

Artemis twists his lips to the side, looks to the floor, and shifts his feet uncomfortably. He shakes his head, careful to keep his eyes away from me. "He went downstairs a few hours ago for rations."

How'd I miss him? I suppose a coincidentally timed bathroom break on my part coincided with his hunger. I must have missed him ducking behind the counter, retrieving his evening rations.

"Oh. Uh…Thanks," I stutter, turning to leave. I'm so caught off guard by Artemis that I can't remember why I'm in Finian's room in the first place. Trying to orient myself, I lift my left leg but freeze when the memory hits. *He's manipulating you.* Mace's words echo in my brain as I stand still, competing with mental images of my and Artemis's friendship, now tarnished by his manipulation.

Holding onto the door, still turned away from him, I can't contain my rage.

I burst.

"Was any of it real?"

The silence is agonizing.

"Was any of *what* real?" Artemis asks.

I stay facing away from him, terrified to make eye contact. "Us. Our friendship. Was any of it *real*?"

"What? Iris, of *course* it was." I hear him rise. "It *still* is. What are you talking about?"

I turn around and find Artemis, only a few feet from me, wrinkling his brow. His blue pearls twinkle beneath his concerned squint, but they focus on the door beside me. *Anywhere but me.*

I look him directly in his wavering eyes. "I know what you're doing. Why you're acting so…distant from me. You won't even look at me for Christ's sake!"

Artemis's eyes finally lock onto mine, and my heart skips a beat. He shifts until only inches separate us, and I momentarily forget to breathe.

The boulder in my throat chokes up my words, but I let my voice shake. "You were my *best* friend, Artemis. I would've done anything for you. And for you to…pretend to feel the same way? When it was all for Mercedes?"

Artemis's eyes widen when I mention her name. "I'm sorry, *what*?" He gulps and scratches his head, stunned into silence. "Iris, I have *no* idea what you're talking about. Are you okay? Please…I don't want to hurt you."

"Then *stop* manipulating me," I fight. "You…you've pretended to be my friend. This whole time! You've pretended to care about me, to have my best interest at heart. Artemis, I fell to my *knees* when I saw you weren't on Death Row last round. I cared *so* much. And for all of this to be…some sort of *game* to you? So you could keep Mercedes safe and use me to get you two to the end?" I shake my head as a tear falls down my cheek. "What kind of person are you?"

Artemis takes another half-step forward, and I shut the door to step back. His eyes gloss over in a trance, and regardless of whether he's manipulating me or not, his lip quivers with heartbreak.

"Iris, I'm not manipulating you. Everything between us has been *real*."

My voice cracks again, and I force the floodgates back up. "Then why are you pretending I don't exist? Why can't you just look at me and tell me why you've been acting differently? What happened to you when I left solitary confinement? If you ever cared about me, for even a *second*…you would tell me what's going on!"

In one swift motion, his gigantic palm cups the nape of my neck, and my eyes shut tight as I'm slammed into his chiseled stomach. There's a loud crash as I'm pressed into the door, and my leg involuntarily slides up his backside, ending just above the crevice in his knees. He takes my breath away, his lips parting mine as they interlock again and again. I grab his arm and squeeze, desperate for the desire throbbing beneath his torso. I pull his lips deeper, the passion somersaulting my heart and pausing time so I can live in this moment for the rest of eternity. The only thing stopping us from being one are the thin, *too thin*, pieces of fabric keeping the skin on our bodies from rubbing against one another.

Finally, the confusing flutters in my stomach around Artemis connect like puzzle pieces in my mind. I find myself intertwining my fingers through his hair and pulling him in deeper, terrified by every breath he takes that he'll separate and end his burst of passion. My opposite hand grips each sculpted crevice in his torso, following the lines as they dip and dive to *exactly* where I want to be. My fingers grip his waistband, and I freeze, violet eyes piercing my blackened vision. I part my lips wide, keeping from sucking on Artemis's bottom lip as a pit drops in my stomach, preventing me from crossing the threshold beneath his khakis. Because despite this moment being the most deeply alive I've ever felt, all arousal fades in a single moment, replaced by one all-consuming reality.

This is all so terribly wrong.

Having nowhere to back away, I duck out of the embrace and break from Artemis's grasp. He jumps back as gravity sets in on what I've just done, nausea twisting my stomach until I'm weak. I stare at Artemis from the floor, hand covering my mouth in disbelief.

I mutter into my hands, barely able to get the words out. "Oh my god."

Artemis's eyes stay focused on me, refusing to budge.

"I've been ignoring you because I can't do this anymore. I can't pretend to be your friend when you've always been so much more than that."

I blink three times and wish the world would rewind. But no matter how hard I squeeze my eyes shut, Artemis still towers above me when I open them, lips stretched into a thin line. My chin quivers so hard my teeth chatter, and I shrink against the wall, consuming myself with the new, all-encompassing guilt.

"Artemis…" I shake my head and cover my eyes. "Why would you do that? What have you done?"

When I peek between my fingers his gaze is still focused on mine, confidence not faltering. "If you're looking for an apology, I'm not gonna give one. I've wanted this for a *long* time, Iris. I don't regret anything."

My breath catches in my throat and one thought pushes through my distress. *Deflect.* "Artemis…I don't…I mean…did you even feel anything?"

Artemis's eyes widen, but his expression remains serious. "With the kiss?" I nod. "Oh yeah," he says. "Did you?"

The hair on my arms rises, and I shiver, envisioning the sensation of his body rubbing against mine and wishing it never had to peel away. He devoured me, leaving nothing but the shameful shell of the girl I was before our lips touched. When he smashed my breasts against his chest, my heart ignited with burning passion and desire that nothing could ever extinguish.

That is what I felt.

But our rebellious embrace left me with the permanent, burning image of the violet pearls of the man I fell for first. So instead of revealing the truth that burns in my core, that I would rather *die* than never taste him again, I squint and put Mace at the forefront of my mind. "Guilt," I whisper, letting the emotion control me.

"Iris." Artemis puts a hand on my shoulder, squatting to the floor.

"Artemis, I'm in love with Mace," I say directly, my vision blurring from moisture. "I…I can't do this. I just…I *can't.*"

We keep at a standstill, my heart pounding in my ears with each second of silence that passes between us.

His bottom lip shakes, but he doesn't deter his stare from my eyes. A burning question torments my heart, and despite every ounce of brain power begging me not to ask, I can't help myself. "Arty," I whisper, leaving a long pause. "Do…do you love me?" The question stammers out of my lips clumsily. Under different circumstances, it would sound childish or feel like an immature grab for attention. But sitting against the cold floor, our bodies mere inches away from one another, his hands only *just* having left my skin…nothing feels off limits.

Artemis bites his lip, his left eyebrow shaking.

"I…I mean, would you even believe me if I said that I did?"

My heart pounds twice. "Yes." I inch closer to his eyes. "I would."

Artemis deflects his gaze to the ceiling, and I can almost hear the gears moving in his head. I scan him for a clue at his thoughts and linger on his lips. Despite my attraction toward him and pulsing *need* to reattach to him, it's not lost on me that he's not a particularly good-looking man. Everything about the pair of us feels unnatural, but his personality negates everything physical. Where he lacks in natural beauty, he more than makes up for in humor and athleticism. His sapphire blue eyes are intoxicating and distract from anything that could divert from their beauty. But down in my heart, regardless of his external person, the magic I felt from our forbidden kiss is sourced entirely by his identity.

A funny, kind, heroic man who would do anything for me.

His eyebrow quivers more severely. He sighs and rushes his hand through his hair, pulling the ends. "Fuck it." He locks eyes with me and cups my cheek. "Yes, Iris." He lets go, letting his arms hang at his sides. "I love you. I'm *in love* with you. It started as a crush I had the moment we locked eyes when you walked upstairs after entering the Enterprize. My feelings deepened as you became my best friend, laughing with me, not judging me for my mistakes…helping me that night when we studied the house. And when we were locked in solitary confinement, and I thought I was going to lose you…" His hands ball into fists. "I fell completely and undeniably in love with you that day. And when you left to vote, and I stood there alone, left with only your blood stains on the tiled floor…I told myself what had to be done. I didn't want to hurt you. You're happy with Mace…I get that. I thought ignoring you would change my feelings, but it only made them deeper. I've just fallen more and more in love with you since getting out of that chamber. And there's *nothing* I can do about it…so I got angry. I became resentful. But you, Iris…you went from being a simple crush to the most important person in my life to the person I love more than anything in the world. *None of this is your fault.* I just…"

He blinks away tears.

"I love you, Iris. Our friendship wasn't manipulation, and I'm not ignoring you because I hate you or I'm done with you, and I pray you don't actually think that." He takes a deep breath, tears streaming down his right cheek. "Iris, I would die for you. I have nothing else to live for…everyone I've ever known is dead. You're the only person I care about and the only person I care to like me. And correct me if I'm wrong, but…I feel like you feel the same way."

I choke on the air and cough. "You *what?*"

Artemis shakes his head. "Iris, you took an entire evening to tutor me when you know as well as I do that only one of us wins this thing." He takes a step closer. "I'm not claiming

234

to know how you feel, but when you agreed to help, I just thought, 'Who does this? Who would actually take the time out of their day to do this?' And I just thought there was no way you would do something like that if you didn't feel the same way about me."

I flashback to approaching him on the stairs despite Ashlea's warning to stay away. *Everybody* told me not to engage with him, and I did it anyway. It's hard to argue his logic, but instead of accepting defeat, I rebound to the only defense mechanism I have. *He must be manipulating me.* But I can't fight back because I'm speechless, gasping for air like I'm drowning.

He stays steady, not advancing any further. "And when me and Sola…when *that* happened…you were the only one that was there for me or made sure I was okay. You were the only one that didn't view me differently."

"Now that's not true," I defend, finally finding words. "What about Mercedes?"

He shakes his head harder, fresh tears falling from his eyes. "Iris, that's *nothing*. I was ordered to get close to her for Dial, and I did." He shakes his head and takes a deep breath. "Look. I knew from the second I met you that I wanted to be with you. But Mace beat me to the punch…he wanted a chance with you. I should've put up a fight, but I knew that if I mentioned how I felt, I'd be dead within the first eight days. I hoped you wouldn't fall for him, but eventually…eventually…" He doesn't even bother wiping his eyes, so tears stream steadily down his face. "It became clear within two rounds that Mace had your heart. So, I tried to forget about you. I knew you were with somebody else, and I wanted you to be happy. I *really* did. So, for a while, I tried to give Mercedes my heart. But I couldn't do it, because *you* had a piece of me. I didn't want to string her along, but I didn't have a choice! In the grand scheme of things, she doesn't mean *anything* to me…she's just a friend."

My jaw drops, and I squint my eyes. "So, she doesn't mean anything to you, or she's your friend? Which one is it?" I sound ridiculous when the words leave my lips and cringe at my bizarre outburst. Our circumstances certainly excuse any strange friendships circulating about the house, but none of that feels important right now. Despite being in a prison where I could be killed at any moment, the only thing that matters to me is forcing out the truth and diverging from his accusation of my love.

"Does it matter? Yes, we're close. But I don't love her…and believe me, I *tried* to love her. But I don't, Iris. Because all this time, I've loved *you*."

I blink away tears. My legs shake so badly I can't stand, so I squeeze my knees together and shake my head, another tear involuntarily falling onto my cheek. "I just…why can't you just interact with Mercedes like you interact with me? Why *me?*"

Artemis doesn't skip a beat. "Because I don't love her, Iris. I love *you*. There isn't a world in which I could've loved her! Because she *isn't* you. There is only one Iris." He gulps and shakes his head. "And you are *everything*. As to why…there's so much. I can't begin to explain to you…"

Thoughts circle around in my head, fighting my focus. His flattery conflicts with my remorse for how my mistake is going to impact Mace. Guilt builds that I've potentially contributed to Artemis's attraction for me, appeasing any mistake he's made while encouraging his occasionally crude behavior. But above anything else, my heart aches, knowing that I've put myself in this situation, potentially compromising anything Mace and I have for each other.

I blink hard until I see stars, stalling for time. Despite every powerful feeling I have for Artemis, it's impossible to figure out whether I'm in love with him or not. Because when I dive into my soul, my love for Mace disqualifies me from developing any solid foundation of adoration for Artemis. As long as Mace exists, there cannot be a life with Artemis.

Of course, the grass could be greener on the other side. But when the patch you're on is this vibrant and luscious, you don't bother speculating what lies across the creek.

I might love Artemis, but the very concept of questioning it leads me to believe that I don't. The jumbled mess in my heart prohibits me from acting on emotion. All central processing is directed toward my brain. So, when tears fall down Artemis's face and he reaches to wipe them away, my gut aches with the realization.

I cannot love Artemis.

Even if I might…I will do anything and everything to preserve my relationship with Mace. So, despite wanting to spill every single adoring thought in my mind and rub my body back up against his, despite wanting to shake Artemis and tell him that kiss was the single best moment of my entire life, and despite wanting to cry with Artemis and say to him that he's *right,* that I *do* have feelings for him, I am left with one option.

Deny, deny, deny.

"Arty," I bite my lip hard, forcing the words out. "I was only there for you…because you're my best friend."

Artemis swallows and sniffles through his response. "You're my best friend, too." He licks his lips and winces in pain. "The only difference is…I want to *be* with my best friend."

My body trembles, and I dig my teeth further into my bottom lip. I fight back emotion, but the confusion and regret trigger tears to pour.

"Artemis…I don't know what to say…"

Artemis holds my chin with his forefinger and thumb. "Then don't say anything." He shifts so his face is just inches from mine. He scans my lips and then my eyes repeatedly, physically asking permission to advance. My gaze lingers on his lips, and temptation bites. My pelvis tenses, desperate for his advance. I squeeze my fists and put Mace at the forefront of my mind, forcing myself to back away and commit to my rejection.

"Arty, you are *so* important to me…one of the most incredible people I've ever met. I don't want to lose you…I *can't* lose you. It's just…Mace."

His head hangs at his friend's name. After the brief motion of defeat, he adjusts his gaze back to my eyes.

"How you feel for me," I force out, my stomach knotting in pain, "is how I feel for Mace." My voice cracks. "*I'm sorry.*" Tears pour down my cheeks, and my throat aches, pushing the words out. "I'm sorry that I don't feel the same way. I love you…but not in the way that you love me."

Artemis's tears flow, but he doesn't stray from my eyes. He sniffs and takes a deep breath, gaze unfaltering. "I just don't believe you."

My stomach drops to the floor, and I shiver, terrified that he can see through my lies. "What do you mean, *you don't believe me?*"

He shakes his head, steadfast in his belief. "The way you looked at me in solitary…the way you laugh with me and genuinely care about me…it's hard to believe that you don't feel the same way."

I push my hands through my hair and groan. *This is absurd.* The Enterprize is life-or-death. Even if I loved Artemis more than Mace, only one of us is making it out of here anyway. I squeeze my palms shut, convinced I'm making the right choice but terrified that Artemis is right.

"You're scared, Iris. Scared of what they'll think of you and afraid of what the consequences might be. But I promise you…it's worth it. I *know* it's worth it."

I shake my head so hard, the end of my fishtail whips my back. Frustration builds that he won't accept my rejection, which is the very thing destroying me. "You're not *listening* to me, Artemis," I spit through my teeth. "I don't feel the same way…I'm in love with somebody *else*." My heart thumps, denying my claims. *But I don't have a choice.*

Artemis breathes through his nose, letting a long silence pass between us. "But if Mace wasn't here, you would feel differently?"

My jaw drops to the floor, and goosebumps erupt across my skin. "You mean if Mace was *dead*?"

Artemis throws his hands up, shaking his head. "No, that's not what I'm…what I'm saying is, you might not know it, but Mace is holding you back. You can't love me because you haven't given it a *chance*." He makes a loud gulp and sniffs back tears. "Please, Iris…*give it a chance*."

Certain that if I stay for another minute I'll falter on my decision, I spring to my feet and run toward the bathtub, trying to get Artemis away from the exit. "I can't do this…" I mutter. I hyperventilate when he approaches me, creating an opening for my escape. I sprint to the door and whip it open, running as fast as I can across the Executive bedroom. "I can't!" I yell as I sprint, my tone warning him to stay away. I wipe the tears from my eyes and don't look back, sprinting past the communal bedroom. I take the stairs two at a time and nearly smash into Mace on the second floor.

"Iris?" His eyebrows scrunch together, and his words are soft. "Have you been crying? Are you—"

I sprint past him, ignoring his alarm. *I need privacy.* I barely recall passing through the living room as I open the metal bathroom stall and lock myself in.

Ignoring the cameras and their *insufferable* red blinks, I fall to my knees and bawl. It's impossible to discern exactly what I'm crying about, but it's something between mourning the loss of my best friend and fear of the repercussions of my actions despite not initiating the kiss. But one realization stands above the rest, and it sends me into a wheezing gasp I can't get a handle on.

Mace is going to kill Artemis.

Chapter 39

I'm wheezing when the pounding begins.

"Iris!" Mace shouts on the other side of the stall. "Iris, it's Mace! Are you okay? Let me in."

I rock back and forth, struggling to catch my breath. Despite wanting to shut the world out and wallow, I know I have to let him in. But how will I begin to explain everything that's happened? I don't want to hide anything but telling him my true feelings could do more damage than lying. I convulse, knowing the repercussions of the truth. *I can't break his heart*, and his reaction to the conversation would almost certainly put Lunar and me in grave danger.

Bang. Bang. Bang.

What's the harm in telling Mace what *Artemis* said? Technically, none of my responses would indicate that the feelings were reciprocated. Who is Artemis to decide how I feel when I've never verbally expressed it? My love for Mace is indisputable, and I said as much when rejecting Artemis. My harsh breaths pause as I convince myself that I did nothing wrong. After all, Artemis promised that none of it was my fault.

I choke on newfound tears when I remember the feeling of his chest against mine, my leg curling around the back of his knees and pulling him in deeper, and my fingers following the path to his desire…

I have to tell Mace about the kiss. But how do you begin to tell the man you love that you had a lapse in judgment? I shake my head and slap my cheeks. *How was I to know that Artemis was going to kiss me?* If I had known, I wouldn't have confronted Artemis about his manipulation. I would never have wanted to compromise my relationship with Mace for something so foolish and impulsive as a kiss.

Right?

I bang the back of my head against the wall, clueless about how I should explain the incident. I take three deep breaths, calm my tears, and blow my nose. Before moving to open the stall door, I silently vow to tell Mace about the kiss when the time is appropriate. For now, that detail can be left untouched. Because in the back of my mind, I know that Artemis meant it when he said he would die for me. And if he would die for me…he would never divulge our secret. If I know nothing else, I know that he would never put me in a position that could destroy my game and end my life. So, I rise to my feet and nod, confident that Artemis won't tell a soul, and I'll be able to tell Mace once the time is right.

One deep breath later, I open the door, and Mace collapses into the stall. His body is slick with sweat, and his face is red with panic. He grabs my torso and hugs me tight, rubbing my back and whispering how thankful he is that I'm okay. My heart simultaneously swells and aches as I curl in his arms, loving the way we fit together but panicking about what to say. When Mace backs away, holds me at arm's length, and looks deeply into my eyes with his violet beauties, I break down into tears once more.

"Iris, stay with me! I can't help you if you don't tell me what happened." His face hardens from relief to urgency. "Who hurt you?"

I sniffle, and Mace hands me toilet paper, keeping one hand always grasped to my arm. I blow my nose and collapse to the floor, and he follows, squatting on his heels. Using his other hand, he lifts my chin, so I look into his eyes.

"Please, Iris. Just tell me what happened."

For the first time since Mace and I kissed in the Executive room, I feel safe.

I nod and struggle for words. "I thought…I was just…" I shake my head and force the words out. "It was Artemis. I…I confronted him."

Mace's jaw drops, and he springs to his feet. His eyes ravenous, he spits in anger, "Where did he hit you? Tell me where he is."

Sola. He thinks Artemis hurt me like he broke Sola. My stomach drops to my toes. "No! He didn't hit me! I'm okay!"

Mace knits his eyebrows together and squats back to my level. "Then why are you crying? What did he do? What did you say?"

I shake my head aggressively, not prepared to provide every excruciating detail. "I just…I confronted him about manipulating me. I just said that I thought our friendship was real and that he actually cared about me. That's all I did! I told him I thought it was wrong that he'd string me along to keep Mercedes safe."

Mace reaches out to touch my cheek, sending a spark down my spine. He keeps his voice level. "What did he say?"

I sniff back more tears. "Well…he denied it. Claimed he had no idea what I was talking about."

"Well, of course, he did. Like you said, he's a coward."

The words pierce my heart. Mace's attack on a person I love so dearly breaks me. But I forfeited any right to defend Artemis when I decided not to express my feelings for him, so whatever judgments Mace has toward Artemis are ones I must mirror.

I nod frantically, overcompensating for my guilt. Mace squints and removes his hand from my face.

"But that's not it. Is it?"

I shake my head and breathe deeply. "No."

Mace rubs his hands together before running them through his hair. "What happened, Iris?"

I look to the floor before meeting his eyes. The violet pierces through my soul, and I know I'll have to pour out every detail Artemis has revealed to me. It's a strange feeling, guilt. On the one hand, I *hate* myself for the events that transpired and even more for my feelings for Artemis. On the other hand, I'm an empty shell, incapable of happiness if I have to pretend that Artemis doesn't matter to me. Feeling remorse for both parties digs me into a deep hole of shame, and it's impossible to determine who deserves more from me. But when I close my eyes and embrace the darkness beneath, the pearls that appear are not blue.

They are violet.

I know what my heart truly wants, and it's the person who's been beside me through thick and thin, even when he barely knew me.

"He…" I stutter. "He told me that he loves me."

Mace looks into my eyes, and for a split second, my heart stops. *He's going to hurt Artemis.* But just when I think he's going to jump from the floor and march to deliver the punch, a smile spreads across his lips, and he bursts into laughter.

"You're kidding?" he fits between laughs. Despite the seriousness of the situation, I can't help but mirror his smile.

"No!" I laugh back, the shame fading. "He really did!"

Mace wipes sweat from his brow, keeping his silly grin. "Okay, what else did he say?"

I get into the conversation, repeating the highlights. How Artemis has allegedly had a crush on me from the beginning before falling for me in solitary confinement. Every detail sends Mace into a fresh bout of laughter, relieving my anxiety with each passing element. When he's curled over, clutching his stomach between wheezes, I get the confidence to reveal one detail that has me uneasy.

"And he accused me of feeling the same way!"

Mace rolls his eyes and wipes his cheek, his laughter so wild that he's tearing up. "He's delusional!" He shakes his head. "That's all it was? Then why were you so upset?"

I shrug. "Mace, he was one of my closest allies and friends. What does this mean for that now?"

Mace puckers his lips to the side. "I guess it means the friendship is over, huh?"

I nod softly, and Mace chuckles. "He's a jerk anyway—you don't want his friendship. Always so aggressive for *no* reason at all. And the way he treats Destry? Disgusting. No integrity to that guy. Trust me, Iris. You're way better off without him."

"But what about what other people will think? What if they find out…how will that look on me? Will I become a target?"

Mace chuckles again. "I really don't think you're gonna be in the line of fire for this. Think about how *Mercedes* is going to react. I wouldn't want to be around her when she finds out about this."

I wipe away tears and get a pang of sadness for Mercedes. She's my enemy, but does anyone really deserve for the love of their life to confess feelings for somebody else and *never* for you? Part of me fears how she will treat me once this information travels her way. The other part is saddened at how she will feel about Artemis using her. After all, their entire relationship was a sham to give Artemis an advantage in this game. He doesn't love her…but has been pretending that he does.

Mace's comfort has given me a new sense of clarity. When I honestly think about it now, without the theatrics of Artemis's bold claims attached…Artemis isn't that good of a person at all. He's perverted and certainly has an anger management issue. He's disloyal to his friends and cowers in fear when faced with moral dilemmas. The more I consider it, the more I am certain that Artemis is not the prince I built him up to be. I love that he saved my life and that he would do anything for me, especially through the horrors of the Enterprize…but I don't love *him*. Laughing with Mace and feeling his heartbeat against my ear when he holds me against his chest, my sorrow at the loss of my friendship with Artemis transforms rapidly to anger at the forbidden kiss. Through one impulsive action, *completely* unprompted…Artemis made me a *monster*.

How in the world am I going to tell Mace?

My mind goes a million miles an hour with images of my relationship with Mace. Him comforting Lunar when Sola was selected for Death Row. Kissing me after my nightmare and promising to do everything in his power to get me out of here alive. Telling me he loves me and hugging me after solitary confinement like I was the only thing in the entire world that mattered. Now, I smile in his arms, my heart swelling with my intense, inarguable love for him. Shortly after, my stomach plummets with terror at the thought of losing him. So, when the love of my life looks me deep in my eyes and asks me if there's anything else I need to share…

I tell him, "No."

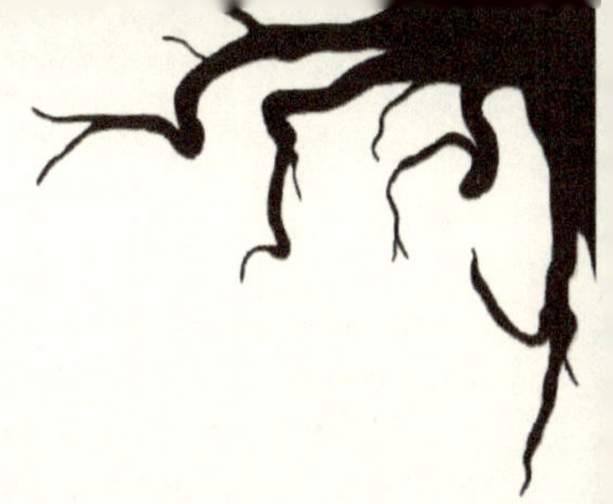

Chapter 40

I step into the living room, not remembering descending the staircase. The air is tense, the only sounds coming from the clunking of my shoes against the hardwood floor. When were the carpets replaced?

I approach the blue sofas, where every one of my housemates is waiting. On the Executive couch sits Mercedes, her face bright red in apparent rage. Once I finally reach the center of the living room, I glance at the Death Row cushions and stumble on the flat ground.

Mace and Artemis stare at me from Death Row, both with pupils so dilated I can't recognize their once-beautiful eyes. Lunar cries in his hands on the blue couch furthest from the kitchen, and I freeze, barely able to find the words.

"What's going on here?" I croak, my throat too dry to speak normally.

"You know **exactly** what's going on, Iris." Mace spits. "Care to share with the group what you so **graciously** let me find out on my own?"

I take a step back, horrified. "I…" I stutter, bewildered at how he could have found out about the kiss.

"How about I catch you up to speed?" Mercedes declares, standing from her Executive couch. She points to me so it's clear to the group **exactly** who she is talking about. "This **slut** decided to come on to **my** Artemis. And then she lied about it all! Wouldn't even come clean to the 'love of her life.'"

"No…I didn't lie…I didn't lie about anything!" I stammer, desperate for the others to believe me.

"But you conveniently left out the part where you cheated on me?" Mace accuses. He rises from the couch and gets inches from my face, so close I can feel his cold breath. "You are pathetic, Iris. You are **nothing**. Do you understand me? NOTHING. And I wish **nothing** but the worst possible shit that could happen to a person on **you**."

Tears pool in my eyes, and I try to stand strong, but I can't take the humiliation. "Mace…please…you don't understand…"

His eyes narrow on mine. "Go to hell, Iris." When he marches away, Mercedes pushes me from behind. I turn to her when she shoves me again, infuriated by my romantic moment with Artemis.

"You will get what you deserve, Iris. I promise you that."

The large iron front door creaks open, begging for my attention. I move to see the entrance clearly and fall to the floor when I see her.

Curi.

She shuffles toward me, green eyes contorted in despair and face puffy from tears. "Iris…how could you do this to me?"

I wake in sweat, my sheets and shirt soaked all the way through. After struggling to find peace in the night, I only managed to find sleep in the first hours of dawn. Even then, my sleep was restless, consumed with nightmares of my forbidden kiss catalyzing endless detrimental consequences. I shoot up from my pillow and search the beds from my spot, finding only a few others still sleeping. Apart from Kylah, Lagiacrus, and Cypher, the rest of my housemates have abandoned the bedroom.

Trembling, I struggle to stretch my socks over my feet and slide into my boots. My fishtail braid no longer holds my hair back, so large chunks of sweaty grease obstruct my vision. Taking a few moments to calm my nerves, I take out my hair and brush my fingers through it. *It was just a dream. Curi is okay.*

But how can I be sure? As far as I know, Curi was shot on her way to school well before we were captured. My heart races as I struggle with rationality. *No.* If they killed Curi, Mace would have seen it. He wouldn't have kept that information from me, letting me live on a hope that was terminated well before I entered the Enterprize. *Mace would never lie to me, no matter how hard the truth was.*

I shudder at the thought. Mace wouldn't keep that from me because he would never keep *anything* from me. I trust him with my life, and he trusts me with his.

So why didn't I tell him the truth?

A boulder lodges in my throat, and I take a deep breath to try and smother it. *Did I just make a life-ending mistake?*

A hand settles on my back, and I jump, my breath catching in my throat.

"Ashlea!" I whisper. "You scared me!"

"Clearly," she smiles, settling beside me. Rubbing her hands together between her thighs, she matches my gaze. "How'd the conversation go last night? I saw you running…I was going to chase after you, but Mace beat me to the punch."

My eyes widen as I remember last night's abandoned mission. "Oh my god, Ashlea. I am so sorry. Finian wasn't even in there. I didn't get a chance to speak to him."

Ashlea puckers her lips and squints. "Weird…I guess we missed him leaving at some point." Silence passes between us until she presses further. "So…what made you run then? Everything alright?" We're both sure to keep our voices down since a few of our housemates are still asleep on the other side of the room. Unfortunately, privacy is a luxury in this house, so we have few better alternatives to where we currently sit.

My brain files through all the possible responses I could give as I debate on telling her the truth. Her friendly brown eyes soften, and I recall everything we've already been through together. Above any alliance, we are friends. And regardless of the situation we are in…I can trust her.

Even if it's just *selective* truths.

"I…it was…" I stumble for words. Finally, I select a path to embark on and bite my lip nervously. "Artemis…he was in the room. I couldn't stop myself…"

Ashlea's eyes widen. "What did you do?"

"Nothing!" I defend too quickly. "Mace had mentioned to me earlier that Artemis was manipulating me. I took offense to it, and…I don't know. I guess I couldn't hold back. With both of us alone in that room, I had to say something."

Ashlea's cheeks harden and she leans closer to me, grabbing my wrist. "Wait, start from the beginning. Tell me *exactly* what happened."

I nod and don't spare any details about his behavior since the beginning. I get into his flirtatious banter starting on that first day. I explain tutoring and solitary confinement and even mention how his eyes linger on mine for too long to be just friendly. After a few motivational breaths, I talk about him avoiding me when we were released and finally get into Mace's idea that I was being manipulated.

"And you believed that?" Ashlea questions, eyebrows raised. I lean back against the headboard, taken aback by her shock.

"I guess so? I don't know, really. When we were in solitary confinement, I was *so* sure that his feelings were real." I gulp. "When Mace told me it was all a lie, I guess I just thought about the repercussions of Mace being right. If Artemis really was using me…" I shake my head. "The idea of him betraying me hurt so much that I believed it. I mean, he was *ignoring* me…I just figured maybe that could be why."

Ashlea looks away and blinks rapidly to clear her vision. As hushed as possible, she leans closer to me and asks, "How much of your friendship with Artemis have you told Mace?"

A pit grows in my stomach, and I shake my head, unwilling to speak the true answer into existence. She lets out a slow breath and settles closer toward me, rubbing my back consolingly.

"Iris, what did you say to Artemis? What happened?"

I look up to the ceiling, desperate not to let the floodgates open. I sigh with extended puffs of air before relaying what happened from the second I entered the bathroom to the moment before our forbidden kiss.

"He was insisting it wasn't manipulation. I was distraught, Ashlea. I couldn't control what I was saying. I just kind of yelled at him, demanding he tell me what's wrong."

Ashlea closes her eyes and interjects, allowing me to stop before revealing the kiss.

"So that's when he told you how he felt?"

I nod, relieved that I could skip over the infidelity. I tell her exactly how our conversation went, with Artemis declaring his love and me not reciprocating it. I omit the feelings I kept inside but convey an accurate script of our conversation.

I expect Ashlea to consol me. Instead, she gives me a look that churns my stomach and makes me feel like it's sinking into the bed. She leans into my ear and whispers so quietly I nearly ask her to repeat herself.

"Is that true?"

I narrow my eyes on her, tilting my head. Matching her tone, I lean into her ear and ask, "Is what true?"

"You don't feel the same way."

My heart skips a beat. *She knows.* Of course, she knows. She's always been skeptical of my soft spot for Artemis and how forgiving I am of his mistakes. She's never supported my commitment to him as a friend, even begging me not to trust him after the incident with Sola. The world starts spinning. *She sees right through my lies.* Enough time passes that simply nodding my head would not suffice, so I resort to the only information I have that could turn her away from demanding an honest answer.

"He...he kissed me."

It's barely audible. Even so, I'm terrified someone's overheard. Tears well in my eyes, and I'm nauseous with guilt. My hands tremble, and I bite my lip hard, doing whatever I can to fight back my tears. If I thought Ashlea would have judged me harshly, I would not have told her. So, when she brings me in for a hug and rubs my back, I finally feel free of the shackles of distrust. Ashlea can be trusted. Ashlea is a true friend.

And there is no way I am letting her die.

While hugging, she whispers reassurances that it's going to be okay. Finally, she cups a hand between her mouth and my left ear to ensure that only I can hear.

"Does Mace know?"

I shake my head so softly I'm sure the cameras have missed it. The floodgates finally break, and tears start individually falling down my cheek one at a time.

"Good. And nobody else does, either?"

I shake my head once more. "Arty won't tell anybody. Not after everything he said. He wouldn't do that to me."

And I believe every word.

Ashlea backs out of the hug and puts all her focus into cupping her hands around my ear without any gaps between her fingers. "If the plan is still to convince Finian to switch sides, you can't tell *anybody* until the round is over. Do you understand? We can make this work, Iris. We'll pin it all on Artemis...it's his fault, after all. And you never said the feelings were mutual, so you're safe. We play on this...it's only a matter of hours before Mercedes finds out. And once she does, all hell will break loose." She shifts some loose hair away from my ear and continues. "This could work. We tell Finian that those boys are falling apart. Without Mercedes and Artemis together, they don't have the numbers anymore. We play on that…make it clear that we will keep him safe until the final six. He's probably disposable to them anyway, right? We use that. But the most important thing is that he does *not* find out about the kiss. Do you hear me?" She takes a deep breath. "Unfortunately, that means you can't tell Mace. The potential for retaliation is too high, and that might steer Finian away from siding with us. For now, we have to emphasize that Artemis is the *enemy*."

I nod, understanding her words but not liking them one bit. Taking advantage of Artemis's honesty and love…it's wrong. But I decided to stick with Mace, and these are the consequences of making that work. It strikes me that to solidify my decision, I will have to do whatever it takes to ensure that I don't go back on it. If that means lying through my teeth and hurting Artemis to the point that he'd never want to be with me anymore…

That's exactly what I'll do.

If this wasn't life or death, the circumstances would be different. But at this moment, Ashlea's life depends on my dishonesty.

Lucky for her, I've been a liar my entire life.

Ashlea rubs a hand softly down my braid, trying to calm me. "I know this sucks, Iris. I am so sorry…this sucks *so* much. But it's the only way."

I nod, but my heart hurts. To make this work, I will have to destroy somebody who means everything to me. Somebody that I can't live without. I'm going to have to hurt him beyond a point of return so that he'll never want anything to do with me ever again when all he ever did was love me.

But I made my decision.

And I will die with that.

An hour later, hunger twists my stomach into a turmoil too powerful to resist. Conceding, I rise from my cot and shuffle across the communal bedroom. I'm on a mission for the kitchen, but no physical cues could distract me from the confusion trapping my mind. I wish my heart had a clearer path forward. My brain understands what must be done, and I am committed to making it happen. But the emotional damage I'll inflict on Artemis is something I don't think I will ever be able to forgive myself for. But in the grand scheme of things, my heartbreak is miniscule. Because despite how hard it will be to hurt Artemis…

Ashlea's life depends on it.

I wipe a bead of sweat off my forehead on the top step and take a deep breath before flexing my legs forward. I rehearse my emotional script and use the railing to guide my steps, my body acting on autopilot.

How can this have happened when there's so much else at stake? *How could I have fallen in love with two people so quickly?* Nobody even knows what's become of my little sister, and I have been neglecting Lunar. Mace and Kylah have been picking up the slack, but my priorities have become foggy. From this moment forward, Artemis's feelings are on the back burner. Lunar is, and always will be, my top priority.

But that doesn't stop my mind from wandering. I shake my head, considering the possibility of all my love being a misattribution of arousal. Maybe I don't love Artemis…I just love the attention he gives me. Even as this thought passes through my mind, I know I don't believe it. But if my love is only real with one of them, it's undoubtedly with Mace. If none of it is real…well, then I've been wasting my time this entire game.

With each step, I mentally repeat my plan to pin everything on Artemis. So, when he locks eyes with me while ascending from the bottom floor, my stomach drops to my feet.

What's happened to him? His hair is slicked back by water, but it shines like there's grease. His body movements are stiff, and his shoulders slump. His ocean eyes are hollow, exposing layers of hurt beneath their sockets. I've never viewed him as particularly attractive, but the grotesque Artemis before me is not the man who kissed me last night.

He's an empty shell of who he once was.

His suffering catalyzes me to abandon any plan I had to foster hostility. I forget about the potential repercussions of my actions when I see a man I love in agonizing pain. My lips spread into a delicate smile, and I nod in his direction, unsure of how to even begin a conversation after the magnitude of what happened last night. Equally hesitant, he matches my smile and whispers, "Hey," not skipping a beat on his walk up the steps.

Pity. That's the first thing that shivers through my body before a pit of second-hand embarrassment overpowers my guilt. But when I hit the bottom step, everything fades to make room for the one emotion that nothing will ever stand a chance against.

Rage.

His moping cuts me in the jugular. Because *I* broke him. His emotional agony is a direct result of *my* rejection. Artemis is miserable *because of me.*

He has to know what he's doing. By enveloping himself in a cloud of depression, he's pulling on my heartstrings and making me feel like the worst person on the planet. He's manipulating me into thinking *I'm* in the wrong for hurting him when *he's* the one that made me a cheater. Suddenly, I hate him. Because of Artemis, I have to lie to Mace. Because of Artemis, I'm going to have to pretend I don't feel the same way and hurt him beyond repair, and I will hate myself forever for it. Because of Artemis, I've lost my best friend and may never laugh the same again. I hate him. I *hate* him.

Am I going insane?

"Morning, *love bird.*" Lunar winks at me then places my ration container on the dining table. Everyone else will think he's talking about Mace, but I know Lunar. *This* is a jab at Artemis.

My eyes widen. "What…why…how do you…?"

Mace approaches from the corner, peanut butter biscuit in hand. He ruffles Lunar's hair and laughs. "Eh, news had to spread somehow." Mace plants a hearty kiss on my lips and hugs me tight, leaning toward my left ear and pushing loose strands of hair from my face. His hot breath tickles as he whispers, "Mercedes can't blow up if she doesn't know, right?"

I force a laugh, fighting the tightness that grows in my chest. I keep my voice low to match his volume. "Who all have you told?"

Mace backs away and shrugs, playing up his nonchalance. "Kylah knows, and Eno was there when I told her. Obviously, I mentioned it to Lunar," he gestures to my little brother. Lunar smiles wide, peanut butter caking his teeth as bits of roll threaten to spill out. I chuckle before Mace is inches from my face again, so close I can feel his lips curving into a smile. "I also may have let it slip to Destry." He winks. Destry is Arty's *closest* friend. Surely, *that* will get the ball rolling.

I contrive my evilest smile before gesturing toward the staircase and taking his hand. Lunar is close behind, and we all perch on the bottom stair so nobody is within ears reach of our conversation. I keep my voice down, mindful of those wandering about the house.

"What's up?" Mace asks.

"I spoke with Ashlea this morning...and told her what happened last night. Obviously, we're all on board to campaign for her to stay. It's just...our talk gave me a few ideas on how we can make that happen."

Mace nods. "We're all ears."

I rub my hands together, organizing my thoughts. "Ok...Finian is probably our only chance, but it's worth trying to get Cypher on our side first, right? Because *as it stands*, the votes to get her out are Artemis, Mercedes, Destry, and Lagiacrus. To keep her here, it'll be us three and Kylah. So, we either need one more vote, or we've gotta have a tiebreaker."

"Wait," Lunar jumps in. "How do you know that's how they're gonna vote? And who's to say Artemis won't just vote in solidarity with you since he's so *in love* with you." He emphasizes "love," intentionally mocking how pathetic he feels Artemis's admission was.

Mace jumps in, carefully steering away from mentioning our involvement in Dial FM. "I feel like the façade has come and gone. Those boys aren't hiding how close they are anymore. They're all any of them talk to. Has Lagiacrus ever talked to *you*, Lunar? What about Destry?"

Lunar shakes his head before whispering, "Dicks," under his breath. Mace chuckles to himself before addressing the second question.

"And personally, I don't think trusting Artemis is the way we should play this. All hell is about to break loose for him, and I doubt our side is the one he's going to align himself with. *Especially* when I make it clear I want nothing to do with him." This last statement brings me pause, and I wonder what Mace is going to do to him. I bite my lip, reminding myself that my dilemma with Artemis is on the back burner for the time being. Ashlea's life is much more important than this elementary love triangle, and her survival needs to be the focus of our mission. "And even if we could get him on our side, is he really somebody we should trust with Ashlea's life? Think about it. Pretend he's *not* full of shit and really *does* want to die for Iris. Is the best way of doing that getting himself out of arguably the strongest alliance in the house when he could play both sides to keep her safe? Obviously not. But pretend he *is* full of shit and continues to manipulate your sister. He won't break up his guy group to help her out, will he?"

Mace is remarkably well-spoken. I purse my lips, impressed with his quick line of logic. Lunar rebounds without hesitation, desperate to exclude Cypher, the Enterprize terrorist, from our plan. "Can't we get Mercedes on our side, then? She'll be so mad at her *lovey-dovey* that I doubt she'll continue to side with him."

This time, I step in. "See, I've thought about that too, but I don't think it's an option. I hardly think she'll want to align with the woman Artemis claims to *truly* love. And even if she would be willing, I feel like she might still have some grudge toward Ashlea. That fight with Jade and Cypher was brutal."

Lunar nods uncertainly but does not raise any further objection.

"So, what I propose then," I begin, "is that we start with Cypher. It's worth a shot, right? Of our options, he's the least likely to tell anybody about our campaign since he's given up on this game." The three of us turn our heads to Cypher at the kitchen table. He's picking at his fingers and biting off hangnails, oblivious to our rendezvous.

We discuss points to bring up with him and decide that Mace and I will speak with him in private. After organizing a script, we move on to the alternative plan.

"And if that doesn't work?" Lunar asks, eyes squinting in apprehension.

I shake my head and pucker my lips. "We approach Finian."

Mace leans forward, hushing his voice even quieter. "It's only a matter of time before Mercedes has a public implosion. *We use that.* Discuss how it'd be silly for Finian to associate with such drama. Tell him it'll put a target on his back. We need to stress that his safest bet is aligning with us, and we'll promise to keep him safe until the final six. He's gotta know that with those guys, he's not even *on* the totem pole – he'll be the first to go when it comes down to it. Destry's obviously been using him throughout the entirety of his Executive reign. The Death Row selections were *not* Finian's choice, and we all know it. We just need to show him he's important to us. It'd probably be smart if all four of us approached him, including Ashlea."

Lunar and I nod, and I hold onto Mace's eye contact far past the end of his monologue. *He got on board with my plan without hesitation. Mace didn't doubt me for a second.* His smile reaches his violet eyes, and my stomach flutters.

"Sound good?"

He really is beautiful. I'm so mesmerized by him that I've forgotten this conversation requires my input. I blink a few times and nod.

"But Cypher comes first," I affirm. "Finian is the most likely to rat out our plan to the others. If Cypher refuses to vote at all, then we'll corner Finian tonight."

Lunar taps my shoulder and grinds his teeth. "And if Cypher's already decided to vote with the other side?"

Mace and I face each other, and I gulp. Mace rests a hand on my other shoulder and answers for me.

"Then we've already lost."

Chapter 41

"**D**on't waste your time."

Cypher stares blankly at the wall in front of him, refusing to listen to any pitch Mace or I have to offer. He tosses an apple toward the ceiling with one hand and nibbles a hangnail on his other.

"You haven't even heard what we have to say," I defend.

"Don't pretend I didn't see you convening on the steps over there. I know you want my vote some way or another, but I've made it *very* clear that my participation in their game is over." Cypher has a complete lack of regard for the volume of his voice, so I'm thankful that the bottom floor is relatively empty.

"Cypher, if you don't vote, they'll kill you. You know *that*." Mace argues.

Cypher slams his apple on the table, and a chunk flings off the side. "They *won't* if you all stand with me. It would defeat the purpose of this show! Want both of your friends to survive? Don't vote. Want to make it to the end and watch every single person you care about die? Then keep doing *exactly* what they want. I'm not participating either way."

Mace tilts his head to the ceiling, and silence washes over us. Footsteps disturb the peace as Destry and Artemis reach the bottom floor. I quickly look away from the duo and focus on the glossy paint of the dining table, sliding my finger over the smooth surface to disrupt my anxiety. Once they finally pass into the living room, Mace brings his voice to a whisper.

"Look, man. I hate this game just as much as you do. But we can help you move forward. We can keep you *safe*."

Cypher whips toward Mace, but the violet-eyed man sits still as a statue, unperturbed by Cypher's sudden movement. Cypher rolls his eyes and rises, spitting a chunk of apple onto the floor.

"Safety doesn't exist in the Enterprize, or in Miasmis, for that matter. So don't make promises you can't keep."

Cypher turns away, stomping toward the staircase. Mace pinches his lips together, and I hold my head in my hands, rubbing my temples. I consider our backup plan as a chill runs down my spine. Speaking with Finian will risk *everything*, but it's the only option we have left.

Mace grips the ends of the table and rises, extending a hand for me to join.

I make it halfway to a stand when the screaming starts.

"SAY IT ISNT TRUE!" Mercedes squawks from the living room, pushing Artemis into the bullet-pierced wall behind Death Row.

My face overheats as I melt into Mace. The footsteps behind me stop and I turn back as a cruel grin spreads across Cypher's chapped and peeling lips. "Now, this is something I'm interested in seeing play out."

Mace grabs my side, and I turn back toward the living room, gripping him for balance. My heart beats rapidly through my chest. The air is sucked from the room, and I struggle to breathe against my raspy throat.

Artemis throws his hands above his head and away from Mercedes. She pins him against the wall and stands on her toes, her face mere inches from his. "Merc, please! Give me a chance to —"

"To what?" she screams, pushing him against the wall so hard the collision reverberates into the kitchen. "Feed me more lies? Not a single thing that comes out of your mouth is honest, is it? *None* of this was real. Not a single part of it!" Lagiacrus and Finian exit the bathroom and gather in the living room, standing on the outskirts. Mace nudges me so I notice Finian, but it's impossible to be relieved that he's watching when my heart is shattering for Artemis. Cypher runs to the living room and leaps onto the Executive sofa, bouncing off the cushion.

"Oh wow! What has your boy-toy done now? Beat up on somebody else half his size?" Cypher's legs are crossed on the couch, so his knees touch the arms of the chair. His hands are interlocked with one another, so he looks like a child waiting for gifts.

Mercedes half turns to acknowledge Cypher but keeps a hand against Artemis's chest. "I don't know. Why don't you ask *that* skank?" She points her other finger at me. The entire room stares at me as I scoot behind Mace, squeezing his arm three times. For some reason, I hadn't anticipated being called out for this mess. With how long it takes Mace to respond, he clearly hadn't expected it either. After an intense silence, he finally jumps to my defense.

"Don't you think you're calling out the wrong person, *Mercedes*? Iris didn't play you. Start pointing fingers at the person who *did*."

Artemis nods, clearing his throat. "Yes…yes, it's my fault, don't blame her…"

Mace steps forward, leaving me alone in his shadow. "Why don't you just shut the hell up, Artemis? And while you're at it, keep my girlfriend's name out of your mouth?" *Girlfriend.* Butterflies fill my stomach at the label, but I keep my exterior stone cold.

Within seconds, the entire house circles the couches. Kylah and Lunar stay on the outskirts of the kitchen by the rationing cabinets, while Ashlea and Eno squat by the Executive sofa. I follow Mace into the center of the living room but keep my distance from Mercedes as Mace inches forward.

"I…you don't understand…none of you understand," Artemis whimpers, trembling against the wall.

"Let me take a crack at it," Mercedes spits at him. "You've been *pretending* to give a shit about me for weeks when your end game was *always* her. You've become my closest ally in the house…*I fell in love* with you! And you never had any intention of bringing me to the end. You're a liar, a manipulator, and a cheat. Everyone sees you for who you really are now, and *you deserve everything that's coming to you.*"

I flash to my nightmare and can't believe it's happening before me with reversed roles. This time, Artemis is the one getting berated. And I wouldn't be surprised if the others started kicking him within the hour.

"And do yourself a favor, man," Mace declares, strutting beside Mercedes and abandoning me on the outskirts of the couches. "Stay the hell away from me and stay the hell away from Iris. Neither of us wants anything to do with you, so take your pity party somewhere else." He gets close enough to touch Artemis. "And don't you *dare* try and apologize when you know it's only to make *yourself* feel better. You're dead to us."

The declaration was made for both of us, but I never agreed to the statement. I don't hate Artemis. I'm not even all that mad at him. I'm flattered by his confession and heartbroken that this is how things must be. But he is not my priority in this game. I need to focus on getting Lunar as far as possible, and this may be the only way of ensuring that happens.

Artemis darts his mourning eyes in my direction, and despite how hard I try, I can't force hatred into mine. My lip quivers regardless of how much I urge it to still, and I fear that it confirms his suspicions of my true feelings. I look down quickly before I ruin the intention of this confrontation, but my heart twists that there's *nothing* I can do to help him.

Suddenly, Artemis bunches his hands into fists and puffs out his chest, no longer cowering behind Mercedes. When he opens his mouth, he speaks without a quiver. "You all can believe whatever you want. I don't care what you think about me. I *really* don't. But Iris," my eyes widen, and I look up to meet his. The others in the room watch as we stare at one another, the tension so thick I can touch it. I desperately try to disguise my sorrow as rage, but the trembling gives me away. "Don't you ever think for a *second* that what I said to you wasn't true. I meant every word of it, and I *promise* I never wanted to hurt you."

Mercedes's jaw drops to the floor. She turns quickly to Artemis and winds her arm back, charging for the perfect slap. She hits him with such force that she leaves a red handprint on his face, and a painful tear falls down his cheek.

"How *dare* you. How *dare* you say that to her when I'm right in front of you. How dare you tell her you love her when you've said it to me *hundreds* of times."

That last sentence gives me pause. *What did he tell her?*

"No, no, I never said that, Mercedes," Artemis defends firmly. A pit grows in my stomach, knowing there's a possibility she's telling the truth. And if she is…

I shake my head, ridding myself of the thought. *No.* There's no way. *Artemis wouldn't do that to me.*

She slaps him again, flinging another tear from his cheek. Slamming him against the wall, her nostrils flare as she stares daggers into his defenseless eyes. "I want you to listen *very* carefully. I don't want to speak with you *ever* again. *Do you understand me?* So, if you want to come and apologize to me, don't waste your breath. From this moment forward, you are *nothing* to me. *Nothing*."

Mercedes backs away and straightens loose chunks of hair from her face. She spins on her heel and stomps to the bathroom, shouting so loud my ears ring. "ROT IN HELL!"

The rest of the group stands in awe, frozen in their places. Artemis still slumps against the wall, face red and tears welling in his eyes. My blood still paints streaks across his shirt and crusts the cuffs of his khaki pants in red flakes. He saved my life…and I won't even *try* to defend him. My chest aches as Destry steps forward, extending an arm around Artemis.

"Alright, everyone…show's over."

He steers Artemis to the staircase. I glance in Arty's direction, but he keeps his eyes glued to the floor, avoiding my eye contact. When the two finally crest the steps, I shiver from the cooled sweat drenching my chest. The Enterprize is at a standstill until Lagiacrus flees to chase the two into Finian's Executive bedroom, triggering the others to scatter. I let out a breath I hadn't realized I was holding when the room clears, and clutch onto Mace to stabilize myself. Despite Mace's support, Cypher's haunting voice still slices my heart in two.

"Secrets, secrets, they're no fun. Until you share them with *everyone*."

Chapter 42

Wanting to stay as far away from Artemis as possible, terrified that proximity to him will expose the kiss and reveal my true feelings to the rest of the house, I keep myself rooted in the living room with Mace. Guilt twists my stomach in a deep ache, so I crunch into a ball on the blue sofa facing the kitchen. Mace rubs my back, falsely attributing my discomfort to Mercedes's outburst.

"She's just angry, Iris," he whispers. "We knew she would explode...there's no way anybody is stuck on her calling you out. And if they are, you're not the one they're mad at." I nod cooperatively, but his words do little to mend my broken heart.

I just stood there. While Artemis was being crucified, I was silent, letting a man that I love get torn to shreds. He took *full* responsibility for our relationship. Above all else, *that* is what destroys me. Because no matter how much he has emphasized that it's entirely his fault, I know better. I encouraged his behavior. I loved his attention, and I welcomed it. I'm not as innocent as everyone believes me to be, and Artemis would not have made such a bold move if there was any indication that I did not feel the same way. The more I question it, the more I believe I'm in love with Artemis. But Ashlea's assessment of love flashes back to me clearly. *Love isn't something that's questioned. If you have to ask yourself...then you don't love them.* But as much as I want to embrace that reality, my heart pierces through my chest, and pain fills every cavity of my body. Regardless of my true feelings for Artemis, I just watched a screaming battle ensue over his behavior when I know the responsibility is shared.

I squeeze my eyes shut as Mace rubs my back and remind myself what must be done. If for nothing else, then for Lunar. Because if there is one thing I know for certain, it's that exposing my true feelings for Artemis would earn Lunar and me one-way tickets to expulsion. So, instead of confronting how I feel and saving Artemis from his downward spiral of heartbreak and suffering, I take three deep breaths and center myself on our top priority.

"It's fine...really." I finally lift my head from between my knees and smile at Mace. "We just need to focus on what's ahead of us...we've got twenty-four hours before somebody walks out that door, and I'll be *damned* if Mercedes's temper tantrum is the reason we don't get a say in it."

Mace smiles back with a gleam in his eye. "If it makes you feel better, she did exactly what we needed her to do." I nod as Mace removes his gentle hand from my back. He leans back and cracks his knuckles one at a time. "Step one: success. Now, for step two."

Step two happens more naturally than we anticipated. We don't wait long for Ashlea to sit beside us on a death row cushion, and moments later, Lunar and Kylah settle at the dining table.

Once the bottom floor is clear of eavesdroppers, Mace motions for Kylah and my brother to join our rendezvous in the living room. Mace puts a finger to his lips, so the two walk purposely but silently to our area and squat to tighten our circle.

Whispering, Mace begins. "Any thoughts on expulsion tomorrow?"

Kylah shakes her head plainly, auburn curls bouncing against her shoulders. "It's weird…usually somebody shares how the house is leaning, but lately, we've just had to wing it."

I can only imagine how uncomfortable Ashlea feels, listening to Kylah insinuate that she doesn't mind how the vote goes. Remarkably, she keeps her calm.

"Is it alright if I make a little pitch to you?" Ashlea questions, clasping her hands together.

Kylah crosses her arms and puckers her lips before answering, "Go for it."

"There's a men's alliance in this house. At this point, it's impossible to ignore. And if you do, it's only a matter of time before they pick you off. They're strong…they're going to win nearly every physical competition there is. So, if we can solidify a group *larger* than them that can be just as competitive with the mental stuff, we'll have a chance. Otherwise…we're all just sitting ducks."

Lunar leans forward, matching Ashlea's discreet volume. "Just to be clear, who's in that group?"

Ashlea nods. "Well, clearly, Destry and Artemis are a pair. Not many people would have the guts to associate with Artemis after that mess, and to *personally* escort him to safety? It's a joke." We all nod, prompting her to continue. "Beyond that, Lagiacrus was close to follow, so he's gotta be with them too. I'm confident Mercedes is somewhat involved…before the Artemis stuff, she could have taken any of those strong men out, but what did she do? Put up useless number one and useless number two. I just think even beyond her outburst, she'd be stupid to stop aligning with them. Because otherwise, she's alone." I'm astounded at how Ashlea is putting this together. I never explicitly exposed Dial. I've only ever hinted at the thought of their existence, and even then, I never revealed that Mace and I were in on it. Her deductive skills are impressive, and I'm proud to have her by my side. "So that's four. I would've thought it ended there, but the way Destry has sucked up to Finian for the past few days? He's gotta be with them to *some* extent." She signs. "And that's where I come in.

"Word is that they want me out. Makes enough sense to me: Eno is the weaker player. They probably only put me up with him because they didn't think anyone would vote him out. But if we fight back and I stay, we may just have a chance to start picking them off."

"Who's to say Mace isn't with them?" Kylah interjects, glaring at Mace. "I've seen you with them…thick as thieves you are. If I remember, you didn't put any of them up when *you* were Executive."

"If you think for one *second* I will be aligning with a group that publicly endorses a man that has betrayed me by coming onto the woman I love, you are out of your goddamn mind." His aggression leaves me on edge. *Artemis has struck a nerve in him that can never be repaired.* "And how stupid would I have been to put up the strongest men in the house in the second round? I'd have been dead *days* ago. Me keeping them safe on day five was nothing more than a game move. There are about to be eleven of us left…ten if Cypher is stupid enough to refuse to vote. We can no longer sit back. Something needs to be done before they pick us all off one by one." Mace is successfully keeping our involvement in Dial under wraps, which is the smartest move if we want the others to trust us.

Kylah considers his reasoning and gives a single nod. "So, what's the plan, then?" she asks. "If those four have the solid votes you claim they do, then all we have is Lunar, Iris, Mace, and me. That's a tie, and as you said…Finian is with *them*."

"That's where you two come in," Ashlea starts, raising her eyebrows. "Not only do we need your votes, but I believe if we all approach Finian together and try to reason with him…he'll *have* to vote our way in the tiebreaker."

"Why is everyone just writing off Cypher?" Lunar asks. I know he *claims* he's not going to vote, but do you actually believe that?"

I put a gentle hand on Lunar's shoulder. "We tried to get his vote, Lunar. He wouldn't budge. He had absolutely no interest in speaking with us at all. We couldn't even tell him how we'd *like* him to vote. He wouldn't hear any of it." I gulp nervously, and Lunar puts his head down, still doubtful. I scrunch to his level and whisper, "It's the best shot we've got, Lunar. And if we fail…at least we tried."

Mace nods. "Dead if we fail, and dead if we don't fight back. I don't know about you guys, but I'd rather die trying."

The group takes a moment to consider. Kylah bites her lip and stares at Lunar until an understanding passes between them. They both nod, and Kylah looks at Mace seriously. "What do you need us to do?"

A smile stretches across his lips.

"I thought you'd never ask."

Mace takes over the discussion, reviewing each intricate part of the plan. Having been the person behind the idea, I occasionally offer additional explanations, but my friends understand their tasks without any struggle.

Ashlea grips the sides of the couch. "Quick snack before we start our stakeout?"

The others nod and rise, taking her lead. Instead of following, I turn in the opposite direction and call over my shoulder. "You guys go ahead. I'm gonna clean up for a sec, then I'll meet you upstairs."

Mace nods before squeezing my hand, and I half-heartedly smile as I shuffle toward the bathroom. With our mission looming, it's difficult to block out the anxiety-filled cartwheels in my stomach. I'm shocked that the others aren't too nauseous to fuel themselves, but we don't know how long we will have to wait before Finian is alone. It could take hours, so I don't blame them for at least trying to satisfy their hunger cravings.

I run my hand along the smooth surface of the bathroom door before shifting it open. Approaching the sink, I tuck my hair behind my ears and take a deep breath. *This is going to work.* One arm clutches my nauseous stomach as the other splashes water on my face. I let the water cool down the heat on my cheeks and dry my skin with the bottom of my shirt. A faint memory flashes of Artemis and I flirting in this very spot, seemingly ages ago. This house is a time warp, with every day feeling like a week, so it may as well have been years ago. I turn away from the mirror before my mind lingers on Artemis for too long and shut my eyes as I push open the closest stall.

"Artemis?"

I freeze in the doorway. Mercedes is slumped in the corner with her arms wrapped around her legs. When she finally looks up from her lap, her hopeful gaze lands on my face. It takes half a second for her to register who I am before she turns away and hides her face, her body racking with sobs.

"Go away, skank."

I'd be delighted to.

But my legs won't acknowledge my urgency to escape, no matter how desperate my brain's cries are. Watching a once formidable, confident, no-bull-shit Mercedes curled on the floor in utter defeat…it twists my heart in a way I wish I could ignore. But as much as I've tried to convince myself that she's a monster, seeing her break down proves that Mercedes is just as human as the rest of us. She isn't an unfeeling, robotic villain.

She's a lonely, heartbroken warrior who, despite her declaration that making friends was foolish, made the mistake of trusting the one person in this house who was never going to save her.

It isn't fair. This entire game, she's isolated herself to spare her heart from this exact anguish. She refused the kindness of any of her housemates but risked it all with the one she genuinely trusted to take her to the end. And despite my jealousy with her inhuman beauty, ruthless honesty, and fierce competitiveness, she just wants to feel reciprocation on what every person desires.

Love.

"What…are you st–still…doing here? I told you to *leave!*"

Her cries break up her words, and an unmistakable flutter of guilt weighs down my chest. I remind myself that she's never accepted my compassion before. But this… it's different somehow. She usually speaks with her heart on her sleeve, but this time, her words lack the confidence she usually exudes. I can't leave her because, right now, I can see just how heartbroken she is. Mercedes may claim she doesn't want my sympathy, but I see right through her. Because Mercedes is many things.

A seasoned liar is not one of them.

Instead of following her orders, my heart wills me forward until I hover over her. With how loud her wails are, there's no way she could've heard me move closer. I know I'm risking everything by staying, but I can't help but imagine that I know how she feels. If I want any chance at survival, my relationship with Artemis is over. My heart has broken a thousand times over losing him, and he actually loves me.

He doesn't even love Mercedes. He's acted like she's been the center of his world since entering this house, but he wouldn't piss on her if she was on fire.

I squeeze my eyes shut, preparing for the worst as I squat beside her and extend an arm across her shoulder. I look away, terrified that she's going to pull through on her promise to end me if I ever touched her again. When she doesn't react, my stiff arm loosens, and I hug her close. She doesn't hug back. Instead, she falls into my embrace and sobs, not giving me a second glance.

My other arm wraps around her so I'm hugging her to the side of my chest. I close my eyes and let her weeps echo around the bathroom as I rub her back. I gulp away my shame at all the time I've wasted disdaining her. Because when all is said and done, Mercedes and I…we aren't that different, really. It's not her fault Artemis gave her the attention I craved from him. All my jealousy blows up into an explosion of empathy. Because she loved Artemis, and he broke her heart.

Just like mine.

Mercedes cries until she doesn't have any tears left. She still avoids looking at me as she wipes her eyes with the back of her hands. I offer her toilet paper to blow her nose, and despite taking the wad to her nose, she still manages to ignore my presence. I can't imagine what kind of hatred she holds toward me, since I am the woman she wanted to be. "You know," she grumbles at the wall. "I *actually* thought he was going to chase after me. After all we've been through, I thought that if I kept this door unlocked, he just might come back and apologize. But I'm just as big of a fool as the rest of you."

My hand pauses on her back, but I know better than to respond. Instead, I stay cuddled beside her, nodding. There's nothing in the world I could say to comfort her, so I don't waste my breath. My presence is the only tangible thing I can offer her. Despite the shallow part of my heart wanting to get as far away from her as possible, I can't leave her like this.

Because she's just as vulnerable and hopeless as the rest of us.

She takes a loud gulp before turning toward me. I freeze as she scans me up and down, but I don't cower. Mercedes bites her lip and shakes her head. "This is why he loves you. You know that, right?" She chokes on tears but doesn't back down. "Sitting here, comforting a monster who's been nothing but cruel to you...of *course* he fell in love with you."

"You're not a monster," I say before I can stop myself.

She laughs without humor. "I've spent this entire game trying to isolate myself so I wouldn't get hurt. And it was for *nothing*."

I keep rubbing her back while she gathers her breath. Once she finally does, her voice shakes. "But you know what I said is true. If Mace hurt you or Lunar was expelled, I wouldn't lift my pinky finger to offer you an ounce of comfort." She coughs to clear her throat, but the tears come anyway, making her voice shake. "Artemis could never love me because I'm not you. I'm not a naïve damsel in distress who would risk her own reputation to help somebody who had nothing left to live for." This time, she looks directly into my eyes, narrowing them with disgust. "And I hate you for it."

I nod, but I don't shy away from her. I watch her as she scans my reaction and scoffs.

"But a word of advice? From one girl to another?" She stretches, making me retract my arms from her. "This doesn't make you special. This doesn't make you the exception to the rule. If he did this to me, he won't think twice about doing it to you. I don't give a shit how he feels about you or what kind of friendship you *think* you have with him. I guarantee that whatever special, unique declarations of love he's given you… he's used the exact same words with me. And, like a child, I believed him." She frowns and looks away. "Do yourself a favor, Iris. Don't fall into his trap like I did."

It's the first time she's ever said my name, and there's no malice behind it. It takes a second to register it, but this is her way of paying back the favor. This is her way of showing that she respects me. I open my mouth to reply, but she beats me to the punch.

"He's going to screw you over, Iris. One way or another. And he'll feel *nothing* for it. Don't forget that."

I stare blankly at the floor, considering her words. My brain urges me to heed to her warnings. But my heart…it knows that Artemis loves me. He won't betray me like he did Mercedes. As much as she wants me to believe that I'm no different, I *know* that I am.

But when she rises, wiping her cheeks on her sleeve and reaching for the door, my stomach turns with uneasiness. She really is beautiful, even at her lowest. How could Artemis *not* love her?

Before she opens the door, I rise to my feet and call after her. "Mercedes?"

She turns toward me with a single eyebrow raised. A shock of nerves flush through me but I push past it. "Don't let Artemis ruin your spirit. You're still the fiercest competitor I've ever known."

Mercedes smiles, then opens the door wide. For half a second, I genuinely believe I've struck a chord in her, and we have a chance at being allies. I take a step forward, anxious for her response.

"Go fuck yourself, Iris."

I sink back against the wall as she shuts the door behind her, leaving me alone with nothing but her warning.

Artemis is going to screw you over. And he'll feel nothing for it.

Once I catch my breath and soothe my racing heartbeat, I rejoin my newest alliance in the communal bedroom, where the four of us lay quietly in our beds, taking turns watching the Executive bedroom door. My mind still whirls from my conversation with Mercedes, but Ashlea's urgency helps me focus on the more important matter of the hour: Ashlea's survival.

We've successfully pinpointed our housemates' whereabouts and wait anxiously for Destry and Artemis to leave Finian's bedroom. But the more time that passes, the less likely it feels that will happen. Privacy is extremely difficult to come across in the Enterprize, but it is nothing compared to the impossibility of staging a coup. As far as Dial knows, Mace and I will vote with them and secure the majority for a landslide victory over Ashlea. So if the four of us rise the second Destry and Artemis exit Finian's room, our blindside would be exposed.

A thought widens my eyes, and I turn to Ashlea, surprised I hadn't considered this before. "What if you just go in and ask to talk to Finian privately?" I suggest. "As far as they're concerned, you'll be dead by this time tomorrow. They'd think you're just saying your goodbyes…then we could wander in one by one. Make it look less shady."

Ashlea chuckles under her breath. "Lovely thought, Iris." She rolls her eyes with a grin. "Let's do it, then." Ashlea rises from her cot slowly, careful not to wake Lagiacrus or Cypher. She may be stealthy, but she still attracts Eno's attention from across the room. He watches her knock on the Executive door as the all-too-familiar pit forms in my stomach. *He doesn't deserve to die.* But if I want any chance at making it out of here alive, protecting a weak player over Ashlea's competitive potential would be disadvantageous.

But that doesn't make Eno's death any easier.

The door cracks open, and she disappears inside. My heart pounds in my ears as I wait for Destry and Artemis to evacuate. Just when I can't take it anymore, the doorknob rotates, and the two sweep out. I keep my eyes away from Artemis's but couldn't miss his miserable slump if I tried. He shuffles behind Destry, his shoulders dipping and his head hung, and descends the staircase to the bottom, gripping the rails for dear life.

The second the two are out of sight, Mace nods in my direction. I rise from my cot before tiptoeing to the iron door and cringe at the volume of my knuckles against the metal. But two knocks later, Ashlea leans through the threshold and yanks my hand into Finian's fortress, sparing me from waking the others.

Not two steps in does my breath catch in my throat. My eyes widen at the gaping hole to my right, directly at eye level. I point to the destruction and turn to Finian, at a loss for words.

"It was there when I came in a few hours ago," he answers, shrugging. I shake my head and lean forward, prompting him to continue, but he just stretches his lips into a thin line. "They wouldn't expand."

This is my chance.

I plop beside him on his bed, careful not to cause too much bounce and trigger pain from his chemical burns. "Doesn't it bother you that they don't tell you anything?" I start, trying to insinuate that he's disposable to his alliance without being blatantly obvious.

"I...I hadn't really thought about it. They've been nice, though. They've helped me through my punishment quite a bit."

I nod, but my mind is swimming. As long as we've been in Dial together, Finian's been a silent, obedient follower. At no point has he expressed an opinion of his own, so his intentions are a mystery. My heart rate skyrockets when I consider the importance of hiding Dial from Ashlea, all while trying to convince Finian that his alliance will turn on him. I just start contemplating how impossible our mission is when Mace's knocks break the tense silence. Finian's eyes widen as Ashlea leads Mace and Lunar through the door. They walk to the front of the bed purposefully, and Finian stiffens.

"Wha—what's going on?" Finian stutters.

Mace squats before him. "Look. Kylah will be here soon." He points to Ashlea and Lunar, standing side by side. "They've figured out that there's some sort of guys alliance. And unfortunately for you, they know you're in it."

Finian raises his eyebrows. "Excuse me?" Navigating the obstacles of our involvement in Dial is tricky, so Finian's confusion is understandable. Before he can out us, Ashlea jumps in.

"They want me out. Am I correct?" She towers over Finian, hands on her hips, but her eyes contort with obvious hurt.

Finian sends Mace a puzzled side-eye. "Um...they?"

Ashlea squats to Mace's level. "The boys. Destry, Lagiacrus, Artemis, and, by association, Mercedes. They're voting me out tomorrow, aren't they?"

Finian flicks his gaze to Mace and then me, desperate for answers. When we don't give them, he shrugs. "I don't know. I'm not them."

Ashlea shakes her head. "Come on, Finian. They've hung out with you the entire round. We *know* you're with them."

This time, I'm the only one receiving Finian's side-eye. He throws up his palms. "Okay...what does this have to do with me? I can't vote, remember?"

As if on cue, Kylah knocks on the door. Once I grab the handle to let her in, our entire squad surrounds Finian. He scans my group with wide eyes and backs away in terror.

"Guys, wait a second," Mace starts. He sends Finian a weak smile. "We're really not trying to gang up on you...that's not what this is. We merely have...a proposition. One which would benefit us all." Finian nods slowly, skeptical but willing to listen. "What Ashlea was trying to say is that she knows she's screwed. With four votes to get her out and you on *their* side, it doesn't really matter what anybody else does…she's gone."

"But she doesn't have to be," I cut in. Everyone turns their attention to me, and there's an embarrassed flutter in my stomach. I pause with a gulp, then scrunch my hands, determined to get the words out. "What I said earlier, about the wall…Finian, those guys don't tell you anything because you're expendable to them." I try to soften my tone so as not to offend him. "These weren't your nominations. You know that. *We* know that. There are no hard feelings on our end because we know they forced you into it. But what are they going to do with you when your reign is over tomorrow? Remember, you can't win Executive next round."

Quick to their defense, Finian interrupts. "Iris…no offense, but why do you care? I didn't put you up. Even if what you're saying is true…that these weren't necessarily *my* nominations…you're not on Death Row. Why does any of this matter to you?"

I look at all my friends and sigh. "Because not only did your selections impact my friends, but they also directly affected *me*. Those boys don't have my best interest at heart, and if they did, they wouldn't have put up the people closest to me." I make a nervous gulp. "Finian…they're coming for me. Whether I ignore it or not, I'm next on their list, and they're accomplishing that by picking off anyone who will protect me. But if they don't have the numbers, it doesn't matter what they want. Because we would control the house."

"Who's to say I don't already control the house?" Finian defends. "Why side with you guys when I'm already safe?"

"Because by this time tomorrow, you won't be," Kylah declares.

"But I will, though. Because according to Iris, they want *you* guys out. That gives me four more rounds of safety after tomorrow."

I take a deep breath. "Finian." I droop my eyes to look weak, pulling on his heartstrings. "Let's pretend you *don't* believe that you're expendable. You know what? Let's imagine that you don't even care if you are. How do you feel about being close to Artemis? Who is *by far* the biggest target in this house?" It hurts to stoop this low, but I don't have a choice. Artemis's crumbling reputation is perhaps our strongest point, and I can't abandon my loyalty to Mace now. "Whether you like it or not, he and Mercedes are *done*. This week, it won't affect the votes. She doesn't like Ashlea, so she'll vote her out on her own. But what about after that? You *know* you can't rely on her anymore, not after the crap that Artemis pulled. So, where does that leave you? In an alliance of four. Four people that, last time I checked, can't do logic competitions to save their asses."

To my shock and relief, Finian nods. *It's working.*

"What we offer is this," Ashlea leans forward, clasping her hands together. "The four of us are voting out Eno tomorrow. Cypher's abstaining, so he's as good as dead." The words leave her lips effortlessly, and a shiver shoots down my spine at how marginalized Cypher's impending death has become. She continues as if the note was nothing more than an inconvenience. "Unfortunately for you, that brings us to a tie. If you side with them, you are an enemy to us, and we will *not* show you mercy." My eyes widen. *Threatening him is not the move.*

"No," I interject. There's silence as everyone stares at me. "S….sorry, Ashlea," I touch her knee and smile gently before turning to Finian. "What she's trying to say is that if you vote with them, you will secure yourself in an alliance of four that will have you at the bottom of their totem pole. When it comes down to it, they will throw you under the bus at the *first* opportunity and will feel *nothing* for it. But if you vote with us…" I look at the others in my group and smile. "If you vote to keep Ashlea, you are one of us. Nothing in the past will be held against you. Your Death Row selections will have been forgotten, and we will accept you as one of our own. You'll be in an alliance of six, and we intend to keep you safe until the *end*. We may not all have the brute force that Lagiacrus and Artemis have, but Destry can't win a comp to save his life. He's been average at everything we've done so far…he won't get you anywhere.

"But with us…Mace is strong. He can compete with those guys, *and* he's smart. So am I." Adrenaline courses through me as my argument gains speed. "Lunar is small…that's gotta be useful in *something*. And Ashlea. She used to knit everything back home. If we need something with precision, she's our girl. And Kylah's strong too—she's proven strength in the physical stuff." I'm less confident in Kylah's usefulness, but I can't exclude her when we need to be a united front. "We won't keep anything from you, and you can make your own decisions. We'll work through things as a team with no leader. Everyone is equal."

Finian scratches his head and sighs.

"How can I trust you when you're betraying Dial?"

My stomach drops. "Dial?" Lunar asks. "Iris? What is he talking about?"

"It was an alliance," Mace starts, "formed in round 1. Those four brought me and Iris in." Ashlea backs away, covering her mouth. Kylah's eyes are wide, but her brows are raised with skepticism. "We were granted safety on the promise that we wouldn't expose the alliance. We named it Dial FM, for the initials in all our names. And we *were* loyal to them until three days ago."

I nod, biting my lip. "We wanted to tell you guys…" I clear my throat. "But we *couldn't*. Not if we wanted to keep you safe. But the second one of us was in danger, we jumped ship. We were loyal until we couldn't be."

"Which, by the way, shows that we *are* trustworthy," Mace says. "We kept our side of the deal until *they* violated it. These selections not only jeopardized our friend's safety but ours as well."

There's silence. Ashlea shakes her head, and Lunar leans back, taking deep breaths. I *hate* keeping secrets from them. I had hoped this reveal would soothe my constant nausea at lying to them, but that pit will never be extracted as long as I hide my last incriminating truth from Mace.

"So...you agreed to putting me on Death Row?" Ashlea asks, water welling in her eyes.

I shake my head wildly. "No...no! That's why we jumped ship!" I argue. "I *begged* them to pick somebody else. Cypher...I suggested Cypher! Then, I begged for Mercedes when they said no! But they wouldn't have it. Destry and Lagiacrus made it pretty clear that if I wasn't okay with it, I wasn't in the group anymore."

Finian tilts his head left and right. "Ehh...more or less."

I nod, scrubbing my palms against my temples. "I tried to save you, Ashlea. I did. But they wouldn't hear me out! They want you gone, and there's no changing their minds. So, when Death Row selections were finalized, Mace and I agreed that we wouldn't let you die without a fight. That's why we're here. It's also how we *know* you're in danger. Because we know how they're voting." Ashlea nods, watching my movements carefully. This isn't the end of our conversation, but there's no other option than to stick a pin in it to focus on the more pressing issue.

I turn to Finian with conviction. "Which is why we also know that *you're* in danger."

Mace sets his palm on the space beside Finian. "Finian, you didn't say a word at our last meeting. They've completely taken over your reign. And correct me if I'm wrong, but I hadn't seen them do anything as much as *acknowledge* your presence before you won Executive." Finian nods, his eyes softening. Mace keeps his voice gentle. "They don't care about you, Finian. We saw it from the beginning, and it's even clearer now. Remember, I was close with those guys at one point. You're not important to them unless you're useful."

Finian rubs his bald, glowing head, then bounces back from the pain of the touch. After a few deep breaths, he bites his lip, considering our offer.

"At the end of the day, it's simple," Ashlea declares. "Vote to keep me, and we'll have your back."

Finian stares at the ground. When he finally speaks, his voice is quivering. "And if they win next week? What will happen to me?"

Mace raises his eyebrows. "Do you really think they're going to come after you when Iris and I were the ones who orchestrated this coup?" I bite my lip, loathing the potential repercussions of our rebellion. But Mace's words are true. Finian won't be in danger. Even if he's on Death Row as a pawn, there's no chance he gets votes out. After winning a competition that was one big trick question, nobody will let him pull that off again. If it wasn't apparent before, it's clear as day now. *He's never going to win anything again.* As harsh as the reality is, the boys in Dial aren't going to target somebody who isn't a threat.

"If it helps," Lunar pokes his head into the circle. "I doubt Artemis is going to be very useful now that he's *blinded* by his love for Iris." He puckers his lips to mock Artemis, and we all smile at the dig. I force my lips to stay curved for longer than the others, but my stomach folds. I'm not only letting Arty suffer, but I'm *encouraging* his mistreatment.

But what other option do I have?

"And let me just say that if anything coming out of that man's mouth is true, he's *technically* more on our side than theirs. You know…if he *actually* loves Iris." Mace's words twist a knife in my heart, but he raises a solid point. When Finian's eyes clear, I bite my bottom lip to keep from another smile. *This might actually work.*

"I need to sleep it over," Finian says, leaning forward and heaving a deep breath. "I see where you guys are coming from…I do. I just…need some time, okay? Can you give me that?" The group of us dart our concerned eyes at one another and nod in unison. With Finian this close to switching sides, pressuring him further would do more harm than good. Now, with the small victory of turning Finian's no into a maybe, there's nothing more we can do but rest.

I rise and lock onto Finian's eyes as my teammates file behind me. "Take all the time you need, Finian. Just remember…we'll have your back. Even if you betray Dial, they'll have bigger fish to fry. But if you stay with them, it's only a matter of time before they dispose of you. Really…they can't keep you safe for long when their numbers are dwindling."

He nods and gives a weak grin, insinuating that our time is finished. I bow my head slightly. "Thanks for hearing us out. Have a good night." My group leaves in pairs to avoid raising further suspicion, so I couple up with Mace. I squeeze his hand as we cross the threshold, and my brain fights to convince me we have a chance. But my anxiety blocks all rational thought, making my teeth chatter against the confines of my sucked-in lips. *If Finian doesn't vote with us, we're dead.* Even if he does, a line will have been drawn in the sand, and all hell will break loose.

By this time tomorrow, nobody will be safe.

Mace kisses my forehead and settles on the bed across from me, having moved his shoes to the pillow earlier in the day to displace Artemis to another cot. I slowly fall onto my blankets and shove my legs between the cool, soft sheets, scanning the room for the most hated man in the Enterprize. Most of my housemates are asleep, so it's difficult to distinguish one heap of blankets from another. But even with the added obstacle of the dark, it's easy to find him.

His bloody knuckle gives him away.

A bullet pierces my chest at the lines of dried blood growing more distinguishable as my eyes adjust. The Enterprize drywall never stood a chance against his rage.

I wince as I watch Artemis on the cot diagonal from mine. He stuffs a pillow over his head, chest rising and falling much faster than sleep would allow. I tremble, trying to force my breathing to calm. Looking up at the ceiling is all I can do to stop the moisture threatening to cloud my vision.

All he ever did was love me. *And all I ever did was lie.*

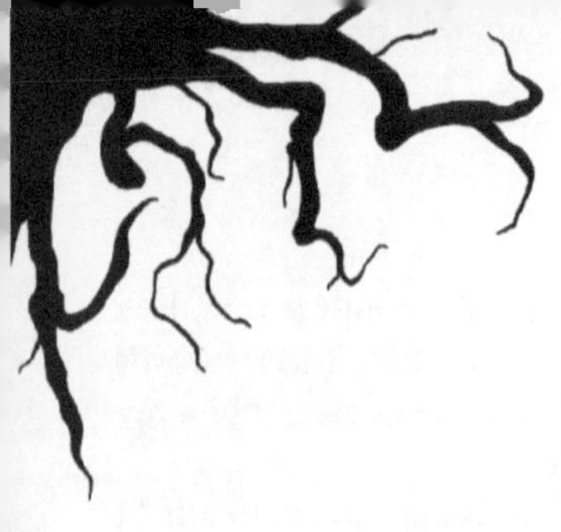

Chapter 43

I wake from cold sweats. Having only slept two hours, it's no surprise that half of my housemates are still asleep. But how can one rest when one of their dearest friends will be dead within the evening?

I gulp, but the boulder in my throat refuses to dislodge. *How am I supposed to look at Eno?* Somebody who has only ever offered kindness and sacrifice. *And I have just rallied a coup d'état to kill him.* Beyond my shame, I imagine every worst-case scenario of our plea and can't escape the plausible repercussions of our defiance. Whatever competition awaits, my side *must* emerge victorious.

I spend the early hours convincing myself that my group is more competitive than Dial, but the pit in my stomach confirms that it's nothing more than a fever dream. If tonight has anything to do with strength, the odds are entirely against us. The only fact keeping me sane is that Ashlea is more competitive than Eno. That is indisputable. Eno would only ever emerge triumphant in a competition about storytelling. But the Enterprize would *never* challenge us to anything of that sort of comfort.

I stretch my legs out of my sheets, abandoning any notion that sleep will retake me. Shuffling through the room, my eyes betray my mind's wishes and flash to exactly where they shouldn't.

My jaw clenches, and I freeze. Artemis hasn't moved since last night, still using his bruised and bloodied knuckle to grip a pillow against his face. If his words to me were true, I'm not the source of his despair. My heart knows his hurt, and he clearly regrets stringing Mercedes along. On top of this, his actions will have disastrous consequences for his friends, specifically for their survival. But as confident as I am in his loyalty to me, each forced step descending the staircase makes doubt creep in further.

How dare you tell her you love her when you've said it to me hundreds of times. As long as I have known Mercedes, she's never been a liar. Artemis personally endorsed her honesty to me in solitary confinement. He went as far as to claim that in the chance of his expulsion, I should shift all my trust to Mercedes. After helping her in the bathroom yesterday, I finally saw the side of her that Artemis must have been trying to emphasize. But even after my efforts with her, she still gave me the cold shoulder in the end. I shake my head, because I clearly don't know the first thing about Mercedes.

She must have been lying about Artemis loving her. I shake my head because none of it matters. Given the circumstances, Artemis's personal life should be the least of my worries. But if he's lying to me about loving her…

What else has he been lying about?

My paranoia vanishes a step onto the ground floor when my eyes land on Eno's. I tense when he waves me to join the others for breakfast. Remembering what I've rehearsed with Curi in the art of deceit, I force a smile and approach Eno casually, letting my legs sway easily before me. Lagiacrus and Lunar are beside him, but I approach the opposite end, where Mace leans back in his chair. He catches my lingering gaze and winks, patting the seat beside him.

"What have I missed?" I grin, grabbing a roll from Mace's ration bin. Eno shrugs and takes a roll of his own.

"I feel like I'm the one who's missed something," Eno raises his eyebrows. My stomach drops to the Earth's core before he smiles. "Looks like kids these days are testing the laws of physics with their chairs." He gestures to Mace and Lunar, only the back legs of their chairs on the floor. "How would I even go about *attempting* such a risk? I'd tumble to the floor and crack my neck on the first try!" Everyone laughs, making my stomach ease. *Of course, he isn't on to us.* He's simply the same kind, optimistic, lighthearted man he's always been. I gulp nervously between cackles and relax when Mace picks up the conversation for me.

"Aw, you'd be okay, Eno. A couple shattered bones in your lumbar spine shouldn't be a problem, right?" We continue laughing and it strikes me how odd our group is. Before long, I remember that Lagiacrus is in the dark about our impending betrayal. Regardless, it's strange laughing alongside him when, in a matter of hours, he'll want us dead. Mace has no problem communicating with him, effortlessly hiding our plan. But whatever Mace's acting does to soothe my crippling anxiety, Lunar's obvious tells negate. My brother's leg shakes against the carpet at unprecedented speed, and no matter how hard he grips his fists under the table, I know it's only a matter of time before he ruins the entire operation.

Desperate not to blow our cover, I grasp at straws to keep the conversation moving. "Say, Eno. Got any other ancient stories for us? How were things back when the Ascendancies were one?" Mace rocks forward in his chair from laughter, making the front legs crash against the floor. Lagiacrus shakes his head with a grin, and Eno smiles with all his teeth. The Ascendancies haven't been together in hundreds of years, so the playful jab calls out Eno's "crippling" age. Lunar laughs forcefully, just ingenuine enough to catch Eno's attention. He watches Lunar for a single second before ignoring the slip-up and addressing the group.

"Well, little one," he begins, placing his chin in his fist, "it was a simpler time. Some might call it *the good ole days*." We laugh in unison, but I can't stop studying Lunar in my periphery. He darts his eyes from the staircase to the bathroom, looking for an escape. Lagiacrus and Mace are totally engaged in Eno's story, but I only allot a portion of my attention to his words. The majority is focused on one reality.

Lunar needs to get out of here.

"You see, Iris, back then, there was this thing called 'food.' You wouldn't believe it now, but *everyone* had it." Eno smiles and holds onto the table for dear life, trying to lean his chair back but only getting the front two legs a couple centimeters off the floor. "And me…well, I was the epitome of health! I had bigger muscles than Crissie, here!" He points to Lagiacrus, who bursts out laughing at the nickname. With the symphony of cackling, it's easy for the others to miss Lunar's breakdown. But when you've known him for thirteen years, it's hard to forget that full-body trembles are his giveaway for *lying*.

My little brother takes hold of the table and spreads a wide smile on his lips. "You've done it, Eno. You made me laugh so hard I've peed my pants. Now, if you'll excuse me," he jokes. Eno dramatically bows over the table as Lunar turns on his heels. My brother walks calmly across the stretch of the living room, but once he crosses the threshold into the bathrooms, I know he's sprinting into a stall.

"On that note," I laugh, "I'm gonna shower." Rising as inconspicuously as possible, I shuffle toward the iron entrance, my insides quivering with every step.

The second I close the restroom door, I search the sinks and showers and confirm our privacy. Running to the only locked stall, I slam my fists against the cold, smooth surface.

"Lunar!" I shout. "It's Iris! Open the door!"

Half a second later, I tumble into the stall with Lunar. He slams the sound-proof iron door behind me, only his quick, shallow breaths filling the otherwise quiet void. He grips the ends of his hair through his fingers as tears stream down his cheeks. He collapses to the floor as his weeps crescendo into blood-curdling screeches. *This reaction can't just be for Eno.* Lunar's been denying his grief since our capture. Eno's death is just the final straw.

"Shhhh. It's gonna be okay, Lunar," I plead, trying to convince myself that the words are true. Regardless of reality, I have a responsibility to protect my brother. The pain piercing my heart is outweighed by my instincts to protect him, so I easily ignore the ache in my chest and force myself to believe in the words. I hug Lunar tight, trying to stabilize the young, innocent boy shaking in my arms. "If either of us wants to make it out of here, Eno has to go. Better to do it now before…" I gulp. "Before it's even harder."

Lunar shakes his head on my shoulder. "No! It's…not…fair!" he cries. "Why are we doing this to him? What has he ever done to us?"

"Shhh, Lunar. We aren't doing anything to him…" I back away and motion toward the camera, which is pointed right at us, a red-light blinking. I grimace. "*They* are."

Lunar's breaths still, and his body turns rigid. He escapes my grasp slowly, inching toward the camera. A nerve in him snaps, and he rises to his feet, screaming and stomping. "Are you *happy* now? I know you assholes are watching…that man's blood is on *your* hands. For what? Rationing out a few extra bags of rice?" His voice is rabid. "You're monsters! All of you!"

He reaches for the camera and yanks, growling as he struggles.

"LUNAR, STOP!" I scream, grabbing his waist and holding him back. "They'll kill you!"

"Who cares! They'll…going…to kill…us all!" He fights my grasp until he's blue in the face. I plead with him to stop for my sake and Curi's, but nothing keeps him from flinging his body toward the far-right corner of the bathroom stall.

Nothing but Eno's voice in the washroom chamber.

"Lunar?" He knocks twice. "You in there, bud?"

My brother's body goes rigid, and his eyes widen with fear. I put a finger to his lips, begging him to quiet down, but there's no point. These rooms are designed so that the occupants on the outside cannot hear those on the inside. Eno's voice may be clear as day, but there's no chance he could have overheard Lunar's temper tantrum. *Then why is he here?*

"Lunar, listen to me," I say directly, locking onto his dilated pupils. "We have to let him in. There's too much risk in locking him out and letting his mind wander. So, you have to get a hold of yourself. Remember what we've taught Curi?"

He nods mechanically, then wipes his face on his shirt. Eno knocks again, his rhythm getting more urgent. Once Lunar shakes out his arms and legs, I grab his shoulders and hold him at attention.

"When I open that door, it won't make any sense to him why I'm in here with you. Just…say that you're homesick. That you miss Curi, you miss the Central Ascendancy, and you wish we weren't at the Enterprize. All of that's true anyway, so you wouldn't even be lying. Can you do that?"

He nods with determination and makes his body slack on command, trembles fading to nothing after three deep breaths. If not for his puffy eyes and flushed skin, there'd be no evidence of his panic attack. We hold hands and nod with finality.

I open the door slowly, painting a smile on my face. I part my lips to insert some fake explanation, but Eno ignores my gesture as he rushes in and shuts the barrier behind him.

"You know, I appreciate your assistance, Eno," Lunar effortlessly quips, his voice only shaking on the last word. "But I really do know how to use the toilet on my own. I *am* a teenager, you know."

Eno smiles and forces Lunar into a hug. Shocked, Lunar's arms hang limply at his sides until he registers the gesture and wraps them around Eno, leaving me with my jaw on the floor.

"Um…thanks?" Lunar laughs. "What's gotten into you?" Eno's lips are stretched into a thin line when they separate, juxtaposed against Lunar's fake smile. Eno scans the both of us, then shuts his eyes and sighs.

"It's me." His pause makes the room so silent that I can hear my heartbeat. Finally, he opens his eyes and takes a deep breath. "Isn't it?"

The world starts spinning. "Wha—what?" I stammer.

"Being old, I've seen a thing or two. And when the legs go…I know what that means."

I step back for Lunar to take the floor, but he's frozen. I wait for him to explain his homesickness, but the longer we stand in silence, the more obvious the lie will be. My heart pinches as Eno's eyes beg to know how much time he has left in this world. And regardless of the necessity of it being a blindside...I cannot bring myself to lie to him. After all that he's done for me and Lunar...who am I to rob him of his last dying wish?

On the same wavelength, Lunar and I throw our arms around Eno and squeeze. Lunar convulses from his tears, but I force my emotions to the back of my brain and clench my fists to fight oncoming trembles. *All I can offer is an explanation.* With my arms around Eno, I ramble, hoping my words will string into coherent sentences.

"Eno...I don't know what to say...they've taken over the house! If we don't take a stand now...oh Eno, I'm so sorry! This is all my fault!"

"Did you guys turn me in?"

His words are calm, which makes them all the more chilling. I freeze at the accusation and then let go of our embrace. "Did I, what?"

Lunar follows my lead and backs away, rubbing his eyes. Eno stares severely in my direction and asks the question again.

"Are *you* the ones that turned me in?"

I scrunch my nose and shake my head. "What? No, of course not. I've never even left my house!"

Eno nods. "Great. And are *you* the one that rationed extra food to hidden families?"

I shake my head again, this time with less aggression. "No...no, I didn't."

"And did you design the Enterprize? Or create the Authority, or engineer the Hage, the death penalty, or anything else in this cursed world?"

I gently shake my head, and Eno nods with finality.

"So, it's not your fault then. Is it?"

As hard as I try to keep a straight face, moisture blurs my vision.

He's not accusing us.

He's forgiving us.

"You two listen to me *very* carefully. I am the one who broke the law. I am facing the consequences of those actions. Neither of you put me here, and neither of you is responsible for my death. I'm here because *I* broke the law. And you wanna know something? If I won this whole thing and went back home, *I'd do it all over again.* I'd find a struggling family and assign them more rations. I'd help each and every Assessment refugee in Miasmis. And with a closer eye on me than before, I'd be dead in a week." He shakes his head. "I will *not* change who I am to stay alive. This world...it was never meant for someone like me. It was only a matter of time before I was expelled...did anyone here actually believe I was going to win?"

A tear falls down my cheek. Eno is such an honorable man that he will proudly march to his death and hold nobody else accountable. His love for human life...it makes me break down. I grab onto Lunar and cry, unable to stop the waterworks from flowing. Letting Eno go is the hardest thing I've ever had to do, and his forgiveness and understanding make it nearly impossible to go through with. But his eyes are intentional and without pity. This isn't a last-ditch effort to keep himself alive. Maybe the audience will think he's manipulating us, but my brain and heart finally agree. Eno's consoling us because he doesn't want us to feel guilty.

He's a great man that should never have been sent to the Enterprize.

"Eno," I whisper, my voice shaking.

"Please. Don't explain yourselves. I understand." He pats my back, forgiving me with his eyes. "I've told you before, and I'll tell you again. I may not be *that* old…but I *have* lived a full life. There's nothing waiting for me back home. As far as I'm concerned, you people here are the only family that I've got. But you two…" he puts his arms around Lunar and my shoulders. "You have your little sister." My heart shatters, and I cover my eyes, my palms immediately filling with moisture. "Curi is watching this right now, and she's so proud of you both. For how you're holding up, for how you're fighting…she needs you. You two have something to live for. You make it out of here, and she'll be waiting with open arms. But please…don't worry about me. I knew the consequences of treason. The fact that I was granted a little extra time, regardless of the circumstances…well, if I wasn't sent here, I wouldn't have met all you wonderful people."

"I'm so sorry, Eno." My mouth is suddenly so dry that I can hardly get the words out. "We're so lucky to have known you. You're a great man…you've made the Enterprize…"

"Less of a death palace," Lunar smiles, wiping his eyes.

Eno grins and shakes his head. "I am the lucky one for having been your friend." He chokes up and blinks his eyes rapidly to keep from crying. "No more tears from you two. You hear me? Let's enjoy these last few hours together. Okay?"

We both nod and even though our plan may fail, I'm grateful that Eno will forgive us regardless of the outcome. We pull him in one last time and hold on tight, never wanting to let go.

Several minutes pass of us hugging before Eno turns for the door. "You're good kids. Don't let this game get to you." He opens the iron barrier, but one final agonizing question escapes my lips just before he passes through the threshold.

"Eno!" I say a little too loudly. He turns around, the door still open, and raises his eyebrows. I take a deep breath and let the words flow. "What Ascendency were you in?"

When Eno smiles, a shiver travels down my spine.

"I lived in the Western Ascendency."

The door closes gently behind him.

Chapter 44

Twenty minutes. That's all the time left before I vote out a man who never deserved to be here.

I've been sitting with the information connecting Eno to Artemis's refugee operation for hours, battling whether to divulge it to Arty before it's too late. I sigh, unscrewing the cap of my water bottle. Should Artemis get a chance to thank the man who ensured years of his survival, even if it means compromising my loyalty to Mace?

Lunar leans back until his head is in my lap, taking up the length of my bed. Despite the comfort and familiarity he brings, my stomach twists with nausea. I reach my fingertips to my lips, but I've already bitten the nails to their stubs.

Within the hour, Ashlea could be dead.

Then why can't I stop thinking about Artemis?

Because I still love him, even if I can't sort out the extent of it. With Ashlea, there's nothing else that can be done. We have our votes secured, and we just have to hope Finian flips sides. But with Artemis…the only thing keeping him from thanking Eno is *me*.

Eno didn't even know Artemis, and he sacrificed his life for Arty's survival. If I wait to tell Artemis until it's too late, I'm no better than the Authority. But telling him could expose our entire operation, with the added drama that Artemis is not allowed to speak with me. However, divulging this *before* the vote would make him think Eno's life was in serious danger…which it is, but Artemis can't know that. He'd catch on immediately. Why would I risk everything to tell him something that has nothing to do with the game?

If I tell Artemis, he'll know the vote has split and the alliance is finished. He'll also feel much more connected to Eno and likely do anything to ensure his safety, even if it means throwing me under the bus. But if Artemis would die for me, why would he try and disrupt my plans when his meddling could get me killed?

Another thought disrupts my panic. *Eno knows that he has a connection to Artemis.* His eyes were a dead giveaway. Since I never told anybody about Artemis's past, Eno must have known about it for years. If that's the case, does Artemis know? I shake my head because if Artemis knew that Eno was responsible for his refugee operation success, he would have told me in solitary confinement. He claimed he didn't know who was helping his family. *And Artemis would never lie to me.*

Despite my brain highlighting the consequences of exposing our plan and screaming at me that Artemis can never know about Eno, my heart wrenches when my best friend rises from his cot, wipes dried blood off his knuckle, and shuffles to the staircase with his head hung.

And despite knowing better, I decide to chase after him.

I rise from my cot, fingers now bleeding from my filthy way of coping. But one step forward, I'm stopped by the image of Ashlea, burying her head in her hands. She's scrunched on her sheets, her eyebrows furrowed as she holds back tears. I stand frozen, looking to the stairs as Artemis descends, then at Ashlea with her inconsolable panic.

And for the first time, my brain beats out my heart.

I sit beside Ashlea and hug her on my left, making it seem as though my intention in getting up was always to comfort her.

"Hey, it's going to be okay," I whisper. Her body heaves in massive breaths as she focuses on keeping her tears inside. I lean in so my lips touch her ear and whisper so only she can hear. "We have the votes. You're gonna make it."

She shakes her head, her black strands gliding across my nose. Ashlea is too bright to blindly accept the elementary reassurances I would typically promise Curi and Lunar. Instead, she sees through my strong exterior and shares in my fear of her possible death. She takes a deep but shaky breath before matching my volume.

"Do you think they're on to us?"

I shrug. "I don't see why they would be. As far as they know, the vote will be unanimous. They shouldn't suspect otherwise."

"But with the drama this week…maybe they're onto us. It's not like you've been hanging out with them as much as you used to."

I swallow hard and force my voice to stay steady. "I never really talked to them much to begin with. I *only* hung out with Artemis. And with what happened…they know I can't talk to him anymore." I rub her back reassuringly. "We just have to hope Finian's chosen our side."

"Ten minutes until the vote!" Lagiacrus's voice echoes from the bottom floor. Ashlea tenses, and her eyes gloss over, so I shake her and smile.

"You're fine. It's gonna be fine," I reassure her. Lunar joins in, moving to her bed and hugging her from the other side. I whisper so many encouragements that I actually believe she has a chance at safety.

Until Destry exits the Executive bedroom with Finian on his heels.

"Oh, god," whispers Ashlea, eyes dilating in horror.

Destry walks mechanically, seemingly on a mission. Finian follows with his eyes on the floor, and a shiver shoots through my body.

I'm too late. Destry got to him.

Ashlea begins to cry, and my body involuntarily shoots off the mattress toward the two guys.

Their pace quickens, but I tap Finian's shoulder from behind.

"Hey, can we talk for a second?"

Destry turns on his heel and stares directly at me, eye contact not faltering. "No, I don't think that will be necessary."

I raise my eyebrows and glance at Finian, but he keeps his gaze on the floor like a coward. I gulp before finding my voice. "I was talking to Finian."

"I know," Destry smiles condescendingly. "He seems to be the popular man of the hour, don't you think?" He tilts his head. "Isn't that *strange*, Iris?"

I step back and force a menacing grin. "*I* haven't spoken to him today. So, if something's strange on *your* end, perhaps you should reflect on why that is? Something fishy going on, Destry?"

He laughs, not at all defensive. "Well, this has been nice." He grabs Finian's hand and pulls. "You can talk to him all you want after the vote. Right now, it can't be *that* important. He's kind of busy."

My jaw drops, and I look at Finian, but he won't meet my eyes. Desperate for his cooperation, I dig in. "Finian has a mouth. Surely, he can speak for himself?"

Finian flinches, but Destry's smile widens. "Why are you so desperate to speak with my friend, Iris? Is something wrong?"

"Why are *you* so desperate to keep him away from me, *Destry*?" I quip without skipping a beat. "*Is something wrong?*"

Destry shakes his head before dragging Finian toward the staircase. Finian slumps awkwardly, unable to keep pace with his puppet master. I don't know how Destry's got an inkling about the blindside, but with less than ten minutes until the vote, that's the least of my worries. I push forward to pursue him but halt as Ashlea sprints past me and yanks Destry's arm.

"You don't have a monopoly on Finian's time. So how about you scoot your ass to the living room and let somebody else talk to him? Or is your head so far up his ass you can't find your way out?"

"Excuse me?" Destry replies, smirking. But his arm gives the slightest tremble, deteriorating the threatening image he's trying to put on.

"I will be dead in ten minutes. *You* will be alive. I don't know why you care so much about who Finian talks to, but maybe back off for, like, ten seconds and let the man breathe."

"Look, *sweetheart*. Finian is following me on his own free will. We were going down together because we're friends."

"If that's the case, why hasn't he spoken this entire conversation?" Ashlea spits back.

"Five minutes, guys!" Lagiacrus calls from the living room. I back away from the confrontation, allowing Ashlea to take charge. I stand near her for support but hide in her shadow so she can say her piece.

The two men stare at her, but Finian has a twinge of regret in his eyes. Destry steps toward Ashlea and puffs out his chest. "Whatever you have to say to Finian, you can say to me."

Ashlea narrows her eyes and smiles. She spreads her stance, hands on her hips. "My pleasure." She turns to Finian and shifts her expression to desperation, pressing her eyebrows together and letting her lips shake. "Finian, I *urge* you to open your eyes. If you've never seen it before, there's no way that you can ignore it now. Destry is *controlling* you. He is not your friend! He's using you to get what he wants! Has he ever paid the *least* bit of attention to you before? Has he ever wanted you for more than your vote?"

"This is ridiculous," Destry declares. "We need to get downstairs before the Authority kill us!"

"Then, by all means, take the lead!"

Destry pulls Finian down the first step, but Ashlea is directly on their heels. I grab onto Lunar so he doesn't get too close, but with how rigid his stance is, I know he's in no rush to follow. We don't let too much of a gap form, though. Regardless of our discomfort, we have to beat the clock so the Authority don't attack us.

Ashlea's shouts don't stop the entire journey to the living room, even as she takes her place in front of her death row cushion. I take the empty seat beside Mace and force Lunar to my opposite side, not removing my hand from his.

Destry sits closest to Finian on the blue settee furthest from the Enterprize entrance. With one glance at the pair, Ashlea erupts.

"Screw this!" With a minute and a half on the clock, she lunges forward and takes the center of the room. I tense at her impending monologue, so Mace slides his arm across my shoulder and pulls me closer to him.

"You can't ignore this anymore. *None of you.*" Ashlea spins, gesturing to every convict in the living room. Her eyes are rabid with fury, and saliva flings from her lips with every syllable. "Destry is playing everyone, and if you don't stop him soon, he's going to take every single one of you down and feel *nothing* for it." Destry smiles with all his teeth and crosses a leg so his heel rests lazily on his opposite knee. Ashlea snarls. "He pretends to have your best interest at heart, but he doesn't! He convinces you all that moves will benefit you when they only help *his* game. He doesn't care about you! Don't you see? He's going to kill us all!"

Instead of shouting a rebuttal, Destry leans back into the sofa, the cushions engulfing him. He looks directly at Ashlea with his cheeky grin and then *winks.* "Better sit down before that clock hits zero, sweetie."

Finally, she drops onto her settee and runs a shaky hand through her long black locks. Jaws around the room are on the floor, and Mercedes creases her brow with a mixture of shock and curiosity. Lagiacrus watches Destry, hoping for an explanation. His master offers him none. Eno sits with perfect posture on his Death Row sofa, refraining from engaging in Ashlea's last-ditch effort for survival. My alliance members are frazzled from the shout-fest, Kylah with wide eyes on the ground and Lunar trembling against my arm. The only person with little interest in Ashlea's meltdown is the one who has the most emotional stake in this decision and doesn't even know it.

He looks at the ground blankly from across the living room, scrubbing scabs away from his bloody knuckle until the clock strikes zero.

"CONVICTS, YOUR VOTING ORDER HAS BEEN SELECTED BY RANDOM DRAW. WHEN YOUR NAME IS ANNOUNCED, MAKE YOUR WAY TO THE SECOND FLOOR. INSTRUCTIONS WILL FOLLOW."

I look at my housemates and count twelve of us. Thankfully, everyone made it in time, and there will be no premature murders for disobedience.

Yet.

"LAGIACRUS."

Lagiacrus exits the living room, climbing the steps one at a time. The air thickens with each passing stride, and the room becomes so silent that thumping heartbeats can be heard bouncing out of my neighbors' chests. I squeeze Mace's palm, and he gives a strong, decisive nod. I smile back, then bite my lip to keep it from quivering.

"MERCEDES."

One by one, my housemates cast their votes. When Mace leaves, I use both arms to grip Lunar tight, not letting him go until his name is called.

With just three names left, a drip of sweat falls down my cheek.

"CYPHER."

I freeze, holding onto Mace to steady myself. With the apprehension of our blindside, Cypher's presence totally slipped my mind. When his name is called, he simply spreads his arms wide across the neck of the sofa and crosses his legs at the ankles. I'd think he didn't hear his name if he didn't roll his eyes at the nearest camera.

My lips part, ready to scream at Cypher that he's just *asking* to be killed. But just as quickly as they separate, my lips crash back together and lock shut.

Cypher's vote would be the flip of a coin and could ruin our plan to keep Ashlea alive. I look at the floor and consider how his disobedience *would* mean one less person to compete against, so fighting for his cooperation would be disadvantageous for not only me, but also my alliance.

A lump lodges in my throat, and a bitter tang spreads across my tongue.

What have I become?

With a minute and a half remaining, Artemis punches the left shoulder of his couch, and then leans toward Cypher. "You've proved your point, man," Artemis shouts. "*Please,* get up!"

Cypher doesn't even acknowledge Artemis's presence. Instead, he takes a deep breath and closes his eyes, falling further into the couch cushions.

"Are you all really gonna just let this happen? Seriously?" Artemis scans the room, but nobody makes eye contact. Mercedes is the only person who speaks up, but even she struggles to keep her voice steady.

"We don't need to take advice from a monster."

Artemis wrings his hands through his hair, bunching his fists so tightly that the scabs on his knuckles reopen. With ten seconds remaining, he scoots away from Cypher and smushes Destry into the couch's arm.

When the clock strikes zero, Mace hoists Lunar over his shoulder, yanks my wrist, and races us to the kitchen island. We hit the carpet behind the ration counter as the iron door flings open, crashing against the wall behind it. The collision pierces my ears, and I tremble beneath Mace's protective arm as five Authority agents march into the kitchen with automatic rifles. I cover Lunar's eyes but fail to shield my own.

My muscles slacken when I see him. I flatten against the floor, jaw gaping. The rest of the living room scatters in my periphery, but I can't peel my eyes from the murderer.

Ethan.

He leads the pack of Authority agents, sprinting into the living room with his rifle yielded. There's screaming as my housemates fling themselves over the sofas, curling up in various corners of the room to avoid the agent's paths. Juxtaposed against the other convicts, Cypher squeezes his eyes shut and leans forward, opening his chest like a canvas for the Authority to paint.

He's so still that only the motions of his chest rising and falling indicate that he's alive.

Ethan leads the agents to the living room, their rifles aimed at Cypher from various angles. I force my hand harder against Lunar's eyes and press mine shut to brace for the bullet storm.

BANG!

CRACK!

BOOM!

I shake as the gunshots reverberate in my bones. The agents shoot until they run out of ammo, so there's twenty seconds of continuous fire. Twenty seconds of shooting at a *stagnant, defenseless* target who *didn't fight back*. Tears fall out of my eyes from squeezing them so hard. My body trembles so intensely that Mace holds my legs down to stop them from kicking the ration counter.

"It's okay, it's okay," he whispers, rubbing circles on my leg with his thumb. "They'll be gone soon. They *have* to be. See? They're leaving now."

Rocking back and forth against Mace, I start humming to block out everyone's screams. But the warped sound transports me to an alternative reality where Lunar had struggled against his cuffs when captured. In real time, Ethan has no remorse marching out of the Enterprize with our housemate's blood on his hands, so I struggle to breathe as I mentally replace Cypher's body with Lunar's. I cover my ears to completely eliminate the blood curdling screeches around me and gasp for air beneath Mace's embrace.

My black eyelids show rewound footage of myself from a bird's eye view, watching my body cower while Mace shielded me from ricocheting bullet shells. Despite every way my heart has been pulled in the last week, the only two people I care about protecting from this massacre are Mace and Lunar. I almost forget Artemis even *exists*. My heart pulses only to keep the two huddled around me alive, and I'm terrified I won't even be able to do that.

Once the coast is clear, the living room fills slowly back up, and I realize I hadn't even heard the door close when the agents left. Out of body, I watch my housemates crawl back to the couch. There's not enough clean space for everyone, so a few sit on the floor around Finian's Executive seat. Kylah hurls on the carpet after one look at the blood-soaked sofa, so I force myself not to look where Cypher sat. The rest of the convicts steer clear of Cypher's couch entirely. Mace rubs my back and mumbles something about returning to the living room, but I can't distinguish any of his words from one another. Instead, I press my hands against my ears and shut my eyes tight, convinced that the brutality isn't over. There's only one voice that can bring me to attention.

One creaky, metallically robotic voice.

"IRIS."

My body stiffens, and I stop breathing.

The vote. I have to vote.

But the second my dissociation started, I forfeited all control over my nervous system. My brain tells my legs to unbuckle and climb to the second floor, but the direction doesn't register. Instead, I continue rocking back and forth until Mace's shouts finally break through my consciousness.

"IRIS!" He shakes my shoulders until I finally look into his eyes. "You have to get up! You have to go! *Now!*"

I climb to my knees and plant my legs on the solid floor, but it feels like the ground is moving beneath me. I wobble until I trip and plummet to the floor, but Mace grabs me before I collide with the carpet. Abandoning any notion that I can make it on my own, Mace tosses me over his shoulder and races out of the kitchen. It's hard to distinguish one feature from another through the spinning house as Mace springs toward the steps. But when I spare a glance in Cypher's direction, my eyes roll to the back of my head.

Blood. The entire stretch of carpeting around the massacre is drenched with it. A stump of flesh sits in the middle, making me gag. Even worse, the whole length of the couch is painted dark red from the blood. My eyes linger a second too long, and I gasp at the pulpy figure in the center of the sofa.

Cypher isn't even human. The flood of bullets removed his humanity entirely, and I can hardly recognize him or locate a single part of him. Chunks of his body lay separate from his torso. His head is missing, having fallen over the edge of the couch. His intestines flood out of his abdomen, and I finally identify the flesh on the carpet as his *forearm*. I'm dizzy all over again and throw up over Mace's shoulder as he climbs the steps.

In any other case, Cypher's remains would have been removed. But the Enterprize is sending us a message.

Disobedience is not taken lightly.

Mace plants me in front of the iron door and heaves it open. He stretches a corner of his t-shirt to my lips and wipes so hard I nearly tumble to the floor. "Iris!" He grabs my elbow, holding me in place. "IRIS, LISTEN TO ME!" My eyeline finally focuses on his face, and a rush of sensation returns to my legs. "I can't go in there with you. We don't know what they'll do to me! You have to go in there alone and vote. One step at a time, but you must *hurry.* You're running out of time, and they *will* kill you if you don't make it. Do you understand me?"

My brain plays tricks on me, shifting from Mace's eyes to Cypher's obliterated remains, burned in my memory. I gulp the image back and force a nod, eyes wide with fear. Mace shifts so he's an inch from my face. "Can you walk?"

I test my legs and manage to pick them up, stretching one forward after the other. I may have regained control over my nervous system, but my limbs still scream with objection. My mouth opens to say yes, but my vocal cords merely croak. I gulp, then abandon the useless attempt at speech. Instead, I nod with exaggerated movement, still getting the hang of motor control. Mace doesn't dare risk another second and turns me around to face the arena entrance.

"I love you, Iris. *You can do this.*" Mace taps me into the room and shuts the door behind me.

Alone, I take a deep breath and dare a glance at the timer.

00:01:02
IRIS VOTE

The blaring red numbers make me gasp for air. My legs nearly collapse underneath me, so I grasp the metal railings and yank my body down two steps at a time. My arms pull me forward, but the strain proves I'm not making any significant progress. Finally, on the turf, I brave another glance at the clock.

Only forty-five seconds remain.

"Come ON!" I yell, grabbing one quad at a time and forcing it toward the pedestal. Drenched in sweat, my legs start sliding beneath my palms. Steps from the black platform, my quad completely slips from my grasp, and I crumple to the turf.

"NO!" I scream, tears blurring my vision. I break into a crawl, my arms hoisting my body so my limp legs drag lifelessly behind me. Finally, at the base, I pull myself to my knees so the buttons are barely visible. But all my focus is on the blaring red numbers, screaming that I have seven seconds remaining.

I whimper and rapidly search for Eno's name. Just above it, I hesitate.

What button am I supposed to press? The one I want to be expelled, or the one I want to live?

281

I switch my hand to hover over Ashlea's blue button and hear the clock blare with three seconds remaining. My chest tightens. *What am I supposed to do?*

At the last possible second, I bash Eno's white button.

The clock starts over at three minutes, and I fall back to the floor. I'm so relieved that I let the tears fall, not remotely interested in wiping them clear. But I only take a second to be relieved because the clock isn't slowing. I crawl to the metal staircase and ascend on all fours, desperate to get out before the next person casts their vote. Only at the iron entrance do I force myself to stand. *I will walk out with dignity.*

I reach for the exit, but the door opens gently before I can touch the handle.

Face to face with Artemis, I nearly tumble back to the ground. He holds onto me before I fall and helps me cross to the other side of the threshold before stepping into the arena himself. His eyes scream, "Are you okay?" for half a moment before they flush with relief. *Mace isn't the only one who thought I wouldn't make it in time.* He blinks at me reassuringly, and there's that same glint of love in his eye as he examines my face and wipes my tears. Despite what my brain screams, when Artemis turns to cast his vote, I grab his shoulder and force him to face me.

His eyes are wide, but his body is obedient. We stare at each other for three tense seconds, and I let the words fall out.

"Eno kept you alive," I spit out so quickly I'm nervous he won't understand. Artemis cocks his head to the side, and I continue, letting the word vomit eject without restraint. "Eno portioned your family extra rations. He kept the refugees alive. That's why he's here." My eyes harden. "It was *him.*"

Artemis sucks in his lips. I watch the gears moving in his head, his eyes reflecting each shift. He feels love, being this close to me. He believes with all his heart that it's reciprocated, me having risked this private moment with him. Then there's a twinge of sadness, having not known about Eno until now. And lastly…confusion. Confusion at why I felt the need to tell him this information *now.*

Then his eyes light up, and I *know* he understands what will happen.

"I'm so sorry," I choke, letting his arm go.

He shakes his head and leans into my ear.

"Thank you."

Then he turns, shutting the door behind him.

I descend the steps slowly, using my arms to support my weight. The coppery scent of exposed blood floods my senses, so I breathe through my mouth to avoid another bout of nausea. When Mace sees me approach, he jumps from his spot on the couch and runs to catch up to me. His body is slick with sweat, making it obvious that he's been running.

He leads me back to the living room and whispers, "There's not much I could do, but I did my best."

When we reach the nearest sofa, I stumble against Mace's chest. Where Cypher's remains were, now lie a pile of blankets strewn haphazardly across the couch. They're already stained with Cypher's blood, but they hide the worst of the massacre.

My body acts of its own accord, pulling Mace into a hug. "Thank you," I whisper. He rubs my back and takes my hand, leading me to the sofa. The second I settle into the cushions, I yank Lunar into an embrace. "You okay?"

He nods, but his eyes are wide. I go to reassure him that it's over, but he cuts me off before I get the chance. "Please," he whispers, "no matter *what*, just frickin vote, okay?"

He catches me off guard, so I can't help but chuckle as I pull him in tighter. "I promise."

Seconds later, the iron door on the second-floor creaks open. I ignore Artemis as he descends the steps. But when he enters the living room, I can't help noticing that he looks completely different. Instead of slumped and defeated, his back is straight and tall, and his eyes are determined. He sits beside Finian's chair, still unwilling to go anywhere near Cypher's annihilated body, but keeps his gaze focused on Eno. Even through the announcement, his stare is unfaltering.

"BY A VOTE OF FOUR TO FOUR: THERE IS A TIE."

"Liars. All of you," Destry spits, glaring at my side of the couch. Lagiacrus's eyes are scrunched, and Mercedes shifts uncomfortably, but it's impossible to distinguish whether Artemis even heard the announcement. All he does is watch Eno, his gaze intensifying.

"AS EXECUTIVE, FINIAN IS INELIGIBLE TO VOTE. WHEN FACED WITH A TIE, THE EXECUTIVE MAKES THE FINAL DECISION ON EXPULSION."

Finian rubs his bald head, still glowing after his chemical treatment. The news shouldn't be a surprise. Still, it doesn't make his decision any easier.

"CONVICT: FINIAN. YOU HAVE SIXTY SECONDS TO CAST YOUR VOTE AT THE HEAD OF THE ROOM."

Red numbers glow above the executive settee, immediately counting down from sixty. Finian lifts himself off his sofa and paces back and forth, holding both arms over his head and locking them over his bald scalp.

"I don't know…I don't know…I don't know…," he mumbles in quick succession.

Ashlea darts her eyes back and forth, terrified of pressing Finian too far but desperate to plead her case. Destry doesn't say a word as he crosses his arms and shoots daggers at Mace. The silence is deafening, only Finian's panicked murmurs filling the room. Finally, when only forty seconds remain, Ashlea jumps from her seat.

"I'll give you anything you want. *Anything*. Just please, *please* don't kill me."

"Don't listen to her, Fin," Destry spits, scowling at Ashlea. He lunges forward and blocks her from Finian's view. "Just lock it in. We're all behind you on this!"

Finian scans the crowd but pauses on Mercedes and Artemis. The two sit as far away from each other as possible. Mercedes has wide eyes, but Artemis is expressionless, only focused on Eno. Finian shifts his gaze back and forth between them, and I can practically see the gears moving.

Artemis and Mercedes really are *done.* Which means that Dial is down to four members. *Three, if Finian jumps ship.*

"LOOK AT ME, FINIAN!" Destry shouts. "DON'T YOU DARE DO THIS!"

My eyes light up. *Destry just made the biggest mistake of his entire life.* And he knows it the second Finian shifts his eyes to Eno.

Eno matches Finian's eye contact and relaxes his hands. Tears fall to my cheeks as I watch Eno delicately nod at the Executive, giving Finian the permission he never knew he needed. Destry and Ashlea's shouts fade into the background, and only once Finian steps forward does the room go completely silent.

Finian squints his eyes before shutting them completely. "I'm so sorry," he chokes out. "Eno, I have to vote to expel you."

"BY A VOTE OF FIVE TO FOUR: ENO IS EXPELLED FROM THE ENTERPRIZE. YOU HAVE THIRTY SECONDS TO EVACUATE."

Ashlea cries with relief, thanking Finian. She quickly peels off toward the kitchen, allowing Eno a silent moment to say his goodbyes. Eno nods again, this time with finality, and rises from his cushion.

"Eno," Finian starts, but he can't get any other words out. He coughs, trying to clear his throat, but the effort to fight tears is too overwhelming to speak. Eno quickly closes the gap between them and shakes Finian's hand.

"It's okay," he whispers, putting his opposite hand on Finian's shoulder. "You're a good kid."

Eno makes for the exit, but housemates stop him every two steps to say their peace. Not a single person withholds from saying farewell, but they're careful not to monopolize his time so he can make it to his execution. Tears now soak my cheeks, and I choke on my sobs. Mace is rubbing my back when Eno reaches us, and I collapse into the old man's arms.

"I'm…I can't…you don't know…," I stammer, unsure how to make peace with his departure.

Eno simply tightens his hug and whispers, "Don't cry. It's been an *honor* getting to know you, Iris. Truly." He releases our embrace and gazes into my eyes.

All I can choke out is, "Thank you," before he moves on to the next houseguest. I cry in my hands, but Mace spins me around so I can sob into his shoulder. When Ashlea hugs me from behind, and we cry together, I know I made the right decision.

But nothing could ever clear my conscience from killing an honorable man who did nothing but save innocent lives.

Lunar is the next to weep in Eno's arms. Mace has to pull him away so he doesn't take up too much of Eno's time. Once detached, Lunar spins into Mace's embrace and sobs against his chest. With my brother latching onto him, Mace simply nods at Eno and thanks him for the fatherly figure he was to us all. But the way he hides his quivers beneath his tense fists confirms that he's struggling to stay strong.

Eno gets around to everyone before stopping at Artemis, who blocks the exit. In one swift motion, Artemis pulls the man into a hug and takes a shaky breath. Nobody else is watching, but I can't take my eyes away from them. I focus on their interaction and can just make out their conversation.

"Thank you," Artemis says. "Thank you…for everything."

"It's been such a pleasure to be your friend," Eno responds.

"No," Artemis pleads, backing away and holding Eno's shoulders. "*Thank you*. For my family, my friends…the village. Thank you from us all."

Eno smiles and shakes his head. "I'd do it again a thousand times." He takes a deep breath and points at Arty's chest. "You're a good kid, Artemis. Don't forget that." They embrace once more before Eno turns to the group, hand on the iron exit.

"You're all good people. Don't let this game make you forget who you are."

Then he pushes the door open, and the gunshots commence.

ROUND 5

Chapter 45

The silence is disturbed by more than a few people stifling their tears. Despite the outcome, Eno was loved mutually by everyone in the house. He didn't deserve to die. If Destry hadn't come for us, Eno could have been spared. But Destry fired the first shots with nominations that blatantly targeted my outside alliances. So, when it came to voting out Eno…we didn't have a choice. Not if we wanted any chance at winning this game. Besides, Eno's lack of competitiveness would have put us in a terrible position for the coming rounds.

Regardless of my reasons for voting him out, I can't erase the crippling disgust and shame that eat my body alive, from my bones to my tissues.

"So, I guess a line has been drawn in the sand then, huh?" Destry towers behind the Executive sofa. He stretches his arms out and claps his hands away from his body in a slow rhythm as if impatient. He tilts his head at Finian, who avoids his gaze. "You really think *they* are gonna protect you better than we can? They'll throw you in the trash just as quickly as they stole you."

Mace shakes his head, his grip tightening around my shoulders. "Come on, guys. Let's everybody just calm down."

"And *you*," Destry shouts at Mace. "You were sittin' *real* pretty with us. What on earth possessed you into thinking you'd be better off with *them*? You're nobody. You really think you'll be competitive with a thirteen-year-old and three girls as athletic as that couch cushion?" Destry purses his lips, shaking his head. "You made a *huge* mistake. We would have brought you two to the end. You know that, right? You and Iris would have been smooth sailing to the final six."

"Come on, man. That's bullshit, and you know it." Mace lets go of me and walks slowly toward Destry, voice raising an octave. "You really think we're stupid enough to believe those nominations were in our favor? You might be able to trick the others, but you can't fool *us* into doing your dirty work for you. Putting up two of Iris's best friends was hardly in her best interest."

"USE YOUR EYES, MAN!" Destry shouts, rushing toward Mace until he's an inch away. "They had to be put up at some point! You really think she would have had the strength to do it herself? I was doing her a *favor*."

"*Excuse me?*" I shout, finally having cleared my tears. My sorrow quickly boils into hatred, and I spit fury. "You controlled those nominations to take out my allies because you *knew* you couldn't get to me until they were gone. I was always the end game!"

Mercedes squints at us, the realization hitting that her boyfriend was in a secret alliance. She's the last to find out, so her confusion is expected. I was less prepared for her sudden bout of anger. She strides toward Artemis and yells, but he won't turn away from the iron exit. "Is there anything you *haven't* kept from me? I mean, seriously, did you even care about me at all?" She pushes Artemis from behind, but he doesn't budge. Whether he's in shock or denial, it's clear he's not registering her.

Ignoring the outburst, Destry takes back the reigns. "Why do you think I'm capable of such manipulation? What did I ever do to you two to make you hate me so much?"

"What haven't you done?" I shout, spit flinging from my mouth.

"You're unbelievable, Destry," Mace throws up his hands. He spins away and does a double take on Artemis before his eyes narrow in disgust. "And to get behind Artemis after *everything* he's done? What more does he need to do to show you he doesn't deserve *anyone's* trust? He will betray any of you the second you give him the chance."

"Damn right," agrees Mercedes, still shooting dagger eyes at her former lover.

Destry stares at Mace in bewilderment, then raises an eyebrow. He gives me a quick glance, and my lip quivers. Then, he takes two deep breaths and looks Mace dead in his eyes.

"How can you hate Artemis so much when it was your *girlfriend* that kissed *him*?"

Time stops. My heart drops to my stomach, then melts through the floor until it hits the earth's core. Simultaneously, it feels as if a knife has been lodged into my chest and is twisting in a circular motion until the entire cavity is sliced out. *Artemis told Destry.* I'm weightless, my fury accumulating into a boulder in my throat.

It was your girlfriend *that kissed* him.

No. The knife isn't in my chest at all.

It's digging into my back, carving enough space for more daggers to launch into my spine.

Mace slowly turns to me and shakes his head mechanically. "Shut the hell up, Destry. They never kissed. If they did, Iris would have told me." He looks into my eyes, and I step back, feeling faint. He catches onto my hesitation and narrows his violet pupils, his voice suddenly empty. "Right?"

I'm frozen. At the same time, my body is weightless, as if I'm about to tumble to the ground. I can't breathe, and when I glance in Artemis's direction and his words echo across the deepest crevices of my mind, I deflate.

I'm in love with you.

I would die for you.

None of this is your *fault.*

And I believed him.

How could he? How could he give such a passionate declaration only to immediately tell the least trustworthy person in this house about our kiss? And the version he gave…it's not the *truth*. Artemis cornered *me*. Artemis kissed *me*. I merely…reacted.

"Five minutes until we need to be in the arena, guys," Lagiacrus announces, trying to diffuse the situation. But nobody moves a muscle or even pretends to be interested in the next competition. Because when Mace steps away from me, and his voice quivers, nobody can look away.

"Tell me it isn't true."

I open my mouth to speak, but nothing comes out. The air has emptied from my lungs, and I can't bring myself to reveal the truth. *I shouldn't have kept this from him*, but I didn't have a *choice*. Ashlea's life depended on me keeping the secret. My face flushes as I grasp for words. Only when Mace wipes a tear from his eye do I finally find my voice.

"I never kissed Artemis," I say. "He…*he* kissed *me*."

Mace deflates as if I've shot him in the heart. Destry merely shrugs.

"That's not what he told me."

My jaw drops as my eyes narrow on Destry. I glance at Artemis, but he's still focused on the front door. I shake, the anger leaving me so ravenous that I shove Artemis forward. *"What?"* I shout, desperate for Artemis to answer me.

He doesn't even acknowledge that I've spoken.

Destry rolls his eyes. "Artemis said his only regret was not resisting *you* kissing him."

"HE WHAT?" My screech is so high my ears start ringing.

"Four minutes, guys!" Lagiacrus shouts, voice shaking.

Mercedes cackles, vile spilling over her lips. "Oh, you are *so* dead!"

She launches toward me with both fists wound, betrayal dilating her eyes. She pounces, but Ashlea catches her just in time. She holds her back, so Mercedes's flinging fists are just out of striking range.

"You shallow, two-faced, attention-seeking, *slut!*" Ashlea doesn't let her go, but Mercedes doesn't relent. "You *dare* try and comfort me when you've been fucking around with him behind everybody's backs? I'LL KILL YOU!"

Shaking my head rapidly, I back away, putting my hands up in defense. "No! That's not what happened!" I grab onto Artemis's hips and force him to face me. His eyes are glossed over in a trance. I know he's not in a mental space to explain himself. But with my heart beating through my chest and my vision turning red, I don't hold back. "Who the *fuck* do you think you are going around and telling everyone that *I* came on to *you*?" I shake his shoulders, screaming. *"ARE YOU INSANE?* Tell them the truth!"

Artemis says nothing. He simply looks at the floor and mumbles something incoherent. We stand like statues as I wait for his explanation.

It never comes.

He merely keeps still, avoiding my eye contact.

I break. "Nothing to say for yourself? *Seriously?*"

My temper rises until it's boiling, and I want to hit him *hard*. But I don't have to. Because just as I wind back my arm, Mercedes escapes Ashlea's grasp and executes the perfect slap on her former lover. The sound reverberates throughout the house, and a red handprint is left on Artemis's face.

Mercedes turns on her heel and sticks an unfavorable finger in my face. "You're next, *sweetheart*. You better fight for your life out there, because I'm ending you if it's the last thing I do!" She sprints toward the second floor, not sparing a glance back as she flees into the arena.

With Mercedes gone, Artemis finally lifts his eyes to meet mine, but there's nothing in them. They are completely empty as if his heart has been shattered and glued back together, just to be wrecked all over again. I would usually grieve for him and yearn for that crooked smile to return to his lips.

But right now, with the wounds still fresh from the bus he tossed me under, I can't think of anything other than how much I *despise* him.

"Great alliance you got there." Destry pats Finian on the back, making his burnt ex-friend recoil in pain. "Good luck in the arena."

Destry and Lagiacrus rush toward the staircase, Kylah following close behind. Finian remains standing, eyes wide. Looking at nobody in particular, he shoves his head in his hands and squeals, *"What have I done?"*

When Artemis reluctantly saunters away, I'm left alone with the people that mean everything to me.

And I can't stop thinking about how I may have just lost them all.

The hike to the arena is a silent march, only the sounds of our shaking breaths filling the calm. Stepping through the threshold, my heart thumps through my chest, and I shiver.

I can't lose Mace. And if Artemis is the reason I do, I will *never* forgive him. Goosebumps erupt along my body as I imagine what my future would look like if Mace wasn't there. And if the reason for that is because Artemis couldn't control his impulse to kiss me, I will make it my soul's purpose to make him feel this pain every moment until the day that he dies.

I climb the rickety steps and hold the ice-cold railing to keep my balance. I gasp as I quickly retract my palm, the ice burning into my fingers. *My rage isn't the only reason I'm shivering.* There may be no contraption sitting for us on the turf, but the temperature in the arena must be below freezing.

Ashlea holds my shoulder, raising her eyebrows. I nod quietly, and she pats my back, doing her best to offer some silent comfort. I keep glancing at Mace, desperate to explain myself. Every time I try to find the words, nothing comes out. But Ashlea knows every little detail about the romantic encounter with Artemis. And despite me not confiding in her about my true feelings for him, I sense she knows those, too. Regardless of the repercussions of our blindside against Dial, I know saving her was the right move. The glint in her eyes as she watches me confirms that she would have done the same for me.

We approach the center, where an instructional card sits limply on the turf. My housemates huddle close together, hugging themselves tight to stay warm. Lunar takes his arms out of his sleeves and hugs them beneath his shirt. His teeth chatter, so I hug him to my chest, shaking. Mace stands beside us, avoiding my eye contact but resting a hand on Lunar's shoulder. The only one not shivering or shrinking into themselves to stay warm is Lagiacrus, flexing his upper arms against the short sleeves of his top.

Destry swipes the card from the ground but quickly hands it to Lagiacrus, opting out of directing those who betrayed him. Once the card leaves his hands, he hugs his body tight, trying not to freeze in the cold.

Lagiacrus's lips move as he reads the instructions to himself. Once he finishes, he squints and tilts his head, scanning his eyes across it again. We look at one another, waiting for him to tell us the orders, when Mercedes spits, "Well? What does it say?"

Lagiacrus looks up from the card and meets her eyes.

"Be the last one in the arena."

And the water starts to rise.

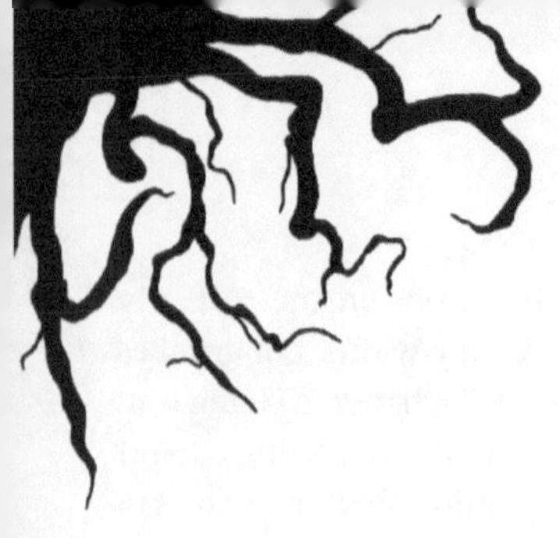

Chapter 46

*S**earing, piercing pain.*

And it's already at our ankles.

"WHAT THE HELL?" Kylah shouts, backing away from the center. My housemates scatter, searching the turf for that water's port of entry. But where once was turf is now a pool of water, temperature just above freezing.

"It's no use!" Ashlea shouts. "It's coming in from everywhere!"

"How high is it supposed to get?" Lunar yells. "Are they going to drown us?"

"I doubt they're *trying* to kill us, but they won't intervene if somebody's going to die," Mace suggests, forfeiting his anger for anxiety. He paces back and forth, squeezing his fingers through his hair, desperate for a solution.

I whip my attention to the metal staircase, where Finian has already perched himself on the top. Not being eligible to compete, he bolted the second the water started rising.

My heart rate races as I back away from the others and grab hold of Lunar. The freezing liquid rises to my knees, and my body burns fresh with each climbing inch. The cold daggers launch into my scorpion bite, and I scream as if somebody is slicing a knife through my flesh.

The water doesn't show any sign of stopping. My breaths start coming out rapidly, and not enough oxygen reaches my brain. *I can't swim.* And if it doesn't stop filling the arena soon, I'll be dead within the hour.

"What do we do?" I shout at Mace. His heartbreak is still fresh; I know it. But my rational brain is shutting down, so I ignore the possibility that he's stopped caring about me.

Without hesitation, he looks directly in my eyes. "Run for the staircase, but don't climb it! Get close enough that you can drop out without drowning!"

Mace, Lunar, and I sprint for the rickety platform, water now at our torsos. Tears build in the corners of my eyes from the biting pain of the current. I force away sobs and focus on pulling Lunar with all my strength, but he slows as if running through honey.

"Come on!" I shout, yanking him forward.

"I can't do it, Iris!" Tears start streaming down his face, and he throws away my hand. "It hurts *so* badly. Go on without me!" Mace lifts Lunar without a second thought and strides for the staircase, keeping my brother completely over the ice-cold water. I trust Mace to get him there safely and instead focus on reaching the stairs myself. Having tunnel vision on the exit, I stumble when a figure sprints past me in my peripheral.

Brown hair flopping with each passing stride, Destry races for the entrance. He straightens his palms and leans forward at a full sprint. The water slows his progress, so his face glows red from the exertion. His breathing is *frantic*. I pause, eyes widening on him as he forces his way through the frigid water. For the first time since entering The Enterprize, Destry's façade of control and collection has cracked.

He's just as helpless as the rest of us.

Mace and Destry make it to the edge of the platform seconds before I do, and both stop before crossing the threshold. My other housemates force their way through the water, following our lead, but nobody reaches for the dry platform. Finian inches as far away from the water as possible, back on the cold iron door, locking him with us.

Once the water reaches my chest, I know we're doomed.

"We can't swim!" I shout, my voice shaking. If Mace hates me, he's doing a great job hiding it. When he sets Lunar down, unable to hold him any longer, his eyes lack any heat or hatred. Instead, they scan my brother and me, compassion and worry contorting his lips. He winces, watching Lunar bob in the water, liquid flowing into my brother's mouth between each passing kick against the ground.

"He has to drop out!" Mace shouts, looking me dead in the eye. "He'll die if he doesn't!" The water has risen to my neck, so Lunar's face is the only thing not yet completely underwater. I kick against the ground until I'm close enough to touch Lunar and grab his wrist.

"You have to drop out, Lunar. LISTEN to me, *please.*"

Lunar shakes his head, unable to stop his tears from falling. "I don't want to give up!"

"I know you don't, buddy," Mace starts, controlling his voice. He pushes himself off the ground every time he falls to the turf, so his body bobs as he pleads. "But I've got this! Leave it to me, okay? You're going to be fine!"

Lunar scans the both of us, purple lips shaking. When he falls entirely under the water, he lunges for the staircase and holds onto the nearest railing, hoisting himself onto the platform.

HONK. "CONVICT: LUNAR. ELIMINATED AT 00:05:32."

Lunar crawls until he hits the furthest wall with Finian, then cradles himself into a ball. Knowing he's safe, I tear my gaze away from him and look at Mace with wide eyes. "Mace, I can't swim!" I remind him. He whips his head left and right before locking onto my eyes.

My heart shatters, seeing the hurt in his gaze. He still loves me; I can feel it. But with what I've done…I don't know how he could ever forgive me. Despite my fears, he gulps the heartbreak to the back of his mind and shifts to protection mode.

"Wave your arms and legs. Like this." He demonstrates treading water, and I do my best to imitate it, but my body sinks faster and faster by the second. "Wave them in circles! Try to keep yourself afloat. If you touch the bottom, kick off the turf to bring yourself back up!"

HONK. "CONVICT: DESTRY. ELIMINATED AT 00:06:15."

Destry crawls onto the metal staircase, heaving. He removes his soaked shirt and sits a few meters away from my brother and Finian. I watch him shiver until the water envelops my skull. I push up from the ground and find air at the top. But the burning sensation of having been completely submerged knocks the breath out of me, and I struggle to get any oxygen into my lungs. I hyperventilate and wave my limbs wildly, straining to stay afloat.

"Mace, I can't do it!" I whine, throat choking as water pours in. "I'm so sorry, Mace. What he was saying," I gurgle more water, "…it isn't true!"

"Iris, we can talk about this later!" Mace shouts. His eyes are dilated, and his voice cracks as he declares, "You need to get *out* before you drown!"

I fall back under the water, and the bitter cold feels like a million needles launching into my skin. My scalp *burns*, and I panic for air, but my limps become sluggish, doing little to get me back to the top. I force myself to the bottom and reach for the ground, but there's so much water in the stadium that it's out of reach. I squeal as I kick ferociously. Just when I think it's hopeless, Mace's hand clasps around my arm and pulls me to the surface. I gasp for air but hyperventilate when I don't float. I start sinking again until only my face is above the water.

"IRIS!" Mace shouts, tugging his hair with his free hand. "I believe you, okay? *GET OUT! I can't* lose you!"

An impossible tear streams down my cheek, but it's washed away when I fall back under. When Mace lifts me back to the surface, I gaze directly into his eyes and let the tears flow. "I love you, Mace."

"I love you too, Iris," he says without hesitation. His arched eyebrows expose his heartbreak, but his worried eyes verify he'd rather *die* than live without me. Even knowing I betrayed him, he's selflessly strained himself to protect my family. I can't take my eyes off him, so they sting into another octave of pain when I sink back under the water with them open. Mace pulls me up in seconds and helps me catch my breath, never breaking eye contact. After a single glance at my purple lips, he pushes his into mine.

My heart warms, and I'm levitating for half a second. He pulls away quickly, the strain of keeping me from sinking too much. But even though the moment was short, it cleared any doubt I had about us.

Whatever treacherous waters are ahead…we can make it through.

I delicately nod at Mace before hurling myself onto the metal platform. It's only just above the water level, but the effort takes the breath out of me. I crawl on all fours and wheeze, jolting when the horn blares.

HONK. "CONVICT: IRIS. ELIMINATED AT 00:10:23."

I spit up water and choke until the freezing air comes in naturally. Finally catching my breath, I tilt my head toward the exit and wince at Lunar in the corner, shivering with Finian. While crawling to them, I remove my soaking shirt, revealing just my sports bra underneath. My arms act on their own, pulling Lunar against me to combine our body warmth.

"You okay?" I whisper, teeth chattering.

"C…co…cold…as…*shit*." he stutters. I bury my head in his hair and laugh, hugging him tighter.

"Of course you are." I can't help but smile despite the circumstances. *Lunar is alive.* And even though I know that shouldn't be enough…at this moment, *it is.*

The competition continues, oblivious to our shivers. I scan the remaining competitors and calculate my odds: Mace, Ashlea, and Kylah against Artemis, Lagiacrus, and Mercedes. At this point, it's safe to say that Mercedes wants me dead. I just hope I don't have to find out if she'll hold this grudge against me into future rounds. I shiver, this time from the way she grits her teeth through each respective tread. There's no chance she'll get out of the water until she's crowned the Executive.

Ashlea trembles so intensely that I can hear her teeth chatter from the platform. She kicks forward until she's beside Mace and searches his face for any sign of struggle. When she can't find any, she starts falling apart. "I'm just so………cold," she complains.

"Try and relax your body!" he yells. "Take deep breaths…try not to panic!"

Behind them, Kylah and Mercedes have lost all color in their faces. Considering how burnt they both are from the Suffering Sanctuary, this is an impressive feat. Now a mixture of scabs and paleness, Mercedes slows her strokes. Lagiacrus and Artemis don't show any sign of struggle, but the latter won't stop darting his gaze at Mercedes. Mace takes slow breaths and keeps his body in control. Despite his strength, I can't help but fear that the emotional toll of coaching his alliance will make him falter.

Ashlea shakes her head rapidly. "I have to get out," she declares. "Wha—where do I go?"

Having finally reached the height of our platform, the water has stopped rising. It does not spill over, so it's clear that the eliminated were always expected to end up here. Despite throwing in the towel, Ashlea starts swimming in the opposite direction to the exit, flailing her arms into a breaststroke.

I know very little about swimming but a *lot* about hyperthermia. In my studies, I have dabbled with the condition. First, confusion takes root, sometimes driving one toward death before the condition can follow through to completion. *Ashlea doesn't know where the exit is.* And if we don't get her out of the water soon, she'll never reach it.

Lunar and I scream her name in unison. I cup my hands around my mouth to raise the volume and lean forward as if that extra inch will make the difference. Mace swims toward her and screams her name, then positions himself behind her, pushing her toward the staircase. Strokes from the platform, a loud bang reverberates throughout the arena.

Both of them turn around despite my cries for them to keep swimming. Soon, everyone stares at the back of the arena, searching for the source. There's a pause. Then, a second, louder boom.

Then all hell breaks loose.

The solitary confinement chamber, once imperceptible from the rest of the arena, bursts open from the water pressure. The arctic liquid rushes into the room, forcing half of the remaining contestants toward the back of the arena. Lagiacrus gets sucked into the prison, but the others resist, desperately swimming against the current.

"GO, ASHLEA, GO!" I scream, waving maniacally for her to swim to the pedestal. Destry stays silent, eyes glued to the open solitary confinement chamber. Lunar, in contrast, springs to his feet and shouts for Ashlea. Our yells echo off the arena, and my ears ring, but I refuse to stop until she's safe.

She struggles with the current pulling her back, but Mace swims effortlessly to her side. Pushing her toward the exit, she progresses more efficiently until she's finally arm's reach from the metal surface. She hoists herself up with Mace's assistance and flops onto the platform.

HONK. "CONVICT: ASHLEA. ELIMINATED AT 00:21:03." Ashlea shivers violently, hugging her knees to her chest. I rush to my friend, helping her remove her shirt to start the drying process. I pull her to the corner furthest from the water and put her at the center of Lunar and my huddle. Our combined body heat minimally assists our hypothermic risk. Still, there's some relief when we hug each other, shielding Ashlea from the frigid air.

I wait for Eno's announcement that five contestants are remaining, and my heart shatters when it doesn't come. I tighten my arms around my group and shield my emotions, hiding my grief that he's truly *gone.* Distracting myself, I watch the last five competitors swim toward our platform. Lagiacrus finally treads his way out of the solitary confinement chamber but takes his time wading toward the staircase. Once the water establishes an equilibrium with the arena, the remaining contestants tread silently. Their panicked breaths are the only sound disrupting the peace.

Inches from the platform, Kylah looks at Mace. "Are you feeling good?" she asks. She's biting her lip, and her complexion is paper-white. She starts sinking below the surface every thirty seconds, barely able to get any words out. "I…I don't think I can make it much longer."

"I'm okay," Mace declares. Despite his confidence, he's paling by the second. He clenches his jaw, forcing himself to withstand the torture and prove to her that she's safe to quit. Kylah has no hope of outlasting him, spitting up the ice-cold water every time she falls below the surface. Mace encourages her to self-eliminate, and Kylah immediately obeys his command. She wades toward the staircase slowly, then hurls herself onto the dry platform.

HONK. "CONVICT: KYLAH. ELIMINATED AT 00:23:40."

Kylah throws her shirt to the wall and hugs the outside of our huddle. She's even more frigid than Ashlea was, so we adjust until she's at the center of our cluster. Her added height and body weight must have helped her last as long as she did, but Kylah's lack of endurance and physical strength could only take her so far. We rub each other's shoulders, the friction helping us thaw. We each chirp encouragements to Mace but stop abruptly when there's a commotion a few yards away.

"NO!" shouts Mercedes, bobbing away from Artemis.

I squint between them but can't make out the source of their disagreement. From physical cues, I can only see Artemis effortlessly swimming toward her while Mercedes desperately tries to move away. But her limbs don't cooperate. Her arms are almost motionless, so her treading is useless. She simply floats, bobbing like a floatation device.

"MERCEDES, LISTEN TO ME!" yells Artemis, voice *booming*. "YOU WILL DIE IN THE NEXT MINUTE, DO YOU UNDERSTAND ME? GET OUT OF THE WATER!"

"NO!" she screams back. "If I quit, I'm the first one out that door! I…I won't leave this arena until I win!"

"MERCEDES, YOU ARE NOT THE TARGET!" yells Artemis, voice quivering. Mercedes doesn't move. She merely rotates from where she floats, eyes shifting in and out of focus. There's no indication that she's even the slightest bit cold, her limbs steady in their rotation. My body goes rigid, and I gasp, remembering the biggest sign of hypothermia…the largest indication that it's too late.

Your body stops trembling.

I bring that chapter forward in my mind, reciting the text.

"One's body becomes so cold that their brain and nerve endings can't transmit signals. The extremities quickly go numb, and the shaking stops entirely."

If Mercedes does not exit the water in the next thirty seconds, there is no doubt that she will die.

"HOW COULD I EVER TRUST YOU AGAIN, ARTEMIS?" she cries. "You've hurt me and lied to me over and over and *over*! How can I trust that you won't do it again!?"

Artemis pleads with her and wades toward her. Mercedes bobs forward, and her eyes widen as she starts to sink.

"Then I'll drop out."

"What?" Lagiacrus barks.

"If I drop out, will you do it with me?" Artemis talks so fast that I can hardly separate one word from another. "I can't put you up if I'm not Executive. Will you self-eliminate if I do that?"

Mercedes doesn't answer. Only her face remains above the surface, but her silence is enough to spring Artemis into action.

"LOOK! I'm leaving! Please, *please* don't do this, Mercedes!" He swims toward the metal staircase and treads water in front of it. "Mercedes, I'm *begging* you!"

Mercedes snaps back into reality and forces her head above the water. Following Artemis's lead, she wades toward the stairwell, but her progress is excruciatingly slow. Her eyes cross while she moves forward, one gentle stroke at a time. Knowing his elimination may encourage her to speed up, Artemis pulls himself onto the metal platform.

HONK. "CONVICT: ARTEMIS. ELIMINATED AT 00:28:51."

He springs to his feet and shouts at Mercedes to hurry. Nobody else speaks, so his words bounce off the walls until there's a chorus of his voice in varying states of desperation. Mercedes treads toward the exit, but her movement gets slower with each stroke.

Inches from the platform, her movement stops altogether.

"MERCEDES!" Artemis shouts. Mercedes doesn't flinch. Instead, her body remains still. Her face turns and sinks beneath the water.

HONK.

"No. NO!" Artemis shrieks, his voice quivering. Mercedes's body rotates until only her back floats above the water. Any exposed skin is sheet-white, and her blonde hair fans around her.

"CONVICT: MERCEDES. ELIMINATED AT 00:29:17."

Chapter 47

BANG.

Ashlea's arms tighten around me as Artemis smashes his fist into the surrounding blue wall. He fails to dent the structure and cradles his bloody hand from the impact. Not even flinching to remove his top, he collapses to the ground with his head between his knees, letting the tears fall.

Mercedes is dead.

Mercedes is dead, and it's partly my fault. No, that can't be right. *Theoretically,* it's Artemis's fault. And if we want to get *really* morbid, it's *her* fault for staying in the water for too long. I shiver, but it's not from the cold. Her death should hurt me, but sorrow is the weakest of my competing emotions. *What is happening to me?* I want to grieve her demise, but I can't help considering how much closer my brother and I are to the end. Her departure from this game has also left me with one less nemesis gunning for my life. Aside from this momentary and shameful relief, my stomach burns as Artemis wails, stomping his feet on the ground. He punches the wall again with his opposite hand, then covers his face to hide his tears. My jaw clenches as I watch him. My stomach hardens when I recognize the one sensation that trumps all others.

Jealousy.

The rational part of my brain screams that Artemis spent so much time with the blonde beauty that it'd be sickening if he didn't care about her. Even if she meant nothing to him, the brutality in which her life ended was undeserved. She never revealed what landed her a spot in the Enterprize, but if it's anything like the rest of us, her crimes were excusable.

Artemis's chest heaves up and down from his tears. I bite my lip to fight the thought from bubbling, but the irrational part of my brain takes over. *Did he love Mercedes?* He's certainly *acting* like it. Watching Mace wave his arms in the water, fighting to stay afloat, I know it's ridiculous for me to care about Artemis's love life. After all, *Mercedes is gone.* Any juvenile competition between the two of us has dissolved. But as much as I fight the sensation, I can't stop my heart from yearning. So, when Artemis punches the wall for a third time, crumbling the drywall beneath his fist, I can't help but part my lips as a weight drops in my chest.

Silence engulfs the arena, and my heart threatens to shatter all over again. Instead of missing him, I force my thoughts on Artemis's betrayal. Not only did he reveal our forbidden kiss, but he perpetrated lies about its extent. When I confronted him about it and begged him in front of the others to explain the truth...he did *nothing* to defend me. After everything he said about loving me, he couldn't even tell the truth. I shake my head and glare at the water.

Artemis might love me, but never more than his own reputation.

When Lagiacrus finally treads side-by-side with Mace, I quiver. My throat constricts as I consider the consequences of Mace failing. I ultimately conclude that my earlier jealousy was a wasteful emotion. Even if Artemis never loved Mercedes, he'll still grieve the loss of her friendship. In that sense, he may be one of the only convicts the Enterprize hasn't yet corrupted.

If only I could say the same about myself.

I hug my friends tighter, overcompensating for my shameful thoughts. Redirecting my focus to the competition, I cuff a hand around my mouth and start cheering for Mace. I narrow my eyes on him, willing him to be the last person to exit the arctic pool. After that, we can confront my mistakes in the safe confines of his Executive bedroom.

Lagiacrus and Mace are the only contestants that remain. My cheers subside as the clock strikes thirty minutes, and the silence is overbearing. Both men are sheet-white, and their breaths come out in fleeting, misty clouds, exposing the true temperature of the arena. I wince, focusing on Mace's trembles as they shift his entire body back and forth. I squeeze Ashlea's hand when I settle on his purple lips, so she takes the initiative to get negotiations moving.

"Are you two gonna strike a deal, or are you just gonna let the other die?" Ashlea shouts. Mace and Lagiacrus look at one another and whisper, but I can't catch any distinct words. My own lips mouth inaudible prayers, hoping Mace talks his way into an Executive win. Striking a deal with Lagiacrus could be worthwhile, but I can't help worrying about the potential consequences. Lagiacrus has given us no reason to doubt his trust, so his promises should be binding. But with nine people remaining and our betrayal fresh on his mind, who knows how the pressure will affect him?

Their conversation takes several minutes. Mace's treads slow substantially throughout, and I nearly jump off the platform and yank him out of the water myself. Even though Mace is muscular and toned, Lagiacrus is brawny. With Lagiacrus having more body mass, the odds are not in Mace's favor.

My heart beats out of my chest when Mace finally shakes Lagiacrus's hand. I look first at Lunar, then Ashlea with wide eyes, praying that Lagiacrus will eliminate himself. From a safety standpoint, he wouldn't have to worry about surviving this round. Destry and Artemis have earned their places on Death Row, so Lagiacrus winning would only benefit his alliance. Having made their decision, the two swim to the staircase together, giving no hint of who will come out of the water first.

With purple lips and pale faces, they stop inches from the metal platform. I rush to the edge to yank Mace out of the arena when he's ready. Once I'm close enough to feel their breaths, Mace turns to Lagiacrus and grabs his shoulder, fingers too weak to form any forceful grip.

"You promise Me, Iris, and Lunar are safe?"

I fight tears when Lagiacrus replies, "You have my word," and Mace reaches for the platform.

HONK. "CONVICT: MACE. ELIMINATED AT 33:48."

I clutch Mace's hand and pull, but his body is too heavy for me to lift. Ashlea races beside me and takes his opposite arm. After several attempts, we manage to slide him onto the platform. I fall to the floor and wrap him in my arms, tears falling down my cheeks. I hadn't even realized they started. But when Mercedes's corpse floats past us, I wail into Mace's hair, pulling him in tighter. He can hardly extend his knees and struggles to wrap his arms around my torso. My tears fall to his shoulders, and I gasp for air.

"You…you could've *died*…," I stammer out.

Mace's voice is weak. "It's okay…we're okay…"

I jerk when the congratulatory horn blares.

"CONGRATULATIONS: LAGIACRUS. YOU ARE THE NEW EXECUTIVE."

I barely notice Lagiacrus pulling himself out of the water but watch as he stomps past us and rips his shirt off. His emotions are impossible to read, but his eyes lack the joy or relief a competition win should bring. Instead, he stares forward and slams a fist against the iron door.

"Let's get the hell out of this place."

The locks creak, and the slab slides open.

I cry into Mace's shoulder and fight Ashlea when she tries to take him from my grasp.

"Iris, stop!" she shouts. "We have to get him *out of here*!" Lunar hops beside her, and the two force Mace from my arms. We may be shivering, but one look at Mace confirms that we should be the least of my worries. When I lunge to meet Mace's face, his glossed eyes show how little time we have left to revive him. I swallow my tears and commit myself to saving him. He's become non-verbal, so I spring to my feet and mentally recite the hyperthermic facts I studied. Eyes darting around the arena, I settle my gaze on Ashlea and shout the first instructions that come to my mind.

"Down the steps…to the bathroom!" Ashlea nods, and we pull Mace across the threshold. We struggle down the plush steps, soaking them with the cuffs of Mace's drenched jeans. He lolls in and out of consciousness, and I grip his arm tight, desperate for him to make it through alive.

We stumble into the bathroom and lean Mace against the sinks. "Get his jeans off!" Ashlea orders, racing for the shower stalls. I loosen my grip around Mace's arm and bite my lip, hesitating to oblige. When Ashlea returns and sees my lack of progress, there are flames in her eyes. "DO YOU WANT HIM TO LIVE OR NOT? Now is not the time for you to be shy!"

I blink rapidly to rid myself of embarrassment before following her orders. Mace slumps like a ragdoll, entirely at our discretion, as we strip his body. I keep my eyeline toward his chest as Ashlea throws off his top.

"Can you hold him up?" Ashlea asks.

"I can try," I suggest. "At the very least, I can lean him on me."

"Then get him in there! It's the same setup as it was with Lunar. Start with the closest showers and work up in heat as he thaws!" Ashlea shouts, pushing Mace's hand in mine. I grip his torso with my opposite arm and shove him into the nearest shower, not caring about getting myself soaked. My muscles strain as I push his body over the silver drains, but I refuse to let his weight falter my progress. Working smarter instead of harder, I sit him on the ground and let the water fall onto him, steaming up the bathroom.

"Come on, Mace. Talk to me!"

"I…I'm here…I'm here."

His speech is strained, and his eyes only open an inch. I desperately whisper that everything's going to be okay. His body trembles, but his motor control starts to return. I pull him into the next shower, focusing on his face and ignoring what I see in my peripheral. After a few progressing rounds, he crawls to the next showerhead on his own, only holding my hand for emotional support. When we're finally in the last stall with the hottest water, Lunar barges in with every towel in the house.

I yank the handle for the shower to stop, and the water obliges. Lunar tosses the bundle of towels into my arms and scuttles out of the bathroom, leaving me alone to lift Mace. He only needs help balancing, so I lean him against the wall and wrap him in the cotton from head to toe. His teeth chatter as I guide him to the sinks, and my heart races as I search for his clothes. My eyes land on his jeans and gray long-sleeve strung over the counter. A soapy fragrance wafts toward my nostrils as I reach for them, but Ashlea swipes my hand away.

"Don't dress him," she commands. "He'd freeze right away. He needs to get dry…get him into the bed sheets. Those will warm him up."

Ashlea lifts Mace's arm around her shoulder, and we guide him across the living room. Religion must claim humanity's most desperate victims because every step of the way, I pray relentlessly for Mace's safety. Our progress and panic warp time, so I don't remember racing past the kitchen or striding up the staircase. I also can't pinpoint when Lunar joined our train, but he's pushing Mace from behind. We emerge into the communal bedroom as if transported there. Whatever housemates we pass blur into the background, and I don't pay them a second thought. The only person on my mind is the man shaking in my arms, wrapped like a mummy in six plush cotton towels.

My mind is frazzled, but I string enough words together to yell for Lunar and Ashlea to bring Mace to my bed. They follow my orders without question and wrap Mace tight into my sheets. Lunar runs toward Mace's bed, strips the mattress of the blankets, and throws them on top of Mace's many cotton layers.

Kneeling beside the cot, my breath comes out in shaky gasps. *Mace is going to make it.* I let the tears fall and don't bother wiping them. I squeeze Mace's hand underneath the sheets and adjust until my back is against the wall. Closing my eyes, I let out a deep breath and whisper, assuming nobody will hear me.

"Don't ever get that close to leaving me again, you crazy person."

My breath catches when he squeezes my hand three times. He doesn't open his eyes, but there's no mistaking the melodic voice that reaches my ears.

"Never in a thousand years."

BANG.

I wake with a start to the sound of an all-too-familiar terror. I search frantically around me, swatting the air with my free hand.

"Wow, calm down! It's just me," Ashlea says, one ration bin in hand. The other sits on my left, *Iris* etched on the side.

It takes me a long minute to gather my composure. "Sorry," I whisper when my heart finally stops racing. "Force of habit."

Ashlea curls her lip. "No, it's my fault. I should know better than to scare you like that."

Silence falls over us as she sits beside me on the plush carpet, once so soft and welcoming. Now it's damp and matted, no longer tricking us with its fictitious comfort. Pins and needles pierce my hand, and I pull it back, realizing I'm still grasping Mace's. I let go and rub the feeling back into my palm. "How long have I been out?"

"A couple hours," she shrugs. "Everyone's been taking their time getting to bed tonight. Most have been sitting in the warm showers for the past hour. It should be a little bit before the others come up for bed, but most of them have eaten by now, so…" She kicks the bin by my feet and places the other on my lap. "Eat up."

I smile and nod at the baskets. "Thanks, Ashlea. For this, and…for Mace."

She puckers her lips to the left and stares at the ground. "It's really no problem…especially after what you did for me today."

"You'd have done the same for me."

She matches my eye contact and curls the corner of her lip into a grin. It's only for a moment, but it's enough to confirm that she would have. "Yeah, well…thanks anyway."

I nod before she turns away, leaving me alone with Mace. I tap his shoulder softly and whisper in his ear.

"Mace….Mace, it's supper time." I rub a finger down his cheek, barely touching his smooth skin. With each stroke, his arm hairs fly a touch higher until a jolt of electricity flicks his eyes open. His violet pupils lock onto my hazel ones, and I shiver at the smile he delicately paints on his lips. I take his face in my hands and plant a kiss on his lips. When I try to pull away, Mace pulls me in deeper, cupping a gentle hand around the nape of my neck. His lips press against mine again and again, and my heart flutters with each passing stroke of his tongue. When he finally pulls away, he simply smiles.

"What did I miss?" he croaks. I laugh as he coughs, struggling to get his voice back. But when the laughter dies down, and I think about Mace helpless in the showers, I bite my lip and avert my gaze. His eyes widen at my bashfulness, and his grin stretches wider.

"Say," I start. "You don't happen to remember what happened after you got out of that arena, do you?"

Mace locks his eyes on mine and transforms his grin into a suggestive half-smile, one lip curled with the other neutralized.

"Every second of it."

I roll my eyes but can't hide my embarrassment when my cheeks start to burn into undoubtedly the deepest blush anyone's ever seen. I know the naked shower was a necessity for Mace's survival, but I'm still mortified about what he knows I saw. I averted my gaze the best I could, but there's only so much a person can shield out of their periphery. His smile says otherwise, but I can't help but feel like I violated him somehow despite having his best interest at heart. Catching onto my embarrassment, Mace laughs and rubs my cheek with his palm.

"Stop. You did *nothing* wrong back there." He pushes a strand of hair behind my ear and kisses my forehead. "Thanks for helping me, Iris. I know it must've been...uncomfortable. I owe you a lot."

I shake my head, and my heart swells. *He never ceases to amaze me.* Especially in times of discomfort, he takes extra steps to ensure I feel entirely safe. My heart swoons with my love for him, leaving me speechless. Without words, I bring forward the only ones I know for certain.

"I love you, Mace."

His violet eyes gaze into mine so intensely that I don't feel his thumb holding up my chin. "I love you too, Iris. *Always.*"

I'm lost in his gaze, transported somewhere safe. My imagination flashes through every little thing I want to do with him, every milestone I want to pass together. His eyes shift their focus from my left to my right pupil, and I get the sensation that he's reading me. *Good.* I want him to see every detail I love about him and every insignificant moment I want to have with him, regardless of the confines of the Enterprize. When I lean in closer, Mace's ration bin crashes to the floor and I jerk, remembering dinner. I cough to break the tension and place our baskets on the floor, side by side. Lifting a sourdough mini-loaf, I stand and lean against the opposite wall. "You reckon you can stomach this?"

Mace raises his eyebrows. "*Reckon?*"

"I don't know, I saw it in some old textbook," I admit. I'd feel embarrassed by my slip, but his smile proves his admiration.

"Well, I *reckon* I'll get it down just fine."

I chuckle and climb next to him on top of the sheets. He sits up, still keeping the sheets tucked around his torso, then pauses, lifting the blanket so only he can see what's under.

"Um...am I naked?"

I burst out laughing. "Do you remember what happened or not?"

"I do! I remember clothes…I guess you just didn't think to put them on me?"

My laughter spikes into high-pitched screeches. "We couldn't! They were so wet, you'd freeze!"

"Sure, they were," Mace responds, closing his accusation with a wink. The suggestion has me gasping from my laughter. I hold my core, trying to contain myself. His violet eyes radiate joy, and I feel a glimpse of peace for the first time in a long time. But my harmony shatters when ocean eyes poke through the darkness in the back of my mind. I erupt in goosebumps when I recall my leg curling around the divots in Artemis's knees, my fingers trailing down his torso...

"Hey…. Mace?" I ask, abandoning the light-hearted tone for a more serious, direct one. He doesn't prompt me to continue, but his clenched jaw proves he knows what I will confront.

"I didn't kiss Artemis. I…I told you everything, I really did. I just…I didn't know how to tell you *that* part. I was confronting him about using me and demanding to know whether any of our friendship was real. There was no prompting…nothing to suggest that the kiss was invited. He just…did it. I was so shocked…I didn't know what to do."

"So, what *did* you do?" Mace asks. His eyes haven't left mine, searching for any sign of dishonesty. I choke on some air, then take a deep breath to get oxygen back into my lungs.

"Well…when I realized what was happening and came to my senses, I pulled away," I explain. "I fell to the floor, and his words just poured out. You know what he said…I told you *everything* he said. I just…I left that part out of it."

"Why?" Mace asks directly. There's no hatred or anger behind his words. Just pain.

"I…I didn't know how to tell you." I stumble for words. "I always planned to. I was going to tell you the *second* I woke up. But I talked with Ashlea and didn't even have to tell her before she realized it herself." I gulp. "We knew how you might react…she said it was too risky to tell you before the vote. So many parts of the plan relied on Finian trusting us. If you knew about the kiss…you might've rolled into Artemis even earlier. And if there was any chance that Finian would find out, he never would've flipped sides. You see how much he's regretting it now that he knows?"

Mace looks away, and I can almost see the gears rotating in his mind. When he finally returns his gaze to mine, his voice cracks within his deafening whisper.

"What made you trust that *he* would keep it a secret?"

The question throws me for a loop. I take a second to clear my throat, trying to navigate a way to answer it. "I don't know…I guess I just thought that if he meant what he said to me, he wouldn't put me in that position. I thought that if he'd die for me…then surely, he'd keep that detail between us. Or, at the very least, not *lie* about what happened."

He shakes his head. "Iris. He's a bad guy. You can't trust him. I don't know what possessed him to say those things to you or if he even meant them. Who knows…who cares?" He takes a deep breath, then stares back into my eyes. "But even if he does, he'd *never* respect a woman enough to take responsibility for himself. He'd *die* before ruining his reputation, no matter what you mean to him."

The accusation hurts, but mostly because it's the truth. Artemis thrives on the acceptance of others. He didn't open up until he scored laughter from the other convicts on day 1. Since then, he flourished only when others supported his words and actions. My eyes dart around the room as it clicks, and my chest deflates. Artemis probably doesn't even love *me*. He just loves that I support his wretched behavior. If I'm wrong, and he did mean the words that he said…

He'd much sooner die than reap the consequences of his actions.

Silence passes between us.

"Why did you stay?"

I tilt my head. "What do you mean?"

"When he kissed you…you could've just got up and left. But you didn't." He takes a deep breath. "Why did you stay?"

It takes me a moment to consider my answer, but I opt for the truth. "I don't know what I was thinking," I whisper. "I just felt so awful for him. I didn't want him to *hurt*."

"What about me?" Mace's eyes are feral, but he's careful not to inch any closer. "Why didn't you think about *me*?"

I shake my head, holding my breath. "I don't know what to say, Mace."

He darts his gaze to the floor and picks his bread apart. His chest rises and falls rapidly as he tries to calm his shaky breaths. *He's holding back.* He wants to ask me one last dying question but is too afraid of what the answer may be. But I love him too much to spare him from the truth. So, despite my better judgment, I lift his cheek until he meets my gaze and force the words out.

"I know you're holding back…*please*….what do you want to know?"

Mace stares into my eyes and drops the half-loaf onto the comforter. His eyes fill with moisture, but he fights back tears, refusing to let one fall. I grip my roll hard, condensing the wheat between my fingers.

"You don't love him back, do you?"

The words pierce a bullet through my chest. How do you answer a question you don't know the answer to? On the one hand, my heart yearns for Artemis. It twists with pain when he's hurting and soars with happiness when he smiles. But when I reflect upon the last twenty-four hours, my brain screams the reality. *Mace wants the truth?* The *truth* is that I didn't even *think* about worrying about Artemis in the Executive competition. The truth is that I never even *considered* his sorrow when his convict girlfriend died. The truth is that when rushing Mace to the bedrooms, I raced past Artemis and didn't give him a second thought. I cared so *little* for him at that moment that my vision couldn't even detect his presence.

I might love Artemis. But what's the point in revealing that when my love for Mace is so powerful that when I'm around him, Artemis is pushed so far in the back of my mind that it's difficult to retrieve his memory.

I might love Artemis. But between the two, I'd pick Mace a thousand times over.

So, when Mace asks the fateful question and my mind flashes through the probable explanations, I gaze into his eyes and answer truthfully.

"No."

At the very least, I've convinced myself it's the truth.

I'm tucked beneath the sheets with Mace when we finish our meals, only his towel barrier keeping our legs from touching. The space is tight, but I don't mind. His warmth makes me feel safe and comfortable. Squeezing his hand around my shoulder, I am truly happy for the first time in weeks.

I think.

My head is on Mace's chest, and I focus on his thrumming heartbeat. It lulls me into a daze, and I smile that I'm the only one who gets to feel it. His loyalty and forgiveness astound me, but I don't question it. He's truly a beautiful man, inside and out.

Which is why I never expected him to be capable of holding such hatred.

He shifts when Destry and Artemis crest the steps, and his pounding heart races against my ear. "Here comes the pity party." Destry rolls his eyes, but Artemis completely ignores him, keeping his stare on Destry's back.

"What's the matter, Artemis? Cat got your tongue?" Mace eggs him on. He hugs me with his opposite arm so I'm still leaning on his bare chest when he sits up. "Come on, big guy. Say something!"

Artemis keeps the pace of his strides, concentrating on the path ahead and blocking out Mace's calls.

"Awfully confident for a man who isn't in power," Destry spits, giving us a side glance.

"Oh, come off it, Destry. When it's me up there next week, you two are *done*."

I'm appalled at how much he's marginalizing death. I'm even more terrified to admit it. So, I simply clutch his chest and inch my head into the crevice between his neck and shoulder. Destry doesn't even look at us when he tries to sneak in the last word. "We'll see about that." He opens the door to Lagiacrus's room and starts crossing the threshold, but Mace refuses to let Destry be the last to contribute to the fight.

"Good to know you aren't physically capable of giving a shit about anyone but yourself, Art! You're a lying, conniving piece of *shit*, and everyone will remember you as such when you *finally* meet the firing squad."

The door shuts late enough that I know the insult has landed. I gasp, realizing I've been holding my breath. My focus is all over the place, but finally, I land on my repulsion for Mace's behavior. Despite the safety and comfort he offers, his anger is frightening. It's a side of him I wish I never had to see, and it's growing more powerful by the second.

307

"Coward," Mace says, shifting back so he's lying down.

"Yeah," I laugh convincingly, my heart breaking a thousand times. My cheeks heat up against Mace's chest when I consider how angry I am with Artemis for telling Destry that I came onto him. But my chest tightens when I acknowledge the part of me that hopes there was a miscommunication. Perhaps Destry is the liar, and Artemis is too consumed in his own trauma to defend me. Regardless of the truth, Artemis's betrayal makes me nauseous. *How could he divulge our secret?* I truly believed he cared enough about me to keep the kiss between us. At least until I was ready to tell Mace. My emotions fight one another: anger, loss, betrayal...

Love.

"What's even worse is how much of a womanizer he is," Mace says, breaking me from my thoughts. "First Mercedes, then you? How many people is he gonna trick into thinking he loves them?"

I laugh forcefully, but the label is valid. "Yeah, I don't get that. He always talked about how much he hated Mercedes but would act like he was obsessed with her when they were together."

Silence passes between us as Mace considers his next words. Finally, he shakes his head. "You wouldn't believe the things he said to her, Iris."

My heart rate picks up, pounding in my ears. "Wha...what did he tell her?"

Mace laughs with no humor. "I don't know if he said he loved her. But the way he sexualized that girl in front of the guys...the way he talked about her body and the things he wanted to *do* to her...it was disgusting, Iris."

My eyes widen in horror, and I sit up straight. "He did that?"

"Yes!" Mace smiles, eyes dilating on me. "Iris, I told you! He's a *terrible* guy! A womanizer, a backstabber...and now a coward too, I guess. The others would laugh, but he always knew how low I thought he was when he'd say that crap. He eventually just stopped saying it around me altogether."

This information shouldn't surprise me, but it does. I knew from my first impression of Artemis that he was crude about women. Still, I never expected that it carried on through the recent rounds. After everything we've been through together...I assumed that it stopped.

Mace drops his voice to a whisper. "I *heard* him tell her she's the only girl he cares about. That she's...what? The best thing that's ever happened to him?"

"*What?*" I drop my façade of holding things together and let my voice *roar.* "*When* did he say that?"

Mace's muscles tense, and his words are slow. "Sometime before Sola's expulsion?"

"It happened that early?" I'm nearly yelling.

Mace slides an inch away from me. "Yeah, but...why do you *care* so much?"

Silence passes between us as I try to compose my thoughts. Finally, I abandon the efforts and let my frustration flow. "I care because he made me feel like *crap* that I didn't feel the same way. I've had to watch him mope around the house for days, making me feel like the worst person in the world…when all this time, he said the same things to Mercedes!"

Mace sets a hand on my shoulder. "I've said it before, and I'll say it again." His voice drops an octave. *"He's manipulating you."*

I know Mace's intentions are not pure. He simply wants me to share his hatred toward Artemis after he attempted to destroy us. Regardless of the objective, I'm overcome with *rage*. If Artemis truly loved me, he wouldn't have told Destry what happened. He *certainly* would not have shared the script he used with Mercedes on me.

I let my top blow. "Who does Artemis think he is? *Screw* that!" I yell, not caring if anyone else hears me. "I trusted him!"

Mace pushes my hair back and leans into my ear, allowing a delicate whisper to reach my eardrum in a whisp of hot air.

"So, let's finish him."

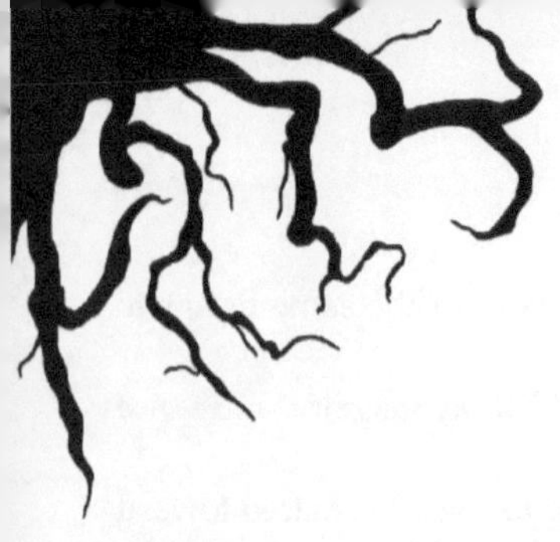

Chapter 48

I lean against the back of the couch and laugh, jaw pointed toward the sky. My sides ache from the intensity of my cackles, but the company makes my heart swoon.

"It's true!" Artemis yelps. "That maggot couldn't get out of Kylah's hair fast enough! Trust me, it wanted out of Kylah's nest far more than she was willing to help it! Poor guy was wiggling his little heart out, desperate to escape that greasy, dandruff mess."

"Stop!" I gasp for air. "She did everything she could!"

"What, shake her head? You should've seen that little man! He was doing some acrobatic shit. I mean, the athleticism on the guy!"

My vision blurs with tears, and I gasp for air. I hold onto my stomach to soothe the soreness, but every time he opens his mouth, Artemis sends me into another bout of crippling laughter. When I finally catch my breath, I smile. Artemis's gaze matches mine, a sly grin stretched across his lips.

"What?" I choke out.

"Nothing," he smiles, stretching his arms behind him so they support his neck.

"Correct me if I'm wrong, but...I feel like you feel the same way."

I blink the memory away and shift my gaze to the ceiling. Wait. Where am I? What day is it?

"Oh, screw it. Yes, Iris. I love you. I'm in love with you..."

No, something's not right. It feels like...

That hasn't happened yet.

Artemis tilts his head, never breaking eye contact. "You okay? It looks like you've seen a ghost. I imagine Sola and Crescentia would be quite the terror to see in the afterlife."

That's the Artemis I know. Marginalizing death and making a mockery of their lives. But somehow...this feels different.

I blink when it hits me.

I'm dreaming.

My heart aches that this banter is nothing more than a figment of my imagination. After everything we've been through, we'll never joke around with each other in this way again. Time freezes, and my chest urges me to do the right thing and wake up. But my head begs me to take advantage of this fantasy and see how far it goes, knowing my actions won't have any consequences.

So, instead of running from fictional Artemis and rushing into Mace's real arms, I embrace a stolen moment with my best friend and see how far I can take it.

"What a fantasy that'd be for you, huh?" I joke.

He leans back and laughs before quipping back, "More like my own personal hell."

I smile and watch him staring back, blue eyes glistening with admiration. His loving gaze makes my next words slide easily off my lips. "You really are something."

"A good something? Please tell me it's not a bad something…preferably I'm an attractive *something."*

I laugh at the suggestion, then remember my predicament. This is a dream. *Nothing I say or do here will matter.*

So instead of holding back or reprimanding his flirtatiousness…

I take it a step further.

"One of those things. And it's not *either of the first two options."*

His eyes widen with shock. We stare at each other in silence until I can't take the tension any longer.

"You really do have the most beautiful eyes I've ever seen."

Artemis smiles and responds without missing a beat. "Not the first person to tell me that and won't be the last." A wink ends the statement. The single sentence spreads a warm sensation from between my legs to the ends of my fingertips. My gaze pauses on his sculpted arms, protruding veins running trails into his chest. When I finally flick my stare back to his eyes, they're scanning my every crevice from my backside to my breasts. He bites his lip when he catches me watching him, and I gasp at my attraction to him. Without a second thought, I'm floating toward him, eyes locked on his suggestive lips. He spreads his legs for me to crawl onto his lap, and I'm steps from pulling him to my chest when the world starts spinning.

In a single moment, my legs are concrete, rooted to the ground. Artemis's shoulders start steaming, whisps of gray disintegrating his outer extremities. I'm pulling my legs from the ground with my arms and wince when I realize what's happening.

I'm waking up.

No. **Please.** *I need more time.*

Artemis finally jumps to his feet and closes the distance between us in two strides. I hold onto my dream desperately as I reach out to my best friend, longing *for his touch.*

Just as my fingers grace his torso, he disappears in a silent wisp of wind, taking the last organic moment between us with him.

I jolt awake on Mace's chest, my fingers grasping his torso.

"You, okay?" Mace tenses, cuddling me closer.

I blink several times, ridding myself of the remaining whisps of my dream. I gulp and wipe a bead of sweat off my forehead. "Yeah…bad dream."

Mace pushes a strand of hair behind my ear and kisses my forehead. His soft lips linger on my skin a touch longer than usual. "Well, you're safe now. Under the eyes of the Authority!"

I smile and roll my eyes at his sarcasm. Wiggling out of his arms, I stretch my back against the bedpost and deconstruct my hair. Halfway through my new fishtail, Mace's gaze freezes time.

"You really are beautiful, Iris." Mace grabs a loose strand of my hair and smiles. There's love in his eyes but also a deep hollowness that only time can heal. Since time isn't a luxury we can afford, I let my heart do the talking.

"Mace," I smile, cupping his cheek. My heart thumps when the words leave my lips. "You really do have the most beautiful eyes I've ever seen."

A pit forms in my stomach at how unnatural the compliment feels. Mace's violet eyes *are* beautiful. And they're certainly more beautiful than Artemis's. However, stealing a compliment meant for Artemis and giving it to Mace crosses *too many* moral boundaries. My throat aches from the guilt, but I don't allow myself to blush. Instead, I move in for a kiss, letting my lips lock naturally into Mace's. He rubs my lower back as my chest melts into his, and I find myself clawing at the blankets, desperate to get closer to him.

Catching his breath, Mace shifts his lips to my neck, slowly kissing the length from my collar to my chin. My eyes are closed when he whispers against my delicate skin. The hot air of his breath sends a shiver through my spine.

"Breakfast before kissing Lagiacrus's ass today?" I laugh against his lips, so he plants one final kiss behind my ear before pulling away. "If only we could be a fly on the wall when Destry's in there. We could really use a brown-nosing tutorial."

I smile. "Let's hope Destry's gotten on his nerves so much that Lagiacrus puts him on Death Row." I roll my eyes. "That'll shut him up."

"We can dream," Mace smiles, following me off the cot. I don't notice that he's ducked back into the covers until he calls for me. "Uh, Iris?"

"What's up?" I spin around, tilting my head.

Mace lifts a single eyebrow. "Uh…could you maybe get some clothes for me?"

We stare into each other's eyes for a silent second before bursting into laughter. I slump over, holding my stomach, having forgotten Mace is wearing nothing beneath his pile of towels.

I shrug, raising my palms toward the sky. "What? Don't wanna strut around the house naked?"

Mace shakes his head. "Wouldn't *you* love that?" When he winks, I'm on my knees laughing, unable to catch my breath. He shifts the blanket until it covers everything but his face and playfully pleads when my eyes land on his.

"Iris, could you *pretty please* get me some clothes? So, I don't have to show everybody in Miasmis my—"

"You just sit there and wait!" I shout, throwing out a hand to cut him off. "I'll go get your clothes, *princess*."

"Thaaank yoooou," Mace says in a singsong voice, purposely extending the vowels. I shake my head and smile as I turn for the stairs. I can't help but flutter my eyelashes as I bounce off each step, my cheeks blushing from love rather than guilt. Still, I can't ignore that sick feeling in my stomach, reminding me of my true feelings for Artemis. I yearn to speak with him again to clear up the misconceptions and rumors floating around. A piercing hurt in my heart brutally reminds me that I'll never get that chance. My dilemma abruptly disappears when I pass Kylah and Lagiacrus in the kitchen.

They scan me up and down, killing their conversation, so there's complete silence.

"Good morning?" I raise my eyebrows, slowing my steps. Lagiacrus nods but swiftly lifts his ration basket and heads for the stairs. I watch his meticulous steps and turn to Kylah, but she doesn't meet my gaze. My heart races as she turns around in her chair, propping her chin with her palm to stare in the opposite direction.

I narrow my gaze on her as I stalk toward the bathroom and retrieve Mace's belongings. I easily locate them hanging off the edge of the sink and bundle the soft fabric into my arms before exiting. When I pass back through the living area, Kylah's still at the kitchen table, picking through her breakfast. She finally locks eyes with mine, and daggers spit out of her pupils. Her demon gaze stops me in my tracks and nearly makes me drop Mace's clothes.

"Hey, Kylah…are you okay?" I ask, stopping in front of the kitchen table.

She raises her eyebrows and tilts her head, auburn curls bouncing with the movement. "I really don't want to get into it right now, Iris."

I scrunch my nose and narrow my eyes on her. "If something is bothering you, Kylah, I'm sure I can take it."

"I don't know, *can you*, Iris?"

I open my free palm to the sky and tilt my head toward the ceiling. A camera with a blinking light zooms in on me, so I shrug. "Did I do something to you, Kylah? What changed in the past twenty-four hours that has you all hot and bothered?"

Kylah smashes her fist on the table. In half a second, she's on her feet, towering over me. "Are you serious right now, Iris? We turned the vote around for *you*. We put our lives on the line for *you*. We rallied around Artemis's vulnerability when *you* catalyzed it all."

Her words punch a hole in my gut, and I step back. "Excuse me?"

Kylah inches forward until her curls fall onto my forehead. "Iris, the only reason we got this blindside to work was because Artemis made a mistake, and we all took *your* side." Her voice raises an octave, making my ears ring. "When, all this time, you forgot to mention that you *made out* with him in solitary confinement! Then told him you loved him the night you got out!"

My eyes are nearly bulging out of their sockets. I can hardly speak, my voice shaking with rage. "Kylah, what the *hell* are you talking about? None of that is true! Where are you even hearing this?!"

Kylah stares directly into my eyes and gulps.

"You might wanna ask your little friend, *Artemis*."

The world is spinning. I choke on the air and nearly fall to my knees.

No. Artemis? My best friend told her these lies?

Kylah rolls her eyes. "Oh, don't stand there and act all *innocent*. You lied about what happened between you two, making your entire alliance a target. And don't you *dare* pretend for even a *second* that you're not after me. It's why you created your little Dial alliance in the first place. You just can't *stand* somebody getting between you and your brother, can you?" Spit flings from her lips. "Well, I'll tell you one thing, Iris. I'm more of a sister to Lunar than you *ever* were."

My jaw drops to the floor. I'm shaking so hard I have to lean against the kitchen table to prevent collapsing. Desperate for the nightmare to end, I squeeze my eyes shut and pinch my side three times. When I open them, Kylah's still scrunching her eyebrows at me, heated rage radiating off her skin. *How could this be happening?* How do I even begin to defend myself when I've never felt these accusations for even a *second*? And worst of all...

Artemis told her this?

"Kylah...I don't know why Artemis said any of this, but none of it's true! I didn't start Dial. They brought me in at the last minute! You've never been my target...if you were, don't you think you would have ended up on Death Row even *once* in the last four rounds? Don't you see how ridiculous you sound?"

Kylah shakes her head, giving her curls a bounce. "You lied about being in Dial. How can I trust anything you say to me?"

I throw my hands up and let my rage *roar*. "You've *got* to be kidding me, Kylah! You're paranoid...I'm not after you! If anyone wants you out, it's the guys! They'll pick us off one by one until they're sitting pretty in the final three! You *have* to believe me! Why would I want you gone if you've been protecting my brother this whole time?!"

Kylah bunches her hands into fists and narrows her eyes. "You don't deserve my respect. After everything I've done for you and your brother? You target *me*?" She throws her remaining rations in her bin and yanks it by the handles. "You disgust me."

Sweat pours down my face, and I'm trembling. But most of all, my stomach twists, and my senses fade. My newfound tunnel vision blocks every competing emotion away. It only lets me focus on the most horrific, heartbreaking feeling of them all.

Betrayal.

"Who told you this?" I ask Kylah calmly and clearly, maintaining eye contact. She rolls her eyes and turns for the living room. My brain tells my limbs to halt-to turn around and lay down my weapons. But my heart dominates control, so I step toward Kylah and raise my voice. "I SAID, 'WHO TOLD YOU?'"

Her eyes narrow on mine.

Then she spits on the carpet in front of me.

Kylah marches to the living room, not giving my question a second thought. I growl and turn for the stairs, tripping over Mace's clean shirt and pants. *I hadn't realized I dropped them.* I bunch them in my arms and stomp up the stairs, letting my feet slam against the carpet. When I reach the top floor, Ashlea kneels beside my bed, smiling at Mace. Lunar's asleep, and Finian is leaning over his cot with his head between his knees.

"About time!" Mace flirts, a grin painted on his lips. As I get closer, his smile fades, and his eyes widen. "What...are you okay, Iris?"

"That lying, womanizing, *manipulating* piece of shit!" I yell, completely neglecting Lunar's peaceful rest. I toss Mace his clothes as gently as my fury allows, then kick the wall with enough force that a boom echoes across the bedroom.

"Iris, calm down! Tell us what happened. Who are you talking about?" Ashlea pleads desperately.

"Artemis, of course! Who else is trying to ruin my life?" I kick the wall again, then pace before my bed. "Can anybody tell me why Kylah thinks I'm after her? Did *any* of you tell her that? Because never, for *one second*, has she even been a blip on my radar! I don't think I've ever spoken about her to anyone, ever!"

"Woah, is everything okay?" Lunar shouts, rubbing his eyes from dreariness.

I try to bring my voice down so I don't worry my brother, but my rage fuels my aggression, and nothing I grasp onto calms me.

"He's gonna get us killed!" I scream. "I trusted him! And he goes around telling people I'm after them? Then *lies* about our relationship?"

"Wow, slow down, Iris!" Mace calls, shoving his shirt on. "Tell us *exactly* what happened."

"I…he's claiming that I started Dial!" I yell. "That I didn't just hide being in it…that I started the entire alliance!"

"Now, that's just ridiculous," Mace complains. "Everyone in that alliance *knows* you and Finian were late additions."

Finian raises his head. He throws his palms to the sky and scowls.

"No offense," Mace directs his way.

"Too late for it to matter anyway," he sends back.

"But that's just the start!" I screech, ignoring Finian's comment. "Apparently, he's claiming that in solitary confinement, I revealed my *secret hatred* for Kylah and my master plan to kill her for getting close to Lunar."

"Are you kidding me?" Ashlea asks, eyebrows shooting toward the sky.

My words come out so fast, they're indistinguishable from one another. "When have I ever said anything about Kylah? All this time, I've *loved* that she's helped Lunar! And she just goes and believes the first thing she's told? From *Artemis*, of all people?" My throat aches, but my following words come out in a scream. "SINCE WHEN HAS HIS REPUTATION SHOWN THAT WE CAN TRUST ANYTHING THAT COMES OUT OF THAT MAN'S MOUTH!?"

Lunar's jaw is on the floor. Ashlea leans back, wincing, and Mace shakes his head, sagging against the headboard. I search their faces for an explanation, but they are speechless.

"I mean, what do I do?" I yell. "He's going around telling everybody we made out in there!" Mace rolls his eyes at the suggestion, not giving it a second thought. "All I've *ever* done is be a good friend to him! *So he hurls my body in front of a train and ties me to the tracks?* Nobody was there for him when he attacked Sola, but *I was*. I looked past it and gave him a second chance. I put my life on the line *for him*. And he does this!?"

"Iris, we've been trying to tell you," Ashlea pleads, leaning forward with her hands clasped in her lap. "He's *bad news*. All he ever wanted was to use you! And now that Mercedes is dead, he's done with you!" She stands and tries to approach me, but I refuse to stand still. Blocking my path, she holds my shoulders. "He's doing damage control and using you as a scapegoat! That's all the coward knows how to do!"

I pound my fist against the bedframe, escaping her grasp. "Well, it's a little late for that now, isn't it?" Ashlea slumps back, biting her lip. My heart wrenches at the fear in her eyes, and I take a moment to breathe. "I'm sorry…I know you're just trying to help…I just…," I shift my gaze to Mace. "You don't believe him, right? All this bullshit about me and him…his claim that *I* came onto *him*. That *I* love *him*." Tears well in my eyes as I step within his reach. "I just…when will he just leave me alone!" I scream, tears streaming down my cheeks.

"Iris," Mace says, pulling me in for a hug. "*Of course*, I don't believe that crap. You've never targeted Kylah, and you didn't create Dial. I *know* those aren't true. Why should I believe there's any truth behind his claims about the two of you?" I melt into his arms and curl my legs around his torso. "You got tricked. That's it. There's nothing more to it, Iris. I don't believe him. Finian shouldn't believe him, considering his late addition to Dial. And I'm *positive* Ashlea and Lunar don't believe him." He wipes my tears with his thumb when I lean away from him. I force a smile and nestle my head between his shoulder and neck.

Ashlea settles on the edge of my bed and puts a soft palm on my back. "I never trusted that guy," Ashlea says. "When you beat a woman to death on the fourth day…that says all you need to know about your character."

I thank Ashlea with my eyes before fluttering them closed. After several deep breaths, I watch Lunar two beds over, waiting for his validation. When he finds everyone watching him, he rolls his eyes. "Of course, I don't believe that crap, Iris. I've never seen you like this before. This…distraught." His voice is raspy, with pity scraping his vocal cords. "Obviously, he hurt you. And we're all gonna hurt him *back*."

I smile at my brother. My muscles feel weak until Mace squeezes my hand. "We're gonna get him back, Iris. Next round…we'll be firing on all cylinders."

I nod and try to force another smile but can't bring my lips to stretch. Instead, I crumble at my newest realization. "Lagiacrus is gonna put two of our group up, Mace." I deflate, so my words are barely a whisper. "What are we gonna do?"

Ashlea raises her eyebrows. "Well, we know you three are safe," she says. "Lagiacrus is a man of his word. I doubt he'd suddenly stray away from that."

I nod, but my fears do not subside. "But what about you?"

Ashlea shrugs. "I got through last week…what's another week, right?" I know she's putting on a brave face for me. But the terror in her tremors gives her away.

"So, what…me and Ashlea then?" Finian interrupts. He stands now, his burned skin peeling around his rage-filled eyes. "And let me guess, you'll keep *her*?"

"We don't know that," Mace shares. "It could be Kylah! And then the decision would be easy! We'd have the numbers." He looks at the others in my alliance, widening his gaze. "They only have two votes. If two of us are on Death Row, it's four of our votes against two of theirs. We'd beat them no matter what."

"*Assuming* Kylah would still be on our team, which she wouldn't be," Finian argues. "We have *no* power. If Kylah switches sides, the vote would be a tie." His volume rises as he steps closer. "We can't decide anything!"

"Does it matter?" Mace interjects, glaring at Finian. "No matter what, one of us is leaving. It's already a lose-lose situation."

Finian rolls his eyes. "I just...what was I thinking?!" He drops back into his bed, rubbing his temples. "We're doomed!"

"Hey," Lunar spits. "We'll know in a few hours. Until then, there's no use getting our panties in a wad."

I open my mouth to respond, but I don't have any reassuring words. I simply nod at Lunar and press my lips together. Before rising, Ashlea pats my back and whispers that everything will be alright. With the argument finally dead, I wrap myself back into Mace's arms, and he wipes the remaining salt from my face.

"It's going to be okay," Mace says. "Everything's going to be just fine. We have each other...we can get through this. I don't care what bullshit Artemis comes up with. I'm not leaving you."

I sniff back tears and lock onto his violet eyes. "You promise?"

Mace looks at me seriously and puts a soothing hand on my cheek, extending the finger furthest from my face.

"I pinky swear."

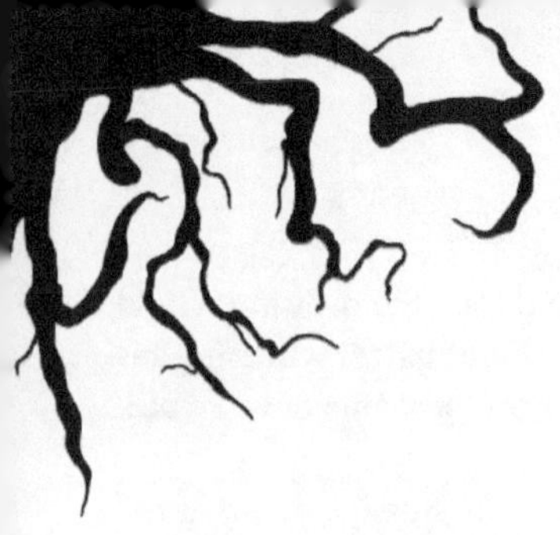

Chapter 49

I swish around my mushy cereal, my shaky arms making it difficult to stop the milk from spilling. Hours after our brief panic in the bedroom, Mace and I checked our safety with Lagiacrus. Without resistance, he promised he was a man of his word. Despite the brief rush of relief soothing my tense muscles, I can't help the fear twisting my chest for Ashlea. The remainder of Dial was so angry she survived Round 4 that I'm confident her safety is at serious risk. I do not want to test my luck with pushing Lagiacrus, so I can only pray that Death Row will be Finian and Kylah.

Then we can get the bitch out without worrying about the other side's vote.

It's all become so rudimentary to me: putting people on Death Row and voting on who gets expelled. Now that I have hatred coursing through my veins for the various snakes in the house, I'm suddenly having no problem sending them out of the Enterprize.

After all, we're all convicts anyway.

I lazily put the spoon to my lips and sip on the milk. Today, I switched my meals around to have something more basic in my stomach. The selections today will not be pleasant, so I'm trying to soothe my nausea the best that I can.

Ashlea, Lunar, and Mace sit motionless around me, nobody touching their food. Despite the front he's putting on, I can feel Mace's terror. I can't tell whether he's more afraid of himself going up or fearful that Lagiacrus will break his word altogether. If he puts us both up out of spite, I don't think either of our hearts could take it. Whatever the reason, I lose my appetite and set my spoon down with a splash.

I push my hands against my eyes and rub so hard I see black dots. I push until there's a light touch on my back and twinge at Mace's hot whisper.

"Stay strong…for Lunar." I nod and wipe the stress from my face. My forced smile twinges at Lunar as I push his cereal bowl toward him. He doesn't register the gesture. Instead, he simply returns a nod and then regains his blank stare at the carpet.

One deep breath at a time, I try and meditate my worries away. But three breaths in, stomps on the staircase disrupt my thoughts. I cringe as Artemis slumps his way through the kitchen. My gaze doesn't stop trailing him until he settles in the living room with a dramatic collapse.

I shake my head a million miles an hour. "I'm gonna kill him…I'm *really* gonna kill him."

"Iris…" Ashlea whispers from two seats over.

"Look at him, Ashlea!" I refute. My voice is hushed enough that the conversation is contained to the table. "He's slumping around like *I* did something to *him*. He's trying to manipulate me into feeling bad for him *again*!"

I grip the side of the table, preparing to stand, but Mace puts an arm out to block my trajectory. "*Please*, Iris. Now isn't the time."

"When *will* it be the time!?" I plead. "He's spreading rumors about me that could get any one of us killed! And he gets to just walk away? With no repercussions?"

Shooting my gaze his way, I scoff at Artemis. He's scrunched on the floor with his head between his bent knees. Several of my feelings conflict with one another as I watch him, and I struggle to identify the most prominent. *Hurt* that he would spread such awful misinformation about me. *Betrayal* that he would share our private moments with others, but only after he's added sexually compromising twists to paint me in a bad light. *Sorrow* that my actions have caused him so much pain that he hasn't been himself in ages. *Manipulation* that he may just be trying to make me feel sorry for him to win me over. *Urgency* to scream at him in front of the others and make him feel the pain that I do. I try to push back the most overwhelming feeling, but it sneaks its way into my consciousness.

Desperation. To have one last real, *honest* conversation with him.

Mace's voice returns in a rushed whisper. "Iris, I don't think he's getting off unscathed. Karma will come back…one of us will put him on Death Row, and he'll get what he deserves." He takes a deep breath. "But you *have to* wait. Causing a scene now could compromise everything."

"But it's not fair," I plead. "You got to yell at him. What do I get?"

"You think I enjoyed that?" Mace raises his eyebrows. "Yelling at him *destroyed* me. You saw how close we used to be. You think I wanted to hurt him? But what choice did I have? He's betrayed you, and that betrays us all." We all sneak a look at Artemis in the living room, and his scrunched body starts to tremble. Mace gently wraps his fingers around my wrist and gazes into my eyes. "I know it sucks, Iris. I know it *hurts*. But the Artemis we used to know…" He shakes his head, dropping my wrist. "He's dead. This…" he gestures toward the living room and lowers his voice to a whisper. "I've never met this man before in my life."

After a fateful gulp, I nod, accepting a reality I never wanted. People are not always what they appear to be. And the Artemis that cowers before me?

He is *not* the man that I fell in love with.

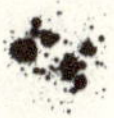

I squeeze Mace's palm on the blue sofa, holding back tears. Lunar clutches my other hand, watching the red numbers descend toward zero.

With two minutes remaining, the final nine convicts aren't taking any chances. We've all been in the living room with plenty of time to spare, only the sounds of our shaking breaths filling the air. Lagiacrus is perched on the edge of his Executive couch, slowly rubbing his hands together and staring at the floor. My team sits on the closest couch to the kitchen. Shockingly, Kylah planted herself on our side. She's either unprepared to make a firm stance on her alignment, or I'm blowing our argument out of proportion. Considering that she's actively ignored me since her accusations, I'm willing to bet on the former.

Our side outnumbers the other. Only Destry and Artemis are seated on the opposite sofa. Finian even placed himself on the rebel couch, whether he's truly happy about it or not.

My legs shake, but I try to control them for Lunar's sake. Instead, I trigger him into a cascade of trembles so severe, the couch sways.

As if the tremors never started, all sensory feelings fade when the clock has ten seconds remaining.

Lagiacrus plants his feet on the carpet and rises when the clock strikes zero. When the horn blares, Lagiacrus doesn't even react. Instead, he turns to face the group and takes a strong breath.

"You know how this goes…I have to choose two of you for Death Row. And having been in this position before, I can confidently tell you that this job doesn't get easier. In fact,…it gets exponentially harder the further into this…*game* we get." I squeeze my eyes, forcing the moisture to stay in place.

"When I stood here before, I was fresh off the murder of my best friend. And with that, I promised myself to stay true to my character and, therefore, true to my word." He looks at Mace, and my violet-eyed hero gives a gentle nod. My rigidness loosens at the gesture, but my heart still pounds in my ears. Lagiacrus looks back to the middle of the room and takes another deep breath, straightening his back and puffing out his chest. "So here we are. Finally, at a place where…people's *true* colors have started to show."

I squeeze Mace's hand, heart beating out of my chest.

"One of you is a person that I thought I could trust. I never had any indication that you would betray me…but with death on the line, the truth *always* comes out." His eyes land on Finian. "Finian…you broke your word. And for that," he gestures toward the black settees, "I'm going to have to ask you to take a seat on Death Row."

Finian rolls his eyes and marches to the seat, successfully staying quiet despite his outright fury. *One down, one to go.* I will Kylah's name to come out of Lagiacrus's lips and nearly mouth it to make it true.

"This next person brings me to my original point." When Lagiacrus exhales, his breath shakes. For the first time, he's unintentionally shed his stoic exterior. He grips his palms into fists and quickly puts his walls back up. "I promised I would never compromise my morals and go against my word. But when it comes down to the final nine, and there are *three people* that will do *anything* to ensure each other's safety…even if that means risking their own? Well…I'd be a damn *fool* to watch them sail by and get me killed. My brother wouldn't have wanted me to target a family…but I know what he would have approved of…"

No.

"I'm really sorry…it's nothing personal…"

I suffocate for air. I squeeze Mace's hand tighter than ever before and feel a tear stream down my face when the words come out.

"Mace…please take a seat on Death Row."

Chapter 50

I cry harder than I ever thought possible. Mace calmly releases my hand and shifts to Sola's bullet-decorated sofa. Mace and Finian sit side by side, but I have to wipe my eyes on my shirt to see them clearly. Finian's nostrils flare, and his muscles tense. Mace simply crosses his legs and spreads his lips into a wide grin.

"Meeting adjourned?" Mace asks, violet eyes shooting daggers at Lagiacrus.

"Yes…meeting adjourned," Lagiacrus answers, turning to walk away.

"Now, where do you think you're going?" Mace asks with mock amusement. "If you wanted to fuck us, you could at least buy us dinner first?"

Lagiacrus widens his eyes at the comment before shrugging, keeping his confident façade intact. "It's strictly gameplay, man. You have to respect that."

"I *have* to respect a hypocrite whose word is less valuable than my morning ration? No…any ounce of respect I had for you vanished ten seconds ago." Mace rises from his sofa and marches toward Lagiacrus. "You suffer in that water with me for over half an hour and *beg* me to give you the win....for *this*?" He slams his chest against Lagiacrus, forcing him to step back. "Your word means *nothing*, Lagiacrus! If I hadn't gotten out of that water, you would be dead!"

Destry leaps from the couch and throws his hands in the air. "Who are you to talk, Mace? *You're* the one who agreed to vote out Ashlea! What happened to that? Who are you to talk about loyalty?"

I shake my head and gasp for breath. Artemis rises from his couch without a word, sneaking behind the confrontation and trying to escape to the bathroom unnoticed. The cowardice of his actions makes my blood boil so hot that I can't stop myself from shouting. "*No*. You get back here, Artemis, and face this decision like a man!"

Artemis turns slowly, jaw on the floor. "I wasn't the one who put your *boyfriend* on Death Row! Why are you yelling at *me*?"

"Oh, shut the *fuck* up, Artemis," Ashlea shouts, standing to join the fight. "You were just as much a part of this decision as Lagiacrus was. Don't you try and pretend that you had nothing to do with it."

Artemis raises his palms at Ashlea. His words come out in a squeal. "Why would I want Mace out? What good does that do for me!?"

Tears still cloud my vision, but rage tears me from my sorrow. I rise with my fists balled tightly, and my voice shakes with fury. "Are you *kidding* me right now? Are you seriously asking that when you know *full well* what you said to me in the Executive bedroom?"

Artemis takes a step forward, blue eyes bulging from their sockets. "What did I say, Iris!? *What* did I say?"

My jaw drops, and I bite my cheek to keep my lips from trembling. I lunge, closing the distance between us so only the long sofa separates our bodies. "You're telling me you don't remember suggesting that life would be easier without Mace in the picture?"

Artemis squeezes his eyelids tight and throws his hands in the air. "Is this a joke right now? That's *not* what I said!"

The ache in my throat is *searing*. I smash my fist into the couch cushion between us and let my voice *screech*. "YES, IT IS! Own up to it, you *coward*!"

"I AM NOT A COWARD!"

The room becomes so silent that I hear Artemis's heart thumping in his chest. Every head is turned toward us, his roar still ringing in our ears. Artemis is red in the face and squeezes his hand into a fist so tight that his veins poke through the skin. He bares his teeth and searches the room desperately. It takes me three seconds to realize he's looking for something to punch. Even with this realization rooting itself in my chest, I don't fear him. Because the entire time we've been screaming at one another, the deep adoration in his eyes has never faltered. Regardless of his lies, I trust he'd never put me in physical danger. But somehow, his betrayal stings exponentially more than any physical abuse could possibly inflict.

"Everybody just calm down," Destry says, feet planted wide.

I take a deep breath before staring directly into Artemis's eyes. "Artemis," I say, forcing my voice to remain steady. "*Please*. If you ever cared about me, *be honest right now*. Did you have anything to do with this nomination?"

Artemis darts his eyes between Lagiacrus and Destry before locking his gaze on me. His face contorts with so much pain I get the urge to cry out. I stamp it down, refusing to let him see my pity.

Artemis gulps. He licks his lips, then takes a deep breath. "Iris, I *promise* I had nothing to do with this."

My lips flatten. My cheeks *burn*. Because I can't stop my heart from accepting his words as fact, even though my love for him has previously led me astray. Regardless, I believe him.

And I hate myself for it.

"Well, now that we have that settled," Destry claps, "how about we all get some shut-eye?"

"Destry, shut the *fuck* up," Mace says, not sparing Destry a glance. My side of the couch erupts in laughter at his nonchalance, but I don't react. Instead, I keep my eyes glued on Artemis and shiver at our connection. I gulp, yearning for the warmth of our bond to remain intact.

But when Mace erupts, it shatters. And all hell breaks loose.

"I don't care who got in Lagiacrus's ear. Artemis says he didn't, which I highly doubt. And Destry is physically incapable of taking responsibility for his actions, so he'll never own up to controlling his alliance. So that leaves me knowing that Lagiacrus doesn't have a truthful bone in his goddamn body." Mace shakes his head, narrowing his gaze on Lagiacrus. "I *trusted* you. I wholeheartedly put all my faith in thinking that you were an honest man. When I saw you dying in that water, *I* forged a *deal*. To keep you alive."

Lagiacrus gulps loudly, then steps forward so he's an inch from Mace's face. "That's your mistake, not mine." He turns away and marches to his room without another word.

Nobody dares fill the silence. Not until Artemis pushes his hands against his face and squeezes the top of his hair between his fingertips.

"Iris, you have to believe me," Artemis urges, his voice nearly a whisper. "They didn't tell me he was going up. I had no idea. And if I did, I would have done *anything* to stop it."

Mace huffs, and I shake my head. My voice is raspy when the words come out. "Arty…how can I believe you when…when you're saying such horrible things about me?"

Artemis tilts his head and steps back. "Wha—why would I…" He moves forward again, reaching out for me. "I love you, Iris. I haven't said a *word* about you."

"For fuck safe!" Ashlea yells. "Would you just admit to something for *once* in your life?" She lunges forward so she's standing directly next to me. "That stuff you've made up about her is *sick*. And we're ashamed to have ever associated ourselves with a soulless, life-sucking jackass like you."

Artemis searches my eyes and quickens his words. "Iris, I swear on my *life* that I haven't said a bad thing about you. Not *once*. I don't want to hurt you, just…*please*. Tell me what you've heard!"

I whip my head away from him, not daring to look at him when I repeat the accusations. Still, I force my voice to keep steady. "That *I* came onto *you*. That we *made out* in solitary confinement. That *I* created Dial…that I was jealous of Shaela and *wanted her dead*!"

Artemis shakes his head so fast that he blurs in my periphery. "I didn't say that. Not once. Never have I said any of those things."

"LIAR!" Kylah roars. "YES, YOU DID AND YOU KNOW IT!"

Artemis clenches his jaw. "Kylah, what the hell?! No, I haven't!"

She purses her lips and slams her palms against his chest. "You lying piece of shit. You can't go back on your words and pin them on me! *No fuckin way*. Those words came out of your mouth. You can deny it all day and all night, but I know what I heard, and I swear on my *life* you said it."

"KYLAH, I'VE NEVER EVEN TALKED TO YOU!" Artemis yells. "When did this conversation happen? WHEN!?"

"You're *sick*. And whoever's watching can see that!" She points to the cameras and marches to the staircase, away from Artemis and away from this mess.

"Iris," Artemis pleads, "I didn't say any of that. You *have* to believe me."

No matter how hard I fight them, tears stream down my cheeks. *This can't end like this.* But when I find Mace slouched on the Death Row sofa, scowling at Artemis, I force myself to shy away from bandaging my friendship with Arty and let it implode.

"Just…why are you doing this, Artemis?" I cough to clear my throat, but my voice cracks anyway, my heart shattering with it. "*Why?*"

He inches closer, the heartache in his eyes gut-wrenching. "Iris…there's so much I want to say to you right now. You have no *idea* how much I want to say to you right now."

"You said you'd die for me…I don't *want* you to die for me, Artemis. I just want you to tell the truth."

He looks at the cameras, then back to me, seemingly considering his next sentence. His face contorts in pain, and his voice shakes when he takes a breath. "You seriously want to stand there and pretend you don't feel the same way?"

I gasp at the accusation and launch another fist into the couch. Ashlea mutters, "Not this again," and Mace strides to my side.

Mace puts a soft hand on my back and leans over the couch, pointing an accusatory finger in Artemis's face. "Dude, would you *let it rest*? She doesn't love you! She never did! What fantasy land are you living in? Just back off already! Leave us alone! Don't you understand? We don't want you here, and we don't want your help! All you do is lie and manipulate! Hear me loud and clear when I say we don't want anything to do with you anymore!" I can feel the heat radiating off his body as the words fling off his tongue. He removes his hand from my spine and leans even closer to Artemis. Mace stares him dead in the eyes and hisses, "You speak to her ever again, and I *swear to god*, I'll put my fist through your skull so hard you won't need a vote to be expelled."

Artemis smirks. He presses his lips together before turning toward me. He snarls, barring his teeth, and kicks the edge of the couch. "Iris, are you seeing this right now?" He points to Mace. "He's controlling you! What about what *you* want?"

"I want you to stay the hell away from me!" I shout, my arms suddenly so heavy I can't lift them. *Of course, this isn't what I want.* But I also don't know if I could ever trust him again. Kylah swears he said those malicious things about me, and even if he didn't, *who did?* One thing I know for sure is that he told Destry about the kiss. And if Artemis would die for me, why would he put me through the hell of Mace finding out about my mistake through someone else? It was understood that it was just between us…telling Destry wrecked my trust.

I need space from Artemis. My love for him conflicts with my pity for not being able to tell him my true feelings. But above all else, *I want him to feel how bad he's hurt me.* I want him to understand that, because of *his* actions, *I will never be the same.* Our friendship flashes before my eyes, and a sudden nausea confirms how much I already miss him. But the pure hatred I have for him and his betrayal overpowers the heavy weight of losing him.

I'm trembling. The truth behind it is that I wouldn't view his friendship as such a loss if I didn't care about him.

I can no longer deny it.

I'm in love with Artemis.

But if you love somebody, sometimes you have to let them go to protect them. The only way I can do this is to make him feel the same way I do.

That I'd do *anything* for him to be dead.

The love in Artemis's eyes quickly transforms into the fire of fury. "Iris, I would *never* do this to you. I would *never* forbid you from talking to somebody. I would make you *so* happy. You have no *idea* how happy I would make you. But you're scared. You're terrified of what will happen if you make this jump. You're sitting on your cargo ship right now in a luxury suite, safe and comfortable with Mace." His voice lowers an octave as he inches impossibly closer. "Jump off that ship, Iris. Join me in the safety raft. I'd make you the happiest girl alive, you *know* that. You just have to be *brave. So* many people would support you. You would be so happy — "

Mace's first storms through my peripheral vision, and Artemis slams into the floor with a loud crack. The breath in my lungs deflates, and I stand completely still, shock gripping my body in its lifeless hands. Artemis groans on the floor, not moving to fight back. Mace waves his hand to get feeling back into it before putting his opposite arm around me.

"*God*, that felt good." Ashlea gives Mace a high five, and the two celebrate by hooting and hollering. But there's no smile on my face. No act of celebration or whoops of success. Instead, I watch Artemis squirm on the ground, holding his already bruising cheek. He crawls toward the bathroom on his hands and knees, and I don't move an inch. Instead, I turn from his body and accept the role I am now destined to fulfill.

Make Artemis hate me as much as humanly possible.

"I need to talk to him…but I need a glass of water first." Once Artemis finally crosses the threshold into the communal bathroom, Mace turns for the kitchen.

"Who? Artemis?" I ask, chasing after Mace.

Mace's laughter booms. "God, no. Of course not!" He points upstairs and whispers, "Lagiacrus."

I nod. "I'll go with you. Safety in numbers?"

He turns the sink on and starts filling his cup. "That'd be great. But just us four, okay?" He motions toward Ashlea and Lunar, who are still in the living room. He doesn't give them a second glance before gulping down his water and shifting the sink back on for more. I turn around to guide Lunar to the stairs, but one look at him sends a shiver down my spine.

His complexion is paper-white, and his eyes are glossed over as they gaze at the ground. I sniff back the remainder of my tears and curse myself for yet again leaving Lunar to fend for himself. I gulp the shame bubbling in my throat and stride back into the living room. Settling on the couch beside him, I'm careful not to touch his tense body. Instead, I mimic his posture and stare at the same point on the carpet.

"You okay?" I whisper. He nods mechanically but doesn't vocalize confirmation. I dare look in his direction and lean forward to be in his sight. "Lunar…I'm really sorry you had to see that. I never thought any of this would happen…I never wanted any of this."

Silence passes between us, so I put a reassuring arm around his shoulders. Ashlea finally joins Mace in the kitchen, so I'm alone on our blue cushions with my brother, side-by-side.

Finally, as quietly as he can muster, Lunar utters, "Do you love him?"

I tilt my head and match his volume. "Mace? Of course I do. He's—"

"Not Mace," Lunar interrupts. "Do you love *Artemis*?"

I squint, but my heart rate undeniably picks up. I shake my head quickly to shut the idea down. "No. He was my friend, and I cared about him. I used to, anyway," I respond with finality, mortified that Lunar will see through the lies I've so carefully curated.

"I'm sorry that he's doing this to you," Lunar says.

My throat aches. I clear my throbbing throat before whispering, "Thank you, Lunar." We sit in silence for so long that our breaths sync up. When Mace calls us over to the kitchen, I put my hand on Lunar's back, insinuating it's time to leave. Before we stand, he grabs my palm and gives me a weak grin.

"Who would've thought an idiot like you would convince *two* guys to fall in love with you?"

I roll my eyes as a flush of relief soothes my system. Shaking my head, I smile.

My brother is back.

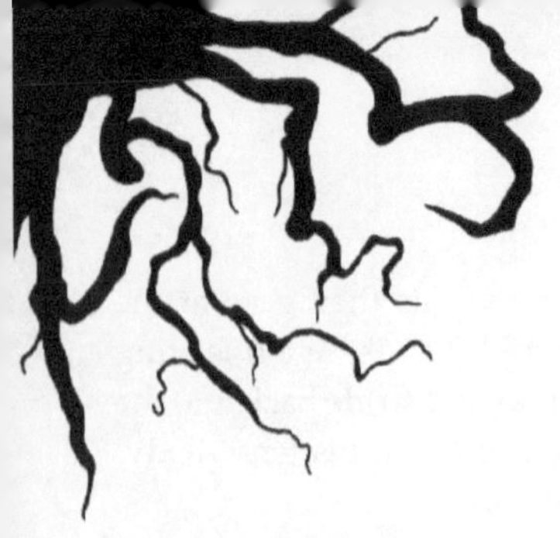

Chapter 51

"Here goes nothing," Mace mumbles. When he opens the Executive bedroom door, the four of us enter behind him in a single file line. I try to ignore Destry sitting in the corner of the room, but his stare feels like a fifty-pound weight on my back. Mace clears his throat. "Mind if we talk to you for a moment?" Once Lagiacrus nods, Lunar shuts the iron slab.

"Can we talk to you in *private*?" Ashlea asks, rolling her eyes in Destry's direction.

Destry puffs out his chest. "Whatever you have to say to Lagiacrus, you can say to me."

Completely ignoring him, Lagiacrus opens the door. "Nah, you don't need to be here, Destry. I can handle it." When Destry gulps back his dejected embarrassment, I don't even try to stifle the cackle that escapes my lips.

"Oh. Yeah…of course. No problem." Destry shrugs, but he's blushing when he exits the room. There's a wave of silence while Lagiacrus settles back between his sheets.

"Are you here to yell at me?" Lagiacrus asks. "Because if you are, I'm gonna walk right out that door."

Mace shakes his head. "No…I just…I want to understand."

Lagiacrus nods and pats the side of the bed. "Have a seat." We all sit on the outside of the gigantic mattress, Mace to my left and Lunar to my right.

"Look…as I said, man. It's nothing to do with you personally. I like you; I really do. But only one of us is making it out of here…it was strictly a game move and a game move *only*."

"I understand that" Mace replies, forcing voice to stay calm. "But I *don't* respect that you broke your word. I put a lot of trust in you, man."

Lagiacrus shakes his head. "I don't want to argue, so I won't raise my voice. I'm just stating this simply as a fact." He takes a deep breath. "You committed to voting out Ashlea. So did Finian and Iris, but I could only pick two of you for Death Row. Now, I can understand why it was hard for Iris to vote against Ashlea. I don't respect her decision, but I understand it. But you and Finian…" He lets out a slow breath. "I really trusted you two. And if you were willing to break up the alliance over a person completely unrelated to our games…why should I trust you? Especially as bigger decisions are made in later rounds?"

Mace bites his lip. "So that's why it's me and Finian, then?"

Lagiacrus nods. "I felt the most betrayed by you two. If I want to make it out alive, I need to eliminate the people I can't trust."

Lunar shifts uncomfortably, making the sheets swish. "Why did you promise to keep him safe in the first place if you were never going to keep your word?"

Lagiacrus shakes his head. "Look, if I didn't make that deal, we both would have died out there. You were struggling just as much as I was — honestly, *more*. If nothing else, I've gifted you four extra days of life." He lets out a sigh. "There are nine people left. Did you really think that deal wasn't too good to be true?"

Mace puckers his lips to the side. He can't even meet Lagiacrus's eyes. "If things were the other way around, I would've kept my word."

"I have no doubt you would've kept me off Death Row. But what if I proposed the deal you gave me? What if I asked you to keep Artemis and Destry safe, too?"

Mace rolls his eyes. "Then I would've put up Finian and Kylah."

Lagiacrus laughs without humor. "Well, I seriously doubt that. But I guess we'll never know."

The room gets quiet as the news sets in. *There is nothing we can do about the selections. My palms start to tremble because, at this moment, I am completely, utterly helpless.* Mace grabs my hand and rubs his finger down it, his gentle touch soothing my shakes.

"You have a good team behind you," Lagiacrus starts. "You have my alliance outnumbered. You have to understand this was the best move I could've made. I really didn't have another option."

"No, don't you dare say that" I demand, dropping Mace's hand. "Every person here has a choice, and you made yours. But don't, for a *second*, try to pretend you shouldn't be held accountable for your actions."

"I'm not going to talk with you guys if you raise your voice," Lagiacrus says, gritting his teeth. I take a deep breath before apologizing quietly, but I struggle to slow my racing pulse.

"Who is the target?" Mace's words are so quiet that I barely hear them.

Lagiacrus twiddles his thumbs before answering. "Doesn't really matter, does it? You have the numbers."

"Let me rephrase that," Mace states, carefully controlling his tone. "Who are Destry and Artemis voting out?"

Lagiacrus doesn't skip a beat. "I don't know, maybe you should ask *them*."

Mace chuckles to himself, but I can hear the frustration under his laughter. He gathers his thoughts before asking the toughest question of all.

"And if there's a tie? Who are you voting out?"

Lagiacrus takes a deep breath before looking directly at Mace. "Whoever is the bigger threat."

My stomach drops to the ground floor. Besides Lunar, Finian is the weakest person in the house. *If the vote comes to a tie, Lagiacrus will vote out Mace.* The finality in his voice makes my shaking crescendo, but Mace doesn't give in easily.

"Is there *anything* I can do to persuade you that Finian is a bigger threat to your game?"

Lagiacrus is still as he lets out a breath. He doesn't break eye contact. "Unlikely."

Mace bites the inside of his cheek. "Is there anything I can offer you to keep me in this house?"

Lagiacrus considers this proposition for an agonizingly long moment.

Then he shakes his head.

"Probably not."

Mace nods twenty times in a row. He looks away from Lagiacrus, so his absent gaze scans the room. His eyes glisten with moisture, but he blinks away the tears and tenses his jaw.

"So, that's it then? Just like that, we're enemies?"

Lagiacrus gulps before giving the slightest of nods.

Mace smiles, but it doesn't reach his eyes. "Well, then…I guess all I can say is good luck." Mace reaches out his hand, and I gulp back a sob as Lagiacrus shakes his palm.

"Good luck, Mace. May the best person win."

Mace squeezes my hand and pulls me off the mattress without another word. Ashlea and Lunar follow us to my corner of the communal bedroom and space out amongst the two cots. Away from the other convicts, my composure crumbles, and my voice *breaks*.

"Mace…what if—"

"Shhhh," Mace says, rubbing my back. Despite his efforts to calm me, I can feel the trembles in his palm. He grips the corner of my sheet with his opposite hand and gazes at the staircase, eyes glossed over. Lunar frowns with an empty stare, and my stomach churns as I consider the worst-case scenario.

"We're not gonna think about the what ifs," Ashlea declares, pillow tucked tightly between her arms. "Because Mace is staying. *That's final.* We just…need a plan, is all."

Her gaze is alert as she sends us a curt nod. Her confidence and determination are infectious, giving me the courage to speak.

"Okay…so what do we do?"

Ashlea takes a deep breath. "I don't like abandoning Finian after he saved my life, but I wasn't the one that put him on Death Row. I…I don't want him dead." Ashlea pauses with a gulp. "But we've gotta campaign against him. It's Mace's only chance."

I clear my throat. "Well, it's not like we lied to him," I justify. "Maybe he would have made it through a couple more rounds if he voted against us. But he really *was* at the bottom of Dial's totem pole. He absolutely would have been the first to go when it came down to it." The others nod, putting the morality debate to rest. I take another deep breath before locking my eyes on Ashlea. "So…we convince as many people as possible to vote against Finian?"

Before we can get too deep in thought, Mace cuts us off. "Most importantly, we *can't* let it go to a tiebreaker. We have to solidify four votes against Finian. If we don't, and Lagiacrus breaks the tie, I'm dead."

Ashlea leans forward. "Is there any possibility Destry and Artemis vote to keep you?"

"Not a chance," Mace and I say simultaneously.

"Artemis wants me dead…especially now that I punched him." Mace rolls his eyes. "But I don't regret it. We don't need his vote. I'm thinking about Kylah…she sat with us for the ceremony. That shows she's more on our side than theirs. And if she is, we'd blow the vote out of the water." We all silently count on our fingers. If Kylah is with us, we've got her vote, mine, Ashlea's, and Lunar's. No further discussion would be necessary.

I nibble on my thumbnail, eyebrows raised. "How confident are we that we'd have Kylah's vote?" Ashlea narrows her eyes on me, so I elaborate. "She doesn't trust me after everything Artemis spread. Mace and I are a pair, really…if she wants to hurt me, she might go through him."

Ashlea rubs her temples. "But what about Lunar?" She motions to my brother. "They're close…and he loves Mace. Surely, she wouldn't do anything to hurt one of Lunar's biggest allies."

"Don't discount anything," Mace replies. "We don't know what she's capable of."

"But if we can lean hard on her loyalty to Lunar, that could solidify her vote," I suggest.

"But can we trust her intentions? What if she's using him?" Ashlea asks.

"Kylah isn't a monster, guys!" Lunar interjects. His outburst makes us pause. I hadn't paid him any attention during this entire conversation. Now that I get a good look at him, I see the sweat on his brow. "You talk about me and her like I'm not even here. I know her better than all of you! Who do you think has been taking care of me the whole time Iris couldn't get her shit together?" I back away from Lunar like he's sent a bullet through my chest. "Maybe shut up and listen to what I have to say for a minute?"

I throw my hands up and lean away from my little brother. "Are you joking right now? Everything I have done in this game has been for *you*, Lunar. To get you out of here alive!"

"So that's why you fell onto Artemis's lips? To save me?"

I gasp, turning toward Mace. His face is expressionless, so I round back toward Lunar and push his chest forward. "Lunar, what has gotten into you? I made a *mistake* confronting Artemis. So, you're turning that against me to convince yourself that Kylah cares about you more than I do? She's known you for five minutes!" I scoff, pushing him harder. "And you weren't even talking, Lunar! How were we supposed to know you had something to say when you've been mute this entire conversation?

He shoves me back, and split flings from his lips. "You never gave me the chance, Iris!"

"Guys, please!" Ashlea yells, standing between us. "We can't afford to fight amongst ourselves! We're all we have! *That's it!* We can't let this game destroy us!"

Mace takes a deep but shaky breath, turning away from us. He's putting on a strong face for the group, but the slight break in his composure reveals how badly he hurts. My disagreement with Lunar loses all traction as I shift to protection mode. After a few deep breaths, I take Mace's hand and rub it softly, offering a shy smile. "It's settled then. We get Kylah on board…if we have her vote, we win." I look at Lunar. "I'm sorry we weren't treating you like a member of the team…but we need you right now, buddy. Can you talk to her? See where her head is at?" I reach out and touch his shoulder. "She's the best hope we've got, and you're the best person for the job."

Lunar smiles weakly and nods. "Of course." Then, he turns toward Mace. "We're keeping you here. I'll get her vote, and if I can't…we'll figure something else out. But you're staying…I promise you that."

Mace ruffles Lunar's hair and smiles as genuinely as he can muster. "I appreciate you, bud. Now, let's all get some sleep, alright? We'll put the plan in motion when the opportunities present themselves. We have two days to make this work." He puts his hand in the middle. "We're gonna get through this. We've done it before," he nods at Ashlea and grins. "We can do it again."

We all put our hands in the middle and bring them up silently to solidify our loyalty. I trust the people around me more than anything, and I believe with all my heart that Mace will survive this round. Because if he doesn't…

"I'm gonna clean-up for bed. Let's reconvene at some point tomorrow…put a status report together."

We nod as he reaches his hand out to me. "Care to join?"

I smile. "Always."

The cold, smooth surface doesn't feel the least bit harsh beneath me. With Mace by my side, anything would feel pleasant, so the sink is welcoming. The silence is peaceful, so I cradle my head on Mace's shoulder and match his breaths as his chest rises and falls. But even in his safe grasp, my mind wanders, and my concern for his survival starts bubbling to the surface. I squeeze his arm and cough, desperate to clear my mind with conversation.

"They're gonna start wondering where we are," I whisper.

"Let them wonder," Mace starts. "I just want to be with you."

I turn slowly to face him and match his violet gaze. He plants a simple kiss on my lips, and his soft pucker successfully wipes my worries away. His smile is weak when he backs away, but his eyes are fueled with love. Mace squeezes my shoulder to distract me, but I don't miss how he cracks his knuckles and taps his fingers against his palm. I grab his hand and rub circles around the outside to calm him. Still, his pulse noticeably quickens the longer we sit in silence.

I adjust so my lips are inches from his ear. "How about I grab you a slice of toast? With that rhubarb jam…we can pretend it's dessert? And have a little picnic with it."

He nods, short strands of his hair tickling my lips. "Don't be gone for long."

"Of course." I smile and pat his hand before dropping off the sink.

I stalk toward the kitchen, slouching the entire way. Exhausted by the positive front I've been putting on for Mace and Lunar, I let my lips droop into a frown. I dissociate from my body and watch myself prepare Mace's toast from a birds-eye-view. My movements are mechanical, and I space out into a nightmarish dream where Mace is expelled on a unanimous vote. I shake my head, trying to rid myself of this terrifying future, and only wake from my trance when I hear disgruntled voices coming from the staircase.

I set my blunt knife on the counter and shuffle forward, crouching to conceal myself. I lean my ear toward the voices, desperate to eavesdrop. They come from the second floor, and I control my breathing when I recognize Kylah's whispers. Her words are urgent and short, but I can't distinguish one from another. Having struggled too long to listen and having nothing to show for it, I'm ready to abandon my useless mission. Rolling my eyes, I straighten my back and turn for the kitchen.

Until Lunar's whimpers stop me in my tracks.

I bolt without hesitation. I lunge up the steps two at a time and halt before the pair. Without a second thought, I yank Lunar away from Kylah and scream, not caring how much my voice will carry. "What are you doing!? Do you get off on making someone younger than you cry? What's your problem, Kylah!?"

Kylah backs away with her hands raised. "How about you mind your own business before going around and making blind accusations?"

My cheeks burn when I turn Lunar away from her. He wipes his tears on the end of my shirt, and I lose control. "I want you to stay away from my brother. Do you understand me?"

"*He* approached *me*!" she shouts. "I was just trying to help him!"

"And *this* is helping him?" I say, pointing at his damp cheeks. "Kylah, I don't know what I did to make you hate me so much, but would you just *let it go*?"

"I TOLD YOU THIS MORNING!" she yells, no doubt waking anyone sleeping. "You are coming after me!"

"ENOUGH!" Mace's voice *booms* from the bottom of the steps. My breath catches in my throat when I turn to him and see the pure, unadulterated *fury* in his eyes. He marches up the steps until he's positioned at my hip. "*Enough.*"

I gulp as he takes a deep breath. Kylah steps back, and Lunar wipes at his tears. Mace shakes his head before leaning toward her. "Kylah, I am *begging* you not to believe that garbage. Iris was *never after you*. Why would she be if you've protected her brother this entire time? You're gonna bring him further in this game…she's not gonna want you out if she wants him to live more than she wants to make it out of here herself!" He's trembling. "I don't know what the hell is going on, but we need you, Kylah. More than ever, we need you right now. And I *promise* we will do whatever it takes to get you to the end. You trust me, don't you?"

Kylah looks from Mace to me before settling her eyes on the former. Her lips are shaking, but she stands tall. "Unfortunately for you, it comes down to trusting Iris. And no, I do *not* trust her."

"None of what you heard is true!" I shout, voice cracking with the threat of tears. "Artemis said it himself!"

"Iris, regardless of what is true or not, *you told us* you lied."

"What are you talking about?" I can hardly stand. Her accusations pierce my chest like bullets.

"You were in Dial!" She throws her palms to the ceiling. "Regardless of whether you created it, *you* were the one who said you were in the alliance! And you kept it a secret for weeks!" She takes a step closer, now pointing a finger at my chest. "You and Artemis kissed, which goes against the entire reason we went after Eno! You manipulated and lied to Finian to get him to trust you, and you kept this secret, *knowing* how badly it would impact the rest of your team. Don't you understand? You've broken my trust *beyond repair*. I can't afford to trust you again, Iris. I *can't*." She presses her lips together when she looks at Mace. "Mace, I'm sorry you're so tangled in this mess. But...I can't keep you here. You're a competition beast! You've nearly won every competition you've competed in! Having you in this game *only* hurts me. I'm sorry, but...you have to understand."

I shake my head, choking up from the tears now falling down my cheeks. "How could you say that? When all he's done is *help* you and Lunar—"

"I've made my decision." She stomps her foot and glares at me. "Now, you stay away from me, and I'll stay the hell away from you." Kylah gives one final glance at Mace and nods. "It's done."

She turns around and marches up the stairs, leaving Mace and me with Lunar in our arms.

I rub the loose strands of hair from Lunar's face and kiss his forehead. His arms tremble as I tuck the sheets against his chest. He's so panicked that he can't articulate his fears, but he doesn't need to. After thirteen years of knowing him, I know he's terrified of losing Mace. On top of Kylah shattering his trust, it's no surprise he can't keep still.

Eventually, his breathing calms, and his eyes shift beneath his eyelids, so I sit back and watch. I don't leave him until I'm sure he's asleep. Without Kylah, it really is all up to me to ensure my brother survives.

As quietly as possible, I abandon my peaceful brother and shuffle down the stairs to meet Mace. I find myself taking slower steps than before, fresh terror coursing through my veins with every heartbeat. *The love of my life might be executed in forty-eight hours.* I clench my fists, unwilling to let the floodgates open and force myself to stay strong for his sake.

"Hey," Mace calls when I reach the kitchen. His voice is lifeless and hits me like a bullet in the chest.

"Hey." I'm completely deflated, but I force a smile to disguise my pessimism. I cuddle beside him on the furthest blue couch, bending my knees to my chest. Before I get the chance, he leans his head on *my* shoulder, settling into the nook against my neck.

"This is a change," I chuckle lightly, seeing that I'm usually leaning against him. He doesn't reflect my laughter. Instead, a chilling silence passes between us.

"Iris?" he whispers, voice shaking.

"Yeah?" When I turn to face him, his eyes are glossed over, staring blankly at the kitchen island.

"What are we gonna do?"

I press my lips together and struggle to catch my breath. We *needed* Kylah's vote. *And we failed to get it.* I shiver because as much as Mace refuses to believe there's another option, the pit in my stomach begs to differ. Despite everything that's happened, all the lies that have been told, and my head screaming that it won't work…my heart knows that Mace's fate may lie in one person's unfortunate hands.

"Mace…" My voice shakes. I rub his hand in a circular motion and take a deep breath. "I know you said we'd never talk to him again…"

"No," Mace says with finality. "*Not him.* We can't trust him."

"Well, who can we trust, Mace?" I argue. "Destry's not going to keep you here…especially after the stunt we pulled last round with Ashlea. He *hates* us, and he *wants* you dead. Kylah is a lost cause and will only get more aggressive the further we push her."

Mace sighs. "What makes you think there's even a small chance we can trust him?"

Images flash before my eyes. Artemis drinking toilet water as I fall to my knees laughing. Artemis saving my leg in solitary confinement and *begging* me to bare the pain. Him kissing me in the Executive room and *promising* that he would die for me. How he looked at me when we played games to get through our punishment…

I take a shaky breath. Regardless of all the terrible things he has spread about me and how his declaration of love may have been a script he had already practiced on Mercedes…my heart urges me to give him another chance. Maybe I trust him because his love is something that I felt deep in my bones…or perhaps it's because, to some extent, despite everything he's done, I still love him too. As much as I fight it, my heart screams one unbearable truth.

If Artemis loves me as much as I love him….he'll do *anything* to make me happy.

"We don't really have a choice, do we?" I rub the back of Mace's head, fluffing up his hair. "He told me he would do *anything* for me…he said he'd *die* for me…if I talked to him, and I mean *really* talked to him, maybe I could convince him to flip sides?" Mentally, I know this proposal has ulterior motives. My priority is keeping Mace alive. But that doesn't mean I'm not *dying* to talk to Artemis. More than anything, I want to clear up what lies have been told and have one last honest conversation with him. And if I can save the love of my life in the process…what's the harm?

"I just…" Mace stutters. "He's been so terrible to you, Iris."

"Which is why he might try to make it up to me." I turn and look Mace in the eyes. "Look…it's not ideal, but it's the best chance we've got. He's the only one who might change his mind…we haven't even asked him who he's voting for. Maybe he didn't want to vote you out anyway?"

Mace's eyes widen. "Iris. I beat the shit out of him."

I wince. "Yeah…but if he'd do anything for me, he'd want me to be happy. And I'm happy with *you*."

Mace stares at me for a long while, contemplating this last-ditch effort to save him. He takes a deep breath before leaning back into my shoulder. "What're you gonna say to him?"

I bite my lip. "I'm gonna beg him to keep you alive." Mace's exhale is shaky, and there's a slight tremble in his palm. "This is gonna work," I assure him. "Because if it doesn't…I don't know what I'm gonna do."

Silence passes between us. Finally, Mace squeezes my forearm and nods. "You talk to him first…then I'll come and…apologize. Then we…we'll make the deal official."

I tighten my grip around his shoulders as he tucks his head deeper into the crook of my neck. His shaking is more extreme now, and he doesn't try to hide it. "Iris?" he whispers.

I lock on his eyes and shiver at the moisture. He squeezes my hand and purses his lips. "I'm terrified."

I wrap both arms around him and squeeze tight, urging the motion to wake me from this terrible dream. I squint my eyes hard before whispering back. "Me too."

I feel his tear fall onto my neck, and my body stiffens. My voice catches in my throat, but I push the words out anyway. "I don't want to live without you."

Mace's body shakes with a silent whimper. "Iris, before you, there was nothing. No humor or light in the all-encompassing shadows. Merely movement for the sake of progress and monotony with no spark. But you struck a match and forever vanquished that darkness. You gave me a reason to survive." He sniffles. "If…if being here is what it took…to meet you…" He wipes his tears and lets his walls crumble. "I'd do it all over again."

My tears fall so heavily I can't breathe. I cup my hand around his cheek and force myself to look into his devastating eyes. "I wish…he…he would've just put me up there…and then…" I can't control my voice. I shatter, my body convulsing as I force the words out. "I wouldn't ever have to deal with losing you!"

We cry together, chests rising and falling in synchronization. I lock my fingers around his back, refusing to ever let go, and shutter, knowing that, eventually, one of us is going to die. Our cries harmonize for over an hour, and we don't release until our tears dry.

336

Finally, I wipe my cheeks and force my breaths to steady. "This is going to work," I declare, my voice raspy. "I promise, Mace…this is going to work."

Mace locks his violet eyes onto mine. Salty tears coat his cheeks, and he wipes the moisture with the back of his hand. "This is going to work," he repeats.

Despite thinking there were no tears left to cry, we weep until we fall asleep in each other's arms.

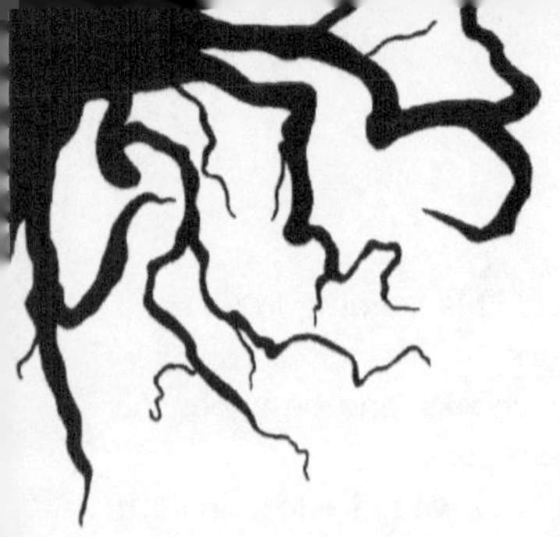

Chapter 52

When my eyes flutter open, I'm inches from the floor. I grip the side of the couch to catch my fall and gently roll onto the carpet with a soft thud. Sitting up, I smile at Mace's curled figure on the sofa. He hugs his legs toward his chest as air escapes his nostrils. He's a portrait of peace, flooding my heart with a warm calmness that makes me back away slowly. I wouldn't dare disturb him, so I shuffle around the couch, smoothing my hair as I tiptoe toward the bathroom.

I walk straight toward the mirrors above the sink, watching myself approach. My fingers run through the streaks of my hair as I undo my fishtail, untangling the knots that consume the nest. I start removing my shoes to prepare for a shower when a crash freezes me to the tile. Without a second thought, I duck under the sink and crawl to the wall separating me from the showers. The toilet stalls are soundproof, so there's no other place the wreck could be coming from than the bathing area. Calming my breaths, I press my ear to the nearest wall and urge my ears to let the conversation come in clear.

When it does, my heart stops.

"You...do this!" Artemis roars. Whoever responds does so soundlessly, so I squat closer and shove my ear so hard against the wall that it flattens against the surface.

"She's not the boss of you!" Artemis shouts.

When the other person screeches, I fall to my knees.

"It's none of your business!" Lunar squeals, rushing a few steps back. His defense shoots me to my feet. I sprint to the shower they've been concealing themselves in and yank the curtain open.

"What's going on!?" I shout, running between them. Lunar's eyes are swollen from crying, so I hug him against my chest. When I turn toward Artemis, his face goes beet red. He cowers from eye contact, so I lock my gaze on his bruised and bloody cheek. My breath shakes as I examine his injury. *His cheek is so puffy I can barely see his pupils.* But the worry is short-lived because the context of our encounter fills me with a rage so intense that I don't have the space to stress over Artemis's ailments.

"What have you been saying to him?" I shove Lunar behind me and step closer to his aggressor. "Why is Lunar crying? What have you done to him!?"

"Iris, I can explain!" he defends, hands up in surrender.

"Iris, it's nothing!" Lunar shouts, making me whip around to him with wide eyes.

"What do you mean it's nothing? What was he saying to you?"

"It's not a big deal! Really, we were just talking like men."

I scowl. "Lunar, you're *thirteen* years old. And you've obviously been crying…somebody needs to tell me why before I lose it!"

Lunar reaches out to me and stumbles for words. "It—it's Mace!" Lunar cries. "I don't want him to die…I was just…*begging* for Artemis's vote!"

My jaw locks and I twist to Artemis. "Is this true?"

Artemis tenses up, every muscle in his body immobile. After a slow breath, he nods.

It doesn't go past my notice that the motion is forced.

"And what did he say?" I ask Lunar. Lunar's eyes travel to the figure behind me, so I leap into his view and push him further from Artemis. "DON'T LOOK AT HIM!" I shout. *"What did he say!?"*

"He said he'd think about it!" Lunar stops to catch his breath. "He said he'd consider it."

Slowly, I drop my hands from his shoulders and let my breathing relax. I gulp back tears and open my arms to my little brother. "Come here." Lunar leaps into my arms and melts into the hug. I force my voice to steady as I ruffle his hair. "It's okay…shhhh, it's okay."

Lunar backs away from my grasp and smiles. "He said he'd consider it Iris…Mace might make it."

I grin before squeezing Lunar's torso and burying my eyes in his hair. "You did great, Lunar. You really did."

When he finally stops crying, Lunar releases his grip around my waist and wipes his tears. I give his hair a final ruffle as I turn toward the exit. Artemis is inches from the door, so I lunge forward before he escapes.

"Wait!" The words leave my lips before I can manage something less desperate. I take a deep breath when Artemis turns and lower my voice when his eyes lock on mine. "Can…can we talk for a minute?"

Artemis stiffens before nodding. "Of course…anything for you, Iris."

I squat and hold Lunar's shoulders. "You gonna be okay, buddy?" Lunar nods and gives a weak smile, but his legs still tremble. "Mace is in the living room…go talk to him. That'll make you feel better, right?" He nods before rushing away.

When the bathroom door closes, silence fills the space. I clear my throat and shuffle forward a step. "Was that true?"

Artemis gulps. "Which part?"

"What do you mean, *which part*?" I step closer so only a few inches separate us. "Are you really considering voting to keep Mace?"

Artemis looks directly into my eyes, and my heart melts all over again. I grip my hands into fists to fight the wild thumping in my chest.

"You know I'd do anything for you."

Instead of thanking him or falling to my knees, I keep his gaze and let my heart do the talking.

"Then why are you spreading lies about me?"

Artemis shakes his head. "Iris, I am *so* sorry that you think that's true. I am *so* sorry that I made you feel that way." He doesn't break eye contact. "But none of it is true. I swear on my *life*, none of that is true."

My heart doesn't let me stop while I'm ahead. The massive betrayal that's burdened me beyond measure urges to be addressed, so I unleash my best attempt to get honest answers.

"Then how did Destry know we kissed?"

Artemis opens his mouth to answer, but nothing comes out. He bites his lip and scratches his head, searching the room while considering his answer. "Iris, *please* try and understand." He stops fidgeting and grabs my arm. "I had to talk to *someone*…keeping it to myself was killing me!"

His touch sends a shock through my stomach. I stare at his hand but don't back away. "What on earth made you think you could trust *him*?"

"Iris," his voice shakes, pulling me closer. "Who else did I have? I didn't know what to do…I needed somebody to…to…"

"To what, *Artemis*?" I spit, using his full name. He looks up at me, moisture in his eyes, the departure from his nickname hitting him like a bullet through the chest.

"To be there for me." He releases my arm. "Iris…you are everything to me. Without you, I have *nothing*. I couldn't keep it bottled inside…it was destroying me!"

"Then why didn't you defend me?" I shout. "You just stood there while Destry made these wild accusations. How could you do that to me?"

He shakes his head. "Iris…it was Eno! I…I was in shock. I didn't realize what was happening around me."

He rubs his hands through his hair, taking a step back. "I'm sorry, Iris!" His voice cracks. "I'm *so* sorry. But all I said to Destry is that we kissed…I don't know where these lies are coming from, but they aren't from me!"

I bite my lip. "Then why did Destry seem to think *I* came onto *you*?" Artemis is speechless, so I inch closer until I can feel his breath against my skin. "You know that *you* kissed me. You *know* that I backed away." Artemis raises his eyebrows. I shake my head and put a hand against his chest. "You know that *when I realized what was happening*, I backed away." I bring my voice to a whisper. "So why does Destry think differently?"

Artemis is completely still. "I don't know why he thinks that."

"So, you want me to believe that he just made it up out of thin air because he hates me? That he has some personal vendetta against me?"

"I don't know what you want me to say, Iris." Artemis narrows his eyes on me. "But I never said that you kissed me, or that you created Dial, or that anything happened in solitary confinement! I never said any of that! You *have* to believe me."

His eyes twinkle, and my gut wrenches. My brain screams at my heart, telling it not to believe him.

But unsurprisingly, my heart wins out.

"Okay," I say with finality. I back away and let my eyes wander around the room. The only thing breaking the silence is our breaths until Artemis's voice returns.

"Iris, I am *so* sorry…I'm sorry for everything. I never wanted to hurt you…but in the process, I ended up hurting the *one* person that I cared about the most. This was never supposed to happen…I just…" He stands up straight and looks me in the eyes. "I wouldn't have kissed you if I didn't think you loved me back. And for that…I am *so* sorry. I'm sorry I disrespected your relationship with Mace by kissing you. I just thought…I thought you never would've noticed or…or *cared* that I was ignoring you if you didn't feel the same way."

My eyes glisten with moisture, but I stay silent, not daring to interrupt.

"The way you studied riddles with me…the way you've always joked around with me…it made me feel so…*alive*. Without you, I don't know who I am. I don't know how to be myself when I'm not around you."

"That's ridiculous," I say, my voice barely above a whisper.

"It's true!" he replies. "I'm only myself when you're right there with me…joking with me…laughing with me…I know this is the weakest thing you'll ever hear anybody say. But Iris, without you, I've lost all of the best parts of myself."

I swallow back tears. "Artemis…"

Artemis leans into my face, only inches separating us. "I love you, Iris. That was and always will be true. I will never love anyone like I've loved you because there is *only one Iris*." He pulls away. "I'm sorry I misinterpreted things on your end. I really wouldn't have kissed you if I thought you didn't feel the same way. I just…" he wipes a tear. "Between you and me. Once and for all with *one hundred percent honesty*." He leans into my ear and whispers. Artemis's voice is so quiet I have to strain myself to listen, but there's no way I could miss the words as they leave his mouth.

"You really don't feel the same way?"

A tear falls down my cheek. My stomach twists as I consider every amazing memory we've shared. As much as I want to embrace my anger and force him to hate me so he won't have to mourn our memories, I can't forget standing in the bathroom, laughing with him about the missing towels. Or pretending he didn't slip up and tell me he loved me for the first time when we were trapped in the tile prison. Or hearing stories of his past when he tried to help me keep my sanity or discovering that his crimes were the most noble sacrifice of anyone here.

The memories *burn* with excruciating pain. It's impossible to remember without shattering my world. But despite how painful the flashbacks are and how agonizing it is to miss him…

I am terrified to forget him.

We stand in silence as I contemplate my answer. I wouldn't be crying if I wasn't in love with the man before me. He will *always* have a piece of my heart. *But my commitment will always be with Mace.* And if Artemis even has an inkling that he has a chance with me, his vote could go against us. So, when Artemis asks me if I will ever feel the same way…

I shake my head from side to side, tears streaming down my face.

He wipes a tear and plasters a fake smile. "Okay." He nods. "Okay."

I tremble as tears continue to flow down my cheeks. Because the only thing more painful than not being loved back? It's not being able to tell somebody you're in love with them, then watching them suffer because of your secret.

Noticing my trembling, Artemis brings me in for a hug. "Hey, hey, hey. It's okay," he whispers. "I won't ask you again, Iris, okay? I promise. I'll take your word for it." This brings me into a fresh bout of sobs because he'll never know the truth.

"I'm so sorry Artemis…I'm so sorry."

"Shhh," he says, hugging me, tears soaking the top of my head. "It's okay. It's okay."

We cry our tears out together, not breaking our embrace. Finally, Artemis breaks the silence.

"I'm voting to keep Mace," he whispers.

"What?" I choke out.

Artemis backs away from me, releasing the hug. "I'll vote to keep Mace." My chest caves with relief as I press my lips together. "I was always going to keep Mace."

"Arty," I start, but he interrupts.

"This conversation doesn't change the way I feel, Iris." He stares at me with intent. "I love you, and I will never love anybody the same. I would do anything for you, Iris. You know this. I've said it before, and I'd say it a thousand times…I'd *die* for you." I smile and wipe a strand of hair from my face. "I wish I was the one that made you smile as bright as the stars in the sky. But if it's Mace…then I'll do whatever I can to keep him alive."

"Artemis…I don't know what to say." I pull him back against my chest, and he slowly wraps his arms around me. "Thank you. *Thank you.*" Artemis doesn't respond, but the tear that falls from his eye and lands on my face gives me all the information I'll ever need to know.

"I was out of line," Mace bites his lip. "I was just so…*angry.*"

Artemis nods under the shower head, watching Mace's fists. My alliance surrounds the two, all crowding behind Mace. Pus starts overflowing from Artemis's left eye socket, and he backs against the wall. I avoid Artemis's eye contact and extend an arm around Lunar.

"What I'm trying to say is…" Mace stumbles on his words. "I'm sorry. The punch was an overreaction…I shouldn't have hurt you." Mace doesn't mean the words, but he's doing a great job of faking it.

Artemis itches the side of his khakis. "No…I'm sorry," he starts. "It was wrong for me to…*you know.*" I wince at the insinuation of our kiss and hope nobody else focuses on that detail. "I'm really sorry, Mace. I never wanted to hurt anybody."

"I wish I could say the same when I punched you," Mace jokes. Artemis chuckles as Mace steps forward, checking out the damage. "We need to get some ice on that, man."

Artemis smiles. "Nah. Makes me look tough, right?"

Mace shakes his head and brings Artemis in for their typical handshake-hug. The whole encounter is bizarre, knowing both of their true feelings, but I bite the inside of my cheek to keep from ruining the truce.

"Do we have your word?" Lunar asks.

Artemis looks at Lunar a second too long before nodding. "You have my word. Four votes to keep Mace."

I smile, and Mace sighs with relief. "You have no idea how much this means to us, Artemis."

Artemis shakes his head. "I'm really sorry for everything that I've done. I know I don't deserve forgiveness…but hopefully, this is a step in the right direction."

I smile. "Are we pinky swearing on this?"

The others look at me and nod. "The pinky swear of the century," Ashlea offers.

We exchange a bout of promises, and a wave of calm washes over me. In this game, I rarely feel safe. But at this moment, surrounded by four people who care about me just as much as I care about them…

I'm at peace.

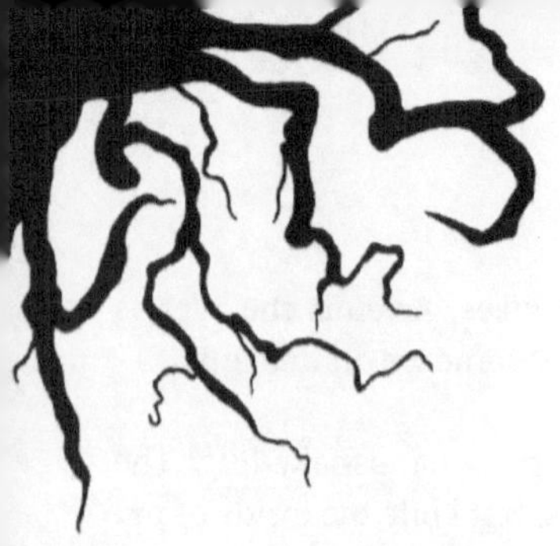

Chapter 53

My new alliance is nameless, but where we lack a label, we more than makeup in loyalty. I'm significantly more confident in my security with Lunar, Ashlea, and Mace than I *ever* was with anyone in Dial. Therefore, I'm careful to avoid those outside of my group. Even with Artemis's promise, I stay away from him, too. Associating with him could risk exposing his agenda to help us. But even more…none of us want his company anyway. Just because we *need* him doesn't mean we *want* him.

That's what I'm telling myself, anyway.

We eat dinner as a team, but despite the promise of Mace's safety, I can't block out the thumping of my heart in my ears. Even if—*when* Mace makes it past the Expulsion tomorrow, the Executive competition still looms over us. And we can no longer pretend that it doesn't present a real risk to our lives.

Even before the aquatic battle, the danger in the Executive contest has been evident. But the reality hadn't set in until Mercedes floated away, the life drained from her limp figure. With the first competition death behind us, the anxiety that accompanies these arena visits has me gulping away more tremors than ever before.

The others eat quickly, but I can't seem to swallow anything. My throat feels like sandpaper, so I struggle to shove any food down. I pick at my lukewarm peas to pass the time, lobbing the pearls off the table as I try to pierce one onto each prong of my fork. When I finally look up, I'm shocked that I hadn't noticed that the others have gone, leaving only Mace and myself on the bottom floor. I turn slowly toward him until my eyes land on the cheeky grin he tries to smother.

"What?" I ask, a slow smile stretching across my lips.

"Nothing," he jokes, lifting a single eyebrow.

I smack his forearm. "Oh, come on. What is it!?" My laughter comes naturally, his mysteriousness fading my worry until it's merely a pesky afterthought.

He leans in and lets out a hot whisper. "I have a surprise for you."

I jolt back, narrowing my eyes on him. "You don't say," I joke, uncertainty in my tone.

He leans back and clasps his hands together. "But…" Mace hops from his chair and extends an open palm. "You need to hide in the bathroom for a while. I need a minute to get it for you, so you have to hide!"

"What is so big that I have to go into another room for you to get it?" I laugh.

"That's the surprise!" he smiles. "Just go into the bathroom. Can you do that for me?"

I stare from his palm to his eyes. His grin flips my stomach in excited cartwheels, so I can't help but smile. Finally, I take his hand and squeeze. "Lead the way."

He's positively *beaming*. "It would be my honor." He swings my arm as we skip past the living room threshold, mixing my gasps of physical exhaustion with laughter. Once in the bathroom, he grabs my waist and squeezes before lifting me onto the sink. My heart twirls, the pressure around my hips sending a rush of warmth between my legs. He plants a simple kiss on my forehead and turns before I can yank him toward me and never let go.

Abandoned in my waiting room, my eyes search the tile walls, tracing the indents between each cemented segment. My brief excitement vanishes as time passes, and I can't stop my mind from wandering on the Enterprize. My gut pinches when I start counting, and I get the sensation that I'm falling when I realize how much smaller our group of convicts has gotten since the start. *Fifteen down to nine.* In just twenty-four hours, that number will be *eight*. I bite my lip and shiver. I may not grieve most of the fallen, but Eno was undoubtedly a tremendous loss. Even with nothing in my stomach, the nausea is all-consuming. Because Eno *had* to go but giving him up broke my heart.

I take a deep breath, but nothing can stop my body from shaking. I miss Eno's stories at the dinner table. I miss him comforting us in a way only a father could, and I miss his wisdom and compassion. And because of me, he is *dead*.

Desperate to shove away my remorse, I let another haunting thought block Eno's memory. *What will happen if Artemis is lying?* I shake my head. *It's not possible.* My heart believes in his promise, and my gut trusts that he's telling me the truth. Technically, he never *specifically* told me he'd keep the kiss between us. That's just something I expected, but who was I to dictate that he was to have no confidant? I rationalize his honesty, but as much as I want to believe he wants the best for me, my head screams that he wants to win this just as much as the rest of us. And if he wants this just as much as I do, there's no telling what he'll do to—

KNOCK.

I jolt upright as the door creaks open. When Mace steps through the threshold with his sparkling eyes and pearly teeth, I instinctively wipe the sweat from my forehead. At this moment, I can't deny that tomorrow's vote is killing me. But even so, as Mace stands before me alive and well, nothing but pure excitement and admiration in his gaze...

I can't help but *swoon*.

"About time," I smile.

"Sorry to keep you waiting," he grins, offering a hand to help me from the sink. "I want you to close your eyes…can you do that for me?"

I shake my head but can't stop from laughing. "Where are you taking me!?" I shout, backing away from him.

"Relax!" he laughs. "You trust me, right?"

I give a thin smile, hiding my teeth. "Of course."

He inches closer to my ear and lets his breath tickle my neck. "Then close your eyes," he whispers.

I shut my eyes but deny his hand, lifting my arms to the ceiling. "Okay. But if I can't see, you'll have to lift me from the sink and set me on the floor. I don't make the rules."

His chuckle sends a shiver down my spine. I can feel his proximity to my neck, and it's absolutely, unequivocally *intoxicating*.

"You know I'll give you whatever you want, Iris."

My breath hitches. His gentle hands touch the skin beneath my shirt, and goosebumps erupt around my torso. He lifts me effortlessly and places me on the tile, letting his soft hands linger as they trail down my waist. Suddenly, all touch is removed, and I'm leaning forward for *more*. But instead of the delicate caress I crave, he interlocks his fingers with mine and puts a stiff palm over my eye sockets. His whisper is positively *infectious*. "Just in case you try to peep."

"What is going on!?" I flirt.

"You'll see," he confirms. I can hear the amusement in his voice. Even though I can't see, I know he can't stop smiling.

He leads me across the bathroom threshold and moves behind me, taking his hand from mine and placing it on my shoulder. Even without his touch, I would feel him. His breath on my neck is enough confirmation that he hasn't left. Mace guides me across the floor slowly so I don't trip or fall. He holds me when I lose balance and hugs my waist when he finally tells me to stop. He's silent while he loosens his grip around my torso. His hot breath on the back of my neck nearly makes me moan, but I gulp to stay quiet.

"You can look now," he whispers in my ear, lowering his hand.

What once was the living space where my friends and enemies awaited their announcements for murder has been transformed into a romantic haven. Instead of terror and bullet holes, the room has become a plush paradise. Every couch has been rotated so the seats point in the opposite direction. Tucked into the crevice of each couch cushion are sheets; the cushions hold the corners in place and create a tented area between the separated sofas, reminiscent of a home. I duck beneath the opening in the sheet and find two mattresses smashed together, fitting perfectly in line with the backs of the settees. It creates a dome of comfort where two people can sleep in privacy, and pillows fill the cracks where each mattress meets the couch, forbidding any camera from spying on the occupants.

"Oh my god," I whisper, palms covering my jaw. "Mace…I don't know what to say."

"Then don't say anything," he replies, grabbing my hips and leading me into a sway.

I wrap my arms around his neck and match his rhythm, dancing in the silence as if we were having our own personal symphony. His breaths are steady, and his lips are soft against my neck. Overwhelmed by his gesture, my throat starts closing, and I melt into his body, following his lead as he turns us around in a slow, meticulous circle.

"This is amazing," I whisper. "*You* are amazing. Why did you do this?"

He smiles, and his violet eyes twinkle. "You've never been on a date before, right?"

I laugh. "Excuse me?"

"What?" Mace laughs, hugging me tighter. "Any boys hiding under that floorboard of yours back home?"

I smile. "Just Lunar."

"Right," Mace replies, shaking his head. "And if you could've lived outside…in the *real* world…well, you would have had men fighting over you every chance they got."

I shake my head and chuckle, keeping the sway. "Shut up."

"It's true." Mace sways his nose back and forth on my neck, giving me an Eskimo kiss. He leans into my ear, stopping our dance, and hushes his words so quietly I doubt the microphones even pick it up. "I'm going to make it through tomorrow. I *will*. But you deserve one date, one dance, one….normal night. And it kills me that you've never gotten one." He leans back and looks me in the eyes, no trace of a smile on his lips. "So tonight, we aren't in the Enterprize. We won't talk about strategy, and we won't talk about what-ifs. Tonight…it's just you and me." The left side of his lip pulls into a grin. "And I want to make this the best night of our lives."

A tear falls down my cheek. Before I can wipe it, Mace kisses it away. When he backs from my face, he studies my eyes, no doubt memorizing every detail like I have with him countless times. Even in the dark, I can recall exactly where the purple deepens and widens, and I'm sure he can account for every flake of brown and green in my own pearls. He finally stares at my lips and moves in, parting mine with his and bursting my world with light. His touch is initially gentle, barely touching my chapped lips. It's me who deepens the kiss, sucking him in deeper so I don't have to resist him any longer. He bites my lip, and this time, I moan, inviting him in. His hand reaches into my hair, and we stay standing, moving our lips with one another and letting our mouths become one. I deny myself anything else because we have the entire night, and I want everything to be what I always dreamed of. So, between kisses, instead of pulling him into the fort and rushing this glorious moment, I smile and whisper, "I love you, Mace." Without hesitation, he answers.

"I love you more, Iris."

"Tell me more about your home." The blanket ceiling makes the dark room feel like the night sky. My head is on Mace's chest, his heart thumping so loudly I can feel it against the back of my head. My hand is clasped in his, and he pulls it to his lips to kiss it three more times. My eyes have adjusted enough to see his outline, but just feeling him is enough to know I'm safe.

"I'm from the Midwestern Ascendency," Mace whispers, drawing circles on the outside of my palm. "So, you know. Lots of grass and animals…" he pokes my side. "And corn as far as the eye can see!" I stare at him with raised eyebrows, and we both burst into laughter. "I don't know, it used to have corn. Apparently, in its heyday, it was the prime jewel for farming. But you know, the Hage and all."

I laugh. "That damned Hage." I kiss his heart and rub the tops of his hair between my fingers, letting them fall when I reach the end of each strand. "You ever wonder what life would've been like if we met back then? If we weren't fugitives, and the Hage didn't exist. There was no Authority, and you and I just met at...I don't know, at school, maybe?"

"I don't have to wonder. I dream about it every night." There's no hesitation or laughter in his voice.

"What do you see when you dream?"

Mace shifts, inviting me into the crook of his arm. I close my eyes and let his vision transport me. "I see us. Growing old together, watching blue birds with Curi while Lunar does cartwheels around a field." He shrugs as if his next suggestion is obvious. "And we have a cat, of course."

"A cat?" I nearly choke on my laughter.

When he kisses my forehead, I feel the smile on his lips. "Yes, several."

"Okay, several cats." I shake my head, not believing his imagination. "And what color are these *cats*?"

"Well," Mace begins, taking his time. "We'd have two. The first one...she takes to you, sleeping on your chest every night. She licks your face to show you her love and purrs you to sleep. That one's a mixture...it's got black and orange. It's a tortoiseshell."

"A tortoiseshell, huh?" I smile.

"Yeah, a tortoiseshell. And the black one with long hair...that one takes to me. Or, at least, it makes me think it does. But at the end of the night, it cuddles on *your* lap, next to the tortoiseshell on *your* chest."

"Someone sounds a little *jealous*," I joke.

"Hardly," Mace whispers, planting another kiss on my forehead. "And its purr...its purr is nuclear."

"Nuclear!" I shake with my giggles. "Where are you coming up with all of this?"

"Hey, my dreams don't lie!" he jokes. "In some reality, that's our life. Just me and you, our family of cats, and your brother and sister. All of us....happier than ever."

When I sigh, he turns toward me so our noses touch. The silence is agonizing, so I let my heart fill it.

"That's what I want." I search his violet eyes and shiver. "I want a life with you. I want a life with you, and two cats, and birds, and Curi and Lunar." He smiles. "I want *everything* with you, Mace."

He looks away, and I swear he chokes back a tear. "I want everything with you, too, Iris." He cups my cheek with his soft hand and moves closer so his lips are resting on mine. I feel them move when he whispers, "And tonight...tonight we get everything. Just for tonight...right?"

I smile. "And every night for the rest of eternity in my dreams." Mace hugs me tighter and touches my heart. He feels it thump with each passing beat and presses his lips onto mine, moving them to the rhythm of my heartbeats. He caresses my back with a delicate palm, so I encourage him by shifting onto his waist. His breath hitches when I draw a line of kisses up his neck, and he slides his hold down to my backside. I tingle when I feel his length beneath me, his desire for me overwhelmingly clear. He pauses as if asking for confirmation. I stretch toward his ear and moan as I shift my weight against his pelvis, and his hold slips below my waist. The words leave my lips without a second thought, confirming that he is the only person I will *ever* want in this world.

"Please."

Finally, he answers my desperate call, carrying true to his promise.

Tonight, I get everything I ever wanted.

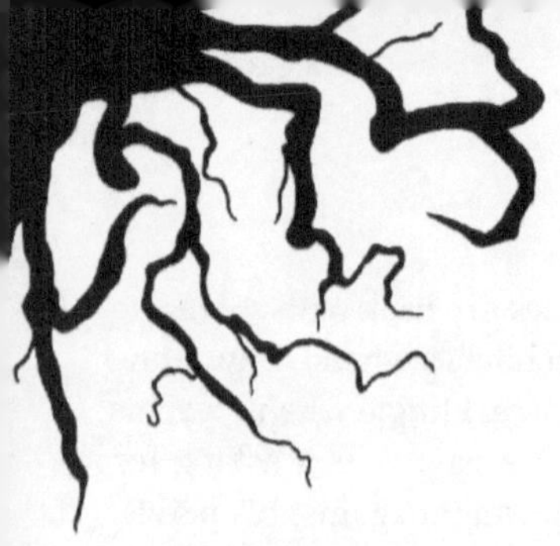

Chapter 54

When I wake on Mace's bare chest, his smile awakens the slumbering butterflies in my stomach. "Good morning," he croaks, voice not having adjusted yet.

I laugh. "Good morning, frog." He smiles before kissing me lightly on the lips. "Big day today, huh?"

Mace gives me a side-eye. "Big day, alright."

I stare at the ground for a long moment before setting a gentle hand on his back. "Well, there's no moment like the present, right?" He laughs, but I can feel his dejectedness when he won't meet my eyes. I rub his upper arm and force a deep breath. "I'll get your rations, okay? You stay put, little frog." He smiles and stretches back against the pillows, leaning away to give me room to exit.

I crawl out of the fort and nearly run into Lunar when I rise. "Well, good morning to you, Mrs. Iris! Or should I say…*Mrs. Mace*?" His voice is sly and drawn out, and he has one eyebrow raised.

"Oh, shut up!" I laugh, slapping his shoulder. "What are you doing up right now, anyway?"

"Iris, it's really not that early," he laughs, pointing at the clock. When I catch the numbers, I feel like I'm drowning. I try to breathe, but the boulder in my throat refuses to let air through. The clock has adjusted to allow only an Expulsion vote countdown, showing just eight hours until Finian is eliminated.

Or…*the unthinkable.*

Lunar jumps in front of the neon numbers. "I…it *just* changed. I didn't know it would…I'm sorry, Iris," Lunar stutters, legs beginning to tremble.

I shake my head. "How could you have known?" I force him in for a hug, holding onto him tight. "I had to come back to reality at some point."

When we break from our embrace, I lead him to the kitchen in silence, only the sounds of his labored breathing filling the noiseless house.

"I couldn't sleep last night."

His voice comes out in a squeak so vulnerable it takes me only a second to turn around and reach for him. His body is shaking so hard that I'm surprised the tears now pooling in his eyes stay in place. "Lunar…it's going to work. We *have to* trust Artemis."

"But what if we can't?" Lunar manages between whimpers.

I shrug as a metal taste fills my mouth. "We have no choice." I grab our bins from the cupboard. "He gave us his word. If he goes back on that…well, we'll give him hell." Lunar nods and takes his bin by the handles. When he plops it down onto the table, I situate mine and Mace's bins beside his. "I'm gonna go get Mace, but you stay right there. A family breakfast will make you feel better." He shutters but forces a smile when I linger with narrowed eyes.

I'm halfway to the fort when Mace crawls out. My grin is forced as I help him to his feet, but my teeth show when he kisses my palm. I gaze into his eyes and give a playful stomp while I squeeze his knuckles. "Do we *have* to get rid of the fort?"

He laughs. "Just because it's gone doesn't mean it'll be forgotten." He kisses me on the cheek and leans in, whispering in my ear. "Our moments in there will replay in my memory until the day that I die." He winks, sending a sensual shiver down my spine. I'm still reeling from his message when he rushes toward my brother and ruffles his brown locks. "What's for breakfast, little man?" Mace's hug is the only thing that calms Lunar's trembling, his legs loosening beneath Mace's arms. Before long, Lunar's swallowing his cereal by the mouthful, the only remnants of his anxiety in the light tapping of his foot against the carpet.

Their conversation carries out with little significance, and the entire day is a drag. My anxiety makes the seconds slow down until it feels like we've been waiting for the vote for three weeks straight. Time freezes when I pass my ex-alliance members, and I don't get more than a nod from Lagiacrus or a "Hello" from Destry. Artemis, for his part, stays completely out of my way, but I know we have his loyalty.

At the very least, I know that *I* have his loyalty.

The rational part of my brain contests my anxiety regarding the Expulsion. When I truly consider how the votes will play out, my nerves minimalize to a pesky simmer in my stomach. But the second I relax about Mace's safety, panic sets in about the Executive competition. My alliance might make it out of this round unscathed, but where will our fates lie if Destry steps into the helm of power? I voice my concerns to Ashlea and Mace about the potential torture awaiting us in the arena, but nobody can imagine a scenario worth serious consideration. Instead, I continue counting the structures around the house and quizzing Mace on riddles I've memorized, trying to freshen our minds for whatever looms.

It's not until the Expulsion clock flashes thirty minutes remaining that the adrenaline in my system refuses to be ignored. My breathing becomes labored as I consider the real danger Mace finds himself in, and I rub my temples viciously to force some sense of calm to ease my tension.

"Mace…" I curl my legs to my chest and bite my cheek to keep from crying. Mace sits at the foot of my bed, watching me with wide eyes. "Mace, what if—"

"It's going to work," he assures me. "It was a pinky swear, Iris. He can't break that."

I let out a single laugh. Pinky swears may be sacred to me, but who knows how seriously Artemis takes them? I nod rigidly, and Mace grabs my hand. "Hey." He looks me in the eye and softens his gaze. "Don't worry. A few hours from now, we'll be toasting with orange juice in the Executive bedroom. Right?"

351

I smile and nod, but I can't stop the shuttering in my arms. I clench and unclench my fists like Sola used to do seemingly a lifetime ago. Mace readjusts so his body aligns with mine along the cot and presses me against his chest. His heart thuds against my ear, and I force my breaths to match the consistent beat.

Ashlea leans over from her bed and pokes my leg. "He's gonna make it, Iris." I smile, hoping for continued reassurance. But nothing comes.

Instead, the three of us sit silently, letting our shaking breaths merge into a chorus of false confidence.

Three minutes from Expulsion, Ashlea, Lunar, and I occupy the nearest couch to the kitchen. I sit on the edge closest to the Death Row cushions, gripping Mace's hand so tightly that I nearly make him lose circulation. He gives the strongest three squeezes he can muster and offers a reassuring smile. I nod, forcing back tears for Mace's sake. Destry and Artemis sit on the opposite couch, officially drawing the line between our two groups. Despite Kylah's declaration against Mace, she still sits beside Lunar, souring our side with her toxic aura.

Nobody dares to speak. Instead, we stare blankly at the carpet, avoiding each other's gazes. The only sounds are my thumping heart and Lunar's trembling, shaking the sofa back and forth against the plush floor. He triggers my own shakes, so Ashlea reaches her arm over my shoulders, squeezing me into her side. Her reassurance offers a momentary flash of calm, but it doesn't go beyond my notice that my trembles are no match for Lunar's. He can barely sit still, terrified of where Artemis's true loyalties lie.

When my gaze finds Artemis, his blue pearls are locked on my palm, interlocked with Mace's. He finally catches my eye, and I raise my eyebrows to confirm that he'll follow through on his promise. He nods subtly, sending another flicker of ease over my body, then looks down at his own hands, clasped tightly in his lap.

Any confidence these insignificant actions have instilled in my unstable mind disappears the second the clock booms and the robotic voice returns.

"CONVICTS." It repeats its usual spiel, and I struggle to focus on the words. My heart beats so loudly in my ears that I barely catch the first command.

"IRIS."

I flinch and jolt my gaze to Mace, eyes widening. He motions for me to take a deep breath and nods, letting go of my hand to gesture to the staircase. I follow his directions and force air through my lungs before marching through the living room. I plant my feet square on the carpet each step up the staircase, propelling my resolved body forward. *Fear will not distract me from what must be done.*

Not like last round.

I force open the iron slab and walk swiftly through. I try and ignore anything but the velvet railings and black pedestal, but I can't help but notice the damage around the walls. The wallpaper peels below the surface of where the freezing water once stood, and an even line separates the damaged area from the fresh cover. I allow myself a single look before descending the metal staircase and marching through the velvet-sectioned path. This time, the railings are merely decoration. I need no assistance in my march, and when I stand at the pedestal and stare at the options, I have no difficulty finding Finian's blue bottom on my left.

"I'm sorry," I whisper, pressing down the blue plastic. Even though my heart doesn't break with this decision like in the past, the remorse doesn't disappear. Finian doesn't deserve to die. *None of us do.* But I can't help the reality we're in. So, when I lock in my vote, I don't give it a second thought before racing the hell out of there.

Destry is next to vote, so he crosses my path when I reach the bottom floor. He ignores my presence and treks into the arena with passionate determination. I roll my eyes when he's out of sight and return to the couch. The second I plop down, I take Mace's hand and press my lips against the back of his palm, lingering a second longer than usual.

The convicts are called one by one. With each passing vote, my heart grows wearier. *This has to work. Surely, it will work. Why wouldn't it work?*

Artemis is once again the last to cast his vote. He raises when his name is called and gives me one final glance, confirming his loyalty. My tremors calm at the look he gives me, but I subconsciously grip Mace's hand even harder. It doesn't pass my notice that I'm not the only one squeezing.

Mace is holding on for dear life.

Finally, Artemis returns to his seat, and I wipe a bead of sweat off my brow.

We sit in silence for what feels like an eternity. I tap my foot against the carpet, and Ashlea leans forward, hands held together in prayer. Lagiacrus chews on his lip, and Finian tugs on his clothes, loosening the collar around his neck. Time passes so slowly that I think they've forgotten about the vote.

Until the robotic voice returns.

"BY A VOTE," it pauses as if it's calculating. I grasp Mace's palm with both hands.

"OF THREE TO THREE: THERE IS A TIE."

My jaw drops to the floor. "No," I try to whisper, but nothing comes out. Mace's hand grows limp between my palms.

"AS EXECUTIVE, LAGIACRUS IS INELIGIBLE TO VOTE." I shake my head on hyperdrive, whipping Ashlea with my hair. "WHEN FACED WITH A TIE, THE EXECUTIVE MAKES THE FINAL DECISION ON EXPULSION."

Lunar's cries crescendo across the room. Lagiacrus stands slowly with his hands balled into fists. There's moisture in his eyes. My vision is blurry, the tears already obstructing it. I don't try to stop them as they fall down my cheeks. I can barely see through the splotches of moisture, but I couldn't miss it if I were blind.

I'd have to be dead to miss Destry clapping Artemis on the shoulder and nodding congratulations.

I bare my teeth, ready to pounce on them. But when Mace's hand leaves my grasp, I collapse against the back of the couch and shut down.

I can't move. My brain can't send messages to my muscles. The motions are getting lost within the tangle of my nerves, so I'm completely frozen against the blue plush, sinking like quicksand. It's like I'm experiencing sleep paralysis, unable to move or speak.

I can only watch the demon before me, threatening to kill the love of my life.

And there's *nothing* I can do.

"Lagiacrus, *listen*," Mace pleads. "You *don't* have to do this."

"I don't have a choice," Lagiacrus says, choking on the last word.

"Yes, you do!" Mace starts to beg. "I can help you. I will commit my *entire* game to you, with God as my witness. I will do anything and everything you want…I'll purposely lose every competition from this point forward if that's what you want. I'll bring you your rations every morning…hell, I'll bring you *my* rations. I'll stop eating…I'll stop trying." He leans forward and puts his hands together. "Lagiacrus, I'll do *anything*."

Finian tries to get a word in, but nobody is listening. Mace begs so loudly, he drowns out Lunar's sobs.

"Mace." Lagiacrus gulps, shaking his head. "I can't win with you here. You have to understand that."

"It doesn't have to be this way, Lagiacrus. I can help you to the end…*we* can help you to the end." He gestures at the group on my couch, ending before Kylah. "We'll give you everything and anything. *You don't have to do this.*"

"Mace," Lagiacrus starts, tilting his head in sorrow.

"*PLEASE!*" Mace shouts, begging for his life. Not a word is shared amongst the rest of the group. Everyone pays their full attention to Mace's pleas. My consciousness leaves my body, and I stare down at them, once again being a spectator of my own life. I watch Mace lunge toward Lagiacrus and put a hand on his shoulder. I watch him pull Lagiacrus's sleeve as he struggles to stand straight, and I watch him beg for his survival and promise his life away. And worst of all…

I watch Lagiacrus decide to kill the only person I've ever unconditionally loved.

"I vote to expel Mace." His voice is barely a whisper. But the announcement registers because the clock resets to thirty seconds.

And the room falls completely silent.

"BY A VOTE OF FOUR TO THREE: MACE IS EXPELLED FROM THE ENTERPRIZE. YOU HAVE THIRTY SECONDS TO EVACUATE."

354

I don't believe it. I *can't* believe it. Because the second Mace walks through that door, so will the light in my soul. Once that door cracks closed, the world will forever be dark, and his candle will never again be aflame. The world is spinning with images of the mahogany flecks in his eyes, circling around the midnight pupil with a ring of magenta around the rim. I'm stuck in a loop of the sound of his heart against my ear, beating wildly out of his chest from my sheer proximity. He's steps away from me, but I *feel* his gentle touch against my thigh and his delicate lips against my forehead. I want to swim in these memories and replay them in real-time, rewinding back to the first time he looked into my eyes or the first time he held me, *truly* held me against his chest. I hiccup from my tears.

I want to remember the first time he *felt* me.

When he straightens his knees and turns in my direction, my nerve endings connect. Every *screaming* message my brain has been straining to send to my limbs is received in an instant. I bound to him as if launching from a trampoline and leap into his arms, burying my face in his neck. He spins me around the center of the room while I wail. When he chokes on his own tears, I go limp. Ashlea helps me stand when he releases me, and I struggle for air as he ruffles Lunar's hair and hugs him tight, whispering his goodbye. When Mace is back in my arms, his shirt is soaked from my tears. Ashlea sneaks in a quick embrace before Mace leads me to the exit with my legs around his waist. With fifteen seconds remaining, we're the only two people in the world.

I gulp back my sobs, if only for fifteen seconds, so he can understand my final words. "I love you, Mace." I erupt but pull the tears back for another moment. "I love you more than I've ever loved anything…I…I…"

"Hey," he whispers, wiping my tears with his thumb as he sets me on the ground. "Iris…*please*…I just want…I want you to *remember me*." His voice is breaking, and he doesn't even try to hide his tears. "Remember…remember that I would do it all over again if it only meant getting to spend a second longer with you. That…that I wouldn't take a moment of our love back, and I'd swing around on a quarter for *fifty* hours if it meant I could feel your lips one last time. Can you do that for me? Can you *remember*?"

"*I would do anything for you, Mace.*" I force him back into my arms while he pleads.

"Iris, promise me…promise…promise that you'll keep fighting."

I struggle to speak with the force of my tears but manage to get the words out. "I promise…I'll keep…keep fighting…for *you*." I hiccup again and shout my next words just to get them out. "*I LOVE YOU, MACE!*"

"I love you too, Iris," he whispers into my neck. The clock starts beeping, indicating ten seconds remaining. Mace pats my head and separates from me, gazing into my eyes with the forty shades of violet I've etched into my memory.

"You have the most beautiful eyes I've ever seen," I say truthfully, somehow getting the entire sentence out in one breath.

He smiles. "You should see yours." He grabs me with five seconds remaining. "Last night was the best night of my life. Don't you *ever* forget that." He plants a kiss on my lips, and I lean into him hard, latching onto his soft touch for the final time. *I never want to let go.* His body makes me feel so safe, so…secure. But he backs away against my mental protest when the clock strikes two seconds. Mace grabs the door with one hand and caresses my cheek with the other.

"Iris." His urgent eyes lock on mine. *"Don't trust Artemis."*

Only when the door shuts does it hit me.

That is the last thing he'll ever say to me.

PART 4

ROUND 6

Chapter 55

The gunshots echo off the house, bouncing off the walls and slamming into me from a hundred different directions. I collapse to my knees and bang on the door senselessly, screaming for the shooting to stop and begging for the Authority to show him mercy. I can't control my muscles, so my body heaves on the ground as I choke on my tears. Ashlea's arms wrap around me as she squats to the ground. She rocks with my aching body as I wail and scream until my throat goes raw. Lunar doesn't join us. He's so distraught he can't remove himself from the couch. Every other person in the house is looking at the ground, not daring to make a sound.

I heave for breath and clear my throat. The single moment of silence as I hiccup back tears exposes me to the sounds of Ashlea's weeps, which only crescendo me into worse shudders. When I look up to the other side of the room and find a pair of blue eyes watching me, I freeze.

Only the eyes of the man who murdered the best thing that's ever happened to me could distract me from my meltdown.

"*You*," I shout, pointing at Artemis. He doesn't look away; he doesn't even flinch. He just stares as I march into the living room, beelining his direction. "YOU!" I scream so loud my ears ring.

I sprint the last few steps until I'm inches from his face, rage blurring my senses and shattering my conscience. I don't care how he feels. I don't care if he loves me, and I don't care if I ever had feelings for him. I don't even care if he hates me.

I only want him dead.

I push Artemis so hard that his back slams into the neck of the couch. He doesn't break eye contact with me. He doesn't even wince. Instead, he keeps his stoic exterior, refusing to fight back.

"You *promised* me." My voice cracks. "YOU PROMISED!" I slam him back into the couch, but he rebounds quickly, keeping his arms at his sides, away from my body. But this time, instead of stoicism, his eyes shift into an image of sadness, moisture thickening the edges. *I growl.* "NO! Don't you *dare* think about crying. You're a monster! A criminal! You're the beast everyone always claimed you to be!"

Finally, Destry pins my arms back, and I kick toward Artemis. I try to break the grasp but only manage to keep Artemis's eye contact. "You are the *worst* thing that's ever happened to me. *Do you understand me?*" Spit comes out with every other word, and I don't try to stop it. "I wish they would've just shot you with your parents. I wish…I wish…" I gulp back my saliva and scream the last words. "*I WISH I NEVER MET YOU!*"

Destry successfully yanks me back, and I fall to the floor. I shove him away and wipe the salty moisture from my face. I look at Artemis from the ground. *He's still watching me.*

"You voted him out," I shout. "You voted him out, and you *promised* me that you wouldn't." He stares at me, not moving a muscle. He has no response, and it infuriates me far more than anything I've felt before. "YOU WON'T EVEN DENY IT!" My ears ring loud, and I fear I may have blown out one of my eardrums. But I don't care. I want Artemis to feel the overwhelming hate that the person he loves most in this world has for him. "I want you to look in my eyes and *know* that I hate you. I want you to hear the words come from my mouth when I tell you that I wish you were dead, and I want you to know *in your heart* that the person you love will stop at *nothing* until you have a bullet through your chest. *DO YOU HEAR ME?*"

A single tear falls down Artemis's face, and I squint in disgust. "No," I shake my head. "You don't get to cry over him." My tears fling onto my shoulders, shoes, and the carpet beneath my body. "You didn't deserve his friendship, you didn't deserve Mercedes's loyalty, and you sure as *hell* never deserved my kindness." When I finally stand, I tower over him, hands balled into fists. "I *never* should've given you the time of day. I should've *listened* when Mercedes told me I was just another piece in your game! I should've listened…to every *goddamn* person here! I should've *listened* to them when they called you a snake…when they called you a traitor…when they called you a *coward*!"

Finally, Artemis shakes his head. He lets a tear fall down his face but doesn't remove his eye contact from mine.

"Well?" I shout, throwing my hands in the air. "SAY SOMETHING!"

Artemis doesn't move. His mouth stays shut, and his gaze switches from sorrow to calm. But his pupils never leave mine.

I back away slowly. "You know," I shake my head. "I *actually* believed you. I actually *believed* that you gave a shit about me. And when you moped around the house after *you* kissed me?" I raise my voice and laugh without humor. "Yes, when *YOU* kissed *ME*." I shake my head and bare my teeth. "I *actually* felt bad for you. But none of that meant anything to you, did it?" He says nothing. He just stares at me with glossed eyes. I lean in one last time and whisper to him as chillingly as possible. "I will *never* forgive you. You deserve to watch every person you care about die slowing before your eyes. And I hope…I *pray*…that I *never* have to speak to you again. You are the worst person I have ever met, and I will do absolutely *anything* in my power to send you out that door. Don't you *dare* ever look at me or *speak* to me again." I back away and narrow on his blue eyes for the final time. "From this moment forward, you're *dead* to me."

I turn on my heel and march to the second floor, not caring what I've left in my wake. The arena door is ajar, so I slam it open against the adjacent wall and let it echo around the Enterprize.

I march down the metal steps in such a rage that I don't even care to look at the structure in the center of the arena. Instead, my feet touch the turf, and I start running to the other side of the arena as fast as I can. The urge to destroy something is overwhelming, and some divine force brings me to the solitary confinement door. The room was once imperceptible from the rest of the wall, but now a section of the wallpaper peels away from the door, making an unmistakable outline. I sprint toward it and wind my hands back into fists. Steps away, I lunge toward the section and wail on the door. I kick with both legs and slam with both fists until a lower section of the door concaves, giving me enough leverage to pull it open. Any lock has been so severely destroyed from water damage that the door is easy to maneuver, so I slam the structure repeatedly, tears falling all around me in a shower of sorrow.

Once I exhaust my anger, I fall to the floor and lean my back against the door, my body convulsing. When I'm finally empty in my chest, my heart having entirely disintegrated into ash, I rest my head in my hands and close my eyes, letting my breath return in steady huffs. I glimpse between my fingers and find two black shoes steadied on the turf, and my stomach twists. I look up slowly and squint, unable to control my anger as it spews.

"What do you want?" I spit at Destry. He stands solemnly with his hands clasped behind his back. His eyes twist with so much remorse that I actually believe he's sorry.

"For you not to give up."

I tilt my head. "Excuse me?"

Destry takes a deep breath. "Look…this game is *meant* to do this to us. This…" he motions to the door behind me, "…*this* is why they didn't just kill us all."

I keep silent and hug my knees to my chest, watching him.

"Iris…don't be the monster they already think we are." I open my mouth to defend myself, but he puts his hand up, stopping me. "The best way to get revenge is by going out there and winning this thing. An eye for an eye."

I shake my head. "I don't…I don't understand." I gulp. "Why are you helping me?"

Destry shrugs. "Losing the people you love…don't we all know what that's like?"

I shake my head, grimacing. "No. Don't, for a *second*, try to pretend like you know how I feel."

"Iris, I'm not pretending to know how you feel." He takes a step forward. "You trusted somebody, and they betrayed you. It *sucks*. But really…you've experienced this before."

I throw my head back between my knees, muffling my speech. "What the *hell* are you talking about? *You don't know me.*"

"But I do." When I look back up, he's even closer. "You're here because somebody knew about you. Somehow, somewhere, somebody knew you existed. You may never know who that was or why they did it…but somewhere along the way, somebody betrayed you."

I shake my head. "Why are you telling me this?"

Destry sighs. "You can hate Artemis—"

"Don't you *dare* say his name," I spit, eyes stone cold.

Destry bites his lip. "You can hate…*him*," he shrugs. "But the real person to be mad at is out there, somewhere, *free*." He points to the cameras. "*They* are the person to blame for putting you here. And the Authority are to blame for what happened to Mace." He lowers his voice. "So don't let them win, Iris. Show them who you really are and make them hurt for what they did to him."

Tears well in my eyes. Despite the absurdity of this change of events, his speech strikes a nerve. Destry reaches out his hand, and I take it, rising off the turf. I nod and let him drag me to the center of the arena by my palm. There's no romance in the gesture, no butterflies. Only purpose. I understand the intent when I glance at the clock and see 45 seconds remaining. One casualty today was enough. I'm sure the others aren't willing to find out what will happen if I'm so far away that I can't hear the instructions. Destry was merely the ringleader to bring me back in.

I briefly ponder why Ashlea and Lunar weren't the ones consoling me, but my thoughts are cut short when Ashlea comes sprinting down the staircase with twenty seconds remaining, Lunar in her arms. *I was so absorbed in my own emotional torment that I didn't even consider what Lunar was going through.* Neither knew about my tantrum because they were dealing with their own crisis.

When we all reach the center, I hug them both and pat Lunar's back. "Hey," I whisper. "We're gonna win this, okay?" Lunar eyes are glossed over, but I shake him into consciousness. "HEY!" I shout at him. He finally meets my eyes, his own puffy from tears. "We're going to win this, okay?" I look at Ashlea. "For Mace."

She nods. "For Mace."

Lunar sniffs back his remaining sobs and can barely get the words out. "For Mace."

Then, the clock strikes zero, and Lagiacrus raises the card.

Chapter 56

"Select a bar and hang…upside down?" Lagiacrus reads the card carefully and then scans the metal jungle gym in the center of the arena. Seven horizontal bars are set side by side, only rising a few inches from the ground. They are separated evenly, with vertical bars keeping them in place. I focus on the bar closest to me and ignore every other distraction, letting my fury stifle my heartbreak. *I have to win this*.

"The last convict hanging will be the new Executive. But…" He wipes his mouth and raises an eyebrow. "Touch the bar with your hands, and you are eliminated from the competition."

I squeeze Lunar's palm and motion toward the bars, signaling where to bolt once commanded. His hand quakes in mine, but he nods with resolved determination. There's a long moment of silence before Finian butts in. "So…whoever hangs the longest wins?"

"Looks like it," Lagiacrus says, looking up from his card. A minute countdown starts on the far wall, so I pull Lunar to the makeshift monkey bars and pat his arm.

"We can do this," I whisper. He gives a half-hearted smile, and I pat his back as I move toward my own gray bar. Ashlea finds a spot on my other side, so I'm sandwiched between allies. Laying on the ground, I throw my legs over and grip the bar between my hamstrings and calves. My knees lock me in place, but I'm still scrunched on the ground, my spine curling uncomfortably against the turf. The second we're all adjusted, there's mechanic clanging, and it hits that, yet again, winning will be no easy feat.

The vertical bars holding the horizontal one I hang from begin extending, lifting us several feet above the ground. We're so high that my arms hang over me, and I still don't reach the plastic grass. My stomach twirls as I consider the repercussions of failure. Because falling wouldn't only be painful…

It could be fatal.

"Let the games begin," Lagiacrus says.

The pain is immediate. Within the first minute, blood rushes to my head, and the pressure is blinding. To my left, Lunar hugs his thighs with his arms, locking his hands around his shins. I study his tactic and attempt to mirror it, but the pounding in my head makes me so nauseous that I struggle to understand the maneuver. I don't give up, though, because his strategy is genius. *I can't win if I lose consciousness.* So, I copy his posture, forcing my head to be level to the ground so I'm not entirely upside down. But the second I stabilize my neck and reach for my shins, my legs sway, and I nearly lose my balance.

"Don't worry about the position," Lunar calls, watching me struggle in his periphery. "If you're not flexible enough, you'll fall…just hang how you were before."

I let out a strained breath and uncrunch my body, letting my arms flail. I jolt when the horn blares and glance between Ashlea and Lunar, quickly confirming that they're still competing.

"CONVICT: ARTEMIS. ELIMINATED AT 00:01:14."

I laugh, grateful for the comedic relief. "Congratulations on one minute, *Judas*. You've really proved yourself useful."

Ashlea smiles, and I fight another cackle. The joy subsides because a minute later, my head is pounding so hard that I can't focus on anything but the pain. Time passes excruciatingly slowly, and each second feels like gravity has compounded tenfold. My muscles ache from the fatigue of locking my body on the bar, and dizziness eats into my crushing headache. I squeeze my eyes shut and focus. But violet pulses in the darkness, reminding me of the reality I'm desperate to ignore.

Mace is gone.

I gulp back tears and shake my head, desperate to wake from this horrifying nightmare. But no matter how tightly I squeeze my eyelids, the image before me doesn't fade. Because I'm not in a dream…I'm in a reality worse than any terror I could've ever dreamed of.

I've never known love before Mace, and he consumes every inch of my subconscious. Even with my eyes open, I see his violet pupils glow. They invite me off the bar, and he waves to me from below, begging me to accept his embrace. I watch the scene play out in my mind and smile as I close my eyelids, letting the image become more vivid. *I sprint toward him, tears running down my face, readying myself to leap into his arms. He smiles, waving me forward, crouching to pick me up and spin me around the arena.*

Then Artemis opens the trapdoor, killing Mace from the noose around his neck.

My eyes shoot open, and I gasp for breath. *It wasn't real.* But it may as well have been because it was Artemis's betrayal that robbed me of Mace's life.

I shake my head, and the physical strain of the competition resurfaces in the form of heartbeats thundering in my ears. I grit my teeth and cross my arms in an attempt to alleviate my pain. But the headache only intensifies, leaving me dizzier than before. Confusion clouds my vision as I watch the turf become a single blob of green. I'm in so much pain that it's impossible to register the horn blaring or feel any relief that it's Kylah who has failed after three and a half minutes.

I lean forward and scan the remaining contestants, desperate for anything to distract from the ache in my brain. I count my odds. *Two against three.* As long as Finian and Destry fall, Lunar, Ashlea, and I can end this competition and get Artemis the hell out of here. *We just have to keep hanging.*

Ashlea locks her fingers behind her neck and presses forward so her head isn't directly below her body. I wince as she grits her teeth, proving her efforts at comfort unsuccessful. I look away to not get discouraged by her struggling and start rubbing my head to try and alleviate the pain. It becomes evident that nothing will help, so I let the blood rush to my forehead until breathing is a chore. I try various methods to get air into my lungs, but even the deepest breaths prove fruitless. Desperate for air, I start hyperventilating.

"Hang in there, Iris!" Ashlea cheers. I want to take her advice, but I'm succumbing to a full-blown panic attack. The faster I inhale air, the worse my breathing becomes. I *feel* the world closing in on me until my terror of suffocation outweighs my urge to get revenge.

I grip my palms into fists and try once more to climb my legs with my hands, forcing my lower half to at least be perpendicular to the ground. I nearly achieve the position when black speckles obstruct my vision. My body shakes so hard that I'm forced to let go of my shins, letting my body hang back toward the ground like an outstretched accordion.

My legs tremble against the bar, and the sweat behind my knees makes me grip harder to hold position. I try to keep myself situated so I'm not entirely upside down, but my arms fail me, and I fling them toward the turf, letting them go numb. I'm still hanging as I imagine prickly nails slicing against my skin, and I can almost feel the blood gushing out of the wounds.

What is happening to me?

I force a few hard blinks in a futile attempt to clear the black specks from my vision. When nothing helps, I finally let my eyes watch the turf absently, forfeiting comfort. A black circle in the center grows slowly, obstructing my sight until there's nothing.

And the world goes completely dark.

"Iris, watch me!" Curi shouts from the top of the attic. I laugh and run to the bottom of her ladder, hands on my hips.

"Just what do you think you're doing, little one?" I call in a sing-song voice, a smile stretched across my lips. Curi positions herself at the edge of her bedroom and peeks over the top of the ladder.

"Are you watching?!" she calls.

"Yes, Curi! Of course, I'm watching!" I shout back, erupting with laughter.

"Okay! I'm coming!" she yells. She shoots down the ladder's rungs at a record pace, laughing the whole way down.

"Wow!" I exclaim. "You're a little speed racer, aren't you?"

"Did you see how fast I went?" Curi says, jumping up and down. "Or did you blink and miss it? Should I do it again? Maybe you can time me!"

I laugh and wrap her in my arms. "You sure can, little one. I could watch you climb down that ladder a thousand times and never tire of it."

Curi chuckles. "Okay, but you better watch me!"

I shake my head. "Curi, of course, I'm going to watch you! I promise you…you will have my undivided attention! Always!"

"IRIS!" Ashlea shakes my shoulders, bringing me back to consciousness.

I wipe the sweat off my forehead and lean into Ashlea's arms. "Wha…" I look up and find Ashlea and my stations unoccupied, which can only mean one thing. "No," I whisper. "I tried…I tried *so* hard."

"It's okay, Iris," she reassures me, rubbing my arms. "You did the best you could, and—"

"But it wasn't good enough!" I huff, not letting her finish. I rub my temples and shut my eyes, furious. *I didn't lose because I gave up. I lost because my body failed me.*

"But Iris," Ashlea whispers. "Look up."

I release my face from my palms and extend my neck slowly. With one glance, my lips stretch into a grin.

Lunar and Finian hang side-by-side, with all other stations empty.

"Oh my god," I whisper. "LUNAR!" I shout, making Ashlea laugh. "GO LUNAR!" Ashlea joins my cheering, and we clap in rhythm. "What happened since I was out?" I ask, disrupting our celebration.

"Destry fell less than a minute after you! I pretty much fell right after him …but Lunar! He could win this!"

I smile and try to stand, but my legs are too weak. My body took a brutal tumble, and when I fall back to my knees, it's evident that my headache hasn't gone away. Stars flood my vision as I roll onto my back, and my abdomen wrenches in pain. Lunar hanging upside down on a single monkey bar is the only thing keeping me from slipping out of consciousness.

Ashlea laughs and cheers even louder. "Look at him, go!"

Finian's body shakes, while *Lunar is completely stable.* My brother's size and flexibility have given him a massive advantage, allowing him to fold himself onto his legs to prevent him from being truly upside down. His organs aren't compressing his lungs as they would if he hung with gravity as I did, and the blood flow to his brain is slow enough that he hasn't gone dizzy. Unlike Finian, Lunar isn't struggling *at all.*

"Oh my god," I whisper. "He's gonna do it!"

We yell even louder, so Finian takes a peek at my brother. His eyes widen when he realizes just how solid Lunar is, so he clenches his fists and looks in the opposite direction to avoid getting discouraged. The Leprechaun is quivering so severely that his bar clanks from the vibration. *Finian is going to fall*. As long as Lunar doesn't touch that metal bar, he will win.

I hold my breath, and Ashlea hugs me from behind. Finian's chemical burns may have subsided, but his face is so red it's as if he's been dunked in another fresh pool of acid. He calls to Lunar, voice quivering. "Am I safe?"

Lunar doesn't flinch. "Wanna be safe? Win."

Everyone watches Finian wince as he tenses his muscles, pushing his body to continue hanging. My focus doesn't shift as he crunches up, reaching for his thighs. I only look away once he slips, and his frame slams into the ground, triggering the elimination horn.

Ashlea screams, and my vision blurs with tears.

"CONGRATULATIONS: LUNAR. YOU ARE THE NEW EXECUTIVE."

Chapter 57

I leap to my feet and scream until my throat is raw. My legs wobble, so Ashlea helps me stand, and we shout in unison, tears streaming down my face. "YOU DID IT! YOU DID IT!" Ashlea drags me, so we're under Lunar. He falls into our arms gracefully, and I squeeze him tight before setting him on the ground.

"THAT WAS FOR MACE!" I scream at the cameras. Lunar smiles and joins as we chant, "MACE! MACE! MACE!" None of us can stand still, so we throw our hands up and let our voices echo around the arena.

Adrenaline coursing through my veins, I force energy into my legs and sprint to the wall of eliminated convicts, pointing directly at Artemis. I look him dead in the eyes, letting my vicious smile shine. "SAY YOUR GOODBYES!" I scream. "THAT WAS FOR MACE!"

"Get ready for the firing squad, 'cause you're OUT OF HERE!" Ashlea yells, launching toward Artemis. He stares at the turf and shakes his head, keeping his facial expression emotionless. I flick a naughty finger in his direction before running back to the middle and lifting Lunar by his armpits. "MACE!" we shout at the top of our lungs, letting the name carry around us.

Destry is the first to approach the newest Executive. "Congratulations, Lunar." He shakes his hand and pulls him into a side hug, giving him a pat on the back. Before stalking toward the exit, he stops next to me and nods. "Proud of you for pulling yourself together. You would've made Mace proud." I stare at him for a long second before wrapping my arms around him, my eyes glossing with moisture.

"Thank you," I whisper, and I mean it. It's a mystery why Destry cared to help me, but the talk had more impact than he probably anticipated. *I won't forget that anytime soon.* Lagiacrus takes his turn congratulating Lunar while Kylah approaches with a soft smile.

"I'm proud of you, kid."

Lunar stares at her stoically before accepting her embrace. Her betrayal is still fresh, so I'm not surprised that Lunar bursts into tears. But I can tell he still deeply cares for her, even though she didn't protect Mace. *Of course, I want her dead for what she's done.* But that's a problem for the future.

For now, we celebrate Lunar's win and Artemis's downfall.

Finian shouts congratulations to Lunar from his stop on the turf. He still hasn't gained feeling in his muscles, having pushed his body almost to the limit that I did. Given his pain, it's no shock that he's making no rush for the exit.

Artemis beelines for the metal staircase with his head hung low. Ashlea and I boo at him and alternate, yelling, "COWARD!" at his back. I smirk as he stalks away, gigantic hands balled into veiny fists.

Once Artemis walks through the threshold into the Enterprize, Ashlea and I force Lunar into our arms and squeeze. "Lunar…I don't know what to say!" I blush. "You know how proud Mace would be right now!?" Lunar winces at the memory of his demise, but I bring him back to the moment. "No…we're not going to dwell on it right now. For this moment, and this moment only…we celebrate."

"For Mace's memory!" Ashlea shouts.

Lunar nods, eyes welled with tears, and we dance around him, whooping from excitement. Lunar's win can't mend my broken heart. But it sure can distract me from it.

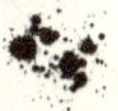

I sink into the Executive mattress and sigh as the plush engulfs me.

"It's just as amazing as it was in the second round!" Ashlea says. We laugh as we bury the blankets around ourselves and lay on our stomachs, facing Lunar on his long sofa. He shakes his head with a grin and stretches his legs over the cushions. I gulp as our laughter fades and prop my chin on my wrists with my elbows on the mattress.

Ashlea adjusts her position and tilts her head at Lunar. "Hey, have you thought much about Death Row selections?"

"Oh, we don't need to talk about that," Lunar whines. "Can't we just keep the celebration going?" He kicks his legs against the opposite armrest of the sofa, but his smile gives his enthusiasm away.

I laugh and slap the mattress excitedly. "Once Artemis gets the firing squad, the celebrations will never end!" It's strange that one decision could make Artemis destroy everything he was to me. But my hatred for him is genuine, so despite how foreign my excitement feels for his impending doom, I embrace it. With the pain he's caused me, I want him wiped from the face of the planet.

A knock on the door draws our attention, and Ashlea rises to answer. My body tenses as I consider who could be on the other side, but my nerves calm when Destry crosses the threshold.

"Enjoying the room?" Destry smiles.

Lunar raises his eyebrows and laughs, drawing out his vowels. "Biiiiig tiiiime."

Destry nods, then leans against the wall furthest from my brother. He licks his lips before crossing his arms. "I'm obviously here because…I just wanted to see where your head was at. Maybe…I can offer you something?"

I'm ready to tell Destry he's safe when Lunar cuts me off. "Here's the thing…regardless of your support in the past twelve hours, *you voted him out.*" My breath catches in my throat. *Lunar is right.* My overwhelming rage for Artemis combined with

Destry's last-minute encouragement to distort my opinion. But I can't forget that he voted Mace out and didn't think twice about doing it. Beyond that, Destry is Artemis's closest friend in the house. Despite his recent kindness and support…Destry is still an enemy of my alliance.

"I understand," Destry begins. "I just want you all to know how sorry I am for that. I take full responsibility for my vote and wish I hadn't cast it." He looks down, taking a deep breath. "Mace was a good man. He didn't deserve what happened. None of us deserve that end, really."

"Artemis does," I declare. "He needs to pay for what he's done." The others look at me as I narrow my eyes on Destry. "Don't you agree?"

Destry reluctantly nods. "Only one of us can win this thing, right?" Silence passes between us. Destry bites his lip before locking on Lunar. "Look, I can't predict Artemis's behavior. He's a ticking time bomb at *all* times. I've tried to help the guy, but he's so impulsive…I can never tell what his next move will be." He lowers his voice. "But I *do* know that he was *never* going to vote to save Mace…he kept Lagiacrus and me in the loop the entire round. His promises to you…they were empty. He was never going to help you, Iris. He made that much *very* clear to us."

My lip quivers, so I chew on my cheek to stop it. I should believe Destry without a second thought, but my heart makes me pause. I ponder Artemis's intentions for the first time since Mace's expulsion. I hate Artemis. I want him gone, and I want him to pay for what he has done. But when I think about it, and *truly* consider what was real and what was fake…

I can't refute that Artemis loved me.

I try to wipe this from my mind. *It was all a part of his game*. After all, he told Mercedes the same things he told me. I feel a fresh wave of sympathy for his ex-lover. The betrayal I feel at this moment…it has to bear similarity to what Mercedes went through just days ago.

And she never got a chance to avenge herself.

Mentally, I try to deconstruct every move Artemis made and struggle to decipher how I could have fallen for his lies. But no matter what I do, I continually arrive at the same conclusion.

He was always telling the truth.

Except when he murdered my best friend.

I ball my hands into fists to escape the pain. *He loved me.* As hard as I try to convince myself it was fake, I saw the look in his eyes and heard the desperation in his voice. And I may refuse to admit it out loud, but this much is true:

I loved him back. It's a hard pill to swallow. Because after everything he's done for me, it's clear that he had goodness within him. Still, he may have been kind at times…

But even the devil had redeeming qualities.

I hate Artemis. Still, as much as I try to deny it, the throbbing in my heart confirms that I miss him. What hurts even more is that the person I miss has already died. The Arty that helped me in solitary confinement and made me laugh until I couldn't breathe…he's gone.

And he's been replaced by a vicious, soul-sucking monster.

Mace wasn't the only person I lost when he was sent out that door. My friendship with Artemis was also destroyed. Arty's vote took two people from my life, doubling my grief. But as always, it's much easier to hate somebody than to miss them. I've become a professional at compartmentalizing my heartache. So, I do as much with Artemis, pushing every happy memory to the darkest crevices of my mind and refusing to feel the tremendous loss that his friendship is. Simultaneously, I bring my hatred to the forefront and fume at the Artemis born this afternoon.

"I want him dead," I say, drawing everyone's attention. "I want him to pay for what he's done."

Ashlea puts a hand on my back. "We all do."

Destry nods. "I understand that, and I encourage you to do what you must to make that happen." He lets the room grow quiet before continuing. "I'm sorry I was on the wrong side of that battle. But if I may…" He leans forward. "I never led any of you to believe that my vote was anything other than what it was. You knew my intentions…I made them *very* clear. I know we've had disagreements…but haven't we all? What I propose to you is this." He gulps loudly. "Keep me off Death Row this week, and if I win Executive next round, I'll keep you off Death Row."

Lunar cringes. "That's it? One round?"

Destry nods. "As I said, I have been and always will be straight up with you. I will deliver on my end of the deal and do anything in my power to keep any of you from touching Death Row."

Ashlea opens her palms to the ceiling. "And why would we believe you?"

Destry shakes his head slowly. "Because I have been nothing but truthful to you." He directs his attention to me, locking onto my eyes. "Iris…I know this hurts to hear…but I haven't lied to you. I accused you of kissing Artemis because *that's what he told me*. I would never have brought it up if he had said for one second that it was the other way around. I was angry…emotions were running high…but that's what he said. I swear it on my life."

I shake my head. "Why should I believe that?"

Lunar straightens his back. "Are you kidding me right now? He lied to your face *multiple times*. What more proof do you need, Iris? He voted out Mace!"

Tears well in my eyes, but I fight them back, not allowing them to fall. "Okay." I look directly into Destry's eyes. "Okay."

"I really am sorry, Iris." Destry leans off the wall and approaches the bed. "This game…it's bringing out the worst in us all. I want to make it up to you guys. Let me keep you safe next round. We reevaluate after that. What do you say?"

Lunar raises an eyebrow before standing. "We need to think about it…is that alright?"

Destry nods. "Of course."

"But if we do keep you off Death Row, I expect that the deal is on."

Destry smiles. "Agreed."

The two shake hands, and Destry puts another hand on top to sandwich Lunar's single palm. "I really am happy for you on your win, Lunar. You deserved it."

A revolving door of convicts beg for their safety, Finian being directly after Destry. He was still weak from the competition but argued that he was always loyal to us from the moment he saved Ashlea.

"I was angry that I was the target for you guys last week…who wouldn't be? But I never went against any of you."

To be fair, he never had the chance.

After him came Lagiacrus. He was stoic. He said very little, making the conversation no longer than five minutes. He promised nothing and showed little remorse. His apology for sending Mace out the door was so insincere that he couldn't even make eye contact when he said it. So naturally, none of us forgave him, and we sent him on his way.

Kylah was the hardest one to manage. Enough tears were shed between her and Lunar that they could have filled an ocean. Apologies were shared, and she could not shut up about how proud of him she was. Despite the grand performance, my opinion of her remains unchanged.

Kylah voted Mace out and will pay for her betrayal when it's my turn to have power.

As night winds down, I crack open the bedroom door to peek at the other convicts. Once glance at Artemis, fast asleep on his cot, confirms that he won't be making a visit.

"What a coward," I joke, closing the door. As angry as I am with him, a tiny part of my heart aches that he never showed. I will never stop talking about how angry I am. But even if all I do is yell at him…

At least I'm still talking to him.

I shake my head, trying to dispose of the thought.

"What are your thoughts, boss?" Ashlea stretches her arms above her head, and I can just see the outline of her legs under the covers. I lay beside her, under the sheets, with my knees to my chest.

"Artemis is the target," Lunar declares.

"Obviously," I joke, punching Lunar playfully. He smiles and punches me back on the arm.

"But as far as who to put up next to him…I can tell you who's not going up there. Finian was honest…he never made a move against us. I think he deserves to be safe. And Destry…he's a tough one, but he was right…he never led us to believe that he had any other intention than getting out Mace."

"Well, he did try and get Ashlea out," I note.

Lunar doesn't hesitate. "Yeah, but he was honest about it." Ashlea and I nod, unhappy about Destry's safety but in agreement that it's fair.

"That leaves Kylah and Lagiacrus," Lunar says. "I don't know about you guys, but I think Lagiacrus is a much better competitor than Kylah."

It's annoying, but it's what I expected. "He *was* also the deciding vote against Mace." I shake my head. "He should pay for what he's done…it could be good to make him shake in his boots."

"I think it's a good idea," Ashlea says. "Even if this round doesn't go according to plan, you'll still get out the most competitive person in the house. That would be huge."

I squint. "You think it won't go accordingly?"

Ashlea shrugs. "I think it will. But I'm just saying that even if it doesn't…we still get a win, right? It's not like we'd be sending Finian out of here."

I smile. "Yeah, that's fair."

"What do you think the votes would look like?" Lunar asks.

"Five people vote this week," Ashlea says. "So, we need three votes against Artemis."

"Well, we have two," I declare, gesturing at Ashlea and myself.

"So, we'd need Destry, Kylah, or Finian's vote," Lunar says. "And we have Kylah's." Ashlea and I look at him skeptically, but he fights back. "Trust me. Kylah will vote with us. Artemis has been causing so many issues…he pretty much broke up our group. She's gonna want him gone."

I shrug before nodding. "And if she refuses? We try to get Finian on our side?"

Lunar nods. "I say we put up Lagiacrus and Artemis, then iron out the details later. Let's give Lagiacrus something to be nervous about."

I smile and nod. "Look how much you've grown, little guy."

Lunar laughs. "Happens when your sister can't get her shit together." I roll my eyes and force him into a hug.

"It's gonna be a long day tomorrow," Ashlea interrupts, stretching her neck. "We may as well rest up." One glance at the clock confirms that it's already one in the morning. Just the thought of the hour makes me yawn.

"I'm *really* proud of you, Lunar," Ashlea says, getting up from the mattress. "You made Mace proud." We smile and watch as she steps toward the door.

"Ashlea, wait," Lunar calls. She turns with wide eyes. "You can stay here tonight if you want. Iris will just sleep in the middle." Ashlea smiles. "We should all enjoy this victory together. And besides…I don't think any of us want to be alone right now."

Ashlea nods and lies beside me. We say our goodnights as Lunar turns off the light and try our best to find a peaceful place to rest our minds.

But silent tears fall from my eyes the entire evening, and I never fall into sleep's loving embrace.

Chapter 58

Every time I close my eyes, I see violet lights…lights that transform into the thousands of bullets that shot through Mace's flesh.

I'd cry, but I've exhausted my tears. Every movement is a monumental task, so I force myself through the motions. Even the single wheat square I shove between my lips refuses to slide down, nearly making me choke. I abandon the prospect of food because I quickly find that the spoon is a thousand pounds when I struggle to lift it to my lips.

My housemates try and lift my spirits to no avail. Even Destry cracks some jokes along the way. But nothing can break through my trance. Every laugh is forced…every smile strained. There's only one person I want to talk to about it…

And he's *gone.*

"Hey," Ashlea says, scratching my back as she plops beside me on the living room couch. I nod in her direction but keep my blank stare on the grimy carpet, letting each stain merge into a single brownish-red blob. I ignore her figure but feel her shift as she leans into my ear and whispers, "This isn't the end, you know?"

I nod but don't believe her. *How could it not be the end when Mace is gone?*

She gulps. "Curi is still out there…watching you. You know that, right?" I take a deep breath and close my eyes, trying to let her words comfort and motivate me. But when Curi's body is also pierced with a hundred bullets behind my eyelids, I force them open and refuse to blink.

Oblivious of my vision, she squeezes my shoulder and continues. "She's proud of you…of how you're fighting…of how you've been keeping Lunar safe."

"Ashlea, we don't even know where she is," I spit out. I know she means well, but her efforts are futile. The rage burning in my chest competes with the ache in my heart, and I have no room for optimism. I grip my fists at my sides and lean forward, desperate to shield her from my anger. But the words come out of me like vomit. "For all we know, they could have sent the troops out to kill her. She could've been dead weeks ago, just like Sola's newborn."

"You can't think like that," Ashlea urges, but I can't help myself.

"Ashlea…there's nothing to live for." I put my head in my hands. "There's…there's no reason to keep going. They broke me…and now, without my spirit…I'm *nothing.* Why…why should I even try?"

Ashlea leans into my ear. "Hope."

My body heaves, but no tears come out. "I…I'm sorry, Ashlea." I can't even summon the strength to look at her. "I just…I could put on a brave face yesterday because of the win…because of my anger at *him*," I say, referring to Artemis, back to rejecting his name. "But now…having to press on these next three days without Mace…" My voice shakes. "And then live the rest of my *life* without him?" I cough, trying to clear my throat, but my words still come out in a whine. *"What do I do?"*

Ashlea hugs me tight, voice muffled from pressing against my shoulder. "You're right, Iris. We *don't* know where Curi is. We can only blindly hope that she's still alive. But you can let that hope drive you forward…you *have to* let it drive you forward. Otherwise…what else is there to live for?" I fold into her arms and choke on my dry sobs. Her arms tighten around me, and she rubs my back softly while I gasp for air. Ashlea doesn't rush me for a response. She simply lets me convulse, allowing me to grieve over Mace, my parents, and Curi's unknown. She can't possibly be as distressed as I am about Curi's whereabouts, but the sincerity is not lost. Her empathy is the only thing that gives me strength, so I let her in.

"I'm just…so…*mad*," I say, Ashlea smoothing my hair back. "How could…how could *he* do this to me? To us?" My voice cracks. *"After everything I've done for him?"*

Ashlea has no response. She simply continues stroking my hair, letting me air out my grievances without interruption. My body tightens as a fresh surge of electricity courses through me. I grit my teeth when I recognize the ugly sensation. I acknowledge that it won't heal my wounds in the long term, but it may be the only thing that can get me through the next few days.

Revenge.

"I'm gonna kill him," I say. "*I'm gonna kill him.*" It may not be healthy, but for the first time since Mace's death, *I feel alive.* My depression fades the more I focus on the fulfillment my vengeance will achieve, and my spirit shifts from an empty, helpless hole to one with overwhelming purpose.

"I know," Ashlea whispers. "And kill, we will."

Ashlea and I take the sofa facing the kitchen as the house gathers for Death Row selections. With a perfect view of the staircase, we watch every convict descend the steps one by one, keeping our eyes out for the traitor as we lace his noose.

Because once he arrives, the real show will start.

Artemis and Destry descend the steps together, the latter obstructing our view of the betraying filth. When I give Ashlea a side eye, we burst into laughter at Artemis's cowardly entrance. Once the two are steps from the living room, my lips stretch into a smile.

"Destry!" I shout. "How are you doing, man? What a beautiful evening for vengeance, wouldn't you say?"

Destry raises an eyebrow and grins, lips barely curving at the ends. "Someone's in a good mood."

Destry sits on the couch across from us, and Ashlea doesn't skip a beat. "It's just *so* great when terrible things happen to people that deserve them. And when we get to be the ones to inflict the damage on behalf of karma?" She pinches her fingers against her thumb and kisses them before flicking them away from her face. "*Delicious.*"

I howl with laughter. Ashlea hunches over, and Lunar smiles. None of us can contain our composure. Destry simply spreads his lips into a thin line and rubs his palms together, watching his knuckles. The attention on Destry is intentional. Anything we can do to make Artemis feel invisible is an effort well spent.

Artemis bends his knees, squatting to sit beside Destry. I focus my wide eyes on the sofa cushion behind Artemis to avoid looking directly at him and spread my arms out in front of me. "Woah, woah, woah there pal! Where do you think you're going?"

Artemis watches me, tilting his head. He's mute, but his hands are balled into tight fists, cluing us into his anger. Ashlea leans forward and narrows her eyes on his figure. "These couches are for the voters…not the *votees*. Why don't you just skip the middleman and take a seat on your throne?" Ashlea gestures toward the Death Row chairs.

I bite my lip and focus on Artemis's chest, still avoiding eye contact. "Preferably on the bullet-pierced one…just a hunch."

Artemis shakes his head and settles beside Destry, not adding ammunition to our revenge-fueled slander. Destry puckers his lips to the side, trying to hide his betraying grin. He may be friends with Artemis, but our performance is signal enough that he's safe, and it's clear that he knows it.

Ashlea clicks her tongue at Artemis's disobedience. "He just doesn't listen, does he?"

"Probably impossible to when all he cares about is himself. What is it you said to me?" I ask in Artemis's direction. "You'd *die* for me?" I lean back in my chair. "Then why don't you just do us all a favor and stop breathing?"

Artemis presses his lips together and looks at the ceiling while Ashlea and I laugh ourselves silly. I smile in his direction so he knows how much joy I'm getting from his despair. But despite the instant and momentary pleasure these insults bring me…

My heart twists a little more with every slight I fling his way.

I clench my teeth because I refuse to let my heart soften for him. So, instead of acknowledging my persistent conscience, I dig deeper into my hatred for what he's done. Leaning my torso in his direction, I scan his face with daggers. I focus on the outside of his jaw, staying clear of his eyes. I promised myself I'd *never* look into them again, and I'll die before I break that oath. "*Fucking* coward."

He doesn't stop looking at the ceiling, even as he shakes his head. He only looks forward once the clock strikes zero and Lunar rises from his throne. Only then does Artemis acknowledge my brother's presence, leaning forward as he narrows his eyes in his direction. I can feel the fire spewing from them and almost shiver from his gaze's animosity. I only get a brief glance from my periphery, but I don't have to see to know that Artemis is furious. The temperature feels like it's risen ten degrees from the intensity of his hatred.

I roll my eyes and scoff. Artemis's hatred for Lunar infuriates me. *I'm* the one hurting Artemis. *I'm* the one calling for his demise. He should direct his fury at me, not the thirteen-year-old boy he just robbed of a brother.

"This decision wasn't hard," Lunar begins, omitting any artificial introduction. He clasps his hands behind his back and leans forward on his toes. "Mace…" He chokes up. "He was a good man. Many of you are responsible, but unfortunately, I can only put two of you up there."

Artemis leans back and looks at the ceiling, the corner of his lip rising into a smirk. A humorless laugh escapes his lips as he raises an eyebrow.

It takes everything in me to not lunge across the living room and smack him across the face.

"Artemis shut the fuck up and pop a squat," Lunar demands, launching a finger at the black couch Sola was murdered on. *Ironic, considering Artemis nearly finished that job for us.*

He rises without a word and marches to Sola's death chair. Artemis shakes his head as he plops into it and locks eyes with Lunar.

And smiles.

"You're ugly," I say in his direction. "Absolutely disgusting." But his smile doesn't fade. Instead, he shifts his gaze to the ground, ignoring my comment.

Lunar claps his hands in front of his chest. "Nice. *Very* classy." He shakes his head before clicking his tongue. "I want to make it *very* clear that if I had the choice, I'd only pick one convict this week. But, given the rules, I have to select another person for the sake of the game. Don't be fooled: I have *no* intention of letting this person leave the house, but what the Authority says goes." Several moments of silence pass before he points at Lagiacrus. "Lagiacrus…you were the deciding vote. And I won't ever forget that."

"None of us will," Ashlea chimes in, nodding in solidarity.

Lunar takes a deep breath. "For that…I'm gonna have to ask you to take a seat."

Lagiacrus nods before shuffling to the black cushion beside Artemis.

A calm passes over the group before Lunar opens his arms and adjourns the meeting. "May the best convict win."

Chapter 59

Minutes pass into hours, and hours pass into days. Minutes, hours, and days without Mace.

Artemis doesn't care. That much is clear. He doesn't seem to feel a touch of remorse for his actions as he stalks about the house with his crew. He spends most of his time sitting mute at the kitchen table with Destry and Lagiacrus, tracing the oak lines with his fingers while the other two converse. He's not even campaigning for his safety. I'd pity him if I still cared.

I spent the rest of selection day replacing my grief over Mace with my fury over Artemis's betrayal. It might not be healthy, but it soothes the gaping hole in my chest. The only time I can manage to feel anything at all is when I let rage for Artemis course through my veins. *This is all his fault.* He's the reason my chest weighs a thousand pounds despite being empty of a heart. He's the reason I don't have the motivation to carry forward, despite the prospect of Curi waiting on the other side. He's the reason that all food is tasteless, and he is the reason for my vacant stare.

And because of that, I want him *dead.*

So, as I sit on Lunar's executive bed twenty-four hours before Artemis's expulsion, I contemplate how to achieve a unanimous vote against the traitor. Some may call it greed. I call it revenge.

"We need *everyone* on board to kill him," I declare. Ashlea leans back and sighs. Lunar stays completely still, only the sounds of his breaths confirming that he's alive.

"Remember, we only need three votes," Ashlea says, watching her words. "We don't need to go overboard."

I squint at her. "How could anyone *not* vote for his death? Who on this planet would want him alive?"

Ashlea's gulp is the only sound that interrupts the silence. She and Lunar share a look before she responds. "Artemis's betrayal…while it may have proven him a liar, the others might view it as a gesture of loyalty. While he was telling us that we had his vote, he was swearing his allegiance to Dial. He may have lied to *us*, but his disloyalty only showed how faithful he is to Destry and Lagiacrus."

Lunar picks at a corner of the bedsheet, letting it slide between his fingers. "Loyalty means everything to Destry. I could see him campaigning to keep Artemis over Lagiacrus…especially considering that Lagiacrus is the stronger competitor."

"You're joking," I say, stifling my gasp.

Lunar continues. "There's eight people left, right? Well, after tomorrow, there will be seven. Yeah, Destry's gonna want somebody to bring him to the end, but not if he doesn't think he can beat them." He takes a deep breath. "Lagiacrus is strong. This is probably the only chance he's gonna get at expelling him."

I sigh, rolling my eyes. "Why don't we just bring him up here and ask? He hasn't lied to us before. Maybe he'll tell us what he's leaning toward."

Ashlea puts her head in her hands.

"What is it?" I ask.

She shakes her head. "I hate to say this, Iris, but Destry's not gonna vote to keep Artemis if he doesn't think he has a chance to stay."

My stomach twists. "You have *got* to be kidding me," I spit.

Ashlea grabs my shoulder and pleads. "That doesn't mean he'll stay, though! Just that he has a *chance*. Look…right now, we have two votes against him. Logistically, Destry will *probably* vote for him to stay. And that's a *big* maybe. But we might not even need him because there's two other voters."

"Kylah and Finian," Lunar says, staring blankly at the wall across from him.

Ashlea nods. "Exactly. We just need *one* of their votes…one! And he's out of here!"

I rub my temples and take a moment to breathe. "So, what do you suggest we do?"

"Kylah's gonna vote with us," Lunar announces. I roll my eyes, but he cuts me off before I complain. "Just hear me out for a second, Iris! I was close to her…*really* close to her. Basically, as close as I am to you!" My eyebrows shoot to the sky, but he doesn't notice. "The way she's been acting…I've never seen her this down on herself."

I stare at Lunar, a frown on my lips. I *hate* that he's compared our relationship to his and Kylah's, but I let it pass so he can finish his thought. "You two have seen her! Every time she looks at me, she bursts into tears. It's destroying her that she broke up our friendship over this." He leans forward. "What I suggest is this. Tell her she can make it up to us by voting out Artemis. She'll do *anything* to get back on our good side. Right now, she's completely alone. She doesn't have a *single* ally. You really think she's gonna team up with Destry over me?"

"What about Finian?" I interrupt. "If Kylah's so lonely, why doesn't she just team up with Finian? Instead of running back to a group that *I'm* involved in. She hates me!"

Lunar shakes his head. "First of all, she doesn't hate you. Second, do you seriously think partnering with Finian will do her any good? He has no backbone and absolutely no talent. He's just as flip-floppy as she is."

I huff. "I mean…I guess you're right. It's just hard for me to get over…" I shiver. "*You know.*"

Ashlea pats me on the back. "I know. But it's the best option we have."

I turn to face my friend. "Why don't we try and convince Finian too? Just to be safe?"

Ashlea reaches toward me, resting her palm on my knee. "Again…I doubt Destry would vote to keep Artemis if he didn't think he had a chance to stay. I bet Finian just went crawling right back to their group. He probably begged for their forgiveness once we put Mace's survival over his." She shrugs. "Technically, they could use all the numbers they can get right now. After tomorrow, they'll only have two people left."

I close my eyes and fold my knees to my chest. The discussion is giving me a pounding headache, and I'm ready to end it. "Alright, enough, guys." They both lean back, giving me the floor. "None of this will matter if we don't *talk* to them. Speculating is just wasting our time."

Lunar and Ashlea exchange a concerned gaze. Lunar is the first to break the silence. "So…what? You wanna bring Destry up here?"

I shrug. "It's a start. Then we can move to Kylah, and if she's with us…well, then Finian doesn't really matter. But…because I don't completely trust her, I think he'll still be worth talking to."

Lunar nods. "Okay. So, speak with Destry and Kylah tonight, then hit Finian tomorrow. Any objections?"

Ashlea shrugs, and I force my lips into a smile as I shake her arm. "Mind getting Destry?"

Ashlea rises without hesitation. "Let's get this over with."

"To what do I owe this pleasure?" Destry asks, plopping onto the blue sofa in the Executive bedroom. Lunar and I relax into the mattress, letting Ashlea take the lead.

"We just wanted to see where your head is at for tomorrow. Are you in on voting out Artemis?"

Destry raises his eyebrows. He twiddles his thumbs, taking a moment to consider before responding. "Look…I will be honest with you as I've always been." He gulps. "Don't count me in for that vote."

Lunar narrows his eyes on Destry. "But…but we kept you off Death Row? Didn't you say you'd have our backs?"

Destry puts his hands up in surrender. "I said that if I win Executive next round, none of you will touch Death Row. I didn't say anything about voting."

I roll my eyes. "Oh, come on! You're catching us on a technicality!"

"No, I'm being honest." He stares directly into my eyes, and I huff with frustration.

"Why would you even want to keep him here? He's a monster!"

"Iris, I know that he hurt you. But—"

"No!" I shout. "He's a narcissist! He will manipulate anyone and everyone to get what he wants and feel *nothing* for it. You really think we're the first people he's screwed over?" I stand up and stomp my way toward Destry. "He played Mercedes the whole game to get himself further. He *lied* to her and pretended to be in love with her, for God's sake! But let's say that was a one-time mistake…if that's the case, then he's done a shitty thing, but everyone deserves a second chance." I take another step forward so I'm inches from Destry's face. "But to look me in the *eyes* and promise Mace's safety?" I throw my hands up. "How many times can a person make the same mistake before people realize they're just a terrible human being!?"

Destry rises from the sofa. "Iris, stop. I'm sorry!" He puts a hand around me. "I'm sorry," he whispers, pushing me to sit on the sofa. "But this game isn't about having integrity. It's about being the last one standing." He turns his attention to everyone in the room. "I've played this game honestly, and I intend to continue doing so. But at the end of the Enterprize…only one of us is going to make it out alive. And if I let Lagiacrus sail to the end, then I don't have *any* chance at winning." He stands. "I am going to keep my promise. If I win tomorrow, you three are *all* safe. But beyond that, we're all trying for the same thing here. We all want to be the last person standing. If Artemis staying here will benefit my game, I *will* vote against Lagiacrus." He backs away. "It's nothing personal…I've just gotta protect myself. Surely…you guys can understand."

The three of us sit in silence until Ashlea answers. "Do you seriously think you can get enough votes for him to stay?"

Destry shrugs. "If you want my advice…I suggest you stop talking to me and start talking to the person campaigning for himself."

He exits without another word. I launch from the couch and throw my hands against the wall. "Of course, he's campaigning for himself! He's pretending that he's not, but he's been manipulating everyone this whole time! How could I not see it? *That's* why Destry thinks he might stay!"

"Calm down, Iris!" Lunar shouts. "None of this will even matter if we get Kylah's vote!"

"But what if he got to her first?" I shout, banging the wall again.

Ashlea runs behind me and holds me back. "Then we'll convince her to switch sides."

Lunar jumps off the bed and pulls on my torso. "Iris, I know you don't trust her. But she's the best hope we've got."

I rub my eyes so hard I see black stars. It takes me a moment to slow my heart rate, but after a series of deep breaths, I finally calm down enough for rationality. I take a deep gulp before locking on Lunar's eyes.

"Bring her to me."

An hour into Kylah being in the room, she still hasn't articulated her remorse. She cries, begging for forgiveness, but her tears muffle her speech so severely that her pleads are incoherent. Once I've finally had enough of her meltdown, I join her on the couch and place a gentle hand on her back.

"You can make it all better if you vote out Artemis."

Kylah nods. "Of…of course! Any…anything to…make it…make it up to…you guys!" She wraps her arms around me, and an auburn curl gets caught in my mouth. I spit it out, but her wails drown out the noise. I widen my eyes in horror. *Get ahold of yourself, woman.*

The conversation is short, but we establish that she's on our side. It's beyond me whether this was a performance or not, but regardless of the gesture, I strangely trust her word. By the time she leaves, we finally relax, each of us stretching ourselves flat on the bed.

"Well," Ashlea starts, "that was something."

I let out a single laugh, not having the energy to give anything more. These meetings have been exhausting, and I can't stomach another one until tomorrow. I'm suddenly grateful that we agreed to have Finian's conversation in the morning after we rest.

I sigh, stretching my arms over my head. My eyelids shut without instruction. Finally, having the confidence that our plan might actually pull through, I flatten against the plush and relax almost enough to fall into slumber. Just before it hits, Lunar's whispers take me back.

"Iris," he says. "We did it. Regardless of what Finian does…we have the votes." When I open my eyes, he's beaming. "This time tomorrow, Artemis will be dead."

My lips curve at the edges as I sit up and bring him into my arms. But as we sit together with Ashlea's celebratory whoops in the background, my eyes are vacant, and my mouth drops into a thin line. Having achieved our goal, I should be celebrating. I should be unable to wipe the grin from my face and be electrified with adrenaline, jumping up and down on the sofa.

But when we settle in for bed, there's nothing. Not even the depression I have for Mace's demise or the anger I feel toward my ex-best friend. Instead, as I lay awake beside Lunar and Ashlea, staring blankly at the ceiling, the emptiness in my chest fills one feeling, and one feeling only.

Turmoil.

Chapter 60

I can't feel my legs. They tremble beneath me so fast I'm afraid they'll take off, leaving my torso behind on the couch. I'm not the only one. Lunar is a mess, darting his eyes back and forth between the two empty Death Row cushions. There are only minutes before the vote will commence, and so far, everyone has gathered in the living room except for Artemis and Lagiacrus.

"Hey," Ashlea whispers. When I turn toward her, her eyes are twisted with concern. "It's gonna work."

I nod, but I can't help my insecurity. This morning, we begged Finian to vote with us, but he refused to take a firm stance.

"I haven't decided yet!" he had pleaded. "I can't make any promises…but if I vote to save him, it's not personal!"

Our conversation replays in my mind. The second Finian closed the soundproof barrier, Ashlea rose from the sofa and kicked the bedframe. "He really has no backbone," she yelled. As long as we've known him, the Leprechaun has never been able to make a decision on his own. If my gut instinct is correct, Destry got through to him well before we had the chance. It wouldn't be surprising if he goes against us, though. We did use him to keep Ashlea alive. The second she stayed, and Mace went on Death Row, we threw Finian to the curb.

"I'll be *shocked* if he votes to expel Artemis," I told her in Lunar's room.

Now, sitting on the blue sofa awaiting the execution, Ashlea whispers in my ear, "Remember, we don't need Finian's vote. Kylah is with us. It's *going to* work." I nod and force a weak smile, but it falls the second Artemis descends the steps with Lagiacrus. As he stalks toward his Death Row settee, my heart sinks. My pulse races so fast that Ashlea notices. She takes a quick gander at Artemis, settling into the black cushion, and turns back to me, taking note of my wandering gaze. "He killed Mace, Iris," she reminds me. "He *deserves* this." I nod halfheartedly and bite the inside of my cheek as hard as I can, trying to remind myself of a fraction of the pain he's caused me.

In this moment, with the countdown having two minutes remaining, I don't have the energy to antagonize Artemis. Now that we're about to vote, the weight of this decision is overbearing. Without the threat of his immediate death, I was able to kid myself into thinking this revenge is justified. My quick tongue had no issue flinging insults his way, and I had no problem with the concept of ending his life. But now, with the firing squad outside with loaded guns, itching at the bit for their next victim…the least I could do is keep my mouth shut. I don't have the wickedness to knock him while he's down.

I'm already killing him. Isn't that enough?

Lagiacrus slumps into the clean Death Row cushion beside Artemis's bullet-pierced one, but I don't acknowledge his presence. Instead, I itch my leg and stare at the ground, waiting for the clock to strike zero. Once it does and the instructions commence, the voting begins.

"KYLAH," the robotic voice calls. She stands and leaves the rest of us at a standstill. Nobody speaks, so the silence is deafening. I commit all my strength to looking away from Death Row and tapping my foot while I await the death of another convict. *It's just a button.* All I have to do is press it, and Mace's life will be avenged.

Destry is called next, followed by Ashlea and Finian. As each person leaves, my trembling worsens. I grip the sides of the couch, closing my eyes to fight my anxiety.

Amid the silence, Ashlea squeezes my hand. She raises her eyebrows, silently assuring me everything will go our way.

My teeth are chattering when the robotic voice says my name, and I squeeze Ashlea's hand so hard I'm surprised it doesn't break.

"IRIS."

I release her hand and take a moment to find my legs. Once I do, I step slowly to the head of the living room, itching my arm to distract myself. When I reach the kitchen, I gulp down my nerves and breathe, trying to soothe the shaking in my chest.

Then, I make the biggest mistake of my life.

I look back.

Gazing into the living room, my eyes immediately find his. Artemis's ocean oases scream at me, begging for forgiveness. But far beyond that, they soften with the one thing that conquers all.

Love.

And I *know* mine reflect it back.

I grip my hands into fists and spin forward, shaking my head as I focus on the staircase. *I'm not going to blow this. His eyes are* nothing. *His love is* nothing. *He never cared about me, and he* never *will.*

I open the door to the arena, squinting my eyes with resolve and marching down the steps to the buttons that await.

Every step of the way, I remind myself why I am doing this. Artemis lied that *I* was the one that came onto *him*. He *laughed* when Lunar called him out for killing Mace. He spread lies about me to Kylah and incessantly poked his tongue into Mercedes's mouth whenever I walked into a room, playing up his physical attraction to her *just* to piss me off.

I march to the pedestal and hover my hand over the blue button marked "Artemis." I bring my hand down to press it, fueled by my hatred for him. *He joked about Crescentia's death and betrayed me with his vote.* I narrow my eyes on the blue plastic and force my hand forward. But centimeters from the button…

My hand stops.

Because as hard as I try to focus on his worst mistakes…the prospect of losing him forever transports my mind down the avenue I've been so adamant to forget. My hand trembles as I remember his eyes in solitary confinement. *His desperation that I made it out of there alive.* His voice *pleading* for me to stay awake and *begging* for forgiveness as he cracked the scorpion jaw from my leg. His vulnerability about his past and the horrors of his capture. Him bowing at the crowd when he fell from his swinging quarter, and him mocking Mercedes during our first introductions. His eyes locking on mine at the top of the steps within the first five minutes of me being in the Enterprize, and him calming my anxiety with stories of his past, pranking the Authority with his best friends. *Best friends that he was forced to watch die.* Him making me howl with laughter harder than I ever imagined possible, and his power to make me think about him every second of every day. His declaration of love for me and how he would do *anything* to get me out of here alive.

I close my eyes and remember the feel of his lips on mine. I freeze, remembering how the world stopped and my brain shut off, letting my heart take control. I *feel* the way the pounding in my chest drove me closer to him, desperate to get the right angle for his tongue to dive into my mouth as far as humanly possible…

Whatever divine force caused me to stop him on the second floor and share Eno's story returns. Because at the end of the day, as hard as I try to hate Artemis and blame him for every terrible thing that has ever happened to me…

I am madly in love with him.

My hatred has been a coping mechanism…a way for me to get through the day without losing myself or turning to much more drastic ways to feel. It's been my heart the whole time, tricking me into thinking I don't miss him. Because losing him was far too painful to bear.

So, despite every unforgivable thing he's done and my promise to hate him forever…I see the boy laughing with me in the living room, trying to memorize the number of steps leading to the top floor. I see him drinking toilet water and laughing as I try to dry my face without a towel. I see his suffering, *knowing* I *am* in love with him, even as I relentlessly deny it to *everyone.*

Even myself.

If only this was as simple as sending him back home. But this is *murder.* And even though Artemis might not deserve my mercy…

I cannot kill him.

So, when the buzzer notifies me that I have ten seconds left to vote, my hand bashes the white button in front of me, labeled "Lagiacrus."

The timer starts over, and I walk back toward the metal staircase. Only once I reach the top, and my legs wobble as I gasp for air, does the gravity set in. Just before crossing the threshold into the house, Mace rubs my cheek in my subconscious, and I can't meet his eyes. But it doesn't matter…because I already know what he's going to say.

"Don't trust Artemis."

What have I done?

Entering the living room, I keep my eyes glued to the carpet. I can't face Ashlea…I can't face Lunar. I can't even face *myself. Not after what I have done.*

The tension in the room convinces me that they already know. That somehow, they saw me debating at the pedestal and failing my mission. So, when I plop onto the couch, I force tunnel vision onto an elongated blood splotch on the carpet, ignoring those who surround me. I clench my hands together in front of me, rubbing my thumbs along my forefingers until the robotic voice returns to announce my betrayal to my own brother.

My betrayal to *Mace.*

"BY A VOTE OF THREE TO TWO."

I squeeze my eyes shut, wincing at what comes next. But there's nothing I can do to stop it. With the votes solidified, it's too late to fix what I've done.

"LAGIACRUS IS EXPELLED FROM THE ENTERPRIZE."

"What?" Ashlea gasps.

"YOU HAVE THIRTY SECONDS TO EVACUATE."

"*No.*" Lunar shutters. "NO!"

Finally, I peel my gaze from the carpet and watch Artemis. His eyes are glossed over; his jaw is on the floor. Much like the rest of this round, he doesn't make a sound. But this time…it's different. There's no regret or shame in the way his jaw clenches shut. This time, for the *first* time, he's completely and utterly *shocked.*

"You *bitch!*" Ashlea shouts, leaping off the couch and launching toward Kylah.

"I…I didn't…it wasn't me!" Kylah pleads, hands up in surrender. "I…I swear on my *life* it wasn't me! I voted him out!"

"We trusted you!" Ashlea yells, pushing Kylah against the neck of the couch. *It's chaos.* Kylah starts bawling so loud it's difficult to hear Ashlea bellow her various profanities at her. Lunar slumps in his Executive cushion with his head in his palms, not daring to look up. Destry hugs Lagiacrus in the kitchen, and I *shake* as the clock ticks down to fifteen seconds.

My head whips around, weighing what damage control to confront first. I could stand up for what I have done, or even better, consol Lunar…but my legs take me to Lagiacrus, and I find myself shouting his name as he reaches for the door.

He turns when I stop before him, my mouth open and eyes wide. "I…I…" I stutter. "I…don't know what to say."

Lagiacrus smirks and gives me a single pat on the back. "You don't need to say anything." He turns around and places a delicate hand on the door. But just before turning the knob, he locks onto my eyes and sneers.

"All is fair in *love*..."

I wait for him to finish the phrase but am left unsatisfied. Instead, he simply turns around and exits the building.

The statement itself makes my heart drop three stories. But it's the *bang* of the bullets against the iron door of the Enterprize that sends an electric shiver down my spine, making my hair stand on end.

ROUND 7

Chapter 61

"**Y**OU LIAR!" Ashlea's shouts are the only thing powerful enough to steal my focus from the door. Without a second thought, I'm running toward the commotion. But every step of the way, Lagiacrus's final words weigh heavy on my chest.

"All is fair in love."

That could mean a million different things. But somehow, I know exactly how it was intended. *He knew.*

How did Lagiacrus know the vote was mine? More importantly, how could he have known I'm in love with Artemis? My stomach drops.

Does anyone else know?

I finally hug my arms around Ashlea and yank her off of Kylah. "GET…*OFF OF ME!*" she shouts at the top of her lungs. "I KNEW WE COULDN'T TRUST HER! I KNEW IT!" Ashlea winds up her fist, and I let go of her, hoping my words break her from her rage-fueled trance.

"ASHLEA IT WASN'T HER! IT WAS *ME!*"

Ashlea freezes, her fist floating inches from Kylah's face. Slowly, she pivots toward me, narrowing her eyes into a scowl.

"*What* was you?"

"The vote!" I scream. "She's telling the truth! I voted out Lagiacrus!"

Ashlea takes a step back, choking on her saliva. "*What* did you just say?"

I cower behind the couch, mouth gaping open. Lunar looks up from his hands, his gaze shattering me. "Iris…" he whines. "How…how *could* you?"

"I…I…" I can't get any words out. I glance between the two of them, their eyes piercing bullets through my chest. *I can't take it.* I can't watch them suffer *again* because of another one of my stupid mistakes. Whether it's trusting the wrong people or playing foolishly with my heart, they don't deserve the pain I've caused them. So, instead of making some poor attempt at explaining myself, I take off toward the second floor, pulling as hard as I can on the arena door. It doesn't budge, so I wail my fists on the smooth surface. Not even denting the structure, I abandon my efforts and sprint to the communal bedroom, hiding behind the bedframe in my corner.

What have I done? What have I done? What have I done?

I rock back and forth, hugging my knees to my chest. I try to convince myself that really, this was the right move. My brain whirls, trying to fabricate a reason I could have made this mistake. Because the truth must *never* come out. I shut my eyes and scramble for something, *anything* to explain my behavior. *Artemis saved me in solitary confinement*…maybe I can convince everyone that this was repayment? And now that my conscience is clear, I don't owe him anything. Maybe…maybe…

"Iris?"

I peek above the mattress and find Ashlea's puffy lips puckering with concentration. I flatten against the floor, desperate for more time. Unfortunately for me, there's nowhere to hide in the Enterprize.

"Iris…I'm not gonna hurt you." She steps closer, finally peeking her head around the foot of the bed. "I just…want to understand."

I shake my head, rubbing my temples with my hands. "I…I just…" *Lie.* "Standing at the pedestal…I couldn't stop thinking about how….how…" I take a deep breath. "Ashlea, *he* saved *me* once…in solitary. I was gonna die…I just couldn't owe him for the rest of my life…I had to repay him…"

Ashlea locks her eyes on mine, stopping my heart.

"Don't lie to me."

My body tenses. "What do you mean?"

Ashlea shakes her head. "You know *exactly* what I mean." She puts her hands on her hips and closes her eyes. "You *know* why you did that. *Lagiacrus* knows why you did that, and *I* know why you did that. It was stupid, and it was a mistake. But you know what?" She taps her foot. "We're all we've got, Iris! We don't have *anyone* else. So…regardless of what's going on in that brain of yours, I'm gonna need you to get off the floor and march your ass into that arena. Because believe it or not, we still need you. Lunar and I *need* you." She reaches out her hand, and I stare at it before nodding. Once I take it, she pulls me to the second floor, careful not to let go of her grasp. Just before entering, she turns on her heel and looks me dead in the eyes, no amusement in her voice.

"But do us all a favor and don't screw up again."

Of the seven remaining convicts, Ashlea and I are the final two to enter the arena. We race down the rickety steps just in time, only having a minute before we would've been executed for tardiness. With each step, I scan the structure in the center, mentally sorting through the possible tortures that await us. A long platform stands on the turf, divided into six chambers, all open from the back. Squinting, I can just make out the blank slates attached to the top of each waist-high pedestal. I look away before getting too distracted and focus on Lunar waiting for us on his Executive stool, instruction card in hand. Artemis is on the outskirts of the huddle around Lunar, but he's within earshot of the instructions. I avoid looking in his direction, but I *feel* him watching me.

"Lunar…I'm *so* sorry…" I plead, but he throws his hand up to quiet me.

"Win this, and all is forgiven."

I nod and step back with Ashlea, giving my brother space. Finally, with 45 seconds left, Lunar raises the card, showing us the black and grey camouflage on the back.

"Convicts. In moments, you will move to the plinth of your choosing. Attached to each podium is a *hologram plank*, which you will use to write your answers." *Oh shit.* I've only ever read about these. Having never used one, I'm unsure how they operate. I only know that once the timer ends, our writing will project in front of us as holograms. I hide my amazement with a stoic gaze and focus on Lunar's words as he forces them out. "With each question, you will select whether the answer is MORE or LESS than the number presented and write your answer on the slate. If you are correct, you will move on to the next round, and your plank will be swiped automatically. If you are incorrect, you are eliminated from the competition and must step down. The person to answer every question correctly will become the new Executive."

With thirty seconds left on the clock, we take our positions behind the pedestals. I barely have time to register that there weren't any punishments mentioned. This competition is too harmless, too…comfortable. *There's something they aren't telling us.* The thought sends a shiver down my spine. If they aren't punishing us for getting answers incorrect…what kind of horror awaits us when the competition ends? The idea slips when Ashlea passes behind me, nodding for encouragement as she takes the compartment to my right. I only have a moment to gather my composure when I spot Artemis entering the chamber to my left. My arms tremble, and I squeeze my eyes shut, forcing away the memories of him that cloud my vision.

Don't think about Artemis. Don't think about Artemis. Don't think about Artemis.

"QUESTION 1." I narrow my eyes on the blank, glowing sheet before me and grip the stylus, releasing it from its magnetic hold on the podium. I'm mesmerized by the mechanism but only allow myself a second to slide my hand over the glossy surface. I shake my head, balancing the mechanical pen between my fingers, and force Artemis from my mind. *I have to win.* The question that follows is music to my ears. "ARE THERE MORE OR LESS THAN TWO HUNDRED CAMERAS IN THE ENTERPRIZE?"

Oh my god. This is a house quiz! I know this place inside and out, like the back of my hand. Every free moment I've had has been spent memorizing numbers, structures, architecture, and times. *Nobody* knows this place better than I do. *More or less than two hundred cameras? Is this a joke?!*

I glance at the clock reading ten seconds and quickly scribble "MORE" on my slate. The house has at *least* two hundred and fifty cameras. *And that just covers the ones we know about.*

When the timer runs out, my answer floats above the screen on my podium. My heart thumps as I resist sticking my hand through the hologram.

"CORRECT ANSWER: MORE. FINIAN AND KYLAH: ELIMINATED."

I roll my eyes. *What do those two do all day? Stare at a wall?*

"QUESTION 2." The projection fades, and my slate resets, leaving a blank screen. "INCLUDING TABLES, BEDS, AND CHAIRS, ARE THERE MORE OR LESS THAN ONE

HUNDRED AND SEVENTY-FIVE LEGS TOUCHING THE GROUND INSIDE THE ENTERPRIZE?"

Oh boy. I count fast because we only have ten seconds to come up with an answer. There are sixteen houseguests and one Executive bedroom. So that's…*seventeen beds, seventeen chairs, three tables…six couches.* It's gonna be close. But…I *know* these numbers are correct. And if they are…that's one hundred and seventy-two legs. There's no time to double-check my mental math, so I trust my gut and jam my stylus against the screen, writing "LESS."

"CORRECT ANSWER: LESS. ASHLEA: ELIMINATED."

Ashlea grunts and steps off her pedestal, storming behind Lunar's stool. My heart rate picks up, knowing I'm now completely alone. But I was also *always* our best shot at winning this competition anyway. With my experience under the floorboards and consistent house memorization drills, nobody can come close to my preparation. If Destry's word is worth anything, and he still plans to keep my alliance safe, I just have to beat Artemis.

Not only to win…but to *survive.*

"QUESTION 3: THERE ARE MORE OR LESS THAN ONE HUNDRED RUNGS ON THE SPIRAL STAIRCASE."

I hold back a scoff and immediately draw "LESS" on my freshly blank screen. Not only do I know there are eighty-seven rungs on that railing, but only an idiot would think there are more than a hundred. I rest my arms on the podium, impatiently waiting for the others to lock in their answers.

"CORRECT ANSWER: LESS."

"QUESTION 4."

I nod as my hologram disappears, noting that Destry and Artemis are both still in the game.

"ARE THERE MORE OR LESS THAN THIRTY STEPS ON THE ROUNDING STAIRCASE?"

I don't even try to stifle my laugh. *Of course,* this is a question. We're being watched…they know about my bet with Artemis in the second round. Not only are they antagonizing us…but they are throwing my complicated relationship with him in our faces. I jot down "LESS," remembering that Artemis had to drink toilet water after betting there were more than twenty-eight steps.

"CORRECT ANSWER: LESS. DESTRY: ELIMINATED."

I roll my eyes. *Artemis remembers.* I cringe, knowing that he's only been competitive at this quiz because of the time I spent tutoring him. But beyond his studies, Artemis is the biggest idiot I know. And two weeks of studying doesn't beat the training I've had my entire life leading up to this moment. Because of that, I'm confident I will win. That, and the fact that if I don't beat Artemis…

Somebody I love will die.

"TIE BREAKER. YOUR ANSWER WILL BE A NUMBER. CLOSEST TO THE CORRECT NUMBER WITHOUT GOING OVER WINS. QUESTION 5."

I take a deep breath. *I can do this.*

"IN SECONDS, HOW LONG WAS THE FIRST ELIMINATED CONVICT AT THE ENTERPRIZE FOR?"

In seconds? The clock glows with twenty seconds, counting down for us to calculate our answer. I give myself a second to panic before focusing. The first convict expelled was Sola. She was here for…four days. There are 3,600 seconds in an hour…that's common knowledge. I reassure myself, knowing Artemis couldn't possibly remember that…he's not intelligent enough. *Now let's see…twenty-four hours in a day…four days…oh god.*

The clock blares with five seconds remaining. I don't even take the time to wipe the sweat from my brow before scribbling my answer. I take a bit off my final calculation to protect my chances of being over. I'm generous in my subtraction because I'm confident Artemis won't be anywhere close to the correct answer. For the first time in days, my chest lifts. I examine my writing and don't try to stop the smile from spreading across my lips.

I did it. I can fix my mistake and do what I should have done twenty minutes ago.

Mace would be proud.

"CONVICT: IRIS. IN SECONDS, HOW LONG WAS THE FIRST ELIMINATED CONVICT AT THE ENTERPRIZE FOR?"

My answer projects over my podium, and I beam. They're drawing out the final question for the audience, but I don't care. Because I *know* I've won this before Artemis even answers. "300,000 seconds!"

I can't stop my giddiness. I'm jumping up and down, the excitement evident in my voice.

"CONVICT: ARTEMIS." The same instructions are repeated, but I barely listen. My ears only perk up once Artemis speaks for the first time in four days.

"Zero seconds."

Huh? What is he doing? Is he purposely losing…for me? *Was I right?* I narrow my eyes ahead of me, trying to decipher what his game is. *Has he loved me all along?* Has he *always* cared for me? I'm halfway between confusion and excitement when the robotic voice returns, announcing the winner.

"THE CORRECT ANSWER IS…ZERO SECONDS."

I clutch the podium to stay upright. *Zero seconds?* I gasp. *No.* Because that means…

"CONGRATULATIONS: ARTEMIS. YOU ARE THE NEW EXECUTIVE."

Chapter 62

By the time I can speak, I'm on my knees. "No....how?"

Destry's voice cuts through like a knife. "Son of a bitch." His jaw is on the floor as he stalks toward Artemis. "Lagiacrus's twin brother...that's genius."

I slam my head against the podium. *A TRICK QUESTION?! Are you kidding me?* A trick question determines whether I live or die?

I can't stand, my chest weighing me against the ground. I throw my fists against the partition to my right, not stopping until I dent the surface. "How is that fair? I knew every *goddamn* question, and they make the tiebreaker a *trick*?" I rock back and forth in my compartment, hugging my knees. "That did *not* just happen. How could that happen?" I jolt when I realize I'm mumbling. But I'm not ashamed of my tantrum. Because all I've ever wanted is to protect the people I love. And now, when a competition was finally *made* for me, I blew it. I blew it because it wasn't fair. I blew it because I couldn't go through with killing Artemis. And worst of all, I blew it because I wasted precious hours tutoring the man who ultimately betrayed me.

My pulse races, and I grip my fists to keep from begging for a rematch because I know I deserve this. None of this would have happened if I just *listened* to everybody. But I *insisted* that I knew better, and now Artemis is going to kill yet another person that I love. There are a million things I could blame my failure on, but only one glues me to the turf, stealing any strength I have left.

This is all my fault.

"Congratulations, man." Destry's voice comes from Artemis's compartment. I still haven't moved from my own, but I'm wrapped in the dark clutches of devastation. Artemis, on the other hand, should be running around the arena by now, throwing his victory in everybody's faces. *So why isn't he?*

Destry clears his throat before continuing. "I don't know what to say...that was incredible."

If I voted Artemis out, I would have won. My alliance would be safe if I had just gone through with it. Lagiacrus wouldn't have lasted two questions in that competition. *I'd have won by a long shot.* But I didn't. *Because I blew it. And now my friends will suffer.*

Artemis doesn't say anything. Even if he did, I wouldn't have heard it. Because Lunar and Ashlea are finally in my compartment, lifting me into their arms.

"That was...I mean...it wasn't..." Ashlea stutters.

"It wasn't fair," Lunar declares. He lets go and steps back, kicking my podium. When I pivot in his direction, his arms are folded over his chest. "It. Was. Not. *Fair*."

I shake my head. "I can't believe it," I say finally. "How…why would they ask it like that? That had *nothing* to do with the house…it was a complete departure from the topic! They *knew* I wouldn't get that! *They set me up!*"

"*APPARENTLY*, they can do whatever the hell they want!" Lunar lunges at the partition separating my compartment from Artemis's and lets loose, wailing his fists against it. "Because they're the Authority! And they don't give a *damn* about us! You hear that?" He runs toward the closet camera and screams at the top of his lungs. "YOU'VE TRAPPED US HERE, FORCING US TO KILL EACH OTHER FOR SPORT! FOR WHAT? TO TEACH US A LESSON? YOU GOT YOUR POINT THROUGH! NOW, LET US OUT OF HERE!"

We let him scream until his throat is hoarse because we know his pleas are useless. One by one, each of us are losing our minds, and as badly as I tried to pretend it wouldn't happen to my little brother, it was only a matter of time before he hit his breaking point. I reach for Lunar but don't have the energy to chase him. Because watching him break was the last straw in undoing me.

What a strange thing rock bottom is. It's praised for being the point where one can only go up, but what happens when I've brought a shovel with me?

I fall back to my knees when Artemis leaves the arena with Destry and Finian. Watching them exit feels like a knife twisting in my heart. I'm already battered and bruised, and now that Artemis is in power, the elite squad of men will kick me while I'm down. Kylah and Ashlea don't entertain Dial. Instead, they opt to stay with me and Lunar. They approach my little brother, but he's inconsolable. He races around the arena, kicking anything in his path. Kylah finally springs into action once he kicks the metal staircase so hard he nearly makes it collapse.

She sprints toward him, blocking the staircase from his reach. "We can't control it now!" He darts around her, desperate for something to take his rage out on. But she doesn't let him close to the exit, holding him by his shoulders so he can't reach the stairs. "We have to face the consequences of…well…putting him up." It seems like she's biting her tongue, but the intensity of the conversation distracts me from dwelling on it. "This isn't over! You can still make it through this!"

He shakes his head so fast that his hair stands on end. "No…no, you don't *understand*, Kylah." He puts his arms up and stomps, tears falling down his cheeks. "He won! He *always* wins! We're not getting out of here because he will *always* win!"

Ashlea rubs her temples with her palms while they scream. Finally having enough, she turns to me and pleads, voice *shaking*. "We have time…we can convince him to switch sides…he *knows* you saved him! You announced it to everyone in the living room! Hell, you announced it to everyone in Miasmis!" She grabs my wrists and pulls me forward. "We can fix this, Iris! This isn't over! We can—"

"Ummm…guys?"

The four of us turn, watching Destry in the doorway. He taps his fingers on the iron door, and his lips stretch into a thin line. He shifts his weight from one foot to the other, too fast to be sheer awkwardness.

"What?" Kylah spits, Lunar in her arms.

"You're gonna wanna come see this…" Destry says, itching the side of his face. "You're gonna want to see it *now*."

Ashlea and I share a tense look, and I roll my eyes. I let Ashlea drag me to my feet and turn to face Destry. "Destry now's *really* not a good time."

"You don't understand," Destry shouts back, barely giving me time to finish my sentence. "They…they…"

"Spit it out!" Kylah yells, prompting Lunar to burrow deeper into her arms.

Destry slams the wall with his palm, loud enough to echo around the arena. Lunar's tears stop as he backs out of Kylah's grasp. I stand completely still as Destry hits the wall again, and Ashlea takes a step back when his voice returns.

"They're happening *now!*"

Silence follows. The only sound is my heart pounding in my ears. "What's happening now, Destry?" I enunciate every word, being sure he won't misunderstand me.

"DEATH ROW SELECTIONS!" he shouts. "Death Row selections are happening *now*."

The tension is so thick I feel like I'm swimming in it. "Excuse me?" Ashlea yells back. Destry jumps from his spot on the staircase, making it rattle against the turf.

"Death Row selections are happening *right now*, so unless you want to become Swiss cheese, I suggest you get your asses to the living room within the next thirty seconds!"

Wide-eyed, I turn to Ashlea and take off. When I get beside Lunar, I grab his hand and pull him up the metal staircase. His body is limp, shock having frozen him to the turf, so the effort is monumental. Catching onto my struggle, Ashlea joins the train and pushes my brother from behind. The four of us run so hard that the arena staircase nearly collapses beneath our feet. Kylah trips and falls on the top, so Destry stops to grab her hand and pulls her through the threshold of the Enterprize. Destry's sudden care for our survival would be unsettling, but I'm in such a panic I don't have time to question it. Kylah slams the door to the arena so hard it whips back open. She hesitates, turning back to shut it properly, but Destry shouts, "NO TIME!" and yanks her into the kitchen.

The second we reach the living room, I hear the unmistakable booms of the final ten seconds on the timer. My group leaps onto the couches with five seconds to spare, so I bury Lunar into a hug, rubbing his back to calm him down. Artemis paces back and forth, holding his forehead, mumbling noncoherently.

Finian cowers on the sofa furthest from Artemis, his arms wrapped around his legs. Shaking his head, I catch Finian muttering, "Won't let me get a word in," before he hides his head between his knees.

As the buzzer blares with three seconds remaining, everything *clicks*, like puzzle pieces falling together. There weren't any punishments in the competition because now, we are playing two days' worth of the game in twenty minutes. *This was intentional*…the producers *knew* that if I had the time, I could convince Artemis to switch sides. But they didn't want to grant me that luxury. Instead, they've subjected us to a shortened opportunity to plead our cases, like a freight train with innocent lives trapped in front of it.

Because there's *nothing* we can do to stop it.

I can't find words, so I stare at Artemis, hoping he'll look into my eyes and have the same revelation I had minutes ago. Perhaps, if he can just *see* me, he'll feel that familiar electricity between us, and everything I've said against him will be forgiven. Then, at the very *least*, he'll have pulled through on his promise to keep me alive.

The final buzzer sounds, indicating that the selections must be made. Artemis shakes his head, now holding his giant-fisted palms at his sides. I try to make eye contact with him…I knit my eyebrows together and wince to look weak. But he doesn't spare me a glance. Instead, he throws his arms up and yells at the ceiling, the first words he's spoken in four days.

First, it's Lunar's name.

And then it's mine.

Chapter 63

My body is frozen, only allowing for the brief shake of my head, sweeping back and forth in denial. *Lunar and me?* I squint my eyes shut ten times to wake myself from this nightmare but continue opening them to the same scene. Artemis towers above us even though he is several feet away. Lunar bawls into his hands while the rest of my housemates lean back, stunned. *What kind of monster would do this?* I force my head on straight and gulp back tears. I can't show weakness. That's what he wants. That's *all* he wants. Artemis wishes nothing more than to see me cry and crumble before him, and for what? Because I rejected his advances? Surely, this isn't equal retribution. So instead of rage, instead of fear, and above all, instead of heartbreak…

I cave to the ever-growing insanity in my chest and *laugh*.

I burst out laughing on the sofa, every pair of eyes falling on me. Using their stares as fuel, I smile at Artemis and stand, tugging Lunar behind me as I calmly place myself on the bullet-pierced Death Row cushion. Lunar's too young to fully comprehend this level of betrayal. He's not as strong as me or perhaps doesn't have the same motivation to stray from weakness because he's having a full-blown meltdown. But the days of Artemis seeing my tears are over. I won't allow him the satisfaction of seeing me cry.

Lunar is dry heaving, curled on his Death Row cushion. Kylah runs over and cradles him around my steady hand on his back. But my eyes aren't on him. The entire time, I keep them locked on one person.

Artemis.

First and foremost, I want him to know that I *despise* him and will regret saving him every day for the rest of my life. But more profoundly, I can hold myself together because I know this is almost over. I know that the living room will disperse in seconds, and I'll take Lunar to the bathroom to cry our hearts out. So, I keep a smile plastered on my lips and tilt my head, willing Artemis to look at me.

But when the robotic voice returns, my lips fall open with my jaw, and I gape at the nearest camera.

"CONVICTS, YOUR VOTING ORDER HAS BEEN SELECTED BY RANDOM DRAW." I allow myself a single moment to let the others see behind my mask of bravery. But the second I realize exactly what's happening, I can't believe it. *This doesn't happen. This has to be fake because surely nothing like this could ever actually happen to somebody. Right?* But the voice continues, repeating the same speech it always has before voting. The world spins at the end of its instructions, and I can only focus on one thing.

I'm about to die.

I wait for the penny to drop. But, for some reason, death doesn't scare me. In fact, it brings forth a fresh bout of laughter, and I finally force my lips back into a smile as the first name is announced. *I really am losing my mind.*

"FINIAN." The other convicts stare at each other wide-eyed, but I don't let my smile falter. I see Finian exit in my periphery, approaching the arena to cast his vote.

Lunar is wailing, prompting Artemis to punch the wall behind him. He pierces a hole through the infrastructure, grunting loudly as the drywall crumbles around his fist. When he removes it, blood runs down his arm, pooling at his elbow. But I don't let the aggression scare me. I can't let it scare me.

I can't give him that satisfaction.

So, I keep watching him, even as the voice calls for Kylah. Ashlea has to push her away from Lunar to vote. I don't even flinch my gaze from Artemis. But my priorities shift when Shaela finally leaves, crying the entire way to the arena. Without her persistent encouragement, Lunar falls apart, wheezing for air. I finally look away from Artemis to focus on my brother and erase my smile, squeezing Lunar's arm before hugging him tight.

"Shhh, it's okay. It's okay." His body heaves as I whisper. "You're going to be okay...it's me he's after...it's *me* he wants..."

"*It's all...my...fault...*" He can barely get the words out, but I hush him. Because it isn't his fault. *It's Artemis's.* Artemis voted out Mace. Artemis put Lunar up against me, and Artemis will be the reason I die. Lunar's merely experiencing survivor's guilt, and I will do anything in my power to ensure that he knows I'm okay with this. I should feel more panic, considering that I'm about to die. But the pain I've felt all my life in hiding...the betrayal and heartbreak I've suffered through in my time at the Enterprize...as long as my death ensures Lunar's survival, my life will feel worth it.

Kylah returns, cradling Lunar, and the others leave to cast their votes. All the while, Artemis doesn't stop his violent tantrum. Instead of cowering in his Executive chair as I would have expected, he continues to pace the floor, banging on the wall every few steps. His punches have less effort behind them, so he doesn't add to his structural damage to the Enterprize. Still, his face grows bright pink, and sweat pools at his armpits. I can't help but wonder why he's so angry if he's the one pinning me up against my brother.

My heart twists, knowing this is my fault. If I had just voted Artemis out, like the plan *always* was, we wouldn't be in this mess. I would've put Kylah and Lagiacrus up without hesitation, and one of them would be leaving through the front door in the next five minutes. Instead...I showed weakness. I fell for Artemis's manipulation and couldn't let him go. But that final look he gave me before I voted to save his life...I really thought he meant it. Now, watching him beat his hand into a pulp while Lunar shakes in my arms, I finally realize the power of loving somebody and letting them go. There's no way Artemis can convince me that this was in my best interest, and he'll never make me fall for his lie of love again. But *my* love was true. *My* love was real. That's what hurts the most. I'm in love with Artemis, and the only way I can cope with him not loving me back is by letting him go.

And now, with the firing squad reloading their guns for my arrival, I'll finally be able to forget him.

When Destry returns, the vote is concluded, and all my thoughts fade. It's too late to regret the past. In my last moments, I want to give my love to those who deserve it. When I'm called to report for expulsion, I will tell them all how much I love them. Then, I will look directly into the cameras and Curi's eyes behind them, telling her I love her with all my heart.

And that I'm sorry I couldn't give her more.

So, when Destry sits, and the voice returns, I close my eyes, ready to walk into death's welcoming arms.

"BY A VOTE OF TWO TO TWO: THERE IS A TIE."

I nod and open my eyes. This wasn't what I expected, but I'm still ready for one final heartbreak. Above all, I'm prepared for the man I love to deny me my life so I can pay for every mistake I've made. I grab Lunar's hand and squeeze it, then look directly at Artemis's face.

I want him to see my eyes when he sends me to my death.

Artemis's ocean eyes finally find mine and lock on. They twist with regret...and sorrow. He shakes his head and mouths an apology. I don't flinch. He's not sorry. If he was, he would *stop* hurting me. But that's life, isn't it? What was it that Lagiacrus said?

All is fair in love.

Artemis mouths that he's sorry one last time then gulps at the ceiling. I grip Lunar's hand and squeeze again, embracing my fate.

I'm ready to get what I've deserved from the moment Artemis and I locked lips.

But my name doesn't come. No name comes...not for a while. It can't be more than a few seconds because otherwise, the Authority would send guards to punish Artemis. But in what little time it takes for him to say a name, it feels like a million years.

Because it's not my name that leaves his lips.

It's Lunar's.

"What's a five-letter word for a person with knowledge?" I tap my pencil on the peeling wood of our kitchen table, closing my eyes to think of an answer to my crossword puzzle. It was a hand-me-down from my parent's office, so I've had to redraw the empty boxes on a separate sheet. Lunar lays on the dusty ground beside me, tossing an apple and letting it fall to his face.

"So...you, then?" Lunar suggests. He catches his apple at the last second and smiles before laughing. "Easy. Dweeb."

I roll my eyes and stifle a cackle. "Nice. How do you spell that again?"

Lunar chuckles, throwing his apple back to the ceiling. "I-R-I-S."

I burst out laughing and step off my stool, abandoning my puzzle. Lunar shifts as I lie beside him, fresh dust swirling around my face. I poke his arm and signal him to throw in my direction so we can play catch together with gravity's assistance. He abides, tossing it toward me in silence as we let the time pass.

Every day, Lunar and I are left alone from the moment our parents leave for work until the moment the sun sets. We've created a routine of eating, playing, and reading while Lunar organizes crazy furniture layouts to practice his gymnastics. It's a simple schedule, but we're sure to embrace every moment we're allowed outside the floorboards.

When the apple lands in my hand, I lean up to scan the windowpane. It's bolted shut, so we don't risk the neighbors hearing us and turning us in. Having no breeze to make them dance, the curtains stand limp at the sides. I sigh before throwing the fruit back to Lunar, and he finally interrupts the silence.

"Iris, what do you think wind is like?"

I grab our makeshift ball and pause the game. Biting my lip, I consider the question. "Hmmm…." I pucker my lips to the side, then smile. "I don't know…" My body turns toward his in one swift motion. "Probably something like this!" I blow wet air onto his cheeks, and he rolls over laughing.

"Ew! You spit in my face!" I spin in the opposite direction, clutching my side and laughing. We stay like that, cackling with one another, until silence consumes us again. I finally toss the apple back toward him as we lay still, letting our game pass the time.

When Lunar finally speaks up, his voice cracks. "Well, I hope that one day, we can feel the real thing." My lips stretch into a thin line, and I nod. Before the pit in my stomach fully forms, Lunar comes back at me, forcing a smile.

"You know…the one without your saliva."

My hand goes limp in Lunar's. All my strength is drained with every second the clock descends, and I don't have the spirit to react. Because how can I truly process the devastation of losing my brother when it's *all my fault*? I can't feel anything except the tears welling in my eyes, but one thing is for sure.

My heart *hurts*.

Ashlea finally takes our hands, forcing us and Kylah to migrate to the front door. I don't remember walking through the kitchen when we stand before the iron slab, but my body springs into action, forcing Lunar into my arms so tight that he can barely breathe.

"It should have been me…it should have been *me*." I take a deep, shaky breath, then bury my head in his shoulder. "I'm…so…sorry…Lunar…" I take another deep breath and search aimlessly for words of comfort, but my mind is stuck in one place, so I repeat it. "It…should…have…been…*me*." Nobody interjects, and I'm glad they don't. Because I only want to be with Lunar, even as the boulder lodges in my throat and strangles my sobs. Swaying my brother back and forth, I jolt as the clock rings with fifteen seconds remaining.

I hold him at arm's length and stare into his deep brown eyes, pooling with fresh moisture. "I'll go instead…maybe they'll take me. I'm the one that deserves it."

"They'll just kill you both," Ashlea says, concisely enough to shut the idea down. Lunar watches me as the tears flow down his cheeks. I know exactly where his mind is because mine is in the same place. *Our childhood.* Growing up, we were all we had. Until Curi came, Lunar and I raised each other. Without him, those first years without Curi…I would have had *nothing.* Even when Curi arrived, Lunar and I spent our days exclusively together. Every memory I have before the Enterprize has him in it. In his eyes, I watch him hop from one rickety chair to another, not daring to touch the imaginary poisonous film covering our wooden floor. I watch him do cartwheels and try to instruct me how to defy gravity with his acrobatics. I watch him laughing as I tumble to the floor, and I wipe my tears when I remember him consistently reaching out a hand to help me up. I watch him jokingly sass my parents, crippling me with laughter, and I watch him cuddle next to me under the floorboards, resting his head on my outstretched arm.

And now, because of *me,* I'll never see him again.

He chokes back another bout of tears and takes a slow breath. Despite his momentary composure, his voice trembles. "Iris…I'm…*I'm scared.*"

I hiccup from my tears and lean forward to make them stop. Taking a large gulp, I straighten my back and *breathe,* desperate to keep myself together. I have to be strong for my little brother in his last moments, even if it *is* impossible. He needs to know how much I care about him…how much I have always cared about him. My voice quivers, and I look into his eyes again, shaking my head. "It'll be quick…painless. *I promise.*" I extend my pinky and he links onto it, both of us kissing our respective thumbs. I swallow, our pinkies still interlocked, and shout to stop myself from bawling. "*You won't feel a thing.*"

He nods but jumps when the clock strikes five seconds. Wide-eyed, I hug him as tight as I can. His racing heartbeat thumps against my chest, and I cover my mouth to keep from screaming. Just when I think I'll never let go, Kylah drags him away from me. I hate her for it, but I'm also grateful. I couldn't be the one to escort him to his death…and despite wanting to stop his execution, I keep my feet planted where they are. I lock onto the brown eyes beneath his bowl-cut hair and stifle a cry.

"I love you, Lunar." I manage to get the words out without a stutter, desperate to save time and ensure they're the last words I'll ever say to him. He looks at me, a tear falling down his cheek, and he gulps.

"I love you, Iris."

We smile at each other, lips trembling, until the door locks shut.

I hope my clogged sinuses will block out the sound that comes next. But the bullets boom and echo throughout my chest, dropping me to my knees as they ricochet off the iron door.

ROUND 8

Chapter 64

I pound my hand on the door but don't throw a tantrum. This time, there's no rage. There's not even grief. I'm so far beyond devastation that there's nothing left to feel. I simply sit on my heels and hold my fist against the door, staring blankly at the silver sliding against my palm.

My heart stops hurting, but only because it's gone. My chest is empty, leaving no motivation to continue to fight. Instead, I stay motionless, sinking into the carpet and hoping I never stop. Because if it never releases me, there's no chance I can get hurt again. *Let them kill me.* I hope the warden himself makes the trip, ending me before anybody else gets a turn to break me. I hear my name, but the voice is so distant it sounds underwater. The others must be trying to grab my attention, but I don't give it to them. I *can't* give it to them. Because as far as I am concerned, my life is over.

Mace…gone. Lunar…gone. Artemis…gone, as far as I'm concerned. Even my parents are gone, and Curi may as well be. Because even if I make it out of here, what good can I do for her? How can I take care of my little sister when I can't even take care of myself?

How can I protect her when I failed to protect Lunar?

I must lay there for ages because when I finally come out of my trance, Ashlea is pulling on my arms, *screaming*. I blink until she's clear in my vision. She's having a meltdown, but her panic doesn't spring me into action. Because absolutely nothing matters anymore.

And what could she possibly be so worried about when we're all going to die anyway?

"What?" I ask, my voice barely a whisper.

Her eyes are so bright they're feverish. "Iris, we have to go *now*. The next competition is starting!" She darts her gaze to the clock across the room and yelps. "We have ninety seconds!!"

I huff and roll my eyes. "Let them kill me. Tell them I'll be waiting here for them."

Ashlea kicks the door and forces me to look back into her eyes. "IRIS, GET YOUR SHIT TOGETHER! There's no time to mourn…not until you're sitting in that Executive suite after winning this thing!" She throws her hands in the air. "You're *so* close, Iris…*so* close to seeing Curi again." At the mention of Curi's name and the hope in her voice, I snap into consciousness. "Yeah, that's right! Curi!" She pulls me to my feet and drags me toward the staircase, voice raising an octave. "You still have her…you still have *me*! If not for Lunar's vengeance, then do it for us!"

Finally, I submit to Ashlea's pulls and force my feet to follow. Everything passes in a blur, and before I know it, I'm standing on the turf, looking at five short, wooden tree trunks in the center. They're large enough for a person to stand on, as evidenced by Destry, who is already in position. Artemis sits on the metal staircase, away from the group. He means so little to me that I don't even remember stepping over him. But as I stare at him, an important realization hits.

I don't love Artemis anymore. I don't even hate him. I'm not angry, mournful, or even vengeful.

I am completely and utterly *indifferent* to his existence.

So, I do as any other logical, heartbroken, empty human would do.

I pretend he doesn't exist.

Seeing that he refuses to speak beyond sending Lunar to his death, Artemis is incapable of reading the instruction card. I rapidly search the turf for the note when Destry raises it to his face, flashing the tree and root symbol on the back.

"Convicts," Destry reads from his stump. "Today, you are statues. You will stand upon your pedestal and be still and silent. Each stump has motion sensors, so anything above our predetermined threshold of stillness will set it off, eliminating you from the competition." He licks his lips as we stalk toward the podiums.

Before he continues, I try and process my chances of winning. Only six people remain, and only five get to compete. *Ashlea is right.* The odds of winning may have been slim at the start, but now that I just have to outlast five other people, two of which suck at everything…I may actually have a chance.

"Speak or change your facial expression, and you are eliminated. Move your eyes from a fixed point, and you are eliminated. The last person standing will be the new Executive."

The clock has twenty seconds remaining, so we take our positions. I shuffle to my stump without urgency, not wanting to lose my breath and set off the motion sensor right as the competition begins. I select the stump between Destry and Ashlea and take a deep inhale. Despite how empty I am, it doesn't pass my notice that this shouldn't be a challenge. I'm so broken inside, so…*destroyed*, that I don't anticipate having any reason to speak at all ever again. All I have to do now is what I was planning to do since Lunar stepped out that door.

Be silent and stare at a wall.

I position my legs shoulder-width apart, creating a comfortable center of mass. After determining what hand position would be the most stable, I let them hang at their sides. I briefly close my eyes, take one last breath, and stare blankly at the wall beyond.

Once the buzzer sounds for the start, I become the silent statue I was destined to be.

There's nobody to update us on our time and absolutely no entertainment. Even Artemis stays silent, destroying the only potential distraction. But I don't need it. Enough is rattling around in my head that I could stand here for days straight, not running out of trauma to revisit. Because every person I care about is dying before me, and there's nothing that I can do about it.

Whether I like it or not, I am *totally powerless*.

As much as I try to fight it, I can't help my mind from wandering to Artemis. He may not be physically dead, but he's dead to me. *Why did I ever trust him?* I've given him chance after chance to prove his loyalty, and he's consistently shown that he only cares about himself. He may have *claimed* to love me, but his actions speak louder than his words. I'm ashamed that a tiny part of me believes there must have been some sort of miscommunication along the way. It's beyond frustrating—what more proof do I need? What good reason could he *possibly* have to pin me and my brother against each other on Death Row? I consider every option, but nothing of validity settles. I clench my teeth because my only answer for his behavior is that he's a traitor.

A traitor who *never* cared about me.

I'm becoming quite familiar with the ache of betrayal. It's much deeper than sorrow, and far more all-consuming than anger. It's a sensation that refuses to be stifled, no matter how hard one tries to push it away. The worst part about it is that it *never* disappears. Even as I mourned Mace, there Artemis's betrayal was…plastered across the back of my mind. Where any normal person would have a healthy silence in the absence of thought, I have a pesky, persistent urge to reminisce on where things could have possibly gone so wrong with him. I think about it every single second of every single day, even as I celebrated Lunar's win and cried over his death. That's the brutal reality of betrayal. One can pretend to be past it and convince everyone on the planet that they've stopped caring. But it never goes away. *Not ever.* So, as much as I try to convince myself that time will heal all wounds, I know the truth.

I will think about Artemis's betrayal every second of every day for the rest of my life. Which, for me…might not be much longer.

My thoughts distort time, and there's no way to know how long we've been standing on our stumps. I assume that a few hours have passed, but if I have learned anything from the needle bed, it's that I can't trust my perception of time. Instead, I focus on everything I'm sure of. For instance, blinking is within the threshold of motion allowed. I tried to keep my eyes glued open, even as they burned with the dryness of the arena air, but I couldn't handle the stinging for long. It killed me to cave, but I was grateful to find no consequence to the movement. Once determined safe, I started blinking so freely that emotionless tears spilled down my cheeks.

With the burning handled, my struggle evaporated. Now, my trauma distracts me from the physical pain of remaining completely still. Still, I can't ignore how tired my legs are. It doesn't make much of an impression on me, considering the events still processing in my mind, but I'm aware of the developing ailment.

Beyond physical ailments, being trapped indoors worsens this competition on the psychological side. The arena may have been designed as a quaint summer scene, but we're as much outside as I was under the floorboards. There's no sun to clue us into how much time has passed, and we have no indication of how our competitors are handling their stiffness and boredom. I don't consider the missing sun for long because it wouldn't have assisted me much anyway. I've never watched the sunset before, so essentially, it would have been useless. I also divert my thoughts from wishing I could watch the others. Of course, they will look just like me. *Completely motionless with no expression.* Eliminating these factors, I slowly let in a deep breath, keeping my eyes glued to the blue wall ahead of me. It's not bad, really.

I've become a professional at blankly staring at walls.

A few more hours pass…at least, I think they do. I barely notice. Artemis has got enough free rent in my mind to keep me entertained for weeks.

I tense when there's a mechanical rumble. Nobody flinches as thin metal poles rise from the ground, halting inches from our chests. None of us can examine the new addition, all being required to keep our eyes on where we selected at the start. In the past, I may have panicked at the new challenge. But now…I don't even care.

The pole is motionless, gaining our trust that it's purposeless. *But I know better.*

A loud, bubbling noise spews from the pole, suggesting that water will soon follow. I make a snap judgment on what is coming and prepare myself, tensing my neck. *I'm going to need to blink at the precise moment the spraying begins.*

The bubbling grows louder until it finally stops. I count in my head, preparing to close my eyes, scared that keeping them shut for too long will set off an alarm. *But a perfectly timed blink should do the trick.*

One…two…*three.*

I shut my eyelids the second the water starts launching at my chest. The water pressure isn't forceful enough to push me from my perch, but it's frigid enough to make somebody stumble. So, when the horn honks, I'm far from surprised.

"CONVICT: KYLAH. ELIMINATED AT 4 HOURS."

The urge to rub my eyes and clear them from the water splatter is outweighed by my shock at the announcement. *Four hours?* My excitement at the update conflicts with my surprise that the first elimination took this long.

Kylah marches in front of me, auburn curls bouncing over her shoulders. She curses loudly, throwing her arms up. The urge to roll my eyes is overwhelming. Still, I fight it, not moving a muscle. *One down, three to go.*

Hours pass without another elimination. The aching in my legs has grown mildly annoying, but I don't mind. My thoughts have been exploring an entirely new avenue since Kylah's elimination. I've been performing a thorough analysis of her actions against me, which has done nothing but worsen my rage toward her. She's been doing significant damage control to get on my good side, but there's no coming back from killing Mace. And with Lunar no longer here to serve as her shield?

If she thinks she'd be safe under my reign, she has another thing coming.

Embracing my newfound need for revenge, my urge to win grows. So few people remain that I finally have the familiar twinge of hope. I can't react to the excitement growing in my chest, so I simply blink. My eyes don't move from the blue wall but narrow on a browned area, peeling from water damage. I breathe and force Ashlea's advice to mind.

Win this for Lunar and Mace. Also, if I want any chance of seeing Curi ever again, I have to outlast the others. And when it comes down to my little sister…

Nothing will move me from my stump.

So, a few hours later, when a door creaks open, and a foreign voice breaks the silence, I don't move a muscle.

"Destry?" The figure moves closer to the neighboring stump, but my competitor doesn't flinch. "I know you can't move," the man says. "*Don't* move."

I force myself to keep my eyes planted on the water-stained wall, but I can just make out the man in my periphery. He's thin, but that's no shock. *Everybody in Miasmis is underweight.* His white V-neck hangs from his skeletal frame, and slim black slacks cover his lower half. Facial features are impossible to distinguish with him this far to my right, but his bald head reflects light like a disco ball.

"I know you can't talk…I…I *know* you can't look at me…" he sighs, choking up. "I just…you…have no…*idea*…how proud I am of you." He leans over and coughs to shield his weeps, but the guttural hiccup in his throat is enough evidence of his tears. When he straightens up, he removes something from his pants pocket and brings it to his cheeks. *Maybe a handkerchief?*

"Your…*Cynthia*…she's proud of you, too." The light reflects from his head when he turns. I urge my eyes to stay on the wall, relying on my ears to eavesdrop. The man drops his voice to a whisper. "You're *so* close, Destry." He sniffs, coherent sentences an obvious challenge. "You can *win* this. There's not much more you have to deal with…just…stay strong, boy. You'll make it out of here. We've been watching…and you're making everyone *so* proud."

At some point, I'd completely forgotten about the cameras. They gradually faded into the background, being a mere inconvenience with their red blinks and mechanical buzzing. And after losing nearly everybody I love, I've stopped caring who was behind them. But this is a reminder that I have to keep fighting. Because people are being forced to watch. Which can only mean that somewhere, if she's still out there…

Curi is watching.

"I have…I have to leave…I wish I had more time." The man sniffs back more tears. "But *please* just…just *know* that if I could do anything to help you, anything at all….*I would.* But you've been holding your own, and I couldn't be prouder of you."

The man from Destry's past retraces his steps without another word.

Who the hell was that? Destry's parents are dead, just like everyone else's. And if all Destry did was avoid going to the Assessment, who could that possibly have been?

Perhaps a grandparent? A door on the right clangs shut, leaving me with a new mission to list everything I know about my housemate. I create a detailed list in my mind, but it doesn't take long to determine that I barely know the guy. *He's 18 years old. He's got brown hair and green eyes. He's a manipulating douchebag possessing few redeeming qualities, if any.*

I sigh as much as I'm brave enough to. *This mission is useless.*

The door creaks open again, allowing another distraction into the arena. A small figure hops into my peripheral vision, and I automatically assume it's somebody from Finian's past. So, I keep my eyes focused on the water stain, ignoring this new guest. But when she gets closer, and her golden-brown blur of hair is nearly in focus, my heart drops to my chest and I nearly faint off my pedestal.

"Iris?"

Curi's voice breaks, and a tear falls down her delicate, rosy cheek.

Chapter 65

*C*uri. I fight movement and immediately break into a sweat. *What have they done to her?* From what little I can see, she's unharmed. This is incredibly fortunate because if there was a single hair amiss, I would leap from my tree trunk and kill anyone who got between us. So, I stay completely still, fighting tears. *She looks just as she did the day I was captured.*

This doesn't soften the blow that my little sister stands before me, and I can't even *look* at her. I can't hug her, talk to her, or properly *see* her. I can't even acknowledge her presence. Every bone in my body tells me to abandon my post. To just forget about the competition, wrap my sister in my arms, and *never let go.* But I know how that will end. *They'd take her away from me.* Curi would either watch me get killed for fighting the guards or watch me get voted out in four days. And after losing Lunar, I know how badly I have to win this. So, when tears stream silently down my face, I do nothing to stop them. I let them pour and stare blankly at the wall ahead of me.

"Iris?" She can barely get my name out. I tense my fingers as she bawls, resisting the urge to comfort her. I want to wrap her in my arms and inspect every inch of her skin for bruises. I want to investigate where she's been and demand to know who she's been with. I want to ask her the millions of questions hardening in my throat, but as she stands before me, wiping her tears, I am left with one harsh reality.

I can't say a word.

Forcing myself to stay still and silent, I focus on the image in my periphery, memorizing every detail. Tears blur my vision, but I can see the orange dress with white polka dots she's swallowed in. *I haven't seen that before.* Who gave it to her?

"I'm okay," she says, reading my mind and sniffing to stop her sobs. "The Authority…they came…to my school…" She must see the short tremble in my lips because she moves forward with a hand up and shouts, "Don't move! I…they didn't hurt me!" I quickly bite the inside of my cheek to stop from setting off the alarms. She spins in front of me, her dress fanning out. "See? I'm fine!" It takes everything in me to stop from lifting her off the ground and giving her a giant kiss on the cheek. I want her to know how worried I've been. I want her to know how she's the only thing getting me through the basic motions of life now. And beyond everything else, I want her to know how much I've loved her and always will, no matter what happens in these games.

Instead, I stay completely silent.

My tears stream heavier, but the sensors don't go off. Even with my heart getting ripped from my chest for the hundredth time, I stand firm. My tears fall to my feet, presumably landing on my shoes. "They took me from class," she continues. "They asked me questions…I…I didn't budge, Iris. I didn't tell them anything, I swear!" She wails, hiding her face in her hands. After a few seconds of weeping, she swallows back her tears and enunciates her speech clearly. "I *promise*, Iris…it wasn't me." She wipes her tears, but fresh ones instantly replace them. "I just…miss you…*so* much!"

I miss you too, Curi.

"But Iris…you…you can win this. You can!"

I will win this for you.

"They took me somewhere…I don't know where…but I have a television. I get to watch."

Please tell me you didn't watch the murders.

"Iris…you can do this. Just…just…" she gasps for air, and I fight to keep from shaking as her tears intensify mine. "They…they told me…I can't help you…I can't…tell you *anything*!" She brings her hands to her eyes and her body heaves. I didn't think my heart could break anymore, but it shatters all over again.

"They're…they're going to take me back…I can't stay…I just…" she wails. "I LOVE YOU!" Her body trembles so violently that she falls to her knees. "I LOVE YOU, IRIS!" She curls up on the ground, wailing, and I don't even spare her a glance.

Finally, she gathers her composure enough to rise. She steps forward until she's inches from my face, so I finally get a clear look at my baby sister. She looks me dead in the eye, and even though I can't match her gaze, I finally get a peripheral glimpse of her emerald pearls. Tears streaming, she whispers with finality. "I love you."

She backs away when three Authority agents enter to escort her from the building. She goes willingly, which is lucky for me. Because if they forced her away…

I would have burned this place to the ground.

I don't stop crying when she's gone. *How can I when the click of that lock finalizes the reality that I may never see my sister again?* How is it possible that for the second time in my life, I couldn't say goodbye to my sister? I consider the possibility that I may have just wasted my last opportunity to speak with her, and I bite the inside of my cheek so hard that I draw blood. The tears stream more steadily down my cheeks, and my sinuses clog, but I don't dare try to clear them. Because if I didn't move when my little sister was here, I refuse to move when she's gone. I no longer have a choice.

I have to win.

So even though the tears fall to my chest, shoes, and knees, nothing escapes my lips.

"Shit." Artemis's voice travels to my stump, and it actually sounds like he's hurting…for *me*. But I won't fall for that again. He's a terrible, evil human being, and I hope he gets the end that he deserves.

The door opens again, but I'm past caring who comes out of it. I ignore the new inhabitant, but he offers another path for my mind to wander. *Where are they all coming in from?*

The realization hits me so hard that I stifle a gasp.

Solitary confinement. When I was trapped in solitary confinement, there was a room…with computers and projections and Authority workers. I only got a glimpse of it before they shut off my access to it, but I saw it clear as day. And now, with people from the outside coming through the entry, it all makes sense. The production room isn't a one-entry area.

It links to the outside.

My thoughts are interrupted when a man with shaggy blonde hair sprints past me, arms wide. He's wearing an Authority uniform, but I can't make out the rest of him. But when he shouts, "Ashlea!" and she leaps into his arms, I don't need any hint at who he is.

The buzzer sounds, informing the rest of us of Ashlea's elimination after six and a half hours.

"SEB!" she screams, wrapping her legs around his torso. She's bawling, wailing into his hair between passionate kisses that I can only see through their exaggerated movements.

"I…didn't think…I would ever see you again!" she shouts between sobs. He laughs and drops her to the ground, and they fall onto the turf together, wrapped in each other's arms.

"I'm so sorry, Ash. I'm *so* sorry! I didn't know!" he tells her. It's less of a plead and more of a reassurance.

"How could you have known?" Ashlea kisses him again and hugs Seb so tight her speech is muffled. But his voice rings clear.

"You're going to make it, Ash. You're so close…just a few more rounds, Ash!"

They stay on the ground for so long that the Authority guards return. Ashlea and Seb don't budge at their request, crying into each other's necks. Without hesitation, the Authority agents peel Seb off Ashlea and pin his arms behind his back, yanking him from the center of the arena.

"No!" Ashlea screams, running after her love. A third guard must have pointed his gun at her because she halts in her tracks, whimpering. Terrified of execution, she cups her hands around her mouth and screams his name. "I love you, Seb! I'll win this for you!"

"I love you, Ashlea! You have no idea how much I love—" The door slams, cutting him off. With the guards having evacuated, Ashlea races outside of my peripheral vision to where I can only assume the solitary confinement room waits.

There's violent pounding followed by the creak of a door opening. Her steps slam further away, and she shouts Seb's name so loud it echoes into the arena. But whatever hunt she starts, she can't complete. Because quickly, she slumps in defeat, realizing there's no escape. *She might be able to cross the threshold of solitary confinement, but beyond that is out of her control.* Whatever door our visitors are entering from, she can't get access. So, when she returns to the arena, the only evidence that she's given up is the wailing of her tears.

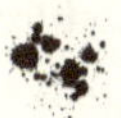

Nothing new is introduced in the hours that directly follow Ashlea's elimination. The final three, Destry, Finian, and I, stand firm on our wooden pedestals, not moving an inch. The only noise to distract us from our thoughts is the harsh whispers of the eliminated convicts.

I can't distinguish words, but I know Ashlea isn't speaking. The hushed voices belong exclusively to Kylah and Artemis. They're so far away that eavesdropping is impossible. Even if I could decipher their speech, I'd be incapable of concentrating on it. Because Curi's appearance has struck a nerve in me. Her mere presence has made me more motivated to win this than ever. Not just this competition…but *everything.* Despite the torture of having to ignore her, the Authority's plan backfired. Not only did I get confirmation that she's unharmed, but I got confirmation that she's *alive.*

So, when Ashlea announces that we're ten hours in, I don't even flinch. I'll stand here for the rest of my life if I must. If it means I'll get to see Curi again.

Much like the past ten hours, I stare at the brown spot on the wall, examining each streak in my periphery. There's not much else I *can* do. The tears have long since dried, so my face is dry from the salt. Snot fell from my nose hours ago, abiding by gravity and exiting swiftly. It's disgusting, but I couldn't care less what I look like. Apart from Ashlea, there's no one else I care for at the Enterprize. *So, if I'm unpresentable, so be it.*

Considering what I would do with an Executive win does make time pass surprisingly quickly. *When* I win this…because I *have* to win this…Ashlea is safe. She is the only person here that I trust. Beyond that…I may have to pick the most threatening competitors.

As much as I want Kylah out of this house, she hasn't won anything. She's far from a competition beast. Perhaps putting her on Death Row wouldn't be the best idea. I quickly alternate convicts because thinking about weak players puts Finian at the forefront of my thoughts. He's not a risk I couldn't handle. I've manipulated him once. Now, with a newfound purpose and motivation, I'd certainly be able to do it again. As for the rest of them…

Consider Artemis *dead.*

"Twelve hours in, everyone," Ashlea announces with a sigh. I've never heard her sound so dejected. Seeing Seb…it must have destroyed her. According to his weeps, I bet it nearly killed him too. I recall Ashlea telling me in the first round that Seb wanted her to avoid the Assessment at all costs. I wonder what he would've said if he had known about the Enterpri—

Boom!

The lights go out. I don't move from my perch, but my balance quality is dropping by the second. I force air through my lungs and bite my tongue, forcing myself to remain calm. After a few short blinks, my eyes gradually adjust to the darkness. I breathe easier once I can make out the outlines of structures like the peeling wallpaper. My heart rate slows once I realize this addition won't serve as an issue—as long as I can faintly see the environment surrounding me.

What *does* become an issue, however, is the light show abruptly projected on the wall the moment I get comfortable.

White and blue lights rotate around the ramparts, making it increasingly difficult to keep my focal point. They dizzy me until I feel like I'm swaying. It must be some illusion because no honk announces my elimination. But the purpose is clear. They're trying to throw us off…make us fall. But I've been in this too long to let a few lights knock me out. I do my best to ignore them and focus on a blank area in the center of the swirls. The darkness eliminates my view of the wallpaper, so I stare where I think the water stain still stands. I hear the eliminated convicts rise, and one or two walk over.

Just when dizziness threatens to throw me from my perch, Ashlea appears from nowhere, inches from my face. *What the heck?* I can't see anything, just her black streaks of hair. One sticks out further than the rest, the frayed edge nearly touching my nose—

And blocking me from seeing the lights.

Genius!

I narrow on that strand among the sea of black and don't let my focus falter. My throat aches with a thanking plea, silenced behind my teeth. But I can't express my gratitude for Ashlea yet—not until I've won.

I don't even move when a contestant on my left crashes to the ground and groans on the turf.

"CONVICT: FINIAN. ELIMINATED AT 12 HOURS AND 2 MINUTES."

Finian's out. Finian's out! One more. Just ONE more.

The Authority, satisfied with the success of their challenge, flick the lights back on, ending the dizzying show. Ashlea takes a deep breath before turning around. Her eyes have so much excitement that they nearly pop out of her head. "You can do this, Iris. One…more…convict…"

I want to nod but keep myself still. Because I can win this. I *will* win this. And *nothing* can stop me.

My legs ache like hell. I can't even shake out my foot, which fell asleep well over an hour ago. My thoughts no longer offer a motivating distraction…the pain is too unbearable. Just after Ashlea announces the passing of sixteen hours, I remind myself of why I'm choosing to continue the suffering when I could easily step off this stump and curl onto the turf.

Curi. Lunar. Mace. My parents.

I mentally repeat their names on a loop. I will not fail them.

I *will* win.

After saying their names in my head for the twentieth time, I'm happily distracted by Ashlea's voice. She's far enough away that she has to shout, so her words echo around the arena, ringing over and over. "Are you gonna tell us who that was, Destry?" Ashlea steps forward, stalking toward our stumps. "You know…who it was that visited you?"

There's no response. Destry and I simply stare at the wall, motionless. I admit my curiosity about who his visitor was, but *surely* Ashlea understands he can't answer her. He can't speak…what does she expect him to say? I keep staring, searching my brain until it hits me.

She's *trying* to piss him off. *She's trying to get him to budge.*

"What's up, Destry? Cat got your tongue?"

I want to laugh, but I keep still. Maybe…*maybe* this could work. *I sure hope it does.* Because with my legs nearing their breaking point, I won't last much longer.

"Come on, big guy. Say something!"

Silence.

Ashlea laughs to herself before stepping closer. "You know what I think? I think you're a *liar*. Come on. *Cynthia*? Give me a break, Destry."

"Ashlea, what are you on about?" Kylah shouts from the staircase. There's an edge to her voice…an *attitude*. As if she thinks she has a better chance at survival with Destry in power over me. But the more I think about it…she *should* feel that way. Even if Kylah's not necessarily a threat to me, I still hate her.

And hate can have a lot of influence when it comes to life or death.

"Destry's here for what…avoiding the Assessment?" Ashlea laughs. "Then who was that?" She leans in closer to his face. "I don't think your parents are *dead*. I think you've been *fucking* lying to us."

"Oh, come *on*, Ashlea." Kylah finally gets off the staircase and rushes to my friend. "That's low…even for this."

The accusation *is* wildly absurd. Even if Destry's crime has nothing to do with avoiding the Authority, his parents will have been killed like the rest of ours. Besides, Lagiacrus had to watch back *every* kidnapping. He wouldn't have kept that secret from the rest of us, not if he ever considered Destry a threat, which *everyone* does.

Despite how outrageous her claim is, I can sense that it's rattling Destry. If she can build enough momentum to piss him off and make him *truly* rageful…he could lose his temper and throw it all away.

"Who would put it past him?" Ashlea throws her hands in the air. "We're all liars in here, aren't we? What about you, Kylah? Ever lied to anybody? To *Lunar*, perhaps?"

Kylah stands totally still, controlling her tone. "Don't you start with me, Ashlea. Don't you start with me, *bitch*."

"Why? What's wrong, *sweety*? Been bonding too much with everyone's favorite douchebag?" She motions toward Artemis on the staircase. "What on *earth* could you two *possibly* have to whisper about for *six hours*?"

"YOU WERE WITH US!" Kylah yells. "You heard the entire thing!"

"I didn't hear *shit*, and you know it!" Ashlea shouts. "You wouldn't move your mouth from his goddamned ear that whole time! What secrets are you hiding, *huh*?"

I can't focus on their figures, but Kylah whips her head so far back I think she's going to tip over. "Don't come at me. I swear to God, Ashlea, I will rip you to pieces!"

Ashlea laughs. "You swear to *God?* You think that means *anything* to me?" Ashlea marches until she's inches from Kylah's face. "Anyone who associates with that lying, manipulating piece of *shit* can rot in hell. That includes you, *tramp*. You think any of us can believe a word you say when you've been plotting with him this entire time?"

"You think we've been plotting?" Kylah yells. "*That's* what you think we've been doing?"

"Kylah, *don't*." Artemis's voice is barely a whisper, but I wouldn't miss it if I were dead. Ashlea turns in Artemis's direction and *laughs*. Kylah's watching him but doesn't respond to his outburst. I'm *shocked* that Artemis even spoke up. If this argument is really the one thing that could get him to break his silence, I really don't know him at *all*. This revelation makes me want to scream, but I can't. Because all I can do is stare at the *goddamn* wallpaper.

"Woah—woah—woah! Somebody *finally* has something to say!" Ashlea yells, the words as snarky as she can make them. "Then come on over and fight like a *man*!" She points a finger in his direction and spits her next words. "Oh, that's right. You're too big of a coward to fight for anything, let alone stand up for what you've done!"

Kylah throws her hands in the air. "SHUT…UP!"

"NO!" Ashlea screams, pushing Kylah backward. "You voted out Mace, and Artemis *betrayed* us! He betrayed *her*!" She motions to me. "You two are the reason MACE IS DEAD!"

"ARTEMIS DIDN'T VOTE OUT MACE!" Kylah screams.

My heart stops. In my periphery, Ashlea halts. For the first time in hours, there's complete silence.

Why would Kylah say that? Of *course*, Artemis voted out Mace. He was the *deciding* vote.

Artemis finally walks into my periphery. He slowly moves toward Kylah with his hands up in surrender, and his voice is soft. "Kylah…"

Kylah moves away from him, choking back tears. "Artemis didn't vote out Mace."

"YES, HE DID!" Ashlea shouts with a blood-curdling screech.

"NO, HE DIDN'T!" Kylah screams at the top of her lungs. "*LUNAR DID!*"

My breath catches in my throat. *I'm going to faint.* My muscles tense, and I'm in such a state of shock that I almost miss Destry's catastrophic error.

"What?" Destry spits.

HONK.

The robotic voice announces Destry's demise. But before it's done, it brings music to my ears.

"CONGRATULATIONS: IRIS. YOU ARE THE NEW EXECUTIVE."

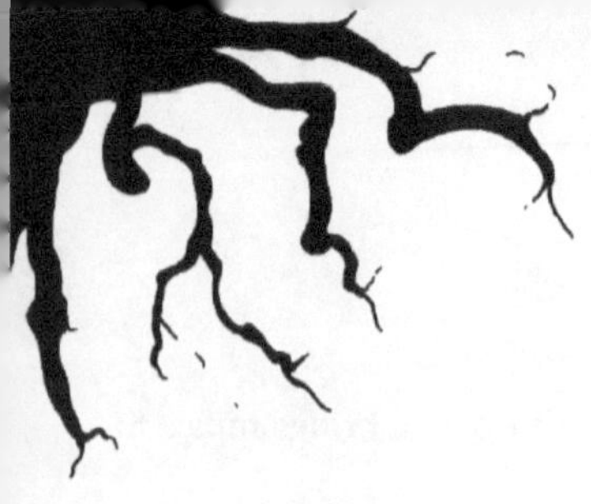

Chapter 66

I *won. I won!* My excitement is cut short by the drowning feeling I get from Kylah's announcement. *Lunar voted out Mace?* Of course, she's lying. But on second thought….the more I consider it, the more sense it makes.

When Artemis cornered Lunar in the bathroom the day before the vote, he told Lunar that "she" wasn't the boss of him. All this time, I assumed he had been referring to *me*. But what if…what if he was talking about *Kylah*? What if Artemis *knew* that Kylah was trying to convince Lunar to vote against Mace? Perhaps she asked for his vote, too, but he refused. But even then, I've known Lunar for thirteen years. I *know* when he's lying. He wouldn't have been able to hide that from me. His legs shake so hard that he can barely stand when he lies, like when he pretended Eno was safe. But on second thought…

When Mace was expelled, Lunar was inconsolable. His body was shaking so intensely that the couch nearly took off. I had assumed he was just heartbroken at Mace's demise. I swallow a sob. *It would have been impossible to know whether his tears were over Mace's demise or for his own lies.* He'd of had the same reaction either way.

When Lunar was declaring his Death Row selections, he announced that he was putting up those responsible for Mace's death. When Artemis laughed, I wanted nothing more than to drop-kick his skull. But now…did he laugh because Lunar was *really* the one responsible?

But Artemis said that he did it. Or…wait…did he? Thinking back, Artemis hasn't said a *word* since Mace left the Enterprize. He hasn't defended himself…and he's *never* apologized. *Because he didn't do it.* But if that's the case, then why didn't he say anything?

The nagging thump in my chest…the one that's been *begging* me to consider that there was a miscommunication somewhere along the line…has it been leading me to the truth this entire time? Has Artemis always been honest with me? I finally remove my gaze from the water stain and lock onto Artemis. He stares back at me, ocean eyes wide.

Destry drops off his pedestal and corners Kylah. "*What* did you just say?"

Kylah backs up until she hits the wall. "I…I…"

Destry's now inches from her face, *yelling*. "How do you know it wasn't Artemis?"

Kylah shakes her head wildly, trying to flatten against the wall. "I…I don't know how Artemis voted! But…but I *know* Lunar voted to expel Mace."

"How would you know that?" I shout, finally gaining my senses. I drop from my stump and nearly fall to the turf, my wobbly legs threatening to betray me. But there's so much rage coursing through my veins that I have the power to march forward until I'm side-by-side with Destry. "Why would any of us trust *you?*"

Kylah wails. "It…I didn't know…"

"Didn't know what?" I yell. "That he'd *die?*" Spit flings from my mouth at the words. The burn in my throat is an unmistakable sign that I'm about to burst into tears.

Kylah only gets a break from the berating because Destry's shouts are louder than mine. He flips on Kylah, taking his hand from her face, and runs to Artemis. Destry pushes him so hard that Artemis, the six-foot giant, tumbles to the turf. "TELL ME IT'S NOT TRUE!"

Artemis puts his hands up but doesn't answer. He desperately searches for an escape before locking back onto my eyes. The look he gives sends a shiver down my spine, his blue orbs glistening with sorrow.

Destry shakes his head, laughing maniacally. "You really are what they've all been calling you, you know." He spits on Artemis and grimaces. "A liar, a manipulator, and above all, a *coward*." Destry marches up the steps, each foot placement rattling the metal structure. He slams open the entrance to the Enterprize and turns one final time, yelling at the top of his lungs. "AND THAT WAS MY TEACHER YOU DICK!" He slams the door behind him, leaving us with nothing but the door's echo bouncing around the arena.

When I turn for another round of shots at Kylah, she's already at the base of the steps. I groan, then pound my foot against the dirt stain I've suffered through watching for sixteen hours. My body depletes of its adrenaline in seconds, and I collapse to the turf. *Despite all the evidence, I refuse to believe that Lunar betrayed me.* Why would he vote out Mace? What advantage would that bring him? It can't be true because I *refuse* for it to be true.

Ashlea approaches my limp figure and takes a deep breath. Before speaking, she rubs her face until it loses color. "Come on…let's get you some privacy."

I lean on her as she walks me to the steps, and I spare Artemis one last glance. This time, he doesn't match my gaze. Instead, he stares at the turf under his shoes and pulls at the brown hair falling into his eyes. I quickly turn away and shut my eyes, taking a deep breath. *This is too much.* This is *all* too much, and I don't have nearly enough time to process it. So, when Ashlea and I reach the Executive room and she shuts the door?

I burst into tears and let them run dry.

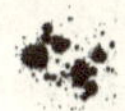

Ashlea and I lay atop my Executive bed sheets, staring blankly at the blue wall ahead. It's nearly midnight, and we haven't left the room since the competition ended early this afternoon. Our appetites are nonexistent, and I don't know if I'll ever get mine back. I haven't slept, even after being awake for nearly 40 hours. My mind wanders to terrifying places, making my heart race. But at the end of the night, when I'm overcome with exhaustion, I have a newfound purpose, which pulls at the corners of my lips and makes me smile.

"Curi is alive," I whisper.

Ashlea takes a deep breath, letting it out slowly. "I know."

"And so is Seb."

Ashlea nods, letting her own tears fall. I put an arm around her shoulder, this time taking on the role of caregiver. Finally, she shakes her head and wipes her cheeks.

"I have to get out of here."

I raise my eyebrows. "You could win."

She takes another deep breath, stretching out her arms as she lets it out. Before long, she's bawling between her knees, heaving for air. I rub her back, letting her grieve for Seb. I don't speak, opting for silence until she can breathe normally. Once she's finally calm, I feel an opportunity to get her to open up. After all she's done for me, the least I could do is get to know more of her story.

"When was the last time you ever saw him? Seb?"

Ashlea looks up, wiping her eyes. "It's complicated."

I nod and pat her back, not wanting to force her back through her trauma. But when we make eye contact and she blinks away tears, the knot in my stomach settles. She doesn't even have to say it.

She wants to tell me her story.

"The last time I saw him was the day I was captured."

I sit quietly and nod, watching her carefully.

"That morning, he surprised me with extra rations. From his trainwreck of a wife, but rations, nonetheless. He wanted to do something special for me...I figured...I don't know."

"What?" I pry. "What did you think he was doing?"

Ashlea deflates. "I guess...I just thought he was gonna tell me he's left his partner...and that he wanted to run away with me."

I shake my head. "But that didn't happen...did it?"

"No." Ashlea laughs without humor. "Not even close. We went to our usual spot in the alley behind the school. It's not romantic, but it's the only place we knew we wouldn't be found. He set up a picnic for the two of us..." She takes a deep breath to stop more tears but can't keep from choking up. "He...he told me how much he loved me...and how *badly* he wanted to be with me. But..." She shakes her head. "He made it clear that above all else...he *desperately* wanted to keep me from the Assessment." I raise my eyebrows. I haven't heard about the Assessment in *weeks.* I'm still nowhere closer to getting behind what's so unusual about it. Still, I know its secret is so horrific that Lagiacrus's parents were willing to *die* for its exposure.

Ashlea continues. "He started going on about how he's *never* seen a person return from it. I mean, he only went a few years ago, and we all know that those who leave don't ever return home…but he said something was off. He tried to find some of his buddies from school…but they *vanished.*"

"They what?" I start. "What do you mean?"

"That's the thing, Iris. *I don't know.* And I'm not even sure if Seb knew either. But the last time I saw him, the last thing he ever said to me…" She shakes her head, closing her eyes to fight back tears. "He told me that he loved me and couldn't stand to see me go to the Assessment." She gulps.

"He said he'd rather see me *dead.*"

I gasp. *He'd rather see her dead?* What is that supposed to mean?

"I don't understand…are you sure you heard him right?"

Ashlea's expression turns cold. She looks at me with dead eyes. "Why do you think I'm here, Iris? What crime do you think I committed?"

Her question takes me aback. My eyes widen as I think back to the first week. "You said you had an affair with an Authority woman's husband?"

Her eyes narrow on me. "Is that a crime?"

I lean back, squinting my eyes at her. *Is it?* I've read Curi's textbooks and Authority propaganda more times than I can count. But I don't recall them *ever* mentioning infidelity. I shake my head and watch Ashlea as she bites her lip.

"They captured me for tampering with ration production."

I tilt my head. "I don't understand…how does that fit into this? What does that even mean?"

Ashlea leans forward, bringing her voice to a whisper. "Iris, I don't even know where rations are distributed, let alone *grown.*" She takes a deep breath. "They said they were given an anonymous tip from someone within the Authority."

Her statement sinks in, and I gasp. "You don't mean…?"

"Seb reported me for a crime I didn't commit. He wanted me to avoid the Assessment *so* badly that he reported a crime he thought would get me killed. Only…he didn't think I'd get sent to the Enterprize."

"But what could be *so* bad about the Assessment that he wanted you killed for something you didn't do?"

"I doubt we'll ever know," she starts. "But I haven't committed a single crime. Not one"

We sit in silence, but my brain is swimming with questions. I open my mouth to speak but can't manage to get anything out. Instead, I rub her back and utter the only words that come to mind. "I'm so sorry, Ashlea."

She shrugs. "Seeing him again…it destroyed me." She chokes on fresh tears. "I can't live without him, Iris. I can't!" The floodgates open, and she covers her face. "I…I have to…have to get back…for *him*…"

I let her cry in my arms and only pry once she's stopped heaving. Finally having enough composure to answer me, I rub her hair and whisper, "Ashlea…if you don't mind me asking…why don't you hate him for what he did?" Her eyes widen, but I don't relent. "If he tried to kill you…why would you still want to be with him?"

Ashlea backs away, jaw hanging open. "Iris, you, of all people, should understand why."

I shake my head. "What do you mean?"

Ashlea sighs, looking me dead in the eyes.

"You don't just stop loving somebody because they betrayed you."

My stomach twists. I back away, squinting. "Why would I know that?"

Ashlea raises her eyebrows. "Seriously, Iris?"

I shake my head, but I know *exactly* who she's referring to. *Artemis betrayed me.* Not only did he tell Destry about our kiss, but up until a few hours ago, I was under the impression that he was the reason Mace is dead. And even then…when it came time for me to enact my revenge…

I couldn't do it.

My heartbeat races, fear rooting in my chest. I shake my head. "Why does everyone think I'm in love with Artemis?"

Ashlea smiles. "Whoever mentioned Artemis?"

My eyes widen at my mistake. But I don't let my embarrassment control me. Instead, I lean forward and clasp my hands behind my neck. "Who else could you be talking about?" Ashlea shakes her head, smiling, but I don't let the subject fade. "No, seriously. What are you getting at?"

Ashlea rests a delicate hand on my shoulder. "I still want to be with Seb for the same reason you couldn't vote out Artemis, even after everything he's done to you." Her eyes sparkle. "You're in love with him."

Tears form in the corners of my eyes. I try to blink them away, but they fall without permission. I haven't admitted this to anybody, but it turns out that I never had to. Somehow…they knew. Lagiacrus knew, Ashlea knew…even Artemis knew. But Ashlea speaking it into the universe somehow makes it more real.

The tears fall more heavily. "I never wanted to hurt anybody."

This time, Ashlea rubs *my* back. "I know." She lets me cry, not daring to rush my tears.

I wipe my cheeks and whisper because I'm too weak to properly speak. "What do I do?" I whine.

Ashlea takes a deep breath. "Unfortunately…that's something you'll have to figure out on your own."

My lungs constrict, making it hard to breathe. "Why does this hurt *so* badly?"

A moment of silence passes before she answers.

"Because when you love somebody…you want to tell them. And it *kills* you when you can't."

I swallow hard, stifling another sob. "Why do I feel like this, though?" I ask. "We don't even know if he kept Mace. It's all hearsay." I stare blankly at the sheet stretched under us. "Why would Lunar vote him out?"

"Iris." She gives me a weak smile. "I think it's time for you to talk to him."

A shiver passes through my body, making my hair stand on end. "But…even if he wasn't lying…he still killed Lunar."

Ashlea purses her lips and looks at the ground. "What if he had to?"

My heart skips a beat. "What do you mean?"

She shrugs. "What if he had to in order to protect you?"

I shake my head. Then I bring my shirt up to my cheeks, wiping the last remanence of tears. The rock in my chest dissolves into determined flutters, and my jaw is set steady when I rise from the mattress.

"It's time to get some answers."

Chapter 67

I've been pacing my bedroom for two hours, biting my nails to their stubs. Ashlea left long ago, and I've been working up the nerve to talk to Artemis ever since. But no matter how many times I force my breathing to slow, my body quakes. I try and convince myself it's from exhaustion, but my restlessness proves it's fear. *What if Artemis doesn't want to talk to me? What if he hates me?* After all I've done to him, I wouldn't be shocked if he did. When I wasn't trying to replace his grief at the loss of our friendship with hatred toward me, I was terrorizing him for the betrayal he never committed. All this time, I've felt he deserved it. But now, after every terrible thing I've said about him…why would he ever want to talk to me again? I don't know if I could bear that rejection. So, I bring every terrible thing he's done to me to the forefront of my mind. He told Destry about our kiss. *He killed Lunar.*

Maybe I've committed some atrocities against Artemis. But he also drew blood. And in the grand scheme of things, a few harsh words are nothing compared to Lunar's murder. Whereas I metaphorically punched him in the face, he carved out my heart and stomped until it stopped beating.

Beyond my fear that he won't give me the time of day is my piercing anxiety around Mace's final words.

Don't trust Artemis.

But that was before Mace knew the truth. *Or did he know the entire time?*

The paranoia drives me toward insanity. The more I predict how the conversation will go, the more nauseous I become. If our time at the Enterprize wasn't limited, I would not force myself to talk before I'm ready. But time is not a luxury the Enterprize offers.

Finally, I slap the side of the mattress and stomp toward the mirror. *Disgusting.* Regardless of the rations, I've lost several pounds. Beyond that, the eyes reflected are unrecognizable. They're the mark of a woman who is beyond saving…a person with trauma that will haunt her forever, never letting me get a whole night's rest. I splash water on my face and straighten out my eyebrows. My hands shake as I re-braid my hair into a fishtail down my back, then tie the end into a knot. Taking a deep breath, I squeeze my fists and hurry out the Executive door before I have a chance to change my mind.

The house is dark, so I stand still until my eyes adjust. Once they finally do, I identify the slumps on the cots around me. I only count four, so when I approach Artemis's empty mattress, I know he's still awake. I tip-toe down the steps, slowing myself to keep quiet. But if I'm honest with myself, it's primarily out of my dread at our impending conversation. My nerves intensify with each step descended, and when I spot the back of Artemis's head on the living room couch, I freeze in my tracks.

My heart pounds in my ears. The pressure in my chest urges me to abandon my mission and race back up the steps. But I refuse to cower from the man haunting my dreams, so I take a deep breath and shuffle into the living room.

Steps away, Artemis turns, making eye contact. His gaze terrifies me, but I'm so desperate for the upper hand that I speak first.

"Hi."

He watches me walk to the opposite couch and plop down. "Hi," he says, shifting his gaze to the ground.

We sit across from each other in silence until it eats me away. All my feelings for him come back at once. Love…trust…hurt…*betrayal*. I'm worried I'll talk myself out of this conversation, so I take a deep breath and force the words out.

"I'm gonna ask you this one time. And after everything we've been through…I'm *begging* you to be honest." He catches my gaze, and my stomach hardens. His blue eyes scream a thousand emotions, but above all, they glisten with *love*. After a loud gulp, he nods.

I force myself not to look away. If I want any chance at reading him, I have to look him dead in the eyes. My body freezes from our connection, but I manage to get the question out. "Did you vote to expel Mace"

Artemis doesn't move an inch, keeping our eye contact.

"No."

I bit my lip, fighting tears. I shake my head, choking up. "Prove it."

Artemis blinks before answering. "I can't."

"Then why should I believe you?"

"You shouldn't."

Despite everything, I laugh. "Great." I break eye contact and stare at the floor. I know my next question won't solve anything…but I have to *try*.

"When you were talking to Lunar," my voice shakes. "In the bathroom…when you promised your loyalty to me and your vote to keep Mace?" He raises an eyebrow. "What were you *really* talking about?"

Artemis bites his lip. "Are you sure you want to know?"

It takes me a moment to answer, but I need to know the truth. I nod. "Yes."

He stretches his lips into a thin line and looks at the ground before answering. But once he begins, he doesn't look away from me. "The day before that conversation…Kylah threatened me." He gulps. "She knew my intentions…she knew I'd vote out Finian." He rubs his palms together. "She was right."

I nod, inviting him to continue. "She said that if I didn't vote Mace out, she'd get Lunar to do it. She…she said she didn't need me…that she already had him under her control." He takes a deep breath. "In the bathroom that day, I was telling Lunar that he didn't have to listen to her. That…he's his own person. That she doesn't know everything." He takes a deep breath. "I told him that she's not the boss of him. But he wouldn't listen." Artemis itches his head. "His mind was made up…and…well, it was clear he was going to pin it on me."

I shake my head. "It just doesn't make any sense. Why would he vote Mace out? He *loved* him."

Artemis bites his lip again and shifts his eyes. "I tried…but Kylah got to him." He scratches his neck. "She said…*she convinced him*…that if he kept Mace, and it came down to you deciding who lives between them…" He coughs. "She made him *believe* that you'd keep Mace over him. She persuaded him that he was in danger."

I sit completely still and lie out of my ass. "I don't believe you."

He shakes his head. "You don't have to." Once again, he stares directly into my eyes. "But have I ever lied to you?"

A shiver goes down my spine and through my arms. I turn my head away from him and gulp loudly, but there's nothing I can possibly do to prevent myself from sobbing. I hiccup from my tears and shake my head, looking him directly in the eyes. "But why did you have to kill him?"

I hide my face in my hands and weep, finally mourning over Lunar's death. My feelings are so complicated that I can't sort them out. But Lunar's death hasn't gotten to settle on me yet, and regardless of how I feel about my brother's betrayal, I am broken that he's *gone.*

Artemis sniffs, and I see that he's crying too. Not only do the tears fall, but his body heaves from the weeps. "I'm *so* sorry, Iris." My name feels unnatural coming out of his mouth, but I dismiss it. I'm too distraught to care if his empathy is genuine, so I weep, our sobs becoming one.

"Why would you do that?" I cry. "Why would you do that to me? Forget…forget about what Lunar's done. He…he's my *brother!*"

Artemis covers his eyes, so I watch his body convulse. He shakes his head. "I can't save everyone…Lunar…he was gonna get you killed!"

"You don't know that!" I screech.

He shakes his head, his body trembling. "I know…you'll never agree…but I had to…in order to keep you safe!"

I have no response, so our cries fill the silence. Even though we're on separate couches, we breathe together, mourning our losses.

Artemis sniffs. "It sounds awful…because it *is* awful," he begins. "But…I also had to prove my loyalty."

My eyes widen. "Are you *kidding* me?"

He puts his hands up. "No, Iris! Listen!"

"You had to do that for who, *Destry?*" I shout, pointing at the ceiling where Destry sleeps.

"Iris," he shakes his head. "He has too much power! Putting you and Lunar up showed my loyalty! And taking the blame for Mace's expulsion only made him trust me more! He was never going to doubt me again after I solidified that I was on his side. And being on his team…I could influence his decisions! I could keep you safe!"

I sniff loudly. "Well, you sure proved your loyalty when you pinned Lunar and me against each other!" He looks at me with deep regret, so I continue. "Why, Artemis? Why would you put us up together? Why would you ever do that to me?"

He rubs his face again, ridding it of tears. "I…I didn't want to." He takes a deep breath, but his words are shaky. "I had two minutes to think!"

"So, what did you think about then? How to hurt me the most?"

Artemis throws his hands up. "No, of course not!"

"Then what was it!?" I shout. My voice cracks, and tears consume me again. Artemis leans closer to me and puts his hands together.

"You were the only pawn that would guarantee his expulsion."

I shake my head. "That's bullshit."

His eyes widen. "No, it's not! Please, Iris! Think about it! He needed three votes to stay…he'd have you, Kylah, and Ashlea against anyone else!"

"You don't know that!"

He puts his head in his hands and leans back to the neck of the couch. Finally, he puts his palms back together and talks patiently. "No, I don't know that. But how did the votes turn out?"

I let his words ring out and consider what he's saying. I would vote to keep Lunar safe no matter who he was up against. If Kylah was beside him, he'd be safe with Finian's vote in the mix. If Ashlea was up there, Destry's vote would have solidified her expulsion, and if Finian was up there, he'd easily be sent out the door. Even with Destry on Death Row with him, Lunar wouldn't be expelled. As much as I hate to admit it…Artemis is right. If anyone else was up there with Lunar, he would still be alive.

I shiver, remembering Mace's warning to not trust Artemis. So, even though I know his logic is sound, I shake my head. "I feel like you're manipulating me again."

He raises his palms to the ceiling. "Is every answer I give just going to make you feel manipulated?"

Artemis stares at me until tears crumple him in defeat. I watch him slump into the couch and my heart wrenches. Because I know he's right. Putting me on Death Row was the only way to ensure Lunar's expulsion.

I cover another weep with a cough, and Artemis rests his cheeks in his hands, finally moving his gaze back to mine. His words are soft. "I didn't want to do it, Iris. It *killed* me to do it." He hiccups from his tears. "But it was the *only* way."

I shake my head, letting another tear fall. He coughs before continuing. "And Iris…I *promise* that if for one *second* I thought you would be in danger…I wouldn't have put you up there."

I hate how much sense he's making. I hate that he was the reason my brother died. I hate how much he has hurt me, and I hate how much I still don't know. But above all else…

I *despise* how much I still love him.

I shake my head. "Why didn't you *tell* me?" He gazes into my eyes, and I continue. "Why didn't you tell me it was Lunar all along?"

He bites his lip and looks away. But when he makes eye contact again, his left eyebrow quivers. "I…because…" His voice shakes. "You know…how I feel about you." His leg is trembling. "And I know…" he laughs weakly, "you don't feel the same way." My heart breaks, and I bite my lip to keep from crying. His eyes glimmer, and a single tear falls. Finally, he shakes his head. "I'd rather you die hating me than die hating your brother. You've known him forever…you love *him*. You deserve to love him always…knowing this all now? It's not going to change that you don't love me."

I shake my head fast, squinting my eyes to keep the tears in. But when I look back at him, my voice cracks. "Do you *seriously* still love me? After all this?"

He takes a deep breath. "Answering that question doesn't change anything. It doesn't change what I've done…and it doesn't change how you feel." My heart breaks further. Because he's wrong. Knowing whether he still loves me changes *everything*.

I look at the ceiling, fighting more tears. Clearing my eyes, I give him my undivided attention. "If you love me, why did you spread those rumors about me?" He sighs, so I keep going. "Why did you tell people I was in love with you? Why…why did you lie about what I said?" A tear involuntarily falls from my eye. Because as little as these details may feel to other people, they mean everything to me. Because I *trusted* him.

He shakes his head. "You're never going to believe me…and that's okay. Really…it is. I'm sorry I made you feel like you can't trust me. But…I didn't spread any of those rumors." I bite my lip. "I didn't say a *damn* thing, and I have no idea how Kylah got that information. I didn't say a word to her." He leans forward. "And I don't want to push my luck here…but has she really shown you that she's trustworthy?"

I know he's right, but the rumors were still painful. What hurts the most is that…I believe him. Everything he's saying makes sense. And above that, I *want* to believe him. Because nobody wants to think that they're in love with a monster. It hurts further that I'll never get to tell him. What Ashlea said was right. One of the worst feelings in life is not getting to tell the person you love your true feelings.

The topper on it all is Mace's last words. *Don't trust Artemis.* I want to reward him with his last dying wish. But I do love Artemis…however, I will *never* love him the way that I loved Mace.

Artemis takes a deep breath, and I'm terrified he can read my mind. At the very least, I feel that he can sense my dilemma. He may claim that he's given up on us…but his eyes tell another story.

He looks to the ground quickly before locking back onto my gaze. "Can I just…ask you one thing, Iris?"

My pulse increases and sweat perspires on my brow. Instead of answering verbally, I nod.

He takes a deep breath, then stares into my soul. "Why did you save me?"

Electricity shoots through my nerves, and I'm frozen without an answer. Because I could never tell Artemis the truth. I'm confident he already knows…but I'll never be able to confirm his suspicions. My silence invites him to continue.

"You had a chance to kill me. You had every right to and did everything in your power to make sure I was expelled. Then…you kept me safe." He blinks and tilts his head. "Why?"

This is my chance. I can open my heart and tell him everything I've been dying to say to him since the day that he kissed me. My stomach floats because I can *finally* be with him like my wildest dreams granted glimpses of. But when Mace's violet eyes pulse through my consciousness, I sit speechless. I grasp at something to say, but nothing comes out. Because even if I wanted to tell him how I feel…I can't.

I could never do that to Mace.

I shake my head. "I don't know."

He laughs softly and smiles. "Well…I'm glad you did it."

For the first time in twenty-four hours, I smile. It's weak, but it's genuine. As strange as I feel on this couch, alone with Artemis…

Finally being able to have a genuine conversation with him without any repercussions feels like a thousand-pound weight has been lifted off my shoulders.

"You sleep well, Iris." He springs up off the couch and starts walking toward the kitchen. I'm alone with my thoughts until he turns around at the base of the staircase and smiles. "And for the record…I do still love you. I *never* stopped, and I never will."

And despite everything I've been through…all the countless losses I have faced in the past 42 hours alone…

I smile.

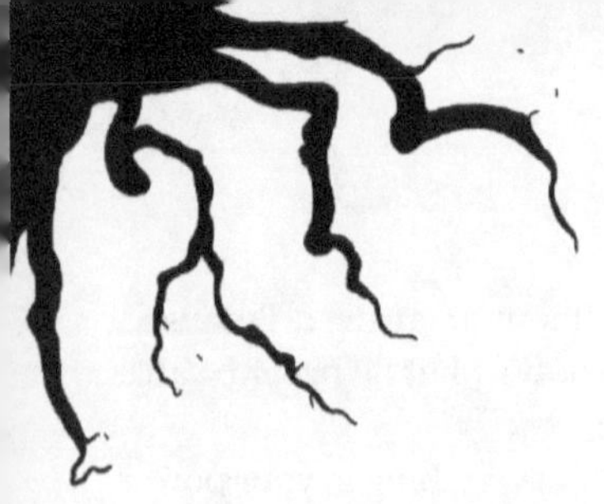

Chapter 68

Curi shoots her hand into the air, bouncing off her chair. "The answer is twenty-five!"

"Very good! Now…somebody who isn't Curi! What is six times six?"

Curi laughs in her chair, grabs her pencil, and scribbles more notes. Her smile is contagious, and I wish I could do something to keep it plastered on her face forever.

The front door of the classroom flies open, and three Authority agents clad in tree-root camouflage stomp to the head of the room. The instructor pauses, stylus on her hologram.

"Hi…can I…can I…help you?" she stammers.

The Authority men separate, making room for the thin figure in a wife-beater and black slacks to enter. My limbs harden into cement, and my throat closes. I try to grab Curi, but I can't move. I can't even shield her body with my own because gravity slams down on me like a solid mass, gluing me to my chair. The more I struggle, the more I dissociate from my physical form. I wiggle until I'm watching from a birds-eye-view, rendering me completely useless. Up here, as a mere viewer, there's nothing I can do to protect my little sister.

"Hello!" The warden beams, swaying his hips nonchalantly as if his presence isn't a death sentence. "Will you please excuse Curi from this class period? We have official Authority-sanctioned business to attend to."

The teacher's blonde hair shifts around her shoulders as she steps back. Her lips tremble as she struggles to speak. "May I ask…what you plan to do with her?"

The warden laughs, holding a hand up while he catches his breath. "No." He shakes his head, beaming. "No, you cannot." He gives the teacher one final glance before approaching Curi. As I always instructed her, she's sitting nearest to the hologram, so it only takes the warden a second to reach her. Once he does, he squats on his knees and rests his elbows on her desk, never removing his smile. "Hello, little lady."

Curi cowers against the back of her chair. She's had little experience with the Authority, but she's been trained to fear their presence. Her terror is concealed in her casual facial expression, but her body tells another story. She's trembling involuntarily, gripping her fists until they lose color. She doesn't dignify the warden with a response, but she watches him patiently.

"We're just going to ask you a few questions, okay? Can we do that?" His smile doesn't falter like he's enjoying tormenting the child. After considering his question, Curi surprises me with a grin.

"No, thank you." I want to laugh, but nobody would hear me. Because I'm merely a spectator of the entire exchange, watching it unfold with no power to intervene. The warden's smile falters, but only for a moment. Regaining his composure, he laughs.

"You're a little jokester, aren't you?" He laughs again, the rest of the classroom enveloped in silence. His cackles echo off the school walls, and the students watch him with wide-eyed terror. Just when I think he'll abide by her polite refusal, his voice drops an octave, and his eyes turn completely black, the whites devoured by a horrifying sludge.

He licks his lips, sending a shiver down my spine. A scream is caught in my throat when he finally opens his mouth. "Guards?"

The Authority agents storm Curi's desk, forcing her into their grasp. Her teacher yells, and the students shout, but nothing is more bloodcurdling than Curi's shrieks.

I wake in a sweat, throat raw from screaming. The room is pitch black, so I draw my knees to my chest and cower in terror. *What have they done to Curi? Are they torturing her? Where is she?*

Curi's real comments in the arena return. She assured me the Authority hadn't touched her, and she didn't seem to have a hair out of place. However, my examination was limited to my peripheral sense. Who knows what I would have seen upon closer inspection? I shiver, because in a pinch, makeup can perform wonders.

My body trembles as my thoughts spiral. My hands naturally travel to my roots and pull, the pain against my head grounding me to what is real. *Curi wasn't violently forced from her classroom. It was just a dream.*

I scream again when I realize the reality of her capture may have been much worse than anything I could imagine.

Not a single soul rises to comfort me. As has always been the case, the Executive bedroom is soundproof. My screams merely bounce off the iron door and reflect back to me, making me the soul audience. Nobody is coming to protect me. Nobody is coming to comfort me. I am completely, utterly alone.

I try to flick the lights on, but my body refuses as if it's detached from my entire nervous system. There's nothing I can do to break from my paralysis, so I take deep breaths, squeezing my eyes shut. But every few exhales, I break into tears, shocking my body back into its frozen state.

Eventually, the paralysis subsides, and my limbs slowly follow their neurological instructions. Every muscle is taut, so my movements are mechanical. After substantial effort, I manage to flick the bulbs on, showering my room with light. Overwhelmed by the sudden brightness, I flashback to my nightmare about Curi and fall to my knees. My shins slide across the carpet, and the friction burn triggers me into a slideshow of heartbreak that was *never* fictitious. Mace promised me I was going to be okay. He *vowed* to protect me. I sob, goosebumps rising up my arms as I flashback to our first kiss. I can hardly breathe as I bring forth the moment I felt his love for the first time.

I weep harder than I ever imagined possible. I slam my fists against the floor and gasp for air until I hyperventilate. I try to curl back onto my sheets, but they are soaked in my sweat, making the Executive bed sticky and uninviting. I roll back onto the floor, drawing my knees to my chest. Squeezing the carpet between my fingers does nothing to soothe

the pain, but I don't stop trying. My breathing is so short and shallow I feel as though I've sucked all the oxygen from the room. *I am going to die here.* Right on this floor, with nobody left to care.

Mace's death has me *ill*. I eventually gather the strength to crawl to the bathroom and hurl onto the shower floor the second I cross the threshold. I'm not ashamed I didn't make it to the toilet. I'm surprised I even made it off the carpet.

My sadness pushes my body to expel everything, forcing me to puke until only acid remains. It doesn't take long, considering my inability to eat much of anything the past few days. Once I'm finally finished, I turn the shower on, not caring about soaking my clothes.

I sit on the marble floor of the shower in my own vomit, letting the freezing water wash over my body. I stare blankly at the other end of the bathroom, allowing the liquid to splash into my eyes, ignoring the searing burn in my pupils. *Mace is gone.* And it's *Lunar's* fault.

I squeeze my fingers back into my hair and scream, letting my voice echo around the tiled walls. A camera whirls, zooming in on me, stealing my last bit of sanity.

In seconds, I'm inches from the camera, soaking the entire floor with my sopping clothes. "IS THIS WHAT YOU WANTED?!" I scream. "ARE YOU HAPPY NOW?" Of course, there is no response. Hopelessly demanding an answer, my voice raises an octave. "ANSWER ME!"

But the camera remains still, watching me descend into madness. Outraged, I punch the side of the equipment, knocking it from its static view of my tantrum. There's no immediate pain. *Only fury.* I watch as, slowly, the camera rotates until it stares at me again. My heart explodes, so I grab the sides of the apparatus and yell, spit flinging from my mouth onto the screen. "If *anyone* is watching this, *please*…make it *stop!*" I inch closer, eyes wild. Strips of my hair flow into my eyes, making me look like the madwoman the Enterprize has created. My eyes dart around the room, and I get so close to the camera that it can only see my lips.

"Help us," I whisper. "Somebody…*please*…help us." The camera hangs motionless, its red light blinding me until I see stars. I shake my head and wipe the snot from my nose before stumbling back toward the bedroom, wondering what the point of living is if there's no one left that you love. *If I lose Curi…what do I have?* I turn to flick off the light but stumble when I catch myself in the mirror.

I burst back into tears at my reflection. I can hardly look, my hair strung out in wet clumps that drip at the ends. Several strands twirl together, knotting my head in cords that resemble barbed wire. My eyebrows are frayed at awkward angles, and my eyes are so dilated that the hazel is indistinguishable from the black. My shirt is wrapped around my torso, so the back is halfway around my front. But water also weighs the fabric, so it not only sticks to my ribs, showing every protruding bone, but also makes my shorts struggle to fight gravity, the waistband bending toward the floor. My eyes travel from my feet to my forehead, examining what I have become.

Destry's words find their way back to me. *Don't be the monster they already think we are.* I can't help but think that it's too late.

I take a deep breath and fall to the tile. I hide my head in my hands and force air through my lungs. *This isn't over yet.* My hands move from my eyes to my chin, letting my head rest upon my knuckles. I stare blankly at the floor as my senses return and tears dry and repeat my new mantra.

This isn't over yet.

I shake my head and jolt at the sound of the water still pounding down the marble shower drain. One deep breath later, I'm on my knees. Another one and I'm on my feet, removing my sticky clothes and tossing them into the sink.

"Okay, Iris. It's time to shower." *Now I'm talking to myself.* But the words are just what I need. I step through the threshold and shut the door, squeezing soap into my palms and lathering my body with the floral scent. It doesn't seem like much…but for the first time in days…

I am accomplishing something. And for now?

That's enough.

Knocks on my door bring me out of my daze. Slowly, I rise from my bed, opening the iron slab and inviting Ashlea inside.

"Hey," she whispers, holding two ration bins. "Brunch?"

Lips in a thin line, I flop back onto my bed. "What time is it?"

Ashlea chuckles, but there's an absence of amusement. "Two in the afternoon."

I nod. "Late brunch it is."

We unpack the contents of the bins, and I fight my lack of appetite. One bland slice of bread at a time, I shove the grain down my throat and chug water, forcing it down. My saliva fights my urgency, thickening the bread like a sponge, so I take breaks to let it dissolve. We eat in silence, a sure gloom settling over us.

"Iris," Ashlea says, turning to me with a grape in her palm. "You know I'm always here for you…right?"

I nod, not looking back. Finally, after a month in this prison, I've let myself grieve. And unfortunately, now that I've opened the floodgates, I can't stop.

The silence stretches, so Ashlea breaks it again. "What are you gonna do?" She pauses. "For Death Row."

I shake my head. "I…I don't know. I haven't really thought about it." It's true. But it's important to consider, nonetheless.

"Well," she says, drawing out the words. "Let's start with who's safe. You have five options. I assume I'm not in the mix?"

Finally, I laugh. It's weak, but it's something. "Shocker." I smile.

She grins back. "So…that leaves four people. Half are safe…half aren't." She scratches her head. "Is there anyone you want to target?"

I shake my head. "I just…what's the point anymore?"

Ashlea takes a deep breath and leans forward. "Hope."

I roll my eyes at this reminder. "Hope for what? They're not coming back. And if I make it out of here…you…you…"

She shakes her head. "You can't think like that." She sets her bin on the ground. "Look, Iris. When we make it out of here…we'll have all the time in the world to dwell. If you want to talk to me about it…I'm here to listen. But right now…we *have* to keep fighting."

I freeze as I consider her words. *When we make it out of here.* My eyebrows raise, and she flinches at my concern. A camera narrows on her, so she claps her hands and purses her lips, ignoring her mistake. "Well…I'm not giving up yet. So, let's go one at a time…Artemis."

"He's safe." I don't look at her when I say it, but her shock is evident in her scoff.

"You can't be serious."

I shake my head. "He wasn't the one who voted out Mace."

Ashlea's eyes widen. "How can you be sure? Iris…he's lied to you *so* many times. He…*he killed Lunar!*"

My temper is short, so I yell. "HE'S NOT GOING UP AND THAT'S FINAL!"

Tears coat the corners of my eyes, so Ashlea backs away. The waterworks begin, and she reaches toward me, no longer scared of my outburst.

"Come here," she says with open arms.

I burrow into her embrace, pushing tears out. But as hard as I try, very few materialize. Dehydration forces me to dry heave until my liquid is replenished. She lets my wheezing calm until silence overcomes us.

I take a deep breath, leaving her arms. "I don't want to talk to anybody. Kylah's going up…and so is Destry. They're the last ones here that voted against Mace, so I'm picking them. Everyone else can decide who to expel."

Ashlea nods. "Okay." After considering her next move, she whispers, "And if by some miracle there's a tie?" Three people are voting, so this is unlikely. But this far into the game…I have to consider all of my options.

So, I think my decision through for all of half a second. Then, I shake my head and look her dead in the eyes. "Then the bitch is dead."

Chapter 69

I shuffle into the living room one cautious step at a time, mentally reciting my Death Row selections. I don't need Ashlea to warn me that my nominations are foolish. I know they don't necessarily threaten the strongest competitors, but I'm too rageful to care. Kylah broke my trust and successfully manipulated one of the strongest people I know. Therefore, she is just as significant a threat as the physical competition beasts. But if I'm honest, this justification is merely a coverup for my real motivations.

I want to make her *pay* for what she's done to Mace.

Not only did she send him to an undeserved death, but she also turned my own brother against me. Without her, Lunar never would have made the mistake of doubting my loyalty, Mace wouldn't have been expelled, and Artemis *never* would have expelled Lunar.

As I fall onto my Executive sofa, a tiny voice reminds me that I wouldn't have had the strength to vote against either of them, even if it came down to Mace, Lunar, and myself in the final three. I don't want to admit it, but Kylah's betrayal saved me from inevitably sacrificing myself to save the people I love. But the louder voice in my head believed in the insane possibility that we could have all made it out alive. That *maybe*, in the end, the warden would have shown us pity.

But with my five remaining housemates planted in the living room, waiting for me to grant two of them a near-death sentence, the odds of us outsmarting the Authority and saving more than one of our group are slim to none. If the warden didn't stop the game when Lunar was expelled…there really *is* only one person coming out of the Enterprize alive.

My eyes travel around the room, and I examine the other convicts as the clock ticks to their dooms. Half the house is upset with me for not getting the chance to plead their cases, but Ashlea made it clear that my decision was made. So, I'm not surprised that Kylah's gripping the sides of the couch like it's the only thing that can save her. Her sobs are strangled, and she tries to fight them, but she knows the mistake she made. I'm entirely unempathetic to her despair and even roll my eyes at her when we make eye contact. I don't feel remorse because I know that deep down in her heart…

Kylah *knows* she deserves this.

Finian's trembling, but I barely give him a second thought. However, without realizing it, I linger on his bald head and note that not a single hair has grown back from his chemical punishment ages ago. I start thinking it never will. He bites his lip to hide his distress, but the way he slumps his shoulders tells me he's more disheartened than anything. Ashlea's the only one who's calm. She sends me an encouraging smile and nods, reaching her hand out to hold mine. I nod back but keep my lips neutral. This selection is *personal*, and I don't want there to be any doubt about it.

For the first time since entering the Enterprize, Destry and Artemis sit on opposite corners of the opposing couches, as far away from each other as possible. I'm heartbroken and *stunned* that Lunar was the vote against Mace, but Destry is nothing short of inconsolable. To expect anything less would be pure ignorance. One can only imagine the pain of trusting somebody with all their heart and standing by them through every terrible thing they have done, just to find out they never had the same loyalty. Only I don't have to imagine it because, for ages, I've been struggling with the pain Destry feels right now. Until yesterday, I thought Artemis had done the same thing to me.

It's ironic, really. That Destry feels betrayed by the same man that screwed me over too many times to count. When all is said and done, I'm grateful that Artemis chose me over Destry. But there's no room for thankfulness when I'm overwhelmed with grief over Lunar's death. So, as much as I wish Artemis's truth bomb fixed everything…

His loyalty doesn't cleanse his hands of my brother's blood.

With thirty seconds remaining, I risk a glance at Artemis. His eyes are instantly on mine, having waited for me to look over, and my breath catches in my throat. He raises the corner of his lip, and his eyes moisten. Despite how badly I want to look away, I can't. His eyes glisten with desperation to *help* me. But even with the truth of his loyalty having been exposed…something within me *knows* he just wants me to make it out of here alive.

I jolt when the buzzer sounds and look away from Artemis as I rise. After a few deep breaths, my body is still. My eyes are straight and emotionless. Every ounce of remorse has disappeared, and I'm left as a shallow shell of a human. There's almost nothing else the Authority could do to hurt me. They've tortured me and played me enough that I'm exactly what they wanted to create: a person immune to the prospect of death. I don't view this selection as a vote. I don't even view it as an undeserved execution. Now, just as everyone expected of us, I look at Death Row, knowing somebody is going to die.

And I don't care.

I lick my lips and tilt my head as if I'm impatient. Then I stare at Kylah and scowl, hoping my words sting like venom. "Mace is dead…because of *you*."

Kylah bursts into tears, throwing her hands up and whipping her auburn curls back so I can see her eyes. "Iris, it wasn't like that! I…I'm just one person! One vote! One—"

"Lunar is dead. *Because of you*."

She shakes her head wildly. "No…that's not true! I voted for him to stay!"

I take a step closer and lean in, watching her tears pour. I glare at her pupils and whisper, letting the hot air suspend around her nose. "Rot in hell, traitor."

I flip on my heel and stalk back to the head of the room. Kylah's wails ring in my ears, even though I haven't announced Death Row selections yet. But she's not that stupid. She knows what's coming.

I fold my arms over my chest. "There's only two of you left at the Enterprize that voted to kill Mace." My eyes dart to Destry, and I glare at him, hoping he will get the hint that I'm speaking directly to him. "And you need to *pay* for what you've *done*."

Destry tilts his head to the ceiling, rolling his eyes. I squint mine on him and rock back onto my heels. "Have something you want to say, Destry?"

He puckers his lips, shaking his head. "You see the irony in this, don't you?" I stay silent, not moving, so he can continue. "We killed Mace, so you want to kill us. But Mace killed Sola. And Crescentia. *And* Eno." He rolls his eyes again. "You can pretend like he's something greater than all of us. Somebody who deserves more than we ever did…but Iris, he was just like everybody else. He voted, he lied, and he *killed*. When Cypher refused to vote, what did Mace do?"

"What did *you* do when Cypher refused to vote?" I shout. "Don't pretend like *you're* above him, Destry."

He keeps shaking his head. "You don't get it. This," he says, gesturing to the room and beyond, "this…place. It's given us no choice. We aren't evil people, Iris. Mace's life wasn't any more significant than Lagiacrus's, Mercedes's, or Jade's. We're all trapped…doing what we can to survive. When it comes down to it…the final two…what are you going to do?" Silence passes as I let his comment fill the air. "If it's you and Ashlea? Or you and Artemis? What are you gonna do then? Let them win?" I glare at him, wanting to knock him out. Because he's right.

And I hate him for it.

"You're no better than the rest of us, Iris. So do what you're told and put us up. Let's hear those magic words…better do it before they decide you've taken too long."

I shake my head. *What does he think this speech is going to do? Change my mind?* Annoyed with him and furious at Kylah, I lick my lips and motion to the Death Row cushions. "As you please," I nod. "I have selected Kylah and Destry for Death Row."

Destry stands up quickly and takes his seat on the bullet-pierced cushion. Spreading his arms out as if in a bow, he smiles. "Now, was that so hard?"

Kylah doesn't cooperate. Instead, she runs to the bathroom, scream-crying the entire way. I should empathize. I've been on Death Row once. But I'm absent of pity. There's not even a smidge of concern for her in any small crevice of my heart. A shiver goes down my spine when I realize how I perceive her fear.

Pathetic.

I shake my head. "Meeting adjourned," I say with no conviction. I care so little that I shuffle past the kitchen and climb to my exclusive room, not giving my housemates a second glance. Ashlea doesn't follow, and I'm thankful for it. Halfheartedly, I shut the door, let it lock behind me, and climb into my sheets. With only my head exposed, I hear the distinct whirring of a camera zoom on my face. Upon second inspection, at least three separate devices are watching me. Fed up with the Authority's games, I cock my head and narrow my eyes on the camera straight ahead. My voice has no conviction. Just resignation.

437

"Congratulations. You win."

The cameras stay still, not acknowledging that I've spoken. I close my eyes and repeat the words, letting them echo around the room.

I twiddle my thumbs, positioning them into a single-person thumb war. I make moves and countermoves, but I can never fully keep one side down. My thumbs always escape the punches thrown, reminding me of the one thing I'm incapable of doing: fleeing. But it numbs my mind, letting the time pass.

I'm still mesmerized when there's a knock on the door, so it takes me a moment to roll out of my sheets. I take long steps toward the iron barrier and crack it open, letting the weight of it fall into my body. Blue eyes peek through the sliver, towering above me. "Can I come in?" Artemis asks.

My body jolts, electricity shooting through it. "Be my guest," I answer, opening my palm to welcome him in. As he passes the threshold, I'm able to attribute the electricity to anxiety rather than excitement. Even so, I have a bit more bounce to my step when he enters. I try and hide it, quickening my pace as he gets seated. He settles on the couch across from the mattress, so I back up to the edge of the bed frame, pulling my knees to my chest.

Silence passes between us as he stares at the floor, gathering his words. After a few deep breaths, he looks at me, pain in his voice. "You okay?"

I let out a long breath. "In what sense?"

He shakes his head, looking away. He lets my mind wander before continuing. "I just…" he bites his lip. "I want you to know…that there's still something to live for."

I laugh. "There's *nothing* to live for, Artemis."

"That's not true, Iris. That's not true, and you know it." Of course, I know it. Curi is alive. She's watching me. I know I can't give up because I need to make it out and bring her to safety. I have to protect her. But my energy…it's depleted. My will to live is running on empty, so I slump my shoulders and take a deep breath. Reading my mind, he continues. "You saw her…your sister. She's *alive*, Iris." Another breath. "You can be with her again. You can go home."

I swallow hard, refusing to let him see me weak. Instead of succumbing to the sorrow that threatens to envelop me, my eyes widen, realizing an opportunity for information. I bite my cheek and meet his gaze. "Did you see her? Curi? Like…*really* see her?"

He doesn't flinch, so I expand. "I…I couldn't focus on her. They…I would have been disqualified." I lick my lips. "But you…were you able to get a good look at her?"

Artemis nods. Goosebumps erupt along my arms. I swallow and tilt my head, and my words barely come out above a whisper. "What did you see?"

"She was fine, Iris. I…it looked like they tried to doll her up as much as they could. Her hair…the curls…it just wasn't natural." *Curls?* I could barely see them, so I have to take his word for it. "I don't think they hurt her. But it felt like they went above and beyond to prove that to you."

My eyes narrow. "What does that mean?"

Artemis shakes his head. "Who knows? I doubt it matters…she wasn't injured. There was nothing…nothing to show that she was."

I nod, relief flushing through me. *Curi is healthy. Curi is alive. Curi is watching, rooting for me.* I close my eyes and thank whoever's listening that Artemis didn't have any bad news to report on her. Silence consumes that room as I let that news sink in.

Once the quiet is too uncomfortable, I probe him. "How're you and Destry?" The answer is obvious, but it's something to fill the silence.

He raises his eyebrows. "I don't think he likes me very much right now." I chuckle softly, and he smiles. "He feels…betrayed. He certainly doesn't want anything to do with *me* anymore."

I shake my head. "It's because he can't control you. He controlled Dial this entire game. The only reason he made the first move against me and Mace is because he couldn't tell us what to do."

Artemis nods in thought. I lean back and bite my lip. "Who do you really think came to visit him in there?" Artemis locks eyes with me but doesn't move. "He said it was his teacher…do you believe him?"

Artemis raises an eyebrow. "I'm not sure how much it matters."

"But you were close with him. Did he ever mention anyone?"

Artemis laughs. "Believe it or not, Iris, we didn't talk much about our dead families."

The awkwardness is unbearable. I stumble for words. "Are…are you gonna try to get close to him again?"

Artemis's lips spread into a wide grin. "I'd rather eat a jean jacket."

There it is. There's the Artemis I fell in love with. I start laughing, and he joins in. My shell opens, and I finally see some light at the end of the tunnel. I let the laughter consume me and burst into cackles, finally getting a glimpse at why I shouldn't give up. I laugh harder than I have in days, insanity taking over me until our eyes meet again. My body freezes, and a shiver runs down my spine. Because when those blue eyes gaze into mine, I only remember one thing.

He killed Lunar.

Without thinking, my voice gets stern. "Stop." His cackles halt with a jolt, and concern contorts in his eyes. "Stop," I say again, no humor in the word. He opens his mouth to protest, but I don't let him in. "You don't get to do that. You…you don't get to come in here and make me laugh. You don't get to come in here and pretend you didn't *ruin my life*." I lean forward and shake my head. "You killed Lunar."

"Iris—"

"You put us on Death Row, and you *voted him out*."

"It was a mistake…it was stupid!"

I shake my head and pucker my lips. "You could've *let me win*. You could've just let me win and let *me* handle the expulsion."

"Iris, I tried to!"

I squint my eyes and tilt my head. "Come on, Artemis."

He throws his hands up. "I'm not lying! Do you really think I'm smart enough to know it was a trick question? I did a number so low I figured I wouldn't have any chance at winning."

I consider it for a single moment before throwing it out. "Then pick a higher number! It would have disqualified you!"

"How smart do you think I am? It was a time crunch…I couldn't make it obvious that I was throwing it. I did what I thought was best."

I laugh under my breath. "That's the same logic you used when you sent Lunar to the firing squad."

His eyes moisten. I don't want to see tears, so I stand straight, walking toward him. "Whatever friendship we had, Artemis…it's done."

His lip quivers. "Iris!"

"We can be allies. We can protect each other from harm's way…but if every time you make me laugh, I see Lunar getting a hundred bullets through his chest…" I gulp loudly. "Then things between us can never be the same."

He stands, and his eyebrow twitches wildly. "Iris…*please* don't do this."

I shake my head, avoiding eye contact. "There's nothing to do. It's *done*."

My throat closes, and I fight back tears. I don't want Artemis out of my life. But if I can't get past what he did to my brother…we can never have a relationship beyond acquaintances again.

His eyebrows pull together before he covers his face completely, wiping oncoming tears. He heaves for a single second before removing his hands from his face and opening his arms. "Can…can I at least have a hug? To say goodbye?"

I watch him, eyes darting with desperation. And despite my heart wanting me to accept the comforting gesture, I shake my head. "No. No, I don't think that would be appropriate."

His eyes droop in defeat and he nods, forcing a weak smile. He makes for the exit, and I follow close behind. He doesn't turn around to say goodbye when he reaches the door. Instead, he puts a palm on the handle and stares at it longingly. "I will never be able to take back what I did to you." He gulps, and his voice cracks. "But I want you to know that I will regret it until the day that I die. And I will spend every last dying day in here, trying to keep you alive." He turns, locking his gaze on mine as a tear falls down his cheek. "I promise."

I bite my lip, refusing tears. "Goodbye, Arty."

He freezes at the nickname, the magnitude of which registers as fresh tears fall from his cheeks. He stares into my eyes and nods, opening the door. "Goodbye, Iris."

When the door shuts, my floodgates burst. I curl against the iron door and bawl, struggling to come up for a moment to breathe. This goodbye meant more to me than he will ever know. Because I wasn't just saying goodbye to him. I was saying farewell to the person I loved. The nickname, Arty, belonged to the person I bonded with in solitary confinement and the man I couldn't kill no matter how badly I wanted to. This conversation was closure...a way to part from the man I never wanted to live without. Because the person that now roams the Enterprize has done too much harm...has caused too much destruction to my life to ever come back from. I'm not only saying goodbye to Arty.

I'm making peace with the fact that Arty is dead, leaving in his wake a traitorous monster.

A villain by the name of Artemis.

Chapter 70

Sleep comes and goes, my exhaustion fighting against my rampant thoughts. When I do finally rise and part with my room for the kitchen, the air feels…different.

With only six convicts remaining, it's uncoincidental that everyone has started keeping to themselves. Any previous alliances have broken, and everyone here is seemingly alone. Ashlea sits at the kitchen table, picking at her food with one hand and bunching her fist with the other. Artemis is nowhere to be found, and Destry slouches on one of the Death Row cushions, staring intently at the wall ahead. Finian is plopped on the living room floor, ruffling his hand through the plush, white carpet. I hear my steps as I walk toward the ration counter and the echo throughout the room as I open the cabinet.

The silence is deafening.

Most concerning to me is Kylah. Yesterday, it seemed like she would never stop crying. I assumed she'd be in tears until the day she was voted out. But now, she leans against the outer railing of the staircase, eyes locked in a gaze on the floor. It's as if somebody has flipped a switch within her.

Like her safety has suddenly been guaranteed.

I grab my bin and sit beside Ashlea at the kitchen table. The silence is killing me, so I lean into her ear and whisper, "What's going on?"

Ashlea whips her head in my direction and shrugs. "I guess the end is setting in on everyone. We're only a few rounds away, after all. And with how dangerous some of these competitions are…*things could end even sooner.*"

Most of her words bounce off my ears, not having a chance for my mind to absorb them. But the last words stick. *Things could end even sooner.* This is the second time she's hinted that the parameters of the Enterprize may not be as set in stone as the creators intended. But…surely, she's referencing what she said just before her cryptic statement. The competitions *have* been getting increasingly dangerous…I wouldn't be surprised if we lost a few people in this next Executive contest. Thankfully, I'm exempt from the next one, making me safe from the Authority's deadly game. But it's equally terrifying not being able to control my fate.

The silence is all-consuming. Not a single person in the house says a word for the entirety of the day. It's so nauseating that I must remove myself from the communal spaces. I even lock myself in my bedroom and curl into my sheets, desperate for sleep to consume me until it's time to vote tomorrow.

When the delicate knocks rasp against my door, I'm awakened with a start. My ears are sensitive to any minor sound, and I've found myself jumping at every little disturbance. I quickly push my hair back, patting it down at the edges. Then, I slide open the door and smile when Ashlea's kind eyes poke through the entrance. She sends me a gentle grin and nods. "Hey."

I raise my eyebrows. "Hey."

She doesn't move from the doorway, so I open the slab wider to invite her in. She shakes her head, putting up a palm. "Look…I'm sorry I've been acting strange. It's just…with the finals looming…and Seb visiting…" She sighs. "It's all been a lot to process. But…I wanted to make it up to you." I tilt my head, waiting for her to continue. "Follow me…I have a surprise for you."

I narrow my eyes, wondering what she could possibly have done to raise my spirits. Resources in this house are sparse, so I don't get my hopes up. She holds my hand, leading me through the communal bedroom. I glance at Artemis, who lies with his eyes on the ceiling, and quickly return my gaze to the back of Ashlea's head before he notices. Oblivious to my slip up, Ashlea leads me down the spiral steps. Once on the second floor, she asks me to close my eyes and puts her hands on my shoulders, guiding me the rest of the way. We slowly descend the final steps and march to the living room in an all-too-familiar way.

Through my dark eyelids, I imagine Mace leading me to our fort, where we spent our last night together. My thoughts end abruptly when Ashlea directs me to open my eyes.

My knees buckle, and I nearly collapse onto the carpet. Before me sits the same structure Mace built for me only days ago. Suddenly, the air tastes metallic. Like rounds ago, the couches are pushed together, and sheets have been stuffed to form a roof. I cover my mouth and peek through the entrance, but no mattresses make up the floor. There are just a few spare sheets and pillows to round out the crevices, so where the fort lacks in comfort, it more than makes up for in privacy. One mattress, however, leans beside one of the longer blue couches. Unlike Mace's fort, it stands as a door pushed to the side, making the fortress a home.

"Ashlea," I whisper. "I…I…why?"

She smiles, voice shaking. "You've just…you've been through so much."

I shake my head, tears pooling in the corners of my eyes. "I can't…not…not without…"

She rests a hand on my shoulder. "I know." Silence reigns, but she cuts it quick. "I wasn't sure how you'd take it…but *please*…can you just give it a chance?"

"Ashlea —"

Her eyes are desperate, and her jaw locks. There's a twisting in my chest, screaming that this is no simple gesture. Her voice might sound stable, but the desperation in her body language tells another story.

"*Please, Iris.* Can I show you what I've put together?"

My eyes narrow on her, and I realize this fort has nothing to do with Mace. It's not just the missing mattress floor…it's the reinforced privacy. *But if she didn't want the others to overhear us, she could have just gone to my room.* Welcoming whatever reasoning she has, I force a convincing smile and oblige with her request. My heart pounds in my ears, fear coursing through my veins at going back to a place where I want my original memory to be forever preserved. But I slouch into a crawl anyway, Ashlea following close behind. I push myself as far back as possible, giving her room to join me.

"See?!" she says, her voice ending with a high-pitched screech. I squint my eyes, flabbergasted at her behavior. "And look!" she shouts. "I bet Mace didn't have a door!" She slides the mattress across the floor with a few huffs, enclosing our space entirely. We aren't in total darkness; enough light bursts through the blankets to see her eyes drop and sweat perspire on her brow. I open my mouth to protest, but she raises her eyebrows, *begging* me to play along. She drops her smile and widens her eyes, forcing one final squeal. "I knew you'd love it! I just wanted to bring you some comfort, that's all! With everything you've been through!"

I lean forward and nod, joining in on her act. "It's incredible…really. It means the world to me."

She nods, her breath shaky. "You relax now…you deserve it."

With the act finally up, Ashlea scoots closer to me and grips my arm, digging her nails into my skin. She watches my lips, so I know she can read my concern. "What's going on?" I mouth. She stretches her lips into a thin line and scoots centimeters from my ear, covering her mouth. She's so quiet I can barely hear her words.

"They can't hear us…in here. If we whisper…the couches will absorb the sound."

I turn to her, covering my lips as she did. "They? What are you talking about?"

Ashlea takes a deep breath, biting her lip. When she leans toward me, her words are so soft that I almost ask her to repeat herself. But there's no mistaking what she says, as evidenced by the adrenaline shooting into my heart.

"We're getting out of here…*tonight*."

Chapter 71

I'm readying myself to gasp but force the noise from exiting my throat. Instead, my jaw drops to the floor, and I sit in awe, eyes wide and palms shaking. I mouth, "What?" as dramatically as I can, and Ashlea quickly puts a finger to her lips.

She leans in again. This time, her words blur into one another. "Everyone's in on it…everyone but you and Artemis." She takes a deep breath and calms herself, ensuring the cameras can't pick up her voice. "Since Seb came in…something switched within me. Kylah knows she's as good as dead, and Destry is terrified the vote could flip. Finian…he *knows* he won't win. We came up with a plan together…Destry took the lead once I told him what I knew."

I shake my head wildly. The information is *too much*. They're trying to escape? *Tonight?* I don't know how to process it, so I let her continue. She takes another breath to check her volume before resuming her explanation.

"The solitary confinement door…it's broken. Ever since you slammed it, it's been impossible to lock. You saw me a few days ago…I walked right through it without any resistance. The arena door is the same." She nods as if confirming it to herself. "The lock to the arena is busted from all the slamming. I guess Destry's last smash did it in." My jaw doesn't rise from the floor. *Both doors are busted?* "Well…when you and Artemis were in solitary…he mentioned a door. A door…*leading somewhere else.*" I recall the wedge in the white cushioned cell. It was barely distinguishable from the rest of the room, but we knew it was straight across from the entrance. "He mentioned computers in there…apparently, there were people in there, Iris. Watching the cameras." I remember this detail as well but squint my eyes, nonetheless, still confused about where she's going with this. "That door *has* to lead somewhere. That's where Curi came in from…and Destry's teacher…and *Seb*." Another deep breath. "And it's also where they all *left* the Enterprize."

I shift, overwhelmed. *There are just too many flaws in her plan.* I move my hand to her ear. "Yeah, but it was *locked*, Ashlea. You even tried to get in…but you couldn't."

She shakes her head, putting her hands back against my ear. "That's where you're wrong. I *could*." I breathe in to speak, but she doesn't allow me to interject. "It's a push door, Iris. One of those futuristic ones. You push it in, and *then* it slides open. I heard them lock it, and I tried everything to get through. After enough effort…I was able to crack it open. I guess the water damage screwed it up or something, but that door *can't* lock. I…the second I realized it was broken, I slid it shut before they could catch their mistake.

As badly as I wanted to risk it, I knew it wasn't the time. How far would I have made it with every camera pointed at me? Whatever sorry excuse for a lock they're using, we could *easily* barge it open." Her eyes glisten, and she covers her mouth with her hands again. "Even though it was only a crack, I saw it. The computers. They're *unarmed* in there, Iris. It's just the producers' offices."

I shake my head, putting a hand up to stop her. *This plan is absurd.* I keep my volume low but can't hide the urgency in my voice. "And after that? Where do you go? You got a map of this place somewhere?" I take a deep breath, widening my hands. "Even if you could manage to sneak into the arena, through solitary confinement, and into those offices, you really think there won't be guards waiting for you in the halls? Where do you think they come from, Ashlea? They'd be waiting for you…they'd see you on the cameras."

She smiles. "Not if we had a distraction." I lean back, but she doesn't remove her hands from my ear. "If you don't want to join us…fine. But…if you could distract the producers…we could end this. We could get you *out*." She shakes her head. "We could get you back to your sister."

I press my hands against my temples. "No, listen!" She covers her mouth quickly, realizing her volume is too loud. She takes a moment to gather herself before continuing. "Your love story…it's been the center of this game. You *know* it. If you could…maybe…add some *flair* to that…it *could* be enough to get them all invested. Maybe…invested enough to *abandon their posts*."

My eyes widen. "What are you suggesting?"

She bites her lip before leaning back in. "Artemis doesn't know about the plan. He's in the dark and won't suspect a thing. If you could somehow…*entice* him…"

"No." The word comes out of my lips before I can stop it. But I'm firm in my decision. I will *not* compromise my morals to entertain a mediocre escape plan that will likely end with all of them getting killed.

"Iris, listen to me," she pleads.

"No…you listen to *me*," I fight back, still hushing my voice. "I've said goodbye to him…it's *done*. I can't…I can't go back on that."

"Iris, this isn't about *you*." Ashlea's voice is harsh and warm against my ear. "If you just…*pretend*…wouldn't *that* be payback for all he's put you through?" I absorb the words, and they sting, so I sit still, dumbfounded. "It's just for the movement of the plan…that's all! When we're all out of here, none of that will matter!"

I bit my lip. "Then he should be in on it, too."

She shakes her head, no doubt in her eyes. "Then it'll be fake. It'll only be convincing if he believes it's true." She's right. If manipulating Artemis can get us out of here…surely, it's worth it. And if he knew it was an act…his heart wouldn't be in it. It *has* to be this way. But her plan is still flawed. Even if we distract the producers long enough to let the others barge into their chambers, where will they go?

"But if you make it into the production room…what will you do? Where will you go…what if they fight back?"

She spreads her lips into a fine line. "Then we fight harder." I shake my head, desperate for her to give it up. But her eyes…there's no changing her mind. If I can't convince her to stay back…the least I can do is get her to reason through her actions.

"Where will you go?" I ask. "You burst through that room…then what? And if you *do* get all the way out of the building…where will you even go? We don't know how to get back home; they blocked out our windows on the way here."

She takes a deep breath. "Once we barge in on the producers…we fight like hell. Then we shut down their computers…and shut off the Enterprize. They can't tell where we are if we force their eyes shut. Then we *run*. As far away from this place as we can."

"What about Seb?"

She stiffens at his name. It takes her a moment, but she coughs up an answer. "We're gonna split up. The others…they're going to run for home. But Destry and I…we're gonna find our captives. And we're gonna do whatever it takes to release them."

I shake my head. "You *really* think this is gonna work?"

She nods slowly. "Kylah and Finian do, too. Even Destry." She pauses. "You may not like them, Iris…but they're people too. If we can all get out of here alive…why not try?" Another deep breath. "And Iris…if you're making out with Artemis…we'll be the *least* of their worries."

The words are a slap in the face. What is she expecting of me? I can't *fix* our relationship in a matter of hours. And Mace…I *can't* do that to Mace. *But he would want me to live*…so what choice do I have? If I refuse this plan, my friends are guaranteed to die. But if I participate…they might have a chance. And after everything I've been through, I will do anything to protect my friends. If that means hurting Artemis one last time…then he better have a Band-Aid ready.

Ashlea leans in again. "When we shut down the Enterprize, the cameras will lose power. The whole house might…that's your cue to run. Do you understand me?"

I shake my head. "And if it doesn't work?"

She looks at the ground before meeting my gaze. "Then you and Artemis are the final two."

My eyes squint, hating that possibility. Because if nothing else, it means that Ashlea is dead. She continues, reading my mind. "Iris…this plan might not work. But if *definitely* won't if we don't have you on board. We *need* you." She looks down again. "If you want me to live…then give the best performance of your life."

A tear forms in the corner of my eye. "There's no changing your mind?"

She shakes her head. "Ever since Seb walked in here…my mind's been made up. I…I *have* to get out of here. And I'm not killing you to do that. You might not agree with the plan…but do we have your word that you will try?"

I keep still for a moment, weighing my options. She's right. If I refuse, they're going to carry on with their plan without a distraction, guaranteeing their death. This might not work…but if it does? We're free. I can rescue Curi…no more blood on my hands. And if it doesn't work…

I'm four steps closer to winning this thing.

"You have my word," I whisper. She smiles, but there's sadness in her eyes. She brings me in for a hug, and her shaky breath heaves against my shoulder.

"I'm so lucky that I got to meet you," she whispers. "Thank you, Iris. For everything you've done for me…for your friendship."

I smile. "Thank you for yours. But…this isn't the end. Because I'll see you soon…right?"

She nods, smiling. "Right." Wiping her tears, she leans in one last time. "You come in at 3:20am. *That's* when you start talking to Artemis. Try to drag him into your bedroom and do whatever shocking thing you can to distract the producers. Twenty minutes later…that's when we begin."

I nod, fighting the tears already streaming down my cheeks. "I love you, Ashlea."

She hugs me tight. "I love you too, Iris. I hope you get the peace you so deserve."

I nod, still smiling. She wipes a tear from my cheek, resting her palm on it for a few seconds. Finally, she crawls out of the fort, shutting the mattress door behind her.

I slump against the couch and breathe my last moments of normal air. Because in five hours, *everything* is going to change.

Chapter 72

I don't move from the fort, even when one of my housemates shuts off the lights. I figure it would make sense to those controlling the cameras if I stayed in here and pretended to sleep. Ashlea made it for me, after all.

The more I consider her plan, the higher my hopes become. There are flaws, of course. But Ashlea's confidence must come from somewhere, and I have to have faith in her if we want any chance of success. That's why I didn't say a proper goodbye, and I didn't let myself cry longer than a couple minutes. Why would I get emotional when this isn't the last time I will see her?

Whenever I doubt her mission's parameters, I envision a future in which we successfully escape. If everything goes according to plan…I can go *home*. Every piece is in place. There's just *one* fatal flaw…Artemis. Not only do I have to speak with him…but I have to do something so drastic that the producers won't have their eyes anywhere near the arena.

The conversation itself is enough to have me weaving my hands through the living room carpet, trembling against the mattress fort. The physical part of my act is almost less intimidating because my words have to be powerful enough to force every person watching to abandon their posts and grant us their undivided attention. It's terrifying, humiliating, and intimidating to have this much responsibility. But if I'm honest with myself, I know the *real* reason I've bitten my nails to their nubs.

I'm going to tell Artemis the truth.

And it's going to destroy me.

Hugging my arms around my chest, I peek my head out of the mattress wall. The red numbers are the only light in the room, so I can read them clearly.

02:50.38

I take a deep breath. *Thirty more minutes.* Leaning against one of the couch walls, my legs become restless. My stomach churns, and my insides quiver. Not only will my vulnerability in this conversation be uncomfortable, but if my words aren't powerful enough and the group in the arena gets killed in the process…I don't know what I'm going to do. I tried to kill Artemis once but couldn't follow through with it. The only thing offering me comfort is the probability that I wouldn't *really* be responsible for his demise. If he loses the final competition…his fate is sealed. I shake my head vigorously. *I can't think about that.* This will work, and when we get out of here, I will deny the truth behind my words to Artemis, and he will understand that they were necessary for his survival.

Once I block that from my mind, the waiting is grueling. When I can't take it anymore, I leave my fortress. Putting the furniture back will make the time pass, so I slowly remove the mattress door, tear down the sheets, and shift the couches to where they belong. I fold and unfold the blankets, trying to crease them to perfection. The viewers will think I'm trying to keep my sanity. Because how could they know what's going down within the hour?

Once everything is finally organized, I lean the mattress against the wall. I don't have the strength or energy to lift it back up the stairs, so I sit on the floor and rest against it. I take my time, braiding my fishtail down my back repeatedly, desperate to make time pass quickly. Once satisfied, a quick twist of my waist shows the numbers on the clock, and my heart catches in my throat.

03:16.22

It's time.

I take a shaky breath and mentally rehearse my script. Only I will know that the words are true. Because when all is said and done, I will deny their authenticity, claiming it was a survival tactic. The viewers will mistake my nerves as anxiety for revealing my genuine feelings. But apart from Artemis, my housemates will know otherwise.

I rise from the floor, forcing one foot in front of the other. I gander into the bathroom, but all the stalls are open. The only person residing in that metal chamber is Finian, and he doesn't take a second look at me from the floor. The kitchen and living room are empty when I pass, so I begin climbing the steps. A quick look at the arena door confirms that it's unlocked. The light from the cracks is more than I'm used to, so there's an obvious malfunction. Once in the communal bedroom, it takes a moment to identify anything in the darkness. Still, I successfully make out the shapes of the others. When my eyes adjust, I even find Ashlea smiling in the corner of the room. Destry and Kylah whisper by Destry's mattress, and Artemis lays on his cot with a pillow over his head. I freeze when I see his motionless limbs and take one last shaky breath before approaching him.

Inches from his mattress, I squat on the floor and poke his hand, hanging off the side. He wakes with a start, darting his gaze around the room before his eyes settle on mine. "Iris?" he asks, eyes widening. "What…is everything okay?"

I bite my lip, letting my left eyebrow quiver. Because as much as I want to put on a good performance, this conversation makes me more apprehensive than I've *ever* felt before. I steer into the skid and whisper, letting my shaky voice reflect my anxiety. "Can…can we talk?"

It takes him a moment to register my request, but once he does, he nods so fast I fear he'll give himself whiplash. He rises from his cot, and a hunch in my chest forces the words out. "Can…can I hold your hand?" The question feels awkward, but I can't help myself. I know the audience will go crazy for it, so when he nods and grabs my palm with his enormous one, I imagine crowds cheering around the world.

His hand is unnatural in mine. Above that, it's fit is awkward. My palm suddenly feels like half the size of his, and the sweat on his fingers instantly coats my knuckles. It reminds me that my oncoming speech to him may be real…but he will *never* be Mace.

I open the door, taking one last look at my housemates. None of them glance in my direction, not even Ashlea. The twist in my chest may suggest otherwise, but I'm grateful for her lack of acknowledgment. With the stakes this high, a simple wave could ruin everything. I bite my lip hard, hoping blood doesn't rush down my face. I pull Artemis into my bedroom and turn the lights on, doing everything I can to get the audience to focus on us *and not on the ones shrouded in darkness.*

Before letting go of his palm, I'm struck with an idea that makes me nauseas. Before talking myself out of it, I pull him toward my mattress and hop on, patting the area beside me. He tilts his head, deciphering my intention. *I* don't even know what I'm trying to do…but I know the audience will love it, so I don't stop.

"What's going on, Iris?" he asks, widening his eyes as he settles beside me. "Are you okay?"

It takes me a moment, but I force a nod. Tears fight their way through, and I let them flow. *But they aren't for Artemis.* As uncomfortable as this conversation will be, I bring the chances of its failure to the front of my mind. *I may never see Ashlea again.* Artemis may never know these tears aren't for him, but what he doesn't know won't hurt him.

I take a deep breath, wiping my eyes. "Look…I'm about to say a lot…and I want you to *listen.*" Another deep breath. "I don't want you to interrupt…just…let me get through it all at once, or I don't think I'll be able to get it out at all."

His eyes narrow on me, and he squeezes my hand. "Iris, you're scaring me."

I smile. "No…it's not bad…not *really.*" He tilts his head before sandwiching my hand with both of his. It's painful, really, how manipulative I am. But when all is said and done…only truth will leave my lips.

"Arty," I start, inviting the nickname back into my vocabulary. He may be dead to me, but holding a grudge doesn't help us escape. "When I first met you…I immediately gravitated toward you." He watches me intently, holding onto my every word. "I remember locking eyes with you upstairs before any of us knew each other. Even then…you had some kind of power over me. I remember you making everyone laugh when you introduced yourself. I remember you falling from your disk in the first round, and I remember colliding with the pole because I couldn't take my eyes off you. I remember…I remember…"

"What, Iris? What do you remember?" For the first time in ages, I get lost in his blue eyes. Finally, the words don't feel like a chore to voice.

They come out like I've been holding them back for *years*.

"I remember the butterflies I got…*every time* you spoke to me."

His eyes contort in pain, but he doesn't interrupt. He simply brings my palm to his lips and plants a gentle kiss on the top.

I glance at our hands, interlocked, and swallow. "I remember you getting close to Mercedes…and when you told me you kissed her…" I gaze back into his eyes. "I don't think I've ever had a worse night of sleep." He stiffens up, inviting me to keep going. "And when the Sola stuff happened…it *destroyed* me. Because everyone told me to stay away from you. But…I couldn't." His eyes glisten. "I knew…somehow, that you weren't evil. Everyone else saw it as murder. But…I saw it as protection."

I rest a palm on his cheek and watch him shutter behind the touch. He quickly rebounds, leaning into the gesture. "And when we studied that night in the second round…I felt so…*alive*. You brought out a new side of me…and I *loved* it." I shut my eyes. "And I could see it in your eyes, Arty. I knew you had fallen in love with me that night. But…I was *with* somebody else. There was nothing I could do. So, I fought my feelings…I tried not to believe they were true. I thought if I convinced you they weren't real, maybe I'd start to believe it myself." This is true, but it's something I would never admit on my own terms. Still, it's worth everything if the audience loves it.

Finally, I open my eyes and see the tears beginning to pour out of his. I scrunch my eyes together, forcing myself to get through it all. "I think about solitary confinement *all* the time. How you saved me. How…how worried you were. And when you basically revived me in there? I thought about how there was *nothing* I could ever do to repay you and how I *never* wanted to live without you."

He takes one of his palms from my hand and wipes his tears. Watching him listen to my confession physically hurts my heart. At the same time, in the back of my mind, I know the operation has begun. My housemates must be infiltrating the arena by now, so I must pull out everything I have to keep the producer's eyes on me.

"In my dreams…you're *always* there." I choke up but don't fight it. *The more drama, the better.* I squeeze his hand hard. "Artemis…that day in solitary confinement…when I thought I was going to die…and you showed up…I…I…"

"What is it, Iris?" The question is delicate. Supportive. *Desperate.* So, I lock onto his gaze and melt into his ocean eyes. Suddenly, my mission disappears from all the files of my brain. The only thing that matters to me is the truth, and something Ashlea said mysteriously fights its way back into my consciousness. *When you love somebody, you want to tell them.* And it *kills* you not to.

Finally, the moment has arrived. Everything around me fades until Artemis and I are the only two people in the world. Every horror and trauma I've fought through for weeks disappears, and I'm in this moment alone with Artemis, only truth standing in my way.

So, when he stares at me with ocean eyes, and my heart explodes, I let the words slip from my lips.

"I fell completely head over heels in love with you that night."

A tear falls down his cheek, and he wraps me into a hug. All my other feelings disappear, relief taking their place. *Finally, the truth is out.* I love Artemis. And for just this frame in time, ignoring everything he's done to me and seeing him weep with liberation…

I feel *extraordinary*.

But one emotion fights from the depths of my soul, and I can't hold it off for long. Once it finally comes up…there's nothing I can do. I burst into tears, succumbing to my guilt that despite this being *real*…it's *also* manipulation.

"Iris," he cries. "I'm so sorry…I'm so sorry for *everything* I've done to you. I love you with all my heart…I'll *always* love you."

Our sobs harmonize with one another as my own knife twists through my chest. Because I know what must be done next. If I don't have everyone's attention yet, I am going to have it now. *It's my last chance to save Ashlea.* And I hate to admit it…but part of me craves it so badly I feel like I'll *die* without it. So, finally, when our weeps die down, I back out of our hug and look him directly in his eyes. My heart breaks with the words, knowing my true love for Mace…but when I force them out, I feel a sick mixture of relief, guilt, shame, and lust.

"I never stopped loving you," I say. His blue pearls make my heart skip a beat, so I give one final blow.

"I'm in love with you, Artemis. I *always* will be."

He smiles, letting a chuckle of joy and relief escape his lips. I match his grin, and when he leans in for a kiss, I don't stop him.

In fact, when he grabs the side of my face, I press my palms against both of his cheeks and squeeze. Our breaths become one, and I arch my chest toward him when his fingers creep into my hair, scrunching it by the handful. Like last time, his lips are intoxicating, and I never want to break from their embrace. And now…*I don't have to.* So, instead of backing out, I grab his chest, feeling for every crevice in his chiseled torso, electricity coursing through me as I outline each individual sector of his muscular trunk. I'm drawn to his body and finally squeeze his bicep, triggering him to twist until his tongue dances around the roof of my mouth.

Not only do I physically never want to let him go, but my heart swells to twice its size at his touch. Finally, every terrible thing that he has done to me fades into the abyss. I know that once we escape…things will be different. The regret and hatred may creep their way back in. But for now, in this moment, I can no longer deny how I feel.

I am in love with Artemis. And I never want to let him go.

Without thinking, I grip the edges of his shirt and pull the fabric over his head in one swift motion. He reaches for mine, pausing our kiss for confirmation. I grab his arms and guide them to force the cotton over my head. The physical consent *unleashes* him, and in seconds, I'm lying on my back with him on top of me, squeezing my chest below my bra.

At the same time, his other palm gently pulls my hair behind me, and I moan from the tingling between my legs. I reach for his pants and pull like my life depends on it, leaving just his boxers to separate his desire from my hands. He pulls me in and shifts his weight against my pelvis, and I *unravel.*

I shift my hips with him, and he gasps against my lips. He pushes harder against me, and I wrap around him, touching every piece of him I can reach. The pressure is so delicious that I forget the purpose of this ploy. The thought is merely a blip as I allow myself to melt into him, the warmth in my pelvis spreading with each thrust he exerts. I shouldn't be doing this. But my *god,* it feels fantastic. It doesn't take much before I reach into his drawers and he flops onto his side, pushing his own hands into mine.

I lean into his hand until it's inches from where I *need* it to be. I never want to leave his embrace, and I *hate* myself for denying his magnetic field for so long. So, when the pounding begins on my door, it takes me a moment to return to reality. He lets go of my lips and removes his hand, backing away from me. "No," I whimper, leaning back toward the deep touch I crave. But Artemis's head is turned, and when he whips his expression back to me, I can feel his confusion and terror.

"What's that?"

We can't hear anything on the other side. The doors are soundproof, so all we can distinguish is the desperate pounding of fists on the cold, metal surface. When I finally realize what this could mean, I jump from my mattress and spring for the door, yanking my top over my neck. Artemis is just pulling his clothes back over himself when I open the iron slab.

"It didn't work," Destry shouts, blood splattered on his tattered clothes. He rests his hands on his knees, putting his head between them. "It didn't work!" he screams at the top of his lungs, kicking the wall beside him.

"What didn't work? What is he talking about?" Artemis asks. Silence ensues, so I touch Destry's shoulder and feel him freeze.

"Destry?" I ask.

He lifts his head slowly, letting the tears fall down his cheeks. When the words come, Artemis reaches out to keep me from collapsing.

"They're all dead."

ROUND 9

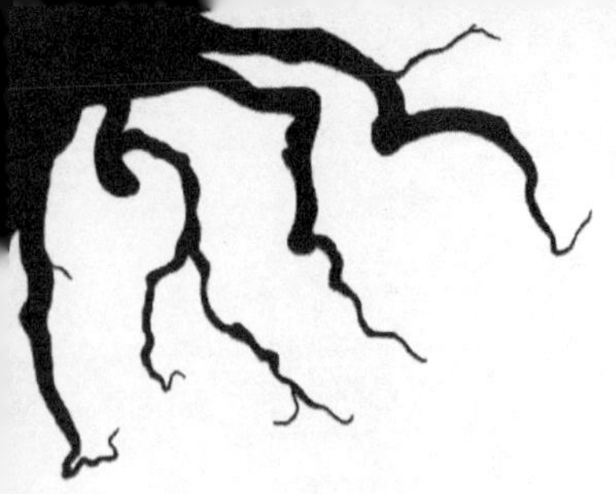

Chapter 73

"Who's all dead? Who is he talking about, Iris?" Artemis asks, eyes darting between me and Destry. I'm in the comfort of Arty's arms, but I still lack the strength to explain. Instead, I ignore him and beg for more information.

"What...happened?" I ask clearly, with determination. "Tell us *exactly* what happened."

Destry rubs his face with both palms and falls to the ground. "We got into the arena no problem...then into solitary...but past then...past then..."

"Tell us!" I shout.

He freezes. "It was a trap. It's like they *knew* we were coming. Ashlea opened the production room door...from there...it was over."

Artemis shifts so he's facing me. "Iris, what is he talking about? Production room? What's going on?" Artemis's eyes are wide, and his tone is aggressive, frustrated that nobody's giving him information.

"There was a plan!" Destry shouts. "We were trying to get out of here! Everyone was in on it..."

"Not me and Iris!" he yells.

Destry locks eyes with me, and my muscles lock up. Artemis feels my shift, so he sets me softly on the ground and gazes into my eyes. "*Right?*"

I bite my lip, and more tears come. *Ashlea is gone. My performance wasn't good enough. Artemis...Artemis...*

His eyes turn cold. "Answer me, Iris. You owe me that." I'm not entirely sure how much I owe him, considering everything he's done to me. But the pain in his eyes shatters my heart, so I reach desperately for him.

"They...they asked me to cause a distraction. So, they could get out...if you knew...then it wouldn't have been convincing."

"Convincing?" His eyes are daggers, and he backs away from my motionless body on the ground. "So, none of that was real? All of it was a game? Some part of your master plan?"

"No...no that's not what it was!" I scream. The plan was to distract the masses from the operation in the arena. But that kiss...

That kiss changed *everything*.

Before I can defend myself further, the three of us freeze from an all-too-familiar metallic sound.

"CONVICTS," the robotic voice commands. I sink into the floor and grasp for something to hang onto, but I only manage to slide my hands against the smooth surface behind me. "YOU HAVE THIRTY SECONDS TO ENTER THE ARENA. TWENTY-NINE. TWENTY-EIGHT."

Destry rocks back and forth on the ground, covering his ears. My jaw drops, and Artemis stands frozen from shock and betrayal. There's almost nothing I can say to get them to move, so I jolt into action, grabbing their arms and pulling them forward.

"We can talk about this later! But if we don't move now, they'll shoot us all!"

Artemis comes out of his daze, but his expression remains unchanged. He yanks his arm away from me and runs to Destry's right. I grab Destry's left side, and we drag him through the communal bedroom and down toward the second floor. We reach the arena door with ten seconds remaining, and I yank it open, letting it slam into the wall behind us. Artemis and I force Destry down the steps, and when we finally reach the center of the arena, we collapse onto the turf in a heap.

Silence ensues as our breaths steady. Once I've regained enough composure, I glance at the solitary confinement room to find it closed, shielding us from our dead housemates. *Thank God.* The blood on Destry's shirt is enough evidence of their murders...we don't need to see their lifeless corpses to believe they're *gone.*

I sprawl on the turf while waiting for the robotic voice to provide further instruction. Only it doesn't.

What *does* appear is *far* worse.

His silky white button-down may not have been enough to put me on edge. But when I see the top two buttons undone and the black pointed shoes shining before me, my heart stops.

"Welcome, convicts," the warden says with a toothy grin. "Congratulations on the final three."

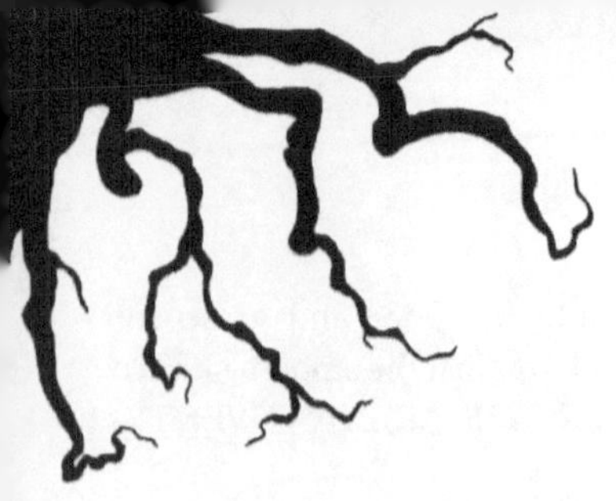

Chapter 74

I'm frozen to the turf. My breath catches in my throat, and adrenaline shoots down my spine. Destry is the first to rise, bolting for the metal stairwell. I want to call after him, but I can't bring myself to move. So, I watch helplessly as Destry sprints away from us.

The warden laughs, hunching over from his cackles. "Why, Destry? You, I have been *especially* excited to chat with." The warden strolls past us, watching Destry stride up the rickety steps. "I wouldn't try that if I were you!" he calls as Destry reaches the top.

The iron door barges open, letting three Authority guards pile through. With guns pointed forward, they crowd Destry down the steps. He shoots his arms up, walking slowly and mechanically, submitting to their commands.

"That's it," the warden beams. The second Destry reaches the turf, the warden approaches with open arms. "Now, let me make a formal introduction." He closes his arms around Destry and rocks him back and forth, the latter entirely still with his arms at his sides. Destry's red in the face and his eyes scream *terror*. "There we go," the warden purrs, releasing Destry from his grasp and patting him on the back. "You, I have been *particularly* fond of."

Destry's eyes dilate, silently urging us to *run*. He grips his palms into fists, keeping himself from making another attempt. The warden keeps a gentle hand on Destry's back, leading him toward the center of the arena. "Let's get you back with your friends. Then we can get things started!"

Destry stares at the ground, sliding his feet along the turf. When he finally arrives, the warden diverts his walk to the wall ahead of us, opening his arms when he arrives.

"As I was saying before your friend got a little...*too* excited." The warden laughs. "*Welcome* to the final three." Smiling, he puts his hands in his pockets and kicks out his legs. "Moments ago, a group of your housemates performed a...*cowardly* attempt at escape, therefore forfeiting..." He stares at the ceiling before laughing. "Well, their lives! But as I said many days ago, if you fail to follow instructions, you will be treated *accordingly*." His smile doesn't fade, adding a deeper layer of terror to his words. Another shiver runs down my spine. I make no attempt at rising from the turf, too frightened to move. *Ashlea's dead. And now, the warden is going to kill us, too.*

The warden takes a big gulp of air, trailing his eyes to the ceiling. He sighs with a smile as he reverts his stare back to us. "Because of the circumstances, it's hardly right to allow the vote to commence. Kylah has been eliminated. As far as I am concerned, she was the one expelled." He claps his hands in front of his torso. "On top of that, it certainly wouldn't be…shall I say…*fair*…to ban Iris from competing today. It's almost as if…" he chuckles to himself. "It's almost as if your Executive reign never happened!"

I stare at him with daggers in my eyes. Nothing about this situation is amusing. In fact, every part of it is horrendous. But I know better than to protest, so I don't interrupt.

"So that brings me to the question I am sure you are all wondering…what now?" He rocks onto his toes, bouncing. "Well, with three convicts remaining, whoever wins this round will have a free pass to the final two. Congratulations!" *He winks.* "He or she will have the responsibility of deciding who will join them. We'll do away with the anonymity of the vote…you'll find out who the winner is sending to the firing squad easily enough with only a single vote being cast." He steps forward, and I see Destry flinch in my periphery. "Win this competition, and you're the Executive." He laughs again, holding a stitch in his side. "As to why *I'm* here? Surely, you didn't think I wouldn't come back to host?" His smile doesn't fade. "Destry knows what I mean. Don't you, boy?"

I whip my attention to Destry, but he simply shakes his head, covering his face with his palms. The warden quickly moves on from him, sidestepping until the wall has no obstructions. Once he stops shuffling, he leans forward, his grin somehow getting wider. "I call this one the 'Reminiscence Record'. You will be shown a series of…*scenes*." He laughs again. "At the end, you will be asked to recall details from what you are shown. Answer the most questions correctly, and you are the round 9 Executive!"

I squint at him, disgusted at how much joy he is getting from tormenting us. *Scenes?* Scenes from *what?* Before I have a chance to think, the lights shut off, surrounding us with darkness. *I can't see my hands in front of my face.* It feels like it takes hours to regain my sense of sight, and I breathe so hard that I start to hyperventilate. I reach for Artemis's hand absentmindedly and find it, gripping tight. There's no passion on his end, his palm limp in mine.

I'm so terrified that I don't even care.

Finally, a projector paints a picture on the wall ahead of us, and my jaw drops from recognition. Every feature is familiar, from the giant mattress to the plush sofa across from it. *I'm staring at a picture of the Executive bedroom.* Rather, I'm watching a *video* from it. In this scene, Lagiacrus sits atop the Executive bed, looking as fresh as I've ever seen him. His clothes aren't tattered, but there's a smudge of dirt on the front. Artemis sits on the couch across from him, and Destry stands between the two. A small timestamp is on the bottom of the footage, labeling the scene as "DAY 1." I try and focus on the details in the photo, but when the speaking begins, I'm sucked into the scene.

"An alliance of us three, then?" Lagiacrus asks, scratching the skull beneath his dirty blonde hair. Destry paces back and forth but claps once at the question.

"Yes. We make up the heart…but we won't achieve much with only three of us." He bites his lip and nods. "We're gonna need some tier-two members."

Artemis leans forward. "So, we get a few more people involved. And at the end…we cut them off one by one." He looks at the others. "So, we'd be the final three."

"Exactly," Destry says, pointing at him. "But we can't make it to the final three without some protection. I'm thinking…we add two or three more. Mace was strong out there…he could be a good addition."

"I want Finian too," Lagiacrus shares. The others look at him with raised eyebrows, so he puts his hand out and shrugs. "He looks weak. We could use somebody on our team who only serves as a number for voting reasons."

Destry flicks his eyes to the corner, considering the idea. Then he shrugs with defeat. "Mace and Finian it is."

Silence ensues while Artemis looks around the room. He seems to be building the courage to speak, and once he finally does, he leans forward and finds his voice. "What about Iris?"

Destry and Lagiacrus share a look. Destry's the first to talk. "What *about* Iris?"

Artemis shrugs. "She's got her brother with her. Could be a two-for-one deal."

Destry considers it, then looks at Lagiacrus, letting him make the final decision. Finally, Lagiacrus nods. "Sure, add the girl."

Artemis nods, biting his lip. I can tell he's fighting a smile, but the others won't have noticed. I glance at the Artemis physically beside me in real-time, but he's watching the film intently, ignoring my gaze. I forget that we're supposed to be taking in the details, so I stand to ensure that I keep my concentration. I whip my attention back to the video just as the Destry in the scene mentions something about convincing the add-ons that we're in the main alliance and encouraging us to string along others.

"Yeah, but let them come up with that," Lagiacrus suggests. "Make them think it's their idea." I roll my eyes at the screen, realizing they *always* planned to manipulate me. I try to move past it, but film Destry's final comment drops my jaw.

"But when all is said and done, the girl is the first to go. Understood?"

"Understood," Lagiacrus says. The film Artemis nods.

The scene fades, and I turn to the real-time Destry, who's only a few steps away from me. "What the *hell*, man?"

He doesn't even look in my direction. "It was *day 1*, Iris." I roll my eyes and look back at the screen. In my periphery, Artemis has risen, towering behind me. He walks forward to get a closer look, still avoiding my gaze. But when the next image shows the communal restroom showers on Day 4, Artemis takes a step back, covering his mouth. The second I look back at the screen, I understand why.

The picture shows Artemis and Mercedes snuggling on the tile. A shower curtain conceals them from the rest of the bathroom, and their swell wounds look freshly shrunken from the second competition. *This must have been taken while I was chatting with Ashlea in the communal bedroom.* And if that timeline is correct…this scene happened only *moments* before I agreed to help Artemis with the riddles. I shake my head, wiping the thought, and focus on the picture before me. In the video, Artemis is leaning against the wall, and Mercedes is sprawled across his lap, her head on his shoulder. Their hands are interlocked when he leans in for a kiss. A kiss with lips that, *seconds ago,* were exploring *mine.*

"I love you, Artemis," she says, beaming. He shakes his head with a grin and kisses her again.

Real-time Artemis says my name, but I put my hand up to stop him. Not only do I need to see what's happening for the purpose of the game…but I'm *dying* to know why he's scared for me to watch this.

"Mercedes," the Artemis in the scene begins. "You know that I would die for you, right?" My eyes widen, and my eyebrows rise so high they nearly disappear into my hairline. Mercedes blinks flirtatiously, grinning at him.

"I would die for you too, Artemis."

She leans in, and in seconds, he's sucking on her upper lip. Their tongues go flying into each other's mouths, deepening the frown on my lips. I ignore the maniacal cackles from the warden on my right and force myself to focus on the scene. *They must be showing us this for a reason.* Artemis backs away, laughing. "No, really, Mercedes." In the scene, Artemis's eyes harden. "Back home…there's nothing left for me there. No reason for me to want to make it back." He pushes a lock of blonde hair behind her ear, and I grip my stomach from nausea. "Before I met you…there was no reason to keep fighting. No reason to try. But with you…" Mercedes's lip quivers. "You're my reason to live."

She fully hops onto his lap and holds his face in her hands, kissing him so hard he *moans.* I close my eyes, desperate to look away. *But I can't.* If I want *any* chance at survival, I have to watch the man I love make out on the shower floor with another woman. My lips curl, and I swallow hard. When the Artemis in the film willingly tears off his shirt, grabs Mercedes's ass, and reaches into her bra with desperation in his eyes, I audibly gasp. Mercedes holds his carved torso like I did *minutes* ago and removes her own top, pulling his hands back to her plentiful chest. Watching is killing me, but I refuse to divert my gaze. If there's a detail in here that I miss because I can't handle these images, I lose. My gaze hardens when it hits me. *That's the point of this competition.* To show us scenes that will infuriate us enough to hinder our senses.

But I'll be damned if *Mercedes* is the reason I walk out that front door for execution.

The scene fades when they finally come up for air, and my throat aches, signaling the onset of tears. I fight them back, not allowing Artemis to see the damage he's done. I swallow as I wait for the next scene to appear, hoping to avoid Artemis's gaze. But in an instant, he's resting a hand on my shoulder, *pleading* in my ear. "Iris…that was nothing. It meant *nothing!* I was just trying to survive…"

I spin toward him with venom flinging from my lips. "Is that why you said all of that to me, too? To *survive?*"

He shakes his head wildly. "No…of course not! It's *always* been you, Iris! Always!"

Suddenly, he's forgotten the chance that my love confession was an act. Unsurprisingly, I forget about it too. Because now that I've seen this…I don't know *what* was real. "You made me feel so bad. So…*terrible* about everything that happened! And

461

this entire time, you really *were* just recycling the same script you used on Mercedes! After all this time, she was right about you!"

"No, Iris! That wasn't it! I swear—"

I put my hand up, ending his pleas. Because as infuriated as I am, there is more to be shown. And I won't let Artemis's antics screw me over *again*.

The new scene projects against the arena wall, and I squeeze my eyes shut briefly, trying to ignore the duplicity of the only ally I have left. He'd been honest with me about his plan to string Mercedes along for as long as possible, accidentally becoming her friend in the process. But ever since his breakdown at her hypothermic demise, I've subconsciously had second thoughts about his true feelings toward her. As self-conceded as it is, my stomach hardens at the thought that the words I've cherished for so long were shared with another woman. And if he's telling me the truth that he didn't love Mercedes…he lied to her so *effortlessly*. I shiver at what that could mean for me. Because with how open he's been about never even having *feelings* for Mercedes, I can't help but wonder if anything he ever said to me was true.

I open my eyes to a scene in the living room. The bottom of the video continues the timeline, highlighting day 8. On a long blue couch, Lagiacrus sits, staring blankly at the blue wall across from him. His back is as straight as a board, and he's motionless against the plush cushions, even as Destry enters the picture, settling beside him. After matching Lagiacrus's posture and gaze, Destry speaks without emotion.

"That wasn't right…putting you through that."

For a moment, it's as if Lagiacrus doesn't even realize he has a visitor. He doesn't acknowledge Destry's comment or entertain his presence. I nod to myself when I recall where this date lies along the competition timeline. On day 8, I was trapped with Artemis in solitary confinement. That can only mean that this footage immediately follows the conclusion of the Suffering Sanctuary. Lagiacrus, being the last convict eliminated from the competition, was granted the punishment of having to watch the capture of every housemate, concluding with his own, looped through thrice. The Lagiacrus on the screen is fresh off the traumatic footage, so it's understandable why he's numb to everything around him.

The on-screen Destry rubs his hands together uncomfortably, working up the courage to say what's really on his mind. Finally, despite there being nobody on the bottom floor to overhear him, he lowers his voice to a whisper.

"You…you watched my capture, didn't you?"

It seems like an obvious answer, but the real time Destry stands 10 meters away from me, rapidly shaking his head. I tilt my neck as he covers his gaping jaw. *Why is he so mortified that this conversation is being aired?*

Softly, slowly, and almost mechanically, Lagiacrus nods his head in confirmation. On-screen, Destry lets out a long huff of shaky breath. They sit in silence once again, the two staring at the blue wall across from them.

Still watching the rampart in a trance, Lagiacrus finally answers. "Your parents are alive….aren't they?"

I step closer, not believing what I am hearing. *What could he possibly have seen that would confirm this suspicion?* I stop moving when Destry answers.

"Yes," he whispers softly, hugging his arms around his chest. He sighs as he readjusts his hands, leaning forward to cover his face. I search the real-time arena, trying to fit this new information together. If this conversation reflects the truth…was it his father who visited him just before Curi was brought in?

"Are you gonna tell me why?" Lagiacrus asks blankly, still in a trance.

Destry shakes his head, his hands still covering his face. "No. I can't."

Lagiacrus nods, not questioning further. Before the footage fades, Destry turns to Lagiacrus and rests a hand on his back. Hushed and rushed, word vomit spews from his lips, explaining everything except why his parents are alive.

"If I told you, it would blow up my game…which would blow up yours because you're associated with me. Look, Lagiacrus. I want to play this game with you until the end. Final two…you and me. If you make it out…you'll see why they're alive—why I'm here. But can you just trust me right now? It doesn't matter what I did to get here. It's in the past. What matters is the future, and I plan to go to the end with you."

After an extended absence of movement, Lagiacrus nods in agreement. Destry extends his hand, awaiting acceptance. Lagiacrus lifts his own palm and shakes, still deflecting his gaze from Destry.

"Until the end," Destry says.

"Until the end," Lagiacrus confirms.

As the scene fades, I fight the urge to stare at Artemis, curious if he knew about that conversation. I embrace my anger at him and keep my eyes on the screen, waiting for the next projection to appear.

The second the image shows, I fall to my knees.

I'm watching the communal bathroom on day 9, but my gaze is far from the timestamp. Mace's violet eyes shine just as beautifully as the first time I saw them. My visibility is fuzzy from the moisture in my eyes, so I rub them to see the picture clearly. On the screen, I'm in the room with him, but…I barely recognize myself. This is the first time I've seen Mace since he walked out the Enterprize door, and now…my heart shatters all over again.

In real time, a tear falls down my cheek as Mace's voice travels back to me. "He's driving me nuts," he spits. "Destry's the biggest kiss-ass I've ever seen. If he doesn't shut up soon, I'm gonna lose it."

It takes all of a second for me to recognize this conversation. I know exactly how it plays out, so instead of studying the small details, I stare at Mace lovingly, wishing I could get him to jump through the screen. I don't move my eyes from him as the on-screen Iris asks, "Was he this bad yesterday, too?" I watch Mace as he meticulously unties my t-shirt bandage and choke on my tears when he apologizes for making me wince.

"It's like he's done a complete one-eighty. His insecurities are starting to show…now he just sucks up to whoever's in power. I know he's close with Artemis, but he almost never left Mercedes's room yesterday. It's just sketchy…if people don't catch on soon, he might win this whole thing."

The scene fades as quickly as it appeared, and I sob on the turf. Nobody comes to comfort me, so I curl my knees to my chest and rock back and forth, hiding my face with my arms. I know the scene was intended to pin Destry against me, but I couldn't care less. Because for one extraordinary moment…I got to see Mace again.

If only we talked more shit about Destry.

I wipe my eyes when the moment of darkness ends, signaling the start of another scene. This time, we're on day 10. I roll my eyes hard when I recognize where we are and unfold my arms from my legs. The enormous bathroom with marble surfaces reflects across the full-body mirrors, creating the illusion that several bathtubs exist. But what clues me into the moment is that only two people stand in this Executive bathroom, both of which were not in power.

On the right stands Artemis.

On the left is me.

I shake my head, ashamed of what comes next. The turmoil comes back to me when the Iris from day 10 stares at Artemis, her voice cracking. "If you ever cared about me, for even a *second*…you would tell me what's going on!"

The past Artemis grabs the back of my neck, and our eyes shut together as he presses me against the door. I always imagined I'd be the only person to feel how magical that kiss was. But as I watch Artemis's lips move with mine, there's no mistaking that my body melts into his. Previous me hooks the back of his knees with my curious leg and yanks his arm forward, pulling him in deeper. My stomach suddenly twists with embarrassment as I catch Destry watching the screen intensely. He narrows his eyes as I'm shown rubbing my hand across Artemis's torso, inching toward the waistband of his pants. Knowing that the previous me is about to pull away, current me stretches my lips into a thin line, waiting for that rejection to set in on Artemis for a second time. I squeeze my fists, eager for the crucial moment that will solidify me as an honest woman.

But just before I back away, the picture fades.

I throw my hands up. "What the hell?" I turn to Destry. "I back out of it. I was just about to back out of it!"

Destry rolls his eyes, ignoring my pleas. Not only is this film intended to turn us against one another…it's manipulating true events, so they don't accurately depict what happened. Everything being shown is *real*…but if there's no context…how is that fair?

The next scene pops in before I have time to throw a fit. It's still day 10, but we're watching the Executive bedroom instead of the bathroom. Destry and Artemis are the only occupants. Artemis sits on the bed with his head in his hands while Destry stands before him. When Artemis peeks up at Destry, his eyes are red, and he hiccups from tears. Destry's posture is straight, but his hands are behind his head, and he's pacing.

"I screwed up, man. Big time, I screwed up," Artemis repeats into his hands, rocking back and forth.

"Artemis!" Destry shouts in frustration. "Pull yourself together, man!"

A fresh bout of sobs escapes Artemis's throat as he erupts into full-body trembles. Destry halts in front of Artemis and leans down so he's inches from his face. Destry takes a deep breath before grabbing Arty's shoulder and yanking him forward.

"Deep breaths, Artemis! You have to stay calm! You've gotta tell me what happened so I can *help* you. It can't possibly be as bad as you think!"

The Artemis behind me shifts uncomfortably in real time, running his hands through his hair. To my left, Destry doesn't spare me a glance, not moving his eyes from the footage.

Finally catching his breath, the Artemis on day 10 removes his hands from his face. His eyes are puffy, and he sniffs back tears, hardly able to meet Destry's gaze.

"I…Iris…I couldn't…help myself…I just had to know what it would be like…"

Destry jumps back, covering his mouth with both hands.

"You didn't."

Artemis nods, squeezing his lips together to hold back tears.

Destry's eyes are wide when he voices his suspicion. "You kissed her."

"You don't understand, Destry! I…I *love* her!"

Day 10 Destry turns away from Artemis, hands still covering his mouth. "You….had…." Destry groans. When he whips back toward Artemis, his voice *bellows*. "*ONE JOB!* Get Mercedes on our team and stay *away* from the drama. Not kiss our ally's girlfriend!"

"I didn't mean to! I…I lost control of myself. I lost control of my emotions! I couldn't stop myself because, in the moment, it didn't feel wrong!"

Hands wide, Destry yells, "HOW COULD IT NOT FEEL WRONG!?"

Artemis rises from the mattress. "Destry, you don't understand! You weren't there in solitary confinement! We had a real connection! I wouldn't have kissed her if I didn't think she felt the same way!"

Destry continues to pace, ignoring Artemis in his path.

"I told you," Destry says calmly, "to *stay away* from her. You *knew* you were falling for her, so what did I say?"

Artemis shakes his head and chokes on his tears. "You said to stop talking to her." I bite my lip and swallow. *Artemis didn't ignore me because he thought it would help him get over me.* He ignored me because *Destry* told him to.

"And what did you do?" Destry asks, getting in Arty's face.

Artemis doesn't respond. Instead, he wipes his tears and leans forward, hands on his knees. Destry backs away and paces until Artemis's voice returns.

"You *don't* understand. Ignoring her was *killing* me. More importantly, it was hurting *her*." He takes a deep breath. "Destry, I can't hurt her anymore. I won't do it!" he shouts.

Destry steps back in a fury. "HER?" He laughs without humor. "We're way past hurting HER. What about me! *Us?* Your *alliance?!* Do we mean *nothing* to you?"

This only deepens Artemis's sobs, but Destry doesn't relent.

"Only *one* person makes it out of here alive, Artemis. You want to know how to *guarantee* that won't be you?" He swallows before shouting. "FALL IN LOVE! With the worst *possible* person here!"

Artemis weeps so loudly that there's no way he can hear Destry. In a bout of rage, Destry runs to the nearest table and launches it across the room. In response, Artemis lunges away from the bed and swings his fist into the wall. In real-time, I take a step back, deflating. Pieces of drywall fall out with his fist, and he crumbles to the ground, palm bleeding.

On the screen, Artemis drops to the floor and hangs his head between his knees, holding his injured palm. Several minutes pass as the on-screen Destry gathers his composure. After a deep breath, he squats beside Artemis and lowers his voice.

"I don't understand...you wanted Mercedes."

Artemis shakes his head hard, making his intentions clear. "It was never Mercedes. From the second I met Iris, it was her. It's *always* been her. Mace just beat me to the punch."

"Why do you think she loves you back?" Destry questions, keeping his voice steady. "Did she tell you that?"

Artemis wipes his eyes. "No...but I can read her. She won't admit it because she's scared of what would happen to her if she did. If nothing else...she won't confirm her feelings for me because she's *terrified* of hurting Mace." I roll my eyes at the screen. *All this time, he's been denying telling others I'm in love with him. He might think his words in this video are sweet, but all they do is prove him a liar.*

Artemis pauses. "Nobody's ever cared about me the way that she does. When I...when the Sola incident happened...*she* approached *me.* Nobody else reached out. Nobody else seemed to care if I was alright. But *she did.* She said her opinion of me never changed, not even after what I had done." Arty shakes his head. "Nobody would even *talk* to me then, Destry! But Iris...she was still in my corner, despite everyone else taking the opposite side. She cared so much, like, actually *genuinely* cared that I wasn't broken up over it." He stares directly into Destry's eyes.

"Before that, I felt so alone...but *not* around her. And when I got eliminated from the second competition right off the bat, she found me. She even gave me *lessons.* Who the hell does that? When this game is life or death, who would ever take the time to help their competitor? And that night she tutored me...you should have been there that night." He shakes his head, the hint of a grin on his lips. "It was one of the best nights of my life. And don't even get me *started* on solitary confinement. She might be terrified to admit it...but I know the feelings are reciprocated. She's *always* been there for me. I didn't just make this up out of nowhere!"

Destry nods, absorbing Artemis's monologue. Softly, he whispers in a trance, "It takes two to tango."

Artemis's eyes widen in the video. "*No.* Don't you blame this on her." He starts stuttering, desperately searching for the right words. "This is *not* her fault, Destry…she's…she's innocent! *I* kissed *her.*" Real-time Destry huffs, not believing a word the old Artemis said. The film Artemis continues, bringing my attention back to the screen. "I just…I guess I thought she wouldn't treat me that way if she didn't love me back. Why would she stand with me through that Sola stuff if she didn't have feelings for me? *Who would do that?*" Artemis puts his hands up, catching himself. "I'm not saying this has any merit. It's just what I thought about at that moment. *That's* why I thought she wanted me to kiss her. And with the way she reciprocated it before backing away…I think I'm right."

I grimace, snarling at the projection. Because Arty's absolutely correct that I initially kissed him back. But to reveal that to Destry, the *least* trustworthy person in the house?

It's traitorous.

In the video, Destry ruffles his hand through his hair, closing his eyes. After a few deep breaths, he turns to Artemis and pats him on the back. "We need a new game plan…this *cannot* come back to us. If you want to make it out of this, you must do *exactly* as I say. Do you understand? That means that whatever happens from here…you need to go along with it. I will take care of this…you're going to be okay."

Artemis nods, wiping away fresh tears. Just as Destry opens his mouth to reveal his master plan, the memory fades, shrouding us in darkness.

Nobody makes a sound as the new image appears. I wouldn't even know what to say if I had the opportunity. I can't decipher whether I'm angry at Artemis for divulging our entire relationship to Destry or touched by his vulnerability concerning his feelings for me. Before I can truly reflect on the scene, the living room materializes on the rampart, day 13 plastered on the bottom right.

Kylah is perched atop a blue sofa, and the clock shows that it's just past six in the morning. Destry is beside her, leaning close to her ear. His words are quiet, but they have been amplified so we can hear their conversation.

"I'm really sorry," he says to Kylah. Her nostrils flare as she shakes her head.

"I can't believe they kissed…after *everything* she did to get me on her side."

I lean forward the second it clicks. *They're talking about me.* This scene…it happens a few hours before Kylah blows up on me in the kitchen. In my periphery, the Destry in the arena groans and throws his hands to his sides. His annoyance only makes me more intrigued by their conversation, so I focus back on the screen.

"You know…Artemis and I are close. He tells me *everything*," he starts, placing a soothing hand on her back. "And the things Iris has done since leaving solitary…it makes my blood curl." I scrunch my eyes. *What did I supposedly do since leaving solitary confinement?*

Kylah just blinks until Destry cups his hand to her ear. Then, the lies *pour* in. "She's *always* been jealous of you, you know. Of how close you are with Lunar. Apparently, that's *all* she could talk about in solitary. Artemis told me himself." He takes a deep breath. "She wants you *dead*."

My jaw drops to the floor. I turn to Destry, but he avoids my gaze. I look back at the screen when Kylah whisper-shouts, "*What?*"

The Destry on the screen nods. "She created an alliance to do it. 'Dial FM,' she called it. We were always meant to make group decisions, but when it came down to you…she's always been…*persistent.*"

I laugh without humor as Kylah shakes her head. "That *fucking* bitch."

In the video, Destry wipes away a fake tear. "It pains me to tell you this, Kylah. It's just so fucked up."

"Yeah, because it's a lie," I whisper under my breath, not removing my eyes from the projection.

"I know," Kylah says to Destry. "But you need to tell me *everything*."

Destry nods, coughing to cover a fake sob. "I just…this destroys me…"

Kylah turns toward him and puts her hand on his knee. He gulps before gazing into her eyes and answering. "Artemis said his biggest regret was not resisting Iris kissing him."

I shake my head as a smile spreads across my lips. "Oh, my fucking god," I say, turning to Destry.

The video continues, oblivious to my commentary. "She came on to him the entire time. It was *all* her. Artemis himself told me. I'm sorry, Kylah…but she lied to your face. You can't trust her." He shakes his head. "But if you ask me, she's screwed over the wrong people. I think it's about time we made a stand."

I don't look away from the Destry in the arena, not even when Kylah's last words are amplified on the speakers. "We're gonna end that bitch." Destry gives her a side hug, but she doesn't flinch. "What else do I need to know?" she asks him. Destry leans back into her ear, and the scene fades, not letting us see what other lies Destry fed her.

"It was you," I growl at Destry. "*You* were the one spreading lies…the whole time, it was *you.*"

"I told you what happened between us because I *trusted* you!" Artemis yells, pressing a finger in Destry's face. "And you manipulated everything I said for your own personal gain!"

Destry grabs Arty's wrist and forces it to his side. "And I trusted *you* to vote out Mace! So, I guess we're both feeling slighted, huh?"

The warden bursts out laughing, sending another chill down my spine. "Perfect," he says, clapping his hands. I ignore him because my mind is doing cartwheels. *Artemis wasn't lying to me…he wasn't the one who told Kylah I was after her, and he never claimed I initiated our romance. The only thing Artemis ever did wrong was trust his stupid friend that he wouldn't twist everything to paint me in a bad light. Artemis didn't* tell Kylah I created Dial. He didn't even tell Destry that I encouraged his romantic advances. In fact, he *begged* Destry to believe it was entirely Artemis's fault and pleaded that he not put the blame on me. This entire time…Artemis was defending me.

This is a terrible moment for the realization to hit because the next scene shows me in a fury. It's another scene from day 13. By the looks of it, I just found out that Artemis "betrayed" me. Mace sits on my bed, and I'm so shaken by Destry's underground manipulation that I barely feel the warmth of Mace's artificial presence. I hardly listen as I stomp into the picture, screaming. "That lying, womanizing, *manipulating* piece of shit!"

I cringe as I say unforgivable things about Artemis for rumors he never started. By the time the video cuts out, my face is burning, and I'm drenched with sweat. I'm so ashamed, but only have the energy to muster a short explanation. "I didn't know Destry planted everything."

Artemis nods, not even looking in my direction. Whether he's too focused on studying the footage or too heartbroken from my horrific insults, my stomach sinks to the floor. I force myself to press forward, but I can't help wondering how much irreversible damage I have inflicted.

The next scene seeps an eerie feeling into my bones. We find ourselves in the communal bathroom on day 14, but that's far from what has me clutching my arms to my chest. Artemis has Lunar cornered against a shower stall, and despite dying to know the truth about this confrontation, I'm terrified. Because the second I get confirmation that Lunar betrayed me, I know there is never going back.

Artemis is pinning Lunar against the tile wall, trapping him in the stall. His grip isn't firm enough to inflict injury but is intimidating enough to establish his dominance. Artemis is baring his teeth when he whispers, "She got to you, didn't she?"

Lunar's eyes dart around the room, and his face is absent of color. "I don't know what you're talking about."

"Answer me!" Artemis demands. My stomach drops the second I see that Lunar's legs are trembling. *He's lying.* Artemis leans in closer. "You're voting out Mace, aren't you? Don't deny it!"

"What's it to you?" Lunar argues. "You get your vote, and I get mine!"

Artemis shakes his head. "You're making a *huge* mistake." He's foaming at the mouth. "Mace isn't coming after you! And Iris will *always* pick you over him!"

"Says the man that made out with my sister and tried to get her *killed* by lying about it," Lunar spits. "Don't pretend to care about Iris now! You're the reason Mace is on Death Row in the first place!"

Artemis winces at Lunar's words. He lowers my brother to the floor but doesn't remove his grip. "But that doesn't mean he has to die. *You* can prevent it."

Lunar shakes his head. "My mind is made up."

I gasp when Artemis smashes Lunar against the wall. "You can't do this!"

Lunar grimaces. "But Kylah said—"

"She's not the boss of you!" The second Artemis lets go of him, Lunar stumbles toward the curtain.

"It's none of your business!"

I finally step into the frame, demanding answers. I only get a few shouts in before the scene fades. The second it does, my throat burns. Artemis not only fought for Mace's survival, but he took the blame for Lunar's betrayal. *All for me.*

The next two scenes flip through quickly, both taking place on day 15. First, Lunar approaches the voting podium with tears streaming down his cheeks. He hovers his hand over Mace's button and covers his eyes, pressing down to seal Mace's fate. I step back, taking the force of a thousand figurative bullets through my chest. There's no denying it anymore. *Lunar is the reason Mace is dead.*

The next video comes and goes as quickly as the last one. As if I needed any more confirmation that Artemis has always been on my side, he reaches the podium and slams down Finian's button without hesitation. When the screen darkens, I look at the real-time Artemis, tears blurring my vision. He simply stares at the ground, rubbing his shoe on the turf.

The next scene is a more significant jump in the timeline. The picture is dim, and day 22 is stamped across the bottom corner. When I realize we're watching night vision, my jaw drops. *This footage is from today.*

"No," real-life Destry mumbles to himself. Gaining his voice, he turns to the warden and shouts, "Shut this off! *Right now*, shut it off!"

The warden leans against the rampart wall and crosses his legs with a toothy grin. "Why, Destry, would I stop the footage when it's *just* starting to get interesting?"

Destry's screams echo as he collapses to the floor. I exchange a confused look with Artemis but quickly return my gaze to the screen. Anticipating Destry's tantrum, the producers have provided subtitles so we can follow the dialogue.

Finian, Ashlea, and Kylah crouch outside the arena door in the darkness, Destry at their rear. My heart pounds through my chest at the sight of Ashlea, but I try and ignore it to focus on the screen. Ashlea counts to three quietly, barely perceptively, as they crack open the arena door. The four of them rush into the dome, tiptoe down the flimsy staircase, and jog toward the solitary confinement room. In the picture, Destry is looking around, *searching* the arena for something. He lags a few steps behind the others but doesn't divert from their paths.

They finally reach the solitary confinement door and regroup, Ashlea taking the lead.

"When we open this door, I'll press the next one in…then we storm in together. Ready?" The others nod, Destry's being so insignificant that I nearly miss it. When the solitary confinement door opens and the lights pour on, real-time Destry pleads even *harder* that the warden shut off the film.

The warden's only response is *chilling* laughter.

In the film, Finian blocks his eyes from the brightness. "Are we caught?"

"Keep pushing!" Ashlea demands. She presses in the door at an odd angle and backs away as it slides open, revealing rows of computers and screens. Half the producers are watching Artemis and I make out in the Executive bedroom while the other half have their eyes on the escape group. Ashlea and Kylah storm in, obstructing our view of the footage. Finian peeks his head into the computer room but opts not to follow the girls. When he turns around to Destry at the exit, Finian's eyes are wide, as if he's just seen a ghost. In the film, Destry hasn't moved from the back of the room, sweat pouring down his face.

The real-time Destry screams so loud, I swear the arena walls vibrate. "STOP IT! NOW!"

We collectively ignore him, so he slams his fists on the ground, trying to distract us from watching the screen. I step forward until he's out of my periphery and narrow my eyes on the projection. My breath catches in my throat when Ashlea and Kylah sprint back into the picture. "Destry, open the door!" Kylah shouts, auburn curls flying behind her. "OPEN THE D—"

The bullets cut her off before she can finish.

Kylah falls to the ground of the solitary confinement room, blood splattering the others. Destry's shirt is painted with her blood, and his face is struck with horror.

"OPEN THE DOOR!" Ashlea yells, only steps away from him.

Real-time Destry jumps in front of the screen, trying to obstruct our view. But the film simply projects onto him, doing little to cover the events that unfold. Even if he could have blocked out a portion of the screen…

It would never be enough to hide what he's done.

In the video, Destry yanks the solitary confinement door open and leaps through. Just when I think he's going to hold it for the others, the picture transforms into a split screen, showing the inside of the solitary confinement room on the left and the arena on the right. On-screen, Destry doesn't hesitate.

He slams his back against the door, forcing all his weight on the exit…*trapping the others in a shooting range.*

"No," I whisper, putting a hand to my mouth to cover my gasp. Tears blur my vision again as Ashlea and Finian pound on the door, begging Destry to let them out. They launch their own bodies against the tiled exit, but Destry's too strong. His muscles flex and sweat pours down his extremities as he forces himself against the door. After a vicious struggle between both groups, five Authority guards storm into the solitary confinement room with machine guns locked and loaded.

I don't need to hear the shots to know they're dead. Because without anybody pushing from the other side, the door slams shut, leaving nothing but a deafening echo.

When the screen goes dark, I fall to my knees. Destry's cries cut through my thoughts, but I'm empty of empathy. I'm just about to yell at him for the death of my best friend but freeze when the warden steps forward, clapping in sync with his slow, malicious march.

"What. A. Performance." The warden only stops once Destry is within his reach. I watch the two from the turf, all my weight on my hands and knees. The warden tries to pick Destry up, but the boy won't budge. "Come now," the warden smiles, pointing at the screen. "You wouldn't want to miss the best one!"

My eyes narrow. *What else could there possibly be left to show?* I watch the wall as the image appears. The second it does, Destry's cries stop altogether.

This time, the date has a longer label. It's so long that it covers the entire bottom of the picture. My jaw drops when I read it.

"2 DAYS BEFORE THE ENTERPRIZE."

We see an empty office with white counters and floors. The only person present sits at the back, clicking away at his computer. At first, I don't recognize him in his gray suit. But the black pointed-toed shoes give him away.

The warden.

A knock sounds on the door closest to him. He smiles, rises, and turns the knob.

A bald man enters. In my periphery, Destry covers his gaping mouth.

"You wanted to see me, sir?" the man asks the warden, hands clasped in front of him.

"Yes, please take a seat," the warden replies, gesturing to an empty chair beside his desk. He has his usual malicious smile, but this time...it's forced. The two men sit on opposite sides of the table in silence, the bald man waiting for the warden to speak. When it strikes me where I've seen this man before, I gasp.

In the Executive competition.

He's the man who visited Destry.

"Randolph, I wanted to congratulate you on a wonderful production," the warden starts. "The Enterprize trials yielded significant results...just the outcomes you predicted. When faced with life or death, the convicts turned on one another without a second thought. It showed...the *true* consequences of crime. Benefit for the self, with death for all else. *Brilliant.*" The bald man nods with a soft smile, expressing mumbled thanks. The warden opens his palms in congratulations. "You'll be happy to hear that my colleagues and I are confident we can start the live show within the next week."

Randolph nods, hands still clasped stiffly in front of him. Silence passes between them as the video warden rises, starting to pace. "I truly believe that, with your creation, we can cut crime rates in half. I mean, torturing their children?" He laughs, spit flinging from his lips. "There's no way parents will continue to commit crimes when their children will be made to suffer on live television." He sighs. "Thanks to your hard work, long hours, and *admirable* creativity, we have the solution...the Enterprize."

My jaw drops. The bald man...that one that encouraged Destry in the arena...he...*created* the Enterprize?

The video warden claps. "But that's not really why you're here, is it?" The warden plants his hands on his desk and leans forward, inches from Randolph.

The bald man backs away. "Sir?"

The warden lowers his voice, still smiling. "We have been working *tirelessly* on this year's selection of subjects. The only thing holding us back from starting is…well, the lack of eligible participants."

Randolph narrows his eyes. "Pardon me, sir, but *surely* that can't be the case. There are thousands of eligible candidates…if you would just let me help in the selection process—"

"No, Randolph, that will not be necessary." The warden is short with his words. For the first time since meeting him, his smile is *gone*. He leans even closer to the bald man, gritting his teeth. "I am going to ask you this *one* time, Randy. It has come to my attention that somebody within the Enterprize Department has…been *hiding* something. Do you have anything you would like to share with me?"

The man doesn't flinch. "No, sir. Of course not. If I knew what you were referring to…you'd be the first person I'd tell. I promise!"

The warden stretches his lips into a smile that doesn't reach his eyes. "Of course." He straightens his back, turns to his computer, and pulls up a photo. I can't see the features until he turns the screen. Once he does, my stomach drops to my knees.

Destry.

Randolph's eyes widen, and his jaw drops to the floor. The warden simply laughs. "Recognize this kid, do you?"

Randolph puts his hands up in surrender, his face glowing red. "Wait…I can explain!"

The warden's smile disappears again. "Explain *what*, Randolph? That you've been hiding an illegal child in your floorboards for the past eighteen years? That you've been creating this experiment for the offspring of eligible convicts when you have been hiding an illicit child in your home all this time?" His eyes dilate with fury. "Cynthia is forty. Tell me, Randolph. How does that math add up?"

Randolph falls to his knees, his hands in prayer. "Please…please don't hurt him! I can fix this…I can!"

The warden ignores him. "In three days, we are going to send your son into the Enterprize to fight to the death with the other convicts. You and Cynthia will pay the price of your crimes, and he will *watch* as you fall to the floor with bullets in your chest." He waves a hand. "That's the end of it. Prepare your wife for this reality, and don't dare think about leaving. We have already set up twenty-four-hour surveillance on your home, so attempt escape, and all *three* of you will be dead with the click of a button."

Randolph cries. "You can't do this to me! We're friends…aren't we?"

The warden's eyes narrow. "We're colleagues. That is until your actions went against *everything* we have worked for." He spits on the floor. "Goodbye, Randolph."

The warden takes a few steps toward the door when Randolph bursts. "WAIT!" he shouts. "WHAT IF I KNOW OF ANOTHER ILLEGAL CHILD?"

The warden turns around slowly, eyes narrowed on the bald man.

"Keep Destry out of the games…and I'll give them to you." He swallows. "There's two of them…brother and sister."

My heart skips a beat, waiting for the final blow.

"They live in the Central Ascendency."

Chapter 75

My ears are ringing. I want to yell, but what would I say? Destry's words after Mace's death float back to me.

The real person to be mad at is out there, somewhere, free. *They are the person to blame for putting you here.*

After all this time…it was Destry.

Destry's parents turned me in.

The air is too thin. I can't breathe. I can only hold my chest, forcing my heart to keep beating. "No," I finally whisper. "*No.*"

In the video, the warden's eyes narrow. "Keep talking."

Randolph crawls toward him. "The parents work in the ration industry…they're how we found a way to hide Destry all these years. Somebody caught wind of our situation when my boy was three…we had a mutual friend. They told me about their kids…well, a single child at the time. There are two of them now…they live under the floorboards. They're around Destry's age." He chokes on his words. "They'd be perfect candidates for the Enterprize."

The warden taps his chin. "And you kept this information to yourself all this time?"

Randolph cries. "I couldn't risk you learning about Destry! He…*he's everything!*" he wails, the tears seeming to never end. After minutes of the warden tapping his foot while Randolph sobs, the warden snaps.

"ENOUGH!" he yells, cutting off Randolph's tears. "You find them for me, and we send them in. Then, and *only* then, do I let you and Cynthia live."

Randolph covers his gaping mouth. "Thank you!" he screeches, reaching for the warden. "THANK YOU!"

The warden backs away before Randy can touch him. "But Destry still goes."

Randy's eyes narrow. "But…but—"

"That's the deal. Take it or leave it." The warden squats so he's at eye level with Randolph. "There will be no restriction on the information you can give him about the game. But as of the second they enter, you are on leave. You are not allowed in the offices until the Enterprize has a *single* winner. If you want to ensure that's Destry, I encourage you to get started on strategy."

Without another word, he turns on his heel and slams the door behind him. The screen fades to black, leaving us with nothing but Randolph's desperate muttering.

The lights flick back on the second the audio cuts off, leaving us in complete silence. I struggle to move. The only motion I can manage is my hand to my eyes, shielding them from the bright lights in the arena. *Destry is… an illegal child like me? His father…created the Enterprize? His family…*

His family is the reason Lunar and I were sent here to die, and our parents were murdered on our living room floor.

"Question 1!" I scramble to my feet so fast I fall back to my knees. The warden watches me, laughing. "Slow down there, girl!" He steps toward me and motions to the other side of the arena. "Booths were installed on the back wall during the presentation. Take your places, and we'll get started." I take a deep breath before forcing myself up and rushing toward the daises. They're the same as the house quiz but with three chambers instead of six. This time, there's no hologram plank. Only a black button sits in the center of each podium. I settle into the middle compartment, the partitions separating me from the others. Once I catch my breath, I notice that my button is *glowing*.

The warden clears his throat. "Very well, then. I'm going to ask you a series of questions. If you think you know the answer, press your button and speak when your name is called. The first person to get three correct answers is the new Executive. Answer a question incorrectly, and you are eliminated from the competition." He pauses, stepping forward with a mischievous grin.

"Question 1," he repeats. "Which day 11 scene was shown first?"

I smash my button, but my name isn't called. "Artemis?" the warden prompts.

"Iris and I kissing."

"That is *CORRECT!*" the warden yells, arms wide. I curse under my breath, but the warden moves on so quickly he cuts off my profanity.

"Question 2: Who was the third person to enter the arena on Day 22?"

What? How could I have concentrated on that when Destry was *screaming* the entire time?

There's a pounding on my right, followed by the warden's voice. "Destry?"

Damn it.

"Kylah," he answers, voice surprisingly steady.

"CORRECT!" the warden shouts again. I roll my eyes at his enthusiasm and smash my hand against the partition. *I'm so close to winning that pardon and seeing Curi…I can't blow this now.* I shake my head, trying to get it on straight. By the time he starts reading the third question, I'm ready.

"What was the sixth scene shown?" I rattle through the options in my head, counting as quickly as possible. Once I have the answer, I hit my button so hard I'm surprised it doesn't break.

"Iris?"

"Artemis telling Destry he has feelings for me."

"CORRECT!" The warden does a sadistic twirl. "The score is tied, every convict with one point!"

I grit my teeth, not letting my anger at the warden distract me. I hover my palm over the button, waiting for the fourth question.

"Who said the following quote: 'You're making a big mistake'?"

Destry did when Artemis confessed his love for me. I bash my button, but it's Destry's name that leaves the warden's lips.

"Artemis," Destry answers.

"CORRECT!" I scoff. *Wait…*Artemis said that to Lunar when he was trying to convince him to keep Mace! I wipe a bead of sweat off my forehead, thankful I didn't get the chance to answer.

"Question 5!" The warden leaps toward us, dancing like a ballerina. "What was the second scene shown on day 15?"

I don't even need to think about it. I bash my button and smile when my name is called.

"Artemis voting out Finian!"

"CORRECT!" *Destry and I are tied…*the next correct vote may win.

The warden clears his throat. "Question 6: What was the first name said in the final video?"

Oh no. I…I don't know! It's silent until there's pounding on my left.

"Artemis!" the warden asks.

"Randolph?"

"CORRECT!" the warden blares, jumping up and down.

My grin is imperceptible to the human eye, but I'm mentally leaping with joy. *Destry can't win this.* Now that Artemis is tied with us, we might actually have a chance at getting Destry out. I stretch my neck side to side, not letting myself get nervous that there hasn't been a single wrong answer yet. I sweat as I settle for a new strategy. Regardless of whether I know this next answer or not, I *must* press the button first. Otherwise…I'm as good as dead.

"Well, isn't this exciting?" The warden smiles, staring at us in silence. "The next correct answer wins!" he says, taunting us as he twiddles his fingers in our direction. Once he finally stops laughing, he continues the game. "Question 7." He waits, letting the silence linger. The audience will love this, but for us, it's *torture*. My heart pounds in my ears. I squint my eyes, scanning the warden's lips as if I'll be able to read them before the words come out. He gazes into my eyes and smiles.

Then asks the question at hyper speed.

"Who wanted Iris in the Dial alliance?"

I smash my button the second the words leave his lips, but the others are doing the same. We all bash our buttons repeatedly as if the first click didn't go through. Once we finally settle down, the warden takes a deep breath.

"You know the light on your button turns off if you're the first to press it, right?"

My eyes widen. I whip my attention to the glowing light on my podium, and my stomach sinks. *It's not me.* I launch my waist over my pedestal, searching for the dim button. I first look left, desperate for Arty's to be dim. I gasp when I see it.

It's glowing like lava.

Destry cheers. "ARTEMIS DID! ARTEMIS WANTED HER!"

The warden smiles. "Congratulations, Destry. You are the new Executive."

Chapter 76

My hand goes limp against the partition. I turn around and sag against my podium, pressing my hands against my temples. *I was so close.* And after everything Destry's done, I wanted to be the one to personally escort him to the firing squad. Nobody at the Enterprize initially deserved to be here, not even Destry. But now, after locking my housemates in a cellar to die, turning his side of the house against me over rumors *he* created, and plotting to kill me off at the first opportunity…

Destry deserves to die slowly, painfully, and without mercy.

It's a shame, really, what the Enterprize has forced me to become. But I feel no remorse at my desire for Destry to experience a torturous death. *He's* the reason I'm at the Enterprize. *And he's the reason I will die here.*

"Boy, am I proud of you!" the warden shouts. His voice gets closer as he strolls toward the daises, but I don't turn to greet him. Instead, I slide down the podium and fall to the turf, wrapping my arms around my neck. I try to ignore the warden's cheers, but the man is persistent. "Bring it in here, boy!"

Destry backs out of his chamber, but when the warden hops around the corner, Destry runs the opposite way. As angry as I am at Destry, it's not lost on me that it was also his first time hearing the conversation between Randolph and the warden. I imagine that watching his father fall to his knees, begging for mercy, wasn't the most inspiring footage to witness.

Too bad I don't care.

"Hey, now!" the warden complains, opening his arms to the sky. "I *am* the reason your parents were given a second chance. That's no way to thank their savior!"

I lean forward and find Destry frozen to the turf, his arms trembling wildly. The warden's smile fades with the silence, and he motions to his guards. "Can somebody *please* remind this convict of the consequence of *disobedience*?"

The Authority agents step forward, aiming their guns at Destry's back. His eyes widen in horror, and he sprints back to his chamber. He leaps into the warden's arms, and they hug for half a minute, Destry's body not moving an inch.

I feel a hand on my shoulder. Looking to my right, I recognize the gigantic palm. "Hey," Artemis says. "We need to get out of here…*now.*"

I don't know where I stand with Artemis now that every secret between us is out in the open. But he's the only person I have left, so regardless of how deep our bond is…it's still there.

I take his hand, and we speed along the outside of the arena. We take the longest route possible, doing our best to avoid drawing attention to ourselves. Only when we're halfway up the metal staircase does the warden acknowledge us.

"Artemis! Iris!" he shouts. We freeze, Arty's hand tensing in mine. We turn together, and I latch onto Artemis's side. He steps forward so I'm half a step behind him, and despite the circumstances, my heart warms. *He's protecting me.* The warden stares at our interlocked hands and smiles, sending a shiver down my spine. Artemis keeps me stable, not letting the chilling nature of the warden make me falter.

The warden shakes his head and laughs. "The nation's favorite lovebirds." He sighs. "Considering Death Row has been selected *for* you…the final vote will be cast in thirty-eight hours. I suggest you enjoy your last few days together." One final wink from the warden, and Artemis and I are running through the arena door.

With too much to say to one another, Artemis and I are silent, slouching on the living room couches. Even if we had the energy to speak, neither of us would even know where to start. *After all this time, Destry was the common denominator in every issue we faced.* Because of this, we don't bother taking our Death Row cushions. We won't give Destry that satisfaction. Instead, we face the kitchen on the same blue sofa, waiting for the traitor to show his face.

When Destry finally descends the steps, I grip my hands into fists. He looks at the carpet as he approaches, and his hands are clasped behind his back. Once he passes into our space, I stand, fists bunched so hard my knuckles lose color.

"Look…I'm sorry," Destry says.

I raise my eyebrows. "How much did you know?"

Destry bites his lip. "What do you mean?"

Artemis springs to his feet and moves in front of me. "About the Enterprize, *dumbass.* The competitions, the punishments…the layout. How much did you know?"

Destry tilts his head. "Look—"

"No funny business!" I demand, moving so I'm side by side with Arty. "*How much did you know?*"

He repeatedly shifts his gaze between Artemis and me, searching for a place to start. After a deep breath, he steps forward with his arms spread wide. "The night he was confronted…my father sat me down and told me everything." Another deep breath. "He told me what every competition was going to be, when they were to happen, and…even the order of the punishments and rewards in the Suffering Sanctuary. He coached me on when to drop out, and…how to act…"

"So, all of that was fake then?" Artemis spits, eyebrows raised. "It was all a strategy your *daddy* told you to follow? Your daddy who is, *conveniently,* still alive?"

Destry shakes his head. "Look, you can be pissed that I lied. But you can't be angry at me because my parents weren't murdered."

I laugh without humor. "Destry, did you ever tell us anything that *was* true? Was everything that came out of your mouth a lie this entire time?"

Destry bites his lip again and shakes his head. After a long pause, he looks me dead in the eye. "You don't win The Enterprize by telling the truth."

Artemis charges forward, and I let him. Destry runs to the opposite side of the kitchen counter, ensuring space between the two.

"Artemis, you really were my friend!" he pleads. "That friendship was real!"

"Tell that to the fist in your nose!" he shouts, jumping on top of the island and running across it. Destry sprints up the staircase, Artemis following close behind. I don't bother to watch. Either Destry gets his face smashed in or not. Either way, in forty-eight hours…

I'll be alone or dead.

Minutes pass before Artemis marches back down the steps. When he finally does, he settles into his original spot beside me and hides his head in his hands.

"Get him?" I ask, not bothering to look in his direction.

"Nope," he answers. "Wouldn't have changed anything anyway. It just…" He shakes his head. "It's fucked up. *Everything* that he's done. It's… unforgivable."

I bite my lip. "Sucks that he's gonna win it all."

Artemis looks at me, but I don't return his gaze. "It's not over yet."

I shake my head, finally locking onto his eyes. "Isn't it, though? He *knows* what the last competition is. The only reason he probably lost all the others was because he wanted to look weak. And he *knew* he didn't need to get extra blood on his hands at the time…not when his *daddy* told him how to manipulate people into doing what he wants."

"You can't think like that," Artemis says, concern in his eyes. "Please…don't think like that."

I turn away from him, pressing my hands to my temples. "In two days, one of us will be *dead*. Regardless of what happens next…we've both lost."

The silence that follows is deafening. Finally, just when I can't stand it any longer, Artemis speaks.

"Do you love me, Iris?"

I turn to him, finally locking onto his eyes. "What?"

He keeps eye contact. No part of his face shows that he's joking around. "Was anything you said up there true? Or was it all…a part of the plan?"

I hang my head, taking his hand. He grips onto mine, allowing the gesture, but waits patiently for my response. Finally, I match his gaze.

In two days, one of us will be dead.

So, when my brain argues the logic of this conversation with my heart…my heart says *fuck it.*

I close my eyes. When I open them, I let the words come. "I do love you."

Artemis's grip tightens. "So, was that conversation real then? Did you…mean what you said?"

I want to lie to him. *But I can't.* Because despite everything, I know how he still feels for me. And I can't let that go.

I nod. "They told me the plan. Before then, I was…prepared to never speak to you again. I told myself it was over…after what you did to Lunar." I take a deep breath. "So, I didn't want to be a part of their plan. I fought against playing along. But…" I shake my head, tears catching in my eyes. "I couldn't let them die, Artemis. I just couldn't!"

He grabs my cheek with his opposite hand, gazing into my eyes. There's instant electricity between us, but I don't let him make a move until I get the words out. To remove the temptation to kiss him, I shift my gaze to the ground and force the words out.

"So, I went through with it. They needed me to cause a distraction. To get everyone to watch us instead of them. Ashlea…she *always* knew how I truly felt about you. I denied it, so she told me to pretend and make a scene…to ensure everyone was watching us. But…" I gaze back into his eyes. "She knew."

He squeezes my palm, urging me to continue. "My intentions weren't *right*. But, as I got to talking…" I shake my head, and a tear falls. "I'm sorry, Artemis. This just…it doesn't feel right."

He caresses my cheek. "What doesn't feel right?"

My lip starts to quiver. "Mace…I can't let him go."

Artemis leans in closer. "You aren't letting him go, Iris. You can love him and still love me. Both things can be true."

"I know…I just…"

He wipes a tear from my cheek. "Shhh," he says, quieting me. He waits until I calm down before letting out one final whisper. "Was. It. Real?"

I gaze into his eyes, butterflies fluttering around my stomach like the first time I heard him speak. My tears fall, but I ignore them. Instead, I focus on him, and *only* him, and answer.

"Every word of it."

He smiles, but I can't see it for long. Because, after what feels like an eternity, his lips are once again on mine. My worries fade now that everything standing in the way of us being together has disappeared. His tongue sweeps the inside of my cheek, and I grip his forearms, *craving* more. I grip the hem of his shirt and force it off his chiseled chest, but the second our lips are apart, everything comes crashing back down on me. As much as I want to ignore every terrible thing we have done to one another, one scene pulses in my mind, demanding my attention. It's so all-consuming that I back away from Artemis. I'm too insecure to kiss him when he has some of his own actions to answer for.

Artemis caresses the nape of my neck, eyes widening. "What's wrong?"

I lick my lips and look away from him, trying to sort out how to express my worry without offending him. I cough before I start. "That scene they showed us…" I look him in the eye. "With Mercedes?"

He backs away, removing his hand from my skin. "Iris, that wasn't real. I *promise* it wasn't real. I was doing everything I could to keep us alive. She was another vote to save *you*. Everything I did with her was to keep you and me alive."

I swallow to keep my voice from quivering. "But that script…"

He shakes his head. "No…no! It wasn't a script! I *promise* it wasn't a script! I just…" he takes a deep breath. "You saw the video, and you saw her in real life. She told me she loved me *countless* times. But I didn't love *her* back. If I ever said I did, I *promise* they would have shown it." He smooths my hair. "Those things that I said…it was to placate her. I…I was never going to tell her I loved her. I couldn't do that. So, I had to think of the next best thing."

"But you said all of those same things to me," I argue. "You used the *exact* same words."

"But I also told you that I'm in love with you. I *never* said that to her." Despite what Mercedes claimed, I know he's telling the truth. If the producers wanted to throw me off my game, there's no chance they would have hidden that footage from me. I gulp, shifting my gaze because, unfortunately, that's not why there's an ache in my core. I'm ashamed to admit the real reason I can't fully commit to our relationship, but Arty refuses to relent.

He grabs my arm, but his grip is soft. *Desperate.* "Iris, I know there's something you're not telling me." His eyes are urgent. "If we only get two more days together, you need to tell me what's on your mind."

I look to the ceiling, trying to stall. But I can't take it anymore. I gaze into his beautiful ocean eyes and let the words spew. "The video cut off before we could see much. But you…you…" I shiver. "You were stripping…for *her*."

Artemis squints. "What are you trying to suggest?"

I look at the ground, embarrassed. Of course, he knows what I'm talking about. And it kills me that he's pretending not to. "I just want to know why you did that. It was a little…forward. Was it not?"

He squints, backing away. "Iris…you and I weren't together. You were with somebody else the *entire* time. Does it matter what happened when the camera cut off?"

I feel like a bullet has pierced through my chest. I stand up, knowing what his deflection means. *If they didn't go all the way, he would have denied it.* But he isn't denying anything. I flail out my palms, trying to distract from the pain. "I just need a minute, okay?" I say, rising from the couch.

"Iris, *please*," he begs, standing. His muscular torso is bare, but I don't let it distract me. Instead, I put a hand up, hoping the gesture is enough for him not to follow me.

"I'm not mad," I lie. "I just…I need to think. Okay?"

He takes a step back. "Okay."

So, when I climb the staircase, and he doesn't persist, I choke back tears. I collapse onto my mattress and let the scene replay in my mind as I bury my head in my pillow. Once the floodgates open, there's no stopping them.

No amount of smothering could ever hide my bellowing cries.

I tremble when I run out of tears to cry. Hours pass while I flick through the bloodcurdling secrets the film helped uncover this morning. *Destry's family turned me in. He knew every competition before it happened and manipulated everyone into helping advance his game. He lived under the floorboards just like me, and his parents are alive.* So, when all is said and done...

The extent of Artemis and Mercedes's relationship is the least of my concerns.

So, when Artemis crests the steps and approaches his bed, I don't give it a second thought.

"Arty?" I ask, removing the pillow from my face.

"Yes?" he says, stepping closer.

I lean my head on the back of the bed frame, sitting up. "Can you stay with me?"

His lips spread into a soft smile. "Of course."

I help Artemis merge Ashlea's bedframe and mattress with mine. We cuddle under the same blanket with his arm stretched around me. I curl onto his chest and listen to his thumping heartbeat, speeding up as I hug my legs around his. I take a deep breath and close my eyes, not letting shame distort my realization.

For the first time since Mace's death...I feel *like I'm going to be* okay.

So, even after every horrifying death and secret revealed today, I'm the first to whisper.

"I love you, Arty."

His heart skips a beat, but there's no hesitation.

"I love you too, Iris."

Chapter 77

My sleep is riddled with nightmares. First, Randolph shoots my parents while Destry hands him ammunition. Then, I'm hiding in the floorboards with Lunar, only to find that Destry is cowering beside us. Countless murders paint my dreams, but every nightmare is interspersed with one more terrifying than the rest.

Mace standing at the end of my mattress, shaking his head in disapproval.

I grip onto Artemis's chest, waking him from the force of my grasp.

"What's wrong?" he asks, shielding me with his back.

I gasp as I catch my breath, sinking into his chest. "Nothing," I whisper, but I'm drenched in sweat. *Mace's body isn't even cold, and I'm nestled against the one person he begged me not to trust.*

Artemis rubs my back, and I loosen enough to breathe deeply, but my body is still as stiff as a board. I grip onto his shoulder and squeeze, hiding my eyes in his chest. "Tell me a story," I urge, voice muffled from his skin against my lips.

Artemis backs away, smiling. "Another story?"

I nod, trying to hide the desperation in my voice. "I like your stories. They…transport me away from here." I shift so I'm looking into his eyes. "I *need* you to take me away from here, Arty."

He stretches his other arm around me, his gaze softening. I shut my eyes and shiver as he whispers, "Anything for you."

I can nearly hear the gears running in his head. Once he settles on a memory, his grip around my waist loosens. "There was a lake by my house," he starts. "My family used to go there every weekend. We'd bring the most random objects to float on, and every time, we'd try different tricks off the dock." My breath slows as I try and imagine the water. "But I loved it most when my friends would join us. We'd make a day out of it."

"Anthony and Jeremy?" I ask, my voice finally steady.

He nods. "Of course. Sometimes, we'd relax, but most of the time, we'd play games in the lake. The best was when we'd make teams and have water wars."

"Sounds fun," I whisper, the hint of a smile crossing my lips

"It was," he answers. "But the best was when Jeremy found Plastyjelly in his parent's medicine cabinet." He laughs, remembering the moment. "He brought it with him to the lake."

I finally turn to him and chuckle. It's weak, but it's something. "Oh god," I say, eyes wide. Plastyjelly was the eventual alternative to petroleum jelly. Once gas was replaced with Plastygas, the byproduct changed to a similar structure designed for an identical purpose.

He shakes his head and smiles. "One second, we're flinging water at each other. The next…" he pauses again to laugh. "The next, Jeremy's launching globs of Plastyjelly at us!"

I laugh. "What?!"

His cackles make the mattress shake. "Before I know it, we're all digging into the can, throwing balls of the stuff at each other. And when that shit sticks, it *splatters*." I wipe the sleep from my eyes and laugh. "We'd chase each other, smothering it down our arms. Before long, our clothes were orange from the stuff. So eventually, we jumped into the lake to wash off." He laughs again. "The only problem is that the dock was the only way out of the water."

I tilt my head, willing him to continue. He can barely get the next sentence out.

"Every time we beached onto the dock, we'd slip right back off! The jelly…we couldn't wash it off! It's resistant to water!" I start laughing, honestly giggling for the first time in ages as I imagine the three boys struggling to grab onto the dock before launching back into the water like a cannon.

"How long did it take you to get it off?!" I exclaim.

He doesn't stop cackling. "The better part of an hour." We laugh in each other's arms until all my tension fades. Once we catch our breath, there's silence, making a solemness flush over me.

My smile drops, and I whisper into his chest, "I wish I could've been there."

He takes a deep breath, his own smile fading. "Me too, Iris." I feel him shift, so I sit up and lock my eyes on his. He stares at me like I'm the most beautiful girl he's ever seen. I shiver as he adjusts a piece of hair behind my ear. "You would've loved it."

Before I can answer, his lips are on mine. It's brief but quickens my pulse from the excitement of it all. When he leans out of it, he shoves his shirt back over his head and grabs my hand. "Shall we enjoy a nice breakfast together? I've prepared something *rather* special."

I laugh, planting my feet on the ground. "Oh, have you?"

He stands, helping me up. "Have you ever tried a multigrain roll? I specifically requested one for you on this *joyous* day." I smile, sarcastically widening my eyes.

"My hero!" I joke. He hits my arm playfully and holds my hand. I don't have to force the smile that paints across my lips as we frolic down the steps, and I can't help but wish this moment never had to end.

Hours pass without Destry in the picture, but I'm beyond caring. Without his hindrance, Artemis and I lie together in the living room, exchanging funny stories from our pasts that seem to get more amusing as they go.

It hurts mourning Mace's passing while connecting with the man he wanted me to stay away from. I can only push on by reminding myself that there's one thing Mace and I had that I will never have with Artemis. *A true, emotional bond mixed with the power of unconditional love.* Artemis and I have a flirtatious relationship that distracts me from reality and puts a smile on my face, even when I have nothing left to be happy about. Artemis may have made me laugh harder than Mace ever had, but there's one big difference between the two. *Mace knew everything about me.* Artemis may care…but Mace knew me well beyond a surface level. I love them both, but Artemis will never know me the way Mace did. Artemis is an escape. Our attraction to one another is undeniable, but I fear that without the boundaries of this game, the spark would have died with the intensity of lust. With Mace, everything was *real*. There was no doubt, no…struggle. Life with Mace was easy.

Life with Artemis may be effortless now…but it wasn't always that way.

I feel better about myself, knowing that Mace has a special place in my heart that Artemis could never entirely fill. But that doesn't mean he can't help sew half the stitches back together. The joy I experience with Artemis is one I have long been deprived of. Mace would want me to be happy. And with Artemis…I am.

This realization sitting comfortably in my brain, I'm able to relax with Artemis in the living room. We're on opposite couches, throwing an apple back and forth, and even though there's silence, I can't deny that I'm at peace. I laugh at the occasional heckle from poor tosses or failed catches until, eventually, the apple is more bruised than red. I examine the structure and shrug, tossing it back at Artemis while he laughs.

I let my mind wander enough that I can't help but breach the topic of elimination. "Are you going to talk to Destry today?"

He holds the apple for a moment too long. "Probably. But I don't suppose there's much of a point anyway." He tosses the fruit back to me.

"What do you mean?" I ask, catching it. He bites his lip before answering.

"He knows what the final competition will be, doesn't he? If it's physical, it's probably a safe bet that he'll pick you. If it's mental…then I'm toast."

I look at the ground. "Destry will pick whoever he thinks he can beat in the final round."

Artemis nods, breathing deeply. "Unfortunately…I don't think there's much we can do to alter his decision."

I swallow the rock in my throat and look at Artemis, willing him to make eye contact. "Can you promise me something?"

He smiles, still looking at the ground. "Depends on what you want promised."

I don't match his grin. Instead, I deflate into the sofa. "Just…promise me you'll beat him. If he picks you, promise me that you'll win."

He ponders the thought before making eye contact. "I promise that I'll try."

I nod. "And if you get out of here…" I gulp loudly. "Find Curi…okay? Take care of her. Make sure she's not alone and can live the perfect little life she deserves."

His face drains of joy. "I promise, Iris. But…" he tilts his head. "You're gonna make it out of here. You'll be able to take care of her yourself. I'll make sure of that."

I shake my head. "Don't sacrifice yourself for me. I can't…I can't lose anybody else."

"I'll never stop sacrificing myself for you, Iris. You know that."

I look at the ground because, unfortunately, I do know. And as painful as losing him would be, now that the threat of death is very real…I'm *terrified*.

Silence passes between us. Finally, he stands up, abandoning our game of toss. "I'm going to talk to him."

I stand quickly. "What? No…I'll go with you."

He puts his hand up. "No…I'll go first. You go after…then maybe he'll take each of us more seriously."

I nod, sitting back on the sofa. He strides forward, closing the gap between us, and squats so he's inches from my lips. "I'm gonna get you out of here, Iris. I'm getting you out of here if it's the last thing I do." He kisses me quickly before fleeing, leaving me alone to consider the true sacrifice he is making for me.

It's not long before I can't take it anymore. Artemis and Destry have been chatting for an eternity, and my paranoia is eating me alive. Finally, I march up the steps, push my fishtail behind my back, and knock on the Executive door.

Destry answers, welcoming me in. His movements are slow and mechanical, as if he's walking on eggshells. *Good. He doesn't deserve to feel comfortable ever again.*

I peek into the room, smiling at Artemis. He nods, rising from the long sofa. "I better head out," Arty says. Before exiting, he stops at Destry with his hand outstretched. "But do we have a deal?"

Destry averts his gaze to the ground and nods. "We have a deal." The two shake hands, and I narrow my eyes on the clasp. Whatever the terms of this agreement are, I hope they are in my favor.

Artemis leaves the room, shutting the door behind him. I don't move to the sofa, opting to stand in front of Destry to make him as uncomfortable as possible. He shuffles to the edge of his bed and leans against it, looking at me skeptically. "I assume you're here for the same reason your boyfriend was?"

I cringe at the label. "He's not my boyfriend."

Destry raises an eyebrow and smiles. "Right."

I roll my eyes. "Let's cut to the chase. You know what the final competition is. What is it?"

Destry's smile fades. "Why would I tell you that?"

I open my palms to the ceiling. "Because I need to know if I'm wasting my time up here. You're clearly picking whoever you think you can beat. So, should I be holding onto the hope that you pick me, or should I be saying goodbye to my sister in the cameras?"

Destry pauses. "You know…Artemis was just in here, *begging* me to keep you alive. Your approach is…admittedly different."

I step closer to Destry so we're inches apart. He backs onto the mattress, not letting me get within arm's reach. I roll my eyes at the absurd idea that I'd harm him. But with my fate in his hands, I take a deep breath to soothe my frustration.

"I have a sister," I argue. "I don't want to win this for me. I want to win this for her."

"All the more reason to send you out that door."

I shake my head. "Look, can you please just…tell me who's leaving? So, I can be prepared?" I rub my shoe against the carpet, swaying the plush in different directions. "If you can't tell me what the final competition will be…can you at *least* tell me who's staying?" I pause for dramatic effect. "After *everything* you've done to me?"

That strikes Destry in the chest. He takes a deep breath, backing up to the head of the bedframe. He looks blankly at the wall beside him. When he speaks, he doesn't spare me a glance.

"Tomorrow is physical." My heart skips a beat, relief flushing through my veins. Before I can speak, he continues. "It's standing on pedestals in freezing rain. The last person on their stump wins." I take a step back. Even if he keeps me, there's no way I would win. No matter what decision he makes, it won't affect anything. Whether I make it past the vote or not…by tomorrow evening, I will be dead.

I shake my head. "You know I can't win that."

Destry's face stays stoic. "Yes, I know."

I look around the room, landing my eyes on his face. He still doesn't match my eye contact, but I ask anyway. "And that's what you told Artemis?"

He nods slowly, not saying a word. I lean forward, eyes widening. "So…you're keeping me?"

Destry finally locks onto my eyes. "Yes. I am keeping you, Iris."

I nod, not letting my emotions show. Because despite my excitement…my heart is shattering all over again.

I pucker my lips, letting the conversation die. "Thank you, Destry…thank you."

He nods, looking the other way. I start pacing to the door, but my stomach drops as soon as I rest my hand on the iron slab.

"This isn't another lie, is it?"

His head rotates slowly until his eyes are on mine. He shrugs. "Have I ever lied to you?"

I shiver at the words that once gave me so much confidence in him. Now, they show him for the fraud that he is. But the thing about cons? No matter how long you talk to them, you never get any closer to the truth. So, instead of arguing with him…instead of losing my integrity by selling Artemis out…instead of punching a hole in Destry's chest…

I nod and close the door behind me.

Chapter 78

I go through the motions, knowing this may be my final night. Earlier, the prospect of death was terrifying. It left me breathless, unable to take two steps without feeling faint. But since leaving Destry's room with his hollow promise of safety, I'm left with a lingering emptiness. *Nothing matters.* Because regardless of Destry's vote, I will die tomorrow.

When I spot Artemis on our double bed in the corner of the communal bedroom, I find my voice. "What did Destry promise you?" I ask, settling beside him.

He takes a deep breath, drawing swirls on my arm with a gentle finger. "He promised to keep you safe."

I squint. "Do you believe him?"

Artemis sighs. "What other choice do I have?"

I deflate and cuddle closer to him, accepting defeat. Sensing my tension, he keeps the circles going.

"Iris…whatever happens tomorrow…" he gulps. "This is the last night we will ever be together."

I freeze. Artemis isn't being pessimistic. He's simply stating a matter of fact. Regardless of who survives between the two of us, we will both be losing the other. I can't move, so I don't interrupt.

"I just…" he chokes on oncoming sobs. "I know that we've only gotten to be together for a short time. I mean, *truly* together." His tear falls onto my cheek, and I look up to match his gaze. His blue eyes are endless, giving the false sense that I'm as free and alive as I'll ever be. But when I look at my hands, I remember that I'm more hopeless than ever.

"I just want you to know that these past twenty-four hours have been the best twenty-four hours of my life. And I wouldn't trade that time with you for *anything*."

A tear spills over the corner of my eye, so I burrow my head into his chest. I love Artemis, but I refuse to lie to him. Being with him in these final hours…it's been magical.

But it could never compare to my time spent with Mace.

Instead of flattering him with false truths, I speak from my heart.

"Curi…" I choke up, knowing I'll never get to see her again. "Curi would have loved you."

His chest starts heaving, so I kiss his cheek. "My parents would have *loved* you, Iris."

We sob together, all our memories crashing down in an instant. *Losing Artemis is going to kill me.* I have no doubt about it. It will cut my heart into imperceptible pieces that could never be bandaged back together, no matter how long a person tried. But the thought of our memories being forgotten? The idea of every moment we've had with each other, *dying* with either of us, just because it's too painful to remember once the other has gone?

It *destroys* me.

The thought of Artemis forgetting about me makes me weep so hard that my words are barely distinguishable from one another. "*Arty.*" He clears my face from stray hairs that are forcing their way out of my fishtail. My chin quivers so hard, it's a monumental task to pronounce my words. "*Please.* Promise me…" I'm crying so hard, my words come out in a shout. "PROMISE ME THAT YOU WON'T FORGET ME!" I weep into his chest, latching my arms around his neck. "You…you are so much more to me than just another convict in this house. I just…" I'm bawling so hard I can't see my hand in front of my face. "*Please* don't forget me!"

Artemis's tears give mine a run for their money. He wipes his eyes vigorously, gasping to get air. "I…I *promise*…I will *never* forget you." Our bodies shudder in unison, and we wipe each other's tears every moment we catch our breath. "I've said it before, and I'll say it again. You are the best thing that's ever happened to me. You…are the most important person in my life. I…I…" he takes a shaky breath. "There is *nothing* you could ever do…to make me stop loving you. No…no matter what happens tomorrow…" he shakes his head. "*I will love you until the day that I die.*"

Our cries are the only sound in the house, making us wail even harder. As Arty rubs my back, every deep regret spills so quickly that I can't stop them from coming. There's just so much shame in my heart, and with our time together coming to an end…I can't help but apologize for every terrible thing I've put Artemis through. "I'm so sorry, Arty. I'm *so* sorry for everything I've said about you…for the *hell* that I've put you through. I just thought…maybe if you hated me…you wouldn't miss me." I gulp. "Then you wouldn't be in pain anymore."

He shakes his head. "I will *never* hate you, Iris. There's nothing you could ever do to make me hate you. You've done so much for me that no matter what happens after this vote, nothing could ever change how I feel about you. There's not a thing in this world that could make me forget the impact you've had on my life. I will *never* let those memories die. Please…remember that."

I nod. "I'm sorry for ever doubting you…if I just *trusted* you…we wouldn't have wasted so much time."

"Iris," he whispers. "I wouldn't take anything back. For this result? I wouldn't change a thing."

I know I still love Mace. But when all is said and done, and I have one final day with Artemis…I have to try and let Mace go. He will always have a piece of me. But I can't change the past. So, when I grab Artemis's cheek and whisper, "I will always love you."

I mean it.

00:10:00
EXPULSION VOTE

Acceptance. After a whirlwind of denial and depression and bargaining with fate…Artemis and I have accepted what's coming.

No matter what we do, we can't prevent the vote. So, instead of making another senseless escape attempt, we let Destry play the game. Then, at least one of us can stand a *chance* at survival.

Destry's been a liar. A good one. But I hold onto hope that he's suddenly decided to tell the truth that I'll be taken to the finals. He promised Artemis he'd do as much and made it clear to me that I'm his choice. But that doesn't make things easier. In fact, it makes everything *so much worse.*

Going through the motions with Artemis, waiting for the evening vote…it's brutal. We both pretend like we're the one going to the firing squad, but we both know it'll be Arty. We've accepted that. More importantly, we've established that we will always have love for one another. And the fact that I finally got to tell him, and we got to be together, even for a short time? It almost makes it all worth it.

Almost.

So, when we sit in the Death Row cushions with ten minutes remaining, Artemis ironically taking the bullet-pierced one that once sat Sola…we hold hands, imagining a life outside the Enterprize. We've pushed the two seats together so we don't have to waste a single moment away from one another.

Not when we only get ten more minutes in each other's arms.

"I'd have a house by the lake, and we'd swim there every evening," Artemis says. "I'd smother you with Plastyjelly, and you'd slide out of my arms into the water. You'd laugh with your melodic cackle, and I'd dive back in to save you, not resting until you were safely in my grasp."

I squeeze his hand, forcing back sobs. "I'd have a bed…not under the floorboards."

He laughs. "I'd have a mansion where we could cook our rations into extravagant meals."

I smile. "Whole-grain stew?"

Our bodies shake from laughter. We accept what's coming. But we refuse to let it take away from our last moments together.

With three minutes remaining, Destry descends the steps. We stop talking, letting him take his place at the head of the room. There's dead silence as my heart pounds. To keep from panicking, I lean my head on Arty's shoulder and shut my eyes.

Pretending Destry isn't there, Artemis picks our conversation back up. "I'd build a home in the woods. Far away from Miasmis, where nobody would find us. We'd start a community with Curi and some others and live our lives together in peace."

I squeeze my eyes even tighter as a tear falls. Nobody speaks another word, it being impossible for me to get anything out. Besides…if these are the last words I ever hear from Artemis…I'd gladly keep them as my final memory of him. When the buzzer goes off, and I open my eyes, Destry stands slowly, staring the both of us down.

He clasps his hands in front of his waist and takes a deep breath. "I'm not proud of the man I've become. I never wanted any of this. I just…wanted to continue living in secret with my family." He stares at the ground before meeting my eyes. "I never wanted to hurt anybody."

I look away. I don't want to be a coward. But I don't have the strength to watch him send one of the only people I have left to his death.

"I want to make a promise to you both. A promise…to never tell another lie." I look back at him, squeezing Artemis's arm. Silence settles while Destry shifts his shoe on the carpet. Finally, he locks onto Artemis's gaze.

"That promise is going to have to start after this. I'm *so* sorry."

I hide in Artemis's shoulder as the tears come. But before I get a chance to say goodbye, Destry turns to me.

"I vote to expel Iris."

Chapter 79

My body goes limp against Artemis's chest. My stomach hardens like a rock, and the world starts spinning. Artemis tightens against me and sits up straighter. "Excuse me?"

Destry shakes his head, choking on artificial tears. "I'm so sorry, Iris. I…I have to do this."

Artemis stands, and I collapse into his cushion. "You don't have to do anything, Destry. But what you *should* do is *keep your goddamn word!*"

I shake my head as the clock shifts from thirty seconds to twenty-nine. I tense my jaw and shoot daggers at Destry with my eyes. "You are unbelievable." I stand, closing the gap between us. "I want you to listen to me *very* clearly. My last dying hope is that every night for the *rest* of your existence…" I let the last words come out in a whisper. "You don't know how to live with yourself."

His eyes fill with moisture, so I turn before I see a tear fall. *Don't humanize him. He's done nothing to earn my pity.*

Artemis grabs my hand and leads me to the door. He squeezes my palm the entire way, but his strength is artificial. I'm positive that without his grip, he'd be on his knees, lacking the ability to stand. When we finally reach the iron slab, I have no time to be scared. I push back my fear and voice my one request, forcing my words to be steady so he understands them. "Win this. Get Curi out and keep her safe."

He nods. "I promise." His eyes are wet. A lump forms in my throat, and my saliva tastes metallic. But I fight the tears. *This is the last Miasmis will ever see of me.* This is the last *Curi* will ever see of me. So, I refuse to cry. I don't even kiss Artemis. Instead, I take a deep breath, turn to the door, and place my hand on the ice-cold knob.

And the world goes dark.

Chapter 80

My ears vibrate. The house is shaking, and I'm *falling*. I can't see anything, but I know I'm alive. Artemis catches me before I hit the ground, and I latch onto him.

"What's happening?" I ask.

"I don't know!" Artemis shouts. "Take cover!"

We run to the kitchen table and hide beneath it, covering our necks. The walls continue to quake, and it's a full five minutes before they stop. Luckily, Destry doesn't try and join us. Instead, he cowers in the center of the living room floor, safe from any furniture collapsing onto him.

The shaking stops, but we don't move an inch. The emergency lights pop on, and it takes a moment for my eyes to adjust. Before long, the room is deafeningly silent. "What do we do?" I ask, terrified to make the wrong move.

It takes mere seconds for Destry to answer. "I assume you should walk out that door."

His suggestion is almost humorous. "I'm sorry, do you see a timer going, Destry?" Even if there was, I know that we're trapped inside. I tried the handle when the walls started shaking, but it wouldn't budge. *Because the lock is controlled by the electrical circuit.* I hide my gasp when I realize it. The door won't open because all the power in the building is out.

I take a peek at the rest of the house and melt back into Artemis's arms. "The cameras," I whisper, pointing. Artemis scans the walls, tightening his grasp on my shoulders.

Every camera is hanging down, no power to keep them straight. None of them are moving, which can only mean one thing.

None of them are watching us.

When we crawl out from under the table, Artemis helps me up. "Hello?" I shout at the ceiling, waiting for somebody to rush into the house and shoot me.

Destry stands, waving a hand in front of the nearest camera. "They're completely shut down."

I turn to Destry slowly. "Is this part of the game?"

He shakes his head. "Not that I was told."

Artemis freezes. "It happened." I look at him, urging him to expand. He doesn't meet my gaze. "Somebody ended it…somebody responded."

I think back to my desperate message to the camera in the Executive room. *Did somebody answer my pleas?*

Quickly, I run to Destry. "Whatever's going on, we don't have much time." I take his arm and yank it. "You know this building inside and out. What is the fastest way out of here?"

He shakes his head. "I don't...I don't understand."

Artemis jerks Destry's other arm, eyes wild with desperation. *"Destry, what is the fastest way out of here?!"*

Destry doesn't focus on us. Instead, he brings a single hand to his temple and starts rubbing. "Solitary confinement. But...that didn't work before...I knew it wouldn't work."

"Why won't it work?" I ask seriously, not giving him time to wonder.

He finally meets my gaze. "It leads to the Assessment Hall. From there...it's a maze. There's no finding your way out."

Assessment Hall? I stagger back. "You mean the Assessment is held here?"

He shrugs. "Apparently. But my father wasn't in that sector...he just controlled the Enterprize. Outside of here...I know as much as you do."

I bite my lip, considering our options. My eyes scan the bottom floor, but no other idea comes to mind. I grunt, frustrated that we're running out of time. "Well, we have to try *something*."

Artemis jogs with me toward the staircase, and Destry yells from the kitchen. "Wait! Are you seriously going to try to escape? After everything that happened with the others?"

I don't even turn to him. "Well, if we don't have you trapping us in there, I think we'll be alright."

Artemis laughs, making me smile. By the time we get to the second floor, Destry has made it to the bottom of the steps. I curse myself for my persistent conscience and pause to yell at him. "Are you just going to stand there or what?"

He stammers over his words, not knowing how to respond. "What if they come back?"

"Then I'm dead either way! I've got nothing to lose!" I shout. I turn for the arena door, but Artemis hangs back, using the logic I've taught him to convince Destry to join us.

"Destry, there was an explosion, for Christ's sake! You heard it...you *felt* it. As far we know, there may not *be* an Assessment Hall anymore."

Destry shakes his head, but he doesn't argue. With no explanation, he runs up the steps, following us into the arena.

This room has no emergency lighting, so the second the iron shuts behind us, it's pitch black. We feel for the metal rails, careful not to let the staircase sway as we race down it. "Was it like this last time you all tried to get out?" Artemis asks Destry. "The video wasn't all that clear with the night vision cameras."

Destry's answer is quiet, but it's audible. "No. It was *nothing* like this."

We race across the AstroTurf, using our sense of direction to find the opposite wall. "Spread out and look for the door!" I yell. The room is so dark we can't even see our hands in front of our faces. But by the sounds of their footsteps, Artemis and Destry scatter, hooking their hands against the wall to find the crevice to solitary confinement. There's nothing but smooth wall as I glide my hands against the ramparts, and I'm about ready to huff my frustrations when Artemis calls to us.

"Here! This way!" Destry and I run toward his shouts and gather behind him. Artemis keeps the door shut, forcing Destry in front of us. "You go first this time," he declares. "Surely, I don't have to explain why?"

Destry grunts angrily before pushing through. With the lights still pitch black, I trip over some kind of log.

When I turn back to move it, my heart stops. *Because it's not a log at all.*

"Ashlea," I choke out, reaching for her. Before I can touch her, Artemis yanks me off the ground. I struggle to escape from his grasp, but he doesn't let go.

"I'm *so* sorry, Iris," he pleads. "*There's just no time.*"

As much as I want to refuse his wishes, I don't argue. Because I know he's right. And if I don't want to end up as another body lining the solitary confinement tile…we have to keep moving.

We run to the other end of the room, careful not to trip over anybody else. The stench makes my eyes water, but I force myself forward. When we get to the end, we stumble into Destry.

"Destry, go! We have to move!"

His body is completely frozen to the tile. "This is the room…this is where they come to kill us."

Artemis pats Destry's back. "Then we better get moving, huh?"

He pushes Destry against the door until he moves to open it. When it doesn't budge like it did in the video, it strikes me that it's another vessel powered with electricity. Catching the idea at the same time, the two boys kick against it until it gives way and force it to the side.

"Go, go, go!" Artemis demands, forcing Destry through. Once Destry stumbles into the room, Artemis pulls me in so he can protect me from behind. I put my fists up in front of my face as we sprint into the production room, then let them fall when the emergency lights expose us to the abandoned posts.

"Where is everyone?" I whisper. Nobody answers. Instead, Artemis keeps pushing us forward. Rows of desks are empty, and not a single computer screen is lit. I try to focus on what's ahead, but the entirety of the production room takes me by surprise.

When we reach the opposite wall, Destry whips open the exit without hesitation. We run through the hallways blindly but stop when we see smoke.

"What…should we follow that?" I ask.

"And burn to death? No, thanks." Destry replies.

He takes off in the opposite direction, and I follow, Artemis beside me. We pass several long hallways, and I try to ignore them as we race through the facility. But when a figure sprints toward us from a hall on our right, I stop in my tracks. "Guys…someone's coming."

Artemis spins on his heel and races back toward me, grabbing my hand once I'm within his reach. "Then we have to move!"

I stand my ground. "No! It's a girl…a teenager." Artemis stops tugging and watches her approach with me. There's smoke billowing down the hallway she sprints down, and I can't stop myself from stepping closer to get a better look. Destry eventually turns around, hopping on one foot before the other, demanding that we follow him.

"Guys!" he shouts. "Come on!"

Neither of us respond. We just watch as the figure gets clearer, the desperation on her face more evident with each passing stride. Eventually, I can distinguish her clothes. Whoever she is, she's got on a gray jumpsuit and black boots. Her brown hair flies behind her like a mane, and she screams once she's close enough to see our faces. "Run!" she says, zooming past us effortlessly. But neither of us budge because the second she turns the corner, our eyes widen at the figure chasing her.

I shake my head. "What…what *is* that?"

Artemis takes my hand. A purple figure stumbles into our view, black patches of hair falling from its head. The girl in the grey jumpsuit stumbles back, urging us to flee. But we stay put, watching, because despite how hideous the figure is, I know where I've seen her before.

"Oh my god," I whisper, covering my mouth.

Artemis's hand tightens in mine. "Iris, we have to go *now*!"

I shake my head, my feet frozen in place. I can barely choke the name out. "*Crescentia.*"

The girl in the jumpsuit groans, leaving us with one final "GO!" before disappearing around the corner.

Artemis tugs on my hand. "Iris, we have no idea where we are, but *she might*. We have to go!" He yanks me into action, and we sprint to catch up with our new guest, Artemis's hand still in mine. But I can't stop from looking back, one thing pounding in my mind with every step we take. *Crescentia is alive.* She eventually gains on us enough for us to stop, and Artemis yells for the others to wait.

He puts his hands up in front of him, hiding me behind him. "Crescentia! It's me, Artemis! You remember me?"

When she gets closer, we find that she's not Crescentia at all. Unlike when she left the Enterprize, her skin is covered in puss-filled boils, popping in rhythm with her breathing. Her hands each miss a finger, and a green substance paints her clothes so densely we can hardly see the gray on her jumpsuit. It's in tatters, but I can just make out the label at the top.

SUBJECT 3E.

It takes a single second for me to distinguish what that means. The "E" is for Enterprize.

"3" is for expulsion number, if Aurelius is included in the count.

Once she's only meters away from us, Artemis yells for her to stop. But whatever's happened to her has also distorted her mind because she doesn't recognize us at all. Instead, she runs straight for Artemis, teeth gritted and claws extended. My breath catches in my throat, and I force out a screech before backing away. "ARTY!"

He doesn't miss a beat. Crescentia leaps at him, face first, eyes hungry for flesh. Midair, Artemis punches her across the cheek, forcing her into the wall. He kicks her several times, each blow forcing more green liquid out of her pores.

I back away in awe. "What the hell?"

Once Artemis is confident she's down, he backs toward me. "Find that girl," he demands, taking off in her direction. I sprint with him as he shouts for her to stop. Deep in the tunnel, Destry taps the new girl's shoulder, pointing toward us. It takes me a moment to decipher whether he's telling her we're dangerous or not, but when the two stop running, I'm flushed with relief.

When we finally reach them, we hide with them behind a corner and stop to catch our breath. Artemis recovers before me and demands answers. "Where the hell did you come from?"

The girl squints, tilting her head. "Where the hell did *you* come from?"

Artemis shakes his head. "We're from the Enterprize!"

She glares at him. "What the fuck is that?"

Destry, Artemis, and I look at one another before Destry joins in the questioning. "Wait, do you work for the Authority?"

The girl throws her hands up. "Work *for* the Authority? Hell no!"

I laugh without humor. "Then why are you here?"

The girl backs away slowly. "You're all pretending like *I'm* crazy when you're the ones making up names!" She locks her eyes on mine. "I'm from the Assessment!"

My breath catches in my throat. Artemis and I speak at the same time. "What?"

Destry explains quickly. "I told you guys before…this building connects with the Assessment Hall." He gestures to the girl. "This is where they're tested."

I rub my hands against my forehead. "I'm sorry…I don't understand." I stare at our new addition. "Can somebody *please* explain what is going on?"

The girl keeps backing away from us. "Yes, but we have to get out of here! I'll explain once we're safe, but the explosion won't hold them off for long."

We start sprinting again, and my mind whirls in circles. Why is she trying to escape the Assessment? Why was Crescentia…*inhuman?* Where is this girl taking us?

We race down hall after hall, following our leader and trusting her sense of direction. We're so far from the Enterprize that there's no way I could find my way back now. Suddenly, my mind puts two and two together.

"WAIT!" I shout. "Where's Curi?!"

The girl doesn't respond, so I stop in my tracks. "I'M NOT LEAVING HERE WITHOUT HER!"

Finally, the brunette turns around and yells. "Whoever you're looking for isn't here! Most of the subjects have escaped, and if she's an innocent, she was never housed here to begin with." Having no other option than to believe her, I start running again, feeling a pit in my stomach.

After a dozen direction changes, the girl finally stops. "In here!" she shouts, yanking the door open. Despite the rush inside, I just make out the plate in the center of the door.

EXPERIMENT CHAMBER

I shiver, running in and letting Artemis slam the door behind me. We collapse to the floor, doing everything we can to catch our breath. The girl wanders the room, scanning the walls, desperately searching for something. The end of the room is blown out, and rain pours onto the rubble. When the girl reaches the end of the space, she falls to the floor, bashing her fists against the tile.

I share a look with Artemis before stepping forward. The girl cries, so I keep my voice gentle. "Please…I just…" I scratch the back of my head. "If you know what's going on, please tell us. What's happening…where are we?"

The girl rubs her temples, then straightens up to stand. She sniffs tears away, then walks closer to us, taking deep breaths.

I shake my head. "Just…start with your name." I point to the others. "This is Artemis…this is Destry." I gesture to myself. "I'm Iris."

The girl stares at the ground, and her voice is weak. "Sierra." I look at Artemis and he nods, encouraging me to continue. I take a step forward, ignoring my surroundings, just focusing on her.

"Why are you running?"

She gulps, then finally looks into my eyes. Hers are moist, and her cheeks are puffy. She nods with resolution and speaks, stopping every few words to fight back tears.

"The Assessment…it's not a test. It's an *experiment*." I take a step back. *What?* "They gathered us the first day. Split us into groups." She shakes her head. "They're not testing us…they're not dividing us into genetic modification factions or whatever *bullshit* they're claiming." She gestures to the rest of the room. "They're performing medical experiments on us. They inject us with…with hormones…from strange syringes…" She shakes her head. "Whatever happened to your friend back there…" she gulps. "That's what they're doing to us."

My eyes widen. "What, so they just put you in chambers and test you…for what?"

She stares at the ground. "Desperate times call for desperate measures."

Destry shakes his head. "No…that makes no sense. How could they ever get away with that? Wouldn't somebody start to wonder why *generations* of teenagers have gone missing?"

Sierra shakes her head. "If half a million kids go missing, but there's a cure at the end of it, nobody in the Authority is going to give it a second thought. Besides…they've already convinced everyone that once a child leaves for the Assessment, they never come back to their Ascendency. Nobody would even know somebody went missing because they'd never think to look for them."

I choke on my words. "I just…I don't understand. Why would they do this?"

Sierra doesn't even look in my direction. "When they're eating like kings, and their dinners go from five courses to three, do you really think they'll care about a few failed experiments? Even failure sustains their resources for longer, having fewer mouths to feed and all. I doubt they ever thought it would take this long, but…"

"Sierra," Artemis cuts in. "What are they trying to cure? Nobody is sick."

Admittedly, I have been wondering this same thing. But my mind is whirring so fast, I can't seem to focus on a single topic at a time.

Sierra gives a frustrated huff before banging her fist on the compartment closest to her. "Don't you see? They've given up on curing the Hage. It's *done*. All that's left are the stockpiles. So…they've turned to human subjects."

Destry gasps. "Surely, they don't think that'll work?"

Sierra laughs without humor. "I don't know, Destry. You tell me." She gestures to the gaping hole in the wall, smoke piling through with a gust of wind. "All I know is what I saw."

I take a step closer to her. "Please…tell us what you saw."

Sierra looks away from me but takes a deep breath. "I escaped that first night. I've been hiding in these halls for months. I got word back to the Southern Ascendency about what was happening here." She looks at Artemis. "The Authority are doing a phenomenal job of keeping this a secret. But once they found out in the South…" She gestures to the gaping hole in the wall. "They weren't happy."

I twist my lips to the side.

Lagiacrus's parents died to end medical experimentation on sixteen-year-olds. Sebastion turned Ashlea in to prevent her from suffering the torture and side effects of these failed experiments. Artemis's family had a refugee operation…to prevent others from enduring this torture.

I shake my head. "I don't believe you."

She gives a brief chuckle, but there's no amusement behind it. Instead of explaining more, she gestures to the walls around us. "Then take a look for yourself."

I look at Artemis and grab his hand. We're surrounded by rows of glass chambers labeled at the bottom with golden plates. We don't recognize the first few subjects, but after a couple strides, we stop in our tracks. Neither of us can speak, so Destry reads it for us.

"Jade."

My arms tremble as I watch her fighting against the glass. She pounds on the walls, screaming to be let out, but nobody can hear her. The cells are soundproof, so she screams her throat dry, begging for release. Her skin is normal, but her eyes…

They're entirely black, with no whites hiding beneath.

I back away, clutching my chest. Without warning, I run through the remaining cells, wildly searching for two potential occupants.

I sprint from glass to glass, looking at the creature inside and scanning the plates. I silently plead with the gods that I'll find what I'm looking for and stumble when I see him.

Eno. Lying against the edge of his chamber, staring blankly at the wall. His hands are green, and the color extends to the rest of his body. I nearly hurl looking at him, and force my eyes shut when I see that his leg has deteriorated into a limp mass of black tissue. I run forward and force myself to look at the other cells, only finding Assessment subjects. With one cell remaining, I verbally plead. "*Please, please, please.*"

When I read *SUBJECT 853A*, I fall to the ground.

Rain blows in from the gaping hole and showers me, blending with the tears falling down my cheeks. I crane my neck toward the sky and fight the urge to howl my frustration.

Behind me, Artemis scans the rows of glass jail cells. Destry follows him, and his words are shrouded in disbelief. "Do you think Sola ended up here? Or Mercedes?"

Artemis shakes his head. "No…we *saw* them die. They're gone."

Thunder roars in the sky beyond, and I can't erase the realization that, for the first time in my life, I know what it feels like to get drenched from rainfall. My nostrils dance with the scent of rain while the breeze clutches me in a warm caress of freedom. But it doesn't have me fooled.

Because without Mace, I will never be free.

Destry and Artemis sit on the ground beside me, the three of us letting the rain pound against our chests. Destry breaks the silence. "I guess if we didn't see them killed…they ended up *here*." Destry lets out a shaky breath. "The gunshots were fake."

Artemis takes a deep gulp before grabbing my shoulder and shaking it with a mixture of hope and fear. "Hey…Mace and Lunar…*they're not dead.*"

Frozen, Destry nods, eyes wide. "But from the look of things…"

I choke back sobs as lightning strikes a nearby hill, the sound so soft amidst the thunder, I'm sure the others will miss it.

"…We're going to wish that they were."

END OF BOOK 1

Acknowledgments

Wow. Here we are, two years after I whipped out my iPhone and drafted the first chapter of *The Enterprize*. All this time, I thought the acknowledgments would be the easiest part of the writing process. But how does one even begin to thank the creative, supportive, talented team that made this crazy idea I had when I was thirteen into a reality?

First and foremost, I would not be where I am without my brilliant mentor, Kevin Wolf. Thank you, Kevin, for welcoming me into your wonderful critique group with open arms. When I first heard that you met with other writers for *three hours* every Monday to compare work, I was terrified I wouldn't enjoy writing enough to commit to consistently attending. But after my first Zoom meeting, I was hooked. So, thank you Kevin, and the rest of the Writers on the Brink, for welcoming me, challenging me, and making *The Enterprize* what it is now.

Thank you to my incredible editor, Adrienne Kisner. Your encouragement was instrumental in getting me to that finish line, and your developmental edits were crucial for constructing the final version of the story. You were the only one on Team Mercedes, and you helped mold her story into one which sends readers into a whirlwind of emotions. You made her so much more than a character, but a complex individual who *feels*, no matter how hard she tries not to. I'm forever grateful for the work you did to improve this story, and I have never been so happy to have somebody tear apart my writing!

My beta readers were also heavily involved in the editing process. I cannot thank them enough for their involvement and contribution to *The Enterprize*. Laura Cook – you provided such descriptive feedback that gave it the final push it needed to get to perfection. Although you weren't entirely on Team Mercedes, you fought for elements focusing on character rather than surface-level bitterness. You didn't hold back and gave me the exact feedback needed to wrap up the story. All my beta readers suggested vital changes that were incorporated one way or another into the story. I am forever grateful for your contribution to this years-long project: Karis Jochen Meyers, Garrett O'Toole, Carlos Fernandes, Katelyn Mitchem, and Maggie Montoya.

I want to express my sincerest gratitude to Brian Barraza, who created every piece of artwork you see across *The Enterprize*. From the covers and house blueprints to the corner chapter art, there was nothing he could not do. No challenge was too daunting, and I'm so fortunate to have had such an incredible artist take my jumbled mess of ideas and make them a reality. Words cannot describe how amazed I am at your work, Brian, as well as your commitment to your craft and supportive advice beyond the world of artwork. Your poetry is soul-shattering and powerful, so much so that you allowed me to incorporate a piece of your work into my own. Here is "Absolution" from Brian's debut poetry collection, *Ashore and Adrift*. It's a stroke of genius.

They may have been kind at times, but even the devil had redeeming qualities.

I would be remiss if I didn't mention the first person I've ever shared my work with, Taylor Dedic. Thank you, Taylor, for your endless support in this crazy journey of writing! You helped give me the confidence to share my art with the world, and you will never know how exhilarating and motivational it has been discussing daily word count goals and holding each other accountable for achieving those benchmarks. Your support kept me going and striving to complete my first draft. Additionally, your extensive knowledge of the world of publishing helped tremendously with the logistical side of writing, which is perhaps the most challenging part of the process. I've enjoyed comparing stories with you and getting your perspective on my most outlandish ideas. Thank you a million times, Taylor. Your writing is a work of art, and I can't wait for it to only continue to grow.

Of course, thanks to every person who helped me along the way in some way, shape, or form. Justin Williams and Alex George were two individuals who encouraged me throughout this journey and read some of the first versions of this story. If I had known how much my writing would grow, I promise I would have spared you from that original draft! I know I'm missing so many others, but from the bottom of my heart, thank you to every person who has picked up a copy of *The Enterprize*, whether I know you or not. This is a story I've been wanting to tell for longer than I care to admit, and to finally have it out in the world is both exhilarating and extremely terrifying.

I want to give a grand acknowledgment to my wonderful parents. Dad, thank you for supporting my dreams. I am so lucky to have been granted the opportunity to have the creative space to put my ideas into the world. Without you, this never would have been possible. Because of you, *The Enterprize* exists. Mom, thank you for being the first person in the world to read my work from cover to cover. I'll never forget you calling me when you were emotional from a particular expulsion or shocked at a dramatic twist. You read the first edition of my work, and how you got through that mess of grammatical mistakes and jungle of adjectives will always be a mystery. But your excitement with my work and support through this process means more to me than you will ever know.

Finally, thank you to my wonderful husband, Thomas George. Thanks for your support, your encouragement, and for constantly challenging me to make *The Enterprize* the best it could possibly be. Your creativity is unmatched, and you continue to astound me with every suggestion you make. From birthing the idea behind the camouflage in the cover's title to the growing and withering branches in the chapter art, you were able to make my creation into a real work of art. I love you more than anything in this world. You are the best parts of Mace and Artemis, and I couldn't write our love story if I tried.

Lastly, I want to thank the 23-year-old girl who refused to give up despite how terribly helpless she felt.

That trauma birthed *The Enterprize*, and I couldn't be prouder of her for pushing through her darkest times to create something so beautiful.

Melissa George is a proud member of the Rocky Mountain Fiction
Writers and resides in the peaceful mountain town of Estes Park. She has
an MPH and enjoys exploring aspects of disaster management, which she
incorporates into her dystopian writing.

When Melissa isn't writing, she's training and racing professionally for
the Roots Running Project. She is an elite steeplechase athlete and graduate
from the University of Missouri, where she currently holds the school record
for the event.

www.ingramcontent.com/pod-product-compliance
Lightning Source LLC
Chambersburg PA
CBHW061852310726
48972CB00004B/994